Twice Upon A Time

FAIRYTALE, FOLKLORE, & MYTH
REIMAGINED & REMASTERED

EDITED BY JOSHUA ALLEN MERCIER

THE BEARDED SCRIBE PRESS
ATLANTA, GEORGIA

"Blood & Water," by Alethea Kontis, originally published in *InterGalactic Medicine Show, Vol. 9,*
Copyright © 2008 by Hatrack River Enterprises.

"Spear Among Spindles," by S.Q. Eries, originally published in *Playthings of the Gods,*
Copyright © 2011 by Drollerie Press.

"The Bone Harp," by Court Ellyn, originally published in *Realms,*
Copyright © 2010 by Black Matrix Publishing, LLC.

"Traveller," by Deborah Walker, originally published in *Horror Through the Ages,*
Copyright © 2009 by Lame Goat Press.

Twice Upon a Time: Fairy Tale, Folklore, and Myth, Reimagined and Remastered
First Edition Copyright © 2015
The Bearded Scribe Press, LLC
Atlanta, Georgia
Joshua Allen Mercier, Executive Editor

Hardcover ISBN: 978-1-942670-02-5
Paperback ISBN: 978-1-942670-01-8
E-book ISBN: 978-1-942670-00-1

DEDICATED to the writers in whose chasmic footsteps we whimsically and reverently trod. Thank you for your stories, whose words echoed loudly, reached deep within our souls, and stirred inspiration. May we bring honor to you, to the originals, and capture the hearts and minds of a new generation of both readers and writers alike; for one cannot exist, cannot flourish, without the other.

D

Table of Contents

Foreword

WHEN I started my writing and book blog, I had it in my mind that I wanted to help other Speculative Fiction writers in some way—whether that be coaching, editing, promoting, or the like. The idea of starting an independent press lingered at the back of my mind, but I hadn't the first clue how to embark on such an imposing endeavor.

Alas, in the back of my mind is where it remained.

Editing and book promotion didn't seem as daunting as publishing, so that is what I did. Over the course of editing a novel for RS McCoy, who had become a client after arranging her book tour through the blog, she and I became fast friends. We shared a great deal—sorry, there will be no beans spilled here—but most importantly, we shared current projects with one another and sought each other for professional advice and suggestions.

As it happened, she had just submitted a short story to an anthology and was accepted for publication. An idea came to Rachel, one that hadn't previously come to my mind; it scared and excited me all the same—but mostly scared. She challenged—dared, even—me to produce my own anthology. It *sparked* something deep inside, fitting (to say the least) given the source of inspiration. Upon further consideration, I realized that an anthology would be the perfect opportunity for me to launch my publishing career, and that which started as a spark quickly became wildfire.

Thank you, Rachel, for helping to ignite my Spark. Thank you for believing in my editing skills, for believing in me.

While watching an episode of *Once Upon a Time*, the theme for the anthology finally came to me (had it been a snake...you know the rest). There's something about fairytales that resonates within all of us—deny it if you must, but I dare say you're a liar!—something that echoes through time and instantaneously releases the child locked deep within. An anthology of Fairytale and Folklore retellings made perfect sense.

Being a lover of all things Speculative Fiction—the focus of my blog and my publishing house—I decided it would be great to have the stories pulled from every sub-genre within its realm. I was soon contacting every Speculative Fiction author imaginable—some I admittedly had no business contacting. But I climbed lofty heights to reach them just the same. *"No,"* was the worst they could say, after all. I was surprised, of course, when some extended a helpful hand; surprised even more when some agreed to contribute without so much as batting an eyelash.

Even though I received a great response among the authors I did contact, I decided to do an open submission call in a few select online groups. The anthology became bigger than I could have ever hoped, receiving a phenomenal 84 submissions! Of course, as much I would have loved to feature all of them, I had to choose those which best met the submission call criteria...

...A horror-inspired *Sleeping Beauty* re-telling? Yes, please!

...A dark fantasy tale about an emperor and his ever infamous new wardrobe? Absolutely!

...Or perhaps you'd love to read a space opera adaptation of Jack and his beanstalk? I knew you would, which is why I had to have it in this anthology!

Though it is my name at the bottom of the front cover, no writing endeavor is a solo act—certainly not this one. Thank you to all the authors. You far exceeded all of my expectations with your thrilling (re)tales. The showcase of talent in this anthology astounds me. How I was able bind it within its pages will remain a mystery, even to me.

There are many others I must thank, too.

Jeremiah, of course; you are my rock. You are the Beauty to my Beast, my Prince Charming, my Happily Ever After. Without your love and unwavering support, none of this would have been possible.

Thank you, Mom. Your love and constant encouragement has always and will always mean the world to me. I am so blessed to have you as not only my mother, but as one of my best friends. You were always my beacon when I was lost in the darkness, and I will always look to your light.

Thank you, Lisa, for your support, friendship, and love, and for listening to me babble on about this project (to the edge of annoyance, I'm sure). I am sincerely grateful for your suggestions and feedback.

Elizabeth—divine librarian, sister of song, tamer of templates, answerer of questions (regardless of their stupidity or the hour), and most-treasured minion—the words "Thank you" fall abysmally short of my sheer gratitude. Without you, my blog would have surely failed not soon after it launched. I am sure I can never repay you for all that you've done—all that you do—but one day I will attempt to settle the debt. (And I will get that novel out of you yet!)

To everyone else who has given their support, their encouragement, their well wishes, or their guidance—the list is far too great to be printed here, but it is forever etched into my heart—Thank You from the bottom of it.

Special Acknowledgements

Rebecca Carpenter | Brian T. Holloway
August Caudle | Jeremiah Jacobs
Rachel Chaltraw | Autumn Jones
Courtney Clifford | Hannah Lesniak
David Danley | Lisa Lowry
Michael Dougherty | Christina Mahaney
Shannon Finnegan | Elizabeth J. Norton
Ken Hagdal | Becky Palmer
Ilana Halupovich | Jessica Schneider
Bill Hiatt | Ila Turner
Brian T. Hodges | Brittany Warman
Cortny Woodworth

I would like to give a special 'Thank You' to the above individuals who stepped forward to offer their financial support to help get The Bearded Scribe Press, LLC up and running. Without your generous donations and belief in both me and this project, absolutely none of this would have been possible.

Your contributions are appreciated beyond words! They've been put to great use as well—from funding a new website, for the expense of LLC formation, for cover design costs, and for the purchase of ISBNs.

I am deeply honored and humbled by your kindness.

Merci beaucoup avec tout mon coeur!

Joshua Allen Mercier

About the Publisher

THE BEARDED SCRIBE PRESS, LLC is an independent publisher of quality Speculative Fiction. We aim to become a platform for emerging writers to get discovered by the mainstream and inversely, through becoming a staple in the literary community, becoming the source for readers to discover emerging talent in the Speculative Fiction realm.

LINKS

http://www.beardedscribe.com
http://www.facebook.com/beardedscribe
https://twitter.com/beardedscribe
http://www.facebook.com/twiceuponatimeanthology

About the Editor

J OSHUA ALLEN MERCIER is the Founder and Executive Editor of The Bearded Scribe Press, an independent publishing house dedicated to the broad genre of speculative fiction. He is a writer, a self-confessed linguaphile and philologist, a proud bibliophile, a coffee addict, and an unrepentant grammar geek. He is also a professional mixologist (a darn good one, thank you very much!) with over fourteen years of cocktail-slinging experience.

Joshua's re-telling of *Red Riding Hood*—titled *Fire & Ash*—is one of the stories featured in this anthology. He currently has two series in progress, but that's all the information he's sharing about the projects at the moment. When he is not working, editing, or writing, he enjoys singing, cooking, and spending time with his family. Joshua lives in the Atlanta area with his partner, Jeremiah, and their two Chihuahuas, Bailey and Chanel.

LINKS

http://www.beardedscribe.com/jamercier/
http://www.facebook.com/author.joshuaallenmercier
https://twitter.com/beardedscribe

About the Cover Artist

L UKE SPOONER, owner of Carrion House, currently lives and works in the South of England. Having recently graduated from the University of Portsmouth with a first class degree, he is now a full time illustrator for just about any project that peaks his interest. Despite regular forays into children's books and fairytales, his true love lies in anything macabre, melancholy or dark in nature and essence. He believes that the job of putting someone else's words into a visual form, to accompany and support their text, is a massive responsibility as well as being something he truly treasures.

LINKS

http://www.carrionhouse.com
http://www.facebook.com/carrionhouse

Twice Upon A Time

FAIRYTALE, FOLKLORE, & MYTH
REIMAGINED & REMASTERED

"Some day you will be old enough to start reading fairytales again."
~ C.S. Lewis

Bog Trade

by Bo Balder

I felt my father's eyes on me all the time. He was becoming increasingly unhappy with me. My hands, already too broad and clumsy for their task of sifting pulses, trembled under his piercing blue gaze as he just stood there. I dropped several good ones in the dirt and his breath puffed out in an irritated sigh. I bit the inside of my cheek to stop my whimper.

I was taller than he was now. And stronger, I suspected. I was his daughter, yet he hated me. Why? Because I was tall and strong, while my sisters were small and weakly with curved spines? I wished he was proud of me instead.

When Father left, I could concentrate on my task again. I finished the beans, pushed myself up, and tipped the bad ones into the pig's trough. Ymke, my favorite, snarfled happily and her silly pink face butted my head. She liked me, as did the chickens. The dogs couldn't stand me, but they feared me as well so that worked out fine.

My mother called out to me. "Gudrun!"

She thrust a piece of old cord towards me, the sprang twists faded and frayed by long use. "Go to the peat hole and gather rushes for the floor."

Although she stood only to my breastbone, she refused to look up to me. I knew she grudged every scrap of wool or linen that went into clothing me, and handed me her worst efforts. Mother didn't hate me, I think, but she mistrusted everything that wasn't perfect or well made, with the exception of my sisters. My fingers weren't suitable for weaving and I could barely even spin, so there wasn't anything I could do about my appearance. My little sisters were dressed in bright-colored wools, almost as good quality as my father's cloaks, although no bright colors could hide their crooked backs.

"Who shall I take?" I asked. "Hildeburg or Lammechien?"

"You shall go alone," my mother said. "Don't contradict me, young lady. Do as I say."

But I never went alone. No woman did. The bog had treacherous places, thick mists, wild animals, and—not to forget—wilis.

She slapped me on the rump. "No dawdling."

I didn't plan to. Although it was still morning, the day before New Year's Day, already the light had a grey, wintry quality that made one long to stay indoors. I stuffed the cord into my belt. All I had in there were an old knife and a leather bag I made myself, unlike my sisters, who had already been gifted with scissors and little mirrors. My father owned two thralls and five cows, three pigs and twenty chickens, a wealthy man. Yet he must have angered the gods for he had only daughters, of which I am the middle one, the only one with a straight spine.

I walked quickly over the boardwalk to the main bog, where no peat had yet been cut. Last summer's rushes still stood, sere and browned, reflected in the film of ice over the dark water. I bent down and slashed them with my curved knife. It was so old it didn't take a good edge anymore, but because I was strong I still managed. My hair kept falling out of my net cap so I took it off to redo my braids. As I stood there with my cap between my teeth, a sheaf of rushes between my thighs, something rustled in the undergrowth across the black bog water. The bare alder boughs parted and a terrifying face stared at me. It was bigger than a man's face, with eyes too far apart to be human, a wide mouth with square teeth opened in surprise. A face as bumpy as a gnarled oak stump.

I dropped the cap. My thighs loosened their hold on the rushes. "Mama!"

As soon as I heard my own voice howling, I lost my fear. Its deep sound reminded me of my own size and strength. I was no timid female with bowed head. I grabbed at my knife, which thankfully was secured with string to my belt or I would have dropped it as well.

"Get away from me, evil monster! Son of wilis! Go away." I wished I'd taken a fire pot so I could have waved a brand at them. Everybody knew wilis could not stand iron or fire, the mark of civilized men.

The thing pointed a finger at me, turned its head, and bellowed something. I risked a glance over my shoulders and found two more standing behind me. My movement cost no more than a heartbeat, yet when my head turned back three more had risen up from between the scraggly alders, two to my left and one to my right. I was surrounded.

They stood like bent old man, their hands nearly dangling to the ground. They wore badly cured hides and carried stout sticks. One of them had no beard, but whether it was female or a male too young for whiskers, I couldn't say.

The only sensible thing to do was run.

But I didn't. I waved my blunt knife at them. "Come closer and I'll stab you straight through the heart!" I yelled, my voice hoarse with strain.

I tried to look belligerent and dangerous, like Father when he'd drunk too much mead.

The creatures melted away as swiftly and inexplicably as they had appeared. I thought about continuing with the rushes as if nothing had happened, but I couldn't face them twice.

I scrabbled after my net cap, which had after all cost me many hours of work, and walked back as fast as I could without actually running. When it seemed I heard no one after me, I looked back. Three of them stood on the middle of the path, sniffing after me. I could only see their silhouettes against the low winter sun and they seemed monstrously tall, with bulges and humps that nothing human ought to have.

I kept looking over my shoulder as I walked towards home. The three figures stood there until a bend in the path hid them from my sight. Who were these creatures? Why had no one warned me of their existence? Why had mother let me go alone today of all days?

Mother stood waiting for me at the edge of the village. She didn't comment on my lack of fresh rushes, but looked avidly up at my face. As if she was expecting something out of the ordinary. I cringed away from the interest in her eyes. Her tongue could lash harder than a whip.

"Are you all right, child?" she said, actually taking my big rough hands in her small cold ones. Small only in comparison to mine, because I believe one would call her a raw-boned woman with big hands, if one were normal-sized.

"Mother, there were things in the marsh. Giants. Monsters. Wilis," I babbled.

Her forehead furrowed like a newly plowed field. "Wilis? Ghostly women in white?"

Oh. "No, a gruesome giant with a face like a wild boar!"

She inhaled sharply. "The Grendels. Hrothgar!" she called. "They're back."

Father practically ran out the door. Mother didn't say, as we hoped, or as we expected, but that was clear from the look they shared that the appearance of the creatures was no surprise to them. Apparently I wasn't going to be punished for not bringing the rushes. I just couldn't grasp what the Grendel sighting meant to them. It made me uneasy, for some reason. It felt as if I'd been sent specifically to spot them. But why?

"We must get ready," Father said. His glance raked over me as if I was a pig ready to be sold at the year market. "Tonight's New Year's Eve."

Tonight all the fires would be doused, and we would wait cold and afraid in our halls, hoping the sun would rise again. I didn't understand what the monsters had to do with that miserable night, and even less with the joyful Midwinter's Day after, when we would celebrate the turning of the year.

My elder sisters visited that afternoon. Unheard of! Taetske hugged me with her face all tight and stern, like mother's, only with more love underneath. She was the elder, married off with the biggest dowry. She had a husband and a homestead of her own, five hours' walk away from Father and Mother's disapproval.

Gieneke cried openly. "You are the best sister a woman could wish for," she whispered. "You know I wanted to take you with me? But Father and Sipko wouldn't allow it."

That made me cry. I had so wished to go with her and look after her children for her, but I hadn't dared ask. To hear that she had wished for it as well was like receiving a wonderful gift. I gave her a handful of chestnuts I'd saved up for the littler girls. It was nothing compared to her generosity, but I couldn't sew or weave prettily like women should, so it was all I had to give.

"Bye," Gieneke said and turned away. She and Taetske hugged each other and walked off.

I remained behind, baffled. They'd walked all those hours for this short a visit?

"Don't stand there gawking, girl," Mother said. "There's work to be done. Start grinding the meal for tomorrow's feast."

My feet started in the direction of the grindstone of their own accord, so used to obeying mother that the full import of the words arrived only later, like an echo. Today was the day before New Year. We weren't supposed to prepare things ahead for the next year. Actually, even weaving and sprang projects should be completed and no new ones started. Carrying projects over was considered bad luck. Of course, everybody cheated. They pretended to stop and picked them up again, but with food it was a different matter.

I noticed nobody else was working. Mother and Father were quietly (but intensely) arguing. The past few days I'd seen them alternately whispering together and pointedly ignoring each other.

"She's no use, and never will be. I want her back, crooked spine or not."

"How can we ask for her back? We have a bog trade with them. They'll be insulted."

"We won't ask. We give her back. We'll say she's a bad girl. We'll make sure she's disgraced, and won't be believed if she tells," Mother said.

The younger children played knucklebones, oblivious of the ebb and flow of the argument. The thralls carried around leftover food and beer and even scraped out the stockpot, which simmered on the hob all other days of the year. I didn't dare stop my work, but Father and Mother's argument worried me. It seemed to be about me, and also someone who wasn't me. What was a bog trade? Who was the other girl? A foreboding settled in the pit of my stomach. As if I wasn't part of the household. As if they were going to send me away. As soon as I'd thought of it, I knew it for a true thought, although some part of me protested. I'd always done my best. It wasn't fair.

The day wore on, my unease increasing by the hour. It seemed as if everybody in the village stopped to chat with my parents a dozen times, staring at me covertly. What in Hell's name was going on? First it had been the women and girls stopping by, even the thralls. Then it was our neighbor and his two sons. They shook hands with my father, but soon enough, they shook their heads nay and walked away.

Then another neighbor arrived. The same thing happened. And again, Mother and Father's ongoing argument got louder. "You are the man of the house!" she screamed. "It falls to you. This is one thing I can't do for you, like I do everything else."

It was unthinkable for Mother to insult father in public. Everybody knew who the real man of the house was, but it was never mentioned.

I had become a woman last year. The only reason I could imagine for this round of inspections was the offering of my virginity, which should have waited for the next May feast. It made no sense to perform the rite at New Year. I bent over my work in an attempt to hide my flaming face and tears. I knew the celebration had been postponed last May for some reason, but why now? Did they fear no one would ask me for a May tree ribbon? I breathed and counted my fingers and toes several times until I felt calmer.

"Does it need to be done?" Father pleaded, sounding desperate. "Why not just the spear? Odin will be satisfied with that. They'll never notice, will they?"

"But Frigg will," Mother said. "It should have been done in the rite of Spring and nobody would. We can't send her back a virgin. We promised to marry her well."

"But you can't ask it of me!" Father said. "She's my—" He fell silent.

"She's not. We are returning our bog trade and we shall be happy with our daughter." Mother folded her arms. "So there is no reason for you to hesitate. You wouldn't if she were a thrall we'd bought."

Father didn't answer but bowed his head.

I knew they were talking about me, but I still didn't get why. I had always wished them to be happy with me, and whatever it was they required me to do, I'd done it to the best of my ability. I had wanted nothing more in life than to be a good daughter, even knowing I could never attain that pinnacle of perfection with my height and clumsiness and slurred way of speaking. What did bog trade signify? Was I not their true daughter? My height and hair and looks had always set me apart from other children, but I had long since put away my childhood fancies of being a lost princess.

Yet I had to be a foster child, nothing else made sense. I was almost relieved to realize that. But that still didn't explain their anger and shame and increasing agitation. Had something gone wrong about the fostering? Were they going to return me to my people? But no visitors arrived, and we weren't going anywhere. A part of the puzzle was still missing.

We only had barley soup for dinner that day since there was to be no slaughter until after the New Year. I spun my bumpy threads mindlessly, poring over the encounter with the creature in the bog. Grendel, mother had called it. Mother and Father arguing. It must all hang together, but I couldn't see how. Until I did, I couldn't act. But I didn't want to die.

I'd always done whatever they asked, but that I wouldn't give. My death was too much.

That evening Father solemnly doused the hearth fire. I knew, as every child older than six did, that there was a fire basket out back that would be used the next morning to start up the New Year's fire, but I felt the chill and the emptiness like every year. We huddled together in the gloomy darkness of the longhouse, deeply impressed by the ritual. Soon it got so cold that we made ready to retire to the warmth of our beds.

My little sisters had clambered in before me and shivered under the blankets, calling out for me to hurry. I took off my wooden shoes. Before I could sit on the edge of the bed to close the doors and curtains and swing my legs inside, Mother sat beside me and shook off her clogs.

"You are in the big bed tonight," she said, not meeting my eyes.

A stone fell into my stomach. "What? Why? Mother, I don't understand."

She shushed me. "Don't make a fuss. You'll scare the little ones. Just do it and keep silent, no matter what happens. Go."

She pushed me off. I walked on cringing feet to the other big box bed, having forgotten to put my clogs with their warm straw back on. My stockinged feet were ice after two steps. It would take a long time to fall asleep with cold feet like that. I couldn't imagine curling up against father as I did with my sisters.

Father was already inside. I could hear him breathe, although I couldn't see him in the darkness. Still, the linen bedclothes felt damp and chill as I sat down.

"Close the doors," he said.

"Shouldn't I get a warming pan?" I said, then realized my foolishness. I'd need hot coals from the fire, and Father had just doused it with a jug of water. I'd even cleaned the hearth myself in the last rays of the setting sun.

"Just get in. We'll get warm soon enough."

I swung my legs up and lay down on mother's soft down pillow. I'd never felt anything as soft, and I wished I was still a little girl who got to snuggle up against mother when she was ill. Not that I'd ever been ill, so I never got that chance. But still.

I stretched my long, long legs out, bumping against the wooden footboard.

"Not there," Father said. "Lie on my pillow."

I didn't want to. I wasn't sure why. Then when his hand started to pull up my shift, I understood.

The next morning I woke, stiff and cold, from Mother's voice. Shame washed over me in a chilling wave. I had brought evil on our house, made Father do wrong. It must be my fault for still having been a virgin, the unmarried one, the unwanted one.

"Don't lie abed, girl," Mother said. "Get up. There's work to be done."

Her voice made me angry. Hadn't she sent me into this shameful bed? Although my heart pounded like a drum, I swung my cold feet out of bed. If mother acted as if nothing was off, I could hide my anger as well.

"Is Father lighting the hearth?" I said, tiptoeing across the floor to the clogs that still stood by my sisters' bed.

"Not yet. We must go to the bog first and make sacrifice. Come. The sun is nearly up."

I tied my wrap more securely about me and tried to neaten my braids while I hurried outside. I just wish my hair didn't curl so wildly, wished it would lay flat and obedient like my sisters'. The whole village, or at least the heads of households, had gathered there, with Father at the head in his most splendid scarlet cloak. He carried the spear of Odin, and the other men hefted unlit brands, also dressed in their best. Mother was there, and our wisewoman, Irmgard.

I could see the pity in Irmgard's eyes, the tight control in my mother's face. I'd almost convinced myself that we would meet my true family somehow, but now it seemed I would be the sacrifice for Odin. Going meekly felt like the dutiful thing to do, and I'd expected praise, or acknowledgement when I pretended to do exactly that. But instead, they acted as if I had done wrong and would be punished. Would I ever understand?

It didn't matter anymore. They had wronged me, and I nursed an ember of anger in my breast, knowing I could fan it hotter in a moment. I would not be the dumb beast of their sacrifice. But there was no way out yet, with people all around. I would wait.

The little procession started moving, the men in front, me and mother and the wisewoman in the back.

"Where are we going?" I asked, as low as I could with my loud, uncouth voice, as we trudged through crisply frozen meadows towards the wild bogs beyond our peat holes.

"Hush," Mother said.

Irmgard took pity on me. "We're going to the bog to make sacrifice."

"To Odin?" I asked.

She waggled her head. "Yes, dear. You must be brave."

Those words struck fear into my heart, as I'm sure they would with everyone. Why do people think saying things about bravery will reassure you? They do the opposite. Spear. Bog. The thing Father had done to me last night. Fathers weren't meant to lie with daughters; one tried to keep one's animal stock free from that taint. What had moved my cautious, law-abiding father to do such a thing?

And now he was deviating from normal New Year's Day festivities. No fires had been lit in our house, and possibly the whole village. Without fire, there was no purification or forgiveness. We were all in a state of limbo. Sacrificing me to Odin wouldn't change that. Something more was going on.

It was a bright morning, a great omen for the next year, but I couldn't feel the goodness of it. I wanted things to be as they had been, peaceful and ordinary and imperfect. I wanted wassail and the strips of pork belly we roast while we wait for the first bread of the New Year to rise and be baked. Not stumble on cold, clumsy feet over icy ground to my death. But even in thinking these things, I was saying goodbye to them. I would act, something would change, although I didn't know how.

We halted where the wooden pathway ended and the peat hole started.

Father said something, and our next-door neighbor and his son grabbed my arms and drew me away from Mother and the wisewoman. The women covered their faces with their shawls and that scared me even more.

Maybe I'd waited too long to escape. But I wasn't going to go quietly. I screamed and kicked and flailed, but the four men managed to wrestle my to the ground, their faces red and angry now.

Two more men hoisted my legs up from the ground, the original two held my shoulders. They pushed me down and lifted my skirts. I thought they were going to do what Father had done, and it seemed it would be more practical to put me down on the wooden path. If I had been virgin, they would have owed him wergild, but now they didn't. I struggled there with my skirts up to my chin and my legs all cold and white under the winter sun. But then Father stepped forward with the spear. The Spear of Odin, I thought. Women weren't normally allowed to even see it, but today he'd carried it out under the open sky.

He was going to kill me.

But then he pointed the spear down. The neighbors positioned me with grunts and complaints so my father could thrust the spear tip into me. I was still sore from Father's own spear, and it was hard not to scream. Father was no rougher than he needed to be. Then he handed the red-tipped spear off, put a sprang cord around my neck and pulled it tight.

I looked up into his eyes, as blue as the sky above. His face was red. "Father," I tried to say.

His eyes turned red and he tightened the cord. I fought him, snarling and biting. I'd gotten a few fingers between the cord and my neck when the neighbors pinned my arms again. I got mad. I felt my anger as waves of heat coming off my face. I swung old Greynt into the air and kicked young Greynt in the stomach. More came at me, hindered by young Greynt being doubled up and bellowing. There was nowhere to go, except into the bog. I'd rather drown than be killed by their self-righteous hands. I jumped backwards onto the ice.

Someone shouted words that seemed oddly distorted as the light changed from cold and bright to beery and warm, and then to black. It took half a dozen heartbeats for me to realize I was sinking into the peat hole through the thin layer of ice.

Something soft beneath me. I breathed in to shout out my indignation, but the breath was more painful than the spear. The shape of a leaf floating above me seemed odd.

I must be under water. I was drowning. I had become the sacrifice, in spite of my determination not to be.

Something grabbed me roughly by the shoulders and dragged me upward into incredibly cold air. I spewed out warm water just before my cheeks were gripped in a spasm and my teeth started chattering. No more drowning, but freezing to death seemed likely.

I opened my eyes. Across a black sheet of ice, I saw my father and his neighbors. They seemed oddly far away. Someone with really big hands wrestled with my clothes and tore them off me. I wanted to protest, my best dress, my only dress, but I couldn't move. Without the wet wool the air seemed less cold, and then a smelly but dry blanket chafed my limbs. The gray shapes around me seemed less real, less interesting than the intent faces of my family across the water.

A white and yellow thing flashed by me. When it rested on top of the water for a bit, floating while its clothes filled with water, I saw it was a girl. A short girl my age with long blond wavy hair, in a colorless wrap and a red and black sprang cord around her neck. Her face looked bloated and surprised while she sank into the bog. The last thing I saw was her strange high left shoulder. She looked just like my sisters.

A shout erupted in the still air. My father turned even redder and screamed words I couldn't understand. I'd never seen him move his hands so much.

"Come," a deep, rough voice said in my ear, a voice so low I felt it in my stomach.

I couldn't move. I couldn't lift my eyes higher than the pale large hand held out to me. A hand even bigger than my own.

"You'll have to carry her," a female version of the rough voice said.

Warm hands shoved themselves between the ground and my shoulders and I was hoisted on something warm and bad smelling. I didn't care about the smell. I lay my head against the moving, warm mountain and soaked up the body heat into my chilled limbs. The person mountain started moving away from the screams of women and the angry bellowing of men. I let my eyelids droop.

Without a word being spoken, I knew I had been rescued. The girl had taken my place as the sacrifice, and I now was no longer father's daughter. I didn't know yet what or who I had become, but as long as I was warm and safe, I didn't care.

The women's keening intensified, and I couldn't help but lift my eyes at the wailing of the woman I had called Mother. Through the branches of the bare alders and birches I saw her. She cradled the limp, misshapen form of the girl in her arms and cried. She must have loved that girl.

In my head, a picture formed. Once before that girl and I had changed places, when we were both much smaller, although I was almost as tall as the woman I would learn to call Mother even then. My parents' foolishness and greed had made them agree to an exchange between me and their true daughter, whose spine was bent. My heart ached for that girl. For her own parents to give her away so heartlessly, just because she wasn't perfect.

Then I remembered to ache for myself. Was I not a daughter? Who had given me away and why? I turned my head and looked into the monstrous woman's face. Her thick lips, so much like mine, I now saw, twisted in a horrible grimace. I flinched, and then I heard her words.

"Daughter."

My whole body flooded with feeling at the sound of that voice. She must be my true mother.

I was a daughter of the Grendels. The man on whose back I rested was my kinsman, and one day I would be mother of a Grendel. I vowed that if I bore a son, I would treasure him and raise him up to hate all men, for they don't care about their children and use them cruelly.

B O BALDER is a freelance writer who lives and works in the ancient Dutch city of Utrecht, close to Amsterdam. When she isn't writing, you can find her madly designing knitwear, painting, or reading anything and everything from Kate Elliott to Iain M. Banks or Jared Diamond.

Her fiction has appeared in *Penumbra*, *Electric Spec*, and quite a few anthologies. Her science fiction novel *The Wan* will be published in 2015 by Pink Narcissus Press.

LINKS

http://www.boukjebalder.nl/
https://twitter.com/boo2305

The Screw-Up

by AJ Bauers

AS Jack stood in a cavernous launch room, getting ready for his departure, he did the only rational thing he could think of when faced with inevitable death: he closed his sapphire blue eyes and mentally prepared his eulogy.

Jackson Wilkes was a good man. Also handsome. Devilishly handsome. And the most gifted Obsolete Engineer to exist in the history of the entire universe. Yes, his death is a great loss to us all. If only he had trusted his instincts to never climb a beanstalk, we might have seen him go on to do amazing things. Like tame a rocknor monster of Planet Echidna or eat a whole G-sized burrito in one sitting.

There was a hiss of a door and approaching, echoing footsteps. "Jack."

But by damming those instincts, those devilishly handsome instincts, he at least got to witness one of the wonders of the galaxy. His last words, "Worth it!" will be remembered by all.

"Jack!"

"Hush, woman," Jack said. "You're ruining my funeral."

"Woman?" the voice replied flatly.

He definitely kept his eyes shut now, feeling the heat of her glare. "It's beautiful, Sasha. Thousands of attendees. Millions watching the galactic broadcast. All of my coworkers, sobbing, regretting they ever called me—"

"Hey, Screw-up!" a high voice called as the door hissed open again.

Jack opened his eyes and sighed to his friend. "That."

Sasha had a ghost of a smirk on the corner of her lip. Not the true Sasha left-side smirk that balanced her asymmetric chin-length black hair. He hadn't seen that smirk for a month and he was beginning to doubt he'd ever see it again. But this half lip was at least more than flat mouth 'Sergeant Chu' persona that she normally projected.

"Screw-up!" the voice called again with a voice higher than Sasha's. Jack turned to see another member of GRIM, the Gargant Response, Infiltration, and Management team. Like Sasha, he was wearing a camouflaging skin-tight suit that was currently projecting the gold, unimatter surface of the warp room. While unimatter, a sub-type of dark matter, was nifty for things like warp travel and protection from anti-matter explosions, it was about as aesthetically pleasing as the skin tight suit on the soldier before him with no neck and arms as thick as Jack's waist. "This is your first time climbing the beanstalk, right?"

"That, it is."

"Well, at least if you soil yourself, we won't notice!" His laughter, or piercing giggle to be more accurate, echoed in the immense room. Jack chuckled as well, pointing at the soldier as if to say, 'Good joke man!'—even if it really wasn't. Yes, Obsolete Engineers were commissioned dark brown jumpsuits as their uniform. Yes, the color resembled excrement. But Jack thought he would experience a higher quality of wit working for the High-velocity Autonomous Rocket Probe (HARP) Earth-based facility rather than farming the blue planet's fields.

"Squeakers is a riot," Jack said to Sasha when the solider had walked away.

"He's also capable of crushing your trachea if he heard you call him that," she replied.

"I'm also capable of shooting a rivet through his skull, yet why am I not afforded a healthy level of respect and fear?"

She raised a brow. "Probably because he doesn't know what a rivet is. To him, you are nothing more than a tall, skinny man-child."

"Better than a short woman who has more muscle mass than my left bicep," Jack said, trying to egg her on. But her smirk disappeared completely and she looked back to the door.

So they were a little different from each other. Probably bad enough that he worked for HARP and she for GRIM, but Jack was motivated to make it work. She had shared dessert with him after all.

...Okay, she was also really hot. But it was mostly the dessert thing.

It had started with her sitting at Jack's table for lunch for a lack of an open seat. The protein bar choices that day were turkey or chocolate. Sasha had made the rookie mistake of choosing chocolate, which tasted like the color of his jumpsuit. Being the gentleman he was, Jack had offered to split his gelatinous turkey bar, which she eventually accepted. The next day, Sasha sat by him again and shared her freeze-dried ice cream as a thank you. Jack solemnly told her that sharing dessert basically bonded them for life and he had earned his first Sasha smirk. And in the six months since GRIM had taken over the HARP facility, they had sat by each other nearly every day with the exception to the last few weeks.

Jack was about to ask Sasha about today's lunch menu to hint that they should eat together when he was interrupted by a hum that made the floor vibrate against his shoes. A green glow emitted from the center of the room where the three harmonic arc gates stood. The place where the magic bean—or split atom of unimatter—grew into the beanstalk, somehow connecting to its identical half instantly across time and space: the warp point. He had actively ignored the arcs since he had come in. But now that the beanstalk was growing, he began to intensely focus on the screwdriver attached to his tool-belt.

Most people didn't know the names of his tools any more, only being familiar with ionic fusion materials. Jack had initially told Sasha that everyone called him Screw-up because they didn't know the actual name for his screwdriver. But when she found out that the previous Obsolete Engineer had no such nickname, the truth had come out. Turns out, little things like causing an anti-matter explosion the first week on the job never really disappear from a person's career history.

Jack withdrew the screwdriver from his belt and began tapping it against the bronze goggles that pushed his brown, bed-head hair away from his face. The little clinks echoed in the room, distracting Jack from the blood pushing against his goggle straps.

"Don't be nervous," Sasha said.

"That's like telling me not be awesome—physically impossible."

The chamber door hissed open again and Sasha disappeared into her Sergeant Chu persona. Commander Grise entered in all his white hair and tanned skin glory. Three soldiers and a man in a maroon jumpsuit accompanied him: the Forefront Technician who would operate the 27th generation gate whose glow Jack was currently ignoring. Sasha threw up a salute. Jack waved his flathead.

"Are you ready?" Sasha asked.

"Oh, absolutely not," Jack said, giving her a wide grin. A loud bang suddenly vibrated in the chamber, and he knew that people had begun climbing the beanstalk. His voice got slightly higher in pitch as he added. "I've told you before how I essentially count warping and death as one of the same thing, right?"

Her lips thinned, "Was that before or after you told me that between climbing a beanstalk and facing a Gargant, you'd rather face a giant, cannibalistic alien?"

Jack often wondered if he was the only person in the galaxy who feared the beanstalk more than Gargants. Yes, he realized it was fully ridiculous. Gargants, the giant alien race discovered almost two years ago, viewed the human race as a delicacy whereas antimatter atomic transportation, also known as beanstalks, were a proven method of traveling across the galaxy. But Gargants were at least tangible. Beanstalks were nothing but flashes of green light, which had the power of a ten-megaton bomb and snapped your body out of existence only to make it appear on an entirely new planet. To Jack, it didn't matter that beanstalk fatalities were about as common as death by polar bears; he would never be able to accept that his body simply transported onto another plane of existence. What happened to your mass? Did it condense? Did it disappear? Or was it destroyed only to be reconstructed? He didn't understand it. And until he did, he refused to climb the beanstalk.

But that stance was doomed to failure the day he was headhunted by HARP. And now, eighteen months later, he was getting ready for his first warp.

"You sure you don't want the Obsolete Tech from the Psamathe HARP facility?" he said, shuffling a bit so Sasha's figure could block out the low green beam that was starting to light up the chamber. "She's got way more field time and experience than me."

"GRIM protocol states that we must utilize the HARP workers available locally before we deprive another facility of their assets," she said sharply, unsympathetically.

"Not that I care," he tried to dismiss casually. "It's just, since this is the first habitable planet that's been discovered since Boreas, I just thought you'd want someone of more experience. For the good of the mission," he added hurriedly. His hands were starting to shake, so he began tapping on his goggles once more. Sasha took a step closer to him and Jack could suddenly see the green glow in its entirety. The energy hit critical mass and the green light was curling and stretching, likes twisted vines. He looked away and tried to remember how to swallow.

"Jack."

Jackson Wilkes died of a heart explosion yesterday. Not just an attack, a literal explosion, showing that, even in cowardice, he was always destined to be great.

"Jack!" Sasha said, touching her fingertips against his cheek. He stopped moving. Sasha really didn't do the human contact thing, so her actions were freeze and stop breathing warranted. "I vouched for you. I told the Commander that we could depend on you. Was I wrong?"

He did his best to relax, pretending he didn't see a halo of emerald around her face. "No, of course not. I just think—"

"Chu!" A deep voice from the GRIM group sounded.

"One moment, Sir!" Sasha shouted. She turned back to Jack, "Wilkes give me a straight answer right now or I will—"

"Not sit with me at lunch anymore?"

Wrong answer. She dropped her fingers from his cheek and clenched the fabric on his jumpsuit sleeve. Jack had a feeling if he had been standing next to a wall, she would have shoved him against it. "You don't get to play that game with me. Not now. Not during these missions. Now tell me, are you going to be a liability?"

He stared at her, grinding his bone-rattling fear away with the gnashing of his teeth. "I can do this." But apparently, that wasn't good enough as she met his gaze. Damn. She could always glare better than him. He sighed and put his screwdriver back in his tool belt. "I got this. I mean, yeah, I kind of feel like I might throw up on you, but I'll be fine once we get there." He took a measured look at her, trying to dig his gaze underneath the piercing stare of Sergeant Chu. "I know what these missions mean to you."

It took a few seconds, but eventually she let got of his jumpsuit and gave him a nod. Jack returned the gesture to the back of her hair as she walked away, his breath torn between a sad sigh and a silent laugh. "Move it, Wilkes," she said with a wave of her hand.

"Yes, Sergeant Chu," he replied, mimicking her salute from earlier.

The green light became too intense the closer they got, prompting Jack to follow Sasha's lead when she put on her goggles. The Commander was alone with the Forefront Tech; the rest of the team had already gone ahead. The tech, who Jack was dubbing as Moron Maroon, treated Jack like all his coworkers treated him—as if he was an idiot who didn't work with harmonic gates every day. But Jack nodded at the right points and repeated statements back when necessary.

"… check on anti-matter energy conversion levels consistently. Will do." Make sure you don't run out of fuel. Jack didn't know if he would have survived without that tip.

"…make sure the harmonic arcs are stable for the return warp, yup, got it." That one was a deliberate sting. It was how Jack had set off an anti-matter explosion the first week on the job. But Jack had no prior experience with warp travel so he hadn't know at the time that this was a golden rule. Without arc stability, the beanstalk would either fizzle out or blow up in your face. Jack's background as a self-educated farm boy was not a saving grace; it was a strike. Most of his coworkers had Master's degrees in Space Travel Engineering.

"… okay, I'm not an idiot. I know not to open the fuel cells and expose antimatter." Every kid of the thirteen, well, eleven planets knew that without unimatter, matter plus antimatter equals death. Like instant, body disintegrating, death. "I also know that I should cover my mouth when I sneeze, just to save you time."

Grise shot an amused expression to Sasha as Moron Maroon huffed and walked away, but Sasha's eyes were stoically fixed on a handheld device she had withdrawn from her side pack. Grise clapped his hands together and gave Jack an easy grin. "Well, let's get going. HARP's anxious to get a crack at the planet once we're done with it."

That was putting it mildly. Of all the effects GRIM had on the facility, HARP scientists were most thoroughly outraged that GRIM got to explore new planets first. Secretly, Jack thought it made sense. Why wouldn't you want the soldiers to make sure it was Gargant-free before mapping out plans of colonization? Boreas might have ended up differently. But HARP felt cheated. After all, had it not been for their probes, humans might have never colonized outside the Earth's solar system. It had been HARP's primary mission for the last 800 years, and of the hundreds of planets discovered, only thirteen had been habitable. They researched all planets possible, habitable or not. But they were especially infuriated today as the probe's readings indicated they were warping to the 14th possible habitable planet. And as the probe was over 700-years old, the only HARP employee allowed on the initial scouting mission with the GRIM team was an Obsolete Tech. The Screw-up. Jack.

Jack stared at the green light he could no longer avoid. It was a violent curl, with lights that cracked and arced like whips, punctuated by random sparks and underplayed with an abrasive hum that had nearly drowned out Moron Maroon's earlier instructions. Jack's skin and goggles vibrated the closer he got. He took a step towards the glow and halted. Desperate thoughts flooded his mind—he had been here long enough to receive full death benefits, right? And what would happen to his things if he died on an alien planet? Would human resources sort through his belongings? Or would it be a game of dibs that—

"Today, Wilkes," Grise said, giving him a "helpful" push in the middle of his back, sending him sprawling into the beanstalk.

It was the most painful experience of his life, and at the same time, the most numbing. There was an instant, no longer than the time it takes for a light switch to darken a room, which Jack's body felt as if it were being compacted, revolving into itself until it was no bigger than a pebble. Then, he had disappeared. Not just from this plane of existence, but from his very life. As if there had never been a Jackson Wilkes who had harvested wheat, planned food fights, or sent checks home to his mother. He was simply himself and then he wasn't.

When he came back, it was as if being born with a stranger's memories slamming into his mind at once. His nerves screamed as he exploded out like a party popper. And before his mind could grasp what he had done or his eyes could adjust to the sudden bright lights, he fell face first into the ground.

Turns out, extraterrestrial mud tasted surprisingly similar to Earth mud.

Hands slipped underneath his shoulders and armpits as he was hauled to his feet. It was only after he got the gunk out of his ears that he heard the laughter surrounding him. When he wiped away the dark black mud from his nose and mouth, he pushed up his goggles and gave a long-suffering look to Grise, who had suddenly appeared beside him. "Thanks for the help, sir."

This got the GRIM team laughing again. But Jack ignored it, finding his mouth gaping at his surroundings. The third generation probe had set up the harmonic gates in some sort of jungle. Not a normal green and brown jungle, but a contrasting blue and orange that made his pupils scream. The surrounding vegetation couldn't be described as trees—not when the exposed insides appeared as broken hoses and the leaves were concave, like deep serving bowls. He rubbed his eyes as he stared at one of the knocked over plants, realizing that, yes, the tubes leaked a thick, grey liquid that had a viscosity similar to mucus. His throat lurched.

"Shut her down, Wilkes," Grise said once Sasha stepped through.

Jack turned back to the landing site and opened the control panel a couple paces away from the three harmonic gates. He winced at the overheating registering on the gauges, realizing the humidity of the planet was already affecting the components. Luckily, it hadn't reached a critical point and he was able to easily power down the beanstalk.

All HARP probes were programmed to find stable ground upon which to construct the harmonic gates, but the wet mud and spongy undergrowth were not very promising. Jack placed his hand on one of the arcs and gave it a firm shake. It didn't give under his strength, which was a small relief. He stamped on the ground a few times, and while it wasn't as ideal as bedrock, it appeared the root structure would provide an acceptable stability for the harmonic gates until a Forefront Tech warped over to set up a new generation gate.

"Sir," Sasha said. She had been calibrating the small, handheld instrument since their arrival and ignoring the other soldiers' chat and laughter. "I think you should look at this."

A GRIM soldier—with a manic smile that barely emerged from his auburn, facial forest—rushed over to Sasha first, withdrawing a pulse weapon from his holster.

The Commander's face turned thoughtful as he looked at the instrument. He pressed a few buttons and swiped a few times at the screen. "Looks promising."

"Gargants, sir?" Squeakers asked, his pectoral muscles visibly flexing beneath his camo-suit, which was now a vibrant mix of blue and orange. The soldier beside him, freckled-face and picking his fingernails, rolled his eyes. Jack crossed his arms and tried to match Freckles' nonchalance.

"Probably not," Grise said, handing the device back to Sasha. "But it's promising."

"How close?" asked a rather unremarkable soldier that stood between Freckles and Beardy. Or at least Jack thought he had no distinguishing attributes he could mentally nickname him until he opened his mouth, exposing an array of missing and chipped teeth. Toothless it was.

"The reading is a few miles away," Sasha pointed at the patch of growth behind Jack. "Probably about two hours by foot if we take our time."

"Does this change anything for me?" Jack asked, withdrawing a wrench from his belt because…well, it just seemed like a good idea.

Grise withdrew an item from his pack and handed it to Jack. "Put that in your ear—we'll let you know when to put supper on the table."

"What about the updated arcs?" Jack asked, doing his best to shove the small, rubber transmitter into his ear.

"No warp travel until we confirm Gargant status," Beardy said, stepping forward to take the transmitter out of Jack's hand, flipping it horizontally and shoving it in Jack's ear canal. Before Jack could yelp at the sudden trauma, Beardy pressed his finger against the device. "Say something."

"What the hell are you doing?" Jack yelped, swatting him away. All the other GRIM members winced and held their hands to their ear.

Freckles sighed before he pressed his own finger to his ear. Jack could barely hear him in his left, unobstructed ear, but he came in perfectly on his right, "The transmitters are sensitive enough to pick up on sub-vocalizations, Screw-up. Anything louder than your normal voice blares the speaker."

Jack grimaced and pressed the transmitter in his ear as Beardy had done. "Sorry," he all but whispered. "But HARP wanted an updated arc as soon as possible. Can we at least open the gate once to bring over a Forefront Tech after I make sure these gates are stabilized?"

"Absolutely not," Grise said sharply, the first commanding note from the officer. "Nothing calls a Gargant faster than a beanstalk lighting up the sky."

"Oh," Jack said, gripping his wrench tighter. "Who's to say they aren't already here?"

"Because the readings would be getting closer, not stabilizing in one location," Sasha said, whose eyes had not moved from the handheld screen. Whose eyes had not looked at Jack once since they arrived.

"Get your stuff boys, we're going hunting!" Grise barked at the other soldiers who ooh-rahed in response.

Jack watched the team head out, led by Sasha and her handheld screen, realizing that they were indeed leaving him behind. He took a few steps after them, and waved his wrench feebly in the air. "Don't worry about me. I'm totally fine staying by myself!"

Against all odds, Jack got bored. It was a common side effect to his job, as Jack found it almost embarrassingly easy. He had grown up with old farm equipment and the stabilizing engines in these arc systems were similar to the hover combines back home. When Grise's transmitter updates indicated they wouldn't be back for a few hours, Jack had even overhauled the stabilizing engine. He was rewarded with a heaping pile of spare parts—junk that the systems didn't even need, as it usually just gummed up the works.

So Jack explored the area. It was wet. The tuberous plants spit grey mush at him if he stepped on their stems or dumped droplets of water on his head when he upset the immense, concave leaves. Or at least, he hoped it was water, considering he had accidentally gotten a mouthful of it. Touching the leaves while stretching and yawning wasn't really the best idea he ever had.

The only life he had come across were small reptilian creatures, colored the same cerulean tone as the leaky stems. At first, they seemed almost exactly like an Earth lizard, except they had a handful of tiny tails instead of one. They seemed friendly enough and they didn't appear to ooze any sort of poisonous excretion. So, boldly, Jack reached to pick up one of them. But before he could even get close, the little beast opened its mouth, exposing dozens of sharp, needle like teeth. As if this and the gargled hiss were not intimidating enough, it had launched its body to a nearby stem, instantly tearing the thing to shreds. When its long, black tongue almost happily lapped up the silver remains of the plant, Jack wondered if this was an herbivore simply eating or a warrior drinking the blood of its enemy. Despite the display of savagery, Jack thought it would be a good pet. Or a mascot. What better way to show how badass the Obsolete Department was then having an alien creature that could eat your face?

One hour later, Jack sat in the tubular jungle trying to construct a lizalien trap. He was in the middle of spare parts and cut off bulbous leaves, debating how to zap his new pet without killing it when Sasha's voice suddenly said, "What are you muttering?"

"Nothing!" Jack said, mildly surprised, instinctively shoving the trap made of very expensive HARP products and alien plant life under a tuber tree. But then he stopped, "Wait, I don't have my ear thingy pressed. How can you—?"

"I switched us on a private line," Sasha said

"Oh," Jack said. "Is something the matter?"

There was a long silence and Jack wasn't entirely sure if he needed to press into his transmitter or what, but eventually she responded. "We spread out to cover the area. Doesn't look like there's anything."

"Good," Jack replied.

More silence.

"… Does that mean I should open the gate to get a Forefront Tech over here?" Jack asked hesitantly, wondering if he had missed a cue somewhere.

"Not yet, we're still combing the area."

"Ah." The leaves tossed in a breeze, spraying water drops. Jack wiped away the liquid from his forehead, turning to focus on reassembling his lizalien trap. "Well hopefully you don't find—"

"Are you doing okay?"

Jack blinked.

"I should have asked how your first warp went. Are you doing okay?"

Jack felt the corners of his lips tuck up to his ears in a slow smile. "Yeah, I'm alright." He wouldn't mention how he had thrown up shortly after the GRIM team had left. Feeling bold by the sudden open communication, he added, "Physically impossible for me to not be awesome, remember?"

She gave a little huff of what might have been laughter. "Still, I'm sorry. I should have asked earlier."

"Don't worry. I know how you get."

"And how do 'I get'?"

"All I'm saying," Jack said hurriedly, at her sudden, hard voice, "is that I understand. This was a potential Gargant mission. Sergeant Chu is on duty. Not my lunch date."

For Jack, Gargants had always been more of a distant boogeyman than an actual threat. True, he had almost gone to the planet where they had first contacted the human race, but only just barely. Two years ago, HARP had tried to recruit Jack for their new facility on the 13th habitable planet, Boreas. But Jack, still clinging to the notion that he could escape the beanstalk, refused the generous offer. A few weeks later when his mom had broken her hip, he really wished had had taken the job and substantial paycheck. His mother had berated him at his initial refusal, but later the hospital, she had waved it off. "Who'd want to be on a planet of perpetual winter anyway?" she had said, patting his leg, trying to make him feel better.

After a few months, Jack was in the middle of harvesting their last field of corn when his neighbors drove up on a hovertruck and started shouting that the end was nigh. They were religious folk, who tended to view technology and moldy fruit as signs of the apocalypse, so Jack had waved them off. It had taken his mother, limping out on a crutch, shoving a portable vid screen in front of him, for Jack to take them seriously.

Snapshots of a frozen wasteland painted in bursts of red. Segments of survivors sobbing in interviews. But the worse was the security footage, showing the destruction the Gargantuan aliens inflicted not only on the new settlement, but also the HARP facility and cities of Chloris—the planet to which the Boreas habitants had tried to flee.

"They just suddenly appeared," one of the survivors had sobbed. "Without the use of a beanstalk. These Gargantuan—the Gargant… oh god." After that day, the number of human inhabited planets dropped from thirteen to eleven.

GRIM had been hastily assembled and were tasked with taking back Boreas and Chloris. But in the last year, when Gargants began to appear at HARP facilities all over the remaining eleven planets without the use of any beanstalk, GRIM's focus had switched from infiltration to protection. The random appearance of Gargants had also resulted in a lot of people quitting their jobs, which is how Jack got offered the Obsolete Tech position at the Earth based facility. The Gargants' random appearances at the HARP facilities had been the topic of Jack and Sasha's lunch one month ago, and Jack kept saying if Gargant transportation couldn't be explained by science, it could only mean one thing.

"They only show up at warp gates. If they were magical," Sasha had argued distastefully, as if the very word tasted worse than a protein chocolate bar, "they would just pop up anywhere."

"Maybe they only show up at warp gates because the first time they did it, they were greeted with a room full of tasty morsels," Jack had shrugged, ready to take another bite of his meal, but was met with a face full of water. Before he could blink it away, Sasha had already left the table.

A week later, Jack found out that Sasha was a former citizen of Chloris. A week after that, he found out Sasha's father had been one of those "tasty morsels" and was the reason why she had joined GRIM. Now, four weeks later, she was beginning to eat lunch again with him. But things had yet to go back to normal.

"I'm sorry, too," Jack said softly. "For...well...you know."

There was a beat. "Yeah. I know"

Jack smiled weakly. "You keep saying that." He swallowed hard, "But you haven't said anything about forgiving me."

"Jack..."

He closed his eyes and began laughing hopefully not too falsely. "You know what? Forget it. I don't even know why—"

"Ah, guys..." Squeakers distinct voice echoed in his ear. Stupidly, Jack moved to hide his trap again, before realizing that the others could not see him through the ear transmitter. "I found some footprints... big footprints."

That boredom Jack was suffering from earlier? Gone.

While Grise ordered the GRIM squad to meet up at Squeaker's location, Jack did his best not to freak out. Wildly, he looked at his lizalien trap, wondering how many he could catch and if he would be able to weaponize them. His breathing became heavy, flaring on his face in the damp, wet air. It must have been loud because Sasha said, "Calm down, Jack. Just because we found footprints, doesn't mean they're here." Her voice had taken on that cold, hard edge, and he knew that it was Sergeant Chu talking to him.

"Yeah," Jack said. He found his screwdriver in his belt and began tapping it on his goggles. "Maybe this is just their summer home."

"Everything will be fine," she said, more firmly. "I'll make sure of it."

"Stop flirting with me, Sasha," he laughed. Or tried to. He kind of choked on his tongue.

"I'm serious, Jack."

"You're always seri—"

A roar exploded, forcing Jack to yelp and rip out the transmitter before it blew out his eardrum. The guttural sound didn't disappear, but echoed in the direction the GRIM team had gone. When it stopped, he held the transmitter up to his ear, "Sasha!" he called out desperately. But he was drowned out by the GRIM squad's status updates and shouts to move, move, MOVE!

Jack was frozen, holding on to his screwdriver in a vice-like grip. Another bellow ripped through the jungle. His throat became thick, swelling up, making him choke on his breath. His body went rigid, unable to break from his half-kneeling stance. Another roar came, this time causing several lizaliens to scamper around Jack, as if thinking he was a good hiding spot from the oncoming destruction. Small voices cracked out from the ear transmitter he still held in his hand. He heard his name, but still he could not move.

I told Sasha she could count on me. I told her that I could do this!

But his mind kept flashing to the bloody snow of Boreas and the security footage of the ravaged Chloris cities and HARP facility. His throat closed and the phrase "tasty morsel" was on an endless repeat. He heard Sasha's diminutive voice yell his name from the distant transmitter. A lizalien crawled up Jack's arm and burrowed under the collar of his jumpsuit. But still he remained, unmoving in his fear.

Then he felt it.

Vibrations. Muted and slight, but still being carried across the undergrowth. With every tremor, he forced his neck to move, feeling the flex of every muscle fiber, the scream of every nerve, the crack of every vertebrate. And only after he had leaned forward past the tubular stem, he finally caught sight of the harmonic arcs.

They were moving.

It flipped whatever switch had gotten turned off by the Gargant's roar. Jack got up, sprinting and diving on his knees. He held the first outward arc, feeling it sway with every pounding step. He glanced over desperately to his pile of spare parts from the stabilizer engine overhaul, but no supporting beams or ionic fusion guns magically appeared. Jack shoved the transmitter back in his ear.

"WILKES!" Grise screamed.

Jack pressed his finger in his ear, "Sir, we've got a problem."

"NO SHIT!" Grise yelled back. "I don't see a beanstalk in the sky!"

"Sir, the vibrations," he swallowed hard. "The gates need to be stable to grow the beanstalk."

"Then make them stable!"

"I don't have any materials!"

"Then warp back to—"

"If I warp back now, I could blow up the harmonic arcs completely!"

A brief radio silence, and then, "Just find a way; we'll be there in ten minutes!"

Jack swore loudly, ripping the goggles from his forehead, grasping clumps of his hair in frustration. What could he do? All he had were spare parts and half made lizalien trap.

As if to punctuate his frustration, a lizalien, which had latched on to his pant leg, launched toward a tuber plant, biting like a little chainsaw into the base of the stem. Grey liquid exploded on the creature, which he devoured, leaving the huge stem laying on the ground.

And then Jack had an idea.

Eight minutes later, he had done the best he could with the tubes the lizaliens had left in their wake. It wasn't perfect, but it was good enough for at least one warp opening. At least, he hoped it was good enough. He had finished wrapping the very flexible, grey gushing tubes around the second arc, tying and securing it to the various other plants in the area. It gave it a wider base of support, which Jack estimated would at least give the beanstalk a few minutes. Providing the Gargant didn't rip up the plants.

By the time Jack moved to the third and final arc, Grise's voice had gone hoarse from screaming about seeing a beanstalk. But when he abruptly cut off, Jack paused to shove his finger in his ear. "Commander?"

"Jack!" Sasha replied instead, her voice out of breath and cracking. "We need that beanstalk now!"

"I need one more minute!" Jack shouted back, his hands furiously tying knots in the tubes, continuously slipping on their grey blood.

"You don't have a minute!" Sasha shouted. Now that Jack was listening for it, he could hear the rubbery sound of the plants knocking against each other. They were almost here. He shook his head dumbly, "But I..."

"DO IT!"

Jack dropped the tube he was working on, and ran over to the central console. He went through the ignition process as fast as he could, holding the gate closest to him, the one he had not finished securing, with his other free hand. When the process was complete, Jack pulled his goggles over his eyes before quickly gripping the last shuddering arc with both hands. With his assistance, the warp gate stabilized, allowing the magic bean to activate and grow into an emerald sprout as it connected to its identical half back on Earth. Soon enough, the vine became a thick stalk, large enough for even Squeakers to step through.

It wasn't a moment too soon. Freckles erupted from the tubular forest first, diving into the warp gate without a word. Jack felt a sudden shudder and was forced to practically hug the damn thing to keep it steady. The vine shrank slightly, but grew back with Jack's support.

Sasha and Squeakers came out next, carrying an unconscious, bloodied Toothless between them. Jack asked, "Where is—?"

"Grise is buying us time and Anderlan is gone," Sasha said, focusing on helping Toothless into Squeaker's beefy arms. A powerful footstep slammed the ground, causing Jack to grip the gate tighter as the vine wavered. "You two. Go!" she shouted.

Squeakers nodded, stepping into the beanstalk with Toothless, disappearing in a curled flash. Jack cried out when the warp light shrank almost to nothing, laughing in relief when it grew back to normal size.

"You next," Sasha said.

Jack nodded and was about to do just that, when he realized he couldn't. It seemed odd that he hadn't thought of that earlier. That letting go of the arc would mean that he would not be able to warp back home. That he would either cut down the beanstalk or blow the harmonic gates apart if he did. How could he have been so focused, so determined to fulfill Sasha's request that he had completely blocked out that simple conclusion? Even now, he refused to face it. Instead, he looked to the ground, and spoke as nonchalantly as possible, as though Gargants weren't approaching. As though his life was not coming to an end.

"I still got some rhubarb bars from my mom's last care package. Make sure you get it before my roommate does," Jack said.

She stepped toward him, her tone still that of Sergeant Chu. "Jack, I'll hold the arc."

"If you don't want them, give it to Toothless. I don't think cavities are going to make much of a difference at this point."

"You will follow my orders, Wilkes!" she shouted over a monstrous step from behind them.

"I still fully expect you to execute that food fight I planned. But remember, you got to wait for tofu and chickpea day. They are the most disgusting and deserve to be wasted."

"Quit talking about food, Jack!" her voice cracked, prompting Jack to finally look at her. He almost wished he hadn't. Her face would be the third thing that killed him today with the first being the beanstalk and the last being... He wanted to reach out to her, hug her, maybe even more. But he couldn't. "I won't let you do this," she demanded, stepping toward him.

He smiled widely, convincing himself that his face was wet due to the water from the tuber leaves. He braced his right leg and lifted his left discreetly behind her knees, "Forgive me, Sasha."

Before she could realize the poor placement of her feet, Jack kicked her low from behind. The mud, which Jack had fallen into upon arrival, assisted him now as it allowed the normally nimble Sasha to slide forward haphazardly. She leaned heavily to the side, trying to avoid the light as she stumbled, clawing at Jack's arm. But then her elbow grazed just a curl of the vine.

And then she was gone.

Jack kept the smile on his lips as he stretched one shaking arm to the console and slammed the emergency shut off switch. The mass of green light disappeared with a shudder. He hummed a little tune as he whacked the arcs and console with the heaviest wrench on his belt, ensuring that it would not become operational again. And when sobs still threatened to overcome his throat at the incoming footsteps, Jack forced out a bark of laughter as he stumbled into the forest, finding cover under a patch of tubers. The footsteps vibrated directly into Jack's brain and he held his hands over his mouth to staunch the peculiar mixture of hyperventilation and laughter.

It was only when half the rumbling desisted that Jack realized that there were two sets of heavy footsteps. One of which had stopped at the warp landing site, the other—shortly thereafter—at the same location. For a moment, Jack heard nothing. Nothing except his crazed breathing. After a few minutes of this nauseating silence, he slowly withdrew his hands from his lips and pushed up his goggles. And when he drew in a gulp of air, he expelled it immediately at a Gargant's scream.

Jack ducked his head into the dirt. But his ostrich equivalent defense mechanism did nothing to desensitize him from the flicks of dirt that pelted into his hair as a Gargant stepped towards him.

After a display of bravery that was most certainly premeditated and not accidentally brought about, Jackson Wilkes sacrificed himself heroically and died by the foot, not hands or even mouth, the foot of a Gargant, making his death probably an official first for all victims of the Gargant wars.

Only upon threat of suffocation did Jack finally raise his head from the soil. A giant toe, roughly the size of his head, was pointed directly at him. The flesh of the giant invaders was normally greyish-brown, but as this foot had been tromping through the same mud-laden forest that had decorated Jack's jumpsuit, it was nearly black. The foot rose clear above him, dripping plops of wet mud and grey tuber juice all over him, setting down safely a couple feet away from Jack's body.

A giggle bubbled up inside of him, but he bit into his forearm to stop its escape. *Not what I thought laughing in the face of danger would be like*, he thought hysterically, knowing he was two steps away from a full mental breakdown.

The Gargants began making sounds. Sort of grumbles and grunts that weaved together with tongue clucks and twirls. Gargant speech. He blamed his oxygen-deprived brain for making his body crawl closer. He ducked beneath a few squashed tubers, using them as camouflage as he finally got a good look at the monsters.

The Gargants towered high above him, gesturing toward the ground where the broken warp gate laid. Their hands fanned the air around Jack, as their huge arms swung about. A bout of silent laughter came up once more as Jack imagined the Gargants swinging their arms around their bodies gleefully, like a child playing jump rope. Their coverings weren't really clothing, more like scales grown on specific parts of their body, reflecting like gasoline in the sunlight. And just like every other Gargant, their coverings only accent was a round, gold emblem at the top of their right shoulder.

The taller of the two, who had been standing quietly as the other had rambled on, suddenly bared its teeth at the smaller Gargant, making a deep throaty noise laced with hisses. The Gargant's razor thin teeth were intimidating enough, but coupled with black-orbed eyes and a red dribbled chin, they were the stuff of nightmares.

The larger Gargant brought a hand to its face to wipe away the blood. Jack swallowed hard, trying not to think of Grise or Beardy, which only made Jack feel callous for not even knowing the name of the dead soldier. What had Sasha said— Amberland? Anderson? But Jack stopped thinking to turn and gag when the monster licked its hand with a swoop of its scarlet tongue.

Jack had thought saving Sasha would be enough. To a point, it was. If he died, knowing that he had at least accomplished that, he would be okay. But now, having lived longer than the fifteen seconds he had estimated, he felt cheated. All of the clever exit lines or dramatic passionate embraces he could have done... heroic actions were apparently wasted on him.

The smaller Gargant squatted, reaching forward into the warp gate wreckage. There was no way it would work again. Even if they were engineering geniuses, their fingers couldn't handle the delicate work to put it back together. But when the giant's fingers grazed the wreckage, it stopped moving.

Jack leaned a little out of his tuberous hiding spot, noting how the taller Gargant stepped beside his squatting companion and placed a hand on its left shoulder. Jack frowned, not understanding why they both weren't moving. Or doing anything for that matter. It was only when a light flashed from the squatting Gargant's right shoulder did Jack notice something strange. The gold emblem had popped off the grey-brown flesh of the giant. Jack's eyes only grew larger when instead of dropping to the ground, it unfurled and revealed wings, flapping sharply in the air as it descended to the wreckage.

What the hell?

The winged creature looked like a duck, or maybe a goose, but without eyes and feathers. It had a long neck and a sharp beak that poked into the middle of the wrecked gates. The sound, while not annoying like the honking of a goose, was grating in its own right, reminding Jack of his roommate's nightly gargling rituals.

Is this golden goose thing going to fix the gate?

The goose gave an abrupt hack and flew back up into the air with something held in its beak. The two Gargants stood up straight, the taller of the two still grasping the other by the shoulder. But instead of flying back to the shorter giant, it flew to other, melding with the taller Gargant's golden goose emblem.

The gargling sound started again, this time twice as loud as it had been before. Jack was starting to feel awkward and grossed out, not certain if he was watching some sort of bizarre mating ritual. He felt that gag reflex especially when the golden geese began to vibrate and the Gargants bared their teeth in wide grins.

Thankfully, the golden goose separated from the other and fluttered back into the nook on the smaller Gargant's shoulder. As soon as the winged creature settled, the taller giant released his grip on his companion and backed away.

Well. I'm completely confused, Jack thought hopelessly.

The smaller Gargant bowed its head and placed its hand over the golden goose. The taller monster kept backing away, until he was about as far away as Jack was from the smaller Gargant. And then they just…stood there again.

In a few minutes, Jack's mud-coated hair began to prickle and stand up straight. Even the tubers seem to lean in towards the smaller Gargant. The lizalien, previously burrowed under Jack's collar, poked its head out and licked to taste the energy in the breeze. The air was buzzing soundlessly, like a mixture of raw electricity underlain with the beat of a heavy bass. Jack stared at the Gargant, not noticing anything different at first, until he looked at its feet. The soles seemed to glow a faint green. But instead of curling and cracking like the green light with which Jack was familiar, it was steady and stable and slowly growing brighter.

Jack realized the moment before the beast screamed what was happening. But before he could do anything or even think of anything, the Gargant disappeared.

Holy shit. Jack scrambled backward in the dirt. *HOLY SHIT!*

The taller Gargant stepped into the clearing. Like the other one before, it clasped a hand over its golden goose and bowed its head.

Is that why they warp near the gates? Jack thought, staring at the wreckage. *Do those geese somehow find and replicate the magic beans from the HARP warp gates? But that's impossible. Only unimatter can replicate other unimatter…right?*

Jack's thoughts became a full-on conversation with himself.

If I assume beanstalks and Gargant travel operate the same way, it would mean Gargants are made of antimatter and this golden goose thing would be made of unimatter. Okay, that sounds completely ridiculous, but… that would allow the geese to copy the magic beans and they would get the fuel they need for the warp jumps from the Gargant. Of course, I'm assuming the geese are sentient and able to consciously lift its absorbing protection when necessary. Wow…I'm starting to think this makes sense, which is a bad sign.

The air was starting to buzz again.

The lizalien in his collar begin to squirm as his hair sparked in static electricity.

I'm probably wrong. And this is all pointless anyway because living beings can't be composed of antimatter or unimatter. The HARP scientists with master's degrees would have discovered that by now. Not some Screw-up. Not me.

The green glow started to appear.

But if I'm right…

The Gargant was grinding its teeth, the process obviously coming to the painful conclusion.

"Screw it!"

Jack exploded from the tubers he had been hiding beneath and ran as fast as his skinny legs could possibly move, straight to the Gargant. The monster noticed and screamed in the air and Jack could only scream back, pushing himself that little extra bit. The light was vibrant now, almost blinding. He was almost there. He just had to—

Unlike the beanstalk, there was no crushing vortex. No vast of nothingness. He was simply in one place and then the next. Had Jack been holding on to anything but a nasty Gargant foot, he might have sat and appreciated the sheer wonder of it. But as the bellowing beast seemed quite irate that it had picked up a hitchhiker, Jack made due with briefly kissing the gleaming gold floor as he skidded across the room straight into the supply cabinets.

Through his hazy OhmigodIcan'tbelievethatworked euphoria and the incredible pain from being thrown across a metal-enforced floor, the shouts of the GRIM response team barely registered. He got up slowly, partly from shock and partly because his knees were about to give out from under him. Eventually, he remembered how to walk and began to stagger his way toward the doorway where a group of GRIM soldiers had erected a barricade.

As Jack half stumbled and half floated toward the door, the distorted air vibrations from the pulse weapons abruptly changed into focused green beams. Antimatter guns. If one of those blasts hit anything but the Gargants or unimatter walls and ceilings, it risked bringing the roof down on their heads. Jack risked a look at the shorter Gargant, which was taking the brunt of the attack. Any human would have disintegrated by now, but that Gargant only howled in rage. But now that Jack knew what to look for, he could see the golden goose nestled into the Gargant's shoulder—glowing.

The golden geese are protecting them from annihilation, Jack thought. *That's why military weapons won't work on them. There's got to be some non-energy based ammunition we can—*

Jack drew in a sharp breath. He abruptly turned around and made his way to the supply corner he had crashed into.

"Someone get the Screw-up out of here!" a voice bellowed.

"JACK!" Sasha's voice cut through the Gargants' shouts and wreckage. But Sasha wasn't the only one running toward him. The taller Gargant had decided that weaponless Jack was much less of a hassle than the GRIM soldiers. "RUN!"

"HOLD ON!" Jack called back, wading his way through a pile of junk he had knocked over to get to the obsolete cabinet. He opened the door and felt a disturbance in the air behind him. His pursuer let out a loud bellow, and Jack turned to see that Sasha had aimed her gold antimatter gun directly into his foot. But instead of a gaping hole, only a patch of smoking skin was left behind. Jack's hands dove into the shelves, throwing things behind him.

"Get out of here now, Jack!" Sasha yelled at him, dancing between the Gargant's huge stumbling limbs, shooting directly into its skin, avoiding its monstrous fingers.

"Got it!" Jack breathed, gripping his hand tightly around the pneumatic rivet gun used for first generation gates. Heavy and dangerous as hell. He fumbled with a portable air compression container, screwing it on as Sasha took on the Gargant by herself. He shouted in triumph when he shot a test rivet into the cabinet, careful not to pierce the unimatter wall. He turned and took a careful shot.

The rivet hit the Gargant square in the chest, not having the power to reach its intended gold target. The Gargant, while not as disturbed by this as Sasha's blasts, still noticed and bared its still red, dripping teeth toward Jack.

He tried to run. He really did. But backed in a corner with two bum knees, all he could manage was to open his mouth and say, "Oh."

As the Gargant's fingers curled around Jack, he resisted his ostrich-defense instincts and raised his arms above his head so his hands, and more importantly, his rivet gun would be free from the monster's grasp. The grip was tight and Jack could barely breathe as he was hefted up to the giant's face. Sasha's screams echoed in his ears, disrupted only by the blasts of her antimatter gun. The Gargant's eyes narrowed into black slits, allowing Jack to see his reflection almost perfectly. Muddied face. Terror-filled expression. And a patch of blue peeking out of his jumpsuit collar.

Huh. Guess I am going to get that mascot after all.

"Well, Shredder," Jack wheezed to the lizalien, aiming the rivet gun to the gold patch in the Gargant's shoulder. "I really hope this works." The Gargant was so close Jack could smell its breath, which reeked of decomposing flesh. Jack took the largest breath he could manage, and pulled the trigger.

The Gargant froze. Jack swore his eyes widened in fear as he craned his neck to look at his shoulder. The golden goose, which had been glowing, was slowly flickering and leaking a white substance by the five rivets Jack had shot into it. Jack, fearing what would come next, began to struggle with every ounce of his strength against the Gargant's grip. But it was Shredder that saved the day by tearing into the grey fingers of the Gargant's hand with same enthusiasm Jack had seen in the tuber forest.

The Gargant howled and dropped him to the floor, almost directly on top of Sasha.

"Jack!" Sasha shouted, helping him to his feet. "How did you—?"

"We've got to move," Jack said, limping as fast as he could toward the doors.

"But—"

"If I'm right, that Gargant is going to turn into an anti-matter bomb in a matter of seconds!"

Sasha, although clearly confused, was very willing to lead him out of danger and not ask questions. She led Jack back to the doors where the other GRIM officers were still pounding away at the shorter intruder. The taller invader emitted an entirely new sound: a high-pitched shriek, almost like a whistle. The smaller Gargant no longer tried to advance on the GRIM team, but rather tried to get to his companion. But the pulse weapons froze him in place.

"Get out and shut the door now!" Jack yelled when they had reached the barricade.

"But—"

"DO IT!" Sasha ordered, nearly throwing Jack into the empty hallway.

The soldiers looked baffled, but did as they asked. They kept their pulse weapons blasting, until the last soldier had gotten into the hallway. Jack kept his eyes on the taller Gargant, who was kneeling on the ground, holding a hand against his shoulder, and emitting that hair-curling shriek. And just as the door closed shut, Jack made out the flash of green light erupting from the gaps of the taller Gargant's fingers as his companion reached for him.

The huge blast registered in Jack's ears for only a millisecond before faint ringing took its place. And although the unimatter-sealed door did its job in absorbing the energy of the blast, it expanded outward, bulging, shoving several soldiers away from it abruptly, knocking them against the wall and, in one case, Jack's skull.

Things were a bit of a blur after that.

Sasha, who had somehow wrapped her fingers between Jack's without him noticing, kept gripping his hand. It wasn't as pleasant as one might think as she only squeezed when he was ready to nod off into unconsciousness with enough force to bruise his knuckles. But she stayed by his side, motioning out what he assumed to be orders, as GRIM soldiers—and eventually, GRIM medics—swarmed the area. At one point, one of the medics tried to give him medical attention, but a black, long tongue shot in the air from his neck, causing the medic to step back abruptly and trip over another soldier.

"Shredder made it," he smiled, hearing his voice as if it were under water and trapped in a box. When a soldier aimed a gun at his shoulder from where the black tongue had emerged, Jack held out a hand and tried to express that this was the Obsolete Technology Department's new mascot and that it should receive some sort of medal for saving his life. But his head got a little fuzzier the more he tried to talk, and soon enough, Sasha's crushing fingers were no longer able to perform its wake-up duty.

When he came to, he was in an all-white room. He noticed Sasha immediately, who perked up and leaned forward in her chair. "Jack?"

His grin cracked the corners of his dry lips. "Hey. I can hear."

"Good. Now you can hear me call you an idiot." She gripped his fingers, which he realized had been in her hand before he had woken up.

This only made Jack grin wider, "Your bedside manner needs work."

She tilted her head. "Do you realize this is the second antimatter explosion you've caused?"

He chuckled and winced at the accompanying pain. "But since it killed two Gargants, people will stop calling me Screw-up, right?" An amused silence was his answer. He frowned and shifted into a more comfortable position, "Is Shredder okay?"

"Shredder?"

"My pet. The one that saved me from the Gargant."

Sasha shook her head, a very small smirk on her lip. "If you're referring to the alien life form that followed you back home, it is currently in the biological research lab. He already bit the Forefront Tech that delivered him."

"Sorry about that," Jack said, his grin so wide and gleeful, it conveyed anything but.

Sasha opened her mouth, apparently ready to reprimand him, but instead, she softened and said, "I forgive you."

Then the most amazing thing he had seen all day happened. Sasha smiled. Not the Sasha smirk, but an actual smile that exposed her teeth and lifted the corners of her eyes. Jack felt the bruised part of his chest, which was basically the entirety of it, clench. He was afraid that if he took a single breath, it would disappear. It was radiant. It was perfect. It was the wonder of the galaxy that he had hoped to see when he had prepared his eulogy. He drew her hand into both of his shaking palms and even though he had been beaten and nearly eaten, Jack smiled back and whispered, "Worth it."

AJ BAUERS finally accomplished her secret dream of writing a novel one year ago. Since then, she has packed her bags and moved from North Dakota to Maine to enroll in the University of Southern Maine's Masters program in Popular Fiction. *The Screw-Up* is AJ's first publication on her path to becoming a full-time writer. Follow her blog, listed below, for short stories and more.

LINKS

http://ajbauers.wordpress.com
https://twitter.com/AJBauers

Forbidden Fruit

by Carina Bissett

The desires of the heart are as crooked as corkscrews,
Not to be born is the best for man;
The second-best is a formal order,
The dance's pattern; dance while you can.
Dance, dance, for the figure is easy,
The tune is catching and will not stop;
Dance till the stars come down from the rafters;
Dance, dance, dance till you drop.
~W.H. Auden

KAREN watched shadows dance on the ceiling as she waited for her clock to sound the alarm. Even though she'd been awake for hours, she refused to get up, to step outside of the rigid boundaries she'd created for living her life. After all, dark thoughts have no place in an ordered world; that's the way she meant to keep it.

The clock buzzed, alerting her of the hour. She ignored it and closed her eyes.

Don't drag your feet, Karen, she told herself. *Get up.*

Calm and collected, she pushed the sheets aside and went through the motions of her morning routine, attempting to distract herself from her afternoon appointment. Her mother would just have to wait.

In the bathroom, she tidied her silvery blonde hair in a tight chignon, firmly jabbing pins into the mass. Neutral makeup and a sweep of nude lipstick finished her severe look, a practiced attempt at dimming her beauty. On the few occasions men had tried to get her attention, she'd had to resort to cruelty in order to keep them away. Better to stop advances before they even started.

She sighed and stepped into the drab, olive green suit she'd set out the night before—properly pressed and accompanied with the exact shade of matching shoes, of course. A final sweep of the bedroom affirmed everything was in its place. Satisfied, she turned off the light and went to retrieve the newspaper from the front stoop.

Once in the kitchen, she looked around in disgust. Spilled coffee, breadcrumbs, and a glob of strawberry jam marked up the white counter tiles. Paintbrushes lay next to the porcelain sink, which was spotted with runny splashes of orange and purple paint. It was as if the chaos of the universe was making itself known in the form of her wild cousin, Ginny.

A memory from her youth sneaked past her borders to taunt her—a sink stacked with dirty dishes, cockroaches creeping in the cupboards, and trash littered on stained countertops. Karen pushed the thought aside and began the process of tidying up her cousin's mess. *Never should have let her stay here,* she thought, upset at the disruption in her well-ordered life. *Only two more days.*

Under her capable hands the kitchen quickly took on its proper guise, gleaming in the early morning light. After everything had been restored to its proper place, she settled herself at the table with a cup of Earl Grey and nibbled a piece of dry toast as she read the business section.

Less than an hour later, Karen sat at her desk, flipping through financials. As usual, the day followed her rigid and methodical calendar. Today, however, she kept glancing at the clock. Time sped up and, with each passing minute, her dread increased. When her phone alarm went off, Karen jumped in her chair.

"Don't be silly," she said to herself as she slipped her shoes on and pushed away from the desk. "You can do this."

Stopping to smooth her chignon, she glanced at herself in the mirror next to the office door. Dark eyes stared back at her from a pale face. She frowned. *There's nothing to be afraid of, Karen,* she reminded herself. *You're safe now.*

The door slammed behind her as she rushed away from her office and the ghost of the girl trapped in the mirror.

"I'm leaving for the afternoon," she snapped at the receptionist.

"Yes, Ms. Klein."

Karen glared at the brunette in her form-fitting red dress. *Jackson and his bimbos.*

"This is an office, not a bar," she said. "Dress appropriately."

"Yes, Ms. Klein." The receptionist lowered her eyes, but the tight set of her mouth displayed amused annoyance even though her tone stayed respectful.

For a moment, Karen thought about firing the girl then and there, but she knew Jackson would intervene. Her boss reminded her of her father, except Jackson never looked at her. He was too busy with the young, dark-haired vixens he plowed through on a regular basis. *If only his wife knew.*

"Tomorrow, Renee," she said. *It's for your own good.*

Karen marched out of the lobby, determined to get her distasteful errand of mercy done and over with as soon as possible.

By the time she arrived at the hospital, the afternoon sun had begun its earnest race toward the jagged mountains in the west. With a sigh, she stepped from the curb and headed towards the floral shop in a nondescript, outdoor shopping mall.

It was because of her mother's failing health that Karen walked the rush-hour streets of this city settled in the Sonoran Desert's harsh climate. Even after a year of living here, she found Phoenix eerily empty and nondescript with its cookie cutter housing developments and stuccoed strip malls caught in a sea of dust and dun—so unlike Boston and its Old World glamour. She heaved a sigh thinking of dappled bridges, sun-warmed brick and profusions of delicate blooms drifting on gentle spring breezes.

At that exact moment she saw them—waiting for her in a storefront window that looked as if it would have been more at home in Boston than this dead city. Redder than newly spilt blood, scales glistening in the dying light of the sun. Never before had she seen anything like them—slippers made from a reptile's skin and stained the truest color of life. The tall heels flowed into smoothly sinuous insteps and then down to the perfectly curved toes. Slinky straps draped into the shoes, waiting for slender ankles to embrace. And the shadowy recesses, deep within the shoes, beckoned with promises of a darker kind.

The vintage store stood next to the flower shop, stopping her progress. It seemed a world away from her mother's bedside. Earlier that afternoon, she had sat watching the life ebb from her mother's overworked body into the sterile air. White upon white, the room seemed broken only by surgical steel and the tiniest bits of pale greens and blues. The face she had both loved and hated from her youth blended with the pillow propped behind her mother's sagging neck. Crisp sheets lay tucked close to her chin. Mottled purple spots flecked fragile skin covering brittle bones. But it wasn't the paleness, the bloated figure, or the bulging veins that made Karen recoil in horror. It was her mother's ankles—ankles that once had seemed so sturdy and weather worn. Now all that was left was swollen, black flesh.

During the short visit, Karen had kept her own legs crossed, as if to ward off a curse. Abruptly, she left with the excuse of needing to get flowers for her mother, needing to escape the realization that one day it could very well be her lying there—a broken shadow of a broken woman.

Dusk began to creep across the street. Shadows grew bolder. Karen shook herself from her dazed musings and started towards the flower shop, but the shoes held her gaze. With a quick pivot, she strode into the shop and demanded the blood-red slippers even as she pulled a credit card from her wallet. The old woman behind the dusty countertop smiled a toothless smile. "Ah," she grinned. "They have caught your fancy, have they?"

The old woman lifted the shoes reverently from the window front, an odd grin crossing her mouth. It was then, when she had stepped from behind the screening counter, that Karen saw that the woman had no feet. Her legs ended in stumps fitted with shiny plastic prosthetics.

Karen's hand fluttered to her mouth, capturing a gasp.

The old woman looked back and chuckled knowingly. "I danced them right off, don't you know?" She lurched back to the support of the counter. "Do you like to dance, I wonder?"

Karen shook her head. "No," she said. "I don't dance." She slid the plastic card across the glass.

"Well perhaps they will make you change your mind. Stranger things have happened, you know?" said the old woman as she slipped the shoes into a black handled bag.

Karen signed the sales slip with a shaky hand and nearly ran from the store. She was halfway home before she realized that she had forgotten all about her mother's flowers.

The shoes sat silently at her side.

Strains of a waltz brought a smile to Karen's lips, which were painted a pretty pink from a lipstick found in her mother's makeup case. She giggled when Daddy took her plump little fingers in his own strong hands. "Dance with me baby," he crooned, smiling a broad grin that crinkled his eyes and showed his even, white teeth.

Sooo happy, Karen thought, dancing with Daddy. She looked at Daddy's big feet and his shiny brown shoes. She grabbed his large hands and delicately placed her own little slippered feet on his and he began swirling her around the room. Her pink dress flared out around her like a pinwheel. "Weee!" she shouted. "I'm a princess at a ball." She looked up and saw her mother watching with a frown. Confused, Karen ducked her head and looked at Daddy's strong feet carrying her around the room.

"Then I must be your prince," Daddy said. Karen looked up questioningly at Daddy's wide blue eyes.

"What about Mommy?" Karen asked. But her mother was gone.

Blaring psychedelic music roused Karen from a deep sleep. She went to raise her hand to her face before realizing that her fingers were entwined in the straps of the red shoes lying at her side. She shook them loose, rubbed her eyes, and peered at the clock on her radio. The glowing lights indicated it was seven minutes past noon.

She looked harder. *It can't be,* she thought. She shrugged back the covers, slipped into a pair of jeans and a white blouse, and gathered up her newest possession before padding out of her bedroom. Ginny met her in the kitchen, dancing in front of an unfinished canvas with brushes grasped in nimble fingers. Her dreadlocks swayed sinuously in time with the music, looking almost as if they had a life of their own. Ginny's sculpted face broke into a grin when Karen caught her gaze.

"Hey. I was wondering about you."

"Humph," Karen snorted. "What in the hell are you doing?"

"Painting."

Karen peered at the emerging figures on the canvas and, for the first time, saw hints of beauty in her cousin's chaotic creation. "I see."

Not wanting to wait for the water to boil, she poured a cup of black coffee and set some bread in the toaster.

"You look like shit," Ginny said as she peered over Karen's shoulder. "Are you sick?"

"No. Would you turn that down for a minute so I can call work?"

Ginny grinned. "No problem."

Karen called in for the day, something she'd never done in her entire working career. After hanging up the receiver, Karen looked down at Ginny's feet where paint-spattered newspapers lay strewn beneath her cousin's newest masterpiece.

"Is it too much too hope for that the paper on the floor is from yesterday?"

Ginny bared her teeth in a voluptuous smile, turned up the volume and dipped a brush into a pot of neon green. Karen sighed.

She sat down at the table, sweeping aside nightclub flyers, art books and CD jackets to create a place for her meager breakfast. She placed the shoes on a pedestal of art books and folded her hands beneath her chin as she gazed at their luster, their sinuous beauty. Ginny peeked from behind her canvas, brush poised in midair as she looked at the red shoes.

"Wicked," she exclaimed before once again dipping her brush.

Karen ignored her, reaching for the knife stuck in a jar of strawberry jam. She smeared the fruity preserves on her toast and took a sweet bite, all the while staring at the red shoes. The desire to wear them made her feet throb.

Ginny stepped aside from her finished canvas and washed her brushes, splashing color across the counter and sink. She wiped her hands on paint-smeared jean cutoffs and plunked down in a chair next to Karen.

"I'm going dancing tonight," she said. "Wanna go?"

"I don't dance," Karen replied, eyes still fixed on her new shoes.

"That's an understatement. You don't even go out, ever—not in high school, not in college and not now. You're twenty-six years old and have never been kissed."

Oh yes, I have. Karen's cheeks flushed. "You don't know anything about me," she snapped. "I'm working on my career. I don't have time for a series of ridiculous relationships. And I certainly have no intention of going to a bar. I don't even drink."

Ginny shrugged her shoulders. "Suit yourself," she said. The kitchen chair screeched as she pushed it back. "See you later. I'm going shopping for a new canvas." She tapped white teeth with a paint-splattered fingernail. "Maybe some new colors."

Karen looked back at the shoes. Shopping suddenly sounded like a good idea. Nothing in her closet would go with the shoes—not even close. So she picked them up, grabbed her purse, and followed Ginny out of the condo.

"Where you going?" Ginny asked.

"Out," Karen said as she slid into her tan Volvo.

"It's about time."

When Karen backed out of the driveway she looked in her rearview mirror to see Ginny watching her with a secretive smile on her face.

All day, Karen went from store to store, mall to mall, searching for the perfect dress to go with her new acquisition. But nothing caught her fancy—nothing could complete or complement the color and style of those snakeskin shoes. Finally, in a frustrated fury, Karen stormed into AJ's Fine Foods with her red shoes tucked beneath her arm. She walked down the aisles looking for something to assuage the insatiable hunger growing within her. At the produce aisle, she stopped and surveyed the fresh and exotic fare. She filled her basket with succulent delights—juicy strawberries, shiny apples, and smooth cherries. Then she added red pears, raspberries, bloodfruit, globe grapes, prickly pear fruit, and pomegranates.

Back at home, Karen lit some of Ginny's candles on the coffee table and rinsed the bag of cherries. Her cousin was off on her rounds in the clubs. Karen plopped herself on the floor to stare at the red shoes. She popped a cherry in her mouth, rolling it on her tongue before biting into the lush orb. Lost in thought, she pulled the seed from between her lips and tossed it on the table. The smell of cinnamon hung in a heavy cloud as the candles tasted the air with flickering tongues of flame. She traced the shoes' exotic, crimson curves, wondering their origin. The delicate stitching and intricate handwork made her think that they were one of a kind. But who had made them and why?

Her feet ached to wear them.

Brow creased in thought, Karen held another dark cherry above her lips, running her tongue across its unblemished skin. And when she finally sank in her teeth, its ripe juices ran down her chin.

Karen leaned forward, running a finger along the right shoe's edge, dipping into the instep. Munching cherries with wicked abandon, she investigated every curve, every hollow of those scarlet snakeskin shoes. Only when her fingertips reached into the glass bowl to discover that all of the cherries had been consumed did she leave off her explorations. Cherry pits lay strewn on the coffee table embedded in pools of melted wax. Karen pinched out the candles' guttering flames, cradled the shoes to her chest and headed to bed—to ancient dreams, to dancing in the dark.

Karen watched the delicate ballerina spinning against the backdrop of her white and gold jewelry box lid. A bright melody tinkled an accompaniment. She huddled in her bed, trying not to hear the noises from the living room, trying not to remember the glass of brandy dangling from her mother's hand or the horrible crash it made when she threw it against the wall in one of her rages. She held her knees tighter to her chest when she realized the only sound she could hear was that of the dainty dancer at her bedside. Then the doorknob to her room clicked and turned. Daddy came in and shut the door behind him. Karen snapped her eyes shut. A moment later, her bed dipped on its frame and she heard the dancer silenced as the lid was snapped shut. She peeked through her eyelashes to see Daddy set his shoes on the jewelry box. In their shiny reflection, she saw his arm reach to pull the frilled covers down from under her chin. Lost and alone, Karen kept her eyes closed, trying to remember the ballerina's song against the harshness of her father's breath.

The next morning, Karen woke even later than the day before, unable to rise from the seductiveness of sleep. Like a force of nature, Ginny slammed open the door and swept into the room.

"I told your boss you were still sick, that you had a fever. He said for you to take as much time as you need," she said. "So I packed a bag for you. You're going with us."

"Going? Where?"

"Burning Man," Ginny smiled. "Let's go."

"I can't...." Karen caressed her shoes. Fragments of her dreams niggled at her. The shoes wanted to go. She could feel it. "Okay, give me a few minutes."

Ginny's dreads swayed as she nodded. "I'm feeling generous. You have ten."

Hours later, Karen sat huddled in the back seat of Ginny's car. Ginny's boyfriend, Ray, drove down the hot Nevada highway. Throbbing music vibrated through blown speakers. Pungent clouds of smoke from Ray's hand-rolled cigarettes wafted into the back seat before being sucked out the open windows. Karen was scraping the white insides of a large, Red Delicious apple with her teeth when they turned off the highway and began the final leg of their journey. As they traveled across the barren desert and onto the dry prehistoric lakebed in the Black Rock

Desert, Karen spotted something on the horizon. The shoes lay silent in her lap.

The car raced across the cracked earth towards the towering figure of a wooden man. Billows of dust rose from the desert floor in the distance. Karen leaned forward, peering between the front seat and out the windshield at the structure looming on the horizon. The late afternoon sun dipped into dusk. She tossed the apple core out the window and licked her fingertips.

As they neared the festival site, Karen saw that the man towered at least six stories high, looming above an impromptu tent city set up at his feet. His wooden frame gleamed in the dusk from hundreds of white, green, and red glow sticks jammed into his joints and orifices. Nudists cycled alongside their car as they passed the entrance. Illuminated by a flickering blue strobe light, a gold-painted woman strapped in a geodesic sphere rolled by them.

They parked, and Karen followed Ginny and Ray as they set off to locate their comrades in arms in South Camp. Karen trailed silently, watching frenzied activities erupting on all sides. A man lit a huge brick of multi-colored firecrackers that flared noisily in the dark. A group of men rode by on a charred wagon that spurted fire from a coned snout mounted on the front. Off to the side, a loud explosion ripped through the new night. Karen clutched her shoes tighter to her chest.

Ginny and Ray entered a dusty tent, but Karen kept on. Slowly she walked, closer and closer to the wooden man. Two women stood to the side watching her slow progress. Karen barely noticed them until one of them grabbed her arm and urged her into a tent. Distanced from everything but the shoes in her grasp, Karen followed. Inside, a bacchanalia raged. Richly colored fabrics hung from the ceiling and draped mounds of pillows, which were scattered on the canvas floor where limbs entwined in a seemingly endless, snaking mass of human flesh and streaming hair. Wine flowed freely from the many bottles passed from mouth to mouth. The musky scent of sex and incense hung heavy in the air. A man sat in the corner, strumming strangely discordant chords on a battered guitar. Wide-eyed and rigid, Karen pressed her fist into her mouth. But the woman beside her just laughed—a rich, throaty laugh promising dark desires.

Questing hands reached from the shadows, pulling Karen into the sultry scene. Garments fell from her, trailing to her feet. Unresisting, she followed the hands as they pushed her down into a pile of pillows. Probing fingers pulled pins from her hair and slipped sandals from her feet, until, at last, she was free of everything but her own skin and the red shoes clenched tightly against her chest. A woman kneeling in front of her attempted to pry those prized possessions from her grasp, but Karen resisted.

"No," Karen said, her voice hoarse and smoky.

A naked man towered above her, a swollen wine skin dangling from rough hands. With callused fingers, he tilted her head back and poured a heady red wine between her parted lips. She gasped, sputtered. A trail of the ruby liquid slid down between her pale breasts and lingered on the slight slope of her stomach. Several pairs of lips followed its path. The man smiled wide, exposing fleshy red lips and a hot pink tongue pressed against a jagged row of teeth. He poured again—a fountain of lust and intoxication. Karen lost all sense of time and place as she was swept up into the relentless tide.

When she came up for air, she found the orgiastic crowd moving out of the tent into the glowing darkness beyond. She stood to follow, only to discover that her feet were firmly trapped in the scarlet jaws of her snakeskin shoes. She wobbled, attempting to find her balance in the arch-stretching heels. She took one hesitant step and then another. And then she was dancing, waltzing into the arms of the night. Past the gathering throng she danced, spinning and spinning in a frantic waltz. Remnants of the day's heat settled on her bare skin, mingling with her sweat, washing away wine and kisses.

At long last, the red shoes brought her to the wooden colossus—a burning beacon in the sultry summer night. In front of his flaming presence, Karen leapt and whirled, swayed and stretched. But when she wrenched her gaze from the fiery face above her, she saw not the scarlet slippers bound to her feet, but the image of her father's shiny brown shoes gliding under hers, guiding her across the desert sand.

Shrieking in rage, she ripped the red snakeskin from her feet, revealing raw and blistered skin beneath. Grasped by the ankle straps, the dangling shoes continued their dance midair. Tangled strands of hair coiled around Karen's neck, choking her. But, even through the matted mass, she tilted her head and listened carefully for the muted song of a distant music box. And there, hanging on the thin thread of memory, chiming notes played for the twirling ballerina and the young princess in pink.

Karen clamped her lips together and limped closer to the burning man. When she was standing so close that her skin felt as though it was melting away from her bones, she launched the shining red shoes into the violent, soaring flames. Cautiously, Karen raised her arms above her head, stretching within her own skin, finding the feel of her heart's rhythm. Slowly, she began to sway to the beat of her body. The moon hung low in the sky. The flames began to flicker as the effigy started to lose his solidity. Turning away from the burning man's slow demise, Karen performed a graceful pirouette. The man with the wineskin stood close by, leering at her. She smiled and winked, falling into a sensual strut, torn feet leaving a bloody map in her wake. Her modern-day Bacchus opened welcoming arms, but she deftly stepped out of his reach. And for the first time in her life, Karen danced for herself, moving to the music of her own making.

C ARINA BISSETT wrote travel articles and books about the Southwest in another life. These days, Carina spends her time crafting twisted fairytales and cross-pollinated mythic fiction. Her short fiction and poetry can be found at the *Journal of Mythic Arts*, *The NonBinary Review*, and other assorted journals and anthologies. She is currently at work on the first novel in her five-book *Elements* series.

LINKS

http://www.carinabissett.com
https://twitter.com/cmariebissett

Before the First Day of Winter

by Rose Blackthorn

IT was the last day of autumn, and the precious hours of warmth and plenty were over. Darker days were coming as the season slid irrevocably toward winter, and all living creatures made their preparations.

Gulls cried as they picked through the receding surf, looking for edible tidbits. The lowering sun brought a glow to cool, misty air, and everything was shaded gold, citrine, and rose. Sea stacks and cliffs were black, jagged reminders of volcanic origins, and the hard-packed sand near the water stretched virgin and unsullied in wind-rippled drifts to the rocky headland.

Naia hurried along the strand, searching for a particular boulder shaped like some bulky four-legged animal crouched on its haunches. She was sure it was close by, but couldn't remember if it rested north or south of where she'd reached the beach. Above, more gulls wheeled and called, flashing like memories through the hazy air.

The mist swirled and pulsed, and the sound of water curling forward and then drawing back was echoed in the beating of her heart. The breeze pulled at her long hair, auburn strands, lifting and licking at the air like flames, and she gripped her upper arms with her hands to warm herself. It was chilly and she wasn't dressed for it, bare feet cold in the sand and legs pebbling with gooseflesh. The sun continued its graceful slide to the horizon, and soon it would be too dark to search. If she couldn't find it, she would have to go back.

"It's here, it has to be here," she whispered, eyes darting among the growing shadows.

At the edge of the tideline, the gulls watched her curiously, no longer searching the sand. It was almost as though they recognized her, knew her as a kindred spirit in this wild reach between sea and land.

"Please," she pleaded, her skirt flapping about her legs. And then, heart lifting, she spotted the boulder that so resembled a pudgy late-autumn bear curled up not far from the cliffs. "Let it be there," Naia said beneath her breath. She hurried to the boulder and knelt near the narrow head, reaching under the overhanging edge. At first her questing hands found nothing, and then something wet and soft gave beneath her fingertips.

"Naia!"

The voice was clear, but due to the breeze and the thickening fog, she couldn't tell from where it originated.

"Naia, where are you?" Jordon stood at the edge of the short basalt cliff, looking out over the beach stretching in both directions below. The sun sat on the horizon, slowly spreading wider and wider as though refusing to drop below the water. The fog blowing in over the surf was gathering along the strand, and he couldn't see anything except darker blurs in the grey. "Naia?"

The last of his batteries had died, making his ancient flashlight useless, but he'd brought a lantern instead. Holding it against his chest with his back to the wind, he opened the hinged door and lit the stub of candle inside. Before the fitful breeze could get at the flame, he closed the door tight. Lifting it by the metal handle, he looked for a safe way down onto the beach.

There was a path down the ten-foot drop of rock, carved as rude steps and handholds that Jordon took cautiously. He was terrified and wanted to rush headlong, but falling and breaking an ankle would help no one. As he reached the beach, the last roseate beams of sunlight made the fog incandesce, rendering his lantern redundant. But the brighter light hid more than it revealed, and his eyes burned and watered as he tried to find some sign of her.

Something moved to his right, and Jordon flinched. As quickly as the sun lit the fog, when it dropped below the horizon the billowing mist immediately became opaque. Shadows darted high, hunched low near the edge of incoming waves, and the sound of wings filled the air as the last gulls lifted from their foraging.

"Naia," he called, desperate now. He moved toward the thicker shadows, lantern held high again.

Crumpled on the sand, safe from all but the highest tide, were a faded red skirt and sleeveless white shirt. Bare footprints led from the discarded clothing to the sea, and Jordon hastened to follow.

"Naia, don't," he shouted, "Please don't go!"

The mist shifted and thinned, giving him a clear view of maybe a dozen yards of wet sand and rushing waves. Standing knee-deep in rising water, Naia pulled something dark and heavy around her shoulders. Her hair lashed in the wind, and she looked back at him for only a moment.

"Naia—"

Then she was gone, and something dark and sleek swam away into the restless sea.

In the early spring of the year that whales were spotted migrating along the coast for the first time in fifty years, a stranger came to the town of Yurka. She was slim and pale, with long, dark red hair and liquid brown eyes. She was dressed in rags, feet torn and bleeding from walking without shoes on the hard packed remnants of the road.

The first to encounter her was Aderyn, the old woman who was historian and keeper of words for the settlement. She had stepped outside to check her garden, for her earliest plantings of lettuce, peas, and carrots were nearing their harvest. The chilly sea wind played through Aderyn's white hair, and she tucked loose strands behind one ear when she caught movement from the corner of her eye.

The young woman walked slowly, gingerly along the rarely used road. Although obviously in pain, her face was untouched by any expression of discomfort.

Aderyn went to meet her, blue eyes still sharp despite her age. "Child, from where have you come?" There were no permanent settlements to the north, the direction from which the girl approached.

The young woman stopped, her dark eyes taking in Aderyn and the garden, with the oddly constructed house in the background. "I have left my home," she finally replied, an odd accent to her words, "for my people dwindle and fail. I come to start a new life."

Aderyn pursed her lips in thought, then asked, "What is your name?"

"I am called Naia."

The name seemed familiar, although she couldn't think why; something to do with the sea. But there was time enough to puzzle it out later. "I am Aderyn." She held out her hand, beckoning. "Come with me, Naia. We will get you better clothes, and something to eat."

Naia followed her back to the house, built of weathered wood and sheets of rusted metal and pieces of translucent plastic that let natural light into the structure. The old woman gave her clean (but much faded) clothing and tended to her wounded feet with warm water and a salve that burned. Then Aderyn wrapped the girl's feet in strips of raw cloth to protect them.

As soon she was finished, Aderyn brought a bowl of warm stew and a piece of dark bread. "There is goat's milk or water, or I can make some tea."

Naia looked up from the small feast before her, seeming a bit bewildered. "Water," she said, then picked up the bread and touched it gingerly to her tongue.

Aderyn raised an eyebrow, watching her guest for a moment. Naia acted as though she'd never had bread before, and then picked up the metal spoon to study it curiously. The old woman fetched a cup of water and brought it back to the table. Naia was using the spoon to pick out items from the stew. A chunk of potato, thin pieces of last year's celery, and bright orange slices of carrot all went into her mouth one at a time. She chewed, thoroughly tasted, mulling over the texture and consistency before swallowing each bite. She seemed quite taken by the small cubes of meat.

"What is this?" she asked, pointing at the brown lump.

"Mutton." At Naia's blank look, Aderyn added, "It comes from sheep."

Naia nodded, and went back to the stew.

"You've never had mutton?"

She shook her head. "You don't eat fish?"

Aderyn shrugged. "We get some from the river occasionally."

"None from the sea?"

Aderyn sat. "Oysters, clams. We have no way to go out into the deep water, and catches are small from the shore. Madoc, one of our young men, wants to build a boat. He has studied all the old records we have of the times before. But the sea has been polluted for so long, many wonder if there are many fish left. It may be just a waste of time."

"There is still life in the ocean, but not what it once was," Naia said, keeping her eyes on the bowl before her.

When she had finished eating, Aderyn took bowl and spoon to the sink. A pump handle drew water from the cistern buried behind the patchwork house. When she turned to set the dishes in the draining rack, she started.

Naia stood directly behind her, looking over her shoulder. "Where does the water come from?"

"There is a tank behind the house. The pump pulls water from there," Aderyn answered, and watched as the girl pulled the pump handle back and forth once, a smile of wonder touching her lips when water gushed forth. "Your people have none of this technology?"

Slender fingers traced the lines of the pump handle, and Naia said, "No. Nothing like this."

"It's left over, from the old world." Aderyn stirred the coals in the hearth, setting her copper pot on the grate to heat. This strange girl had interrupted her plans for the day, but she didn't mind. It had been years since she had spoken to anyone who didn't live in Yurka or the two settlements farther south along the coast. "We find things in the ruins, made of metal or sometimes wood or plastic. We have found books, a few here and there that were not completely destroyed in the Great War. We learn from them what we can. My nephew, Jordon, is gifted with mechanical instinct. Many of the things we've found, he has studied and been able to work out their functions. He ran the pipes from the cistern into this house, so that I might have water without carrying it from the communal well."

Naia listened with her dark eyes full on the old woman's face, as though absorbing every word and flicker of expression. When the kettle began to hiss, Aderyn made tea for them both in heavy earthenware mugs.

"And your people? Where are they?" Aderyn asked when they were settled with tea and a crock of golden honey.

"North." Naia seemed reluctant to speak of them, but Aderyn just arched a brow at her and waited for more. "They are diminished. Once, we were strong. We lived on the bounty of the sea. But now, there are not many left."

"Such is the fate of all the world, child," Aderyn said gently. "I've found records that say this part of the world was once teeming with people, so much that there was overcrowding and not enough resources for all. That was part of the reason the war came about—people trying to take food and supplies and space from other people. Now, because of pettiness and greed, we have all been made to suffer. This is why I search for the records, and teach our children to read so they can see with their own eyes. We are so few, yet someday in the distant future we might once again grow to be too many. Spoiled and decadent, our distant descendants might make the same mistakes all over again."

"You are a Teacher, then," Naia stated.

Aderyn shrugged. "I am the keeper of words for my people. But yes, I try to teach those who would learn."

"Will you teach me?" Her eyes were intent, her question sincere.

Aderyn smiled; she was a teacher in her heart and so her great joy was to find someone who wanted to learn what she could share. "Of course, Naia. Whatever I know, I will gladly pass on to you."

Jordon came to see Aderyn the next day, carrying with him a basket of small heavy cylinders. He came in without knocking; he had spent as many hours at his aunt's house as his own growing up. He halted mid-step upon seeing the stranger.

"Ah, Jordon," Aderyn said, smiling at his surprised expression. "I was wondering when you'd appear again."

"I—uh, I found some more batteries with a little power left," he said, and then stopped again when the girl turned to look at him. "I thought some of them might work for you," he added, a bit breathless.

"Jordon, this is Naia. She's going to be staying here for a while."

"Oh." He didn't resist when Aderyn took the small basket from him, just continued to meet the girl's deep brown eyes.

"He's usually not so rude," Aderyn said to Naia, her tone a bit sharp for

Jordon's sake.

"Hello, Jordon." Naia's voice was soft, silken-smooth; but it was her eyes that still held him.

"I—I have more stuff to unload," he muttered, backing toward the door that still stood open behind him. For a moment he seemed unable to decide his next move; then, with a jerk, he turned and broke eye contact, hurrying back outside.

Aderyn sighed. "Don't let first impressions ruin him. He really is a talented and kind young man. But maybe he hasn't seen a girl as pretty as you since reaching adulthood."

Naia tipped her head to one side, eyes down as she thought of Jordon's hazel eyes and windblown sandy hair. He was tall with wide shoulders, sensitive hands and a mouth made for smiling. "He studies with you?"

Aderyn was going through the batteries, separating them by size. "Rarely. He's read everything I have. But he brings me what he finds in the ruins of the old cities; it's all stored in the big shed behind the house, until we can determine what their function was and if there is any way we can use them now."

A few days later, Jordon returned to Aderyn's house with a cart full of strange odds and ends. He had gone south and east looking for any buildings from the old civilization still standing, in which he might find more relics of the past. There was also the ongoing search for books—ones that hadn't been reduced to cinders and ash or bloated and molded by water damage.

When he got there, after putting the carthorse in the small lean-to to eat and rest, he started pulling items out of the cart. Rather than going into the house to announce himself, he decided to unload the cart first. That would give him time to figure out what to say to his aunt's houseguest. He yanked open one of the heavy wooden doors on the storage shed, blinking when he saw a light inside.

Naia turned to look at him. She was seated on a high stool near the central workbench with a lantern burning beside her. "Hello, Jordon."

He paused for a moment, then closed his mouth when he realized it was hanging open. "Hello." He made himself continue through the door to take the box he was carrying to the counter. "What are you doing out here?" He winced when he realized how gruff the question sounded, but she seemed unaffected.

"I offered to sort through the things you brought the last time." As she spoke, Jordon noticed the neat piles of junk that she had gone through. Strands of wire had been wound into loops, nails and screws separated by size, and pieces of machinery that she obviously didn't know what to do with were placed together. "I hope you don't mind. I restrung the chimes."

"The what?"

With a soft tinkling, Naia lifted a collection of slender metal tubes. She had strung them together with twine going through tiny holes drilled in the top edges, and hung a flat washer in the center as a clapper.

Jordon smiled, an expression of wonder crossing his face. "So that's what they're for," he said, coming closer to admire her handiwork. "How did you know?"

Naia shrugged. "I've seen something similar, a long time ago."

"Have you shown it to Aunt Addie?"

"No, not yet." She held it out to him, her fingertips brushing against his hand as he took it. "Do you think she'll like it?"

"Yes, of course." The chime seemed to have broken the ice, and he'd lost his shyness and tendency to stutter around her. Or maybe it was the swift touch of her fingers against his. "Let me bring in the rest of what I've found and we'll take it in to her."

As he brought in three more boxes filled with leftover technology from before the war, Naia picked through them. Most of it was mismatched pieces of junk, as far she could tell. The last box was full of pieces of glass. Bottles, jars and colored pieces of flat glass shared space amongst rounded bulbs of frosted or clear glass with metal threaded ends. In the clear bulbs, she could see fine metal filaments. She said nothing, but saw in her mind's eye the soft glow of electric lights.

"That's all of it," Jordon said, setting the box of glass items down gently. "I'd better let Addie know I'm back."

Naia nodded in agreement and got down carefully from her seat. Her feet were still wrapped in strips of cloth to protect the healing abrasions from further damage.

Jordon watched with brows drawn as she began to pick her way across the floor. "What did you do to your feet?"

"No shoes," was her short reply.

"Huh." Without asking, he stepped forward and picked her up. "Put your arm around my neck," he said, and when she did, he carried her out of the shed and through the garden toward the house. "You should stay off your feet until they heal."

Cradled against his chest, Naia closed her eyes for a moment, breathing in the scent of him and enjoying the warmth of his body against her. "Aderyn can't carry me," she replied, and smiled at him.

"She probably could," he retorted, but grinned. Then he dipped to let her turn the doorknob, and carried her into the patchwork house.

The warm season from spring through early autumn was when Jordon did most of his exploring, traveling along the old roads that were now mostly covered in windblown debris or broken apart by weather and the passage of time. He used an old map Aderyn had given him, along with a compass, and marked off the names of those places where there once had been towns or cities filled with people and all their possessions. Most of them had been destroyed in the war and the following natural disasters and climate changes, leaving nothing behind. The great forest of ancient redwood trees north of Yurka had been burned to the ground, leaving miles of charcoal and ash. The sea, corrupted with chemicals and airborne pollutants, had risen in its bed. Taking over miles of coastline. Jordon had tried going north more than once—when he first began his scavenging trips—but the devastation was too much and he didn't go that way anymore.

To the south were other settlements like Yurka; likeminded folk and families working together to survive in a world that had become very harsh. Traders traveled from Fortune and Kingrange and occasionally from as far south as Fort, named for Fort Bragg, which had been relocated to Willits when the Pacific Ocean rose in her bed. These traders carried cloth and food, tools for woodworking or farming, and news from one small town to the next.

Because there were still permanent settlements of people to the south who had already picked clean nearby caches of ancient artifacts, Jordon spent most of his time searching inland. According to his map, there were some really big cities to the east, but they were far enough away that he had yet to reach them. A trip to places like Redding, or even farther to Sacramento, would mean journeying for the whole season. He didn't want to be gone for so long when there might not be anything to find.

He returned from his latest trip after being gone for a couple of weeks, coming straight to his aunt's with the cart full of finds. He looked forward to sharing his scavenged treasures with Aderyn, but even more he wanted to see Naia. He had thought of the young woman often while he was gone, even dreaming of her at night. No other woman had ever insinuated herself into his mind before, and he had missed her. When he came into the house, she was the first thing he sought. She was there, at the big table in the back by the bookshelves that Aderyn kept; but she was not alone.

Sitting close beside her, pointing out specific areas on an ancient schematic of a boat, was Madoc. The dark haired man, the same age as Jordon, was intent on the drawing and she seemed engrossed in whatever he was saying.

"Ah, Jordon. You're back!" Aderyn met him with a motherly embrace and an affectionate smile. "You must have found some wonders to have been gone so long."

"Yes," he replied, dragging his eyes away from the two at the table. "I wanted to let you know I was here before I started unloading."

"Jordon."

He turned from his aunt to find Naia within arm's reach, a smile on her lips and warm light in her dark eyes.

"I'm so glad you've returned," she said, and with no hesitation she stepped forward to hug him, her cheek pressed against his for a sweet moment.

Madoc had crossed the room as well, and with a grin he held out a hand to take Jordon's when Naia stepped back. "Good to see you back safe. Do you need help unloading?"

Jordon nodded curtly, trying to rein back the uncharacteristic surge of jealously that gripped him. "Thank you, yes." Before going back out, he pulled something from the inside of his jacket. "I found this in the remains of a building, and it made me think of you." As he spoke, he handed a small hardback book to Naia. "There is a little smoke damage, but it is otherwise unharmed."

Naia took the book, a puzzled slant to her brows, and then a kind of understanding touched her expression as she opened the cover. She raised her eyes to his again and smiled. "Thank you, Jordon. It's wonderful."

The two men went out to unload the laden cart, and Naia returned to the table to roll up the boat plans with the book tucked beneath her arm.

"What is it?" Aderyn asked curiously.

Naia smiled but made no move to give up the book. "Fairytales," she answered. "Ancient legends of the fae folk of the sea. Jordon already knows me too well."

Aderyn nodded. Madoc had been spending a lot of time here with Naia once he'd learned of her love of the water. She wondered privately if there would be a problem between the two young men, friends since childhood, because of the girl. Aderyn was fond of them both and would not take sides one way or the other, but she secretly hoped that Naia would find favor with Jordon. The keeper of words had come to admire the swift intelligence and gentle ways of the young woman. She wouldn't mind at all having Naia as part of her family.

It was late in the evening, after a shared dinner and Jordon's tale of his travels over the previous two weeks. He had found plenty of old books, which brought a flush of pleasure to Aderyn's face. There were parts of machines—all metal gears and plastic-coated wires. Jordon had found undamaged flashlights, but no batteries for them, which was disappointing. But the most incredible find was a small, flat rectangle of battered plastic and metal. After finishing their food and clearing the dishes, Jordon presented this last find.

"It runs on batteries, but not like any of those I've found. I don't know how long they will last, or if I'll find replacements," he said as he touched a small lever on one edge. The top part of the rectangle swung upward on tiny hinges, revealing a glass panel in the top half. "I had to mess with it for a while, before I figured out how to work it." He touched a button on the lower half. There was a soft whirring sound and a red light blinked in the corner.

Then, like a portal to another world, a moving picture appeared in the dark glass. Clear blue sky with a few puffy clouds, and below that waves rushing onto the sand; in the foreground, two children in brightly-colored brief costumes ran along the closest edge of the surf. They shrieked laughter, and white birds with black-marked wings hovered above them shrieking their own calls.

Jordon looked at Naia with a smile on his face, expecting to see an expression of wonder. Instead, her eyes were filled with tears and her lips were pressed tight to keep from trembling.

"A recording of the times before the war," Aderyn guessed, her eyes sparkling. "Is there any way to date it?"

"There may be, but I haven't found it yet," Jordon answered, still looking at Naia.

"Don't go out too deep!" The voice was an adult's, coming from out of view on the screen.

"Come swim with us, Daddy!" The older of the two children, a girl with long blond hair, beckoned toward the screen.

"Go ahead, I'll keep recording." The woman's voice was softer, and the tableau on the screen tipped and shuddered before becoming steady once more. A man wearing dark blue shorts and black lenses over his eyes appeared to one side and jogged away toward the water. "Give me a smile!"

The man and both children flashed bright grins at them, then began chasing each other through the shallow water, laughing and chirping like exotic birds.

low batt appeared at the bottom of the screen, and Jordon touched the button to turn it off.

"Amazing," Aderyn whispered, reaching to squeeze his arm for a moment. "I wonder if we could convert it to use the kind of batteries we already have? I would love to see the rest of the recording."

"I'm not sure; maybe." Jordon closed the screen, and glanced back at Naia who was as calm and composed as ever. Before he could say anything to her, she got to her feet and went to get another cup of tea from the kettle.

Madoc took his leave then, pausing only to speak softly to Naia for a moment before making his farewells. When he was gone, Aderyn made a point of giving them some privacy.

"A lot to go through tomorrow," she said, nodding as she got to her feet. "I'm for bed. Now, you two don't need to hurry on my account. I'll see you in the morning," and she disappeared through the narrow doorway to her bedroom.

"I think I'd like a walk, to stretch my legs," Naia said, setting her steaming cup on the table. "Would you care to accompany me?"

Jordon nodded, following her out of the warm, firelit room and into the breezy dusk outside. He noted that she no longer limped, her feet protected in soled leather shoes. The light wind pulled at her long hair, tossing it behind her; and then she took his hand to keep him beside her.

"It's not too far to the beach, if you're willing." She looked up at him, her pale face a ghost in the coming darkness. "I already know the path well."

He said nothing, just nodded and went with her. The feel of her hand in his was a touch of warmth, one he hadn't known he was missing. The flowery scent of her hair filled his nose, and he admired the easy way she moved along the path. When they reached the sand she stopped, slipping her feet from the shoes, and turned to face him. The wind, still playing with her unbound hair, pushed it toward him so the ends tickled his face and throat.

"Isn't it beautiful?" she asked. She might have meant the stretch of untouched sand, the midnight blue waves touched with creamy foam, or the livid sky faintly touched with flickering stars.

His answer, though, was for her. "Yes, beautiful."

He wanted to ask her why she'd been brought to tears by the sight of those long-dead children in the glass. He wanted to ask if she favored Madoc, who loved the sea as she did. But before he could ask her anything she was in his arms. Her slight form pressed against him, her hands caressing his face and then sliding into his tousled hair. Her lips touched his, warm and sweet, and Jordon forgot the barb of jealousy that had pierced his heart when he saw her with his friend. The wind blew her hair around them, curtaining their faces, and her sweetness filled him.

"I missed you," she whispered.

"I was afraid you'd chosen Madoc," he replied, unable to completely let go of that momentary glance, the two of them side by side at the table, with their heads leaned together.

"I chose you."

Although nothing was said, it became clear over the next few weeks that Naia and Jordon had reached some kind of understanding. Aderyn didn't ask, not wanting to pry, but she smiled when she saw them together. Invariably they touched hands, or brushed arm to arm. As they worked through the load of findings that Jordon had brought back from his latest foray, they began to finish each other's sentences, and quiet laughter became commonplace.

As it became more obvious that they were committed to each other, Madoc came less often. He still spoke to Naia about the ocean, and the best kind of boat to build for sailing on it, but he had lost some of the spark that had jumped between them in the beginning.

"You know that I love her," he said to Jordon one day after Naia had left the storage shed to return to the house, leaving the two men alone for a moment.

Jordon was silent, gazing at the face of the man who he had considered his closest friend. "I know. But you're not the only one to love her."

"We have more in common, she and I, than you do," Madoc went on, determined to have his say. "She loves the ocean as I always have. We spoke of building a boat together, to sail out into the open water, as our ancestors did long ago."

Jordon sighed. "You are the closest thing I've ever had to a brother. I don't want to lose your friendship, or your respect. But I cannot give her up. She chose me, and I won't let her go."

The silence held for a long time, and at last Madoc nodded once—not in agreement, but in understanding. He left the shed, not bothering to close the door behind him, and Jordon sighed again. He meant what he'd said. He didn't want to lose their friendship, but he would not give up what he had with Naia.

Jordon turned, catching movement out the open door, and saw Madoc standing just past Aderyn's garden. Naia stood with him, close but not touching as they spoke. The air was still, but he could not hear what was said. After a while, Naia reached up to touch the dark-haired man's face gently. Madoc put his hand over hers, leaning closer, but she pulled away. Finally, the other man turned and left, with Naia watching after him.

Late that night, after Aderyn had gone to her bed, they retired to the room where Jordon stayed when he was home. Beneath the blankets required now that the season was winding toward winter, Naia lay with her head pillowed on Jordon's chest. She listened to the steady thud of his heart, fingertips drawing cryptic designs over his skin.

"Is everything all right?" Jordon asked, wondering if she would tell him what Madoc had said to her.

"I think we should go on one more gathering journey before the season ends," she said, surprising him. "You told me there was nothing to the north, but I passed at least two fair-sized ruins on my way here. I could show you where they are."

"You—you want to go on a trip with me?" he asked, cocking his head so he could see her face.

"Yes." She sat up, leaning on one arm so she could look squarely into his face. "By next spring, I will be too big to travel. I want to go once before the cold comes and we must stay close to shelter."

He gazed at her, brows crooked together as he tried to make out what she was saying. "Too big?"

Naia didn't smile, but her deep eyes were filled with a mix of emotions. She reached to take his hand and placed it on her belly. "Too big," she repeated.

Jordon's eyes widened as he understood, but she shook her head.

"Say nothing to Aderyn. I will tell her when we get back, but I don't want her to try and talk me out of going. I want to take a journey with you, Jordon; I don't want anything to stop it."

He held her close then, as close as they could be without becoming one person.

He thought about the old customs he had read about in Aderyn's books, when people in the times before the war had bound themselves to each other with vows and symbolic rings. People didn't do that now. When two people wanted to be together, they just were, combining their lives and possessions with no fanfare. But Jordon found himself wishing he could give Naia vows and physical symbols of what he felt right now. He would be a father soon, and would pass on all that he had learned in life along with his genes and heritage. It seemed there should be fanfare.

They traveled north in blustering fall winds and the salt scent of the sea. The cart was light, and the horse made good time without having to hurry. Sometimes they walked, and sometimes they rode on the narrow seat, Naia's head resting on Jordon's shoulder. Her dark eyes sparkled and she smiled often, with one hand resting on her belly.

In the evenings they would camp with a fire for light and to heat their dinner, a simple canvas cloth on stakes to protect them from the weather. Jordon would consult his maps, trying to determine where these ruins, which Naia had passed on her trek, might be. They skirted the burned remains of the ancient redwood forests, and Jordon was surprised to find saplings rising among the blackened stumps and fallen trunks. Rust-colored ferns carpeted the ash-enriched soil, turning the place into an autumn wonderland of bronze, umber, and burnt sienna.

A week had passed before they found the first abandoned town. Because of the change in the coastline and no sign of any highway, Jordon was unable to determine which one it might have been.

"It could be Orick," he said, his expression confounded. "I don't think we've gone far enough north to be at Klamath."

"Does it matter?" Naia asked, looking around at the tumbled remains of old buildings and buckled pavement.

"It helps to mark on the map, for future reference. If we find some good things, we'll know how to get back and how long it will take to make the trip."

"We'll have to look for signs, then," she responded, "but we haven't reached the bigger town yet, the one I wanted to show you. It's still a couple of days ahead."

Jordon glanced up at the sky. Clouds had moved in, darkening the day so it was hard to determine what time it was. "You walked a very long way."

"Yes." Naia turned her head to the west. They were within sight of the sea, a blue-grey waste that stretched to the horizon.

"I only brought enough food for two weeks. Maybe we should look around here tomorrow, and then head back to Yurka the next day."

"Not yet," she said, putting her hand on his arm. "The larger ruin will be worth the extra days. There's plenty of food to last us until we get back." She leaned closer, putting her head on his shoulder once more. "I'm not ready to go back, Jordon. Just a few more days?"

He put his cheek against the crown of her head and stroked her soft auburn hair where it cascaded down his chest. "A few more days," he agreed, and kissed her when she raised her face to him.

Two more days brought them out of the remains of the redwoods and into regenerating pine and deciduous trees. None of them were very tall or robust, but they were there interspersed amongst lichen-crusted granite and acres of dead grass. The groaning skeleton of a bridge crossed a river too deep to wade, and Jordon almost turned back there. But Naia slipped down off the seat of the cart and walked across, unconcerned at openings in the surface.

"I crossed this on my way south," she said, reaching the other side without incident and turned to beckon him forward. "It's stronger than it looks."

Teeth worrying his bottom lip, Jordon acquiesced and led the horse across the expanse on foot. Once on solid ground again, he shook his head at her. "You need to be more careful, Naia. What if you had fallen, or the bridge collapsed?"

She just smiled and climbed back into the cart.

As the sun dropped toward the horizon, they came to the large town of which she had told him. Like all the old cities he'd found, this one was piles of collapsed masonry, rusted metal, and broken concrete paving mostly overgrown with vines or weeds. They made camp near one of the few structures still standing, a brick and mortar single-story building with a steel framed portcullis along one side. Jordon unharnessed the horse and put down some oats as a treat while Naia started a fire.

"I'll get some more wood," she said while Jordon unloaded their groundsheet and blankets for sleeping.

He spread the heavy canvas and blankets beside the cart, then stretched the tent cloth from cart to ground as a lean-to for shelter. The fire was crackling merrily, and he added another branch to it. The breeze from the west was cool and tangy with salt, and he could hear sea birds calling. He put a kettle with water beside the fire to heat, and sat down with his map, trying to locate the rickety bridge that they'd crossed to get here.

After a while, as the lowering sun cast shadows over the map, Jordon looked up. Fog had appeared, sliding in over the water, and scant rags of mist swept through the open streets between ruins. "Naia?" he called, realizing suddenly that she'd been gone for a while. "Naia, where are you?"

He hadn't paid attention to which direction she'd gone, and the humped asphalt before the building took no tracks. Worried, he folded the map to replace it inside his pack. Fluttering from beneath the pack were the pages of an open book.

With a frown, Jordon pulled it out, recognizing the book he'd given to Naia weeks before. *The Sea-Maiden, and other tales of Mermaids, Selkies and Merrows* was written in faded gold leaf across the cover. The book was open to a story about a

Selkie woman who fell in love with a human man. A folded piece of paper protruded from the smoke-stained pages.

Jordon pulled it out, tucking the book back beneath his pack, and opened it. Naia's spare handwriting caught his eye.

"I came here to start a new life, although not in the way you might have expected, my dearest Jordon. Poisoned by human refuse and the destruction of your wars, my people have perished until only a handful survives. My two sisters and I agreed to try the old way, to bring new life to our kind. And so we have each taken human form and come to land to find mates.

"I saw this as a duty. I never thought to lose my heart. I wish I could tell you everything, my love. But all I can do is leave you this letter to explain. Before the first day of Winter, I must return. I will don my sealskin and return to the depths, and there I will bear and raise our child in the ways of my people.

"I am sorry, Jordon. I never meant to hurt you. But I promise, our child will know of you from his very first day."

It was a terrible joke, too much to believe. And yet he remembered her odd ignorance of things that everyone knew, and her inordinate love of the sea. She had been gone too long. She wasn't coming back.

He picked up the flashlight he'd brought along for extra light. Switching it on, he scowled at the dim yellow glow. He hadn't brought any more batteries, as they were in such short supply. Even though the sky was still bright, it wouldn't be long before the sun dropped below the sea and then darkness would come swiftly. Leaving the flashlight behind, he took instead the glass-sided lantern with a candle fixed inside, hanging it from a loop at his belt.

Then he went searching for Naia, calling her name into the wind and stopping at every shift of windblown mist that caught his eye. There was no point in searching for her among the ruins. Her letter had said where she'd gone. He hurried toward the foggy beach and swift sunset, praying under his breath only that he might find her before she disappeared.

Spring finally arrived after a particularly harsh winter. The storms had been merciless, lashing the coast and covering everything in sheets of glistening ice. Now that it was finally warming up, Madoc spent as much time at the beach as he could. He had spent the winter in the cramped shop behind his dugout shelter, working on the boat he had dreamed of sailing all his life. After speaking with Naia last year, and taking her surprisingly sound advice regarding changes to his plans, he had at last completed his first seaworthy vessel.

It was small, only twenty feet in length with a single mast. He didn't expect to make a long voyage in it. But if it worked as well as he hoped, then he was sure he could get some of the other men in Yurka to help him build something bigger. With the help of Randon, the tanner's son, they loaded the wooden boat onto a long, two-wheeled cart and transported it down the winding narrow path to the beach.

Madoc spent all his free time there, finishing the process of sealing the wood and smoothing the joints. He had tried to get Jordon to come down and see it, but his oldest friend refused to come near the water. After losing Naia last fall, he had become morose and monosyllabic.

Now, on the first truly warm day after winter had passed, Madoc prepared to launch the boat for the first time. He arrived early in the morning, with oars and sail in place, and bottles of water and a basket of food in case he should be gone for the day. When he reached the boat, he was surprised to find it wasn't alone.

A girl with long reddish-blond hair stood beside the prow, her fingertips tracing the smooth wood. She wore ragged clothing and her feet were bare, but she was lovely nonetheless.

"Hello?" Madoc called, halting a few feet away.

She turned toward him, her dark liquid eyes filled with warmth. "Hello."

"My name is Madoc," he said, rather at a loss. He had never seen her before, and yet she seemed so familiar. "Who are you?"

"Madoc." A smile touched her lips, changing her from merely pretty to beautiful. "I am Maris."

"Do I know you?" he asked, puzzled.

"My sister told me about you. And your love for the sea." She held a hand out toward him. "You're going out onto the water. Could I go with you?"

ROSE BLACKTHORN lives in the high mountain desert of Eastern Utah with her boyfriend and two dogs, Boo and Shadow. She spends her time writing, reading, being crafty, and photographing the surrounding wilderness. An only child, she was lucky to have a mother who loved books, and has been surrounded by them her entire life. Thus instead of squabbling with siblings, she learned to be friends with her imagination and the voices in her head are still very much present.

She is a member of the HWA and has been published online and in print with *Necon E-Books*, *Stupefying Stories*, *Buzzy Mag*, *Interstellar Fiction*, *SpeckLit*, *Jamais Vu* and the anthologies "The Ghost IS the Machine," "A Quick Bite of Flesh," "Fear the Abyss," "The Best of the Horror Society 2013," "Enter at Your Own Risk: The End is the Beginning," "FEAR: Of the Dark and Equilibrium Overturned," among others.

LINKS

http://roseblackthorn.wordpress.com
https://twitter.com/rose_blackthorn
http://www.facebook.com/RoseBlackthorn.Author

Wonderland's Nightmare

by S.M. Blooding

"If I had a world of my own, everything would be nonsense. Nothing would be what it is, because everything would be what it isn't. And contrary wise, what is, it wouldn't be. And what it wouldn't be, it would. You see?"
— Alice in *Alice's Adventures in Wonderland*

SHORT, squat trees rambled by, their long roots entwining beneath their bulbous trunks in such a manner as to make a person wonder how they didn't simply topple over. Green leaves topped the handful of branches, appearing more like a man with a military hair cut than a tree.

Red closed her eyes, her heart twisting cruelly in her chest. She didn't want to think about her late husband, or how badly he'd returned from the war with the Nazis, fighting for a freedom she hadn't lost. She'd lived above the tyranny that had lodged on the other side of her country's borders.

She shook her head and opened her eyes again, watching as small globs of fuzz dangled off the branches of the moaning traveling trees.

"Are you quite entertained, sister?"

Red didn't turn away from the large, balcony window. She raised her chin and ignored the person who'd entered the room behind her, ignoring the lilt to the other woman's words that reminded her so painfully of home. England.

"Dottie," the woman said with a breath of a laugh. "Surely this childish behavior can cease. Can't you see this wonderful place I've brought you to? Can't you see I was merely trying to help?"

"Help?" Red asked, refusing to acknowledge the name her sister had called her. When she'd died and awakened in this doubly cursed place, she'd done more than merely change her name. She'd accepted a new identity.

"They were trying to turn you into a nightmare, Dot."

No. Red laid her well-manicured hand on the cool tile wall next to her. This land had brought her there to bring hope to the hopeless. They'd thought she had it within her heart to brave the darkness of the soul, to banish the defeat, and to guide others along the same path.

What they hadn't counted on was that there was nothing left inside her worth saving. The woman she'd been during the war, Dottie, was gone. That woman had died with her husband, so brain damaged and deranged that death had come gladly for them both. The rest of that woman was destroyed with the deaths of her two children, and the complete abandonment of her sister who couldn't be dragged away from her perfect life and hero of a husband.

No. The elders, whoever they were, had determined there was nothing left inside her to salvage, and so they chose to end her existence.

She'd been quite understanding and had felt no end of relief. She was tired of living, and for what? Was life so great a thing? No. It was not.

But then her sister had swooped in, like the heroine everyone thought she was, and saved her.

"Dottie, please talk to me."

"Don't call me that. My name is Red."

Muggs sighed deeply, the clipping of her heals sounding on the pale blue tile. "I don't understand why you had to change your name. You've been Dottie my whole life."

A woman like her, so talented, so protected and shielded and naïve, couldn't possibly understand what it was like to feel one's soul die within her living flesh, to feel it rot inside like a cancerous sore. Explaining would only waste breath.

Muggs set her hand on her sister's arm.

Red flinched and backed away, swatting at the hand that offended her. She stalked to the wall of mirrors and watched her scarlet-swathed reflection in wonder and contempt. "Why are we here?"

"Dreamland has given us another chance. She's given me this land, this wonder-filled land. You should see it, Dot. It's so beautiful."

Red gestured to the window outside. "Oh, yes. You get the land and the sunshine and the wonder. What makes you so special, dear sister, you are handed everything?"

Muggs walked slowly toward her sister, meeting her reflection in the mirror. "I was not handed anything, Dot. I worked hard for this. I always have."

The two didn't look like sisters. Muggs had the fair skin, and the perfectly coifed pale hair. A flowing white dress of feathers and lace, which reminded Red of a swan out of a fairytale, swathed her slim figure.

Red, on the other hand, had long, dark hair that gleamed in the bright light of never-ending day. Her dark eyes narrowed, taking in the sight of her blood-red gown of the finest silk she'd ever laid eyes on.

"What's really going on, Dot?" Muggs' blue eyes softened, the corners falling minutely. "I thought you'd be happier."

Red didn't even know if she *could* feel happy again. Anger was a distant memory. Anguish, closer yet. Happiness? What would it feel like to laugh again?

Muggs touched Red's hair with a ginger hand, a soft frown furrowing her pale brow. "I just want you to be happy, Dot. Just be happy. Okay?"

As if it were a choice. Red closed her eyes and pulled away from her sister's touch, a frigid sweep of cold sweeping through her chest and into her limbs.

"My queen," a male voice said with a snap of his heels.

Red watched in the reflection of the wall of mirrors as a footman in white and pale blue livery stood in the doorway to the large room. He held his short hat that reminded her so much of her husband's. She swallowed and looked away.

Muggs paused, then turned, pushing her slim shoulders back. "What is it, Tweedle?"

Red sighed. "Do you ever come up with more realistic names for people? Are they always whimsy and make believe?"

Muggs glanced at her sister with a quirk of her lips, but returned to an otherwise attentive expression toward her footman.

"We have lost a dreamer, Your Majesty."

Muggs frowned at the man. "How did we lose a dreamer?"

"I would ask Dustman Finn, were I you, Majesty. He understands the dustman ways much better than I ever could."

She bowed her head in acknowledgement and turned back to Red. "I'll be back later tonight. We'll have dinner and we'll talk."

Red rubbed the back of one hand with the thumb from the other, and said nothing. Night never fell and they never talked.

Muggs walked two steps then evaporated into thin air.

Red turned and stared at the spot where her sister had been only moments before. When would she learn the secrets of this land? How this teleportation worked, this Place, as they called it. Why the trees walked and why the grass sang.

Try as she might, she couldn't dredge a single morsel of energy to partner the curiosity as she walked to the pale grey couch in the middle of the large and otherwise bare room. Her mind traveled down corridors she recognized; avarice, envy, wrath. Images of what she should want—should crave—teased her mind.

Nothing followed. A deep ache of emptiness overwhelmed her soul, stripping her heart of any emotion.

At one point, she'd welcomed it, this apathetic approach to a life that refused to allow her to leave it.

But now, she craved more. She needed one moment, one spare second, of feeling.

A whisper of a pop filled the air behind her. Red raised her gaze to the wall of mirrors.

Her sister stumbled as she appeared out of the air. She brushed back a runaway strand of strawberry blonde hair. Her posture was slumped, her expression marred in folds of confusion.

Red rose carefully and faced her sister, waiting.

Muggs' blue eyes drifted upward. She blinked furiously, her lips parted. "Something terrible has happened, Dot, and I don't know what to do."

"What?"

"I—" The hand at her head shook.

Red raised her chin, waiting for something to tick inside her chest, some worm of infestation, some inkling of emotion.

"I lost a dreamer. A hole appeared, and he fell through."

"How far could he have gone?" Red pushed her silk gown out of the way and walked around the couch. "It's a hole in the ground."

"No, Dot. It doesn't work that way here." Muggs' blue eyes unfocused and her hand fell to her side. "He fell into a space I cannot reach."

Red narrowed her eyes. "Are you being overdramatic?"

"No. He—He's in a land of nightmares." Her gaze latched onto her sister's. "I don't dare enter so dark a place, but—but you might be able to. No. You're the only one who *can*."

Red blinked a long, slow draw of the eyelids and rose to her full height. "I am in no mood for your childish games, Margaret."

"This isn't a game, Dottie." She reached up and cupped her sister's cheek. "My big, brave sister. You're the only one who can help him."

Red's cheek twitched under Muggs' touch, but whether it was from the warmth of her sister's hand, or from the weight in her chest that threatened to drag her down, she was unsure.

She only knew on thing.

It would be best if no one ever *counted* on her again.

Really, it came down to one of two choices: remain in the castle as a veritable prisoner, or wander this crazy land in search of a child.

Red opted for the latter.

Muggs met her at the large front door to the castle, her dress immaculate, a white and silver parasol in hand.

Red stopped, her boots clicking a fine clomp on the gray tiles. "I had thought we were on a mission to save a child, sister, not an outing to the garden."

Muggs winced a pretty smile, but looked deeper into the large room behind them. "This is Wonderland, sister, not the English countryside."

Red rolled her eyes and gestured to the door. "Shouldn't we be going, then?"

"Not quite as yet." Muggs took in a large breath and let it out. "You need a guide."

"A guide?" Red smoothed her scarlet and leather tunic over her dark pants. It felt quite remarkable to be in pants again. She wasn't entirely sure why her sister had relegated them to a Victorian era of fashion, but Red much preferred the twentieth century, thank you very much. "Are you afraid you'll get lost? I thought these were your lands by design, though I don't understand what that means entirely."

"They are, but I am not going with you, if you must know." Muggs paced away. "I have other things to which I must attend, dreamers to take back home and such."

"Oh," Red said, pulling her head back, her hands out, a dark twisting of inferiority spiraling like a vacuum in her chest. "Lah-dee."

Muggs let her parasol fall as she slumped her shoulders. "Oh, Dot."

Red rolled her eyes and headed for the open door.

"How are you going to find the child on your own?"

Red didn't stop. "I'll figure it out, I suppose. Or I won't. Either way."

"Dottie!"

Red stopped and thumped her fist against the metal door. Why did she pause? Why did she care? The best part of feeling nothing was not caring. *Not* caring. So, why wasn't she leaving?

"Am I la'e to the party?" a man asked behind her.

Red turned and saw a man in brown trousers and a green jacket with long tails. His dark hair curled up and around the brim of his wide-topped hat.

He raised dark eyebrows at the White Queen.

She flattened her lips and tipped her head in Red's direction.

He pushed his shoulders back and bowed with a flourish of his hat. "Hatter, at your service."

Red blinked coolly. "Your name is Hatter."

"No." He straightened and put his hat back on. "But it's wha' I allow people t' call me."

"And what would your real name be?"

"Would ya prefer I called you by *your* real name, or by the name ya chose for ye'self?" His dark eyes held hers.

A corner of her lips rose in a half smile. "Indeed." She turned to her sister. "Can we be off now? Or must we wait for an entire circus to join us?"

"I'm the only guide you'll require." Hatter brushed past Red on his way out the door. "Now, then, if you're quite ready, I'd say we should be off. Yeah?"

A full smile found its way across her lips as she followed, a slight saunter to her gait. "Where are we going?"

He stopped at the last silver step and scoped out the countryside.

The bulbous trees from earlier were gone, leaving a rolling hillside landscape of green grass and tall flowers of varying colors, mostly yellows, reds, and blues. Bugs flew about, buzzing from one flower to the next.

Hatter clucked his tongue then cleared his throat. He pointed to his left. "In that kind o' direction, I think. Yeah. It should do."

Red frowned and headed in the direction he pointed. "Do you know, are you guessin', or is this some fragile attempt to 'save' me?"

He gave her a rakishly cocky grin as he passed her. "Why in the world would I want t' save you? I quite like ya the way ya are."

"That would make you the first," she muttered under her breath.

They walked over quite a few hills when she saw another castle on the horizon, off to their right. "What is that?"

He glanced at it, but didn't alter his course. "Tha'd be your castle, should you wanna take it." He frowned. "You're sister is one strange apple."

Red threw her head back and laughed, something strange and light filling her chest. "In that, we can agree."

He sidestepped a particularly large flower that roared at his passing knee. "You should do tha' more often."

"What?"

His lips curled as he shot her a look over his shoulder. "Smile."

She scoffed at him, but her smile remained. She paid attention the flowers they passed, listening to them chatter and yell at they passed. "What is this place, anyway?"

"Dreamland? Or this tiny island o' it?"

She dodged a wide bush of magenta horn flowers. They plucked at her tunic as each trumpet blew at her, filling the air with noise and ranker. She had to raise her voice to be heard. "Yes."

Once past the tangle of trumpet flowers, they shushed, the air almost ringing with quiet.

He held his hand out for a pixie that passed by.

The little thing, no bigger than a large dragonfly, was the brightest, clearest blue Red had ever seen. The little thing chittered and carried a fuss, tossing glitter this way and that. A small poof of it rose when she stomped her foot. Red leaned in to see if she could understand the daft, little thing, but was disappointed to discover she could not.

"Hmm," Hatter said, then lifted his hand with a slight bounce.

The pixie flew off in quite the huff and nearly knocked a flying rocking horse out of the air.

Red stared at the buzzing bit of equine wood in consternation. What was her sister thinking to create something as ridiculous as that? "What did she say?"

"What would ya like answered first? The bit about the world? Or the bit about the pixie?"

She narrowed her eyes and pressed her lips together.

He smirked and continued. "Well, this here's Dreamland. What that means to the likes o' us is that we're meant to protect the dreamers."

A bitter tang covered her tongue and singed her throat. "I hate to disappoint you, but I'm not the kind that protects poor, innocent, little children."

"Yeah. Knew about that already. That daft sister o' yours won't hear none about it, though. Says you'll come to yer own soon enough."

Red cupped the head of a singing, yellow rose. "So, why are you in Dreamland? What do you do?"

"Well, we're not real sure about that, really. All we really know is that I came on m' own. I'm not a dustman like her." He held out one hand as if representing the sides of a scale. "And I'm not a dreamer. More'n that, we just don' know."

She frowned, watching the forest they approached. Long, spindly arms pierced the air. Gaping maws hung open along their wide trunks. The roots didn't move, didn't shake, or quake, or give any other indication of living.

"The dreamplanes, as the people what actually live here call 'em, are built from the imagination of their dustman. In this case, that's yer sister. However, apparently, this one's a bit different in the fact that we seem to be gatherin' the likes of you and me. Those who don't belong nowhere else, but they can't seem to get rid of either."

"Where did you come from?"

He shot her a long, dark look over his shoulder as he breached the perimeter of the wood. "From nowhere."

"The accent?"

"Always had it."

Right. "If you didn't want to tell me, all you had to say was it was none of my business."

He turned back to watch his progress. "I would never be so rude. No. I simply don't remember is all. Now, you asking leaves me with a funny feeling like you do remember where you come from."

She didn't reply for a long moment, but finally nodded.

"Right like. I read ya. The White Queen mentioned they'd tried to make a nightmare of ya. Didn't take, I see?"

Her hand trembled slightly as heat found its way to her cheeks. "I'm not the nicest person I've ever met, but I couldn't become that dark." She didn't want to admit out loud that she'd failed because she was too dark to be a nightmare, that there was no light of hope in her rock of a heart.

"Hmm," he said. "Well, and I read ya there, too." He stopped.

She skidded, nearly falling into him.

He stayed where he stood and didn't move. "Red, do me a favor."

She raised her chin and looked at him warily. "What?"

"You decide right now. Are ya saving that child, or are ya saving ye'self?"

Red ran her tongue along her molars.

"Because what we're about t' do can't be done if you're only in it fer yeself."

In the short span since she'd met this man, slight shifts of emotion had rattled through her existence, but even she doubted it was enough to say she cared about some nameless, faceless, lost child.

He nodded, his lips flat. "That's what I thought. Ye'd best work on that. Otherwise, the elders *are* gonna find ya; and this time, there'll be no escapin'."

"Wait." Red jogged a few steps to catch up, the slick soles of her low-heeled boots making it a bit more difficult than it should have been in the damp grass. She glared at the drooping flowers and the bowed heads of the blades of grass. Everything had just been dry, hadn't it? "Escaping the elders? They can't know where I am."

He narrowed his eyes to the sky and stopped. "Yeah. They've been searching for ya since ya arrived. They know you're here. Now, what's goin' on over there?"

She stared at him in consternation as he walked away from her. "How did Muggs get them to go away?"

"Muggs?" He shot her a glance, but returned it to the sky again. "We need ta be looking t' more pressing matters, Princess."

"I'm not a princess." She stepped in front of him and placed her fingertips against his chest. "The White Queen. How did she make the elders go away?"

"Same as any dustman does, I reckon." He took her shoulders and moved her out of the way. "She told 'em to go."

Red stumbled back two steps. No one touched her, much less moved her aside as if she were a doll. "Then if all she has to do is ask them to leave, I don't understand what all the ruckus is about."

"Oh, she can tell 'em to leave, but they own this land more'n she does. They allow her to live. You, too, for that matter."

"Oh," she said, expelling a puff of breath that clouded before her. When had the temperature dropped? "But not you. So, I suppose you're immune."

"I am, of sorts, I guess." He glanced behind him, then back to the sky, tipping his head as he frowned. "I'm a dream walker. I wasn't invited by them, wasn't brought here. I'm here by my own rights."

She shook her head, completely perplexed and turned her eyes upward. The light of day had dimmed. She couldn't quite say the sun was setting as there was no sun, at least none as she'd seen yet. However, the outer edges had grown darker. Stars would be out soon if she were home in England. She sighed and flopped her hands to her sides. "It's night time, Hatter."

"Dreamland doesn't have night, Princess."

"I'm not a princess."

"Course not." He grimaced and gestured for her to follow. "We need t' pick up the pace a bit. Whatever happened with the child, it's changing the dreamplane, altering it so's like. We're gonna be in a bit of trouble if the elders come in force."

A tremor rippled through her, startling her as she put a name to the emotion that accompanied it. Fear. "What do you mean?"

He rounded on her, thunder filling his body. "What I mean, Princess, is that yer sister's been out of her mind trying to protect yer ungrateful backside to her detriment."

Red curled her lip, but stood her ground.

"Someone ripped a hole in her dreamplane. That's an anomaly on a good day. But now there's night. They're fixing to storm the place, kill your sister, and destroy you. Don't be thinkin' any different."

Hadn't she been the one who'd noted only hours before that this place had no night? Something *was* wrong. Something *was* different. The elders made sense.

"Are ya getting it yet?"

Red took in a deep breath, filling her abdomen as much as her tight tunic would allow. She raised her chin, her hands clenched at her sides. "I get it, Hatter." She turned away, watching the spindle-armed trees rise like shadow wraiths in the gathering darkness. "I'm a danger to this place."

"Just like a woman t' make it all dramatic." He rolled his eyes and headed deeper into the woods. "Now, what happened to these trees? They were green just yesterday."

"You just finished telling me I bring danger to this place by being here, and now you're saying I'm being dramatic?" She gritted her teeth, but followed, staying close to him.

The trees reached out, tugging at her clothes, her hair. Whispers filled the air, though if from the trees or something else, she couldn't say. They didn't touch Hatter, or move to interact with him at all.

"Why are we chasing a child, Hatter? Why aren't we going after the real problem here?"

"The only problem here," Hatter said, spinning on her, "is you. We have to find a solution to the problem that's you."

"Fine." She was used to this argument. She was a bother to everyone. Well, she knew the solution. "I'll leave."

"That's what ye'd like, isn't it?"

The muscles in her shoulders and arms quivered as her heart rate sped up.

He turned, ducking to miss a low-hanging branch as he stepped over a high root. "What about yer sister? Eh?"

"What about her?" Red touched the branch. It shivered and shrank away from her. "I couldn't care less."

"Well, that's obvious. Is there anyone you care about so much as ye'self, love?"

The sting his words left behind reminded her yet again why she preferred her emotions turned off. "It has nothing to do with that."

"Oh, really. Tell me your sob story. See if my heart'll bleed for ya."

Heat rose to her cheeks and rolled down her arms. "I don't need to be judged by you—or anyone else."

"Who said anything about judging?"

"That's what you lot do." She stopped and blinked into the shadows of the whispering wood. "What am I doing here?"

He took in a deep breath and let it go before he turned to her. "The White Queen wants t' save you. She thinks you're something worth keeping, I reckon."

Red flinched, pulling her lips back.

He scratched his chin and advanced. "The elders are coming to destroy her world because she helped you, and there's a child out there what needs your help."

Two things with which she couldn't assist.

He pointed to the world behind him. "That's what I'm doin' here. Trying to keep that daft woman of yer sister alive for her dreamers, for all the little boys and girls out there she gives hopes to. That's her job, ye see."

Red took a step back as he pressed his body close to hers.

"And you, I think, understand what that means more'n most. Ye've had yer heart near ripped out. You barely survived with any of yer muchness intact."

She took in a sharp breath.

His dark eyes, mere shadows among shadows, gripped hers. "And I think you know what these kids, these dreamers really need. Yer sister? Not so much. But you?"

She shook her head, denying what he was about to say.

"You do."

She swallowed and breathed in his scent of leather and wood smoke.

"Finding that dreamer, that child you couldn't care less about, could be the one thing that saves you, saves yer sister, and saves this land."

Her heart folded, or unfolded. She couldn't quite tell. It hurt. It twinged with a pain she'd hoped to have forgotten, a pain the understanding in his eyes awakened. "What if... " She let that sentence trail off. She didn't want to finish it, didn't want to say it out loud.

He nodded. "In order to help others, ye have to allow ye'self to be vulnerable."

She shook her head.

"Vulnerable," he said, his words feathering against her lips, "doesn't mean weak, Red."

Experience told her otherwise. Flinching, she re-erected the walls around her emotions, and shut off the pain in her heart. "If you're counting on me to do all that, you're in a sorrier state than you thought."

"Oh, no, Princess." He turned and walked away. "I don't expect you t' do any of that. I'm quite expecting ye to fail. That's what ya do, right?"

Red jerked away as if she'd been slapped, her abdomen clenching in the sheer truth of his words. "Then why are we here if you think all I'll do is fail?"

"Because learning happens with the failing, not with the succeeding."

Red rubbed the back of her neck, the spindle trees poking at her ribs and thighs. It was stupid for anyone to count on her. Muggs really should have known better.

A picture floated in her mind's eye of a rosy-cheeked boy, smiling for all the world, his arms moving wildly about as he told of some grand adventure. Her arms grew heavy with the remembered feel of her daughter's body, her breast recalling the comfort of her warmth.

Red blinked back tears she thought had deserted her long ago. Her gut twisted as her heart filled with the lead weight of her sorrow. She doubted she could help anyone ever again, and she didn't know if she had it in her to want to.

Hatter stopped on a knoll and looked back, the light of the rising moon masking him in silhouette.

She'd failed her children, her husband. How could she ever overcome that?

Her feet moved, one in front of the other, and a tiny voice sounding shockingly like her own whispered, *I dare you, Red. Try.*

Red picked up the pace, her heart fluttering in her chest along with a few rather uncomfortable emotions and sensations. She couldn't name them all, didn't know if she wanted to.

Why had she wanted to feel again? What had been the point? To be miserable? Because that's exactly what this was.

With her emotions turned on, however, she *did* want to help the child and her sister and this crazy world. Why? What was in it for her? She'd just end up disappointing them, being disappointed by them, but at the moment, she didn't care.

Someone's boy was out there, scared, lost. She had to help if she could. She remembered what it felt like when she couldn't find her son, the desperation, which had been hammered in the moment she found him buried under the rubble of a building that had been bombed. No mother should have to suffer through that.

"How far away is this child?"

Bright light from overhead lit up a thick frown along his brow. "We should be there already."

Where was all the light coming from? Red looked to the sky and stumbled backward.

From the three moons, perhaps? "How many moons does this place have?"

He gave her a look that asked what kind of crazy she'd had for breakfast, and then looked up. His expression widened in wonder. "We've never had moons before, much less three of them."

One was a crescent moon, but large and, surprisingly, the source of most of the light. The second one was either waning or waxing, but at the half mark. The third one was blue and full, but small, riddled with pockmarks and scars, and reminding her of home if not for the color.

"You think this is the work of the elders?"

He nodded, frowning at her waistline.

"What are you looking at?"

He gestured to her with an upraised eyebrow.

The spindly arms of the forest behind them wrapped around her. To shield? To protect? She touched them lightly. "I have to be off now," she said as softly or politely as she could muster, which was a lot nicer than she'd spoken in... Over a decade. Possibly two.

The branches paused, but released their hold on her.

Hatter narrowed his eyes at her. "What affect are ye having on this place?"

She rolled her eyes and flung her hand to the lands in front of them. "Why don't we just disappear and reappear where we want to be? Wouldn't that be faster?"

"Indeed, it would." He stepped off the hill, his hand extended toward her. "Place hasn't worked well for some time now. The dustmen are able t' use it on a fairly consistent basis, but only fer the carting away of the children. For everything else, we're best served going the long way."

She ignored his hand. The decline wasn't so steep she couldn't handle it on her own. "I thought we were concerned over a boy, a lost child. Why are we dilly-dallying?"

"To be honest, love, it should've been no more than an hour's walk."

"An hour?" She grunted as she reached the bottom of the hill with a not-so-graceful dismount. "We've been at it for longer than that."

"I know." His gaze flitted wildly about.

"Are we lost?"

He shook his head, his cocked top hat making the motion look lopsided.

She stopped, folding her arms over her chest. "What is this really? She honestly thought a mocked-up quest would turn my heart?"

He held up a hand to shush her.

"Or maybe she thought your pretty face would melt me, turn my head, bring me round a bit. Is that it?"

He jerked his hand to reinforce his shush.

She wasn't the kind of woman to be quieted so easily. "Is there really a child out there?"

He nodded.

"And is that child really lost in a location only I can go?"

"Yes, Red. Now, just let me think for a moment!"

The one moment turned into several. Anxiety built in her chest, an emotion that made her squirm with discomfort. "Hatter, we need to leave now."

He turned to her, his head tipped to the side. He gave her decidedly long blink and his lips parted as if he were about to speak.

When no words issued forth, she flared her fingers and stalked off. "Some guide you are."

He stopped her, his grip soft on her arm.

She could have kept going, could have broken the hold, but something in the pit of her soul stopped her. "What?"

His dark gaze pierced hers. "How are you affecting the plane?"

"I'm not."

"You are." He glanced back at the forest, returning his gaze to her. "Somehow, fer some reason, this plane's responding to you."

"Why would it?" Anger-fueled fear thrummed through her. "This is a place of hope, of dreams. I can't even become a nightmare."

His lips parted as understanding lit his eyes, tiny shards of gold flittering through his irises.

She took a half-step back.

"So that's it? Isn't it?"

"I don't know what you're yammering about."

"Yes, you do." His lips crept into a smile as he closed the gap between them. "There is no place in Dreamland for terror. Even in the Nightmare Realm, hope is the key to existence."

She shook her head. "You don't know what you're talking about."

"I believe I do. Nightmares are chosen because they understand how to use darkness to bring hope. They comprehend diseases of the heart. They know how to battle it in ways dustmen can't. They can reach people your sister cannot."

Red swallowed hard. "Use darkness to bring hope. Do you know how brain blasted you sound?"

He brushed a strand of hair away from her face. "You're lost to the darkness." His whispered words feathered across her cheek. "You've lost hope, lost love."

She closed her eyes, her heart twisting as she pulled away. "Hatter, I thought we had a boy to save."

"We do." His hand didn't allow her to go far as he tightened his grip on her arm.

To be truthful, his grip still wasn't that hard. She could break away if she wanted to.

The power of his will shooting from his gaze stayed her feet. When was the last time someone had looked at her and actually saw her? Yes. People had laid their eyes upon her, like her sister. They'd viewed her, condemned her, and asked what was wrong with her. And why? Because none of them saw her for whom she truly was.

"You prance around like an angry princess."

She raised her chin as the anger he mentioned cooled. The fear fell away with it.

"All anyone sees is an independent, stubborn, self-centered woman."

She flinched and looked away. She'd heard that enough, but they didn't understand. They didn't know.

He cupped her chin in his hand, his eyes soft. "You're hurting."

To hear those words said out loud made everything seem so... Real. She had barely kept it together when her husband left. She'd pushed down her fear, pushed down her worry, pushed down anything that would make her weak. She'd empowered herself with anger because she had an endless supply of that.

And when her husband had come back, his brain injured, his personality shattered, there'd been no time to grieve. She had to support herself, her two kids, and her invalid husband.

When he'd died, she'd had a slight sense of relief, but it was shattered the moment she'd discovered her little boy buried in the rubble. She should have mourned. She should have, but there were still too many things to do. She had a daughter to care for. So she'd pushed it all down again; the sadness, grief, the heart-wrenching, spine-stiffening fear. She'd charged on.

Then her daughter fell with the sickness. She'd soldiered on all alone. She'd had no one to talk to, no one to share with, no one to grieve with as she watched her daughter slowly slip away.

And then?

Then, she'd had time in the world; time to grieve, to rest, to think.

He nodded as if he could see everything racing through her. "What I'm guessing is that there really is something left in you, something even you don't realize. The plane sees it."

"What does that," she whispered around the lump lodged in her throat, "have anything to do with the missing boy?"

"The dreamplane has connected with you, which means that Place now works through you."

"You speak like a natter. What do you mean?"

His lips dipped then blossomed into a smile. "It means the path to the boy is in your heart."

Red shoved Hatter away. "You're wrong."

"He's depending on you." He spread out his hands, taking a step back.

"Then he's dead," she yelled, all the emotions she'd battened down to survive rising to surface. Her hands balled into fists. Her eyes laced with tears her thick eyelashes refused to release.

"He's not, Red. Can't you see? There's still hope. Dreamland believes in you. You can—"

She slashed the air with her hand and advanced, her heart raging with grief. "Everyone I held dear died because they relied on me."

He stilled, his hand halfway extended. His eyes searched her face in the power of the moons' light.

"Everyone." The words clogged her lungs. She shook her head unable to say anything else.

He took a step forward and carefully grasped her hand. "Dreamland's given you a second chance." His voice was soft as silk as he placed her hand over his chest. "She believes in you, Red. Dreamland believes in you."

She couldn't take her trembling hand out of his. It was as if her entire existence had been robbed of heat. She imaged she could feel the pounding of his heart under the palm of her hand, but in truth all she felt was the rise and fall of this breathing.

That was enough, though. For one moment, for this fleeting moment, she felt as though she existed, existed with this strange man in this strange land.

She blinked, raising her gaze to his.

His grip tightened on her fingers as his worried expression melted away. He smiled, revealing thin crow's feet along his eyes.

Life fluttered within her soul, opening battered wings, flinging bits of light and hope into the far reaches of the deepest caverns of her mind. She closed her eyes, feeling something shift inside her. Her ears captured the voices of the sleeping flowers, the blades of grass, the spindle trees. The tiny hairs on the backs of her arms caught the whispers of the wind as it raced around her.

Around and around it spun until she felt she must be lost in it, but not desperately lost. Blissfully lost. Lost and content. Not happy.

Content was bliss enough and she could accept it.

She opened her eyes to Hatter's grinning face. She raised her eyebrow, feeling... Well, not lighter, so much, but more able to bear the weight.

"Shall we see about saving a boy?"

She knew what she had to do. The wind caressed her with the knowledge, bathed her with the certainty of knowing. She felt the fear of the boy coursing through her system, a fear she could master for she'd felt far worse.

In her mind's eye, she saw what he saw. Darkness. Whipping wind. Oblivion.

Her heart knew where he was, though she'd never been there, had no idea what it was called.

Hatter's hand latched onto hers as cold stabbed into her like a thousand darning needles. The air froze just beyond the reach of her nose, just past the break in her lips. Pressure built in her ears, blanking all sounds.

Then the daggers were replaced with a shrilling wind and the air was no longer frozen. It was forced away from her gasping lips.

Red opened her eyes and flung out her arms to keep herself from falling. She stood on what might have been perceived as a tall cliff, but was unlike anything she'd seen in her life. She stood on grass. The long blades bent all the way to the ground, forced along the torn and ragged edge.

A brilliant night sky stared back at her from the tear in the dreamplane. Night sky shined from beneath her feet.

Red shook herself and looked to her left where Hatter hung onto her, his other hand on his hat.

His expression folded in confounded consternation as he stared at the hole at their feet.

A few meters away, the grass rolled in happy hills as though nothing was amiss. From the edge of the crater, Red could hear nothing more than the deafening roar of wind, but she saw flowers bend and nod to one another, their piston lips moving as if casually conversing.

Hatter grabbed her gaze and widened his eyes, his lips moving.

She couldn't hear anything he said, but could guess. They were there to save a child and standing there helped no one. She studied the hole to see what she could do to lower herself inside. No walls of dirt or rock. Just a ragged edge like a torn bit of cloth.

She shook her head. She stood on cloth? That seemed a little unlikely.

The boy was in that hole, though. That much she knew even though she couldn't see him. So, if she couldn't see him, how could they save him?

A sharp sound she couldn't quite hear stabbed her ear, making her eardrum throb in pain.

She clapped her hand over her ear and turned sharply.

A fragile creature that could have been a man jerked toward her, his gait uneven and awkward. His fluttering blue robe was nearly as ragged and torn as the gaping wound in the dreamplane. He reached out with a long, bony finger looking like a great, walking corpse.

Hatter tugged her, hugging her close behind him. The wind lit with his hat, tossing it high into the brilliant night sky. For one fleeting moment, its shadow raced against the light of the blue moon.

Electric fire hit her in the arm. She returned her attention to the decrepit man stalking toward them, her lips twisted in distaste.

Hatter turned his face toward her, his lips moving. She caught the barest of sounds over the wind, comprehending mere syllables.

Power?

What did she have?

Darkness. She had an entire soul filled with darkness.

If dreamplanes were made of hope and dreams, her soul was a veritable arsenal of weaponry.

She reached into her heart, not having to reach very deep, and dug out a tiny handful of an inky substance, holding it in the palm of her hand. Tugging Hatter with her, she sidled away from the creeping ancient man. Her soul called for the boy.

His fear answered it like a moth to a lantern.

She knelt in the smashed grass and rubbed the inky sludge into the dirt. It scuttled toward the elder.

He didn't seem to notice, his cataract-ridden eyes peeled on her. He opened his gaping mouth to reveal a ragged set of yellowed teeth.

She reached with her soul, not knowing what else to do, and leapt.

Hatter's hand had left hers, though when, she couldn't recall.

Red's dark waves of hair floated around her. Her booted feet rose as if to let her know they'd found no purchase. She twisted around. "Hatter?"

"... Atter? Ha... Tter?"

Her call echoed around her in crystalline perfection, rising in pitch as if it were going through a chimney.

"Re... Re... Ed," his voice echoed back.

"Do you see the boy?"

"... The boy... The boy?"

Red kicked her feet. A world of broken blue shards surrounded her. Twinkling bits of light shown through. Stars? It seemed the likeliest of answers as they'd been standing on the precipice of the night sky when they'd leapt.

"I'm... Here," a younger voice cried. "I'm... Here!"

Where? She couldn't see a thing and couldn't make out from where any sounds originated.

How had she discovered him in the first place?

His fear had connected with her own.

Taking a deep, steadying breath, she reached into the pit of her heart and tugged. The fluttering light from before rang out in a high peel of bells, traveling away from her.

She kicked the air and paddled, swimming in the great nothingness.

The blue shards drew tighter around her, constricting. She grabbed onto them and pulled herself along them. They dug into the palms of her hands, injecting her with something cool and tingly.

They fell away and she found herself floating in the night sky. Ragged threads dangled from the tear in her sister's dreamplane just ahead. Hatter floated beside a boy, his gaze searching wildly.

As soon as he saw her, his entire expression exploded in a grin. "You found him, Red. You did it."

She swam toward them.

The boy couldn't be much older than twelve. His blonde hair was disheveled, his blue eyes round as saucers. "Can I go home now?"

She used Hatter's shoulder to push off of and gazed at the tear in the dreamplane. Turning, she pushed her hair out of her face, staring. Billions and billions of stars stared back at her.

Hatter floated up to her.

"Who was that man?" she asked.

He quirked his lips, pulling the boy up with him. "An elder, and it didn't look like he was much in the mood to negotiate."

She shook her head. "We can't go back through there. He'll be waiting for us."

"Well, we can't go back through unprepared." He tipped his head at her. "We have weapons. We simply have to defend ourselves."

She kept her lips closed as she lowered her jaw, staring up at the tear in the plane. It really was like a sheet of material, but on this side, it was brown with strings of roots fluttering about.

Movement caught her eye.

She turned her attention toward it, but couldn't quite make out what she'd seen.

"Come on, Red. Let's take this boy to the White Queen so he can go home."

"Yes!" the boy nodded fervently.

She saw it then. The brown slowly slithered away as something dark, something inky overtook it.

No. She gasped. What had she done?

The tear above their heads began stitching itself back together.

Hatter swam toward it, the child in tow. "Come on, Red. We have t' go now!"

She kicked with her feet and paddled with her arms. The opening grew near. The strings flapped tantalizingly just out of reach. With another kick, she grabbed one and pulled herself up.

Hatter had done the same. He and the boy climbed, reaching the top, pulling themselves through the hole.

Red stopped, watching them both disappear.

This could be her end. All around her were stars and darkness. She could float out into the great nowhere and disappear. She could finally find rest.

Hatter's head appeared through the ever-shrinking hole. He shoved his hand through it, reaching for her, while the other struggled to keep the edge at bay. "Red!"

She was so tired. She could let go and simply drift.

He jerked his hand, so close to her own. "Grab hold. Come on, Red. Don't go out. Not like this."

She looked up at him, everything in her soul ready to say good-bye.

His gaze latched onto hers. His eyes pleaded with her to stay. "Red," he said softly, wind buffeting his ragged brown hair. "Stay. Don't go."

How long had she waited to hear someone ask her stay?

Experience told her she'd live to regret it, but her free hand latched onto his. He hauled her over the edge and the hole sealed up behind her.

She found her feet, staggering and tripping as if walking on solid ground were suddenly foreign. She spun, searching for the elder.

"He's gone." Hatter lay on the grass, one arm sprawled over the ground, the other resting on his chest. His thick lashes framed his eyes in the cascading light of the triple moons. "You did something, Red, and whatever it was, he's gone."

She frowned, spying a lump of black in the midst of green. She took three hesitant steps toward it and stopped a meter away. The darkness she'd released lay there, burping purple gas. A fragment of blue robe disappeared within the ball of it.

She turned away, unwilling to look at what she'd done. A tiny bead of darkness had devoured an entire man. Or, perhaps, he'd been a creature, for he hadn't appeared entirely human.

A bead of her soul.

Her breath escaped her as a slight pop sounded in the air.

Her sister's bright, white dress seemed to glow as she appeared out of thin air. She beamed a smile at Red, taking the boy's hand. "I knew you had it in you, Dot. I always knew."

Red blinked as the White Queen disappeared in a flash of mist, taking the young boy with her.

Hatter sighed, folding his hands behind his head. "You saved that boy, you know."

Yes, she had, but at what price?

"And you saved that woman."

That was rather unlikely.

"You saved this dreamplane and all the people who live in it."

"I did not do all that."

"I assure you, Red." He pressed his head into the palms of his hands and released a long breath, turning his face to the sky. "You did. What say you stick around and create a little havoc?"

She frowned at him.

He sent her a mischievous grin. "I believe Wonderland could use a bit more of that. Don't you?"

Something settled in her like a happy cat. Mischief was exactly what she could bring to this world.

S.M. BLOODING

lives in Colorado with her pet rock, Rockie, and Jack, her bird. She likes to hike the beautiful Rocky Mountains and has decided to investigate the fascinating world of microbiology. It's a bit daunting—but amazing! She's dated vampires, werewolves, sorcerers, weapons smugglers, and US Government assassins. Oh, yes. She has stories.

She loves to take the real world, find a singular line of truth, and wrap a complex fiction of reality around it.

LINKS

http://www.smblooding.co
https://twitter.com/smblooding

Tailored for the King

by Rick Chiantaretto

E DEN was well-spoken for a seven-year-old peasant, but I suspected her clear diction and royal accent was a playful act. She even held out her pinky while pouring tea into two crown-shaped teacups that were laid out on my bed coverings.

She picked up her tea and blew on it as wisps of purple steam danced in her golden hair. The sunlight that streamed through a nearby window (hadn't I closed those damned curtains before bed?) lit her from behind. She looked soft and angelic.

I sat up, propped against the headboard. I reached for my cup.

"Careful, it's heavy," Eden's trilling voice echoed through my chambers.

"I am King, my child. Kings are always strong men," I smiled, pretending as though I was struggling to pick up the cup.

Eden's face twisted to a look halfway between expectation and the look my own daughter gave me when she knew I was lying to her. It caught me so off guard that my smile widened.

As a king, not many things caught me off-guard, but children always had their way.

My prepared expression was not so pretend when I actually struggled to pick up the cup. It wasn't only heavy, it was impossible to lift.

Eden's eyes brightened. "Maybe you aren't as strong as you think you are," she chuckled, picking up the cup and forcing it, along with the rest of her tea set, down the mouth of a small teddy bear.

The fact that I could actually see the bear *swallowing* the cups and pot seemed perfectly normal.

"What made you so strong?" I asked. "Stronger than a king?"

Eden's smile vanished and her gaze fell. Instead of answering, she pressed her light pink lips into a hard line, her rosy cheeks flushed.

"It is against the law not to be truthful with the king," I said gently, feeling an overload of anxiety. Something wasn't right. Who was this child anyway?

"It was heavy when my daddy..." she stopped.

"When your daddy what?"

She didn't answer immediately but crawled toward me on the bed and wrapped her glowing arms around one of my royal pillows. She began to cry. "He took a pillow like this. I don't know why."

"Come now, child, don't cry. Let me fetch the nanny to dry your tears and get you something sweet."

Eden considered my offer. "You don't understand," she said. "It felt like *this*."

She lunged at me, the weight of the pillow on my face knocking me over. Damn children. This was exactly why I hired nannies to play with my daughter. Sometimes they were too much to handle, too much to control.

I was not good at these games, and I pushed her off my body. At first, I was careful not to hurt her, but when she didn't move, I struggled harder. When I realized that I couldn't breathe with the pillow over my face, I screamed and thrashed. I clawed at the hands that held down the pillow. How was she so strong?

The pillow was as heavy as the teacup.

I woke with a start, bolting out of bed and gulping air. My lungs burned as I choked, but at least I could breathe.

It was a dream.

I had barely composed myself when there was a knock at my chamber door. The door cracked open and a man dressed in a grey robe poked in his head. "Your Majesty," he announced himself. "I bring news."

"Yes, yes, come in Flynn," I responded. "You know, I prefer for the guards to announce you."

"I do, sir," he stuttered, quickly entering the chambers and bowing his head in submission. As soon as he closed the door, he noticed how dark the room was with the drapes drawn. I sat patiently and watched the expressions on his face while he decided whether to risk my anger by saying something.

Flynn certainly wasn't the most social, cordial, or proper of all geniuses, but he was the most trusted advisor to the royal court for a reason: he was always right.

Finally, I grew impatient, got out of bed, walked over to the window, and pulled open the curtains so we could see each other. "Come now," I said, coarser than expected, but not any coarser than he expected from me. "Out with it."

"Tonight you will receive Vladimir and Balor, quite late. They will arrive after sunset, but before sunrise. Beyond that, I do not know."

I looked at him, stupefied. "Why don't you tell the court to receive them and the guards not to shoot them? What concern is it of mine?"

The look on Flynn's face was judgmental, as if I had said something stupid. Had anyone else dared look at me like that, I would have him locked away until his face was too old and fragile to make that expression again.

"You've sent them all away, Majesty. The court, the guards, your wife... they are all getting the country ready for your procession," he said.

"My what?"

Now his face faded to concern. "Your procession. To England. To claim the throne." The last word trilled upward, unsure whether or not it was a question.

"I won the war?"

Flynn sounded like he was choosing his words carefully, "Yes, sir. England has fallen to your armies. Vladimir and Balor will fit you with royal attire for your procession to the castle where you will claim the seat of England."

Of course. I knew this. Didn't I?

"As the cooks are out," Flynn paused, then added hastily, "also preparing for the procession, I will lay out some fruit and cheeses for your morning meal. I'm assuming you still wish to spend the day in celebration with your daughter? Shall I arrange a seat at the table for her, as we discussed?"

"Yes, yes. That would be lovely."

"Very well, then. I will leave you to make yourself ready."

He bowed a little too low before heading toward the door.

"Wait," I said. "Flynn, I know sometimes my wife asks you things... mystical things."

Flynn didn't answer, only turned to look at me from behind dark eyes.

"I had a dream last night about a little girl. Everything in the dream was too heavy for me to lift. How would you interpret such things?"

"My Lord?"

"Dream interpretation. Are you any good at it?"

Flynn paused, his hand resting on the doorknob to my chambers. The worry behind his dark eyes made me wonder if he contemplated running away instead of answering my question.

He chose to respond. "May I speak freely, without fear?"

I laughed. "According to you, I sent all my guards away. What do you have to fear?"

Flynn's gaze slid to my sword, which I always kept either on or near me. It was leaning against the bed frame. "You are quite gifted with a sword yourself, Majesty."

I put my hands on my hips and laughed again, a deep throaty laugh. It felt good to laugh so hard, but I could see real concern behind Flynn's expression. I answered him in a friendly, casual tone. "Yes, yes. Speak freely."

"Since the battle—since you were injured—" his gaze wandered again. A nervous tick of his, I recalled. "It's just that sometimes, when someone has been that close to death, they start to see things. Things that are also dead."

"I don't recall being injured."

"I know, My Lord. The doctor's have explained it to you. Her Majesty, the Queen, has explained it to you, too. It seems your memory has been affected as well."

I thought on this for a moment, deciding to take Flynn at his word. "Yes. Well. My wife tells me you also see things that are dead. Have you seen this girl?"

"Yes. That's how I know she is dead. Sometimes the dead cling to things they desire most. Her spirit is drawn to things she didn't have in life. The nannies, your daughter's toys, a loving father..."

"Does she pose a threat?"

"No, sir. She should cross over after her wake. Most spirits wait around so they can attend."

"I want her father to be found and beheaded."

Flynn looked surprised. "On what charges?"

"Murder," I responded, pulling on a robe and reaching for my sword.

"Is there proof, Your Majesty?"

The dream of the girl replayed in my head, but I chose not to share how I knew—too well—the girl's fate. "I am the king. Do I need any?"

"How will you find him?"

"Tell the guards her name was Eden. Have them interrogate the peasants after the procession."

"As you wish."

"You are dismissed, Flynn."

"Yes, Your Majesty."

He had just stepped outside of the door when I added, "Oh, one more thing. No tea at breakfast."

"As you wish," he repeated, subduing a grin, his dark eyes a little too knowing.

To say my daughter was the most important thing in my life was not a lie. Not exactly, anyway. I loved her dearly, as any father would. Her raven hair reminded me of her mother, and there was so much of it springing from her head that it all looked too heavy for her small frame—and that reminded me of her strength. So, of course, I loved her. She represented all the important things in my life, even if she wouldn't look at me while she ate her fruit.

The fact was, I didn't dote. I made a much better king than I did a father. If only running a child could be the same as running a kingdom.

I sighed. "Well, what a joyful morning this has turned into."

She still didn't look at me, just poked at a banana.

"I'm sorry I'm not good at playing games with you. I'm a man of strategy, and—"

"Cunning," I heard Flynn's voice. He was standing against the wall of the dining hall, ready to wait on us, his eyes downturned.

It's rude to watch people eat. It's even ruder to eavesdrop. But I supposed since it was only the three of us in the room, he couldn't help it. He couldn't see the sharp glare I gave him either, since his eyes were trained on the ground.

I sighed again. Usually my daughter was not this hard to impress. "I suppose, if you would prefer, I can have you sent to your mother."

"Would you like that, Emilie? Shall I send for the carriage to take you to the Queen?"

For the first time this morning, my daughter's eyes brightened, but Flynn's interruption caused anger to boil inside me. I hit the table so hard a plate went flying, hitting the ground and spraying shattered porcelain across the floor. "I do not need you to help me speak to my own daughter, Flynn!"

The brightness of my daughter's eyes faded to black as fear crossed her face. She tensed and pushed her back against her chair.

My fatherly instincts failed me. I had no idea what to say or do to comfort her. This was her mother's role.

Finally, I stood to leave. I wasn't hungry anyway. "Call the carriage, and clean this up."

My sleep that night was restless. I tossed inside the inky blackness that swirled through the room, so much that it felt like my entire body was moving. The sensation made me dizzy, even while I slept. The air around me was so hot and heavy that I dreamed of being held down while demonic creatures breathed on me. I couldn't see them in the darkness. I only knew they were there because they swirled while spinning me 'round and 'round.

When I first heard the pounding, I assumed it originated from within my dreams. It accompanied a pounding headache, so rhythmic and regular that it sounded otherworldly.

Pound. Pound. Pound.

One, two, three.

Eventually I opened my eyes, registering that the pounding wasn't going away.

Lighting my oil lamp and slipping on my boots while still clad in my nightclothes, I wrapped my baldric around me and snapped my sword and scabbard into place at my hip. I regretted dismissing my guards, even if I were only here for one more day.

"The walls are secured and the gates are locked, as are the castle doors," I reminded myself out loud.

Pound, pound, pound.

I was an exceptional swordsman. I drew my blade to feel its balance in my hand again. I used this blade mere days ago to gut the king of England and claim his throne as my own. "I am capable of protecting myself," I said to the blade, swallowing the pit that was rising from my stomach. I set off to find the noise.

It didn't take me long to trace the pounding to the front door. Was I being invaded? The pounding was much too strong for a normal knocking, but much too subdued to be any type of battering ram. How did somebody manage to make it inside the castle walls? Past the drawbridge or the gatehouse? I set my lamp down in the middle of the floor so I had enough light to see by, but so I also had both hands free... just in case.

Pound, pound, pound.

Where was Flynn? The idea of having him around would put my mind at ease.

I watched dust shake loose from the door with the next *pound, pound, pound.*

I drew my sword, and slid open the lock.

Half-expecting the door to burst open, I clenched the hilt of my sword so tightly that my knuckles were white.

However, the door didn't move; the pounding stopped.

I stood there in the silence for what seemed like a long time, watching the flicker of the lamp cast shadows against the heavy door. Finally, when I was sure that whatever was making the pounding noise was gone, I inched the door open.

My sword was at the neck of the first of two men before I even remembered putting it there.

He made a sound that resembled a screech as his muscles tensed. "Uh, well. Sir. I am Vladimir and we are invited guests of the King."

Vladimir. Oh, yes, yes. Flynn told me he and his friend would be arriving tonight.

As if reading my thoughts, the tall and slender man motioned to his short and chubby cohort. "And this is Balor."

He tried to smile, but the grin looked nervous.

I lowered my sword and considered giving an apology, but I am the king, and I do not apologize.

"You are *very* late. How did you get into the courtyard?"

Vladimir was as still as the statues that flanked the door; his nervous grin seemed as permanent as the expressions carved upon their stone faces.

"Do you make it a point to ignore the questions of the kings who employs you?"

Vladimir seemed to wake up, or something (was there something seriously wrong with this guy?). He gave a quick bow, rambling, "Of course, of course. Forgive me, Your Excellency. I must admit, His Majesty has never before greeted me at a castle door. The drawbridge was down and the gates open. A man met us in the courtyard, attended to our horses and cart, and suggested we knock... um... here."

"Here," the short chubby man repeated, his voice much deeper than I expected.

Flynn. That made sense. Someone would have had to receive them.

"Well, come in. Are you aware you are *exceedingly* late?" I realized my question wasn't coherent, but I would not take blame for being on edge when they arrived in the middle of the night. The more I thought about it, the more I wondered if I was trying to justify my own fear—fear I probably shouldn't feel as a king fresh off a conquest.

Vladimir and Balor gazed around the castle with curiosity as they entered, although at what, exactly, they were looking I didn't know. The light from the oil lamp didn't give off enough light to see either the expansive halls, or the ornate detail of the room.

"I will show you to your room..."

Ugh, I really shouldn't have let all my servants leave for England. I hated catering to people. They were supposed to cater to me.

"...which you will be locked into for the night. Security, of course. Flynn will see to you in the morning."

"Yes. That will be wonderful," Vladimir said, stressing the word 'wonderful' enough that I was sure it was meant to be sarcastic. Not that I cared.

"Not to doubt your work," I started as I twisted my way to the rooms furthest from my own, careful not to add what I really wanted to say, which was that I doubted their work, "but how do you intend to dress me in time for my procession. It's the day after tomorrow."

Balor snickered, a reaction I didn't appreciate.

"Most of the work has already been completed, Your Majesty. Tomorrow I will just need to take some measurements to finish assembling the pieces."

"And what if I hate what you have decided to do?"

Vladimir paused before he spoke, his voice softer than it had been so far tonight, "Sir, I dress the finest men in the entire world. If someone didn't like one of my designs, I would have surely been dead by now. I have something for you that is cutting edge, exciting, and worthy of a ruler of your power and renown."

"This procession marks my transformation from King to Emperor. I need something worthy of more than just power and renown. It must... frighten."

Balor and Vladimir now flanked my sides, clinging to the light. I saw them pass a knowing glance, but the fact they were willing to die for their work did put my mind at considerable ease. Not many men were so devoted anymore.

"I will show you what we have planned for you in the morning. I believe it is more than worthy, and more than frightening. I believe these clothes will define you forever."

A smile curled my lips. As I turned the key in the lock of their room, I thought that, for their sake, they'd better be right.

The following morning I stood with my hands raised while Balor invaded my personal space with a measuring ribbon. Whenever someone was this close, especially a stranger, my anxiety grew. I kept my gaze glued to his pudgy face, almost daring him to try something. I had already planned the movements required to snatch the ribbon and pull it tight against his throat.

Unless standing here with my arms out meant to weaken my muscles to the point where they couldn't react. How long had it been already? My shoulders burned.

Vladimir chatted incessantly about things like the silk of the East (and how it stained too easily), and the furs of the North (and how they were too heavy for any 'practical' royal to wear, especially when needing to maneuver, like in times of war). I wasn't really paying much attention to him until he started talking about his new chain mail and how it would be incorporated into my new clothes.

"Wait," I said as he rambled about 'fineness' and 'flexibility.' "Show me."

For the first time this morning, Vladimir's eyes met my own and beamed with pride.

Balor pushed my arms down to my side and threw himself around me in a bear hug. At first I thought it was some sign of affection, which made me nervous again, but it turned out he was only wrapping the ribbon around my body so he could measure my chest. I flexed instinctively.

"No need to puff up, Your Majesty. I know you're a large man," he joked while his arms were still around me. He was so close that I could smell his breath as he spoke: oranges and cinnamon. It was more pleasant than what I expected, which would have been something like rotting bacon or whiskey, perhaps. The look in his eye, however, made the comment a bit awkward. I let out a breath of my own... and 'unpuffed.'

Balor lingered a moment longer than necessary, but finally murmured, "I'm finished. The pieces we've cut will be sufficient. We may need to take in the breastplate a bit at the ribs, and loosen the waist. Do you dress to the left, or to the right, Your Highness?"

Flynn, who had been standing close by with my sword, had an amused look on his face all morning. Now he smirked.

I didn't know what games this man was playing, but I refused to be embarrassed. My cheeks flushed with color and I felt a scowl coming on. I don't know why I felt this flush: every pant maker I had ever encountered asked me this same question.

"To the right," I answered, my voice gruffer than usual.

Balor stepped back and eyed me up and down, raising an eyebrow. "We'll need to let out the right pant leg another inch or two—"

I grunted.

"Fine. Three."

Vladimir looked amused, but nodded his agreement before hastily bringing me a piece of material. "This, Your Excellency, is my greatest accomplishment in fashion so far, and I am excited that you will be the first to wear it."

He handed me a piece of black cloth, which looked thick in appearance, but otherwise not out of the ordinary. Yet, when Vladimir placed it in my hands, it was heavier than I expected.

Vladimir smiled, giddy, when I couldn't control the surprise on my face.

"See," he said, flipping the fabric over, and pulling back an unsewn edge, "between two pieces of the finest blend of cottons is this new type of protection. It's made from steel that has been spun very thin, and then woven together like traditional chain mail. But because it is so small and light, and the weaving done so expertly..."

The way he said the word I knew he had come up with the expert weaving technique himself.

"... It presents itself as both strong and flexible. You could wear this every day, unlike your regular armor, and be protected from any sword I've encountered. In battle, it is more flexible, giving you an advantage over your enemies who will barely be able to move in their traditional battle gear."

I examined the interwoven steel threads more carefully, flexing them in my hands. I was impressed.

"My entire procession clothes will be made out of this?"

"Of course."

"Am I the only king to possess this material?"

Vladimir's eyes glimmered. He looked like he was about to cry tears of excitement and happiness. "You're the only *emperor*," he said with reverence.

"If this wears as you say it should, comfortable and flexible, I will employ you and your household full-time."

Vladimir flushed. "The honor, Your Majesty, would be mine," he said with a bow.

"Now," he continued, "I believe we have what we need, but I want to tell you my vision. I have made for you an asymmetrical jacket, which will cut diagonally here and here," he said, making crisscrossed markings over my chest.

I had no idea what he was talking about, but I let him continue.

"Some pieces of chain mail will be exposed, accenting the hems and linings of the clothing. You see, the chain mail will not only be practical but decorative as well. No one but you, and those in this room, will know the steel runs through the entire suit. I will accentuate the black material with a few large silver buttons. Finally, the cuffs of the sleeves will be free of material, exposing the chain in a manner that is both masculine and dignified. Your Highness, people will be talking about these clothes for ages. You will inspire artists and poets to dream, and there will be no woman who won't want to ravish you. In the end, you will be feared."

I knew he was playing to my vanity; it worked.

That night, I dreamt of women. Women who desired me. I knew I was a powerful man. I could command any woman to do whatever I wanted; but this was different. They came to me without coaxing. Their eyes were full of lust.

One climbed on top of me and pinned my hands above my head as her lips met mine. She licked down the side of my neck and asked me to remove my shirt. I reached down and felt metal, tightly woven strands of finely spun steel. This woman writhed on top of me, begging me to undress.

But I couldn't find any clasps or zippers. I panicked as the metal grew tighter and tighter.

I awoke, sweat beading on my brow. I had kicked the blankets and bed coverings to the floor, but it was still unbearably hot. My parched throat burned as I tried to calm my breathing. I pulled off my shirt, which had become covered in sweat and tangled around my neck—most likely the real reason why I felt constricted in my dream.

Sword in hand, I exited my chambers and set off to find water and cooler air. The castle was dark, but I knew my way around. The brightness of the moon made the stone hallways glow with a bluish hue.

I went to the kitchens first, pumping the handle on the sink until I was rewarded with cool water. I didn't bother with a cup; I just stuck my face under the faucet and let the water wash away the shadowy images of beautiful women that lingered behind my eyelids. Now I regretted not only sending the court away, but my wife as well… and my mistress… and my other mistress. I considered for a moment that Vladimir and Balor wouldn't refuse me, but then I'd have to kill them so they wouldn't start rumors. They had to stay alive long enough to dress my army in the new armor.

The water on my face had the side effect of waking me up and causing me to be more alert than I desired. Now I wouldn't be able to fall back asleep easily.

I made my way to the courtyard. The nightly breezes would cool my body and, hopefully, coax my eyes back to dreariness.

Sitting on a bench near a small babbling stream, which the original landscapers had carved off a large river miles up the hill, my eyelids drooped until I heard a rustling noise that popped them open. A surge of adrenaline woke me up again.

"Damn animals," I said aloud, instinctively drawing my sword closer and resting my right hand on the hilt. I peered toward the noise, but one of the castle spires shadowed that corner of the courtyard. Several large trees stood by as silent sentinels on that corner.

Slowly, a white face appeared out of the shadows. It was close to the ground, too short to be a man, with a long nose and two black eyes. It inched forward into the moonlight, revealing itself in a calculating manner, never taking its eyes off me.

I was about to stand and draw my sword when its horns appeared in the light. The small, white goat bleated at me.

I laughed and stood anyway. The castle grounds were full of goats. One of Flynn's past-times was raising them. He did it a little too well, based on their numbers.

Then something odd happened. The shadows shifted, and I watched something glimmer in the moonlight behind the goat. At first it looked like a sword, metallic and reflective in nature, but then there were more than one of these metallic objects, each casting its own glow as they inched toward the goat.

As the wind picked up, the metallic objects moved faster and faster until they clicked against each other. The click didn't sound like metal against metal; instead, it was like someone was making the noise with their mouth, like someone was trying to call to the goat.

Click, click, click.

The goat's head swung back toward the noise, and the metallic objects flashed. I watched in horror as the goat's head dropped from its body, the carcass snatched back into the shadows.

The whole thing happened so fast that I couldn't be sure what I was seeing. Fear raised the hair on the back of my neck. It also made the shadows around me come alive. How could I convince myself I was seeing things when the sound hadn't stopped?

Click, click, click.

I drew my sword, inching toward the darkness.

I was at the line where the shadows met the moonlight before I was able to make out the body of the goat... or what was left. It had been completely mangled and sliced. The only pieces that remained were a few internal organs and the skin lying in a pool of blood.

My eyes widened as I felt a gaze on my back. Everything moved in slow motion. My mind registered that something was behind me. I spun with my sword, ready to strike.

My eyes lifted upward toward the creature. It was easily twice my height and girth, hairy, with cloven hooves for feet, and long, sharp fingers on its hands.

I aimed for the hand that reached toward me. To my utter horror, I realized my sword was gone. I didn't know how, and I didn't understand. It was in my hand just moments before, but now my hands were empty. My slash toward the creature was useless.

Pain tore through me as the clicking, claw-like fingers ripped into my chest. I fell onto my back.

The creature positioned himself over me, his hollow, black eyes staring down into mine as I gasped and gurgled blood. His face was smashed and sinewy, not human, and the skin on his forehead was dry and cracked.

He raised his claws to his mouth, a forked tongue tasting the blood that dripped from them... my blood.

This creature was a devil. Something sent from Hell. I knew it when it looked at me, and a hungry grin broke the skin of his rotting lips.

I heard the noise again as he clapped his claws together.

Click, click, click.

Then I screamed as he tore into my flesh.

I woke myself screaming, thrashing, kicking, doing whatever I could think to do to defend myself from the creature. I bolted out of bed, and my feet hit dirt.

Where was I? I wasn't alone. I heard Flynn's voice cry out, then felt his hand on my arm as he shook me and practically yelled, "Your Majesty! Your Grace? Sir?"

I think he slapped me, but I can't be sure. My arms were flailing, so I could have hit myself.

"Are you okay?" he asked, his hands on my shoulders, his dark eyes staring into mine with real concern. I could tell he had just awoken.

The familiar smell of tanned animal skins and herbs filled my nostrils. I tried to calm my breathing. I was in Flynn's room. There were cloven foot marks in the dirt that made up the floor.

"What are those? Where did they come from?"

Flynn looked at them, then back at me, confusion furrowing his brow. "I let the goats come in and out as they please. They often sleep here with me for warmth." He motioned to the corner of the room where a white goat, just like the one I had saw get sliced up by some monstrous creature, laid curled next to the fireplace.

Flynn's room was underground, always cold and always damp, with a dirt floor and his own private entrance from the courtyard, but he liked it down here. He claimed it kept him grounded, connected to nature.

"How did I get here?" I demanded.

"I was about to ask you the same thing," he said, finally dropping his hands from my shoulders.

When he did, I almost fell over. I didn't realize how much I was relying on him to keep me steady. I looked down at my stomach, and then felt around for any sign of attack, any sign of injury. There was none.

"I was sleeping, and then you were here thrashing. You woke me," Flynn said, with irritation in his voice.

I glared back at him.

"I mean..." he fixed his tone, "what can I do for you?" He smoothed his nightshirt, which had come untucked in the scuffle.

My breathing slowed, but I still couldn't shake the prickling feeling that raced up and down my spine, giving me goosebumps.

"I don't know," I finally answered.

"You don't know why you came down here?"

"No," I answered, confused.

Flynn moved swiftly, setting a pot of water to warm on the fireplace. "I'm going to make you some tea."

"I don't need any of your potions."

"Just some ginger and ginseng root. It will help calm your nerves. The ginseng will help with your memory. You haven't been the same since—"

"I came back from the war. I know," I finished.

"You can't run a country, let alone two, if you can't even remember why you came down here." He sounded annoyed as he muddled some herbs. "God forbid someone start questioning and find out you're not in your right mind."

"Now that's a little extreme," I defended, annoyed—a feeling that didn't mix well with the fear I was still experiencing (some of which was caused not from the dream, but from the possibility he might be right).

"Well, it doesn't matter much now," he said, pouring hot water into the herbal mixture. "Your procession is in a few hours. When you get to England, we can call in a doctor to perform a physical."

"I don't need a doctor." I took the cup from his outstretched hand.

"I won't be responsible for you," he said, a look of worry in his eye. "You need to take better care of yourself. Calling a doctor after your procession to England will be easy to sell as *preventative*, not *suspicious*."

"Fine," I said, gulping down the tea. Flynn certainly was exercising my patience, but since I was in this castle alone with him and the two fashionistas upstairs, I decided I would cut him some slack... for now.

"Would you like me to escort you back to your room?" he asked with impatience. His eyes grew hard.

"No. I'll find my way."

I didn't want to look like a coward, but I knew I would have to cross the courtyard. I did want Flynn to escort me. Normally, I'm the kind of man who would face his fears head on. I would march straight into the courtyard, straight into the dark and shadowy corner where the moonlight didn't touch, just to prove to myself there wasn't anything there. If there was, I'd prove I was stronger than it.

Tonight I barely stole a glance in that direction, and ran—not walked—back to the safety of my room.

Tonight I would allow myself to be a coward.

I began my procession at sunrise, mostly because it would take all day and all night to get to England. People from both countries would line the entire way so they could see the strength of their new and united leader. Vladimir and Balor would lead the way, as was customary for them to receive credit for their hard work on my clothing... my clothing, which, by the way, was exactly as they had promised. Even if the right pant leg was a touch too big.

The armor was brilliant. It was heavy enough to let me know it was there, while being light enough to move as if it weren't there at all. The cloth was cut to perfection, hugging my body in a way that made me feel protected. I could sense the morning breeze flicker through the cotton, which was refreshing and unexpected.

Oh, the cheers! The cheers I got as I walked down the street were unparalleled.

Vladimir and Balor were right about the women, too; I saw looks of desire in their eyes—their men were obviously not being attentive enough.

The men were so impressed, they looked like they were about to revolt. They shouted at me with envy and adoration. They coveted my position. The crowd chanted excitedly, "Long live the Emperor!" I couldn't help but pick up on their enthusiasm.

Vladimir and Balor occasionally stole glances at me, their lips curved into satisfied smiles. When they did, I nodded my approval.

Flynn, who walked behind me, didn't enjoy the jovial occasion. He walked in a heavy wool robe that hooded his face. He kept his eyes downward.

We reached a curve in the road, where the mountainous terrain only permitted a single row of people to stand on the road. As I marched, my eyes picked up on a woman in the crowd. Her golden hair and bright blue eyes reminded me of the little girl that had appeared in my dream a few nights ago.

But this woman was no child. Her corset was tied so tight that her chest was practically spilling from her blouse. A boy no older than eight stood next to her... no doubt a bastard child from one of her dalliances. This woman was bad, and I immediately craved her.

I called a stop to the procession and drank in her ample bosom.

"My Lady," I said, "you must come with us to the castle. I would love the pleasure of the company of a distinguished woman such as yourself."

I waited for her response, but she said nothing.

Flynn cleared his throat. "Do you have nothing to say to your king?"

She curtsied and said softly, "Long live the King."

I took that to mean agreement, but her young son turned to her with a scowl on his face. "Long live the King? Long live the King!" he screamed angrily. "How can you say that? He was horrible to us. He was supposed to protect his people, and he did nothing for us!"

I motioned to Flynn, who quickly stepped between the boy and me.

"It would be unwise for you to continue," he said.

Not as direct or as firm as I would have been, but I supposed it would do.

"I'm glad he's dead!" I heard the boy scream. He peered around Flynn, right at me... no... *through* me.

"This procession, his funeral," the boy continued, actually physically pushing Flynn, "it's stupid. You *forced* us to come."

"Flynn," I laughed, "the boy is obviously insane!"

But as I turned toward him, I caught sight of a casket in my procession. I hadn't ordered a casket.

My face fell. My royal seal was carved into the wood, and my favorite horse was pulling it.

"Flynn, what's the meaning of this?"

"I believe I can answer that, Your *Majesty*," I heard Vladimir spit. I spun toward him. "You see, Balor and I are known for dressing all sorts of people from all over the world."

There was something wrong with his voice. He was talking too loudly, too pridefully, not how one should speak to a king.

"We dress them in a way that will help them endure Hell," he said, and as if on cue, the steel-woven threads started to glow... glow red hot.

"Flynn!" I screamed. A chain appeared between the two glowing cuffs, the metal becoming tighter. Not like armor, but like a straightjacket.

Flynn looked at me with knowing in his eyes, but no softness.

"You didn't win the war," he said. "You fell to the King of England. He is the living Emperor now—not you."

The burning sensation caused spots of darkness to appear in my vision.

"I'm dead? How long have you known?" I asked. "Why wouldn't you tell me?"

"Sometimes the dead cling to things they desire most," he said, as if he were reciting a line. As if it was something he had said before... when he said it in my chambers after I had the dream about Eden. "The nannies, your daughter's toys, a loving father, or..." he hesitated, "a desire to rule over and dominate others."

I fell to my knees as pain overwhelmed me. The skies filled with shadows. I felt Vladimir and Balor pull me forward with a set of chains that I couldn't remember them fastening to my wrists.

"I'm sorry," I whispered. "I'm so sorry."

"No. You're not," I heard Flynn say. But I couldn't see him anymore. My vision faded to black. "But you will be."

Somewhere between the sizzling of my skin behind the red-hot straightjacket and the sound of hooves that roared in my ears, I heard a menacing, *click, click, click.*

R ICK CHIANTARETTO has often been accused of having done more in his life than the average person his age but if he were completely honest, he'd have to tell you my secret: he's really 392. So after all this time, he's a pretty crappy writer.

Rick is the author of two books, *Death of the Body* and *Facade of Shadows* (Crossing Death Series), and has a bunch half-written (when you have eternity, where's the reason to rush?). He's been favorably reviewed by horror greats like Nancy Kilpatrick, and his how-to-write-horror articles have been quoted in scholarly (aka community college freshmen's) papers.

Rick enjoys the occasional Bloody Mary, although a Bloody Kathy or Susan will suffice.

Mostly, he just tries to keep a low profile so people don't figure out who he REALLY is.

LINKS

http://www.rickchiantaretto.com
http://www.facebook.com/rickchiantaretto
https://twitter.com/ricktheauthor

After the Bombs

by Richard Chizmar

THE old man was blind and had crumbs in his beard. He sat in a rocking chair with a half-eaten biscuit resting on a paper towel in his lap. His left hand was shaking, but he still felt dangerous.

I sat down in the chair opposite him and watched him and waited.

He took another bite of the biscuit and returned it to the paper towel. I noticed that his right hand was steady. His gun hand, if this was the man I believed him to be.

He chewed slowly and I watched crumbs tumble from his mouth and join the others hiding in his untended whiskers. I could hear men working the field outside the cabin, and farther away, the sound of a child crying.

Finally, after one more bite, he spoke and his voice was that of a man much younger:

"I apologize for not offering you something to eat. We plant these fields but nothing grows now. Like everywhere, the soil is tainted. But we keep trying."

"No apology is necessary. Your daughter kindly gave me water. That is more than enough."

"My daughter is still beautiful, isn't she?"

I hesitated before answering. "Your daughter is very beautiful, yes."

"She had a birthday last week. Do you know how old she is?"

I couldn't even begin to guess his daughter's age; everyone looked older than they were. The "old man" before me was probably only in his fifties. We were all lucky to be alive.

"She is younger than me, that is all I know."

The old man laughed. "A politician's answer. Or maybe just a kind one."

"An honest one."

"My friend told me you were an honest man," he said, nodding. "And a historian."

"Nothing that impressive, I'm afraid. I write down the stories I hear. It is up to those who read them to decide whether they are history or mere campfire tales."

"And today's story...*my* story, for which you have traveled all these miles...which shall it be?"

"I have a feeling it will be a little of both, no?"

The old man slammed his palm down on the rocker's armrest and bellowed laughter. Again, the strength of the sound coming from within did not match the frailness of the body outside.

"I *do* like you, young man. By all appearances, you are every bit as wise as I have heard." He readjusted himself in the chair with a grimace of pain. "Although, I *am* blind, so I am limited in that capacity."

I laughed before I could stop myself. "I have another feeling...that perhaps you *see* things better than most men with healthy, even watchful, eyes."

The old man nodded again, his tired smile fading.

"It wasn't always this way..."

Before the bombs, I was a schoolteacher. Middle school English. The most "watchful" matters I attended to were keeping my eyes on students passing notes in class or trying to cheat on vocabulary quizzes.

For a time after the war, if you can call what actually happened a war, I was like so many other survivors. Scared. Angry. Confused. But, unlike many others, I was fortunate enough to have family that survived the initial catastrophe. So, despite the hardships, I considered myself doubly blessed. I wasn't alone, and I had something to live for.

We lived in rural West Virginia, far away I suppose from anything of even moderate tactical value, and as a result, we were able to avoid most of the bombs' impact zones and the heaviest radiation levels. As laughable as it now sounds, I once believed our little town to be one of the few safe havens to still exist after the bombs.

Not that our remote location mattered to many of the townspeople. Most of the others chose to leave, and they were never heard from again. Not even a single one of them ever returned.

My wife and daughter and I decided to stay, along with eleven other families, and here we still remain all these years later. A bit the worst for wear, but most of us survived, and that is something I doubt many of the others can lay claim to.

We lived underground in the mines for the first year. Like starving ground hogs. We believed it to be the safest option, and over the course of those first twelve months, we lost only a total of sixteen people and took in strangers totaling twenty-three adults and thirteen children.

We ate canned foods and drank bottled water that we were able to scavenge from abandoned stores and homes in town. Everything was rationed from Day One; we knew what kind of a future we were facing.

Benjamin Travers and Frank Dodd assumed mutual roles of leadership, Benjamin having been a police officer before the bombs dropped and Frank a retired Master Sergeant in the Marines. They assigned duties to both men and women. Cooking. Cleaning. Scavenging. Scouting. Weapons collection. Even guard duty.

This hierarchy seemed to work well, until we were awakened one night by a gunshot near the mouth of the mine. Benjamin had killed himself without warning nor explanation. Frank took over after that, and I still remained in the background, doing my daily chores along with the others.

But that all changed in the weeks leading up to the ambush.

"Do you mind if I write some things down?" I asked, reaching for the notebook inside my satchel.

He waved a wrinkled hand. "Just don't expect me to slow down or repeat myself. This story is once for the telling."

It was fifteen months after the bombs dropped, and the main group of us was still living like animals in the mines; but we had recently decided to rotate a group of ten of us above ground. Human guinea pigs to determine how harmful the remaining radiation might be, and what other factors might affect us if we decided to move ourselves back into town.

After much discussion, ten of us—nine men and one woman—had volunteered to take part in the experiment. Two groups of five, alternating for shifts of one month each. I was one of those to volunteer, the first of many decisions that would anger and worry my loving wife. But, after more than a year underground, something had ignited inside of me; a kind of restlessness that could not be quieted regardless of how many tasks I took on or how many miles I traveled. My Annie called it recklessness and a death wish; I called it living.

The five of us in my group—all men—lived under one roof during our month spent above ground. The old Tanner cabin on the north side of town. The cabin was perched on a tree-lined ridge and offered a scenic view of the valley below. More importantly, if you didn't know a cabin existed on that ridge, it was nearly impossible to find.

All of us crowded into the same three-room cabin wasn't exactly appealing after living in such close quarters for more than a year; but it was deemed safer this way, and it was also thought to be the best environment in which to observe any subtle changes that might occur amongst ourselves.

As it turned out, radiation didn't end up being much of a short-term issue at all. Other survivors—outsiders—proved much deadlier.

At first, in the months right after the bombs fell, it was mainly groups of men, women, and children, much like those from our own town who had chosen to pack up and move on with the hope of finding something better, perhaps even a government-managed safe haven. There were many such rumors in the early days.

These folks proved to be no trouble at all. They crossed the hills into town in tired, ragged groups, looking like settlers from the Old West. A handful of them chose to remain with us, but most moved on with a friendly handshake and a hopeful promise to send back help if they found it.

Occasionally, a lone man or woman staggered through town, more often than not mad as a hatter and twice as noisy. One time when Randy Conners and I were moving through town on a scouting patrol, we witnessed a stark naked man zigzagging his way down Main Street with a pistol in one hand and what looked like a dead rat in the other. His body was covered with bright red scribbles from what appeared to be a permanent magic marker. We always left those folks alone to their wanderings.

But as time wore on, we noticed something more troubling.

More and more of these roving bands consisted solely of armed men. Usually moving through the valley in rowdy, noisy, and more often than not, drunken disorder. We hid from these men and watched them pass with silent gratitude.

But the day of the ambush was different.

It was two weeks after the five of us moved into the old Tanner cabin, and Doug Lawrence and I were resting on a boulder the size of a school bus, smoking homemade cigarettes and watching the sunrise over the horizon, when we both spotted them at the same time.

There were eight of them. Moving fast in a staggered line, as one. Using hand signals. They snaked their way through the valley with the discipline, speed, and stealth of a military unit.

We stayed hidden and followed them the best we could and once we observed them crossing the river, we high-tailed it back to the cabin to tell the others, thinking we were safe.

But we were wrong.

We were no more than a half-mile from the cabin when we heard gunfire. The quick, loud bursts of automatic weapons. Maybe thirty seconds, and then silence.

We ran as fast as the ground would allow, but we were too late. We smelled the gunpowder before the cabin came into sight, and then we smelled blood.

Randy was sprawled facedown in the dirt in front of the cabin, his back peppered with bullet holes, and the other two men were crumpled on the blood-splattered porch, no sign of their weapons anywhere.

Once we made sure that our friends were beyond saving and the outsiders were gone, we searched the cabin and discovered the food and water missing and the three men's' weapons destroyed. They had somehow been lured outside unarmed, and then ambushed.

Doug and I collected what we could carry and returned to the mines to tell the others. The next morning at dawn, five of us returned to the cabin and buried the dead.

"Is that when you decided to go off and help the others?"

The old man shook his head. "That was later...when it became absolutely necessary." He took a deep breath, and I could tell the memories were becoming painful. "We lasted in the mines for another six weeks after the men were killed but then we had no choice but to move above ground. Food and water were running low, and people were starting to act funny. The crazy kind of funny, if you know what I mean. We needed change. Most of all, we needed *hope*."

"Weren't you worried the outsiders would come back again?"

"Yes, the same men," he nodded. "Or others even worse."

I stared at the old man and realized I was no longer afraid of him. "What did you do?"

"We worked in shifts, constructing bunkers and walls, and turned the town into a fortress. We posted lookouts along the ridgelines to warn us of travelers. We still welcomed anyone with good intentions and helped those we were able to. But we were wary now, even paranoid."

"So why did you decide to leave?"

"I left because my daughter was sick and my friends were starving."

Elizabeth was twelve at the time. Even, after the bombs, she was an angel. Unlike many of the other surviving children who passed their days feeling understandably helpless and in tears, Elizabeth spent most of her time reading and helping others. By the time we left the mines and moved into town, she could cook, sew, clean, and administer first aid as well as any adult in camp. All without a word of complaint.

But then she got sick.

At first, we were afraid it was the radiation making her lose her appetite and strength and causing her fever. A handful of us had started to show some minor effects—hair loss, teeth falling out, skin rashes and blistering—but the majority of us remained, on the surface at least, unaffected.

It was Gwen Sanderson, the old school nurse, who soon made us realize that it wasn't radiation at all; instead, it was some kind of virus raging inside our little girl's body, as well as the bodies of another dozen or so of the townspeople.

More and more of the others were getting sick.

And we were out of antibiotics.

And running low on pain medication, canned goods, and bottled water.

That evening, we held a town meeting in Memorial Park and took a vote. It was decided that a search party of four armed men would be sent out immediately to look for medicine and supplies.

When the time came for volunteers to step forward, my hand was the first to go up. Annie cried at first, and then later once we returned home, she got angry. When it was apparent that her hard looks and even harsher words weren't going to change my mind, she started crying again.

But I never faltered. Elizabeth was sick and my town was slowing starving to death; someone needed to find help, and fast.

We left at dawn the next morning. The four of us on horseback. Armed with rifles and pistols, lugging mostly empty knapsacks we hoped would be stuffed full upon our return. Despite the early hour, much of the town turned out to wish us luck and say goodbye. Annie blew me kisses, tears streaming down her cheeks, but Elizabeth remained at home in bed.

We waved goodbye and headed East.

"Excuse the interruption," the old man's daughter said from behind us. "I thought you might both be thirsty." She handed me a plastic glass of water without making eye contact, then placed a second glass on the small table next to her father's chair.

"Thank you," he said, smiling and feeling for the glass.

"Thank you, Elizabeth." I noticed the smile on the old man's face falter and knew it had been unwise to call her by name. He might be old and blind, but there was nothing more dangerous than a protective father.

Elizabeth left the room without another word, and he continued:

"We were gone for nine days…"

The first few days, we searched houses, stores, sheds, schools, even an abandoned police station and came up empty. We were exhausted and dejected and stank worse than any human beings in the history of human beings. We smelled worse than the horses. We decided to give it one more day and then head back.

And then we got lucky.

One of the men spotted a lake in the distance and we all agreed it was time for some rest and a bath. We cut through a meadow and then a thick stand of trees to reach the lake, and it was amidst those trees that we stumbled upon the abandoned camper. The camper was old and covered in Grateful Dead bumper stickers and had four flat tires—it's funny the things you remember—but we searched it anyway, not really expecting to find anything of value.

Boy, were we wrong.

Inside, we found boxes of canned foods and cases of bottled water. More than all of us could possibly carry. We also discovered a mini arsenal of automatic weapons, more than a hundred paperback books, and best of all, two duffle bags full of medical supplies and assorted drugs.

I was the one who found the body curled up in the camper's sleeping bunk. Most of the flesh had decomposed, but we could tell it had once been a man with long gray hair pulled back in a ponytail. His skeletal hands still held a tattered leather bible.

We buried the man at the edge of the meadow, under an old maple tree, and joined hands in a prayer of gratitude. Then, we skipped our baths in the lake and packed as much as our horses could haul and set off for home. It took us two days of around the clock riding to get there, but we made it in time for the medicine to help Elizabeth and the others.

The food and water were inventoried and organized in the town pantry, and the medical supplies went under lock and key in our makeshift hospital.

Three days later, I led a party of six men back to the camper and we brought all the remaining supplies home with us.

At the time, it felt like a miracle.

"Did you see anyone else?"

"Not those first two trips, no. We *heard* someone one night. A man screaming in the dark. But he was far away and we never went looking for him."

"During later trips?"

"Later...yes, we did."

"Good guys or bad guys?"

"Both." The old man scratched his whiskers, dislodging a shower of crumbs onto his lap. "We tried to help as many as we could. If we found six cases of water and ran across others in need, we gave them a case with our blessing. The rest went home with us. But many others...we hid from."

"Did you ever see the men from the day of the ambush again?"

Nodding. "We did...but that was years later, and another part of this story."

I itched to ask more but knew it was best to move on for now.

"How often did you leave town on these...missions?"

"At first, only when necessary. When something was needed. But later..." He stopped and reached for the glass of water. Took a drink.

I waited for him to continue. When he didn't, I asked, "Later...what happened?"

He carefully placed the glass back on the table, and then I could feel him staring at me with those sightless eyes.

"A stranger came to town. A nearly dying man. With a story to tell..."

His name was Joseph and he was the biggest man I had ever seen. At least six-six and two hundred and seventy pounds. A mountain of thick, black muscle. But he was bleeding to death from a gunshot wound in his stomach. How he walked the miles he claimed to have walked is beyond me; the pain he must have endured.

At first, we kept him under armed guard as we administered first aid and allowed him to recover in our hospital. His brute size and obvious strength frightened us. But it was something else, too: he was too quiet, too aware. Even in the haze of pain medication, he seemed—borrowing your word—*watchful*.

A week later, he was amazingly back on his feet, still weak but able to walk with a cane for short periods of time. We had already decided to ask him to leave once he'd fully recuperated when he found me in the fields one evening and, with great difficulty, told me about Camelot.

At first, I misunderstood, and thought he was telling me a good thing. An entire city protected by concrete walls—with an abundance of food and water and supplies; even luxuries such as real doctors and scientists and rudimentary electrical and irrigation systems—all of it guarded by a private security team armed to the teeth.

It sounded like heaven.

But then he explained in greater detail and I understood that the news was anything but good. Camelot was controlled by power hungry men and women, whose cunning and ruthlessness were matched only by their cruel ambition. They allowed no strangers inside their precious walls. Any survivors who approached were either killed or captured and turned into slaves to work in their fields or do other manual labor. But that wasn't enough. They sent out search and destroy missions and executed and robbed any other survivors they could find. They burned entire settlements to the ground. Killed men, women, and children without remorse. Anyone living outside of their walls was considered a threat and an enemy.

When I asked him how he had come upon this knowledge, Joseph explained with great shame that he had once been a member of this city. A high-ranking officer in charge of dozens of men, but that as soon as he'd realized the true intent of the city leaders, he'd stolen away in the middle of the night and escaped. He'd been wounded by a sharp-eyed sentry, but had managed to get away on horseback. He had ridden until his horse, also wounded, had died, then walked the rest of the way.

He estimated Camelot to be located some fifty miles to the Northwest of our town. He believed it was only a matter of time before they found us…and destroyed us.

"So he stayed?" I asked, leaning forward in my chair.

"He never left. In time, Joseph became my best friend, my brother."

"And he did great things?"

The old man slowly nodded, remembering. "Until the day he died."

"How did he die?" I asked.

"I rather tell you how he *lived*…"

I decided to share the news of Camelot with only a handful of others in town, and Annie wasn't one of them. I felt horrible about this, of course, but I didn't want to cause unnecessary panic or worry. Besides, I had an idea.

While Joseph continued to recuperate, we quietly posted double sentries and did our best to solidify the town's walls. Mostly constructed of dirt and timber, the walls had served well over the years at providing sufficient protection from disorganized stragglers that happened upon our town; but we all knew they would be useless against an army of any size. Still, we did our best.

Each evening after my work duties were completed, I would sit outside and smoke and talk with Joseph. I grew fond of him very quickly, as did my family. He often played cards with Elizabeth and taught her how to read the stars at night. He insisted on helping Annie clear the table after every meal and told her stories about his own mother, a single mom who had raised him and his three brothers while working the day shift at a hospital and the night shift at a Dunkin' Donuts.

Joseph had a contagious laughter and a generous spirit. He didn't talk about a wife or children of his own, and we didn't ask. This was a lesson we learned very quickly after the bombs.

By the time Joseph was strong enough to travel and I told him about my plan, it felt like we had known each other for a lifetime.

Two days later, we rode out alone. The black giant and the schoolteacher.

"And that's how the raids started?" I asked, scribbling in my notebook.

The old man ignored my question. "My plan was for Joseph to lead us to Camelot, which we would survey from a safe distance. Along the way, we would keep our eyes open for any sign of a Camelot raiding party or—our biggest fear—an advancing army. It was predominately a scouting mission, meant to make us feel more secure in the knowledge that no one was looking in our direction for Joseph. But I had other things in mind, too…"

We stumbled upon the raiding party at dusk on our third day of riding.

Joseph estimated that we were within fifteen miles of the city by then. His initial guess that Camelot was some fifty miles northwest of our town had now grown to seventy miles; a fact which brought me great relief.

There were six men in the raiding party. Armed and on horseback. Joseph recognized two of the men from Camelot, even from a distance.

We tracked them West for a number of miles and watched them take up positions along a grassy bluff. An hour later, hidden in a treeline, we watched in horror as they swooped down from their hiding place and surrounded a group of unsuspecting survivors on foot, most of them women and children.

A pair of survivors—a man and a child—broke free and tried to escape, but they were gunned down in cold blood. Shot in the back.

As the men dismounted and began to ransack the survivors' belongings at gunpoint, Joseph and I quietly circled behind them on foot, nothing but shadows now in the moonlight.

We stopped some thirty yards behind them and with guns drawn—a rifle for myself, a pistol for Joseph—we looked at each other and nodded. I know it sounds brave; I know it sounds heroic; but it wasn't. I was scared shitless; but more than that, I was angry.

I broke cover first, walking on my heels the way my father had taught me to move in the forest when hunting deer. I hadn't taken but a handful of steps when I sensed Joseph at my side. I stopped and raised my rifle and sighted in one of the men.

"Black hat," I whispered, marking my target.

From the darkness beside me: "Skinny asshole on his left."

Then we both pulled the trigger.

The old man started coughing then, a harsh sound that I could feel deep in my own chest. He fumbled for a sip of water, but it seemed to make the coughing worse. I noticed that both of his hands were shaking now and his face had gone pale.

I was just getting up from my chair to call for help when Elizabeth hurried into the room. "Here, try this." She held a baby blue breath inhaler to his mouth. He immediately closed his lips around it and she pushed the button. There was a hissing sound, and when she pulled the inhaler away from his mouth, the old man's coughing had stopped. He sat in his rocking chair, eyes closed, taking slow and steady breaths. After a moment: "Thank you, darling. I needed that."

"You need to rest. I knew all this would be too much. You need to—"

"You know who you sound like, don't you?"

She smiled in spite of herself, and I think that is the moment I fell in love with her. "I sound like Mom."

"Right as rain. Spitting image."

"Don't try to sweet talk me, mister. It's not going to work this time."

"Ain't sweet talking anyone. Just telling the truth." He turned in my direction. "Right, friend?"

I was still smiling at Elizabeth. I couldn't help it. "Right."

She rolled her eyes at me. "Dad, I really think you should—"

"What I need is for you and my new friend here to help me out onto the porch so I can finish this story and eat me some supper."

So, that's what we did.

It's not easy to kill a man. But that's what we did that night. All six of them.

My plan all along had been for Joseph and me to start intercepting their raiding parties and to return what they had stolen to the folks they had taken it from. If those folks couldn't be found, and quickly, then we would bring the supplies back to town for ourselves.

That first time was an accident the way it happened.

The next dozen or so times were not.

We learned how to set up an ambush; how to flank an enemy with superior numbers and firepower; how to booby-trap a trail; how to strike fast and disappear into the wilderness without leaving a trace of our passage.

And we learned how to kill without mercy when necessary. It never got easier and I never learned to like it, like some men did, but for a schoolteacher, I found that I was extraordinarily good at it. I had a steady hand and a true aim.

Joseph and I learned to trust each other with our lives—and to believe that what we were doing had purpose and meaning.

We took back food and water. We took back weapons and ammunition. We took back hope. And, all of this, we either gave to others in need or we hauled it back to town for our own.

It was months before the higher powers at Camelot figured out what was happening, and by then, it was too late.

"So that's when the stories started? That's when they started calling you Robin Hood?"

There was a nice breeze on the porch. The setting sun felt warm on my face.

"Some folks started with that nonsense, yes. But that's all it was."

The old man was propped up on a straight back chair, ankles crossed on the ground, a thick blanket thrown over his lap. Most of the color had returned to his face.

"'Course, the fact that it was nonsense didn't stop me from calling Joseph 'Little John'—just to get a rise outta him. It worked, too."

"The two of you became legends..."

He scowled at that. "For a lot of survivors, we represented hope and maybe some goodness left in this world. But that's all it was. Yes, we took from the haves and gave to the have-nots. But that's where any comparison stopped."

"What do you mean?" I asked, looking up from my notebook.

"The Robin Hood in the movies and books never did much killing. He fought with the evil sheriff and he stole from the rich to give to the poor and he got the beautiful Lady Marion and all that business; but he did it all with a swashbuckling smirk on his face and a fancy little kick to his step. Errol Flynn in green girlie tights.

"But this was real life. It was dirty and bloody and just plain ugly most of the time."

I didn't say anything. Just stared at him.

"Sure, we made a lot of people happy, even saved some lives, but it cost us. I wasn't there the night my Annie passed on. Elizabeth held her hand as she drew her final breath, but her other hand was empty. Instead, I was running around in the valley helping strangers I would never see again. I still have nightmares about some of the things we saw and did. And we lost a lot of good men ourselves. Some of them died in my arms."

I looked down at my feet. "I'm sorry."

He waved a hand at me. "What do you have to be sorry for? You weren't there."

"I just meant that—"

"I know what you meant. What say you hush and let me finish now?"

After the first half-dozen or so raids, it became too difficult to keep what we were doing a secret.

First of all, we had to keep coming up with stories to explain why we were leaving town and then even more stories to explain where in the heck we were finding all the supplies we were lugging back with us.

Secondly, there were too many people running their mouths by then. After awhile, any stranger that crossed our path was more likely than not to be blabbing about this mysterious Robin Hood fellow and his giant of a companion.

When we finally explained the truth, my wife didn't speak to me for three straight days. Annie was a sweet old girl, but nastier than a pack of yellow jackets when she was angry. And, boy, could she hold a grudge.

It was Joseph who finally convinced her to forgive me. To this day, I don't know what he told her, but whatever it was, it worked, and I was forever grateful. Six months later, I would lose her to the sickness. One week Annie was fine; the next, she was gone.

That was just like Joseph, too. He was always keeping the peace in town. He went out of his way to be kind and helpful to folks, and they loved him for it. Especially the children. We called him the Pied Piper, because he always had a line of happy kids trailing behind him wherever he went. He was also the first to step up and volunteer for any job and he worked twice as hard as any man in town. People respected him. And not just because of his size and strength and willingness to work. He was a good man, with a good heart, and we learned a lot from each other.

As the next few years passed, Joseph and I—along with other men from town—continued the missions; we always gave some of what we captured to those less fortunate than us, but over time, we saw less and less of Camelot's guns-for-hire. We ran across other bad guys now and then, including the group who ambushed us at Tanner's cabin all those years earlier, and we took care of them with the same swift and merciless efficiency.

But Camelot remained a quiet mystery.

"Why didn't you just go to Camelot and see for yourself? Joseph knew the way..."

"We were days away from doing exactly that, Mr. Smartie Pants," the old man said, adjusting himself in his chair. "When the answer came to us instead."

On the last day of Spring, a group of nineteen survivors approached town from the Northwest. They carried with them enough supplies for a small army. They said they had been held captive inside a walled city for a number of years and made to work as slaves; but that an uprising had taken place and the soldiers had been overthrown. Much of the city had been burned to the ground, but the warehouses storing food and water and medical supplies had survived. Some folks had decided to stay and rebuild. Others left to find a new place to start over.

We welcomed these newcomers into town, and within a week they had decided to stay. Joseph, as usual, was one of the first to make them feel comfortable in their new home.

Now I reckon I've rambled long enough about my life after the bombs, and I doubt you've heard what you came for. So, now, I will try to help you, my friend.

The years from then until now have mercilessly been quiet ones. Very few moments of blood and violence. It seems that people are finally tired of fighting each other. Now we fight only to live. Death and sickness still blanket us like a dark cloak, but there is nothing we can do about that. Each sunrise is a gift. We live or we die. The dirt no longer yields fresh crops the way it once did. No one understands why it suddenly stopped last Spring. But the world is like that now. Full of mystery and more questions than answers. Some give birth to healthy babies now. Others to monstrosities. Some animals have returned in great numbers. Others have disappeared. One evening, I sit by the fire and my eyes are tired but fine. The next morning, I awake with the sun and I am blind. Again, there seems no reason for any of it.

Your father, Joseph, died three years ago. He went peacefully on a Thursday evening not far from here. I held his hand and together we stared at the setting sun; Elizabeth held his other hand. The sunlight touched his face one final time, and he smiled that wondrous smile of his and closed his eyes.

I stared at the old man in shock. Tears in my eyes.

"How did you——?"

"I knew from the moment you walked in and sat down and started talking."

"But *how?*"

"I lived and breathed with your Daddy for a lot of years. I knew the sound of his voice as well as I knew my own. You sound just like him, son."

I wiped the tears from my eyes.

"He talked about you, you know. It took him awhile to trust us with your name and your memory, but once he started, he never shut up. He had a favorite story that he told over and over again. I used to love to listen to him talk about you…"

He told me your name was Noah and that your Momma had died when you were just a baby. So, it had always been just the two of you. He said you took care of each other; you and him against the world.

You lived in Baltimore. He was a police officer during the day, a security guard at a factory after you went to sleep each night. He worked hard to earn enough money to send you to a good school outside of the city.

He told me you were away on a field trip with your school the day the bombs fell. A field trip to Washington, D.C. The city had been leveled. He thought you were dead. He searched for you for years, just in case, but he never found you.

He said you came to him in his dreams, and I believed him. I used to hear him cry out for you in his sleep sometimes when we were on the trail together. It was one of those dark nights, sitting by the fire, that he told me this story…

He said one of your favorite things to do together was watching baseball games before bedtime. Sometimes you would fall asleep, your head on his chest, and he would carry you to bed and kiss you goodnight before heading off to work at the factory.

He told me that for your ninth birthday he surprised you with box seats for the Orioles game. Right behind home plate. He described to me what your face looked like when you walked up the ramp and saw the field in person for the first time.

"It's so green!" you said. He would always laugh and laugh at that part.

And then he would tell me every single thing you ate during the game. Peanuts and hot dogs and pretzels and ice cream. He remembered everything you said that night. Everything you did.

He said the game went into extra innings and that one of the players fouled off a fastball into the stands and he stood up on his seat and caught it and gave it to you. And you smiled so big and hugged him so tight.

The Orioles beat the Yankees that night, four to three. And the two of you walked home holding hands and singing silly songs. He said it was the happiest day of his life.

Tears were streaming down my face now, and I made no effort to stop them.

"He remembered..." I said.

The old man leaned forward in his seat, his face drawing close enough to mine that I could smell his breath. "He remembered *everything* about you, son. He said you were his compass in the night sky."

I reached down to my side and took something out of my satchel. Placed it in the old man's hand, so he could feel it. He closed both his hands over it.

"The baseball," he said with a beautiful smile. Tears slid from his eyes.

He reached over and placed a rough hand behind my neck and pulled me closer until our heads were touching. I felt his tears on my face. I closed my eyes and remembered my father.

We were still sitting like that, the old man and the black giant, when Elizabeth came out onto the porch. I looked up at the sound of her footsteps and had to smile at the surprised expression on her face.

"Are you two okay?" she asked.

The old man laughed through his tears. "We're better than okay. Set another plate for supper tonight."

He took my hand in his and placed the baseball back into my palm. "Joseph's long-lost son has finally come home."

RICHARD CHIZMAR is the founder/publisher of Cemetery Dance Publications. He has edited more than 20 anthologies, and his fiction has appeared in dozens of publications, including *Ellery Queen's Mystery Magazine* and *The Year's 25 Finest Crime and Mystery Stories*. He has won two World Fantasy awards, four International Horror Guild awards, and the HWA's Board of Trustee's award.

LINKS

http://www.cemeterydance.com
https://twitter.com/RichardChizmar

The True Bride

by Liz DeJesus

J ANE'S calloused hands trembled as she reached for a glass of water on the table. She had been working on the garden all day with the hot sun beating against her back without a moment of rest. There was also half a loaf of stale bread on the plate in front of her. This was her dinner. More than she was given on a normal day. Her stepmother, Clothilde, must have been pleased with the work she did today. It was the only reasonable explanation.

She brought the wooden cup to her parched lips. Jane took a small sip and let out a minuscule sigh of relief.

"Have you nothing to say? No thanks for your stepmother, who was kind enough to feed you?" a shrill voice next to her said.

Jane nodded and whispered, "Thank you, Stepmother. You are so kind to feed me my dinner this evening."

Clothilde lifted her upturned nose and looked away.

Jane ate her meal in silence and as fast as she could. Clothilde could take her dinner away in a moment's notice just because she didn't like the way Jane breathed. She ate everything on her plate, down to the last crumb, and she drank every drop of water. It would probably be the only thing she would eat until breakfast the next day.

"Thank you for my dinner, Stepmother. All my chores are done; may I please be excused?" Jane asked, making sure she kept her eyes downcast. Clothilde hated eye contact.

"Hmmph. I suppose I can let you rest." Clothilde then pointed her twisted, arthritic index finger at Jane and said, "But don't expect this treatment from me every day."

Jane nodded and whispered, "Thank you."

She went to the furthest corner of the house next to the window. There was a straw mattress that was filled with old hay and it always poked and dug at her skin. And a white blanket that was so thin it was practically transparent. It did nothing to keep her warm at night, but it was better than sleeping outside. One night, when Clothilde had drunk too much wine, Jane moved her things in front of the fireplace and she was able to sleep in the warmest spot in their little house. She draped her whisper-thin blanket over her shoulders and looked out the window. The bright silver moon clung to the inky sky and shone down upon her while she waited for her stepmother to fall asleep.

Jane took a deep breath and closed her eyes. She imagined that she was far away from this pitiful place, someplace where there was no winter and the vegetables grew on their own. Where there was someone who could take care of her instead. Jane thought it would be strange to have someone do her chores for her, but she would welcome that change—or someone who loved her unconditionally. These were the things Jane dreamed about.

Once she heard Clothilde's soft snore, she grabbed one of the books on the bookshelf (the ones she dusted every day but was never allowed to read) and sat down in front of the fireplace. She cracked the book open and read the love story between a lowly servant girl and a handsome prince. This was her favorite book; she loved losing herself in this imaginary world.

Only within the pages of this worn book could she pretend to be the beautiful-but-lowly servant who catches the eye of the handsome prince and proves that she is worthy of his love. Only inside a book is she able to forget about her life.

Once she was sufficiently warm, she carefully placed the book back on the shelf and returned to her corner of the house. She lay on her straw mattress and went to sleep. In her dreams, Jane was the servant girl in the story she'd just read, and she lived happily ever after with the prince. If only she lived in a world where dreams come true.

The following morning Clothilde woke up in a foul mood.

"Good morning, Stepmother," Jane said.

"What's so bloody good about it?" Clothilde snapped.

Jane said nothing. She got up and folded her blanket and set it neatly on her mattress.

"What would you like for breakfast, Stepmother?" Jane asked.

"I've already had breakfast," Clothilde replied.

"Very well. I will get started on my chores for today."

"No. I have something more important for you to do."

Clothilde stepped out for a moment and returned with two giant sacks filled to the brim with white feathers. "You are to make pillows and sell them at market tomorrow morning."

"Tomorrow?" Jane whimpered. There was no way she would ever be able to do it in time. Even if she worked all through the night, it was an impossible task.

"Is that a problem?" Clothilde asked.

"Stepmother, I will do my best to make these pillows for you," Jane replied.

"Make sure you do. I do not want to see a single feather in this house when I return or you will get a beating so severe you won't be able to walk for a week," her stepmother hissed.

Jane felt the promise of tears stinging her eyes. She took a deep breath and forced herself not to cry. Clothilde would make her day even worse if she were to shed a single tear.

"I am going to visit my friends and then go to the market for a new gown. Remember what I told you. Not a single feather," Clothilde said. She slammed the door behind her and left Jane alone with an impossible task.

Poor Jane set to work as soon as Clothilde was gone. She opened one of the feather-filled white sacks and they all spilled onto the dining room table and floor. Soon, there were feathers everywhere.

Jane filled several small pillowcases with the white feathers and stitched them as neatly as possible. It was a fine pillow once she was done with it, but it took her approximately ten minutes to make each pillow. She wasn't fast enough. What she wouldn't give to have the nimble fingers of an elf or a fairy. Or someone to sit with her and help her make the pillows. Large, round tears streamed down her cheeks. She knew that there was no way she would be finished by the time Clothilde arrived. She would certainly not get anything for all of her hard work, not even a pillow. Jane would surely receive a beating come sunset. A lump formed in her throat as she continued to fill the pillowcase with feathers. Jane wiped her tears away with the back of her hand and then burst into a fit of sobs.

She looked up at the ceiling and cried, "Is there no one who will have pity on me? A shred of kindness? Mercy?!"

A soft voice spoke. A voice that was like a warm embrace after a long winter. A voice that was everything she didn't have in her life: kind, gentle, and comforting. "Worry not my child. I have come to help you."

Jane gasped and looked to her right. Sitting on the rocking chair was an old woman. Jane frowned as she gazed into the stranger's periwinkle blue eyes. They were vibrant and playful.

The old woman stood, her salt and pepper hair nearly touched the ceiling. Jane had never met anyone so tall. She wore a simple dress that was a bright indigo and an apron that was as white as bleached bone.

"You can trust me, Jane. I'm here to help you," the old woman said.

Jane remained silent and kept her eyes on the stranger in her house.

"What troubles you?" the old woman asked.

"Who....who are you? How did you get inside my home?"

The stranger gave her a kind smile and adjusted her half-moon glasses. "My name is of no consequence. But if you must call me something, you may call me Old Woman. As for your second question, I appear when someone has great need for me."

"I'm Jane."

"I know...it's lovely to meet you, Jane," Old Woman said.

Jane's heart leapt to her throat as she tried to explain what has happened to her, but all that came out were sobs. Jane covered her face with her hands and felt as her tears trickled from her wrists all the way down to her elbows.

She heard Old Woman's footsteps as she walked toward her. Old Woman knelt down beside her and placed a gentle hand on Jane's knee. Jane looked up and met her steady gaze.

"M-my stepmother, Clothilde, hates me," Jane whispered. "I do all the chores around the house, and still she beats me for no reason. And gives me impossible tasks...I hate it here. I hate her. But I have nowhere else to go. No one who will care for me. So I must stay here and endure her abuse."

"I see," Old Woman whispered.

Jane wiped her eyes and sniffed. Could this woman be the miracle she was hoping for? Perhaps she could help her with the stuffing and the sewing.

Jane whispered, "Can you help me with these pillows? I can do everything much quicker if you could help with the stuffing."

"Dry your tears, Jane. Go rest while I continue with your work," Old Woman said.

"But it's too much work for one single person. The two of us together will be much faster," Jane suggested.

"Shhh, worry not. I'll get started while you get some rest," Old Woman said.

Jane frowned but did as Old Woman asked. She sat down on the rocking chair and told herself that she would only rest for a few minutes. Then she would go back to work. But the moment she closed her eyes she was fast asleep.

Jane woke up with a start. She was certain that she had hallucinated the entire thing. Meeting a strange, nameless woman, falling asleep... leaving a mountain of work unfinished.

"Stepmother will beat me for sure," Jane muttered. She took a deep breath and got up from the rocking chair. She took a few steps until she reached the living room where she expected to find all of the white feathers waiting to be stuffed into pillows.

She cried out in surprise. All of the feathers were gone... save for one. It fluttered in front of her, suspended in the air. Carefully, Jane grabbed it and studied the feather as it rested in the palm of her hand. She half expected it to vanish in a puff of smoke, but that didn't happen. There it remained. Like a well-kept promise. She placed the feather in her pocket, looked around the house, and in Clothilde's room she found that all the pillows were made. Stitched to perfection. Each one in a different fabric. Colorful. Vibrant. Sapphire. Emerald. Sunflower yellow. Amber. Cranberry red. Rows and rows of pillows neatly stacked on top of each other on Clothilde's bed.

"How is this possible?" Jane wondered aloud.

The old woman!

Where was she? All Jane wanted to do was wrap her arms around the stranger's waist and thank her until she lost her voice.

Clothilde arrived moments later. Jane's heart hammered against her chest as her stepmother inspected her work. Clothilde narrowed her eyes and flared her nose in frustration. It was as if she had expected Jane to fail and was amazed to see that the exact opposite had happened. Her stepmother let out a huff of air in frustration.

"Do you see, Simpleton? What you can do when you set your mind to it?"

Jane lowered her gaze and whispered, "Yes, Stepmother."

"Don't just stand there. Go cook dinner," Clothilde snapped.

Jane ran to the kitchen and with trembling hands did her best to cook a meager meal. She tried hard not to cry from relief. It was the first time in many days that her stepmother had not given her a severe beating. She hoped her good luck would continue.

Clothilde woke Jane the following morning by kicking the corner of her straw mattress. "Wake up, simpleton. I have a new chore for you."

Jane yawned and nodded.

Her stepmother walked and Jane followed in a daze, still not completely awake. She wondered if she was dreaming the entire thing when Clothilde's shrill voice confirmed that she was very much awake. Jane looked at her surroundings and saw that they were at a nearby pond, not too far from their cottage.

Clothilde handed Jane a spoon. "Take this and empty the pond with it. Expect a beating if I see a single drop. I'll come back to fetch you in the evening."

Jane sputtered and searched for the words to express her distress, but Clothilde walked away. She held her spoon up to the sunlight and saw that the spoon had several holes in it.

Even if it didn't have holes in it, there is no way I could ever empty this pond.

Regardless of the challenge, Jane got on her knees at the edge of the pond. She caught a quick look at her reflection since it was the only time she could remind herself that she indeed had a face just like everyone else. She had a heart-shaped face and large green eyes that always looked sad, on the verge of tears. Her dark blonde hair was in a loose bun—and in need of a good washing. She remembered that she had her father's prominent nose and her mother's full lips. She forced herself to look away; she didn't want to gaze upon that sad face any longer. All it did was remind her of all the things she didn't have and would never get. She focused on the task she was given and tried to do as she was told. After several very frustrating minutes, Jane threw the spoon into the pond. With a soft splash, it vanished underneath the water. The surface rippled and glimmered as the sunlight touched the pond.

"Impossible. Why does she hate me so? Why does she give me such impossible tasks?" Jane cried.

"Worry not. For I am here," Old Woman's warm voice said.

Jane gasped as she turned to her right and saw that the strange old lady had returned.

"You're here," Jane said as she threw her arms around Old Woman's waist and embraced her.

Old Woman patted Jane's shoulders and said, "I heard your grief. I thought perhaps you needed my help once more."

"I do. I don't know how she expects me to empty the pond with a ruined spoon."

Old Woman gave her a kind smile and kissed her forehead.

"Go. Lie down. I'll take care of this nonsense."

"But surely I can help. Do you have a bucket? Perhaps two? Then together we can empty this wretched pond," Jane said.

"Shh. Worry not," Old Woman said.

Jane was reluctant but did as she was told. Except that this time she kept her eyes wide open, for she wanted to see what magic she would use. Old Woman's eyes shimmered as she touched the pond water with her index finger. Jane's mouth hung open as the water evaporated and hovered over their heads in a large white cloud.

Impossible.

Old Woman turned around and gave Jane a playful smile and a wink. Then she vanished in a puff of smoke.

"Wait!" Jane got up and ran to the place Old Woman had stood. "Take me with you," she whispered.

A lump formed in her throat, and she swallowed several times in a futile attempt to push it back down. "Please...come back," she whimpered.

Jane sat on the edge of the now empty pond until sunset. She heard the leaves rustle behind her letting her know that her stepmother was nearby.

When Clothilde appeared, her jaw dropped. "How did you...?" she sputtered.

Jane wiped a single tear away and walked to the middle of the empty pond. She bent down to retrieve the spoon. She wiped some of the dirt off using the edge of her blouse.

"Here, I don't need it anymore," Jane said as she handed the spoon back to Clothilde.

"Who helped you? How did you do this? There is no possible way you could have done it on your own," Clothilde said.

Jane narrowed her eyes at her stepmother. She was exhausted in every possible way. Physically. Emotionally. Spiritually. If someone were to crack her open, all they would find is a shriveled, dried up tree. Barely alive. She was tired of feeling that way. Day in and day out.

"Someone did help you. Who? Tell me," Clothilde said between clenched teeth.

"It has been a long day, Stepmother. I'm hungry, tired and dirty. I'm going home," Jane replied.

As Jane walked away, she heard Clothilde shout, "I will find out who has been helping you."

Jane ignored her stepmother's shrill cries and walked back home.

When morning came, Clothilde dragged Jane back to the now-empty pond. Jane tripped over her own feet and landed with a heavy thud on the ground. Her hands were covered with grass stains and dirt. She wiped her hands on her apron and stood, making sure that she kept her eyes downcast. No sense in making Clothilde more angry.

Clothilde pointed to a nearby field and said, "Right there, on that spot, you will build me a castle."

"What?" Jane asked.

"You heard me. If you can empty a pond with a spoon with holes in it then you can certainly build me a castle."

"Stepmother, I cannot build you a castle all alone in a day. Please understand."

As if perhaps she was doing her best to search for something that would finally allow her to take pity on her stepdaughter, Clothilde studied Jane's face. "If my castle is missing a kitchen or a cellar, you will be sorry."

As her stepmother walked away, Jane wondered if she should run away. Where would she go? Who would take her in? What if she came across someone worse than

Clothilde? An ogre or a troll—perhaps a giant? Jane took several deep breaths while she decided what to do next.

What if Old Woman doesn't appear this time around? What if her magic isn't strong enough to build a castle in a day?

So many questions running rampant in her mind. None of which had a definitive answer.

Jane found a few stones and tried to lift them in the hopes that Clothilde would spare her if it looked like she tried to build a castle. She was able to lift the smallest of the stones a fraction of an inch. Its weight was too great, and a sharp edge of the rock sliced her index finger as she released it back to the ground. Jane hissed with pain and inspected the wound. Bright red droplets of blood dripped down her hand.

Her bottom lip quivered, she looked around the empty valley for a sign that her magical friend would soon appear.

Nothing.

No one. I'm all alone.

Her eyes moistened with the promise of tears. Jane pulled on the cleanest part of her skirt and pulled at the hem until it ripped. She used it to wrap it around her finger to control the bleeding. The bones on her hands and lower back groaned in agony as she bent over to pick up another large rock. A single tear escaped her eyes and landed between her feet with a soft splat on the ground.

"Do not cry, my child. For I have come. I am here for you," Old Woman whispered. She placed a warm hand upon Jane's calloused, overworked hands.

Jane looked up and let out a soft gasp. She threw her arms around Old Woman's waist and allowed herself to cry from the relief she felt.

"Oh, thank you. Thank you for coming. Please help me," Jane said between sobs.

Old Woman patted Jane gently on the back and made soothing sounds until Jane's body stopped trembling.

"Now, now. Worry not. How can I help you today, my dear?" Old Woman asked.

Jane took a step back and pulled herself away from the only person who cared about her.

"My stepmother wants me to build a castle," Jane began, "in a single day!"

Old Woman took a step back, disturbed by Jane's words. She adjusted her half-moon spectacles and frowned. "She wants you to build a castle? Has she lost her mind?"

"She hates me. I'm certain of it. But I don't understand why. I've done everything she has ever asked of me. Ever since she married my father, I have done everything to please her, to be a good daughter. Even after my father passed away, I was still a good daughter—even when she didn't deserve it and all she has ever done is hurt me. I don't understand..." Jane said.

"Poor, poor girl. It's not your fault. Some people just like to watch others bleed.

Sometimes that's the only explanation there is. But it has absolutely nothing to do with anything you have said or done," Old Woman said.

"What are we going to do?" Jane asked.

"Worry not. I will take care of it."

"But…you can't build a castle all by yourself in a single day. Please, let me help. What can I do?" Jane asked.

Old Woman turned her periwinkle eyes at Jane and gave her the kindest smile she had ever seen. "I need you to lie down on the softest grass you can find. Close your eyes and dream of something pleasant. And if you're lucky, I can make that dream come true."

Jane's lips quivered, she almost smiled at that statement. But even she knew all of her dreams weren't going to come true. The only thing she wanted more than anything was for someone to love her just as she was: simple, poor, and plain. Jane took a deep breath and did as she was told. She knew there was no arguing with Old Woman. She found a soft patch of grass nearby, and she slept soundly knowing that the old woman would perform another miracle just for her.

She did her best to dream of something pleasant. All she wanted was someone who would love her. Someone who was honest, faithful and kind, loving and true. She knew there was no one like that in all of Everafter. Perhaps in another world. In another life. But who was she to dream such a dream? All she could ever hope for was a soft mattress to sleep upon, a blanket that provided warmth, some clean clothes, and a nice bowl of soup wouldn't hurt either.

And with those thoughts in her mind, she drifted off to sleep.

Jane's hazel eyes fluttered open. Her mind was foggy; for a moment she had forgotten where she was and what had transpired. She yawned and stretched her limbs, lazy like a cat. Jane rolled to her side, ready to go back to sleep when suddenly it dawned on her—where she was, what she was supposed to do, and how Old Woman had taken over her impossible task. Jane sat up and scrambled to her feet.

Jane's mouth fell open when she saw the castle in the distance.

She did it. She actually built a castle in a single day.

Old Woman waved her hands back and forth as she put the finishing touches on the castle. It was as if she were commanding several thousand invisible hands and they obeyed her every command. Down to each opalescent tile, which was placed in its exact perfect place upon the roof; they shimmered and glinted under the red-orange sunlight.

Jane walked toward the castle without knowing that her feet were moving. By the time she realized she was in fact walking, she was standing next to Old Woman, who was still hard at work on building the castle.

"Ah, I see you're awake," Old Woman said. Never once did she take her eyes from the new castle.

"You really are magic," Jane said in awe.

Old Woman smirked at the comment.

"Magic is a simple matter of knowing how to ask for help from the right sources. The wind, the soil beneath your feet, rocks, moss, the sun and all of nature. They are all friends of the Earth Mother. You simply have to learn how to ask for their assistance. Mother knows what you need before you do."

"Is that how you know when I need you?" Jane asked.

"That is correct."

"Can I learn? Can you teach me magic?"

"I could if you want me to teach you, but that is not your destiny at this particular moment," Old Woman replied.

"What? Why not?"

Old Woman parted her lips as if to speak, but then she tilted her head as though listening to someone whisper in her ear. After a long moment she finally spoke. "Your stepmother is on her way here. Now hush, I must finish soon and be on my way before she arrives."

Jane nodded and remained silent while Old Woman finished her work. She moved her hands at a quicker speed and muttered something under her breath in an unintelligible language. Jane watched with amazement as the castle was completed.

"There. All finished," Old Woman wiped her hands on her white apron— even though Jane witnessed no dirt or grime on them—with a satisfied grin on her lips.

"Jane! Where are you, simpleton?" Clothilde shouted from a distance.

"I must hurry away. Good bye, sweet Jane," Old Woman said.

Jane grabbed Old Woman's wrist and held on as though her life depended on it.

"Take me with you," Jane begged.

"I can't," Old Woman replied.

"Why?"

"It is not your destiny to come with me. You must stay here and see how everything plays itself out."

"Please. Please don't leave me here," Jane whimpered.

Old Woman looked over her half-moon spectacles at Jane and gave her a soft smile.

"There is something much greater for you in the near future. If I take you with me you will always be a simple girl. If I leave you here now, there's a chance you can become much more than you could possibly imagine. I promise you, if it doesn't work out the way I intended, I will fetch you and bring you with me. In the meantime, be a good girl and stay here. No harm shall befall you."

"Do you promise?" Jane whispered.

Old Woman looked deep into Jane's eyes and in a voice that was both young and old all at once she said, "I swear on the magic of the Earth Mother that I will keep my promise to you."

With that solemn vow having been spoken, Jane released the grip she had on Old Woman's wrist.

Old Woman patted her gently on the shoulder and gave her a warm grin. "Good girl. Just play the part for a few more days. All will be well."

The kind lady gave her a tender kiss on the forehead and, in a puff of smoke, vanished.

"Jane! Where are you?" Clothilde shouted as she pushed a bush out of her way and sidestepped an overgrown tree root.

"Hello, Stepmother," Jane said. She wiped away the tears that gathered in the corners of her eyes. She took a shaky breath and did what Old Woman told her to do: play the part and hope for the best.

Jane grabbed a fistful of soil and rubbed it through her hands and face to make it look as though she had done some work for the day.

"I cannot believe it," Clothilde all but whispered. Her eyes were wide with a mixture of surprise and awe. Clothilde gazed upon the new castle and then turned her attention to Jane.

"I don't know how you did it or who helped you. This is truly remarkable," Clothilde said.

And that moment was all worthwhile. Those were the kindest words that Clothilde had ever spoken to Jane.

"Thank you, Stepmother," Jane said. She lowered her head and felt her cheeks grow warm. She wasn't used to receiving compliments from anyone, much less her stepmother.

Clothilde pursed her lips and looked away, as though embarrassed for having been thoughtful enough to give Jane well-deserved credit for everything she had done thus far.

"Well...there had better be a cellar filled with many bottles of fine wine—or you will surely pay dearly for it," Clothilde said.

That was certainly short lived.

Clothilde stomped her way toward the glittering castle while Jane followed closely behind her.

"See how easily it was done? I wish I had given you a more difficult task," Clothilde goaded.

They walked into the castle and Jane let out a soft gasp. Old Woman created a castle in which only a king and queen would live. Jane did her best not to look so surprised. She didn't want to give away the fact that she had absolutely nothing to do its construction or design.

"You will be sorry, Jane, if you've forgotten a single thing," Clothilde warned as they made their way downstairs.

But every room they explored in the castle was pristine. Not a thing was out of place. Copper pots and pans hung near the kitchen hearth; the drawers were filled with silver utensils, and the cabinets housed the finest china. An inspection of the pantry revealed bread and jam, salt and sugar and spices, fish and fruits, herbs and honey, tea and coffee—everything you could possibly need.

Clothilde, however, was determined to find something wrong with the castle. She let out a huff of frustration and said, "Aha! There's the cellar door. There had better be wine in those bottles waiting for me."

"Wait, don't go downstairs in the dark. Let me find a candle," Jane said.

Clothilde waved her hand as though Jane were a nuisance, a buzzing little fly and opened the cellar door. "Hush. I'll be perfectly fine."

From where Jane stood, she noticed that there weren't any stairs that lead down to the basement.

"Stepmother, wait!" Jane warned.

"I said be quiet, simpleton," Clothilde snapped.

Jane bit her lip and did as she was told.

Just play the part…

Clothilde muttered some unintelligible words and turned back to the door. She walked through the threshold and all Jane heard was a loud *whoosh*. Jane covered her lips and gasped. It felt like an eternity had passed before she finally heard a deadly *thump* and *crunch*. Only then did Jane allow herself to scream in shock.

Her hands and legs trembled as she lit the candelabra. She walked as fast as she could to the cellar door and looked down. There, at the bottom was Clothilde. Her arms and legs at awkward, twisted angles, blood spilled through her nose and mouth, around her head there was a pool of blood that surrounded her like a crimson halo. But she wasn't an angel, at least not one Jane had ever imagined.

"I knew I had forgotten something," Old Woman said as she appeared next to Jane.

"She's dead! My stepmother is dead," Jane cried.

"I know," Old Woman said. She looked down below and clicked her tongue against the roof of her mouth.

"B-b-but…now I'm all alone," Jane whispered.

"No, my dear. Now, you are free," Old Woman said.

Jane shook her head. She never wanted her stepmother to die, but she knew that Clothilde would never have let her have a life of her own. She was always given too many chores. And even if she had met a young man that loved her, Jane knew that Clothilde would've ruined any chance at happiness.

"What happens now?" Jane asked.

Old Woman shrugged her shoulders and replied, "The possibilities are endless."

Jane nibbled on her thumbnail while she thought for a moment. She didn't know what she wanted and she certainly needed time to think.

Perhaps I can stay here until I've decided...

"This is a beautiful castle," Jane mused as she looked around.

"It's yours if you want it," Old Woman said.

"But what about Clothilde? We can't just leave her there."

Old Woman waved her hands and Clothilde's body and blood vanished. She waved her hands once more and stairs appeared.

"Better?"

Jane nodded.

"She's buried where the pond used to be, in case you want to bring her flowers. I certainly wouldn't... but I know you're a sweet girl and will do those things."

"Thank you."

"You're very welcome, my dear."

"Will I ever see you again?"

"I'm not sure. But I do know that my duty here is done."

Jane pouted and did her best not to be too sad. She had been given everything she could possibly want.

"Good bye, sweet Jane," Old Woman leaned forward and kissed her gently on the forehead.

"Good bye, Old Woman," Jane said.

Old Woman gave her a playful wink and a mischievous smile. "Remember, all you have to do is play the part." And with those words having been said, the mysterious woman vanished in a swirl of smoke.

The place now belonged to Jane. She couldn't quite believe she had the incredible castle all to herself. In every single room, there were coffers filled to the brim with gold and silver coins. There were trunks filled with dresses in every color imaginable—some she couldn't name. Soon villagers approached her with the hopes of finding work in her beautiful castle. That was how she was able to fill her home with friendly faces and helpful servants to wait on her every whim. The callouses on her hands and feet vanished after several months, leaving behind soft, supple skin, as if she had been a princess her entire life.

Soon stories of her vast riches, kind heart and beauty were told in all of the corners of Everafter. What surprised her the most was hearing about her supposed beauty, for she had never considered herself pretty. She felt as though they were describing someone else. One day she passed her reflection in the mirror and, for a moment, she almost curtsied; she didn't recognize herself. Who was that striking young woman with golden honey hair that shone in the light? Who was that lovely lady? Jane smiled when she realized that it was her. She blushed and walked away.

Play the part and all will be well, she reminded herself.

She had Princes, Dukes, and Lords visit her nearly every day with the hopes that they could win her affections and earn her hand in marriage. Jane was overwhelmed by all the attention and her quickly growing popularity.

After many, many suitors, she finally met the man that made her heart flutter at the mere sound of his name. Prince Stephan. He was the only one that looked at Jane and saw her as a person. He didn't look at the jewels, gold, castle, or rich lands that he would gain through their betrothal.

They met on Sunday morning and spent the entire day together.

On Monday, he brought her a large bouquet of bright pink peonies. On Tuesday, they spent the day baking sweet cakes with blue frosting. On Wednesday, Prince Stephan wrote her a lovely sonnet about how he wanted to spend every waking moment with her at his side. On Thursday, there was a terrible thunderstorm, so he was unable to visit—Jane spent that entire day sitting by her window and praying for the rain to go away.

When Prince Stephan returned on Friday, they spent the entire time in the garden.

"I want to know everything about you," Prince Stephan confessed.

Jane blushed.

"Your cheeks are as red as these roses," Stephan teased.

Jane covered her face with her hands and willed herself to stop blushing.

"Tell me something about yourself. Something nobody else knows," Prince Stephan said.

"I wouldn't know where to start. No one has ever been interested in knowing anything about me before," Jane said.

"We'll start with something simple. How about your favorite color?"

"Pink." She remembered the peonies she had in a white vase by her windowsill. They were beginning to wilt but she would never get rid of them.

"Ahh, lovely color. Feminine, and it suits you perfectly."

"And you?"

"On most days? Green. Sometimes I like blue, and other days I like black. But more often than not—green."

They told each other their greatest hopes and fears, what they longed for out of life.

They kissed on Saturday, and on Sunday, Prince Stephan bent down on one knee and asked her to be his wife.

"Yes! Of course!" exclaimed Jane.

Prince Stephan beamed with joy at her response, lifting her high in the air—as if she weren't high enough already—and spinning her around in delight. "I will go home and tell my father at once. We shall make an announcement as soon as possible. Wait for me. I shall only be gone a few hours."

Jane smiled, unable to mask her joy. Oh, how she loved her handsome prince.

She felt as though she could fly if she truly wanted. She wrapped her arms around his waist and gave him a tight embrace. She couldn't wait to start their new life together. Jane stood on the tips of her toes and gave him a gentle kiss on the cheek. She caressed his cheek and said, "Keep true to me, my love. And let no one kiss you on this cheek until you return to me. I will wait for you."

Prince Stephan beamed as he looked upon his bride-to-be. "I will return shortly, and then we will never again be apart."

Jane watched him leave. She frowned when a strange feeling came over her, as though something wicked had cast a shadow over her happy day. She shook her head, doing her best to push away those negative feelings.

All will be well. Prince Stephan will be gone only a few hours and then he will return. He will come back...he promised me that he would.

Jane waited under the tree until the last of the sun dipped below the horizon, but Stephan never returned. Reluctantly, she went back to her castle and continued to wait. She watched the sun rise and fall for three days. On the fourth day, she thought something horrible must've happened to him that kept them apart.

I must find him.

She resolved to leave as soon as possible in order to find her beloved Stephan. She grabbed a large sack and filled it with three of her favorite dresses. Jane put on her old dress, the one she wore the day Clothilde died. She also packed a handful of gold coins, jewels, and some bread. As Jane walked out of the castle, no one bowed or curtsied. No one recognized her, which was exactly what she wanted.

She walked for countless miles and stopped at every town, shop, farm, and castle. Everywhere she went, she asked if anyone had seen her betrothed.

No one had seen him. No one had heard of him.

She began to wonder if perhaps she had been wrong about Stephan. Perhaps, he was nothing more than a thief, a liar, a man who had made a fool out of her—a charlatan.

She replayed every moment they had together and thought perhaps she had missed something he said or did. A clue that perhaps she had been wrong about him. A clue that she shouldn't have trusted him so quickly. But nothing she remembered gave her any hints that Prince Stephan would abandon her and break her heart the way he did.

Jane came across a picturesque little farm. She knocked on the door and hoped for the best. A kind-looking old man opened the door. He had tufts of white hair sticking out of his head at odd angles. He smacked his lips and squinted at Jane.

"Yes? May I help you?" he asked.

"Kind sir. I am a simple girl, lost and hungry. I was wondering if I could do some chores around the farm in exchange for food and a dry place to sleep for the night," Jane asked.

The old man scratched his balding head and thought. "I'll tell you what. You look like a good, strong girl, if you stay and work as a shepherdess you may have room and board here for as long as you like."

Jane burst into tears. "Thank you so much for your kindness."

The old man smiled at her and patted her gently on the shoulder. "There, there, all will be well. Come, sit by the fireplace and tell me what troubles you."

"I should warn you, some of the sheep will bite from time to time," he said.

"I've dealt with sheep before. I know how to get them to follow me and listen to my calls," Jane said.

"Oooh, even better," he replied. "What's your name, my dear?"

"I'm Jane. Jane Silver."

"Pleased to meet you, Jane. My name is Albert Cane," he replied.

Jane followed him inside his home and joined him by the fireplace. Moments after she took a seat, Jane told him everything that happened to her, from the moment she met Old Woman, until the moment she knocked on his door.

"That is quite a tale," Albert admitted.

Jane nodded.

"You left behind a castle, servants, and riches—all for a boy?" Albert asked.

"Not just any boy. A Prince. My Prince," Jane said.

"Anyone mad enough to leave your side for even a moment is not worth all this trouble."

"But," her voice fell away. "I love him."

"You have a choice to make. You can either go home and return to your beautiful castle and your servants or stay here wallowing in your misery searching for a prince that might not want to be found."

"I don't believe that. I know in my heart that something awful has happened to my dear Stephan. He promised me he would return."

"Some promises can be broken," he countered.

"Yes, but not this one," Jane said.

Albert let out a long sigh and shook his head, almost as if he pitied Jane for the decision she had made. "I see that you will not be swayed. Come, have some vegetable stew and then I will show you to your room."

"Thank you, Albert. You are far too kind."

"You're a good girl, Jane. I can see it in your eyes. I'm happy to help."

And that was how she came to live with Albert on his little farm.

Albert tried to cheer her up by giving her a little calf. It brightened Jane's mood but only briefly. Jane loved the honey-colored calf and its large brown eyes.

"I shall call you Honey," Jane whispered as she stroked her new pet on its velvet-soft head.

Little Honey followed Jane everywhere. Whenever Jane went out in the field to tend to the sheep, her darling calf was closely behind her. Jane thought it was the funniest thing she had ever seen in her life. A calf that thought was a sheep, Honey even tried to bleat from time to time. But, being perfectly content to sit beside her, Honey provided Jane the company she needed.

"Little calf, little calf, kneel you down. Forget not your mistress, dearie. Like the king's son, who his sweetheart left under the linden, dreary," Jane sang the sad tune to Honey when she was feeling particularly melancholy. It had been three long months since she decided to stay with Albert on his farm and make a home for herself there. And still, she had not received any news…not a word or a whisper about her dear Prince Stephan.

Jane let out a sigh and picked at the sole of her shoe. That was when she noticed that she had a hole on the bottom of the shoe.

"Will you look at that, Honey? Just when I think that things can't possibly get any worse I discover a hole in my shoe," Jane muttered.

Honey mooed in response.

"No, you can't eat my shoes. Don't you remember the last time you ate something you weren't supposed to eat. That wasn't exactly the best day of my life, I can tell you that much."

Honey looked away from Jane, as though embarrassed.

"Now, now. I know it wasn't your fault. You didn't know any better," Jane said sweetly. "Come now. Time to finish our chores and see if the shoemaker can fix my shoes."

After Jane was finished with her chores, she went into the village (without Honey, who mooed in protest) to visit the shoemaker. It only cost her a penny to have the shoes repaired, and it was done very quickly. The shoemaker was handing Jane her shoes when she heard the sound of trumpets being played in the distance.

"What's all the fuss about?" Jane asked.

"Haven't you heard? The Princess is getting married," the shoemaker said.

"Princess?" she whispered. She remembered when people thought she was royalty. If they only knew that she was but a poor girl who had the good luck and fortune of having a kind old lady for a fairy godmother.

"Yes. Princess Marie."

"Who is the groom?"

The shoemaker became pensive. He tapped his lower lip with his index finger and muttered to himself. "Prince Steven…or something or other. I can't seem to remember."

"Stephan?" Jane blurted out. She counted the seconds until the shoemaker replied.

One…two…three…

The shoemaker snapped his fingers and lit up. "That's it! Stephan. Prince Stephan is the fellow's name."

Jane clutched her stomach as though someone had kicked her.

"Are you all right, my dear?" he asked.

"Yes, quite all right. Thank you," Jane muttered and forced a smile on her face.

She grabbed her newly repaired shoes, slipped them on, and left his store. Jane stood on the sidewalk with the other villagers, hoping to catch a glimpse at the local royals. She needed to see him with her own eyes, needed to confirm if it was the same man that had stolen her heart and then shattered it into a thousand pieces.

Then she saw him. Prince Stephan on a top of a white horse waving at the villagers, looking more handsome that she remembered.

"Prince Stephan!" Jane cried.

Please hear my voice.

Jane called his name once more and he turned toward the sound of her voice. She smiled and waved at him, and a glazed look came over his eyes, as though some magical force was keeping him from recognizing her.

He saw right through me. He didn't remember me. Why?

When Princess Marie rode by, Jane was finally able to get a good look at her. Marie wore a light blue gown—with a corset so tight Jane wondered how she was able to breathe—and a white wig that was half as tall as she was. Princess Marie felt Jane's gaze upon her and gave Jane a dirty look. That was when she became suspicious. Was she some sort of witch or evil enchantress? Had she cast a spell on her beloved and taken him as he prisoner against his will?

Are you going to the ball?" a young woman with bright red hair asked.

"What ball?" Jane asked.

The young woman handed her an ivory colored piece of paper. Jane read the words, which swirled and flourished intricately upon the invitation. It was a celebration of Prince Stephan and Princess Marie's engagement, which would last three days and three nights. Everyone was invited to attend as long as they were properly dressed.

"I have a gown that I can borrow from my mother. It needs a little mending here and there but nothing I can't fix," the young woman said excitedly.

"I have the perfect dress for this event…three dresses in fact," Jane said. She thought of the sack she had buried underneath the large rock not too far from Albert's farm. Three nights. Three dresses. She would shine like the sun, glow like the moon, and shimmer like the glittering stars in the heavens.

Perhaps there is still hope for me.

"Thank you very much," Jane said.

"You're very welcome," the young woman replied. Her eyes were warm and kind and immediately reminded Jane of Old Woman.

Before Jane could utter another word the young woman vanished. She rushed back to the farm and told Albert what she had seen.

"A ball?" he asked.

"It's an engagement party—and anyone is welcome to attend as long as you have a proper gown to wear," Jane said.

"Why would you want to attend such a thing?"

"I can make him remember me," Jane said.

"How?"

"I haven't quite figured that part out just yet. But I know that it'll come to me at the right moment."

"How can you be so sure that he even wants to be with you? What if he's a coward? What if he wasn't man to tell you that he didn't want to marry you?"

"I understand what you are trying to say, Albert. You are trying to help me avoid another heartache. But I can promise you that we loved each other. If he truly does not want to see me ever again, then I shall leave this kingdom and return to my castle and forget all about my Prince," Jane said.

Albert shook his head and was quiet for a moment. "Very well. How are you planning on getting inside the castle? You can't go to an engagement party dressed like a shepherdess," Albert said.

Jane gave him a mischievous grin. "I think I'll manage."

Jane's heart hammered against her chest. She was fairly certain that it would burst out of her ribcage and leave a bloody mess everywhere. Luckily for her, that didn't happen, and she took a step forward and walked into the ballroom.

It looked as though everyone in the village was in the castle. Jane brushed up against everyone—feeling quite claustrophobic—as she tried to make her way to the table laden with the sweet cakes and chocolates. She thought Albert may have been right, that the ball was a bad idea.

When she finally reached the table, however, she grinned when she looked upon the beautifully decorated desserts. Chocolates with pink polka dots and swirls, cupcakes with white frosting and blue sprinkles, corn bread and other baked goods. Jane went straight for the chocolate. She took a small bite and let out a soft moan. It had been a long time since she had a taste of her favorite dessert.

"I'm glad to see that the chocolate is as good as it looks," a male voice said.

Jane turned around; she was ready to say something witty, but the words died in her mouth. Standing behind her was the man for whom she had searched for the past four and a half months.

Stephan.

"Are you all right? You are white as a sheet," Prince Stephan said, his blue eyes filled with concern for her.

Jane nodded and stammered, "I'm...I'm fine. Sorry, I got a little lightheaded for a moment. I must have been hungrier than I thought."

"Please, wait here. I will bring you something to eat," Prince Stephan said.

He walked away before Jane could utter a word in protest. A few minutes passed and Stephan returned with a large plate filled to the brim with every type of food imaginable. Two drumsticks of chicken, cherry tomatoes, a large helping of mashed potatoes, a biscuit, corn, and green beans.

"I didn't know what you would like...so I brought you a little bit of everything," Prince Stephan said.

"Thank you so much, that is very kind of you," Jane replied.

"Here, have a seat." Stephan handed the plate to Jane and then pulled out a chair for her.

Jane thanked him once more and sat down next to him.

"This is an awful lot of food. Would you care for some?" Jane asked.

"I'm quite all right,"

"I'll have to insist," Jane teased.

Prince Stephan grinned and grabbed one of the drumsticks from the plate. Jane picked up the fork and ate some of the mashed potatoes.

"This is a lovely party," Jane said.

"I'm glad you think so. I had absolutely nothing to do with the planning that went into it," Prince Stephan said.

Jane smiled and tried not to think too much about what she really wanted to say to him.

Why didn't you come back to me when you said you would? Who is this Princess Marie and how did you end up engaged to her? When can we go back home? Do you recognize me at all? Please kiss me. Let's run away together and get married. I'm your true bride—not this princess that has bewitched you!

But she didn't say any of those things. She sat beside Prince Stephan and basked in his company like a sunflower yearning for the sun.

"Would you like to dance with me?" Prince Stephan asked.

"Are you sure your bride won't mind?" Jane asked as she placed her now empty plate on the table next to her.

"She won't be thrilled to see me dancing with such a beautiful girl, but I think it can be our little secret," Prince Stephan said.

"Won't be much of a secret if everyone here is staring at us," Jane whispered.

"Nobody is staring at us," Stephan said with a chuckle.

"Are you sure?"

They looked around and all eyes were on them.

"Oh my...well then...now you must dance with me. You can't turn me down in front of all these people. It would be humiliating."

He extended his hand out to her. Jane's heart skipped several beats at his kind gesture. He truly did not remember her. Jane took a deep breath and accepted his hand.

"All right. If only to avoid you further embarrassment," Jane grinned.

Prince Stephan guided Jane to the dance floor and they began dancing the moment the music began. For a glorious moment they were the only two people that existed in Jane's mind. Everyone else had vanished and the only thing she could see was Stephan. Then she noticed the look her prince was giving her, it was a look one would reserve for a friend. It wasn't a look you give someone you loved.

"How did you and Princess Marie meet?" Jane asked.

"She was visiting my kingdom and my father introduced us. I remember being a little flustered because I had something important that I wanted to tell my father. I can't seem to remember what it was I needed to tell him. It was a bit of a blur after that. I don't even remember asking her to marry me. I simply saw her one day and the very next moment I'm leaving my castle and my family to be with her," Stephan explained with a frown.

"Are you all right?"

"I just thought it was rather curious. Don't you think you would remember the most important moment of your life? The moment you asked someone to be yours forever and ever?" Stephan posed.

Jane gave him a sad smile. "I would certainly remember every single detail of that moment if you had asked me to be your wife."

Stephan shook his head as though trying to shake cobwebs out of his mind. He stopped dancing with Jane and pressed the heel of his palms against his temples.

"Are you all right?" Jane asked.

"I suddenly have a splitting headache," Stephan said.

"Excuse me. What is happening here? My dear Stephan, are you ill?" Princess Marie asked as she pushed Jane further away from Prince Stephan placing herself between them.

"Nothing, darling. The pain has suddenly gone away. Miss Jane and I were dancing. Isn't she an enchanting young lady?" Prince Stephan said.

"Yes...quite...enchanting," Princess Marie said and then gave Jane a tight lipped smile. "You looked like you were having far too much fun. Can't fault a girl for being a little jealous." Marie gave Jane a deathly glare and grabbed hold of Stephan's arm.

"Jane and I were going to dance one more song," Prince Stephan said.

"I'm sorry, darling, but we have other lords and ladies to whom I simply MUST introduce you," Marie said.

"But..." Stephan said.

"That's quite all right. My shoes were bothering me anyway," Jane gave Stephan a kind smile and walked away.

Jane maintained her distance from Stephan since Princess Marie stayed glued to him for the remainder of the evening. Anytime Stephan snuck a peek at Jane, Princess Marie would yank on his arm and pull him closer to her.

After a while Jane decided that it would be best to leave the party and try again the following evening.

"What happened?" Albert asked when Jane walked through the door.

"We danced for a little while, but Princess Marie interrupted us and forced him to stay by her side all evening,"

"Did he remember you?"

Jane shook her head. "No, it was as though some sort of wicked magic was stopping from remembering me. He tried so hard to remember me that it gave him a splitting headache. I hated to see him in so much pain and unable to do anything to stop it. I felt helpless—useless, even."

"Worry not. You will find a way to bring him back," Albert said.

"If only I had more time. If only I could get him away from that awful woman, I might be able to break whatever spell or curse she has cast over him."

Jane spent most of the night worrying about the following evening. Would she be able to get a moment alone with Prince Stephan? The only thing she could do was try.

Jane returned to the castle the following evening; once again, it seemed as though the entire village had managed to attend. The ballroom was buzzing with excited chatter and laughter from every corner.

She did her best to stay away from Princess Marie and Prince Stephan, but something happened that required the princess elsewhere. Jane didn't care. The whole castle could've caught flames, and the only thing she would've cared about was her prince, Prince Stephan, who was now completely alone.

This is your chance. Don't ruin it, she said to herself.

"Hello again, Your Royal Highness," Jane said.

"Jane, how lovely it is to see you again this evening," Stephan replied as he beamed with joy as he looked upon her face.

Jane's cheeks grew warm as she blushed.

"It is good to see you again as well. I saw Princess Marie dashed away. Is everything all right?"

"Yes, some trouble in the kitchen. It seems that there are some sheep running loose, eating everything in sight," he explained.

"Oh, dear," Jane covered her lips to hide her smile. She knew that Albert was behind that little incident.

"I thought it was rather funny…obviously the princess and I don't share the same sense of humor," he tried to make a joke out of the situation, but Jane noticed the sadness in Stephan's eyes.

Jane wished she could think of something to say that would make his sadness go away. All she wanted more than anything was to close her eyes, make a wish and that when she opened them once more that they would be back home in her castle.

"Are you thirsty? I can fetch you a glass of wine or champagne if you like," he said, as though trying to change the subject.

"I'm quite all right, thank you. I'm just happy to be here, talking to you."

Stephan studied Jane's face and said, "Me, too. I can't explain why it is that every time I see you I get a jolt of energy in my heart. As if it were trying to tell me something that I already know…"

"I can tell you why," Jane whispered.

"Really?" he leaned forward as though waiting for her to whisper her answer.

"Yes."

"Please tell me," he pleaded. "Tell me why is it that I look into your eyes and feel immediately at ease. I feel like I'm home. Yet I look into my fiancée's eyes and all I feel is a vast emptiness that seems never-ending."

Jane looked into Stephan's eyes and held his hands.

"Prince Stephan, we've met before."

The prince smirked, "I'm certain I would've remember you, Miss Jane."

Jane caressed his cheek. The same cheek she kissed before he left her underneath the linden tree. She parted her lips to say something else when she felt a sharp tug on her hair.

"Owww!" Jane shrieked.

"You evil little wench! How dare you touch my fiancé?" Princess Marie cried. She turned to Stephan and said, "And you are no better! Is this what I will have to look forward to once we are married? Am I not able to trust you with another woman unless I am always by your side?"

"Princess Marie, darling, I can assure you nothing happened," Prince Stephan replied. He reached out to hold her hand but Marie quickly pulled it away from his grasp.

"Don't touch me," she hissed.

"I'm so sorry if I caused any trouble," Jane whispered.

"I want you to leave and never—ever—return to this place. Do you understand?" Princess Marie growled.

"I—I…yes, I understand," Jane fumbled.

"He is mine, and I will do everything in my power to keep him," Marie hissed.

"Please, don't do this," Stephan said.

"It's quite all right, Your Highness. I should go," Jane said.

Prince Stephan locked eyes with Jane and frowned. She gave him the best smile she could muster at that moment and walked away. She cried and sobbed the entire way home.

When she walked through the door of Albert's little farmhouse, he saw the look of pure devastation on her face. "What happened?"

"I was so close. So close!" Jane cried.

"Then we will try again tomorrow," Albert said.

"I can't. I've been banned from attending," Jane explained.

"You cannot give up, dear girl. Not when you are so close."

"But how?"

Albert sat down and thought for a moment, "Perhaps a note. Do you have any gold coins left? Perhaps we can pay someone to deliver a message to him?"

"Do you think that would work?"

"We can try," he replied.

Jane smiled and said, "Yes, we can try."

She paid a young boy to deliver a message to Stephan. She wrote a note and handed it to the boy.

> *Meet me under the big oak tree by the river. I will tell you everything you need to know. Please...tell no one.*
>
> *J.*

She wore a black dress, which had thousands of shimmering crystals sewn in; it looked as though it was a dress made out of the night sky. Every movement she made caused the dress to sparkle like the stars that shone above her. She hoped that the boy had given her letter to Stephan and that Marie hadn't somehow intercepted it.

She was moments away from giving up and going back home when she noticed something moving in the darkness. She squinted, hoping that it would somehow help her see who or what it was. All she saw was a dark figure in the distance approaching. He was headed straight toward her. For a moment she thought that this was all a mistake. Maybe she should have followed Albert's advice and forgotten all about him?

"Miss Jane?" Stephan whispered.

Jane let out a sigh of relief. Her plan had worked after all. "Stephan?"

"I'm here," he replied.

Under the light of the silver moon, they were finally able to see each other. Alone at last.

"I'm so glad you're here. I never got a chance to finish what I was going to tell you last night," Jane said.

"I received your note. I slipped away as soon as Marie fell asleep. I apologize if you have been here long," he said.

Jane held his hands and said, "Before I lose my nerve...I must tell you that we have met before. I have been searching for you for months. I left my castle, my gowns, and my riches just for the hope of finding you to at least have the chance to look upon your face one last time. I want nothing but your true happiness, my dear Stephan. Even if you don't remember me, I will remember every smile, every act of kindness you showed me. Every loving embrace and smile we shared. I will love you always."

Jane took a deep steadying breath. She felt a lump forming in her throat as she thought of the next sentence that she was going to utter. "If you....if you truly wish to marry Princess Marie, then I will respect your wishes and I will walk away."

"Jane...I don't know what to say," Stephan said.

"You don't have to say anything."

"I wish I could remember you."

"The last time we saw each other was underneath the linden tree. Immediately after you asked me to marry you. I kissed you right here, on this very cheek," she caressed the place where she had kissed him. "I said...keep true to me, and let nobody kiss you on this cheek until you return to me."

Jane stood on the tips of her toes and kissed him on the exact same spot. As soon as she did this, a sickly, olive-colored mist left Stephan's body and floated up to the sky. The young prince fell onto the ground on his knees and pressed his hands against his temples.

"Stephan! Are you all right?" Jane asked.

Prince Stephan shook his head and said, "Jane?"

She knelt down beside him and put her arm around his shoulder. "Yes, I'm here."

Prince Stephan lifted his gaze and locked eyes with Jane. Her heart skipped a beat...there was something different in his eyes—something familiar, too. He smiled at her and that was when she knew that he knew who she was. She finally got the one thing she had been searching for all this time....recognition.

"My darling Jane," he whispered.

"Do you know who I am?" she asked as her voice trembled.

He leaned over and kissed her on the lips. That was all she needed in order to answer her question. All doubts were pushed aside and the only thing that existed was Stephan, Jane, and their kiss.

"What about the princess?" Jane asked.

"Who? Marie? That awful witch can rot in hell for all I care. It's her fault.

Everything that has happened has been her entire fault," Stephan said.

As they made their way back to Albert's farm they planned their escape back home to their land. Jane walked through the door of the little farmhouse she had begun to call home. As usual, Albert was sitting by the fireplace reading a book. He turned toward the door and smiled when he saw Jane.

"How did it go?" he asked.

"The spell is broken," Jane replied unable to hide the grin on her face.

Stephan stepped inside the farmhouse and said, "Hello."

"Will you look at that? You finally did it, my dear girl," Albert said.

"Albert, my wonderful, kind friend—we must go. But I came back because I wanted to thank you for your kindness," Jane said.

Albert gave Jane a warm embrace and said, "It was my pleasure. It was very exciting to be a part of such an amazing adventure."

"I will be sure to write to you, and I will send someone to fetch my little calf when Princess Marie has forgotten all about us," Jane said.

"How will you get home?" Albert asked.

"We were wondering if we could purchase a horse from you," Stephan suggested.

"Yes, yes, of course," Albert said.

"Thank you so much," Jane said.

Stephan handed Albert a sack full of coins and Albert immediately protested. "This is far too much. Lady is an older horse and not worth this much."

"We insist," Stephan said.

Albert shook his head but accepted the payment. They bid each other farewell one last time and then Jane and Stephan hurried away on their new horse. It took them several days, but they finally made it home. Jane was amazed that her castle was still standing, still as beautiful and splendid as she remembered it. The tiles shimmered under the setting sun and the windows were glowing with a soft, warm light.

"Home at last," she whispered.

Stephan dismounted and helped Jane down from the exhausted mare. He gently patted Lady on the neck and said, "Good girl. Go get some rest."

Lady quickly obeyed his command and trotted away.

Jane rested her head against Stephan's chest and closed her eyes. She focused on the sound of his heartbeat. The steady rhythm of his heart was all she needed to make her feel anchored to the world. To make her feel as though she belonged somewhere.

L IZ DEJESUS was born on the tiny island of Puerto Rico. She is a novelist and a poet. She has been writing for as long as she was capable of holding a pen. She is the author of the novels: *Nina* (Blu Phi'er Publishing, October 2007), *The Jackets* (Arte Publico Press, March 31st 2011), *First Frost* (Musa Publishing, June 22nd 2012), *Glass Frost* (Musa Publishing, July 2013), and *Morgan* (Indie Gypsy, Summer 2014). Her work has also appeared in *Night Gypsy: Journey Into Darkness* (Indie Gypsy, October 2012) and *Someone Wicked* (Smart Rhino Publications, Winter 2013).

She is also a member of The Written Remains Writers Guild.

Liz is currently working on a new novel and a comic book series titled *Zombie Ever After* (Emerald Star Comics, Fall 2014).

LINKS

http://www.lizdejesus.com
http://www.facebook.com/lizdejesus
https://twitter.com/lizdejesus23
http://www.writtenremains.org

The Bone Harp

by Court Ellyn

THE cold fists of the floodwaters tugged Angharad's skirts. Twigs, leaves, and hawthorn petals gathered in swirling eddies. Her toes deep in the mud of a still pool, Angharad realized one of her shoes was missing. Her hands shook. She couldn't make them stop. Her fingers held the memory of thrashing waters, a pulse.

A garland bobbed in the pool, and the white flowers haloed a blue eye. Gwyneth's blue eyes, laughing, lovely, dead. A cloud of golden hair swayed a seaweed dance, and mud clung to a white cheek. One silver bubble escaped the parted lips, flitted to the surface and burst. A breath? A word? Silence.

Poor Gwyneth had slipped. So fast. Right into the swift waters, struck her head on the tree roots there. That's what Angharad would tell them. Would they believe her? Father loved Gwyneth best. Would he blame Angharad? She heard voices through the trees. The men were to choose a tree for a Maypole this morning, the maidens to gather flowers for wreaths. Would they believe her?

Gwyneth had been laughing, then she was choking. *Help me!* Over so quickly. The finality of it made Angharad sick. She retched in the mud. There... On the bank, the deep groove where Gwyneth's heel had slipped. Yes, she would show them. They would believe. She had to make them believe. She didn't want to spend the rest of her life locked away in the nunnery at Llanllugan. What she wanted was approaching through the trees. She could hear his voice. Whose name did he shout?

The water tugged at her sister's feet, but Gwyneth's skirts and wine-red cloak anchored her to the bottom. Angharad unlatched the cloak's silver-and-ruby brooch. Gwyneth's shoulders floated; the tip of her chin and pretty nose broke the surface. Sand in her mouth! Choking back the urge to scream, Angharad gave the shoulder a shove. The body drifted but a few inches. She kicked it hard—harder!—and Gwyneth glided toward the middle of the river. The floodwaters seized her. A glimpse of yellow hair, a white hand, nothing.

"There you are!" called Father through the damp forest-quiet. Red-faced and rotund, Lord Gwilym, Baron of the southern cantrevs, approached through the brambles, flushed from excessive wine. He lived for the festivals when he could laugh and drink with impunity. How could Angharad tell him? "We've chosen our tree, daughter. Come and see it."

Beside him, Sir Llyr looked resplendent in new spring silk, golden hair catching the thin rays of sunlight just so. Angharad's heart felt too big for her chest. Oh, to run to him, to nest in his arms while she wept for Gwyneth.

"What are you doing so near the flood, daughter? Come away, it's dangerous."

"Where is Gwyneth?" Llyr asked, looking at the brown, roiling waters

Angharad lifted the cloak, so heavy now that it was empty. "I could not save her."

The day she had met Sir Llyr, Angharad took special care before her mirror, brushing her dark hair until the waves shone like deep water in the sunlight. She had never liked her hazel eyes, preferring the forget-me-not blue of Gwyneth's, but Father said Llyr was a hunter, so perhaps hazel would remind him of the woods and fields he favored. She chose the dark green gown she'd saved for a holiday and felt beautiful until the banquet was nearly over.

Father had gone to rare extravagance for his guest. A pair of swans adorned the table, dead and brilliant, breasts and beaks touching so that their arched necks shaped a heart that made Angharad's sisters sigh. Angharad herself didn't care about the birds. She could hardly eat for sight of their guest. As golden as the noon-bright heavens, he seemed to wear the halo of a saint. He wore lightly the sword and dirk of a knight, and the pearls ornamenting the baldric across his chest appeared to have been carefully polished, for they glittered like stars upon the sea. His wit caused the Great Hall to ring with laughter. Still, Angharad pitied him; his father, the baron of a neighboring cantrev, had been shortsighted, it seemed, knighting both his sons though he could ill afford it. So as the younger, Llyr was forced to seek his path and his fortune.

Finally, the servants brought the dessert wine, and while they served the upper and lower tables, Lord Gwilym wrapped a heavy arm about Llyr's shoulders and said, "No, no, don't go north. Stay here. Choose one of my daughters."

Angharad's stomach flipped exquisitely. The girlish chatter at the lower table hushed. Llyr glanced from face to flushing face. Angharad's heart could hardly soar higher; as the eldest, she would have precedence.

"See there, Angharad, my firstborn," Father went on. "Though Gwyneth, beside her, is the fairer and more pleasant-tempered. The other three are too young yet... ."

Like a dove speared from above by the falcon, Angharad's heart plummeted. Had her own father just slighted her? He had always favored Gwyneth, fair and blue-eyed and adoring, but why should he try to ruin Angharad's chances? Her face burned, her stomach sank, but she wore a smile for the rest of the evening.

Retiring brought no escape. She shared a bed with Gwyneth. And how smug the little ninny looked.

"He smiled at me, did you see?" On and on she prattled: Did you hear him say this? Did you hear him say that?

No doubt Gwyneth dreamt of him that night; Angharad dreamt of bleeding doves.

The next morning, Angharad glimpsed a sliver of hope when a servant brought word that Sir Llyr wished to meet with her in the garden after breakfast. She had to look especially fine, to undermine her father's assessment. All her day-dresses were drably colored, so she chose one of Gwyneth's. A pale pink with long narrow sleeves and a neckline that revealed her collarbones. She stepped into the garden, confident that she could win Llyr's suit. But the moment she saw him, pacing impatiently beneath the spreading ash tree, Angharad's confidence withered like leaves before the fire. It was as if her father's words had cursed her tongue to foolish silence. Their meeting was amiable but brief. Angharad thought it a complete disaster until Llyr extended a gift to her. A brooch. A lovely thing of twisted silver. A knot... A bird... A swan, it was! She blushed, lightheaded, as Llyr pinned it upon her shoulder.

Later in the day, Gwyneth ran to her crying, "Look what he gave me!" A brooch. Silver. Studded with rubies. She ran to show Father. Humiliated, Angharad tucked hers into the bottom of her clothes chest. She never wanted to see it again.

Now she had the ruby-studded brooch. Hers... Hers forever.

One year later, the Great Hall rang with the exuberant notes of a pipe. At the high table, Angharad filled the bottom of her goblet. A polite, ladylike amount. Only the flush in her cheeks and the heaviness on her eyelids hinted that, altogether, she may have drunk a flask all to herself. Father didn't notice; he was far more inebriated, chuckling at Angharad's three younger sisters making missteps in the Maypole dances. A week before the May Day celebration, Arwyth, Lily, and Olwyn decided they'd be wise to practice.

Llyr didn't notice either. Sullen and silent, he was too enrapt watching Lily spin about her sisters. Arwyth tripped into Olwyn, and Lily laughed, her throat like white silk. She was sixteen now, with golden curls and eyes as blue as forget-me-nots. Angharad thought Llyr might have the decency to disguise his interest. He brought to mind a wolf lapping at the blood of one kill and desiring another. Lily saw and flushed, then made a turn about the imaginary Maypole, just for him. What girl didn't have eyes for Sir Llyr? His golden beauty was renowned throughout the cantrevs; his hunting prowess and skill with a sword had won him the admiration of the king himself. He was glorious to behold, riding his charger, cloak rising on the wind of his gallop like an angel's wings. Yes, his peers, servants, and tenants adored him, almost as much as Llyr adored Llyr. Could even Gwyneth have made him fall out of love with himself? Angharad doubted it. At least, she liked to think that Gwyneth would now be as miserable as Angharad was herself.

She gulped the wine. Though they had been married less than a year, she felt as though it had been a decade. She was so tired of feeling suspicious and hurt and lonely. What happened to the joy she'd imagined? The romance? Drowned in the floodwaters.

At the center of the high table, Lord Gwilym stopped chuckling. "Gwyneth."

Angharad's hand paused halfway to the wine flask.

"Doesn't Lily look like her sister?" he added.

"Please, Father. Don't do this again tonight."

Lord Gwilym's wine-blurred eyes welled. "Tell me, Angharad. Tell me how we lost her."

Overhearing the request, Llyr groaned and left the table.

Angharad rose to follow him, but Father's fingers clenched her wrist. Bruising. Insistent.

"It only hurts you, my lord," she said. "Why resurrect her every evening?"

"She might still be alive," he said, a plea in his eye. "We never found her."

Angharad tugged against his grasp; his fingers were hot and clammy with too much wine. "No, Father. You saw the river that day. She couldn't swim."

"Tell me." How pathetic he was, pining for the little harlot he'd idealized into a saint.

Angharad sank into her chair and told the story she'd told hundreds of times. She knew it word for word and never varied in the telling: "Gwyneth dropped her garland into the river. She leant over to pluck it out, but the bank was muddy and she slipped. I grabbed her cloak, but the current was too swift."

"Did she scream?" The same question. Every night.

She was laughing... . "There wasn't time."

"She didn't suffer?"

Coughing, choking, thrashing... . "No. She struck her head. No pain."

Father's fingers released her, drifted heavily for his goblet. "She loved the May Day celebration. She loved it best of all."

Arwyth and Olwyn danced among the lower tables, the pipe sounding frenzied, a thin scream in Angharad's ears. Lily was gone.

Angharad fought off the wine as long as she could, lying awake in a wide, cold bed. But Llyr did not come.

She woke late in the morning, a taste as rotten as spoiled intentions in her mouth. Llyr stood before the copper mirror, pinning on his green traveling cloak. Angharad bolted up from the pillow. "Where are you going?"

"To court."

"But you just got back."

He dusted his recent journey from his hat. "Is it my fault your father is incapable of handling his own affairs?"

Llyr rarely consented to take Angharad to the king's palace with him. He was often blunt in his reasons: "I'd rather go alone," he told her once. "You embarrassed me last time, weeping openly when Lady Mathilda asked about your sister." At other times he was more diplomatic: "You should look after your father. Don't let him drink too much."

This morning, Angharad didn't bother asking. It was clear that Llyr had hoped to slip away before she woke. How like the sunlight he was. The tighter her grasp, the more shadow she held. "To which one are you rushing off to make love?" she asked.

He glanced at her in the mirror.

"Let's see," she said, wrapping her arms about her knees, "Lord Gryffydd's daughters are of age now. And Lady Rhys was widowed this year. And the king has always favored you."

Llyr's expression of amusement slipped, like a shaky foot on ice. "You're a fool, Angharad. I don't have to ride so far as that."

"Then stay."

He harrumphed. "You don't have it in you to be lonely."

Was he so blind? Or did he take pleasure in hurting her? He set the narrow riding hat on his golden head, tilted it, smiled, pleased with the reflection. A red feather wagged at Angharad like a finger. "I'll be back in time for May Day," he said. "I wouldn't miss it this year. I met a harpist at the palace, did I tell you?" He approached the bed, flung out his cloak, and sat next to her. "He has the most marvelous magical harp. I invited him to come play for us on May Day. And such a song he sings. I've requested that he sing it just for you, my dear." His fingers lay gently against her cheek. Angharad's heart rose into her throat, and she regretted accusing him. Llyr was so often cool and short with her, but at moments like this, she felt he might love her after all.

The sun failed to shine while Llyr was away. Heavy, late April rain flooded Lord Gwilym's green valleys, and the baron complained that the rain would drown out the festival, but the skies cleared in time, as if in honor of the old traditions. The youths and maidens abandoned the castle and the town for the forest; upon a sun-strewn May Day morning, the girls returned to town wearing hawthorn in their hair. The youths carried on their shoulders the tree they had chosen for the Maypole, shorn of leaf and limb, and set it up in the town square. Families from across the cantrev arrived in droves throughout the morning, feet churning the roads into a muddy slough. Merchants carted in wares from far-flung villages and set up shop under striped tents. Mummers and musicians competed on the stage. The town danced with colorful ribbons, garlands, and laughter. Angharad mimicked the lightheartedness of her father's people, but all the while, a shadow lurked on the edge of joy. A memory so tangible she felt she could strike it with her fists. When Father had set out from the keep in his finest velvet, he'd looked anything but festive. "A year ago," he'd whispered. "A year ago this very morning."

"I know," she'd replied, stopping him as gently as she could. "Take joy in the day, Father, for her sake. It was her favorite."

Now, seated in the lord's box, his laughter and cries of approbation sounded a trifle too exuberant. Angharad sat between him and Llyr, watching the dancers and smiling and wishing she were anywhere else. On the square, the youths had painted their faces black and brandished swords and sticks in intricate steps about the Maypole. The maidens joined them with the wreaths they had woven from the hawthorn branches. Lily was by far the loveliest; the boys vied for her attention, but she modestly shunned them all.

Llyr slouched in his chair, arms over his chest, irritated that he was relegated to the spectator's box. How many maidens had he taken into the green over the years, and none of them Angharad? She smiled with spiteful glee.

In the afternoon, the mummers claimed the stage to perform the traditional May Day play. Face hidden behind an elaborate bearded mask, the mummer doctor poured elixir down the slain hero's throat. The hero sat up with life renewed, and the audience cheered. Lord Gwilym applauded the loudest and tossed a handful of coins at the players. They scraped up their earnings, then emptied the stage for Llyr's harpist.

Nissyen ap Hedydd—Nissyen, son of the Skylark—had accompanied Llyr when he returned from court. Though he had dined with Lord Gwilym and his family, Arwyth and Olwyn hanging upon his every word, the bard had refused to play for them. Saving his voice, he'd said. Nor had he removed the velvet cloth from his lap-harp when Lily begged to see it. He'd satisfied their yearning with tales of Tristan and Isolde, Lancelot and Gwenhwyvar.

Angharad didn't like him. The moment he entered the keep with his harp bundled under his arm, the balmy spring air grew close and cold, like a hand of the dead poised before her face. She had dreamt of Gwyneth both nights the bard slept under Lord Gwilym's roof. The choking of a mouth sucking down muddy water. "Forget me not," she heard, and a swan wreathed in hawthorn landed on still waters and paddled among the reeds. Its black eyes never left her, no matter how grotesquely the long white neck had to twist and contort, like the silver wire of a brooch. Angharad ran along the bank, but the swan was always there ahead of her, staring, watching, accusing.

On the second night, she screamed at the swan, "I couldn't save her! She laughed and slipped and went under. I couldn't save her!"

During the day, Angharad avoided the bard. "Can't you try to be polite, sociable, *something*?" Llyr cried, taking her aside. How could she make him understand? When Nissyen ap Hedydd looked at her, it was as if he were looking at her with the swan's eyes.

Though the bard and his bundled harp took the stage among hundreds of eager listeners, he gazed only toward the baron's box, and—Angharad was sure—at her in particular. "At the request of my host, the gracious Sir Llyr, and in honor of his lady, I shall sing for you a new ballad. One of betrayal most unnatural, of tragedy most grievous, of murder yet unavenged." The audience approved the preamble with applause. The bard pulled away the black velvet.

Sight of the harp filled Angharad with revulsion. She was not the only one who felt it. Murmurs sifted through the audience like wind through leaves. Rather than wood, the instrument appeared to be fashioned of bone, palest yellow, polished to a shine. Ribs and femurs shaped the frame, tiny finger bones were the delicate tuning pegs, and the strings themselves looked like spun gold.

"There, my dear, what do you think?" Llyr whispered into Angharad's ear. "Just wait till you hear it. It's more marvelous than angel song."

Instead of occupying the stool set out for him, Nissyen set the harp in the center of the stage and stepped away.

"What under Heaven is he doing?" muttered Lord Gwilym, lifting an empty goblet toward a servant who waited on hand with a flask. "It's a strange one you've brought us, Llyr."

"Play, bard!" shouted a man in the audience, inciting a rumble of laughter from the crowd.

All at once, the golden strings vibrated, shimmering in the sunlight, and haunting ripples of music coursed over the town square. Members of the audience scurried away from the stage.

"Possessed!" cried an old woman.

Others cheered, perhaps thinking it a clever trick. Nissyen's clear tenor voice joined the notes:

"There were two sisters sat in a bower.
A knight there came to be their wooer.
He courted the eldest with glove and ring,
But he loved the youngest o'er all things.
The eldest said to the youngest one,
'Will ye come and gather garlands in?'
She took her by the lily hand
And led her down to the river strand.
The youngest stood upon a stone
The eldest came and pushed her in..."

Blood rushed from Angharad's head, causing her ears to roar. The sound gushed over the delicate notes. Floodwaters gushing... She caught Llyr watching her from the corner of his eye.

"'Oh, sister, sister, reach me your hand,
And ye shall inherit half of my land.'
'Oh, sister, I'll not give you my hand,
And I shall inherit all of your land.'
'Oh, sister, sister, reach me your glove,
And sweet William shall be your love'..."

Lord Gwilym groaned, brow falling into his fingers. "God, man, have pity. Llyr, is this your doing?"

"Surely not mine, my lord. The harp plays its own song."

"Aye, but the words belong to the man!" Angharad retorted.

"Do they, my love? Are you so easily offended by them?"

"As should you be!"

"I *am* offended."

"Then *why*?"

The bard sang on:

"Sometimes she sank, sometimes she swam,
Until she came to the miller's dam.
A famous harper passing by,
The sweet pale face he chanced to spy.
He made a harp of her breastbone,
Whose sounds would melt a heart of stone..."

Angharad fled the box. Her sister's laughter was a golden note pursuing her through the crowd. She avoided the castle where questions would only catch up to her. The forest, so close under the castle walls, offered seclusion. Angharad broke through the branches, stumbled over ferns, but she kept running. Eventually she outran the notes of that hideous harp. But the laughter remained close behind.

How Gwyneth had laughed. "I *told* you he'd choose me. I asked him to go into the green with me, and we were together all night in a bower of hawthorn branches. You never had a hope, Ang. You silly, heartsick thing. Destined to be passed over. By Father, by Llyr." She turned in a wistful dance of triumph.

Then she was in the water. Slipped right down the rain-slick bank in the middle of her boast. Angharad reached for her. Yes, reached as far as she could. What right had that bard to sing of murder? What if they believed him? Surely Llyr already believed. Of course, he wanted to believe he had good reason to get rid of her and marry Lily.

They would lock her in the convent! Yet what cell could be more bleak than the one she shared every day, every night with Gwyneth? She slowed, chest burning, cheek stinging where the branches clawed into her.

She found herself on the riverbank. Rust-brown floodwaters churned, thick as cream. There it lay, the still pool where Angharad had reached, reached—*Help me!*—and pushed Gwyneth under. *No, don't look! Look!* Waters thrashing, mud clouding, fingers squeezing a gasping throat. And there had been no begging, as Nissyen ap Hedydd sang. Only choking, half-formed curses, silence.

And this harp. Had the bard really found Gwyneth's body and fashioned a harp from her bones? Or was that a lie, too? No, Gwyneth's spirit lived in that enchanted, grotesque thing, Angharad was sure of it. How else could it play by itself? Why else had Angharad dreamt so vividly of her sister after the bard arrived? And how could Nissyen fashion his song so close to the truth unless Gwyneth's ghost had breathed it into his ear?

Angharad sank to her knees beside the empty pool and wept. After a long while, the leaf-crackle of footsteps announced Llyr's pursuit. Had she once thought him the sun? How dim and small he seemed as he stopped to stand over her.

"So it *is* true," he said.

"Will you prey on Lily now? Spoil her, too?"

He scoffed. "All you've ever had is petty jealousy."

"Petty, yes. But well founded. I see so clearly now. What you are. What I am." She rose without hurry, without rage, and selecting a sodden alder branch, struck Llyr in the head. He reeled and cursed. She hit him again. He fell hard. She hit him again.

When he lay still at last, she dropped the branch and sat at his feet. Caught her breath. Listened for voices in the trees. Only birds. And the river. The river's endless voice, calling. Sunlight flitted through the swelling leaves, fell on heedless rushing waters. Would there be a bard for Angharad, too? Would he shape her into a fiddle, a drum? Or would there be only crows for her, and the slimy things that dwelled on the river bottom? She hoped for silence, for an end of memory. Graceful as a swan, she waded into the water and embraced the current.

C OURT ELLYN defines herself as a dreamer, a cynic, a klutz who loves cats, a homebody who roams. She started writing historical fiction when she was fourteen but slowly gravitated toward the fantastical. Now, somewhere between dragon dens, haunted bogs and battlefields strewn with otherworldly foes, she moderates the LegendFire Critique Community.

Her fiction has appeared in *Kaleidotrope, Silver Blade, A Fly In Amber, Explorers: Beyond the Horizon*, an anthology by Dead Robots' Society, and a number of other publications. Her novels, The Falcons Saga, are available at Amazon.

LINKS

http://www.courtellyn.com
https://twitter.com/courtellyn
http://www.legendfire.com

Spear Among Spindles

by S.Q. Eries

THE news rocked Skyros like a magnitude-9.0 quake. One moment I was yawning over my algebra assignment in the Sunday evening lull, and the next, banshee screeching jolted me out of my seat. Deirdre, who was working on an oceanscape, was startled so badly that blue paint splattered all over her smock and raven hair.

As one, we scrambled for the door, but instead of a fire or a rampaging madman, we found girls dancing giddily about the hallway. Bewildered, Deirdre grabbed one of the other juniors and yelled over their racket, "Maya, what's going on?"

The petite redhead squealed so shrilly I thought my eardrums would burst. "It's Helen! She's run off with a lover!"

"Who did what?" I said, confused.

"Keelie, you dunce! Helen! *The* Helen! Gah! Just come!" Before we could protest, she hauled us through the crowd and into the dorm lounge.

To my astonishment, the room was packed, girls straining against one another. Fortunately, I was the tallest person in the crush and had a clear view of the TV screen where the anchorman was announcing that Helen, Queen of Sparta, had abandoned husband and country for a Trojan prince.

Everything clicked at once. Skyros Girls' Preparatory catered to the daughters of the upper echelon, and the glamorous Queen Helen was the idol of every debutante. Most girls here found inspiration in the tiniest minutia of her lifestyle. As shots of their heroine with a sexy foreigner flashed across the screen, they erupted into ecstasies.

Meanwhile, the dorm matrons clucked disapprovingly from a corner. They considered it their duty to guard our innocence, and as such, confiscated gossip magazines and had more security controls on our computers than deadbolts in a locksmith shop. Still, there was little they could do with every network headlining the celebrity queen's brazenness.

The evening news seemed like a soap opera as reporters and eyewitnesses related how Prince Paris recently visited Sparta for trade negotiations, how the couple eloped while King Menelaus was abroad at his grandfather's funeral, and how Helen emptied her husband's Swiss bank account as a parting gesture. Her worshipers gobbled every tidbit. But I couldn't say I wasn't getting caught up myself, especially when the newscast turned to the Spartan king's press conference.

Outrage burst from the screen. It was so vicious I could almost feel the man's spit spraying on my skin. Red-faced, the jilted husband vowed revenge, that he would use all means to exact retribution from the Trojan and his country.

His oaths sent a chill up my spine. They were tantamount to a declaration of war—a declaration that went largely unheard in the lounge. Helen's fans were too busy comparing Menelaus' looks with Paris'.

For the inhabitants of Skyros Prep, this wasn't so much an international crisis as a fairytale come true, as evidenced when late-breaking footage interrupted the king's tirade. From a luxury yacht, Paris swore that he would never give up Helen, sparking a chorus of delighted gasps in the room. Clearly, they found it wildly romantic—a sentiment I did not share.

Bile rose in my throat at the image of the golden woman clinging to her young lover's arm. *Selfish bitch.*

The chattering stopped. Suddenly everyone, even the matrons, was staring, and I realized I'd uttered my thought aloud.

My face burned, but it was too late to take the words back so I figured, *What the hell.*

"If she was going to have a fling, she could've kept it quiet. But she had to turn it into a spectacle, and if it gets as ugly as he says—" I jabbed a finger at Menelaus' picture on screen, "—people are going to die."

"Keelie," Deirdre gasped, her dark eyes wide. Beside her, Maya paled beneath her freckles.

"It's true, and I for one would rather my father not go to war on account of another man's marital problems."

My condemnation struck like a knell. Everyone looked away, the girls from other military families especially shamefaced.

"Idiots," I muttered and flounced off.

I slumped forward on my desk. Through the walls, I could hear that the chatter had resumed in the lounge, but I had a feeling they were talking about more than Helen's new beau. I'd made a point never to say anything contrary to the group mentality at Skyros Prep, but this time...

I shoved a hand through my hair in frustration. In accusing Helen of causing a spectacle, I'd managed to raise one myself. But contrary to what everyone thought, it wasn't the ravings of the offended king that sparked my outburst.

It was Helen's daughter.

I doubted they even noticed her, but there was no way I could have overlooked that little girl, silent in the background as her father seethed vengeance to the world. The sight of her, so confused and vulnerable, had sent anger flooding through my veins, and before I knew it, I'd blown up.

I knocked my head against the desk. It was dumb of me to lose it. I didn't even know those people. Still, that girl's forsaken look haunted me, and I found myself staring at the framed photograph sitting on my desktop.

It was a family picture, taken what felt like a lifetime ago. To one side, a laughing child clung to a burly, graying man, who hugged back with fierce affection. As I gazed upon my younger self in Dad's arms, a wave of homesickness washed over me.

Dad and I were close. As close now as we were during that long-ago trip to the beach. Though the years had brought many changes, our love was the one thing that remained constant. Some of my friends back home found it odd that we were so tight, but I genuinely looked up to Dad, just as he took pride in me. I wondered sometimes how much of that was our coping with the indifference of the other member of our family.

My gaze shifted to the third figure in the photo. Anyone with eyes could tell she was my mother. Her fine features, her cerulean eyes, her corn silk hair—all of those reflected back every time I looked in the mirror.

Stunning in an elegant turquoise dress, she stood a little apart from my father and me. Though her glossed lips were smiling, her eyes were not.

Mom had always been like that, keeping her distance despite our efforts to draw her in. Six months after this picture was taken, she left. Dad and I were devastated. But the truth was that she'd checked out long before then.

I could count on one hand the times she'd come to see me afterward. That kind of neglect would make anyone resentful, and bitterness grew to be a familiar companion as time stretched long between visits.

The weird thing was that every time she resurfaced, all that resentment disappeared in a flash. One glimpse of her and I was four years old again, frantic to please her so she wouldn't abandon me.

And that was what landed me here—in the middle of freaking nowhere.

My jaw tightened at the memory of that last visit. She'd popped up, unannounced as always, and, without fail, I'd dropped everything to fawn over her like a star-struck groupie. But my elation came to a crashing halt when Mom said she wanted me to leave home for Skyros Prep.

"Girls' boarding school? In Skyros? Are you crazy? No! I'm staying with Dad!"

"I know it sounds strange, but trust me," she wheedled. "It's all to keep you safe."

"Safe? I don't need protection! You know I don't!"

"Keelie! Just do as I say!"

Mom's words struck like a lash. Anger and desperation resounded in her voice, sending an avalanche of disapproval on my soul.

I had caved immediately.

I groaned, cursing myself for the thousandth time for giving in to Mom's whims. *Maybe I've got a complex—*

"Keelie."

I yelped, jolting so badly that Deirdre stumbled back several steps. "Deirdre! Don't sneak up on me like that!"

"Sorry," she said, equally flustered. "But I called you a few times and you didn't hear me."

"Oh," I said sheepishly.

"Are you okay? You were... Really upset back there."

My face warmed as her expression turned from annoyance to concern. Considering how pretty and popular she was in the Skyros crowd, you'd think she'd be at the head of the Helen Fan Club. But she was actually quite down-to-earth and caring enough to worry about her grouchy roommate.

I pressed a hand to my forehead. "I'm not okay. Not even close."

She pulled up a chair beside me. "You're really worried about your dad, aren't you?"

It would be easy to let her believe that. She knew my father was an officer and would naturally attribute my outburst to a hysterical daddy's girl moment.

But somehow, her sympathy tugged at my heart, still raw from reminiscing, and I found myself saying, "Yes, but that's not really it. All that about Helen... It just reminded me how messed up my own family is. Pathetic, huh?"

Deirdre blinked. I didn't blame her for being surprised. Despite two years of rooming together, I'd never shared anything remotely personal before. Mom had cautioned me against it. So while I got along well enough with my classmates, I kept mostly to myself.

I just couldn't take it anymore. Mom never once made good on her promise to visit, and though I received letters from Dad through Mom's assistants, she forbade me to reveal my whereabouts or have any contact with him. I was tired—tired of isolation, tired of holding back, tired of secrets. My soul ached to unburden itself, and I knew that Deirdre, who had respected my reticence for so long, could be trusted to be discreet.

"You want to talk about it?" she asked carefully. "I'll understand if you'd rather not, but—"

"I need to get this off my chest or I'm going to go crazy."

Deirdre nodded and drew closer, all ears.

"It's complicated." I paused, trying to decide where to start. "Actually, it might be easier to show you."

Deirdre looked on as I fished through my drawers. "This should do it," I said, pulling out a letter opener.

I rolled a shirtsleeve to the elbow and laid my forearm against the desktop. "Watch," I said, taking the letter opener in my free hand. Without further preamble, I plunged the blade into my bared flesh.

Deirdre shrieked. "Keelie! What are you—"

Her words ended in a gasp as I held out the knife, its tip completely bashed in. Deirdre's disbelieving eyes shifted to my arm. There wasn't even a scratch. "What are you?" she whispered.

"I'm a demigod," I said, rubbing the spot I'd stabbed. Just because the blade didn't penetrate didn't mean it didn't sting.

"My mom's an immortal," I explained as Deirdre struggled to take it in. "But my dad's not. Neither am I. That's the problem."

Folding my arms behind my head, I stared at the ceiling. "I don't know all the details, but my parents had an arranged marriage. Dad fell in love with Mom at first sight, but she resented his mortality. Even worse, that it would pass on to their kids. She couldn't stand the thought of raising children only to have them age and die. So when she had her first, she took measures into her own hands.

"She arranged for an operation. It was supposed to burn off his mortality, but it was too much. He didn't survive. Neither did the next five."

"They died?" Deirdre's voice came out strangled. "But she... How could she..?"

"I don't know. All I know is that when I came along, she was still hell-bent on doing the same thing. Fortunately, Dad figured out what was going on and stopped the procedure before it finished me off. So I made it, but the operation only half worked. Meaning I'm still mortal, but invulnerable skin makes it damn hard to kill me." I poked myself with the now-ruined letter opener.

"They had a huge fight after that," I continued, tossing the dented blade into the trash. "Mom nearly walked out, but Dad somehow changed her mind. So she stayed, pretending to be a part of the family—until Dad's accident."

I closed my eyes. "Dad was riding, showing off his new Ducati. He was taking the turns way too fast and lost control."

In my mind, I heard it all over again, the squeal of tires and the heart-stopping impact that followed. "It was a complete wreck. The bike was totaled, Dad wound up with a broken leg and cracked ribs, and Mom...lost it. She screamed and took off like all hell had broken loose. She never came back."

"She just ran away?" Deirdre was stunned.

"It's weird." I sighed, my gaze drawn once more to the image of the family that never really was. "Mom won't ever have to worry about dying, but anything that hints at death sends her into hysterics. So as long as Dad was healthy and strong, she could pretend nothing would bring him down. The crash ended that. There was never an official divorce, but it was as good as one. It didn't matter how much we begged. She wanted a new life that wasn't contaminated with age and death, so she abandoned us—the way Helen's abandoned her family."

I heard a sniff and to my surprise found Deirdre on the brink of tears. "Keelie... I don't know what to say."

I shrugged as I tipped the picture facedown. "There's nothing to say. It's just how it is, and it's stupid I'm not over it. I mean, she turned her back on us. I wish I could do the same, but for some reason, I can't. Nothing I do will ever turn me into the child she wants, but that doesn't stop me from trying any chance I get." I gave Deirdre a wry look. "Like I said, it's stupid."

Sorrow misted Deirdre's eyes, and before I knew it, she'd thrown her arms around me.

My breath caught. For Deirdre, who used hugs and pecks as a form of greeting, the gesture was nothing, but it nearly gave me a heart attack.

Since coming to Skyros, I hadn't had any physical contact beyond a handshake; anything more felt too risky. But once the initial shock passed, I realized how starved I was for another person's touch, and suddenly, I was hugging back. Her dark hair tickled my cheek as I leaned closer, finding comfort in her warmth.

And abruptly, my face flushed hot as I realized I wanted more from her than comfort.

I pulled away at once. "Keelie?" Confusion tinged Deirdre's voice as I retreated for the bathroom.

I halted by the door and smiled awkwardly. "I'm fine. It's just... I'm still working through stuff."

She nodded. "I understand. It's complicated."

"Yeah. Complicated." She didn't know the half of it.

Within weeks, my prediction came to pass. The few attempts at negotiations between Sparta and Troy went nowhere, and war was officially declared. Still, the conflict had no direct impact on Skyros, and life here went on as usual. So while Menelaus' allies gathered like impending storm clouds at Aulis, I posed under the same October sky in the school arbor before a half-dozen would-be artists.

As I held my stance, I made a mental note to demand more specifics the next time Deirdre asked for a favor. The Art Club's subject was Artemis, goddess of the hunt. As such, I was wearing a green tunic with a tiny crown and a fake bow and quiver to complete the illusion.

I felt utterly exposed in the flimsy outfit. The knee-length garment did meet the requirements of Skyros' strict dress code, but compared to our wool uniform, it felt like nothing. As the afternoon breeze sent a draft between my thighs, I hoped I wasn't revealing too much.

I revealed enough for the others to make remarks though.

"Y'know, Keelie, you really ought to shave," said Maya.

I nearly jolted out of my pose. "Excuse me?"

"Your legs. They're so hairy." She waved her pencil at the offending fuzz. "They're like gorilla legs."

I swatted her hand away with a growl. "Well, it's not as if you usually see them." Even for athletic meets, my legs stayed modestly hidden beneath loose-fitting sweats.

"Doesn't matter. You never know when you'll have to show off some skin, and you don't want to be the one scaring off the guys because you look like an ape in a bikini."

"Maya's right," said Iris, her plump roommate. "Honestly, Keelie, you're probably one of the prettiest girls here, but nobody's ever going to notice because you keep yourself such a wreck. Your hair for instance—"

"Is fine," I snapped.

"It's not! It's an awesome color, but you've got tons of split ends, and do you realize how hard it was to style earlier? If you just tried some conditioner and..."

My eyes glazed over as Iris rattled a litany of grooming must-haves. I'd never seen human beings so obsessed with primping and preening as I had at Skyros and often wondered if the phenomenon was endemic to this place or universal across teen girldom.

"Yeah, and if you stopped wearing sports bras all the time, you'd probably grow some boobs," Maya chimed.

I almost gagged. "What?"

"It's good to be fit," Maya went on, "but guys like a little bounce, and if you keep them squashed, you'll stay flat as a —"

"My boobs are fine," I hissed.

The duo merely shook their heads. "Such a waste," said Maya, "she'll never get a man if she keeps that up."

Iris agreed. "No kidding. What are you going to do with this girl, Deirdre? She's practically an Amazon."

Deirdre shrugged. "To each their own," she said and continued sketching.

"Thank you, Deirdre," I said.

Iris frowned and opened her mouth to continue the argument when a crash rocked the campus. Shattering and smashing slammed our ears, and the Art Club screeched, dropping their sketchbooks.

That can't be good. I sprinted to the arbor gate for a look and stopped cold.

A heavily armored truck rumbled at the campus entrance. Half submerged in the reflecting pool in front of it were the mangled remains of the school gates, completely torn from their posts. From their booth, the security guards gaped in shock.

Suddenly, men in sunglasses and fatigues spilled out of the vehicle. The guards instantly fled. As they retreated, an invader pulled out a rifle and fired—

"Bandits!"

Even as I yelled, I could sense the mayhem erupting throughout the school. I dashed back to the Art Club girls, who clung to one another in terror.

"Don't just stand there! Move!" Grabbing the nearest girls by the wrist, I dragged them from the garden.

By the time we exited the arbor, the intruders had already fanned out over the campus grounds.

"Coney! Hawkeye! By the garden!"

"Dammit!" I swore as two of them bolted after us. "C'mon, this way!"

I broke for the cover of the ancient pines along the campus perimeter with the others streaming behind me. From the looks of it, the bandits were focusing on the area around Lykos Hall and the dorm. But they might have overlooked the equipment shed at the rear of the campus...

My hunch was right. There wasn't a soul near the prefabricated metal shed behind the lacrosse field. I ran for the door and fumbled open the combination lock as the others caught up.

"Hurry!" I waved them inside, scanning the trees for our pursuers, and jolted. Lagging far behind was a chubby figure with two large shadows rapidly closing in.

"Iris!" Adrenaline surged through my veins, and I doubled back.

My bare feet flew, skimming over the needle-carpeted earth like they never had. I'd nearly reached Iris when the men raised their rifles.

"Look out!" I dove as gunfire shattered the air. Three shots thudded against my back, and I landed heavily atop Iris.

Pinned beneath my weight, Iris writhed in terror. "Keelie? Keelie, no! Somebody! Help!" In the distance, I could hear the other girls screaming.

"Coney, take care of these two. I'll get the rest."

Iris' panic redoubled. "No! Get away!"

"Shut up!" snapped Coney. "No one will get hurt as long as you do what we say. So be a good girl and—"

The bandit gasped in agony as my elbow slammed his groin. He doubled over, and I jumped up, smashing my knee into his skull. He collapsed like a clubbed ox.

Suddenly, shots fired, and I whirled to find Coney's buddy unloading his rifle at me. "Sorry," I said, as his ammunition bounced off my chest, "you'll have to do better than—"

My smug smile fell as he dropped his gun to whip out his radio. I lunged, desperate to stop him before he could call for reinforcements.

CRACK!

The man crumpled, radio still in hand. Behind him, Deirdre held a wooden bat aloft, prepared to take another swing if necessary.

"Good job," I said.

Deirdre dropped the bat and burst into tears.

"Oh gods, oh gods! We're going to die!"

"Iris, shut up! No one's going to die."

"Deirdre's right. Nobody's killing anyone. Not with these." I held up our attackers' ammo between my fingers. The feathered ends of the tranquilizer darts made them look like a bizarre kind of shuttlecock.

"If they wanted to kill us, we'd be dead already," I said, reloading a rifle. "They're obviously out for ransom money."

"So what do we do?" squeaked Iris, her face chalky white.

That was the ten-million drachma question. We were safe for now, all seven of us in the shed with our assailants trussed up in jump ropes. But it wouldn't be long before their pals came looking for them, and we had no way of calling for help. Skyros Prep forbade personal mobile phones, and the school lines were undoubtedly cut.

"Maybe we should make a run for it," Deirdre suggested.

I shook my head. I could make it, but the others didn't stand a chance. "Even if we get to the road without getting caught, it's more than twenty kilometers to town, and the mountains are full of bears and wildcats."

The anxiety in the room heightened at the mention of wild beasts. A few girls began to cry.

"We can't run, we can't hide forever," Maya despaired. "Maybe we should give ourselves up."

"What?" I goggled as if she'd lost her mind.

"They need us alive to ransom us. So it's not like it's not safe—"

"Are you kidding me?" I exploded, sending Maya shrinking against a storage cabinet. "They won't kill us, but there's a whole lot they could do to us."

"Like what?" Iris stuttered.

"Rape us, maim us. I hear Italians cut off fingers to deliver along with ransom notes."

"Keelie, stop it! You're scaring them!" Deirdre cried as Iris fainted dead away.

"They should be scared," I retorted as I finished reloading. "These men are dangerous. We can't afford to mess around with them."

"So what do we do?" Maya wailed.

"*We* are not going to do anything. *You* are staying here." I shoved the rifle into Deirdre's hands. "Stay quiet and away from the door and windows, and if someone does break in, let him have it, Deirdre."

Deirdre nearly dropped the gun. "Me? Why me?"

"Because you won't lose your head. And on the off chance Deirdre misses, the rest of you finish him off with these." Pulling down a bag of softball bats, I shoved them at the nearest girl.

"What about you, Keelie?" Maya asked as she tentatively reached for a bat.

"I," I said, tugging the Artemis crown from my head, "am going to bring those guys down."

There was a moment of stunned silence, and suddenly everyone was screaming some version of "Keelie, are you crazy?" And of them, Deirdre's was the most strident.

"What are you thinking? You just said they were dangerous!"

"So am I," I said darkly.

That shut everyone up. Some of them began to tremble, as if I'd transformed into an entirely different being before their eyes.

"That was not a fluke," I said, pointing at the man I'd taken out. "I can do this. I know I can. They can't do anything to hurt me, and I sure as hell don't want to go down without a fight."

"What about the others?" Deirdre protested as the rest of the girls looked on in fright and confusion. "They might threaten them if you try something."

"They won't. Like I said, they're out to catch us, not kill us. And besides, what man is going to resort to that much trouble to catch one harmless little girl?" I said with a wink.

Everyone stared in horror. Finally, Maya broke the silence. "You *are* an Amazon."

I grinned. "Something like that."

Ridiculous as my costume was, it served me well as I surveyed the campus. It afforded more ease of movement than any of my school clothes and practically blended into the foliage of the tree in which I perched.

A strained quiet had settled over the school. Some bandits guarded building entrances while others patrolled the grounds in twos and threes. I counted twenty of them.

I gnawed my lower lip. *How am I going to do this?*

Although I assured the others that nothing could happen to me, that wasn't quite accurate. They couldn't get me with their darts, true, but that didn't mean I couldn't be stopped in other ways. Impenetrability aside, I was a weakling compared to those guys. I'd have trouble fending off one; two could easily overpower and tie me up.

I couldn't let that happen. Fortunately, I had two more things in my favor. One, this was my home territory, and two, I was fast. Whether short or long distance, I'd never lost to anyone in a foot race. The tricky thing was leveraging my advantages well enough to offset the odds.

As my mind racked, my eyes fell upon the high hedges of the arboretum labyrinth, and inspiration struck.

A few minutes later, the circuit of a three-man patrol neared the arboretum entrance. Once they got close enough, I blundered out the gate like a disoriented waif, directly into their path.

"A straggler! Get her!"

I screeched, throwing up my arms, and dove back into the garden with the trio in hot pursuit.

I kept up the panicky girl act until I reached the labyrinth and then poured speed to disappear within its twists. Behind me, I heard, "She went into the maze. Savage, go right. I'll go left. Xander, stay outside in case she comes out."

Exactly what I wanted.

A minute later, a bandit found me wringing my hands in the middle of one of the longer runs of the maze. I screamed and took off.

"Stop or I'll shoot!"

I didn't slow, and his rifle fired. The dart struck my shoulder, and I went down flailing, tumbling around the corner.

"Savage!" came a voice from the opposite side of the labyrinth. "You get her?"

"Yeah," Savage said, sounding bored.

"Good. Stay put. I'll find you."

"Right." Savage's voice dropped to an irritated mutter as he tramped over to collect me. "Stupid, noisy girl. Now we'll have to carry her back—"

A fleshy smack to the face cut short his complaining. He reeled for a moment, but a second blow from my shovel put him out cold. Flipping him over, I bound his wrists with garden twine.

"Savage? Where are you?"

Savage's pal was getting close. Shoving the unconscious man into the shallow hollow I'd used to hide my shovel, I grabbed my weapon and prepared to strike again.

"Damn maze... Savage!"

I swung as he rounded the bend. He never saw it coming.

Within minutes, a third bandit lay senseless in the arbor.

Divide and conquer, that was the name of the game. Having figured it out once, I knocked out my adversaries at an increasingly fast pace. I did have one close call. A bandit pulled a stun gun, and I nearly got zapped. I made sure to take careful note of their weapons after that.

It was only a matter of time before my activity drew the enemy's attention. Shortly after I bagged my tenth man, his radio crackled with the message, "All units, initiate Plan Omega. I repeat, initiate Plan Omega."

At once, the campus bustled with activity as everyone moved towards the school cafeteria. Through the open doors and high windows, I watched the ten remaining bandits herd their hostages to the center of the hall.

They're going into lock down mode. This would make things a lot harder. There'd be no getting away with my helpless girl act with all of them within sight of one another. Not to mention the bystanders I had to worry about.

As the intruders took up defensive positions, I noticed that one of them wasn't so much in concert with the rest as he was orchestrating the whole thing. A barrel-chested guy with a coppery beard, he had his radio glued to his ear when the others weren't reporting directly to him.

My eyes narrowed. I knew who my new target was. He'd changed the playing field, but that just meant changing my strategy. With one last glance, I slinked off to collect the ingredients for a decisive checkmate.

Although having all my opponents in one place made them harder to pick off, it left that much more territory unguarded, including Lykos Hall, which housed the school's classrooms and teaching labs. I got in and out and over to the campus entrance in less than ten minutes undetected.

My nose wrinkled as I opened the jar I had swiped from the science storeroom. Inside were about fifty sodium metal pellets immersed in an organic fluid.

Chemistry wasn't my strongest subject, but even the most apathetic student took notice when the science teacher dropped one of these pellets into a pail of water to send white flames spurting into the air. Nothing like an explosion to grab people's attention.

Considering the amount in my hands, no one was going to miss this.

I carefully released the jar into the reflecting pool and hurried back under the trees. After stopping briefly to drop a second jar into a bucket by the gardeners' shed, I raced to Lykos. I had no idea how long it would take for the water to disperse the oil and trigger the reaction, but I had to be in place before then. I sped to a classroom on the second floor and peered out a window.

Outside was a covered walkway. A couple meters above where the walkway connected with the cafeteria were the wrought-iron rails of a fire escape. Fixing my eyes on my goal, I pulled the fire alarm.

Girls and teachers screamed at the clanging that resounded throughout the school. Their captors didn't flinch. Two men stepped out to circle the cafeteria cautiously, while the rest coolly maintained position.

Suddenly, an ear-splitting barrage tore the air like gunfire. Within the cafeteria, everyone hit the floor while the pair outside jumped at the smoke and flames spurting around their vehicle.

They and two others took off. Meanwhile, the remaining bandits attempted to calm their hostages, only to have panic erupt anew as the next round of explosions went off.

Three more left, and I sprang out the window. Between the shrieking girls and clanging alarm, my approach went unnoticed. In a flash, I made it across the walkway roof and scrambled up the fire escape.

I kicked open the door and hastened inside the audiovisual booth. Through its wide glass windows was a view of the entire floor. Directly below, the copper-bearded man shouted at the frenzied crowd for silence. His flunkies were nowhere near him.

I burst out of the booth and leaped over the guardrail. I could hear the other bandits shouting a warning, but it was too late.

I landed right on target, knocking him to the ground. Whipping out the kitchen knife strapped to my thigh, I held it to his throat. "Freeze!" I yelled, "Drop your weapons, or I'll kill him, I swear!"

As the men stared in shock, the body beneath me began to shake, and to my bewilderment, my hostage burst into raucous laughter. "You heard the boy. Weapons down, everyone!"

At once, rifles clattered to the floor, and the bandits began applauding. "Well played," the leader chortled. "You far exceeded my expectations, Achilles!"

I jolted as if electrocuted. *What the hell?*

A setup. It was all a setup.

Lying on a bench by the lacrosse field, I stared skyward, struggling to wrap my brain around everything that had happened. In the distance, I could hear the clanking and scraping of Odysseus' men as they cleared debris from the campus entrance. In addition to their destroying the gate, my little diversion blew apart half the pool and flattened two of their tires.

What a mess.

That Odysseus must really be something, to not only track me down but lure me out. Being impressed was not the same as being flattered, though. When he revealed his little ploy, I got so mad I grabbed his rifle and fired three shots point-blank into his leg. Bet Mr. Mastermind didn't see that one coming.

Speaking of whom, I could see him limping across the field.

I scowled at his approach. A couple hours had passed since I stormed out of the cafeteria, but I was still prickly as an offended hedgehog. But I stayed put. I wanted answers, and he was the only one who could give them.

"Hey, Achilles," he said, sounding all buddy-buddy. "You cooled off yet?"

I snorted. "You attacked me and my entire school just to blow my cover. What do you think?"

"I guess I deserve that." He chuckled, which only irritated me more. "But it's not like you would have raised your hand if I waltzed in and said, "I know one of you is actually a boy in disguise so why don't you save me some trouble and come along quietly."

"Well, you've found me, and I hope you get your ass handed to you for it. Do you realize who these girls are? What kind of families they're from?"

"Subordinates and vassals of the man who sent me," Odysseus said evenly. "I'm sure some will be upset, but I doubt anyone will press charges. General Agamemnon's already agreed to take responsibility for the damages."

I startled at his words. General Agamemnon was high commander over the forces going to Troy, the most powerful man in the region, and *not* an individual to be trifled with. My voice dropped to a harsh whisper. "What do you want with me?"

He blinked. "You don't know?"

"How should I?" I snapped. "You came after me, remember?"

He studied me with genuine astonishment. "Wow... You really don't know," he said, scratching his head. "I can't believe Thetis got you to go along with this without telling you anything."

I bolted upright at my mother's name. "What are you talking about? You better not be lying about my mother or—"

"Calm down!" Odysseus threw up his hands. "Give me a minute, and I promise I'll explain everything."

I shut up at once, and he sighed, his demeanor turning serious. "Basically what it boils down to is that you're a child of destiny. Happens a lot with kids of immortals. In your case, the prophecy said you'd take one of two paths. Either you'd live a peaceful, boring life and die of old age in obscurity, or you'd go to war to achieve glory everlasting—and die young."

My blood froze. His words sounded unreal, but I couldn't discount them, especially because so much finally made sense in light of them. I could easily imagine my mother's reaction to such an oracle, and in that context, disguising me as a girl to prevent my enlistment was a logical one.

Part of me was touched she cared enough to protect me. The rest of me was livid. Again, she was calling the shots without any regard for my feelings. She couldn't even tell me the truth. That hurt.

As I grappled with the emotions roiling in my chest, Odysseus patted my shoulder. "Sorry to break it to you, Achilles."

I jerked away from his touch. "So what's it to you? I doubt Agamemnon went through all this trouble just to tell me what my mom didn't."

"You're right. He didn't. After agreeing to lead the Trojan expedition, Agamemnon received his own oracle. According to it, we need you fighting on our side to win."

"Are you kidding me?" I sprang to my feet. "I'm not even eighteen! I don't know the first thing about fighting!"

"You are a kid, that's true," Odysseus said calmly. "And personally, I don't like the thought of minors on the battlefield. But as for you not being a fighter, there's nothing further from the truth. What you pulled off today proves that."

"Humph. And why should I fight for you?" I folded my arms across my chest. "I don't have much incentive." It didn't take a genius to add the two prophecies together and figure that a trip to Troy would be a one-way ticket for me.

"True. But what are your alternatives? You look cute in that dress, by the way."

My face flamed. I was still in that stupid Artemis outfit. "Obviously, since everyone knows I'm a guy, I can't stay here."

"But would you if you could? After discovering what you're capable of, would you want to spend the next few decades in some sleepy place attending cotillions and art shows? That's what your mother wants, but is that what you want to do with your life?"

His question jolted me. The future wasn't something I thought about. My mind was usually too preoccupied with my wretched past and present.

"Tell me something," said Odysseus. "How did it feel when you fought today?"

"You attacked. We were defenseless. What do you think?" I said sarcastically.

"Ah, but you didn't let fear get the best of you. Instead, you stepped up and faced the danger head on. Didn't that stir something inside you? Didn't you feel a sense of purpose?"

That gave me pause. While the girls' instinct had been to hide and flee, mine had been to defend and fight. And despite the fear that flooded my senses, I had never felt so alive.

But fighting another man's war wasn't the same as protecting my own.

"Even if I did, I don't see why I have any stake in your fight."

"You don't care about your father then?"

My breath hitched in my throat.

"Agamemnon's already called up Commander Peleus and the Myrmidon

Squad," Odysseus said, settling onto the bench. "I imagine going back into combat's going to be tough on the old guy, especially considering the shape his heart's in..."

My eyes turned hard. Age had not been kind to my father. From what I knew of his condition, simply leading his troops into war could be more than his heart could handle. While my father could dodge a bullet, he couldn't dodge this, and Odysseus knew it.

"You're a manipulative bastard, you know that?" I growled.

He shrugged. "Perhaps, but it's the truth. Old man Nestor's eighty-five, and there's no exemption for him. He's already at Aulis, cataracts and all, as will your father. That is, unless another man from his family is willing to take over his command."

"Are you crazy?" I exploded. "Even if I wanted to, what squad is going to let a kid who's been wearing skirts the last two years tell them what to do?"

"The very squad you beat today. Those weren't just any men you defeated. Those were your father's Myrmidons." He leaned back, ignoring my shock. "What we did wasn't just to find you, but to see what you were made of. See, Agamemnon is the superstitious sort. If a seer says thus and such is necessary to win, he'll get it done so fast you'd get whiplash.

"But not everyone puts the same store by oracles, and some of us were skeptical, especially your father's men. You were young, way too young, for it to make sense. If you ended up being a dud, they'd be left holding the bag."

"You were testing me," I said flatly.

He chuckled. "We decided to consider you passed if you managed to take out two of us. Never dreamed you'd defeat the whole squad."

"Fine," I huffed. "I passed. Now what? You slap on a bow and haul me over to Agamemnon?"

"No. You get to decide what you want—as a man."

He stood and looked me full in the face. "Crucial as you are, I'm not taking you if you're not willing. An ally with a grudge is more dangerous than the enemy, and I prefer not to die by friendly fire. However, if you choose to join us, I assure you that those men and I can think of no one they'd rather have fighting by their side. You're a natural, Achilles. You have the makings of a legendary warrior. Whether you fulfill that promise, though, is up to you. But whatever you decide, I will honor it. As will your father." With that, he turned and left.

My heart pounded as I watched him hobble away. And suddenly, I was running after him.

My days at Skyros were like a drug-induced dream. I moved and breathed but was merely sleepwalking through the motions of another person's existence. And now Odysseus had literally crashed through to jar me awake. His stunt sent all I knew into disarray, but it also gave me a glimpse of another life. One with freedom and purpose. One where I was needed.

There was so much I didn't know, so much that was unclear, but having caught sight of that future, I didn't want to lose it.

"Odysseus!" I cried. "Wait!"

He halted and turned, smiling broadly.

Single-handedly taking down a squad, having your biggest secret revealed, and volunteering for a detail guaranteed to lead to death was a lot for one day, and I wanted nothing more than to crawl into bed and pass out for a week.

Unfortunately, life wasn't so accommodating.

I stared glumly at the cot I'd set up. It barely fit in the aisle between the island and the sink. As I tossed a lumpy pillow onto the narrow frame, the ice machine began to grind and rattle.

I sighed, anticipating a long night. With my secret out, no way they'd let me back in the dorms. All things considered, I should probably be grateful the matrons were letting me sleep in the kitchen instead of turning me outdoors to bivouac with the Myrmidons.

As I contemplated a future of cold nights on hard ground, my hand lifted to run through my hair and touched stubble. Odysseus had clipped my hair shortly after I agreed to go with him. My neck and ears felt strangely bare without the excess length, but I was glad to be rid of it, along with a few other things.

I scratched my chest, reveling in the fact that I'd never have to wear a bra again. That alone was worth running away to the army. I'd had to wear the damned contraption even to bed and the chafing from the padding and straps just about drove me insane. How women could wear those things was beyond me—

The creak of floorboards interrupted my musings, and I saw Deirdre at the door.

My mouth went dry. Only hours ago I was one of the girls. With my new crew cut and the olive T-shirt and shorts Odysseus loaned me, I couldn't be taken for anything but a boy.

But Deirdre's face showed no emotion as she held out a toiletry bag. "Achilles." Her tongue stumbled over my name as if it was a foreign word. "I brought you your toothbrush."

She was acting as if I was a stranger, and really, I deserved it. I wasn't Skyros schoolgirl Keelie any longer. But somehow, coming from Deirdre, it felt like ice being shoved into my gut.

Desperate to have her old warmth back, I said, "Deirdre, it's okay. Call me Keelie."

She looked at me strangely. "That's not your name."

"Keelie's my mom's nickname for me. She registered me under it because she thought it would be easier to use a name I was already used to."

The temperature dropped several degrees as Deirdre stared, her expression an absolute blank. I'd never seen her like this. "Deirdre, are you okay?"

"Am I okay?" The quiet vehemence in her voice stopped me cold. "Am I *okay?*" she repeated, angrier with each word. Her mask cracked, and suddenly, a torrent of fury erupted.

"I just spent all day hiding in a shed with a gun getting worried sick about you only to find out that the roommate that I've been living with for the past two years is actually a guy! So, no! I am not okay! I am not even close to okay, and it's all your fault!"

"Deirdre—" I said, reaching for her.

"Don't touch me!" She flung the bag at me and fled.

"Deirdre! Wait!"

I caught her easily in the hallway. She was crying so hard she could barely see where she was going. Grasping her by the shoulders, I said, "Let me explain."

"Were you sneaking looks when I was in the shower?" she snapped.

I jerked back as if slapped. "What?"

"Did you?" Her eyes flashed dangerously.

"Deirdre, I swear I never did anything—"

"You swear? Why should I believe you?" She shoved hard against my chest. "Everything you've ever said was a lie! Nothing about you was real!" Her voice broke, and she burst into tears again.

I'd never felt worse in my life. I'd hurt her. Badly. It wasn't my fault, but if I didn't fix it, I'd regret it forever. "Deirdre, please," I pleaded. "Don't be like this. I don't want to leave tomorrow knowing that the one real friend I made here hates me."

"I don't hate you," Deirdre hiccupped between sobs. "But I... I don't know who you are anymore."

"That's not true," I whispered, brushing her hair from her face. She flinched, but to my relief, she didn't break away. "You do know me. Better than my own mother does. You know what I love, and you know what I hate. You know how I'll run the trails for hours, rain or shine, and you know how I can't iron pleats to save my life. You know how grouchy I am if I don't get my coffee, and you know how I nearly flunked math last semester."

Deirdre let out something between a sob and a laugh. "Yeah, you do suck at math."

"And..." I tilted her chin up. "You're still the one I'd choose to share my secrets with. I'm sorry I didn't share all of them with you. I wanted to. I did."

"I know," she sniffled. "It's just a lot to take."

She let me hold her then. For several moments, we simply stood, her head on my shoulder, her tears soaking through my shirt.

At length, she pulled back. "It's so weird," she murmured, her eyes searching my features. "You're so familiar one second, and the next, you seem a completely different person." She shook her head. "I think I understand now what you meant when you said things are complicated."

"Yeah. Well, hopefully things will start getting simpler from here on out."

Deirdre's expression grew taut. "Keelie, is it true? Those soldiers are taking you to Troy?"

I nodded, and her eyes filled with anguish.

"Why? You're not old enough to fight! They can't just make you go because you have a power! There's got to be some way—"

"Deirdre, they're not forcing me. I'm volunteering."

Her mouth fell open. "They say if I go, my dad doesn't have to. Given the circumstances, it's better if it's me," I explained. "But there's more to it than that. An oracle says they need me to win, and... I feel like I'm meant to go."

"It's war." Deirdre's voice was barely a whisper. "You'll have to kill people. Can you do that?"

It was a hard question, one on the forefront of my mind. The worst I'd dealt my opponents were concussions and broken bones, and now that I knew that they were actually Dad's men, I was glad I hadn't inflicted worse. But the battlefield wasn't going to be nearly as convenient when it came to people's lives.

"I don't know," I said honestly. "But if I've learned anything today, it's that I can't stand by when others are taking action. If my going will protect my dad, that's a good enough start for me. Who knows?" I went on, trying to sound light. "These people have already decided they're going to fight. If I go, maybe I'll end it faster."

But instead of being reassured, Deirdre began to tremble.

"Shhh..." I drew her close as tears spilled down her cheeks. "It's okay."

She shook her head forcefully. "No, it's not. Keelie, I'm scared for you."

"I know. But I've got to go. I have to."

"Then promise me...come back alive, okay?"

My spine stiffened. I couldn't bear to tell Deirdre the full extent of my fate.

All at once, the gravity of my decision struck like a blow to the stomach. I thought I knew what I was getting into when I gave Odysseus my assent, but it didn't truly hit until Deirdre spoke those words. Urgency, unlike anything I'd ever felt, flooded my body as my mortality pressed as keenly as if Death gripped me in his bony hand.

I broke our embrace. Deirdre blinked as my gaze grew intense. "Keelie?"

My hands tightened on her shoulders. If I didn't seize the moments I had now, I'd never get another chance.

"When I said I never did anything inappropriate, I meant it. I have never once tried to take advantage of you. But... I have always wanted to do this." Leaning down, I kissed her.

When our lips parted, Deirdre's eyes were wide with surprise. "Keelie," she breathed.

"Hush," I said and kissed her again.

Zipping my duffel, I made a final check of my belongings. A glance showed that all was accounted for, so I shouldered my bag and paused. For so long, I'd wanted escape, but now that I was actually leaving...

My eyes lingered over every part of the suite—the twin beds against the wall, the blazers and plaid skirts in the wardrobe, the cracked tile of the closet-sized bathroom. A breeze wafted through the window, and the tang of pine mingled with the smell of Deirdre's paints in my nostrils. My fingers traced the coffee rings staining my desk, and as the belfry at Lykos Hall chimed the hour, a lump formed in my throat.

The dorm was quiet as I left. All the girls were in class. After yesterday's mayhem, I figured it would be better to get my things when no one was around and disappear quietly. Saying goodbye to Deirdre last night was hard enough.

I touched a finger to my lips. Remembering the warmth of her mouth on mine, I couldn't help wondering if something could have developed between us. I guess I'd never know.

As I reached the foyer, the front door slammed open. I jumped as Deirdre burst in, her hair flying. "Keelie! We've got a situation!"

She flung her arm in the direction of the campus entrance. Parked in front of the Myrmidons' truck was a cherry red sports car. Oddly, the soldiers made no attempt to approach it. They hung back, milling uncomfortably while their leader argued with the driver. The exchange was so heated students poked their heads out the windows to see what the commotion was about.

The car door opened, and a tall woman in a fur-trimmed coat stepped out.

I gasped. "Mom?"

In an instant, I sprinted across the grounds.

I wasn't prepared for this. I wasn't prepared for this at all. Although the school was required to notify my guardian on record of any change in my status, Odysseus somehow convinced them to let him handle it. "Handle it" meaning him getting me out of Skyros before Mom could interfere.

Apparently, Mom had her own ways of keeping tabs.

The Myrmidons parted as I approached, but Mom was so busy fighting she didn't notice. As I reached the car, she slapped Odysseus hard in the face.

Odysseus staggered back, holding his chin. "Nice right hook you've got, Thetis. Hey, Achilles."

Mom whirled, her expression a mix of surprise and relief. "Keelie! There you are!"

The sight of her face sent longing and dread rushing over me, and my breath constricted as she swept me into her arms.

"Keelie, you crazy boy, what were you thinking going after those—never mind. I've got to get you away from these madmen." Taking my arm, she hauled me toward the car. "Let's go."

Her tone was imperious, and my tongue felt like lead as I forced out, "No."

"Did you say something?" she asked, not looking up.

I pulled free of her grasp. "No," I repeated, louder this time. "I'm not going with you, Mom."

"What?" Shock swiftly darkened to anger, and she rounded on me, her voice a low hiss. "What did you say?"

The air around her crackled with wrath, and I was plunged into it once more— the desperation to please, the weight of inadequacy, the compulsion to obey. My hands fisted at my sides. "I'm staying with Odysseus," I said, determined to resist. "I'm going to Troy—"

"Are you insane? No! Now get in that car!"

Her rebuke slammed like an icy squall. I struggled desperately to maintain resolve, but it was no use. I crumbled completely.

Seeing that she'd won, she headed for the car. I followed, head hanging. I was vaguely aware of others calling, but to my ears, it was just static. Everyone and everything had faded into a fog, leaving only my mother and her will.

As I opened the passenger door, it scraped against stone. The sound startled me, and I looked down. For some reason, the edge of the reflecting pool was charred and cracked. I blinked at the damaged marble, and suddenly, the Myrmidons, Odysseus, Deirdre—everything flooded back into my consciousness as I remembered what I wanted, what I was capable of.

"Keelie, get in." My head jerked up to see Mom frowning from the driver's side, but somehow, she lacked the authority she had before.

I closed the door. "No."

Her forehead wrinkled in consternation. I'd never disobeyed her before. "Keelie, I mean it. Get in now!"

"Why?" I stepped away from the car. "So you can ditch me somewhere else while you take off again?"

My retort caught her off guard. "How dare you!" she sputtered. "I did not raise you to speak to me like that!"

"No, you didn't. You didn't raise me at all." As she gasped, I backed off another step and pivoted to walk away.

"No!" In a flash, Mom threw herself on me. Long, painted nails clawed my arm as she held me back. "What do you think you're doing?"

"I'm going to live my own life. I've had enough of you controlling me."

"But Keelie, everything I've done has been for you—"

"The hell it was!" I exploded, thirteen years of resentment erupting to the surface. "All you wanted was to keep me trapped here so you could feel good about yourself while you walked off. Do you have any idea what it's been like living a lie the last two years?"

"I had to!" she wailed, hysterical now. "There was no other way to protect you!"

"From what? Living?"

I shook her off. She threw her arms out in silent entreaty, but my heart was immovable. With an aplomb I never thought I was capable of, I said, "Life is too short for me to simply exist. I know what I want, and I'm going to do it."

"You'll die!" Her shriek pierced the air like a blade. "The prophecy says you'll die if you go!"

"And if I stay," I replied icily, "Achilles of Thessaly might as well be dead."

Her face crumpled, and she fell to her knees. "Keelie, why? Why are you doing this to me?"

As she broke down, compassion swelled in my heart, and I saw my mother more clearly than ever. She never wanted this. Nothing prepared her to bear a child that would eventually pass on and leave her behind. Her immortal body was capable of enduring the ravages of time, but her soul wasn't strong enough to endure an eternal loss.

But I couldn't let her weakness stop me from fully living. My mouth pressed in a firm line. I turned from her and stopped short. Deirdre stared back at me, her face ashen.

My heart lurched. I'd hoped to save her from this, and now she'd learned my fate in the worst way possible. With heavy steps, I went to her and bowed my head. "I'm sorry."

She didn't say a word, but the grief in her eyes spoke volumes. With a trembling hand, she caressed my face for what we both knew would be the last time. Then she walked off. Without a backwards glance, Deirdre went to my weeping mother and kneeled beside her.

My face was grim as I marched up to Odysseus. "I'm done here. Let's go."

With those words, the men, who'd been transfixed by the drama before them, jolted to life. Odysseus barked a command, and the Myrmidons boarded the rear of the truck while I followed Odysseus into the cab. The company was silent as it filed past the girl and goddess huddled on the ground.

I stared fixedly at my shoes as we rumbled away. I didn't dare look out the windows. The burden was heavy enough without having to watch those that I was leaving disappear in the distance.

"It's always hard on the ones left behind," Odysseus remarked, sensing my thoughts. "At least we're doing something. They can't do anything but wait, and having only time on your hands is rough."

Having been one of those caught in the endless wait, I silently agreed.

S.Q. ERIES was an engineer, once upon a time, who wrote dry technical reports. Then one day, she discovered anime fanfiction and has been writing fiction ever since. She also contributes book and manga reviews for The Fandom Post website. Currently, she's hard at work on a novel-length manuscript about the first woman to win the ancient Olympics.

For more about her and her writerly research, drop by her blog.

LINKS

http://sqeries.wordpress.com

Patient Griselda

by Steven Anthony George

I am an ant in honey, drowning in sweetness. The dusty, stillness of this space is as comforting as the scent of old books. Many years ago, there were books in this house, and I once entertained myself by reading them. My husband, being the aesthete that he was, stocked his shelves with classic novels, by Austen and Dickens, which I read voraciously and multiple times. There were also several sets of atlases, encyclopedias, and other reference materials. There were a few books in his collection that were extremely difficult to read, such as those by Woolf and Faulkner; I got through them, however, because—aside from housekeeping (and eventually he had hired servants)—I had little else to do with my time, and I discovered that I eventually enjoyed them. He owned a couple of ancient manuscripts, which he said were very rare. Of course, I was forbidden to touch those, although he did once allow me to read a few pages while he turned them over with gloved hands. The books and the shelves on which they were displayed have been since replaced by costly and complex electronic equipment.

He tested me in an attic room across from this one, and so during the summers it was nearly too warm, as it is this evening. I dislike the summer; it brings with it horrible creatures: houseflies, centipedes, and mosquitoes. I used to see all sorts of frightening things, or so I thought at the time. He only rarely takes me out to the yard anymore, although he realizes that sunlight is important to my health, and so he demands that I sit by the open window during the day—when I remember it is day. Within the past few years, the months have begun to blend together and I often look up at the night sky to consult the stars rather than the earth or the branches of trees. I learned, for example, that if the nights had gotten long and I can see Orion after my testing, then Christmas must be near. I can't look back fondly at Christmases, because I never had them in the traditional sense, but at least it was cooler and I enjoyed seeing the lights sparkle in the distance.

When the nights were hot, the barrel of the revolver felt comfortingly cool as he glided it along the closely cropped bristles of hair on my head. My head is regularly shaved, because he enjoyed the prospect of clearly seeing the entry wound should the bullet fly into my skull. When my husband tested me, I could never see him because he came in from the door behind my chair, which faced the opposite wall. I'm not sure where his Masters crept in; even now, I only catch a glimpse of a claw or the glint of a reflective red eye from time to time, but I wondered why they appeared to me all. It is only my husband who requires my loyalty. Sitting obediently in the wooden chair, I would hear the unlatching of the door. I only knew the appointed time to sit and wait because it followed dinner, which in turn, came soon after sundown. On some days—and increasingly with time—dinner is delivered to me through the slot in the door. I had no communications to give me a clue to the date. I only knew that I could be killed on any day. This had been the situation for a very long time and once my mind began to feel numb, I thought back to my childhood for a hook on which to hang my fading memory.

An elderly woman who lived down the street when I was a young girl had given me her old sewing machine after she bought herself a new one. With it, I taught myself how to design and sew my own clothes. My mother approved of this hobby, not only because we were poor and the fabric was inexpensive, but because, as she would say, knowing how to sew well might attract a good husband. She was eager to have me out of the house. Reading and making elaborate and detailed dresses were my two passions. I educated myself well, though I did poorly in school, as I spent most of my time daydreaming and writing adoring love letters to boys I had not even met. A tall, blonde boy who played basketball was a favorite. He was two years older than I was. I would write poetic notes of my undying devotion, which I would never show to him but save, and as I lay in bed at night, I pretended that I was falling asleep with my head on his chest as he stroked my hair. I would write secret letters as well to the repairman who came to fix out furnace one winter. I would watch him work and imagine that I was his dutiful wife baking cookies for him and our children until the work was complete.

It may have been as much as twenty years ago now since this world first absorbed me. I have no mirror; my husband insists that his Masters will not allow mirrors, clocks, or calendars in the house, but I can look at my own hands and see that I have gotten older, and there is, of course, a reflection in the window at night, even if it has become grimy and is now obscured by the candles. I was in a club called The Blue Light when he chose me. There were wooden booths and red cushions, postcards stapled to the walls around the mirrors behind the bar. I would sit atop a barstool in order to watch the various types who came in groups of four or five, showing their IDs on busier nights. The club was packed with college students when school was in session, and older, local people drifted in and out during the summer. Just spending time there made me feel a part of society, though I rarely spoke to anyone.

I was showing off the periwinkle halter dress I had made the just night before. New Order was playing, the song was "Blue Monday"—I can still hear the lyrics in my head from time to time, though I have not heard music since that night aside from solemn chanting or what might drift in from town. I was underage for a nightclub, but the manager realized that I had nowhere else to go, so he was being kind to me. He'd let me sit at the bar and drink cherry soda. The young men thought I was older than I was, and so I would tell them I was drinking a sloe gin fizz. I wasn't sure what one was; I only knew that they were red and bubbly. I had to decline if they offered to buy me another with an, "Oh, I can't. I've had too many already." And then I would act all tipsy and laugh. That was where I saw Dr. Walter Salvatore. He was older then—a plump, balding man with bushy eyebrows and a few grey hairs poking up from the top of his shirt. He looked like a little frog. That is how I thought of him: The little frog. He sat alone also at a table in the corner of the room.

Dr. Salvatore watched me closely for half the night before gesturing for me to come and sit with him. When he asked me my name, I hesitated to tell him that it was Griselda, because, as I told everyone who asked, it is a name for an old woman. As soon as I sat down, he touched my knee. Men often touched me while chatting at the club and I did not mind it, but Dr. Salvatore was interested in knowing who I was as well. He asked about my parents, and if I had any disorders or illnesses in my family, I supposed at the time that this was because he studied medicine. Then he took me to the beach, which was only a few blocks away, to talk until morning. Even before that first night was over, he told me that he needed children and I responded with joy at the prospect of being a mother. He was not handsome, but he showered me with attention and was a practicing doctor, so I felt very special.

Dr. Walter and I were married within days in this same house, a grotesque late-Victorian—with balconies, front-facing gables, and overhanging eaves—on a hillside at the isolated edge of town. We gathered in a room set aside for an altar. He had given me the words on a card, to read when he nodded toward me. The room was lit by rings of black and red candles. A silver orb of burning incense lay on a table next to a dagger, and other items that I could not then understand. There was also a painting of a winged demon that hung on the wall behind the altar.

I realized what this might have meant, but it did not matter to me then; I was falling in love with this man, and he assured me that he would be my husband forever. At that time, I was skeptical of such absurdities as demons lurking in the corners. Even if he was in league with some kind of evil, it had nothing to do with me—so I thought. His odd beliefs did not affect my love for him or my ability to be a good wife to him. Although I had begun sewing a wedding dress, he informed me, weeks in advance, that I would be married naked, and so I was on the day of the ceremony, wearing only an amulet of another demon of some kind around neck, and hanging from a leather cord that caused me to itch.

A man in black struck a gong four or five times and the ceremony began.

The man I will call a priest chanted in a shrill cry, "I call upon the forces of darkness and the infernal power within! Consecrate this place with the power and light of our hellish Masters! Join with us, we ask, in the binding of these two beings."

There followed a long pause during which the six or seven guests present bowed their heads. My groom looked to me to bow my head as well.

"We call now upon the element of fire to come serve us!" continued the priest. "Flame the passion of Walter and fill him with all-consuming desire and hunger for his bride, Griselda!"

At those words, he took me, pushing me down onto a leopard skin rug that was under our feet. Two boys, I believe, in horned masks, took my arms and pinned them up over my head, and two women, who were also nude, held my legs as he ravished my body. My husband was rough and the act was painful, though I did not cry out. He bit me several times and scratched my breasts before kissing my lips and then biting them until I could taste blood. That was when he released himself into me with a howl. The boys pulled me up to a kneeling position and my husband knelt next to me. I could feel the blood dripping down my chin.

The priest then resumed his shrieking chant, "Hear me, you mighty watchers who lurk in the darkest recesses of this house! Be attentive of these lovers and swiftly provide our ardent groom with what he requests for that which he offers!"

My groom then startled me when he closed his eyes and abruptly shouted, "I bid you provide me energies from my wife, Griselda, to make my life again whole!"

The priest then passed the dagger to my groom, who took my hand, and then cut my palm and sucked the blood from it. When he was finished, he nodded to me to read what was printed on the card.

Trembling, I read, "I pledge my soul to my husband, to be ever in his service. My love for you shall pour forth so that your life shall be forever nourished. Accept this, my beloved, and with it, all that is mine now becomes yours."

My groom then replied, "Griselda, I take you into my mind and my heart as my wife."

Finally, the priest spoke again. "By the secrets of earth and water is this pledge unbreakable and irrevocable. By the law that created fire and wind is this bond written in your souls. Your vows have been made before the Eternal Spirits of Darkness and all the Masters of the Infernal Abyss! This ring, like your vows, is without end. It is the physical sign of your promise."

The priest gave my husband a ring to place on my finger. There seemed to be a sharp edge on it that felt as if it had cut me as he slipped it over the knuckle, by I saw no scratch.

"Welcome to the home of our Masters!" cried the priest.

"Thanks be to our Masters!" cried the others in the room along with the naked women and the boys in black.

My husband shouted, "Welcome potent creatures! Welcome my new Masters for eternity! Welcome to my home," and then he began to weep.

Suddenly I felt overwhelmed by it all; I fell over onto my side, unable to right myself.

With the passing of time, my dear husband grew thinner and taller. He has a clear, olive complexion, unlike when we met. I suppose his eyes may have been blue when he chose me, but they are now nearly black. His hair, even on his body, is dark. He is lean and finely muscled. He smells of musk, like a forest animal, and over the years he has had gotten tattooed with the nude figures of the girls he may have loved before had he had the chance to love whomever he wished in his youth—but certainly he must have done so in the years since. Yet, he married only me because he thought that I could be loyal and it was obvious that I could be just that. I would never run away to a supportive mother or the arms of a lifelong girlfriend from school, because I had never had them and so, as alone as I was, I would never reveal his secret.

He was delighted to find that I was pregnant soon after the wedding. I had a daughter first, born in the springtime in the basement of this house, where my husband had arranged a room for the occasion. His Masters' midwife fed me herbs through the labor. I thought that I might die, but I did not die, though the sweat poured from my face in rivulets. The girl was born many years ago, but it is difficult for me to remember exactly how many years. The girl was a bundle of softness I could kiss to all ends, but he would not let me even name her, nor would he let me keep her longer than a few days. He said that she was intended as seed for his Masters and there were many to appease.

He took my face forcefully in his hands and asked me, "Do I come first? Do I come first?"

"Yes, my husband, you always comes first," I responded.

"In your heart and your soul?"

"Yes, Husband."

"And what else?"

"You are continually on my mind and my body belongs to you."

"The Masters will feed upon my child, the greatest sacrifice I can offer."

I asked only that her remains be buried beneath a tree that flowers in spring in her honor, but he gave her that instant to his Masters, who would consume her, he said, and feed on her essence, in turn, keeping him beautiful.

When I again became pregnant the following year, I wondered if his Masters would require that baby as well. I bore a boy under similar circumstances, also in the spring.

"Do I come first?" my husband asked, his eyes wide in anticipation of my answer. "The demons will consume our child. This is the greatest sacrifice I have to offer," he said again as I held the boy in my arms, as if he had never spoken the same words two years earlier.

Again, the baby was taken from my arms as I nursed it, but out of my love for my husband, I asked only that he be dispatched with as little pain as possible and that any remains be buried where no animal could disturb them.

"He will be one with the Masters," was my husband's only reply.

Long after, when my husband told me he would soon be marrying another, I felt certain I would die. He told me that every day I would be tested, but that day I believed that it would be true. A few weeks before the wedding date, or so I supposed, he announced to me that I was no longer needed and that I should prepare for both his new bride as well as for my own death. He demanded that I sew for her a honeymoon gown, as well a very simple cloak with the leftover fabric in which I could be buried. I began immediately, of course, as my love commanded. For his fiancée, I created a fine-looking black draped nightgown. I requested crystals to sew into the bodice so that it sparkled for him in the candlelight. I sewed a final bead into the skirt before finishing my dinner.

He brought his newly betrothed to see me the night before he would be again married. I bore the two children he needed to repay his Masters, but he now he needed a proper wife, he explained, who was as young and beautiful as he was. He said that she had come from the same bar that he met me so long ago, but I knew that could not be true, because she was far too young to have been there. She was only a child of probably fifteen or sixteen, which was a proper age for induction. There was also with them a boy of about fourteen, who I imagined may have been one of the acolytes.

When my love stooped to me and whispered ever-so-softly into my ear that his new wife was, in fact, our daughter, or rather his daughter, for she is and always has been his, I felt such joy for him. His blood and flesh to do with what he chose had not been devoured by his Masters. What a relief it was to see that she was alive and had emerged from a cocoon as a sweet adolescent, looking the way I remembered I had looked at the same age when I could see myself clearly in a lighted mirror. I asked my husband then, while my head was nearly spinning to the floor, if the boy was also his son. I knew in my heart that he was, because he resembled Walter so in his former state with his bulging eyes and frog mouth, a younger image of the old Dr. Salvatore who put the children into me.

So, they are with him now, moving about other rooms of this enormous house. I hear their sweet voices at certain times of the day, but I see them less and less, and I wonder if they have had babies of their own. I see my husband only occasionally now. He even has a nurse come up to my room to give me the needle in a good vein and I am always so thankful. That perfect, still-handsome man no longer tests my devotion with a revolver to my head, though he insists upon keeping my head shaved and certainly I have no reason for a head of hair. The Masters needed to be paid, after all, and I, for my husband's sake, suffered for them—not he for them. Was that not clever? I am now confined to just one room at the top of the house and, so when looking out of the window at the world as I know it, I feel like Rapunzel, but that is the soul of irony.

I see now that the gun would have never been loaded. He needed to keep me alive, but I feel that I am never sure that I am really alive. I often do not know if I am awake. Have I wakened or am I still asleep? I light votive candles and place them in loops in wires I've salvaged from my sewing things when I had them, or so I can see myself doing so. They dangle from the window frame by pushpins so that they appear to me from the far side of the room to be the brightest of stars gathering just inside my little space. The tiniest lights from candles are the most brilliant of fireflies, too delicate to touch, or perhaps butterflies; colorful, glowing Chinese butterflies, fluttering toward me in groups of three or four, their soft, dusty wings lightly kissing my cheeks and brushing my lips and I find that I am in ecstasy.

S TEVEN ANTHONY GEORGE is a poet and short story writer who resides in Fairmont, West Virginia. He finds inspiration largely in historical events, visual art, and film. His work has appeared in several online and print journals and is also forthcoming in the anthology *Diner Stories,* to be released in late 2014. He operates an online murder mystery game and he is active in the autism community, often speaking on the topic of self-advocacy.

LINKS

http://www.stevenanthonygeorge.com
http://www.facebook.com/sageorge.writer

My Name is Melise

by Dale W. Glaser

MELISE. *Melise.* Her name was Melise. The thought rebounded in her brain, around and around, an echo of itself. Melise, Melise, Melise. In her mind, she heard her own voice repeating the words, *My name is Melise,* but they felt like an idea given to her by someone else, thoughts left to her on another's deathbed, parting words.

Her eyes opened, twin butterflies newly emergent, hesitant and trembling.

A star, cold and white, was suspended above her head, close enough to touch. Her hand reached out, almost of its own accord, fingertips brushing the point where the five rays met. Angular panels lifted away from her, fanning outward, the star exploding in slow motion and revealing behind it a blindingly bright light. She sat up, looking around at her cradle, like a steel flower with razor-edged petals unfurled. Warily, she climbed out.

Her bare feet met a chill surface, polished steel as smooth as glass and almost as reflective. The floor, featureless except for her cradle, extended in every direction for many yards before dropping off sharply, the hard edge the last distinct feature visible before an abyss of shadow. She gazed around—unsure for what she might be looking—for some time before the realization fully formed: she was looking for help. But there was none to be found, only the low susurrus of a wind she could hear but could not feel. She walked in a circle around her cradle and discovered several cables attached to its base and snaking off across the floor, leading her toward the edge. She followed them to the drop-off, lowered herself to her hands and knees, and peered down. The cables tumbled off the precipice and doubled back under the floor to a distant point she could not see. Vertigo tilted the entire chamber, and she closed her eyes and drew back her head, curling on her side into a little ball atop the steel surface, terrified at any moment she might roll off like a glass marble, spin and fall and shatter below.

She opened her eyes again to the harsh light, coming from a source overhead too bright to look at directly. The sterile illumination fell straight down, sparing nothing to reach the farthest corners of the massive enclosed space, too large to still be properly called a room, practically a coliseum. She could remember what a coliseum was but not whether she had ever been in one before. *My name is Melise;* that was all that she knew of herself. On the edge of her perception were more memories, like beacons obscured in heavy, swirling mist.

More powerful than indistinct memories was her growing sense that she could not remain where she was, that this featureless space was somehow inimical to her. She circumnavigated the entire platform but found no exit; one edge of the steel surface abutted a barrier constructed of gigantic concrete bricks, towering higher than the suspended light source, but the wall held no doorways. The other three sides of the platform anchored no stairways or other means of descent aside from the dangling serpentine cables.

She straddled a cable, hugged it, inched herself along its length off the platform, shifted her position to remain atop the cable as it snaked under the floor. It bore her weight without complaint, even as her ragged breathing shook her entire body. The cable angled downward, passing above an expanse of steel mesh. Through the mesh, she could see huge, branching club mosses, primordial jungle plants rising from a floor of dark soil. Again she felt that profound dissociation; she knew plants of such size, even greenhouse born and bred, must be remnants of an epoch hundreds of millions of years gone, yet she did not know where she had been the day before, why she had fallen asleep within a steel flower, how she had come to be in this enormous desolate vault. *My name is Melise,* she thought, as if that could account for anything.

She had no explicit reason to believe the greenhouse room below her would be the site of a doorway to the outside world, but it was the first sign of life she had seen since awakening. She dropped from the cable to the mesh, and searched it until she found access through a small trap door. She lifted it open, lowered herself through. Hanging by her fingertips, falling to the floor of the greenhouse, moist loam squishing between her toes. The club mosses were arranged haphazardly around the glass walls, while a large plastic pool full of water stood near her, a massive tree stump on the opposite side. Strange for a greenhouse, but then its purpose had been only an assumption. Perhaps a terrarium, some kind of habitat, was closer to the truth.

The tree stump had a hole, large enough to be a doorway, and a huge limb emerged, splayed webbed digits, mottled green-black skin. A frog, airsac pulsing, bronze-bowl eyes bulging. Melise pressed herself back against the glass wall between two club mosses. The frog was the size of a hippo, nearly as tall as she but longer and wider, easily outweighing her fivefold. It crawled forward, turned, and in profile showed Melise that a section of the top of its head had been removed, an open window through skin and skull exposing the ghostly white lobes of the brain. Slender wires, coils and antennae protruded from the cranial nodes, and a technical diagram assembled itself in Melise's mind: multi-channel neuromags, non-disruptive scanning electrodes, axonal proton flow ... Was she a scientist, or had she been before she slept?

She lacked the luxury of time to consider chance encounter with what might be her own memories. She noticed a few fist-sized rocks lying on the ground, and slowly moved to pick one up, trying not to appear as a threat. If the giant frog attacked her, she would be able defend herself using the rock as a crude weapon. The frog's eyes would be especially vulnerable.

No sooner had she found the best grip for wielding the stone than another frog squeezed out of the hole in the stump, barely able to pass through the opening. The two frogs were nearly identical, except for the first being a mere fourth of the size of the second. The larger frog was also crowned with electronic components, increasing the parent-child resemblance.

She wanted to scream herself awake from her nightmare of gargantuan frogs, but deep in her heart she knew this was no dream. She dropped the stone, all but useless in the face of the titanic second frog, into her pocket. Both frogs turned and looked directly at her, and began to lumber toward her. Melise ran. She ran around the glass-walled habitat, looking for the door, but found none. The hatch in the mesh ceiling was the only way in or out. She had left it open, but it was too high overhead to be reached.

She reached the plastic pool again, and stepped up onto its edge as the frogs closed in on her. She waited as long as she dared, so long her nerves grew hot and seemed to consume themselves like bomb fuses, until the larger frog waded halfway into the water. She jumped, and landed on the slick surface of the frog's back. Her fingers clutched at the only handhold they could find, the lip of the incision around the frog's brain.

The frog reared up out of the water and hopped wildly around the habitat. Every leap of the gigantic amphibian brought her tantalizingly close to the mesh ceiling. She braced herself on her knees and stretched at the apex of one jump, catching the steel grating with her fingertips and tightening her hands into desperate fists. She dangled from the ceiling, with the hatch several feet away as the larger frog hopped away, blinking agitatedly.

She had to swing toward the hatch, and the mesh bit into her fingers while her shoulders burned from the strain. Three more swings and she would be at the edge of the hatch. Two more.

A sticky warmth encircled her left shin, tightened and pulled. Her left hand lost its grip and the right reflexively tightened, deeply slicing her palm. She looked down, and saw the smaller frog had shot out its tongue to snare her as easily as it would a juicy cricket.

She reached up and grabbed the mesh with her left hand. She kicked her leg, flailed it violently, lifted and swiveled it to dislodge it from the slimy coils, but the tongue was tenacious. She swung her body toward the hatch, arm over arm, stretching the frog's tongue but not escaping it. She grasped the edge of the hatch and pulled herself up onto her elbows, her stomach, her right knee. The frog followed her, the tongue held fast.

She fell to her side, rolled onto her back, and felt for the hatch door. The angle was bad, offering her no leverage, but she lifted the hinged section of steel mesh upright, then let it fall over the open hatch as she jerked her left leg out of the way. The hatch door crashed onto the frog's tongue, which finally recoiled.

She wanted to cry, at the stinging pain of her lacerated palms, at the viscous and sour jelly clinging unpleasantly to her leg, at all the other indignities she could not name. But she yearned to reclaim her freedom more than she needed to shed tears, so she rose to her feet. The giant frogs' habitat had not concealed an escape route, but she remained determined to find one.

She walked along the top of the mesh grating until she came to the edge of the giant terrarium. The platform extended to another tank, uncovered, half full of murky water. The tank was wider than the platform, with no way around it. If she jumped from the top of the terrarium down to the platform, she would be unable to get past the open tank, and would have no way to climb its sheer glass walls to cross over it. She would have to jump from the top of the habitat to the edge of the water tank.

She backed up, ran, and threw herself into the air. Her chest struck the upper edge of the water tank and her arms clamped over it. Her breath was knocked from her and her arms immediately protested with throbbing pain. She pushed with her bare feet against the glass side, but they found no purchase. She pulled with her arms, heaving her stomach to the edge of the tank, dangling like a ragdoll half in and half out of the tank. She raised one knee, enough to push it over the lip and drag the other leg up. She planted her foot, stood up, and immediately slipped on the remnants of frog tongue slime coating her lower leg. She flailed her arms for balance but teetered forwards and fell with a splash into the cloudy water below.

She came up gasping for breath, wiping water out of her eyes with both hands, scissor kicking to keep her head above the surface. Her eyes stung, and she realized she was smearing her face with blood from the ragged wounds on her palms. Crimson ribbons swirled through the water around her.

Something underwater moved toward her. She could not make out any details of it, only evidence of its passing, as it cut an undulating furrow through the semi-stagnant liquid. Then it reared up before her, a sinuous shape, spectral and translucent, a horror with no limbs, no face, only a pale tubular body ending in a fanged oral cavity, flexing silently and obscenely.

She pulled the rock from her pocket and hurled it at the grey water-worm, desperately hoping to choke it. Her aim was true, she struck the mouth of the worm, but the creature ejected the rock a moment later.

Seizing on the distraction, however momentary, she dove under the surface of the water before she had a chance to wonder if she knew how to swim. *My name is Melise, and I don't have any choice.* She pulled herself through the water blindly, frantically, hoping that she was eluding the worm but with no way of knowing if she were swimming straight into its maw. Her fingers grazed the flinty surface of her rock weapon, grabbed it. She would need it to escape.

She swam one-armed until she reached one of the sides of the tank, and smashed the rock into it near the base, again and again. Her blows began to feel as if the impacts were driving deeper into the glass when the fangs of the worm sank into her ankle. The pain shot through her entire leg as she kicked away on instinct, dropping the stone.

The worm pursued her, she was certain, and she was tiring. She thought of death and felt an eerie sense of déjà vu. Her mind was as tired as her body as she came up for a deep breath that might very well be her last. As her mouth cleared the water and she inhaled, her toes brushed the bottom of the tank. The level had gone down, was continuing to go down, as water leaked from the cracks she had made in the side of the tank.

She saw the wake in the water left by the worm's passing, and swam away from it, always in circles around the enclosure of the tank, although soon enough the water was so shallow that it was faster to run than to swim. The water fell from her chest to her waist to her knees. When it was barely puddle-deep, she risked a look back over her shoulder. The worm twisted helplessly on the other side of the drained tank's floor.

She retrieved her stone, returned to where she had begun smashing the glass wall of the tank. She hammered methodically at it until the cracks spiderwebbed and fragments fell loose, then struck at the edges of the hole to make it wider and wider until she was able to step through onto the narrow lip of the platform below the tank. She could not retreat the way she had come, and on the opposite side of the cuboid from which she had just emerged was an identical tank, doubtless home to another ravenous worm. She braced her heels, jumped, fell to the bottommost floor of the chamber, and lay there, bleeding from both hands and one leg. She coughed pitifully, cold and wet and in pain in a puddle that made the chill cement slick.

After a few moments, she forced herself upright. Her back was to the only source of light in the chamber, and in the shadows surrounding her she could only make out muted colors and faint outlines. She limped toward a lighter hued area, looming like a pale monolith.

Some details began to resolve as she approached, although she felt unable to accept their reality until she had drawn close enough to reach out and rest her hands against the white vertical surface, panels six feet wide and four times as high, covered in soft, clear vinyl film, with markings near the tops. Legible markings. Handwriting.

The panels were the spines of binders, ordinary office supplies lining the shelves of an ordinary bookcase, unremarkable in every way except for their enormity. But their very nature as commonplace items caused a seismic shift in her perceptions, her perspective. She had been able to believe that the frogs and the worms were giant creatures, freaks of nature collected in a menagerie. But from where would giant books have come, and what purpose could they serve? In fact, the binders were perfectly proportional to the frogs, the worms, their tanks, everything she had seen. Everything except herself. She was the anomaly, the miniature woman. The frogs were normal-sized frogs, their brains implanted with monitoring devices because they were part of a neurological experiment. The nematode was larger than usual, because it was part of a growth experiment, but still small. This was no zoo, this was a laboratory.

And she? What kind of experiment was she?

My name is Melise, she reminded herself, although she was beginning to doubt even that.

Beside the bookcase was another white shape, this one rounded, oblong and opaque. It floated above the floor, supported by apparatus that hummed softly, only audible as she came close to it. She walked the length of it, finding tubes a the far end that she could clamber up. Ignoring the screeching pain in her hands, the dull ache in her bones, she ascended.

The top surface was smooth, uninterrupted except at the end closer to the bookcase, where a steel ring rose. She made her way toward it. She gauged it was as high as her waist, but she was learning to compensate in her mind; knowing that she was only two inches tall meant the ring was no more than an inch thick. A horrible dread filled her as she reached the ring and placed her hands against its surface, leaning over it tentatively, as if it were a deep well and she feared plummeting to its bottom.

But there was no way to fall in, not with a glass window encircled by the steel ring, flush with the surface she stood upon. The glass was laced with crystals, which partially obscured what lay beneath: a face, a hundred times the size of hers, as pale and still as a statue. Not stone, but skin made coarse and pitted and hard by frost, not marble but flash-frozen flesh. And recognizable, instantly, shockingly, for the face was her own face, a terrible reflection monolith, a monument to her in final repose.

She backed away from the window, fast, too fast, and her feet slipped on the unfeeling, unyielding lid of the cryogenic tube. There was nothing to grab on to, no features at all to the smooth surface, and so she fell once again, and when she hit the floor stars exploded behind her eyes, but even their intensity was not enough to drive the vision from her mind: her face, her true countenance, appropriately sized. A deathmask.

She was tired, so tired, utterly unable to go on. She retreated toward the lab animals. She could see the frogs' terrarium, the shattered nematode tank, its intact counterpart, and to the right of that, a mouse cage. She was easily able to slip between the bars of the cage. As soon as she entered its domain, the mouse approached her, sniffed her, retreated to its burrow in the cedar shavings, unimpressed. She understood. Despite the similarity in size, she felt no kinship with the animals, nor they with her. She laid down and pulled shavings over herself. She coughed, for so long she feared she might never stop, until finally the spasms subsided.

Light flooded the lab. She shut her eyes tight against it. Footsteps echoed down wooden stairs, then stopped. "Melise?" A voice of concern. It moved around the lab, with the footsteps resuming in counterpoint, "Melise? Melise, what...? Oh there you are." The last directly overhead, and then she was being cradled in giant hands, lifted gently out of the mouse cage. "Are you awake?" the voice of the hands asked. She made no move to answer, did not open her eyes. "Oh, Melise, why didn't you wait for me?"

Curiosity overwhelmed her. She opened her eyes, saw the giant's face: haggard, bleary-eyed, tragic. "There you are," he said with a weak smile. "No hello?"

She said nothing, regarding him wearily and warily.

"Do you ... you don't remember, do you?" he sighed with foreknowledge of the answer. "Did you use the mantra I suggested? You'll have to try harder this time. But the good news, my darling, is that this should be the last time."

Holding her as if she were something both fragile and precious, he turned and carried her back to where her memories began, the steel flower cradle. She could see two more steel flowers on either side of it, their unbloomed petals tightly closed, half the size of the flower from which she had emerged. One of the smaller flowers was connected with cables and tubes to the larger, while another set of unmoored wires dangled from the last flower. He laid her in the open cradle, his huge fingers lingering along her back as they reluctantly let her go.

He picked up a digital tablet from the nearby table, swiping its screen to life and scrolling through its electronic contents. "Your name is Melise Thomson," he explained, in a tone that sounded rehearsed and fatigued. "You died, tragically, far too young, and I couldn't bear to live without you. I cloned you, with DNA from your cryonically frozen remains, and I recreated the spark of your mind with brain patterns you had recorded for our database. That was our great stroke of luck, my love; it was how I knew that it was right for me to make you live again, despite the taboos of some so-called ethics panel. It was fate, wasn't it? Fate that you and I would be research partners, and that the means to reconstruct you, the real you, body and soul, would be in my basement.

"The methods were untested, but I believed in them. The amnesia was an unfortunate side effect, but one which I believed would reverse itself in time. Unfortunately..."—here his voice hitched, as the memories overwhelmed him— "...the new body was too unstable to provide that much time. The rapid growth matrix allowed the replication of an adult body to house your adult brain patterns, your personality and memories... in theory, at any rate. But the cells suffered catastrophic replicative senescence and decay.

"But you see, that was when I was inspired. Smaller cells, fewer cells, faster growth with less oxidative stress...if I could bring you back in any form, even on a smaller scale, I had to try. You do understand that, don't you? I *had* to.

"My hopes were high when you emerged from the matrix perfectly proportioned and three feet tall. But the systemic collapse had only been delayed. I tried again, and your one-foot tall clone lived a bit longer, and your six-inch tall clone longer still. I hoped your two inch tall clone would finally achieve telomere stability." He peered at the tablet screen. "It's close. So very close. A one inch tall clone should be perfect, I'm certain of it."

He stabbed the screen in a series of keystrokes, and in response tiny armatures arose from underneath her seat in the cradle, chromium insect limbs with needle tips that bit into her neck and hips, then deeper into her spine and pelvis. Her mouth twisted into a grimace of pain, because she could not scream. She wanted to, to protest, to howl that he had re-made her as a creature with no proper place in the world, a world that was now terrifyingly monstrous and out of proportion. She wanted him to know how devastatingly lonely she had felt. But all her half-paralyzed throat could manage was a single, creaking word: "Alone."

"No, no, no, my love," he said, setting aside the tablet and bending over her steel cradle. "You will never be alone. Because this time I am going to join you. If the only way for you to live out the full lifespan fate should have intended is to do so as an inch-high woman, so be it. And if the only way we can be together, as we were destined, is for me to become an inch-high man, so be it as well. Don't you see? After all you've been through, we've found the solution. Now I can clone you and clone myself as well, place our recorded consciousnesses in two tiny new bodies, and we can live out the rest of our lives."

"How...?"

"Don't worry, no one else will find us. No one else needs to know. No one else would ever understand," he added darkly. "And all we need is each other, isn't that right, my love?" He returned his attention to the tablet once more, and continued in a half-distracted way, "Technically we need food and shelter, as well, but I've laid enough of those by in a secret place we can call our own."

Rolling up his sleeve, he continued, "But the important thing is that you hold on to yourself, Melise. Do you understand me? If I clone you at half your current size, and clone myself at one sixty-fourth my size, and you don't remember me, then what is the point? The world is dangerous enough, and at that size everything will be a deadly peril. As perhaps you already know," he mused, pausing and looking questioningly at her. He picked up a modified syringe, attached it to a cable which ran to one of the smaller steel flowers. "We need each other, all the more so when we are small. So please, promise me you'll focus on the mantra for as long as you can, even as you feel your consciousness ebbing away. Your name is Melise. Names are important, meaningful, the keystones around which we build our sense of self. Say it again and again, tell yourself 'my name is Melise' and the brain pattern recordings will do the rest."

He pierced the skin of his bare arm with the syringe's needle. "I'll be saying my mantra, too, my love. Don't forget yours. Don't forget me." With that he closed his eyes, laid his arm carefully along the worktable, and lowered his head beside it.

She did not remember him. She had no knowledge of the man other than their brief strange interactions of the last few minutes. She did not even know his name. She had remembered her own name, the mantra had worked, but only as a single word, one iota of her essence, not some magical key to its entirety.

Melise. Melise. My name is Melise.

Melise tried to remember the life the man had been describing to her, their work together, their relationship, the life before her death. Her first death, apparently, if the man was to be believed. He had raised her from the dead, and death had reclaimed her, and he had tried again, and lost her again, and continued wrestling her out of the grave, smaller and smaller gobbets of her each time. Was that love? Or jealousy? Did she love him in return?

Melise, Melise, my name is Melise.

He seemed to feel as if he owned her, as if he had always been entitled to claim her as his own and had only strengthened it in deed by re-animating her, forcing her to live again and again through recursively diminished copies of herself.

My name... my name...

The worm, Melise. Remember the worm. Take him to the worm, Melise. Guide him there, push him in, into the water, in with the worm.

The worm, the worm, the worm.

D ALE W. GLASER is a lifelong collector, re-teller and occasional inventor of fantasy tales. His short stories have previously been published in *How the West Was Weird* (Volumes II and III). He currently lives in Virginia with his wife and three children, none of whom have been definitively proven to be changelings (yet).

LINKS

https://twitter.com/sunnydwg

A Taste of Winter

by Jax Goss

GERDA was dancing. She seemed to be doing that more and more, he thought, as he watched her through the window. It was early autumn, and the leaves were just beginning to change. The roses were in their last bloom, and she had been pruning them for their winter rest, but now she was spinning out on the grass, her face alight, her arms wide. Two crows sat on the fencepost watching her, and she laughed, and gestured with her hands like she was talking to them as she danced.

He shook his head. Gerda had always been a bit like that, ever since they were children, living in opposite houses. She had always loved roses. And summer.

He remembered a time when she had loved winter, too, loved snow and snowmen and sledding, but that had changed at some point as they got older. Now she hated it, and the closer they got to winter, the more withdrawn and sad she would become. He'd catch her watching him with fearful eyes, like she thought he was going to disappear. He didn't understand what the problem was. It was just the turning of the seasons, and it had its own cold, magnificent beauty.

He watched her dance in the late afternoon sunlight, glancing down through the trees, lighting up the fading colors of the roses, illuminating her face. He smiled, and shook his head a second time. She wouldn't come in until sunset, when it started getting cold. He'd better start dinner.

When she did come in, her cheeks were rosy with the exercise and the evening cool. He was stirring a pot of Bolognese on the stove, and she wound her arms around his hips, standing on tiptoes to peer over into it. She breathed deeply.

"Smells amazing," she said.

He smiled, turning his head to kiss her cold face. "Your favorite."

She grinned cheekily. "I know."

She extricated herself, and started pulling down bowls from the cupboard and cutlery out of drawers. She pulled out two wine glasses, and poured them each a glass from the bottle of red he'd been using in the sauce. She sat at the kitchen table and sipped at it.

"It's definitely starting to feel autumnal out there," she said ruefully.

He turned and smiled, took a sip of the glass she'd left on the counter beside him. "Summer will be back before you know it," he replied.

She sighed. Swished the wine idly in her glass and stared at the colored liquid as it spun.

"One day she's going to come back," she said very softly.

"She?" He frowned. "Who?"

She glanced up, eyes wide. "Did I say that out loud?"

He smiled, bemused, and nodded. "Who did you mean?"

She shook her head, gave him one of her brilliant smiles and said, "Never mind. Shall I put on some music?"

It was mid-winter, and they were curled up on the sofa together, under a blanket, reading, while a fire burned brightly in the hearth. Gerda had her legs stretched across his lap. She was reading Robin McKinley's *Sunshine* again, one of her favorite books. He was reading a history of Scandinavia. Snow fell outside, thick and heavy. He looked out at it for a moment, watching it flurry and swirl and settle against the windowpane.

He'd been watching for a while when he realized that while his book lay neglected in favor of staring at the snow, hers lay neglected because she was staring at him. He cocked his head questioningly at her.

"What is it?"

"You love watching the snow."

He smiled. "Sometimes, yes. It's...there's something strangely mesmerizing about it. Like you can forget who you are in the patterns it makes."

"Don't say that, Kai."

He frowned at her. "Why does it bug you so much?"

She shook her head. "I just...I don't like the snow."

He laughed. "Is it because of that old story my grandmother used to tell us as children? That the Snow Queen would come and take us? That always used to scare you more than I thought it should."

She peered into his face, frowning. Then she made a wry grimace with her mouth and shook her head. "Yes. It was that. That...story."

"It's just a story, Gerda. You take that sort of thing so seriously."

She pursed her lips. "Maybe you don't take it seriously enough," she snapped.

He was taken aback. It was very unlike her to snap. This winter must really be bugging her. He reached over and ran a strand of her hair through his fingers, and softened his voice. "Hey. I didn't mean it like that. I'm sorry."

She nodded, and returned to her book, but something in her face made him strangely uneasy, like he was missing something.

A couple of days later, he walked into the living room and she was on the phone. She had her back to him, her feet up over the back of the couch, like a little girl. He smiled, then stopped as he heard what she was saying.

"I don't get it. The rest of us remember, but he doesn't. He acts like it was just a story he heard as a kid. How is that even possible? How do you forget something like that?"

She paused, listening. He could hear the tinny sound of the other voice, but not who it was, or what it was saying.

She sighed. "I know. I just find it frustrating. And scary. He'd have no..."

Another pause.

"I guess. Okay. I'll try. So we'll see you Saturday morning?"

Another pause, and then she chuckled. "Fine, afternoon then. I can't wait. Bye."

He backed off, and then came in again loudly, so she'd know he was there.

"Were you talking to someone?"

"Yes. It was Vilda. She's coming for lunch on Saturday."

He grimaced. "I'm really not sure why you're still friends with her. She's so... Boorish."

"She's real. And she's always been there for me. She may lack elegance, but she makes up for it in heart." Gerda grinned. "Just hide the silver. You know she can't resist that, even though she's reformed."

"That girl will never be reformed." Kai grinned. "She does keep things interesting, though, I'll say that for her. Any particular reason for the visit?"

"She always comes in winter. You know that."

He nodded. There was no way to ask her about what he'd heard without revealing he'd been eavesdropping. Maybe with enough wine in her, Vilda would give something away. The girl sure knew how to quaff a mulled wine. And Kai's mulled wine was the best.

That Saturday, lunch was a sumptuous winter feast. Gerda had slow-roasted a leg of lamb, drenched in olive oil, rosemary, and garlic cloves, and accompanied by a tray of roasted winter vegetables—potatoes, sweet potatoes, carrots, onions, all golden and steaming. Kai had made his amazing mulled wine, and the three of them sat around the table eating happily and chatting comfortably.

Vilda was a character, Kai had to admit. He'd never quite understood their relationship. He knew Vilda had done time, and she was supposedly reformed, but she still had a wild streak—a tendency to anger swiftly and forgive just as quickly, a penchant for expensive things he was sure she shouldn't be able to afford. She laughed easily and boisterously, and while he knew there had been men, none of them ever lasted longer than a month or two. Vilda was a wild thing, and no one was going to tame her.

And yet she and Gerda had been friends since childhood. Kai had no idea how they'd met, or how sweet, kind Gerda and boisterous Vilda had even become friends, but Vilda had suddenly just started showing up. She always swooped in like a force of nature, and then vanished again just as inexplicably. While Kai and Gerda had been studying and trying to get through school and university, Vilda had lived wild on the streets, weirdly untouched by the harshness of that environment. The world just seemed to bounce off her as she thundered through it.

The only person he knew of that she cared about was Gerda, to whom she was fiercely loyal. When they'd moved in together, Vilda had pulled Kai aside and told him in rather colorful imagery just what would happen to him if he ever hurt Gerda. And he had no doubt at all that it wasn't exaggerated—he absolutely believed Vilda totally capable of everything she'd said she'd do.

Now she was downing the mulled wine and eating the lamb with her fingers like some kind of barbarian Viking girl. He chuckled, knowing that if he said anything she'd just look at him nonplussed. Vilda was the only person he'd ever met with absolutely no shame—she was who she was, and it had never occurred to her that there may be any issues with that at all.

"You're going to have to stay the night, Vilda," Gerda was saying.

"I'm good with that," Vilda agreed cheerfully. "Can't even ride a reindeer with this much wine in me, I suppose."

Kai laughed, and Vilda looked at him, a cheeky grin on her face. "You still don't think I do that, huh? Gerda knows better, don't you, girl?"

Gerda smiled and nodded. "Vilda let me ride one of her reindeer once when we were children."

"I don't remember anything like that," Kai teased, and watched as Gerda's face did a strange thing, passing through something like hurt and sadness—just for a minute—and then back to the shining smile, though there was still a trace of something in there.

"There's a lot you don't remember, Kai," Vilda said, poking his shoulder with a finger.

"Vilda..." Gerda began.

Vilda just snorted and took another swig of her wine.

"Sometimes I don't know what you two are talking about," said Kai, as he stood up and began to clear plates for dessert.

He was standing in the kitchen, listening to the murmur of their voices and laughter, and stirring the hot syrup he was going to pour over the pecan pie he had made. And then the world shifted.

He staggered a little, and rested his hand on the windowsill for just a moment. Then he pulled it back sharply. It was ice, ice cold. He looked at the window, which was ajar, and reached up to close it when it swung back suddenly, letting in a blast of cold and snow and ice.

His small cry of surprise brought a worried call from Gerda in the other room, asking if he was all right.

"Yes, I'm fine..." he trailed off, staring out the window.

Out in the garden was the figure of a woman, all in white, furs and silk, staring at him with eyes like ice and frost and the taste of her lips, he knew somehow, was like the first touch of icicles against stone, like the moment water becomes ice, like the transformation of one thing to another, like a world turned clean and beautiful.

There was a fluttering of black wings that broke his reverie. He shook his head and looked confused at the crow that perched on the windowsill. It cocked a head and flew away. Kai looked out into the garden. There was nothing out there but snow blowing in cold flurries.

"Kai?"

Gerda was standing at the door, that strange look on her face. He shook himself again and pulled the window closed.

"It came loose, I suppose. It's okay, it seems fine now." He turned back to his sauce. "And this is ready. Let's eat."

Her smile was small, and afraid, but she followed him back, where Vilda was merrily pouring herself another cup of mulled wine.

Later that evening, Kai stood just outside the back door staring out into the darkness, thinking about what he'd seen. *What I thought I saw*, he corrected in his head. It must have just been his imagination. It was odd though, it felt strangely familiar to him.

He stared out, and saw her again, just outside the line of the trees. He could see her clearly, despite the dark, standing there watching him. When she knew he'd seen her, she smiled a cold, inviting smile full of promises, and a voice echoed inside his head.

...You'll never be cold again, my love, you'll be mine, and mine do not feel the cold; you'll ride the stormwind, sing the snowflakes out into the world with me, you'll be the night and the whiteness and together we'll freeze the seas and the rivers and the rain until the world is ice and I will make you know such things, feel such things, as your little mortal heart can only imagine...

He knew her. He didn't know how he knew her, but he did—of that he was certain. He remembered something, a cold, cold touch, something that hurt all the way to the depths of his soul, but only for a moment, and then it had been silence and quiet and perfect clean white.

He took one step towards her, and saw her raise a hand, a gesture of invitation to go with that smile.

...Remember my love, you were just a boy, but a boy with such promise, I wanted you as son and heir, but this is better, so much better, now you can love me like you love your little mortal woman, now you can feel all my magical power, imagine it, throughout you, flowing through you like a blizzard, imagine how you'll scream, how you'll be mine, how you'll beg...

Kai cried out then and, just for a minute, he knew—knew deep in his soul, almost in his memory—what it would be like, how she would take him, and have him, and he'd be destroyed, frozen, broken, and yet he'd beg, *more, more, my lady, my...*

"No," he said, hoarsely, his throat parched. He tried to back away, to pull away, to turn and return to the warmth of his house, the warmth of Gerda. But he couldn't look away. All he could see were those ice-blue eyes, pulling him, and the smile of triumph as he took another small step towards her despite himself.

Just then the kitchen door flew open, and he felt Gerda's hand slip into his. He couldn't turn to look at her, but he felt the warmth of her hand flow into his and slowly up his arm.

"No." Her voice was strong, firm, like a hearth-fire, like the sun. "Go away. You can't have him. I took him from you before, and you know I always will. You know I'll never let you keep him. You know he wouldn't want you if you gave him any choice. Go away. He is not yours."

MINE!!

It was like a blow, like all the power of the strongest winter blizzard blasting them at once, and Kai felt he would fly away in it, lose himself, but Gerda held his hand and kept her feet. He could turn his head now, and he looked at her, saw the strength of her, the fire in her face, the determined power as she stared out at the woman in the snow.

"No," she said, her voice hot and firm and certain in the darkness. "He is not."

Then Vilda was there, too, taking Gerda's other hand, and staring out in her turn at the woman.

Robber Girl.

Vilda grinned a feral, angry smile that looked like a threat, except Kai knew that Vilda only threatened if she liked you enough to give you warning.

"You bet. You couldn't beat us as children. Why do you think you can now that we're adults? The thing that makes us strong is something you won't ever know, Ice Bitch."

Two crows fluttered down from somewhere in the sky, one on each of Vilda's shoulders. Without letting go of Gerda, she took one step forward.

"Go on. Give me a reason. You know I'm at least as much of a brat as you."

The Snow Queen roared then, like a storm, like an animal, like the power of winter. And then she was gone, and Kai reeled as the power withdrew and fell to his knees in the snow, that now was just normal winter snow.

"What..? I..?"

Gerda helped him to his feet. "Come inside, Kai."

"Will I forget again?"

He looked from one face to the other.

Gerda looked at Vilda, who shrugged. "I don't know how it works. My guess is she could make you forget as a child to give herself another go. We always knew she'd come back."

"Did we?" Gerda said.

Vilda shrugged again. "You always said..."

Gerda nodded. "I know I did."

"Is it over?" Kai asked. "Will she stay away now? Without you, I'd have gone. Without you..." He squeezed Gerda's hand.

"You won't ever find out. I'll always be there. I came and got you last time, and I would again. Always."

Kai nodded. "I still don't remember that. I mean, it's coming back. But it feels like a story I heard, like something that happened to someone else."

Vilda downed her drink. "Well, I'm glad I was here. Not that I don't think you can handle it, Gerda-lass, but I'd have hated to have missed the show-down."

Gerda kissed her cheek then, and then turned and kissed Kai's as well. At the window two crows cocked their heads, watching, and, satisfied, flew away into the night.

"I don't know if she'll come back, Kai. But if she does, we'll be here."

Kai nodded.

Later that night, Kai stood and looked in the mirror. The edges were frosted, but there was nothing in the mirror but himself. He looked carefully in each eye. They looked normal. His eyes looked normal and his heart felt normal, but he knew that's how it had started the last time.

He sighed.

As Kai turned to go to bed, where Gerda waited, he saw—just out of the corner of his eye—a glimpse of something, like a snowflake twirling, and thought he heard just a whisper, like the sound of wind in snow-covered trees.

you remember don't you, how it felt, how you knew it would feel, lover of winter, you want it, don't you

NO.

don't you..?

No.

don't you?

no

Don't you?

It was late, and Kai was fast asleep, curled up in their bed, warm and safe. Gerda stood out in the snow, barefoot and gloveless, like that night years ago when she was a child. The cold bit at her, but she ignored it, standing there, knowing *She* would come. Some things had to be done face-to-face.

Eventually the gusts of snow began to flurry with something like intent, and took on the shape of a woman in a long white coat of fur. She smiled at Gerda, a smile full of certainty and ice.

Gerda stepped forward, further into the cold night.

"You're just a child," the Snow Queen said. "How can you possibly hope to beat me. His heart is mine. It has been mine, always, since he was a boy. You see it when he watches the snow. You know it is true."

Gerda nodded. "I know that part of him will always be drawn to you. To your power, to the things you promise him. I know that he longs for the things you're promising. I know that sometimes he aches for it."

The Snow Queen smirked.

"But I know this, too." Gerda's voice was warm, with all the power of her summer love. "It doesn't matter."

The Snow Queen laughed, her laughter like the sound of icicles falling to the ground, shattering. "How can it not matter? When everything in him pulls him to me? All I have to do is wait."

Gerda smiled again, and her smile was triumphant. "You forget, though, that he has choice. And he chose that day when he walked out of that castle with me. And he chooses every time he closes the door on the snow. And he chose today again. The only way you can have him is by taking away his will. And that's not winning. Because even if you took him, even if you beat me, he will never be yours. He cannot be yours. Because every moment he will fight to be free of you, and if you let your grasp go for one second, he'll run. And when he runs, he'll run to me."

"You think he is yours? Poor little mortal..."

"No." Gerda's voice was strong in the night, like a light in the dark. "He is not mine. He is HIS. And he chooses me. That is more powerful than all your magic."

The snow flurried again, and for just a moment the outline of the woman wavered.

"You can't win with that." Her voice was like ice, melting, dripping.

Gerda raised her hands and the Snow Queen recoils slightly, just slightly at what was in them. "On the contrary. That is the reason we've already won."

Gerda lit the torch in her hand, and the darkness and ice flees before the flame, leaving her standing alone and lit up in the night.

J AX GOSS is an editor and writer. She is a wandering South African who has settled in New Zealand. She lives in Dunedin—for the moment. She is currently employed full-time as the mother of a very small human and writes and edits on the side. She expects this situation to stay the same for a while, but she has long ago learnt that nothing ever goes the way she expects.

She spends a large amount of her time gathering tales and poems and art and sending them out into the world in various forms, and thinks that this may be her vocation. She has edited a number of anthologies for Solarwyrm Press, and her stories have appeared in a variety of places. You can learn more about Jax and follow her wayward journey at her website.

LINKS

http://jaxgoss.wordpress.com
http://www.facebook.com/writerjaxgoss
https://twitter.com/belgatherial
http://www.solarwyrm.com

The Night of Awen

by K.R. Green

MORFRAN had worked hard to bring about his failings. That didn't stop his family from expecting him to be his father. The two women moved through the crowds below, graceful despite the frantic bustle of the streets.

His sister had so much—her beauty, her countenance, and her wit. His mother, Ceridwen, escorted her through the streets of the marketplace, looking back and forth through the stalls. Morfran knew she had begun to struggle again, slipping out at night on some secret ventures, and the servants were concerned. So, he had given up feeling guilty for spying, instead embracing it as his duty. Since he became man of the house, he'd been pushed into the boxes of what was expected and had clung to the small pride in never quite living up to their expectations. Where they wished him to act proper, he would sneak off to read mother's diary and watch her dealings with the town crier. Being so unaccomplished gave him a gift no one else in his family could taste: invisibility.

Other sons had to learn history and understand warfare. Despite their wishes of him to be a well-educated, charming gentleman, he was left to his own devices, a lost cause, and thus a free man. His mother's pitying looks were taking more and more of his thoughts; and so, his freedom had turned to unraveling that mystery.

Was she disappointed *in* him, or did she truly feel sorrow *for* him?

Morfran pulled back from the windowsill for a moment, clenching his fists. He knew how the kingdom saw him—he spent time indoors, failed at archery and fencing, lost arguments in debating, and ignored diplomacy. He had nothing to be desired in a King, leaving him free to use his real talents.

He grinned as his sister slipped back under the cover of their mansion's porch, taking the cue. His mother headed down an alley across the courtyard, veering towards the river. Time to find out just what she had been doing for the past few months.

Having leaned out to check his mother's direction at the end of the alley, he hopped down from the sill, sneaking out of his room and along the hallway. Her diary had given him glimpses, but never enough detail to capture the full picture. And Morfran loved to know a good story.

He made it to the streets without glimpse of either palace guard or civilian. His parents had clearly never thought to check the tapestries for secret passages. Or if they had, they'd assumed Morfran would not be so clever as to find them himself.

The thought concerned him, bringing up the same worry he'd had since Ceridwen's weeklong disappearance a year before. She had gone to the druids for some potion, claiming his name in reason—of that, the birds had told him. But he couldn't shake off the feeling of uncertainty: did she love him enough to want something for him, or could she not face him without it?

Either way, he was going to find out.

The shadows crept around him as Morfran reached the fisherman's cottage beside the river. It was a little derelict; the struts holding up the porch leaned to one side, and the corner of the roof closest to him was missing tiles. He wouldn't have been surprised if it leaked. The light was fading, and he shivered. He might soon be missed back home; but his mother's voice told him that she was still here.

"You have done well, child. When Morfran is king, you shall both be rewarded."

King? He was barely fourteen, and he'd already failed the skills that were necessary. Besides, he didn't want to be king. Didn't that matter?

"Thank you, my lady."

What exactly had his mother done?

Morfran crept forward, pulling himself up at the window of the dark cottage. A small fire shimmered beneath a massive cauldron, one certainly too big for the fire over which it rested. His mother's figure blocked out its light, casting shadows upon the window.

A young boy, perhaps ten years old, sat beside another adult; someone resting in a rocking chair with a blanket draped across their knees. A cane leaned upon the edge of the chair between them.

The boy was short and skinny, but he held his head high in the presence of the enchantress.

"Remember, I shall bring him tomorrow—when it will be ready. Be polite and step back when it is his turn to drink. Do I make myself clear?"

The boy nodded, though Morfran caught his eyes glancing towards the bubbling mixture.

"Very well. Continue your vigil until I return."

The old man in the rocking chair spoke, his low voice shaking. "Yes, my lady. Gwion is my best caretaker. We will not let you down."

"See to it that you do not. It's important Morfran drinks the first sip, which I shall measure out. The rest of the brew will be poisonous."

Morfran's heart hammered in his chest. She'd made a poison for him? How would that make him king? The snippets he'd gleamed over the months failed to connect; his brain closed down at the idea of his mother harming him. But the part about the 'rest' gave him a small measure of peace. The poison wasn't meant for him, although, he couldn't explain how any liquid, even with magic, could contain some parts poison yet other parts not. Before he could contemplate entering—his hands shaking and head in a panic—his mother turned on her heel, sweeping out of the cottage and up the lane towards the city.

Morfran sat back on his haunches shaking his head to force his mind clear. She wanted him to drink a potion, to become king somehow. Perhaps his failings had gone too far. Too far for her to love him as he was. On the edge of tears he barely understood, Morfran turned back to the palace.

Ceridwen came for him just before breakfast, knocking on his door just as he was dressing.

The wood creaked in a quiet manner as she opened it, as if it sensed his fear. A small smile covered her face, spurring the fear already threatening to choke him. "Morfran?"

He hoped she wouldn't notice how much his voice shook. "Yes, Mother?"

"I hope you don't have plans today—I have a little surprise for you."

He debated ruining her surprise, about asking her about the mixture, but he feared the answers. Taking a slow, steadying breath, he shook his head. She rarely spent time with him, and he couldn't change tonight. He would savor this moment of quiet family time, almost like he deserved to be her son. He shunned the voice commenting on betrayal, and plastered an inquisitive smile to his face.

"Oh?"

"Come down and break your fast. We'll do whatever you want, and then tonight we're heading to the river."

He feigned confusion as best he could. "We're... fishing?"

She chuckled, a response he'd rarely seen since his father's death. Perhaps she did love him, at least in some way. She didn't answer, merely closing the door in response.

He took his time eating, trying to enjoy the attention. But even his calm-and-collected mother seemed frazzled today. Was she concerned the potion wouldn't work? What would it do to him? He wouldn't get answers until they arrived, however, so he swallowed his anxiety alongside his porridge and went along with her idle chat.

She watched him eat, and he pretended not to notice. "How have you found the book?"

He resisted a snort. "A bit dry, and pretty darn long. I don't understand why politicians can't get to the point already."

"Morfran." There was her disapproving face; even though he looked into his bowl, he could feel the gaze.

"You asked. I answered."

"I'll be more specific. What have you learned?"

He met her gaze. "That to rule fairly, one must act like a heartless, spineless monster."

"Morfran! Enough."

He frowned into his lap, forcing himself into silence. Perhaps he hadn't managed to bury that anger and anxiety as much as he'd hoped. But, if she knew anything about him, it would be nothing less than her expectations.

The space between morning and evening shot by in a blink of chess (which his mother won easily), interruptions from his sister Creirwy, and stony silence as they shopped—where he would watch her, and she would watch him. The sky began to darken as the afternoon sun became covered in cloud.

She wrung her hands together, a mannerism he'd never before seen in her. It took all his strength not to bolt then and there.

"Time to go, Morfran. I hope you like it."

Nodding with a sick feeling in his stomach, he pulled his cloak tighter around him and followed her into the light rain.

By the time they arrived, the rain had stopped, and the clouds grew brighter as the sun began its descent. The cottage looked different in daylight.

The river shimmered under the semi-sunshine, and he caught sight of a couple of otters on the far side of the river. Smiling as he recognized the female to be his friend Mara, he stopped on the bank. Ceridwen didn't appear to notice, already heading up the steps to knock on the door.

Morfran hadn't asked any more, and his mother hadn't brought up the subject of his surprise again. It had been a worrying day though—with clothes shopping for suits he'd never wear by choice and then a fancy lunch where people referred to them as their *Majesty*. And now they'd come to an old cottage. The creepy day just kept getting creepier. His mind wouldn't stop sifting through possible potions his mother could wish upon him.

What would she change if she could?

Everything. He snorted, flinching as he realized she may have heard his noise, or worse, the thought itself. He'd managed to temper his powers around the home, but today had unnerved him a little too much. He exhaled slowly when she failed to respond; already speaking to the old man from the rocking chair, not attending to him. He took the moment to inhale deeply and forcibly relaxed his shoulders. There were witnesses here. But to be safe, he called out on his mental connection.

"Mara. I'm afraid. Watch out for me?"

A splash sounded, his concentration on an answer broken as his mother summoned him.

"Morfran."

Here went nothing. He bowed his head towards the otter, hoping she'd understand, and followed his mother into the fisherman's cottage. The door shut behind him with an audible click.

"This is Morda." He bowed his head at the old man, his cheeks reddening after a moment as he realized the blind man would not see it. Ceridwen then pointed to the young boy who'd tended the fire. "And Gwion."

Morfran nodded towards Gwion, hoping he didn't look overly suspicious. "Uhh.. Nice to meet you both."

"Morfran, come here." Ceridwen pointed at the fire, the cauldron bubbling softly. "Tell me what you see."

Morfran swallowed as he looked into the pot. It simmered gently, though he couldn't detect anything specific. "I see a fireplace... with a cooking pot on it."

"And in the pot?"

He peered in, trying to discern the item's color. It appeared to be a dark blue, although that didn't feel right, and it had no smell, despite him being close to it. "Some... potion, I guess?"

Ceridwen smiled at him; and for a moment, he felt a tingle in his chest. He'd impressed her by not saying soup, most likely. There was actual pride there— without him even having drunk anything. But this was the end of the road.

Morfran cleared his throat. "What's it do?"

"It's called Awen."

His mouth dropped open. Of all the things he'd fear and considered, *that* had not even entered his mind as an option. Perhaps he'd misunderstood. "As in the druid's elixir?"

She grinned again, this time he could see the satisfaction at her own genius idea. So she did want to change him. *Everything* about him. No, he must be mistaken. He was a failure in the eyes of the crown, yes, but could she not love him as he was? The potion couldn't be for him. Not if what he'd heard about it was true.

"Why do you need that?"

She laughed again, but this time, he couldn't feel it. "It's not for me—but you." She stepped forward. It took all his will not to step backwards. "This is my gift to you—education and money did little to fulfill you. I've seen your sadness, your worries that I don't love you like I love Creirwy. It's the best I can offer you, and you only have until sundown until it's ready."

Morfran frowned, his mind spinning with words and half-understood letters. She meant it as a proof of love? His mind would not accept such a reason, already whirring with its lightning speed to conclusions. What spurred such *love*—guilt or compassion?

He sighed, glaring back over at the cauldron. "Do you know what it will actually do to me?"

She put an arm around his shoulder. Perhaps she meant it reassuringly, but it felt like a restraint, like she was afraid he'd bolt and not take her damned potion. "Not specifically. But it won't change *you,* only how you're presented and are seen."

That sounded like a quick-fix king formula to him. But he had to tread carefully. His mother was not great at criticism, and even her weirdly misplaced gifts would not save him a beating if she thought he questioned her judgement. After all, she was his mother, and she knew what was best. He fought back the urge to grimace.

"Why... why did you... Feel the need to do this? It seems very complicated."

She smiled, that slightly pitying look to which he was accustomed. She always assumed him to misunderstand, which gave him an excuse for accidental rudeness, but that didn't stop the assumption infuriating him. "Morfran. You are to be a great man one day—there are legends you could be part of, great lands to traverse, and social change to ignite."

A great man... if he were to take this concoction. Morfran glimpsed at the blind man, whose head was bowed, and to Gwion, who just watched the conversation openly. Did he think Morfran mad for not instantly jumping at this opportunity?

Perhaps he was.

Still, his mother continued, now pacing across the room. "I... I fear I have failed you, in some ways. You have not the skills that will give you the best life. This was the best course of action. After dusk, it will be ready, and you may enjoy your reward."

Of course. To her, his life was a route to be plotted out. And this, clearly a reward because he had survived despite her failings. Not that he cared for travel or politics. His sister could take over the family lands and he enjoyed his freedom. He rummaged in his mind for something else to say, another question to ask, anything that would allow him an opt-out.

He reached out his hand to rest against the wall as he sought out the presence of Mara. Their connection thrummed, providing some comfort, though they weren't speaking at this point.

Could he stop the potion from working?

The idea entered his head without much structure, just a seedling. But with the silence offered until sundown, it grew. He perched himself close to the window, whispering in his mental voice, and hoping only the otter would hear him.

"*Did you hear that?*"

"*Yes.*" Her voice came across as a small squeak, likely too quiet for his mother to notice. Whatever happened with this potion, he wanted to keep his common language secret.

"*Any ideas?*"

"*Do you not want to take it, or do you believe it to be a fake?*"

I... He hadn't even thought about the poison part again. He took a moment to contemplate the ideas. There would be no real reason to kill him. "*I don't want to take it.*"

She didn't hide the surprise in her voice, though she said nothing about it. "*In that case, knock it over. Spill it all. Or offer it to someone else.*"

He didn't reply, looking at the heavy cauldron with its burning liquid that would surely harm anyone who got too close. Perhaps he could drop the cup, or spoon. Especially if it was only the first sip that gave power.

The glimmering mixture brightened as the sun set; the potion turned a bright blue, which lit the whole room. There, beneath its warmth, the seed of Morfran's thought germinated. If he could take it, but ensure nothing really changed, he could remain as he was. But then, would he be beyond a failure in her eyes? What kind of person couldn't be fixed by the Awen?

Morda's snoring was off-putting—the thought that he had worked to provide such a potion and now slept idly.

That was unfair.

It was a positive that he wasn't alone in this strange place. His mother had also fallen asleep, clearly exhausted by her late night.

Perhaps it wouldn't work—it was just a myth—but he could see the glow, feel the thrum of power. He glanced outside, standing up as the panic set in. The sun sank below the horizon. He had to think fast.

"Arrgh!" Gwion's scream shattered the silence, breaking his concentration. He tried to ignore it as the poor boy sucked at his scolded fingers. Some of the mixture must have splashed out. The blue glow faded, darkening the room in an instant.

"YOU!"

Morfran's head snapped around at the sound of his mother's howl. Her head twisted, ugliness contorting her face. Morfran shrank back, heart pounding against his ribcage. He'd never, ever seen her so enraged. Even in the mild darkness, he could make out the reddening of her face. Morfran shook his head, trying to understand the problem, and yet not wanting to remind anyone that he was there.

The boy's face glowed yellow, his blond hair lighting up as he raced towards the doorway. Morfran didn't blame him—Ceridwen had already thrown herself into the hunt.

"Run, Gwion!" He couldn't help himself, the fear for the poor boy overwhelming everything else.

The boy's hair glowed; his body shrank as the glow faded, and he raced out, melding into the shadows. As his mother flew out, screaming in her rage, Morfran pulled himself out of his chair and ran out of the open door, standing beside the riverbank. A hare darted across the grass, now chased by the favored animal of his mother. A hound.

Morfran dropped down, uncertain that she would recognize him in her shifted form, and almost touched noses with a mouse.

"What's going on?" the mouse asked.

Morfran swallowed. "I don't really know. Ceridwen's hunting."

"The enchantress?"

"Aye, though I hope she doesn't win."

"Who's the prey?"

"A hare called Gwion."

"The fisherman's lad? He will need help!"

The mouse scurried off before Morfran could stop him. The night had darkened around them, but he heard the scurries of the creatures around him, rumors passing around the fields. He scurried around to the window, looking for Mara. She'd probably fled in fear of the chase. He crossed the river, seeking out any of his otter friends. Someone would know what had happened.

If Gwion was now creature, he may hear Morfran. But then, so might his mother.

He forced his shoulders to relax, whispering in a pitch they would hear.

"Mara... It's Morfran. I need your help."

Though he felt no response, he waited, releasing a held breath as an otter shot past him, a large fish leaping from the river. On the third leap, it glowed—not in the way that moonlight reflects, but in the way of magic.

Gwion!

As the otter gained speed, the boy-fish shimmered past, until wings sprouted from his body. As it leapt free of the water, the otter's jaws snapped shut on the air, but before she fell back to the water, she also shimmered; the red glow of his mother's power. Fur turned to feather and a hawk flew up into the sky, chasing the smaller bird towards a barn upon the other bank.

Morfran scuttled across the bank, fear rising in his stomach. His mother's power and strength would be waning, but even untapped Awen in a new host couldn't last much longer. He snuck around to the open doors, peeking around the edge, startling a small bat from its home above the doorway. Otherwise, only a black hen stood inside.

"Psst! What's happened?"

The bat turned mid-flight, fluttering over to hang against the brick of the barn wall. *"The bird became a seed, and the hen ate every grain!"*

It flew off without another word, and Morfran felt the terror descend. He peered into the barn, but saw nothing now. Even Ceridwen had moved into the shadows. He'd best head home—hanging around here was unlikely to do him any favors.

He didn't think as his body took him home; he kept to the shadows and hoped this had all been a dream. But something in the way his bed had been made when he arrived home—with curtains draped across the usually bland posts and a silky satin sheet beneath the covers—stopped even his imagination from saving him.

The darkness crept around him as he watched his mother's belly grow. He knew his eyes blazed each time she came past him. She'd wrecked their family, not content to leave him be, to accept Morfran as he was. And now she was having a child, despite his father's death a year before.

Only when the child was born, did he understand—putting together the pieces of that grain and the timing of her swollen belly. Morfran followed the sound of screams, creeping along the passage behind a tapestry that hung beside his mother's bed. He squinted through the gap, uncertain what he was seeing as her servants bustled around the room, the crumpled duvet covering his view of anything but her sweat-covered face.

"Leave us!"

She cast out her arm to dismiss the two maids, who had presumably delivered the child. They bowed their heads, not openly questioning their mistress. But he saw the uncertainty in their eyes.

The babe had a glowing forehead, and Morfran couldn't help but smile as the baby's crying ceased, a shrill chuckle escaping lips that should be too young to express it. He had green eyes, just like Morfran.

His mother had not yet left her covers, yet he saw the shimmer of a blade from under her pillow. He closed his eyes, awaiting the sound of the silence, but it didn't arrive. He opened a single eyelid, daring to push the edge of the cloth to see. His mother stood, cradling the child for a moment, gazing down into its eyes.

Then he watched as she pulled out a leather holdall, placing the child within, bloodstained rags still around it.

What was she doing? Then his heart wobbled in his chest. She would take the young boy to an orphanage or a church. She would not let him affect their family. But his stomach clenched as he saw her pull out her sewing box. She was not going to follow any rules. With her quick and steady hand, the leather bag was sealed shut: Morfran frozen in horror.

This couldn't be happening.

But no amount of pinching helped, and he found himself close to wailing; the small sounds he couldn't stifle were muffled behind the curtain. Unable to watch anymore, nor face her and demand something be done, he turned, folding in on himself to turn around and flee to his room. He'd always been too weak to be a king, to make the decisions that had to be made.

But he could not rest, and so headed down to the fisherman's cottage, abandoned since the old blind man, and his young helper went missing. There, he caught Mara's voice, and called to her with apprehension bubbling in his stomach.

"*She came. I saw it with my own eyes,*" she replied to his questioning look. "*She threw a bag into the sea, crying erupting from its seams. I tried to follow it, but the current was too strong.*"

Morfran swallowed, thinking of his father as his fists clenched by his sides. He had to remain matter-of-fact, else the hurt could destroy him.

It was done, then. He turned back to the town, looking up at the turret where his mother would be. This incident would fade with time, and his mother could relax her silence. Perhaps they could move on now—after all, his mother had no choice but to accept him as he was. Morfran hoped that would be enough.

But could he accept her, as the person who had led a child to its demise?

He didn't think he would. No matter how much his situation demanded he must.

In time, his skills brought him news.

His mother's tarot cards, he knew from her journal, spoke of a great meeting and much going wrong in the future of the child. Then, the birds spoke of the western coast of Wales and the miracle child who had sung until rescued. When he could stand the rumors no more, he crept down to the riverside, whistling for the otters who had always brought him the truth.

The grass on this side of the cottage was blackened; a faint smell of stagnation coursing through the air. The poison had left its mark on this place, claimed its heritage.

"What news? These tales of a bard sprout throughout the isle."

Mara hopped up to the bank, her wet whiskers touching Morfran's ear as he spoke. Her partner, a male Morfran didn't recognize, remained in the stream, but watched them. *"Master, it is true. A fisherman claims to have rescued a child in a leather sack, naming him Taliesin for his bright forehead."*

"And he is well?"

The otter smiled, already sliding back into the water. *"Oh master, he is wise and as charming as you are talkative."*

The otter faded into the swirling river, and Morfran was left only with his black cloak and a heavy heart. Nothing could fix the sorcery of his mother's restlessness. And his heart would thus never forgive her betrayal.

But the child lived, and seemingly thrived. He had deserved the chance the druids had given him.

Morfran lifted the hood of his cloak, standing upon the bank and heading into the coming darkness, towards the mountain of the Druids. Perhaps they could find something of which he was worthy.

K.R.

GREEN writes about dragons, falconry, mythology, and sorcery. She attends a local writer's group and, outside of writing, enjoys herbal teas, reading, and gazing up at the stars. When she isn't painting pictures with words, she works in the Mental Health sector in London and Children's Health Services in Sussex.

LINKS

http://www.krgreen.co.uk
https://twitter.com/K_R_Green

Blood Medicine

by Kelly Hale

FATHER returned from his summer rendezvous alone, on foot, with dried blood in his hair and a darting terror in his eyes. For a long while, he could not speak, so we brought him into the lodge and warmed him with blankets and broth. In his hand, he held a scrap of soft leather about the length of my thumb. There were three brass pins stuck through it.

I'd once seen a Kuyadikka woman fasten her shawl with a brass pin and so brass pins had come to mind when he'd asked what I wanted from the white traders.

My sisters would tell it differently. I should have asked for a kettle or a good knife. My sisters believe my head is filled with cottonwood fluff.

When our father was recovered enough to speak, some of the men came into our lodge to hear what had happened to him. He told about losing his horses to a band of Crow, of falling off the mountain into a ravine. About taking refuge in a cave. When he got to the part about the cave his eyes moved sideways, as if to keep some secret from shining out of them. My sisters and I knew this look, and we looked at each other. There was something about the cave Father wasn't telling. But the men seemed not to notice it. Whatever happened within the cave he said only that as soon as he left it he was set upon by numedeka.

Numedeka. Man-eating little people. They shot at him with their poisoned arrows. He showed us a hole in his shirt and small wound in the hollow of his arm, scabbed over but inflamed all around. It looked like a spider bite to me. And the hole in his shirt looked like the hole I hadn't mended before he left.

But Father's story was far more exciting than a spider bite and a neglectful daughter. His face, gray and lined from exhaustion, grew livelier as he regaled us with his tale.

There he was, surrounded by cannibal dwarves. He fought bravely, fists and feet, whoops and war cries, but there were too many of them and he knew they would kill him and eat him and so he began to sing his song for dying. It was a powerful song. He sang a little of it so we could get the flavor of it—

Oh hear me, Great Spirit, my people
Hear me, my ancestors. I fight.
I will be eaten by monsters.

But the Ice Giant appeared before he could finish his song.

"Tam apo!" the men in our lodge cried. "From bad to worst!"

From lie to bigger lie I was thinking.

The Ice Giant's roar caused a wind strong enough to topple trees. Little people fell from the trees like pinecones. The Ice Giant threw lightning from his hands, killing many. Those that tried to flee the lightning were caught and tossed into the sky with such force they did not fall back to earth.

That was Father's story. Saved from the evil little people by an evil ice giant.

His fingers tightened around the scrap with the brass pins. He cast his eyes to me, dark with shame. I knew then that the Ice Giant had demanded a price for his life. I knew, without his saying, that price was me.

The Ice Giant would come before the Rutting Moon had passed and claim me for his wife.

There followed much discussion for many days and nights about whether an ice giant could demand such a price, being evil magic and not human. There was also discussion of honor and if my father owed anything and if he did, was there was an honorable way to get out of a promise to an ice giant? Everyone knew ice giants had a terrible sense of smell, and bad eyesight. Some of the women thought we should trick the Ice Giant—put a dog in my good dress, or make a woman out of reeds and sticks, also in my good dress. I wondered why my everyday dress wouldn't suit if ice giants couldn't see or smell?

A successful illusion requires some sacrifice, I was told.

In the end, the people decided it didn't matter what my father had promised, for my father had not asked to be saved by the giant. My father had been prepared to die—he'd made a song for it. All the men of our band would fight the monster if he dared come for me. They kept watch in all direction with weapons ready until the Rutting Moon was just a sliver in the curve of my left hand.

But when the monster came, he came with three packhorses and a pony-drag piled to the sky with all manner of goods. He'd brought gifts of guns and shot and powder. Chisels and knives, hooks and horns. Scrapers, fire steels, cups and kettles.

Tobacco. Barrels of strong water and gallons of brandy. Looking glasses and burning glasses. Pony beads, snake beads, seed beads. Blankets and scarlet cloth and blue cloth and folds of sprigged calico. Scissors! Needles! Ribbons! Rings! There seemed no end to the wonderful things he'd brought.

The Ice Giant of my father's story had shrunk himself down to the size of a very large, very hairy white man wrapped in pelts and his own white-man stink.

Father seemed astonished at the man's appearance there in our camp. Had he really thought his crazy story could never follow him home? My sisters and I knew our father too well. Still, he'd got a blow to the head—that was obvious—and had perhaps been poisoned by spider venom as well. It was possible that a sickness dream caused him to make an Ice Giant out of a fur-trading white man. Possible it was *not* a lie told to explain away his gambling losses.

There was dream-truth and everyday-truth and the truth-in-between. Father knew the difference. His expression of confusion and wary disbelief troubled me. The trapper who was not an Ice Giant was also not quite human. My father knew it in his heart, and so, then, did I.

The beard hair and the head hair were all grown together on his face, so that his mouth could not be seen through the brambles of it. The hair shifted when he spoke, moved by his breath, perhaps, but that was the only indication he might have a mouth to make speech. And he spoke our tongue *too* well. Most Shoshone bands spoke the same tongue but made the words a little differently. Yet this person, claiming to be a white man, spoke like a Watatikka born among us. No one else seemed to find this odd.

Not only was his mouth invisible but his eyes were as well, hidden behind green goggles even though the sky was overcast and the snow sparse on the ground. There was no reason to wear green goggles. No natural reason.

My people, in the way of people everywhere, saw what they wanted to see: a white trader who had brought great wealth to my father in exchange for me. One woman. And not even an exceptional woman.

I was not the hardest worker. I was not the prettiest girl. My beadwork was uninspired, my cooking barely edible. I couldn't cut skins for a lodge to save my life. I was not the best at anything. Ask my sisters, both exceptional women. Both of them married to the same man, a tested warrior, who gave father a musket with a ball mold and ten boxes of shot for my sister, Cloud in the Water, and gave three horses for my sister, Fat Otter. Me? I am Fluff-Headed Dove, and no one has ever tried to give him anything for me. Until now. Father had so much to share it was embarrassing.

There was a feast, day into night and day again. A ceremony. My hand in the hand of a man whose knuckles are covered with hair.

I received a new tanning kit, a sewing kit, nesting kettles, two horn spoons and wooden wares, winter robes, blankets, fur lined-moccasins, rope, twine, packets of healing plants, dried berries, two baskets of pine nuts, a parfleche of pemmican—

But the man, my husband, refuses these gifts. We were only taking one of the horses.

I could carry all of this on my back easily.

He refuses. He says I won't need any of these things.

But woman *is* the home and everything in it is hers. My sister, Fat Otter, puts her hands on her hips and speaks to him with the sort of boldness she wouldn't dare with our own men. "What good are your efforts if your wife has no scraper, flesher, bone, or rope? If she can't cook or dry the meat? If she can't sew skins together and keep you warm in the night?"

"She'll have no need of these things where I am taking her," he says.

I can feel what all the people are thinking now. Thinking but not saying. *I* am thinking it. I will not live long enough to use any of these things anyway. Because I have married a monster who will kill me and feed me to the little people.

My husband grabs me around the waist with his big, hairy hands and lifts me onto his horse. He takes the lead in hand and starts walking. Suddenly, my father comes running after us, crying, "My daughter, my daughter!" His new striped blanket falls to the ground as he reaches for me. I lean down to embrace him. I can smell the smoke in his clothes. The bear grease in his hair softens my cheek. My monster husband looks away. Father has counted on this, and while the man is looking elsewhere, the scrap of leather with the brass pins is pressed into my hand. He closes my fingers around it, squeezes my closed fist hard so that the pain will sear his whispered words into me. "This is medicine I took from him. As long as you keep it close you are safe." Then he steps back, wiping a tear from his eye. "Do not forget us, Little Dove."

"Never," I tell him. I hide the pins in the bag around my neck, tucked inside my dress, between my breasts and over my heart.

There is magic in this place where I am. There are little people here, but they are not cannibals. I think they never eat at all but only glide along the polished stone, always going somewhere, always busy. Some dart through the air like large dragonflies. Once, one of these got tangled in the fringe of my sleeve. When I tried to bat it away, it crashed to the ground and broke into pieces. Little people swarmed and scuttled around it and carried the pieces away.

Mostly these creatures pay me no attention, except at the command of their master, my husband.

He once commanded them to have me spit into a hollow reed.

The first indication of my husband's sorcery was on our journey to this place. He'd been leading me on the pony, and so sure-footed was that pony I fell asleep. When I woke it seemed no time had passed at all though the sun was high overhead. It was only then that I heard the rush of water and saw we had come to Bear River.

I swung my leg over the back of the horse and slid to the ground so that I could gather fire wood, start a fire, kill something for him to eat so that he would not eat me. But he told me not to bother, we weren't stopping. We were going to make the rest of the journey by water.

My people don't travel by water much. I had never done so in *sixteen* winters! I knew the best crossings of this river in different seasons, though. The place I knew of was a good walk upstream, but if you had to swim part of the way across it wasn't too hard to manage with horses and bullboats for the goods.

But I had also never made a bullboat, and even if I had, they were made to carry goods not fully-grown people. And it didn't matter whether I had made one before or not because I had no rawhide with which to make one, no rope, no fire to shape it, and no pitch to seal the seams. What could I, a poor woman equipped with a small knife and a strike-a-light pouch, accomplish in the short time between the sun high over my head and the sun setting over the mountains?

My husband removed the rope lead from the horse and sent it on its way with a slap on the rump. The horse wandered a short ways off to graze, unconcerned about its welfare. Unlike me.

I looked at the man with no visible mouth, whose eyes were hidden behind green goggles. His face shifted, revealing a curved gap in the bush of hair. I think it was meant to look like a smile. I was not comforted by this.

From inside his coat he withdrew a fold of slick cloth, the color of pine pollen. He shook it out and tossed it onto the ground. After a moment it began to *unfold itself.* I watched in wonder as it puffed up and filled out so that when it was finished it had become a yellow boat, round and flat on the bottom with raised sides, large enough to carry two people. It bounced a little on the ground when the wind touched it, as if anxious to get on the water and begin the journey. My husband pulled two small shields from a pouch, twisted and tugged at them until they turned into paddles. He handed one to me.

I learned to paddle a boat as quick as I've ever learned anything. Thus we traveled swiftly over a great distance to his home inside a mountain.

My husband is called Asa. When he told it to me that first night, I thought he said *Issa*. Oh well, that's not so bad, I thought. I have married the wolf god. When he steps out of his furs he will be handsome. But Asa assured me he was no god. That his layers of fur and hair were for my protection. I wish he could protect me from the smell.

And isn't that something a god *would* say? How the sight of his true self would blind a humble woman like me? That I would swoon at the sight of such perfection in manhood? Best accustom myself to the cage of smelly fur that surrounded him.

I have many furs myself now, capes and hoods and cushions. They don't stink and I didn't have to skin or tan a single one. Beautiful dresses, too, with beadwork on the shoulders and down the fronts in patterns of flowers and doves, willow and cattails, blue, red, yellow, purple, white on black, black on white. Fringes cut so fine and long they are almost like hair. I have a belt with silver disks, and a belt with copper disks. A knife-sheath worked with seed beads in a pattern of lilies. Jingles of tin that make music when I walk. Moccasins so soft they seem not made for walking at all. Head bands with feather crowns of turkey and spotted grouse, flicker and hawk, blue jay and cardinal, heron, duck, and crow. There is a looking glass in my room as high and broad as a grizzly. I spend hours putting on dresses and taking them off. I have nothing to do but dress myself.

I never thought I could miss sweeping and scouring pots.

My husband commands I join him for a meal each night. Or day. I can't tell because I have not seen the sky since we arrived. I don't know which time of the moon it is, or whether the sun stays long or leaves early. My room darkens when I wish to sleep, but many parts of this place are brighter than day—*always*.

I do not prepare the meals we share. I don't do anything but sit across the fire from him in a beautiful dress, with feathers in my hair and my feet tucked beneath me. There is so much food! Once there was a bowl filled with maple sugar and I ate so much that my teeth hurt the next morning. Emboldened by hours of idleness, I ask relentless questions: Why do the little people serve you? What are they doing? Why do you live in a mountain? How can you speak the tongue of my people so perfectly? Are your garments really your skin, is that why you can't take them off? From what do your furs protect me?

The answers he gives are all the same. *Magic.* But I suspect that is only the word I *hear*. That his mouth is saying something else. If only I could *see* it. I can see his eyes though. He doesn't wear the goggles when we eat together. His eyes are set deep into his bushy brows, and glittering pale with no discernible color, like the eyes of a wolf in a thicket watching his prey.

One night he asks me, "Can you save us, Little Dove?" I don't know what he means. I don't think he expects an answer, but my head is sick with boredom and makes me rude. "Ask your magic, why don't you?"

Then I flee and hide in my bed, afraid—but angry, too.

My bed is a luxury of buffalo hides, three or four, piled with so many woolen blankets and robes of fine, thick fur that sometimes I don't bother to get up. I lie there all day, swaddled like an infant, drifting in and out of dreams. I dream of my father and my sisters. The smell of smoke, the smell of hot blood when the knife goes in, the taste of fresh elk. The sound of voices, of water, horses snorting, watchers whistling down warnings. I dream of people I didn't even like that much. The ones that teased or mocked me, even *those* people I long for somehow, and ache with love for them. In my dreams.

Sometimes, after I awaken, there is a red mark in the bend of my left elbow that is sore and a little bruised. When I dream all day I suspect it is because I have been made to dream. I wonder if that is what happened to father.

My husband has never come to my bed nor asked me to his. I don't know where he sleeps or if he sleeps. Or if he has other women. My sisters told me he would be on me constantly, that the white men traders are more ardent than our men because they are not warriors. Warriors have many tests to prove their strength and one of those is how long they can abstain from relations with women. I have heard some men can go as long as two or three years. Or so women often complain.

But my husband is not really a white man. He is not a man at all, I think.

There are doors in this place I can open with thought! If I move towards a door with purpose and think 'open' it does. So I have been exploring. There's nothing and no one to stop me from it. I never see my husband except when we take a meal together. I've tried to spy on him. To catch him unawares, but so far we meet only when he wishes it.

There is great industry happening here. If you have ever seen inside an anthill or a beehive then you know what I mean. Busy, industrious creatures moving with intention, each to its own task, never bumping into each other, or doing something over that another has already done. Some of these creatures I know—the metal little people, the dragonflies—but others not only act like insects but resemble them as well. There are metal grasshopper beings ranging in size from the length of my thumb to big as jackrabbits. Other kinds have gleaming appendages—a single arm or as many as twenty, twisting and turning and lifting and moving things. And the things they move! I have no words to describe these things.

I have walked amongst these creatures unheeded, unnoticed. I have watched carefully the tracks they make, the patterns they follow. The air crackles and vibrates around them, sometimes it's so loud it's like a constant thunder and I have to cover my ears and flee. But as soon as the doors slide shut behind me the noise is sealed inside the room and all without is silent.

In stories it is Grandfather Thunder who lives inside a mountain. Not *Issa* the wolf. And when Grandfather Thunder's many children beat the drums and dance and sing the whole world trembles.

But this is not even the most important discovery! What I found, what I realized, is that my scrap of leather stuck through with brass pins is not that at all. The three brass pins are really delicate traceries of metal set into a material that is smooth and flexible without grain or weave. The traceries are embroidered patterns. There are grooves between each set of patterns. The grooves and the patterns match the same grooves and patterns in a slot in the side of the large looking glass in my room.

Now that I know how to use it, the looking glass shows me pictures of other lands, of other worlds, of all the stars in the night skies, and—most importantly—it also shows what has already happened.

Part of my father's story was true. A band of Crow stole his horses and he fell off a cliff. What he didn't tell was that he was tended by the little people. What he didn't tell was that he saw the magic here, tried to steal some of it for himself and was caught. The only thing he came away with was this thing in my hand.

I saw spirit people in the glass, too, and watched for a long time. They are beautiful people, with shining dark hair, golden brown skin, tall, and strong limbed. Their clothes are strange. The animals they hunt are not like ours. They ride in boats that travel beams of sunlight or moonlight.

Are these my husband's people?

My foolish father lies sweating alone in our lodge stricken with fever. My sisters, too, are ill. Nearly everyone at our winter camp has fallen ill. I can see them through the glass, how they suffer. I call out to them until I am hoarse and weeping. But they can't hear me and I can't reach through to help them.

Asa has agreed to let me go to my people and tend the sick and dying. He has powerful medicine that will save any who are not too far-gone. In exchange, I have promised to go away with him to the land of his people. I will never see my people again.

He gives me a looking glass as thin as leaf, which folds up very small. "You will be able to see me and talk to me when you look into it." He demonstrates. I put it in with the flint and striker in the pouch at my waist. He says I am to speak with him every day I'm gone. He has also given me three skins of special medicine water to sprinkle where the sickness has touched sleeping robes and clothing, and a pouch of medicine pellets, enough for each person to swallow three times in a day for five days.

"You must swear never to reveal the source of this medicine," he tells me. I swear it, of course I do. "And you must promise to return when the moon is full. That is all the time I can give you. If you don't return by then...it will be very bad."

But I don't know how I can possibly get there in time to save anyone. In a boat on swift water moving downstream, the journey took no time at all. But I'll have to go over land for days. They could all be dead by then.

My husband takes my hand in his. His palms are the softest part of him. "You can trust your journey to my magic." And then he presses a fingertip to my brow and I close my eyes.

I awaken in a grove of cottonwood, there is snow thick on the ground beneath me. The same pony we abandoned at Bear River is hobbled close by and loaded with packs. I can see all our lodges in the distance, but only a few feeble threads of smoke curl up into the grey sky.

"I thought you were a spirit person when you walked into camp," says Cloud in the Water. She holds up the two-hide dress I wore when I arrived. The one with pond lilies beaded up the sleeves. I have given it to her, though she won't be able to wear it until after she has her baby.

Father sits up against the cushions looking like a grumpy bear himself. "I thought you were a ghost."

Fat Otter shushes him as if he is a child. She's got her youngest at her breast. I have saved my close family but many others were lost.

I remember when I was little how the wails of grieving women at night frightened me. I thought they were ghosts and covered my head and cried at the sound of them.

I am not a ghost, yet I feel in need of reassurance. I want to touch everyone, taste and smell everything, so the memories of my home are painted in my mind when I leave it again. I will not return. I will never come back. That is the oath I swore my husband.

I catch Fat Otter staring at me. I've got my nose buried in an old moccasin, inhaling greedily. "One of the dogs chewed on that," she says. I stop sniffing but press it to my breast like a favorite doll.

Cloud in the Water lays the dress on the bed. "Are you back for good then?"

"No. I must return to my husband tomorrow."

"Can't you stay a bit longer?" Fat Otter says. "Surely he won't begrudge you another day with the loved ones you nearly lost."

"I've *promised.*"

"You used to promise to fetch fire wood and then not do it," Cloud in the Water says.

"Look at our poor sister with her big belly," Fat Otter says. "She could have that baby any day now. What if the sickness has caused trouble in her womb?"

Cloud in the Water puts her arms around her belly and gives me a face with big-eyes and her lower lip stuck out. I know they're playing me, but I can't help laughing. And then we're all laughing.

I miss them already and I haven't even gone. Maybe another day won't hurt.

I'll tell my husband I was too busy tending to my pregnant sister to use the looking glass leaf.

A day and another day, three all together since I last spoke with my husband. Cloud in the Water's baby is in no hurry to arrive. When I take the folded looking glass from the pouch, I can't spark it to life. I am filled with a sudden sick dread, and I rush to my lodge to pack.

Father grabs me by the arm and won't let go. "Listen to me, you must not go back." His voice shakes with fear. "They are going to eat you."

I pulled from his grasp as gently as I can. "If anyone was going to eat me they would have done it by now."

"I beg you, child, do not go with him to the land of his people. There is bad medicine in that land."

How did he know I'd promised to go to the land of my husband's people? I told no one. "Stop now, father. I know he cared for you when you were injured. And you tried to steal his magic." In fact, the magic he stole was in a bag down the front of my dress. "You *did* steal it."

"No. Well, yes, but that's not why I tell you this. They drink our *blood.* They steal the marrow from our bones."

"Father—"

He turns and lifts his shirt. For a moment I am annoyed at the sight of his flat, wrinkled buttocks, and then I see he's pointing to little scars at his hip, fading bruises around tiny punctures. Too small to be made by an awl or knife. Certainly not an animal.

Pins. Needles. Metal not bone. Strong metal that can go into bone.

"Listen," my father says, his eyes piercing into me, his voice low and urgent, "please listen to me. When I returned here, my mind was clouded, but I think I was *made* to dream of the numedka, of the giant, so that no one would hear the truth of what I'd seen. But I tell you now, when I left that place I witnessed a battle of a kind we could not dream. I saw a great metal beast shoot lightning from its hands, I saw creatures thrown into the sky with such force they vanished into the sun. Their power is too great. If you go you will never return."

My poor father. He could never know that never returning was the price I'd paid for the medicine that saved his life. And he'd never know how or why his words served only to strengthen my resolve to do the very thing he begged me not to do. It pained me to think he would believe he'd failed me, that his words were not strong enough to make me stay. It was true, what father said, I realized. My husband (and by extension his people) *had* stolen our blood, father's and mine, and maybe the blood of others. But they hadn't killed us. They'd even pulled marrow from our bones. For medicine. To make medicine. To save their own people.

I had to get back to the mountain! My husband had once asked if I could save them. I still didn't know the answer to that. I only knew that I would try.

Would the medicine of the pins work with the looking glass leaf? I take each out of their bags but I can find no way to fit them together, so I just press them between my palms. A prayer, an entreaty, a message. I don't wait for a sign. I get on the horse and ride to Bear River.

When I get to the place he made the boat, I can already see the metal dragonflies coming. They carry me in a flying basket back to my husband.

Inside the mountain, the little people and other metal creatures are packing to move camp—but quickly, like a Lakota raiding party is headed their way.

I find my husband collapsed in a heap before the looking glass in my room. But when I touch what I think is him I see the furs and hides, the ragged bush of beard and hair, leggings, boots, hairy knuckles and the hair covered body within are all of one piece. As if whatever was inside had undone a seam and flown out, like a moth from a cocoon. Where is my husband?

What is my husband?

"My disguise was meant to keep you safe." I hear the words behind me, but I don't turn. I can see him in the looking glass, propped up in the beddings.

The women in the winter camp had spoken truth. Successful illusion requires sacrifice. I see now how much my husband sacrificed to keep himself hidden. To protect me and mine from danger. The shell he wore has left his true body wasted and shriveled. He has sacrificed his vigor, the strength and beauty of his limbs, to hide in that skin. In the looking glass I can see the shades and shadows of his people, what he must have been like once.

"There was a terrible war in the land I am from, and after, a terrible sickness. I was sent here in secret to find a cure. If I failed in this mission, no one would know we had tried. But we were discovered. People think we're keeping the cure to ourselves." His chest heaves and rattles. "People are crazy when they're afraid."

"That is true. Warriors use that craziness to fight. Are we going to fight them, husband?"

"I don't want to fight my own people. I want to bring my people medicine. But I don't have medicine yet. Only the hope of it."

Me. I am that hope.

"Husband. Are there earth and water and sky in your land? Or do you all live inside mountains now? I would like to see the sky sometimes."

He groans and hides his face in his hands. "I should never have made that demand of you, Dove. And I can't ask it of you now."

I almost laugh. Who asks a woman? We are given to strangers all the time. For the sake of our tribes, ours families, our fathers, to add wealth or bring honor. And women go off to strange lands all the time, make homes there, make new families. Not for love, though a woman may come to love.

There are reasons greater than love.

I am the woman of the blood medicine. I am the woman of the bone marrow medicine.

This is the medicine I will bring to my husband's people.

KELLY HALE lives in the beautiful Pacific Northwest where the streets are paved with espresso beans and the garbage recycles itself. She is the author of a bunch of short stories in a bunch of anthologies, and a couple of novels (including the award winning *Erasing Sherlock*). She has loved science fiction and fantasy for so long that the characters from the original Star Trek represent archetypes in her dreams.

LINKS

http://kellyhale.blogspot.com

Thirteen Petals

by Tonia Marie Harris

"As a rose among the thorns, so is my beloved amongst the daughters." ~ Songs 2:2

YELLOW stars abbreviate the vapors of fog and their cold breath while men stomp gleaming boots. A mother whispers to her daughter, "Stand still and look up. We are not cattle." A small child clings to her father's legs. He wraps one of her curls around his fingers and prays for her. Stifle your cries, look in their faces. Remember that what they believe does not make it so.

Stories of lives turned into numbers inked into arms. All they know is the freight rail cars wait for them, and when they board, life becomes one long night. Someone takes a stranger's hand, and then they are all linked. It is not enough. An old woman fights the terror in her bones passed down from her ancestors and can't find the room to breath. A door opens, and the grey light and shouts stun them into moving again. A hand snaps under the heel of a shoe and they only gasp for clean air, for the freedom of muscles unbound.

A White Angel lifts his arms to him and the girl wants to look into his face but someone pushes her into a line. Right. Left. Left. Right. The father shouts his little girl's name, reaches for her dark curls as a soldier forces her to the left. The White Angel smiles kindly.

"Shoot them both," he says.

Bang. Click. Bang.

Even the bare trees hold their breath as the bodies are dragged away.

In the silence, the White Angel's herald is made clear—left is death.

I am Rebecca, the girl says to herself. Her gaze meets the Angel's. His eyes are like those of a trapdoor spider. She fights not to fall in, to become his prey. He is the end of all things.

She suppresses a shiver and wants to touch her mother's shoulder. The want is an ache worse than the smell of urine on the train car. Everyone faces forward, biting their lips, and tears fall like prayers. Shame and gratitude intermingle like the ash and sky above them.

Weeks pass before the sun shines again, long after they lose count of the hours. They stare at their thin fingers and the gaunt hollows of their cheeks. At dinner, they pick the bugs out of bread while they listen to Rebecca tell them of a miracle.

"I saw the girl with the curls today," she says.

The women can't look at her mother. This girl will die soon, they think. If the SS soldiers hear these tales, she will die.

"Hush," Mother says.

"It's true. She ran right past me and I followed her to the fence. Then she was gone." Rebecca jiggles in her seat. "She looked more alive than any of us."

"I suppose you saw her father, too," one woman remarks.

Rebecca shakes her head no.

"This is no place for fairytales," another says.

Everyone hushes when the White Angel saunters by. He passes out candies to some of the children. "Call me Uncle Mengele," he tells them.

Saliva fills Rebecca's mouth, but she resists the urge to spit on his clean coat. He stands before her and holds out a chocolate. The candy smells like home—bitter coffee brewing and supper in the oven. She wipes her face and eats the candy in one bite.

"Thank you," she whispers.

"Thank you, Uncle Mengele," he urges in a gentle voice.

"Thank you, Uncle Mengele," she says.

No one looks at her through the rest of the meal. Bile churns her stomach; she wants to tell them that fairy tales aren't real, but monsters are. Three days later, she sees the little girl again. Rebecca washes blood out of sheets and pretends not to notice. Still, the girl's smile causes a fragile ribbon of hope to unspool in her chest. She says nothing to her mother or the other women.

Until the day the spirit calls her name.

The women often choose Rebecca to run the laundry to the hospital, the one that does not cure the sick but sends them up the chimneys. Her mother learns to swallow her protests. Death and fear turn them all into living ghouls. Rebecca pretends to wear a cloak of invisibility, and the SS soldiers look through her. She is a window through which the cold draft of time slips.

The little girl holds something in her hands. First, Rebecca thinks it is a bird, the girl cusps it so carefully, as though tiny bones would shatter in her dimpled hands.

Then, she spots a flash of crimson and thinks it is spilled blood. Rebecca kneels before her, pretending she drops something on the ground.

"This is for you," the ghost says, and opens her hands.

Rebecca blinks; it is like the sun coming through the dense cloud that hangs above the chimneys of the prison, or like the startling taste of candy after weeks of moldy bread. Vivid green sepals cradle the tiny rosebud. It is a hot pulse of life in a world turned colorless by nightmares. Rebecca remembers joy, but the smile is pain on her cracked lips and dirty cheeks.

"When the rose blooms, I will return for you and my people," the little girl says.

When Rebecca hears the rustle of a starched uniform behind her, she slips the rose under her shirt, next to her flat chest. "What is your name?"

The ghost answers and disappears as a bayonet strikes the back of Rebecca's skull. But the camp hardens her day-by-day into a stone version of herself. Old Rebecca died the day the White Angel fixed his gimlet eyes on her. She is nothing but a statue presiding over the place of her own ending. Still, her eyes sting and her ears ring. She stands on quivering legs and the soldier moves on.

Inside camp, the women laugh and cry over the tiny bud. Her mother finds an old cup and they fill it with precious water. The rosebud becomes their secret axis upon which life's wheel spins.

"Tell us what she said again," they ask.

"When the rose blooms, she will come back for us," Rebecca says.

Her mother stands apart, clasping and unclasping her hands. She pulls her daughter aside. "What is her name?"

"Deborah."

"No," her hand reaches for her heart. "It can't be."

"What does it mean?"

All the women go still when they hear the name. "Judgment is coming," they whisper among themselves.

"Mother," Rebecca pleads. Snakes of fear slither inside her skin. "Tell me."

"As a rose among the thorns, so is my beloved among the daughters," her mother quotes. She takes a risk by embracing her only daughter. "You've brought hope into our hearts again. We must guard it as our most precious treasure." Her mother pointed to the tight green leaves that protected the deep red of the bud. "There are five sepals. Our people are the thirteen petals of the rose. When the rose opens, we will know for sure." She smiles and Rebecca remembers what a handsome woman her mother once was. "For now, we have hope."

The women kiss Rebecca and use the scarves that cover their shorn heads to wipe their eyes. Days pass, and they watch each other turn into skeletons—or disappear. They rustle and stifle their cries in the dark, so tired that sleep is a hobby for those not caged in barbed wire and despair. When they do sleep, they dream the soldiers are shadows that devour them and they wake in the morning counting their dead. Right. Left. Left. Right.

Only the rosebud remains untouched by ash and sorrow. It draws each slant of light to it—their sacred sentinel. Rebecca wakes one morning, hot and blind with visions. She sees green fields all around her, and rose petals falling from a blue sky. Their perfume fills the air.

No one meets her mother's gaze as she brushes Rebecca's hair from her forehead. She will not say goodbye to the only one left to her. Outside, the soldiers grow mountains from flesh and bone. Here and now, a mother tries to draw the fever away from her daughter's face with kisses and calloused hands. She prays to the spirit of the rose as Rebecca whispers about red rain. Her voice stirs through the crowded, dirty room like the wind through the bare trees outside.

"It's so beautiful, Mama," Rebecca says.

The white harbinger of death stands in the doorway.

His thumbs rest on his pistol belt and he smiles.

A woman nudges a cup under the bunk.

A bird trills in the stillness.

Left.

"Please," Mother says before she screams.

Her screams do not stop as a blur of hands and faces lift the child away. Her screams do not stop as they drag her out and beat her. Her screams do not stop until she falls facedown in the mud.

Rebecca smiles.

The White Angel shudders as though he feels the weight of humanity bearing down on him. He smells roses and silk tickles his cheeks while the soldiers carry the fevered child to the ovens. His thoughts go mad with ideas of salvation and all the pounds of flesh he calls for like numbers in a lottery. No relief sates him as he watches a slender arm reach for him while the men slam the grate down. He hates the smell of burning flesh but does not cover his mouth. The White Angel returns to his bedlam of syringes and endless screams. They are not human. No matter what they believe. He pushes back his sleeves and raises his hands like a conductor. Doctors in white coats raise their instruments and play a symphony.

The moon lowers her face over a small group of women that night. They pull a cup from under the beds. Tears fall like dew onto thirteen red petals. It is their beating heart, their promise of victory. They do not forget how to pray.

The White Angel eludes the new soldiers. These are men, not specters, who remove their helmets and wipe tears from their eyes. Skeletons rally and grin before them. Some fall to their knees in horror and grief. They do not forget how to pray, either. The chimneys stop belching and children laugh as hot food fills their swollen bellies. Women fall against their men who have survived. Mothers try to meld their children back into their flesh. Many stand alone, but they smile anyway.

One woman holds a rose in her shaking hands. She watches two children walk away, one with dark, curly hair. They hold hands and carry their heads high as the woods and fog embrace them. The woman counts the thirteen petals and gives them each a name. She names one Rebecca, one for the mother who couldn't say good-bye, and the others for her husband and children who flew into the sky in a curl of smoke.

The survivors bear their marks and tumble back into the world. Alive. They listen to their hearts pound in their ears when the night comes. The tattooed numbers along their arms fade, but their memories do not. Some plant stories in the dark, fertile soil of their ancestors. They watch roses bloom in the faces of their children and grandchildren. Someone laughs; and when they realize the sound comes from their own mouths, they laugh harder until the tears come. Imagine a woman aging. Her back is straight and narrow and she remembers the red perfume of hope. She turns a corner and sees the face of a monster loose in the street. His coat is brown, but she sees the arms of the Angel of Death cloaked in white. A fist presses to her lined mouth and her belly growls as though she were hungry. Out of the corner of her eye, a girl smiles at her.

Rebecca.

A monster who calls himself Wolfgang swims into the warm currents of the Atlantic Ocean. The balmy air stirs his thinning hair and the salt water braces his limbs.

"Uncle Mengele," a child's voice says.

Bodies sodden with cold press against him. He can't escape their hollow cheeks, their staring eyes. Fingers like white matchsticks pull him under. His head bobs up once, surrounded by rose petals like drops of blood on froth.

"Take your candy and say thank you, Uncle Mengele."

After thirty-four years of life as a ghost, his heart stops.

TONIA MARIE HARRIS writes YA speculative fiction and poetry. She wants to be a ghost hunter when she grows up. Chocolate is her Kryptonite. You can follow her on her blog or connect with her on Twitter, links below.

LINKS

http://passionfind.wordpress.com
https://twitter.com/TMarieHarris

Eyes of Wood

by Brian T. Hodges

MAGGIE willed herself to be invisible, tried to make herself as small and insignificant as a mouse in a shadow. She sat in an empty doorway, clad in black on black, knees held tightly against her chest, watching the street from behind a fringe of dyed-black bangs. She wouldn't sleep tonight— she couldn't. There were too many dangers that slipped the skins of humanity and prowled the city streets after all the day folk had thrown the bolts on their cozy homes. She had to be ready. Nighttime, she knew, was waiting with watering jaws.

She'd seen many dangerous things on the streets. Most common were those lumbering, dead-minded beasts; corruptions that she could evade, outrun if she stayed alert. But then there were those dangers that were driven by a soul-hunger—lurking in holes and corners, opportunistic, famished. Their predaceous hands seemed to materialize from behind walls, from under pavement, overwhelming their marks. It had been a soul-eater—a hueless wisp of emptiness—that had forced her from her home. The grasp of its winter-chilled hand had rent a hole through the fabric of her being, left behind a seed of darkness, driven her onto raveling streets where chaos provided a camouflage of sorts. She was lucky though. The soul-eaters would eventually demand payment from anyone they marked. She had escaped at a relatively low cost—a cost she could endure at least.

Maggie counted the seconds as they drifted into the night: it would be ten hours, thirty-six thousand ticks, before the first rays of dawn would chase the dangers back into their daytime lairs. She scanned the streets through heavy, tired eyes—*dusk eyes* her mother had called them when she was young; eyes so dark, so inscrutable, that they seemed to be made of night itself. Maggie smiled at the memory. Although her mother was just remarking on their color, Maggie had always fancied that her eyes were magic—dark coals that could see into the night worlds of her bedtime stories. Her mother, she had thought, had sea eyes because she saw the world through a streaming pane of tears. Her father, so distant, unattached, blind to his family, had eyes of stone, of granite.

Dusk eyes would have proven most useful, Maggie mused, as she watched the dark hours pass by. It was a weary duty, and yesterday's kohl stung her eyes—each blink felt as if her lids were made of splinters. But she wouldn't allow fatigue to overcome vigilance.

Nothing moved. Nothing happened. The air was still and thick with the smells of refuse and damp concrete. Still, she watched. She knew that nothingness was a prelude to somethingness. She was right. After a long wait—several thousand ticks—she caught sight of movement all around her. The curb began to churn then, all at once, hundreds of wildflowers pushed their way up between curb and sidewalk like a hedgerow, erupting in yellows and whites and pinks and periwinkles. The verdant smell of freshly turned soil drove the rank odors from Maggie's stoop. She watched in wonder as flowering vines snaked their way up parking meter and lamppost. The iridescent dance of dragonflies followed, their alto buzzing drowning out the hum of streetlights. Then, an army of great old trees—oaks and elms— shouldered their way from behind brick walls and marched onto sidewalk and street to lay claim to their root-homes. There, the trees shuddered, scattering a blanket of leaves on the grass and underbrush that had worked its way through the asphalt.

Maggie rose from the doorway and took a hesitant step onto a patch of soft grass where a curb had been. *Step lightly*, she thought, *you're walking on a dream*. She half-expected the grass to break apart like cobwebs, but it was soft and spongy.

A long, golden braid fell lazily over her shoulder, startling her. It had been years since she had worn her natural hair color, but there was no mistaking its color. She looked at herself. She was dressed in greens and oranges and plaid, rather than her uniform blacks. It was as if her child-self hadn't been lost after all. She was once again that innocent girl, untouched by the hands that had forced her to seek refuge on the streets. She felt a playful urge to go and investigate, so she hoisted her skirt just a little above her knees—she had always loved plaid as a girl—and climbed over a vine-encased newspaper bin into the wood.

Maggie ran from tree to shrub to tree, touching each to make sure it was real. But, just as she bent to sniff a flower, a shadow shifted in her field of vision. Maggie snuck back to her doorway and crouched in the shadow, still as stone. She watched a figure, bent and hulking and misshapen, as it scuttled up the sidewalk, pushing a squeaky, three-wheeled shopping cart. A scraggly beard trailed between its legs like strands of seaweed, streaking the pavement with a greasy stain. The creature stopped and scooped a glistening slab into the cart, then snuffled at the air. It stiffened like a dog catching a scent, turned toward Maggie and chuffed three times. Spittle misted the air, obscuring its wide frog's mouth. Then, all at once, the creature shuffled forward, sweeping its head in long arcs to sniff the ground and air as it closed the distance with Maggie.

Maggie bolted into the woods, running as fast as she could through underbrush and over root. She could hear the creature crashing through the brush as it labored to keep up, rasping breath, snapping twigs, and heavy footsteps. The sounds grew fainter, more distant, then disappeared. But Maggie kept running. She ran until she found herself in a clearing lit by stars and crescent moon, where she stopped to catch her breath. She couldn't go back to her doorway—not anymore. The creature had her scent and would be snuffling around, looking for her, waiting for her. She had to find a new place to pass the night—so, why not here in this starlit meadow? She looked around. Rose bushes rambled through the glade with no regard to the type of orderly design demanded of the gardens her mother had kept. Red and pink blossoms called to her with joyous voices, but it was another rose that caught her eye. Next to a crumbling stone well grew a rose so white that it whispered to her with the moon's silvery voice. She answered its call, plucking a single fragrant blossom and tucking it into the top of her braid.

"Are you a thief, then, Lady Margaret?" a man's voice called from behind her. "Dare you pluck a blossom without leave?"

Maggie spun to face her inquisitor. The man sat on the lip of the well, tossing a stone from hand to hand. He was dressed in the green and gold coat of a knight. But she could see that he was thin—too thin—and strangely angular. His skin had a grey cast and hair was so pale that it seemed to disappear where it brushed his shoulders. He looked as though he were wearing away from the edges. Still, the man had a fiery presence, an intensity that demanded her attention.

"I see no fences, no signs," Maggie snapped at the man's presumption. "I have just as much right to be here as you. These are wild roses, after all."

"Wild or not, you didn't ask leave." The man's words were shaded by the hint of an accent—one that Maggie found frustratingly unplaceable.

"I'm free to do what I want," Maggie said. "I certainly don't need permission from the likes of you."

"True enough. But did you ask leave of the rose?"

"A rose can't give consent. It…it's just a *rose*."

"There's the problem, Margaret. For isn't a rose like love itself? And like love, there's a story it must follow: it must bud, then bloom, then wither away."

"If so, then I suppose I've done the poor thing a favor by plucking it in full bloom, no? It'll never know the disappointment of love's downward arc, feel the pain of loss."

"Is blossoming truly a blessing?"

"If the only other choices are desire and death, then yes."

The man sat in silence for a long moment, apparently weighing her answer. Then, all at once, he rose from his perch and approached Maggie. Without further word, he took hold of her milk-white hands. Maggie looked into his eyes—pale blue, almost gray, translucent like a cloud on a summer day. His eyes seemed to look into her, to call to her from the depths of his being with a rhythmic pulse—a heartbeat, a distant drum. He leaned in and kissed her on the corner of her mouth. A wave of joy—golden and warm—washed over her. She wanted to fall into his arms, lose herself in him.

"No!" Maggie cried out, pushing him away.

The word ripped through the meadow like a thunderclap, echoing upon itself, growing louder and louder until it became a screaming feedback loop. The forest shook and shuddered. Maggie clamped her hands over her ears and watched as the flowers retracted petal and bloom then disappeared into the cracks in the pavement. The vines disentangled and the trees uprooted and marched back to their hiding places. The wood was gone, so too was the fading man and the golden-haired girl. Maggie stood in the street, alone, a black figure illuminated by a flashing red light.

Maggie wrapped her leather jacket around herself for warmth. Still, she shuddered, trying to forget the fading man's hands, the memory of his kiss. *Tenderness is a weakness*, she reminded herself—the lyric of a song she liked. She couldn't let herself think of him, couldn't let herself get lost in him. Not here. Not now. There was so much to lose, so little to gain. Infatuation was a faithless pilot that would only lead her astray, distract her, and make her drop her guard.

She focused her attention back to the street, now slick with rain. The pavement was a dark mirror, interrupted here and again by the broken reflection of streetlights. This was her life: the monochromatic landscape of night in the city. The wood wasn't real. *He* wasn't real. It was all a game of make-believe—a way to bridge the long dark hours. But she knew that it was more than that. The night world had meaning—it provided a canvas upon which her story could be told. Without her little reveries, the fear and despair of the street would grow blacker and blacker until it became a burden so dark that no light could penetrate the shadows in which she hid. She would have to suffer—rather than live—every moment, watching the darkness to deform her spirit until she became one of those misshapen corruptions that prowled the streets. And that just wouldn't do.

As far as squats went, the old blue house on Madison was a dream. It was two stories tall and had an unfinished cellar—enough space to room the growing number of guests, if they doubled up here and there. Maggie, for her part, had claimed the sewing room all for herself. It wasn't much more than a closet, but it was perfect. The walls were decorated in a yellowing paper crisscrossed by fading roses, baby blue and cotton candy pink and daffodil yellow. A streetlight shone through the dormer window, casting a sterile light over her nest of clothes and old blankets. It was the most comfortable bed she had slept in for ages.

Maggie traced her fingers over the paper roses. It had been several months since she had visited the wood, several restful months tucked away inside her house. Memories of the fading man lingered, but she didn't dare look for him. The dangers that had chased her into the wood were still there; they pressed against the walls. She could feel their winter cold seeping through plaster and board, reaching for her. She rarely left the security of her little room.

There was a knock, then the door opened. It was Dave—one of the latecomer, cellar dwellers. Maggie hadn't spent much time with him, but he was a nice enough guy, tall and rail-thin with a pinched face that reminded her of a kid sucking on a sour ball. The effect wasn't all that bad; it gave him an unimpressed, disdainful look. It worked for him, Maggie thought, it gave him a punky edge.

"You comin' down, Mags? We lifted some beer from KwikMart, and Ken's got his guitar." Dave leaned against the doorframe and ran his hand through his long, dark hair.

"I'm fine," Maggie said, smiling. She didn't really know anything about him besides the fact that he always carried a skateboard, but never rode it. But who was she to judge? She obsessively carried a key ring despite having left her home.

"Don't you get lonely being up here by yourself all the time?" he asked.

"Not really," Maggie lied. "I like to think about stuff, you know."

"What kind of stuff?" Dave sat on the floor next to Maggie.

"I don't know…Stuff like, do you think this world is all we get? I mean, is this the only place we can go? The only world?" Maggie gestured at the window.

"Wha' d' you mean? What we've got is all we got, y'know. You've gotta do all you can before you die 'cause there ain't nothing more. If you can't touch it, it ain't real."

"That can't be right. It just can't—not if life's going to have meaning. There's got to be more. There's got to be magic and beauty…somewhere." Maggie thought of the starlit meadow and the fading man. She wondered if she would ever see either again.

"Yeah, that's just what I was thinkin'." Dave pulled Maggie close and kissed her—a hard, bruising kiss—more desperate than passionate. Maggie wanted to turn away, but she felt the great black maw of loneliness open in her belly. Memories of why she left home would follow in an unrelenting storm. She didn't want to be alone. She didn't want to remember. So, she kissed him with the same foggy desperation. Street kids didn't ask why you were here. They all had their own reasons—abuse, neglect, bourgeois ennui—they didn't care so much about your particular story. Life was about the here and now.

Maggie's eyes fell on the floral wallpaper while Dave bit her earlobe and neck, pawed her. The roses moved under her gaze, slithering from the walls and taking root around the little room. A large white rose bush burst up from the floorboards. Creepers pushed through the window and wound around the radiator, where they turned their flowery faces on the pair. Trees crowded the yard in front of her room, tapping the window with branches and leaf.

The fading man was there—in the sewing room that was now a sunlit clearing in a wood.

She crossed to him. Neither said a word. Her eyes shone with a soft luster, like flowers wet with dew. They kissed. His mouth tasted of summer—of mint and honey and sunlight. He didn't close his eyes. Instead, he cradled her in his gaze. His hands were kind; they lacked violence and desperation. He held her, comforted her, and stoked her into a blaze that consumed all thought.

Her breath quickened as he led her to a bed of moss. She unbuttoned her blouse and let it slip from her shoulders. Leaning close, he placed a kiss on her neck, on her collarbone, his lips as gentle as down. She could feel his breath, feel her body rising to meet him.

"This is terribly awkward, but I don't know your name." Maggie plucked a moon-white blossom for the fading man. But when she turned, he was gone. So, too, she realized, were the forest sounds. There wasn't a woodnote, croak, or buzz. Even the scents of grass and bloom were gone. It was as if all life had vanished. Then, all at once, the sun plummeted from the sky, falling behind the trees. Dark fingers spread across the clearing, like a giant grasping hand. The shadowy tendrils reached for Maggie, roiling and churning and grasping at her bare ankles. She tried to run, but she couldn't. The shadows held her fast, winding around her legs and dragging her into the dark wood.

Maggie came to in the sewing room, sweating with panic, chilled to the core. Darkness had found her and was laying claim to her.

Maggie was with child; there was no denying it. Day after day, she had risen in her little room pale and wan and sickly. Dave wouldn't be any help. He had vanished with her panhandled earnings shortly after visiting her room. She couldn't keep the lurking dangers at bay in this condition, not alone. If she had a babe, both of them would be forfeit to the soul-eaters, for whom innocence was delicacy—a mother's love, dessert. She had to be rid of the child. For the babe's sake. For her own sake.

The clinic turned Maggie away. Sure, there were plenty programs to help people like her, but she had to be *someone* to claim them. She couldn't just walk in the door, flesh and blood, and ask for help. No, without ID, she wasn't a person and wasn't entitled to any services. She didn't exist. She didn't belong to this world.

The fading man was the father. It only made sense. The babe was of another world. She could feel it pulling her to the wood. It was as if a black hole had opened in her belly. She could feel herself growing thinner, transparent. She had to return to the clearing. If she stayed in the house, the baby would tear her apart.

She wrapped herself in an old army blanket and ran to the cold wet street, looking for any sign of the wood. There was none. The old willow tree stood alone in front of the house, where it had always been, branches waving lazily in the breeze. Orderly gardens lined the streets in every direction. Maggie paced back and forth, hands on her head, sobbing breathlessly.

"No, no, no," she cried.

"Mags, babe, what's the matter?" It was Emily, a 15 year-old who, despite her spiky bleached hair, had taken on the role of house mother, nursing her roommates through sickness, guiding them through bad trips, and comforting them through hook-ups and break-ups. "Come here. Talk to me."

"I have to find the forest." Maggie wept. Mascara ran down her cheeks in shadowy streams. "I can't find it...It's not where it's supposed to be."

"Oh, baby, it'll be okay." Emily took Maggie's hand and stroked it gently. "Just sit here with me. Everything will be alright."

"You don't understand. I'll die if I can't find the clearing. I'll be ripped in two."

"It's okay, Mags. Just come inside. We'll take care of you. You'll come down soon."

"You think I'm high?" Maggie screamed, pulling her hand back. "You don't get it. I need to take this baby to the forest. I need to get rid of it."

Emily nodded to herself. "You sure of that?" she asked in a calming voice. In the long silence that followed, she took a step forward and touched Maggie's elbow.

"Mm-hmm." Maggie nodded. She kept her eyes on the ground, refused to look at her friend.

"You couldn't get help at the clinic?"

Maggie shook her head. She had no words.

"You know, there are other ways I've heard of."

Maggie retuned to the doorway where she had first seen the wood come to life. The floorboards were torn up and the door was tattered and scarred. Splinters the size of blades protruded threateningly from the wounds. The stoop reeked of vomit and piss, a smell that would sink into her skin and settle in her clothes if she stayed long. But that didn't matter so much to her anymore. She climbed the steps and sat with her back against the brick wall, watching the street just as she had months before.

The night dragged; each second labored to turn over to the next. Maggie's eyelids grew heavy but she kept her dusk-eyed vigil. After what seemed like hours, she saw the bent, frog-faced creature shambling toward her, its seaweed beard dragging like a pendulum on the ground, and its unbalanced shopping cart raising a racket in the still hours. Another figure appeared from behind it—unlike its colleague, this one was tall and thickly muscled with a long neck of a horse and antlers on top of an oval head that reminded Maggie of an angelfish. Then, to her right, Maggie spotted a third figure making its way up the street. A rust-red carapace limiting its use of arm and leg, making it scuttle rather than walk. She would soon be surrounded, cut off. But the creatures were approaching her at a measured pace. It wasn't the chaotic free-for-all of a feeding frenzy. It was deliberate. They had something in mind.

Maggie pried a long, jagged splinter from the door and waited atop of the stairs, brandishing the shard like a dagger. The three corruptions stopped when they reached the curb, snuffling the air with their impossible faces and stamping like antsy thoroughbreds at the gate. The smell of rotten tide filled the doorway, thick as toothpaste. Maggie stepped gingerly onto the landing and edged down the stairs, looking for a crease in their line. Then, just as she was about to step onto the sidewalk, the concrete fractured with a loud crackling noise, spiderwebbing then buckling and turning over on itself. Trees and bushes and vines burst from the fragrant soils. The creatures fell back several steps. Maggie saw her opportunity and ran into the nascent wood as fast as she could tear through the tangled brush and bramble.

The creatures followed, spreading out into a triangle that swept Maggie deeper into the forest. She could hear them crashing through the brush, their garrulous whoops and yips lending strength to her tired legs. Everything, it seemed, was fighting against her, trying to hold her back. Thorn dug into hem, root twisted around foot, and branch slapped at face. But she pushed through until she stumbled into the clearing, cloak and skirt torn, legs bleeding from a hundred scrapes. The creatures came to a full stop, once again, at the clearing's edge, whining and stomping and chomping at the air. They threw shoulder and hip forward to no effect—it was as if they were trapped behind a wall.

Maggie retreated into the clearing, keeping a watchful eye on the trio and a tight grip on her splinter.

The herb Emily had described wasn't hard to find with its velvety leaves and yellow pinwheel flowers. But when she tugged at a cluster of blooms, the bush tugged back; it didn't want to yield its secret without a fight. Maggie tugged again. She needed to taste of the bitter herb that would twine the babe from her belly, rip it from her womb, deliver it to heaven without first touching foot to the terrifying streets.

"Leave it be, Margaret." It was him again—the fading man. "Let our child grow and live and laugh and love."

"Our child?" Maggie spun on her heels, ready to scream, ready to slash out with the shard, ready to cry. But when she saw him—his eyes clouding with sadness—the words turned to ash in her mouth. She knew she shouldn't trust him, but she couldn't trust herself either. She ran to him, threw her arms over his shoulders, and buried her face in his chest.

"There's no place in the world for our babe," she said between sobs. "There's hardly place enough for me. I can't do this."

"I can protect you, if you let me," he said. He had the conviction of a fool, Maggie thought, of someone who predicted effects without knowing their cause. He knew nothing about her, about her circumstances.

"How could you possible protect me?" she said, taking several steps back. "You aren't even real. I mean, what are you? How could we have made a child? You're not even from my world."

"Oh, but you're wrong, Margaret. I am just as much a part of your world as you are." He closed the gap between them and placed a hand on her shoulder. "It's just that the queen of shades has taken hold of me. And if I don't break free, I'll become one of them. I'll hunger for souls instead of love. I'll hunt in your world rather than live in it."

"Why didn't you tell me this before? When you first came to me?"

"I didn't know if you were real or just another of the queen's illusions. How could I trust what I saw when she could so readily turn my eyes to her service?"

"But, certainly, you realized I was no illusion when you lay with me. Why wait until now?" Maggie wondered why chivalry so often turned to self-interest when tested.

"I was fading." He gestured at his face. His eyes had darkened, like mirrors whose faces were turned to the wall. Gone was their light, their transparency. Before her stood a desperate man. "I was afraid you'd take me for one of them, that you'd fear me. And I couldn't risk losing you. You were the last thread binding me to my person. If I lost you, I'd have turned."

"So, you thought you'd bind me with a child? That you'd force my return?" Maggie could feel the fading man's trap closing around her just as quickly as his glamor disappeared. He had tricked her, toyed with her imagination. But she had no time for regrets, no time for recriminations—no, those were luxuries best left for the comforts of suburbia. She had to play out the scene that the fading man had set.

"It was the only way." He wouldn't look her in the eyes. "I have to break free from the queen."

"Why didn't you just run from her? Apparently, you can come and go and do as you please—the queen has no hold over you."

"I'm afraid she does." The fading man looked at Maggie, twisting his face into mask of dread. "And her hold on me will play out tonight. For it's the seventh year since I was caught, and the shadow court must pay tribute to hold their fates at bay, to forebear the calls of hell. I fear her, Maggie. I fear that I'll lose my life tonight. That I'll be conscribed to the shadows."

"Can't we just leave, return to our world?"

"No, if I try to leave, they'll catch me for certain and I'll be bound to my fate."

Just as you bound me with a babe, Maggie thought. She pulled herself free from his hands and stood silent, watching a patch of grass between them. After several long moments, she said, "If you're doomed, then leave me be. Let me take the herb and be done with this, be done with you."

"No, Margaret, didn't you hear me? I'm not doomed. Not until you taste of that herb. You can break the queen's hold over me. Tonight, when the court rides."

Maggie felt a tugging in her belly. The snare had been tripped. She had no choice.

"What must I do?" Maggie braced against herself against his words, against her own words.

Maggie crouched behind the wheel of an old mill, watching the stone bridge for a sign that the shadow court was approaching. Her mouth was parched and her heart beat against her chest like a bird trying to escape its cage. It happened just as the fading man said it would: a clamor of bridles and hooves announced the court's arrival. Then she saw them. First there ran a black horse, then there ran a brown. The third was white as snow. Hundreds more followed. Maggie waited for the first two to pass then took a deep breath and launched herself at the rider of the white horse, dragging him from his saddle and holding him tight as they tumbled down the embankment to the edge of the creek, a tangle of arms and legs.

A commotion erupted from above and all around. Orders echoed down the shadow court's ranks, harsh and clipped. Horses whickered in protest against their tightened reins. A single voice screamed, shrill like steel being drawn across glass, "He is away! Stop them! Get them!"

It was the shadow queen. She sat mounted upon a stallion that was as red as a burning ember and stood several hands above all the other steeds. Her face was heavily lined birch bark, riddled with holes, and her hair was strands of moss. A colorless fog wove its way angrily in and out of the rotten bark that made up the queen's body. She pointed a twig-like finger at the pair and screeched, "Don't let her take him from me."

At the queen's command, the shadow court spread across the top of the bank, at least five score across and a dozen deep. The line held its position, fire-hardened spears raised like hundreds of angry quills. The black rider nudged his horse to the base of the embankment, where he dismounted in one smooth motion.

"Fear me not," whispered the fading man. "Hold me tight, whatever they might do. Remember that I'm the father of your child. I'll do you no harm."

The black rider glowered at the pair with his wide frog face, then stooped and picked up a twig. He held it above his head, chanting a throaty ululation and tracing symbols in air. There was a loud noise, like a fuse popping, and then the twig began to wriggle. Immediately, the fading man cried out. His body warped and bent and stretched—arms and legs shrinking, neck elongating, head pinching—until he became a snake as black as oil. Maggie struggled to hold the slick serpent that twisted and hissed and snapped at her face with dripping fangs. Venom stung her eyes and she felt her muscles burn and stretch and tear, but held on. She held him close, she didn't let go.

"I won't give him up," Maggie yelled at the rider.

The rider screamed a cry of frustration then fell to his knees, his hands shimmering and translucent. The twig slipped through his ghostly fingers and fell dead to the ground. So, too, did the rider.

The rider of the brown horse dismounted and craned its long horse neck toward Maggie before taking a position next to his fallen comrade. He produced a feather from his bag and recited a charm in a thin, metallic warble, then tossed the feather in the air. The serpent writhed in Maggie's arms, contorting and crying out. Massive wings sprouted from its back, thrashing against Maggie's head in a fiery blur. The hawk fought to break free, to take flight, clawing at her breast with hooked talons, opening a gash below her neck. Maggie's leather jacket hung in shreds from her shoulder and her chest throbbed. Still, she held him close, hands wrapped around the hawk's neck.

"I won't let you take him back," she cried though her pains.

The rider's fish face showed no emotion as he picked a pinch of dandelion fluff and recited the charm again. Maggie felt the feathers turn to rough fur under her hand. A pitiful cry turned to a roar and the fading man became a lion. Claws and teeth flashed before her, tearing at her arms and legs, opening new wounds.

But still, she held him close.

"You won't break me," Maggie snarled. Her eyes fell in and out of focus as she fought to push the pain from her mind. After several long moments, she locked eyes with the rider and repeated herself in a low growl, "You won't break me."

The rider stumbled; his spell was all used up, his will broken. Like his comrade, he fell lifeless to the ground, where the fluff escaped his hand and danced on the gentle breeze.

"Enough of this," the queen said, urging her horse forward. Her body groaned like a tree in a strong wind as she dismounted. She took several steps toward Maggie, rubbing her knotty fingers over an acorn until it burst into flames. "He's mine."

Maggie's hands began to burn as the lion transformed into a bar of red-hot iron. At once, she gathered the bar into the old army blanket and dove into the river. There, the bar hissed and bubbled and bent and twisted, slowly taking the shape of a naked man. Maggie dragged him from the water and wrapped him in her blanket. She threw herself across his body.

"Leave us be! Your spell is broken. You have no claim over us," Maggie shouted.

The queen stood wavering above the couple. The colorless haze churned beneath her bark skin. Her mouth contorted, foaming, turning into a hideous mask of hunger and rage. She spoke with a faint voice, "Had I known that you'd betray me, I'd have plucked out your eyes. I'd have blinded you and bound you."

Maggie thought of the fading man's dull eyes. They had been eyes of wood all along, she mused, decorative, changeable, but not meant for seeing.

"It's over," Maggie said, rising from the fading man to stare down the queen with her dusk eyes. "I can see you. You're a shadow, a shell of a memory. You have no claim on him—no hold over me or my babe. You're nothing." With that, she lunged and drove the splinter into the queen's chest. The queen staggered backward; her body split open, wet like a rotten log, releasing the angry fog. Then, one by one, the members of the court took flight into the woods, leaving their horses to wander aimless in their fine tack.

"You're free," Maggie said, her voice hoarse and strained. She refused to look at the fading man, refused to be drawn-in by his promises or sad eyes. Instead, she walked up the embankment, ignoring his calls. *I'm free.*

B RIAN T. HODGES lives in the mossy forests of the Pacific Northwest, where he works as a lawyer, researcher, and non-fiction writer. He is also a musician, having released several albums of esoteric and ethereal music under the moniker, the Blue Hour. His fiction has been published by New Lit Salon Press, Liquid Imagination, The Strange Edge, received an Honorable Mention from the Writers of the Future contest (V31 Q1 2014), and was a finalist in the 2013 N3F Amateur Short Story Contest.

LINKS

https://twitter.com/brianthodges

All That Glitters

by Tarran Jones

"GUNTHER, you cannot do this! She is your daughter." Nadja's desperate voice reached up into the attic where Sigrun lay on her bed listening. Her mother had always cautioned the girl to never show her father her talent, but he found out the previous week when he saw it by accident. A tear ran down the side of her face as the wind rocked the shutters outside, a sound that echoed what was in her heart. She prayed to God that He would protect her, but it seemed her father had made a deal with the Devil and she was the prize.

"Woman, I can do whatever I want with her. Although, I might have to wonder about her being my daughter, as sorcery doesn't run through my line." Her father's harsh voice cut through the protests of her mother. "Have her ready to go by high noon."

She heard heavy footsteps for a few seconds then the door slammed, making small dust motes float through the air. The girl turned her head and wished with all her heart that she hadn't taken off her gloves that day by the river.

Lighter footsteps and soft sobbing broke through her thoughts as her mother's head poked through the small attic hatch. "Sigrun, my daughter." Her mother climbed into the attic and bustled over to the bed and pulled her into an embrace.

"Your father has gone mad. He has promised you to Junker Risteard Von-Hislenad. In return, he will grant your father a lesser title and we will leave the mill."

Sigrun nuzzled into her mother's neck for a moment, appreciating the comfort of her embrace, then pulled away. She was sixteen summers now; old enough to be married—old enough to accept what was coming. "Mother, God will protect me. Junker Von-Hislenad, while cruel, will value me for my abilities."

She did not see the slap, which had enough force to twist her head around, coming. "Where is my daughter? Where is the girl I raised to be a strong Hessian woman? God will not protect the weak, my girl."

Sigrun's cheek throbbed; her hand came up shakily and caressed it. Her mind started to clear of the fear that had plagued her since the discovery. "Mama, what can we do? We only have until high noon."

Nadja pulled back and rubbed her forehead, and Sigrun could feel the despair in that gesture. Her mother then reached into a small, red woven bag, which, before then, Sigrun hadn't noticed. "When you first turned my comb to gold, I went to the church and prayed all night. An angel came to me and told me that you were special and had a destiny. That no one must know of your power—it was a gift from God. She gave me a potion to paint on your hands, but only if times were dire."

Tears ran down Nadja's face as she pulled out the blue glass bottle. "If you were to ever use this, then you must go away from this place and never come back. It meant it was time for you to go and create your place in the world."

Sigrun's hand shook as she accepted the bottle from her mother. It felt cool and the glass was smooth in her grasp. "Where would I go?"

Nadja shook her head sadly, "That I don't know." She reached back and pulled Sigrun towards her again and whispered into her hair. "Don't let him sell you. He wants status more than wealth or he would have kept you and locked you away. Run from here my daughter, and don't ever come back."

Sigrun nodded, her heart pounding with fear. Her mind was awhirl with possible destinations to go. Where would she fit in? At least she wouldn't have to worry about money—not when you can change objects into gold.

"Now get dressed to play your part. Paint your hand sparingly now. Be prepared for trouble." Nadja pulled away and gently caressed her daughter's pale cheek and left Sigrun to get ready.

At high noon, Sigrun was ready. Nadja gazed at her daughter, sadness warring with pride. Her dark brown hair was beautifully braided down her back, the tip reaching just to her waist. She could remember the feel of the fine, grey velvet on her fingertips as she embroidered the blue flowers. Nadja had been saving the dress for Sigrun's wedding day—and even though she knew what was coming, a part of Nadja was glad to be able to see her daughter dressed in her finery.

Sigrun had painted her hand with the potion, and now they waited. The sky had cleared up from the windy weather of the morning, and the sun now shone weakly through the clouds, the brisk air gently swirling the leaves throughout the courtyard. She prayed to God that he would protect her and help her find a safe place. She already had a place she wanted to go—Marburg, the university town. She would get lost in a sea of people and hope to never see her father again.

Sigrun's stomach jolted when her mother tightened her grip on her upper arm. She looked up and saw a closed black carriage with the arms of Junker Risteard Von-Hislenad displayed on the sides. Two jet-black horses, their mouths flecked with foam, pulled the carriage fast. Her throat dried up and she started to pray for the strength to go through with this deception.

Remembering her mother's admonition this morning about weak people, she straightened her back and raised her face as the carriage pulled up. Strength was called for—not weakness. Her right hand, the one she used to turn objects into gold, was numb; and her left hand, her secret hand, was tingling.

Dust billowed around them, causing mother and daughter to step back as the coachman jumped down from his seat and opened the carriage door for her father and Junker Risteard Von-Hislenad. The women watched as Von-Hislenad alighted.

He was an older man of forty summers. Sigrun noticed that his eyes were the lightest blue, like a sun kissed sky. His blond hair carefully oiled and clubbed at the back. He was the epitome of fashion for a Junker, and his shoe buckles proved it: wide and made of high-quality silver and lined with small gemstones. His black coat and breeches were cut low and tight. Very much the dangerous dandy, as there were rumors of cruelty in the house of Von-Hislenad—and his bearing declared him a hard man. The girl saw there were no smile lines on his face, his eyes were narrow and his mouth tight.

Next to him, Sigrun's father, Gunther, was dressed in his best clothes, yet still came up looking shabby. For a moment, Sigrun felt pity for her father, but she squashed that thought when she caught him looking at her with revulsion on his face.

"At least she is somewhat pretty. That will help with the marriage bed, at least till I get an heir." Risteard Von-Hislenad walked over to Sigrun and circled her. His walking cane came up and prodded her on the chest. She let out a held breath as the metal bruised her flesh through her clothes. A slight smile whispered across his face, and Sigrun knew the rumors to be true.

Panic filled her being and it was only the gentle touch of her mother that kept her from striking out and fleeing now.

His hand came up and gripped her chin; he lifted her head and stuck his finger in her mouth. "Good teeth, strong features. Padding in all the right places and not too tall. Excellent! Now to seal the deal, I want the girl to transform this—" Von-Hislenad clicked his fingers sharply and point to the ground. His carriage driver quickly brought over a small chest and placed it at his Lord's feet, opening it. Von-Hislenad reach in picked up a medium sized stone cross. Beautifully crafted Sigrun knew it would make a fine gift for the Church. "I want the girl to transform this cross and then I will take her off your hands, miller, and you will get your status."

Von-Hislenad stepped back; Gunther took the cross from him, placing it in front of his daughter. "Daughter, do as the Lord asks and turn this into gold."

Sigrun calmed herself by counting to ten and then stepped forward. Sound left her for a moment then came back with force. "Father, how do you expect me to turn stone into gold? I am not a goldsmith."

Ranges of emotions crossed her father's face, settling on rage. He stepped closer to her and whispered, "Don't test me daughter. I know you can do it for I have seen you do it. If you turn me into a fool, I will make your life miserable."

Von-Hislenad started to look bored. "What is the matter?"

Gunther smiled over his shoulder, "Nothing milord. She will do it now." He pointed to the cross and glared.

Sigrun closed her eyes and prayed that the potion worked. She reached over to the cross with her numb right hand and touched the stone. She opened her eyes and felt relief with the stone's unchanged state.

"Touch it again! Now!" Her father barked at her.

So Sigrun touched the stone again and again with the same result. Nothing.

Junker Risteard Von-Hislenad narrowed his eyes even further and said to her father, "What is the meaning of this, Miller! Do you seek to mislead me? There will be consequences if you cannot deliver the gold you promised."

Gunther paled. Sigrun could see his mind working on how to save himself from the angry Lord. He squinted at the sun and pronounced, "My, Lord Von-Hislenad, the sun is in the wrong position. If you come back tomorrow, just before sundown, I swear to you the girl will be able to perform her skills."

Junker Risteard Von-Hislenad stared hard at the sweating miller, then he turned to Sigrun. "Is this true girl?"

Sigrun knew she was stalling for time to escape. She curtsied deeply and forced a smile upon her face. "Lord Von-Hislenad, my father tells the truth. My skills are attuned to the rising and the setting sun. Sometimes they work at high noon, but if you come back tomorrow night, I am sure they will work perfectly then." She kept her eyes down and waited, still in a deep curtsy.

Von-Hislenad sniffed then growled, "At least you have manners, girl. Fine, I will be back tomorrow." He turned to Gunther, "If the girl fails again you will suffer."

Gunther gave a sharp nod. "Do not worry, My Lord, she will perform." He glared at his daughter, and Sigrun dreaded the wrath of her father when the Junker left.

Her mother patted her daughters' hand.

Von-Hislenad clicked his fingers once more and the driver collected the cross and returned the box to the top of the carriage. "Right. Tomorrow evening, just before sundown. *Be ready.*" He spun on his heel. Strode over to the carriage, and climbed in. The driver gave Sigrun a pitying look, which made her feel furious inside, then he clucked at the horses and the carriage started moving. Risteard Von-

Hislenad stared straight ahead, not glancing at them.

Nadja put her arm around Sigrun's shoulders and started to pull her inside, but Gunther had other ideas. He grabbed his daughter's arm and ripped her from her mother's grasp. "You seek to defy me! I will show you the error of your ways." He threw her onto the ground and started to take off his belt.

Nadja leapt at him and pleaded, "Gunther! No! Risteard Von-Hislenad will not like it if you damage her."

Her father stood there, trembling in fury. The need to hurt her glowed out of his eyes, and Sigrun felt such a profound sadness that tears swept down her face and she sobbed. For a moment, the father she used to know glimmered under the surface, but then the illusion was gone, replaced with this hard shell of a man who restrung his belt in agitation. "Wife, you are right. Sigrun, you will spend the night in the root cellar. Tomorrow I will do more than beat you if you fail to impress Junker Von-Hislenad."

Sigrun struggled as he father laid hands on her again and dragged her over to the cellar door. "No. Father, no. Please don't do this to me."

He looked at her and simply said, "It is already done." Then he pushed her into the darkness of the cellar and locked it.

Sigrun beat at the door above her head until her right hand was bloody, washing away the potion. Her hand started to tingle again until she placed her left hand over it, subduing the magic. Sigrun sat down on a pack of potatoes and did the only thing she could: she prayed until she fell asleep.

Someone was listening to Sigrun's prayers that night. He sent an angel to watch over her until dawn, keeping her healthy and warm. Sigrun woke, curiously refreshed and aware of what she had to do next. She sat still and cleared her mind, meditating all day, stopping only to eat the food that Nadja pushed through the tiny window close to the house.

When the time came for Junker Risteard Von-Hislenad to come back, Sigrun poured the last of the potion onto her hand and waited for the numbing to begin. Soon, her father unlocked the doors and pulled her out. Even though the sun was setting, the light was still too bright for Sigrun's eyes. They started to water and spill onto her cheeks; she absently wiped her face with her right hand, smearing the potion.

Von-Hislenad's carriage drove up to the mill and stopped. Once again, he was immaculately dressed, not a hair out of place, and dust billowed around them as he got out.

"Bring the cross." He commanded, his voice sending shivers down Sigrun's spine. The same driver as before placed the box in front of her and opened it. "Now, girl. Show me your skills. I do not have all night. Remember, if you fail to impress me, I will cut off your father's hand."

Gunther paled. That was not part of the deal he had made.

Sigrun swallowed hard, her stomach a hard ball. She reached for the cross, increasingly alarmed by the feeling returning to her hand. The one she had numbed was now tingling, as if the potion was never applied; her tears had washed it away.

Just as she was about to touch the cross, sealing her own fate to Junker Risteard Von-Hislenad, a strong male voice sharply shouted, "Stop!"

A light started to glow in front of Sigrun, which grew bigger and brighter until all had to cover their eyes or risk going blind. When the spots cleared from their eyes, an angel with large, midnight wings stood tall and proud. A steel sword was strapped to the angel's belt while his breastplate gleamed gold. "By the command of God, this girl is to come with me. You shalt not have her or her power, Junker Risteard Von-Hislenad."

Everyone had fallen to their knees in the presence of the angel. The angel turned to Sigrun and held out his hand. Sigrun noticed that his fingers were very long and, when she touched him, his skin was smooth. The angel pulled her closer to him and held onto her tightly. He snapped his wings together and then they were gone.

Suddenly, Sigrun was airborne, her hair streamed out behind her as the wind pushed her skin tightly against her skull. The ground receded quickly, and she started to panic as they got higher and higher. Sigrun started to wriggle uncomfortably and cling tighter to the angel who held her.

"Relax and enjoy the view. You will not fall, little one," he whispered with a slight chuckle. With those words echoing inside her head, Sigrun found the courage to open her eyes and see the world like a bird does. She felt her whole world changing, opening up something new inside her. No longer would she let anyone step on her, she would be the master of her destiny.

The land looked like a patchwork quilt, all different colored squares sewn together. Clouds streamed by them while birds looked at them strangely, momentarily forgetting to flap their wings and nearly falling from the sky. Soon, though, the journey ended and they descended to the ground, gently alighting in a beautiful garden filled with pear trees.

"Sigrun, you must now make your own way. We have helped you as much as we can; now the rest is up to you. Find your happiness, but be mindful, the greed of man does not ever go away. Lords and Ladies like Junker Risteard Von-Hislenad will always seek to use and abuse you. Be good-hearted but aware. Now, fare thee well."

Sigrun nodded, speechless at the faith God had shown in her. As she curtsied to the being that had helped her change her life, she wondered about her family, mostly her mother, and wept for the loss, for she knew that Von-Hislenad would have made good his promise to chop off her father's hand. After a few moments she wiped her face clean and thanked God for sending the angel. Her stomach growled and she realized that it was in the middle of the night.

Sigrun walked over to one of the pear trees and reached for one of the sweet, supple fruits. She took only one, and when that was finished, she looked around for a place to sleep. Only finding a bush, she curled up under it and slept the hardest she had slept in a very long time.

Sigrun woke to a foot gently prodding her.

Quickly sitting up in fright, not noticing the twigs in her hair or the dirt stains on her clothes, Sigrun stared into a pair of green eyes. Blond hair, loosely tied back in a rough crop, framed the face. A week's worth of stubble graced the man's chin and Sigrun felt her stomach clench at the sight of him. Her mouth went dry and she had no words to say. She was trapped. The man smiled at her and held out his hand. She hesitated, remembering the angel's words.

"I will not hurt you." It was his tone, soft yet commanding, that helped her make up her mind. Sigrun carefully placed her left hand into his, which he used to pull her up gently.

"Now, who do we have here?" His voice was like honey, it slid over her skin and she wanted to hear more.

He was dressed like a lord and he spoke like one of the nobility, so she addressed him accordingly, "I am Sigrun, My Lord."

The man raised an eyebrow. "Just Sigrun?"

"Yes, My Lord."

He laughed. "Very well, *just Sigrun*, come and tell me why you are in my father's gardens."

He took her arm and tucked it into his and she felt a bond between them. It grew stronger each second. Sigrun knew he could feel it, too, and was puzzled as to why she felt this way.

"That is a strange story, and I do not know if I can trust you yet. Apologies, My Lord."

The man shook his head, amused. "You do not think you can trust your Prince?"

Sigrun felt the world go out from under her feet. She was in the Royal Gardens of Kassel, and she had just insulted Prince Alarik.

He took one look at her face and instantly told her, "Do not be alarmed, Sigrun, I know you meant no offense. I will not take your head for an imagined slight. I am sure you have your reasons for silence."

Relief flooded her body and she put away the words of the angel, for now, and followed Alarik into a pavilion set for breakfast. The Prince hustled over to a chair and pulled it out for her. Sigrun had never seen so much food and finery. She caressed the red, wooden chair with her hand; this could feed her family for two years.

"Now, Sigrun, talk to me."

And the two of them talked. They talked for hours, breakfast turning into midday meal, then into dinner. Finally a servant came looking for Prince Alarik and he felt strangely loathe at letting her go. He insisted she have a room in the castle so he could find out the tale of how she came to be in the garden.

Weeks passed and they grew closer. This was the first time that Sigrun had ever really felt happy. Alarik never yelled at her or became impatient. At first, she was wary and froze up when he was around her. Gradually, her feelings thawed and she allowed herself to be happy.

One day while they were out in the garden, Alarik couldn't contain himself any longer.

"This is madness. I burn for you, Sigrun. You are all I think about. My father has given me some advice. Either I send you away or I ask you to be my wife—and I can't bear to send you away."

She was momentarily speechless; she had hoped he felt the same as her but never felt she was good enough for the Prince. "Alarik, what about your station? You father won't allow you to marry a miller's daughter. It just is not right." Sigrun turned her head away as she spoke the words that broke her heart.

He turned and grabbed a pear off the tree—a beautiful pear that reminded her of how she arrived in the Royal Garden and of the angel's words. He knelt in front of Sigrun, whose heart was in her throat. He looked up at her with his emerald eyes, so strange for a Hessen man but wonderful to look at. "Sigrun, will you please be my wife. My father has given his blessing; he, too, once felt that way, but he has seen the goodness that shines so bright within you and has come to think of you as his kin." He offered her the pear and her pulse leapt.

She took the pear with trembling hands and, feeling overwhelmed with that knowledge, nodded.

Alarik shouted and grabbed her and held her against him. He cupped her face and gently kissed her lips. Love filled her being; she had never felt this way before.

Sigrun knew it was time to tell him the truth and to show him her power. "Alarik, I must tell you something."

She pulled him to their pavilion and seated him before her. He gazed at her with a questioning stare. Sigrun bit her fingertip and started to pace slightly. A few times she stopped and opened her mouth, but nothing came out.

Alarik started to grow alarmed. He caught her hand and pulled her against him. "Sigrun, my love, nothing you have to say will ever change my opinion of you. Now, please, just tell me what you need to."

A bright feeling welled up inside her and she suddenly felt better. It would be better to just show him and go from there. She reached for the pear he had given her and carefully placed her right hand against it. Before his eyes, the pear turned to solid gold. He quickly glanced at her, then the pear, then back at her. Curiously, though, he didn't look panicked—just intrigued.

"That is why I was in the Royal Gardens. I had fled my home when my father tried to sell me to a Junker. One of God's angels brought me here, and that was when you found me."

She watched him carefully, looking for signs of the greed she had seen in Von-Hislenad's eyes.

He reached over and touched the pear, carefully picking it up. "How did you learn to do this?"

She shrugged. "It is something I have always been able to do. I can control it more now than when I was a child."

He grinned at her. "You must have Midas's royal blood flowing through your veins. I had wondered why you never touched anything with your right hand. I thought you might have been lame in that hand, but never this."

Sigrun pushed to see if he meant to now use her. "When will you want me to start turning things into gold for you?"

Her prince grew still and silent. He let go of the golden pear and sighed. "I do not want to use your gift, Sigrun. That is yours and yours alone. If you want to turn things to gold, then do so, but I am not going to ask you to. God has given me something to cherish in this life—and that is you. I wanted you before I knew your gift."

Sigrun felt so happy she could burst; she threw her arms around his neck and held him tight.

"We need to fix it so you can touch me with that hand, though. If you touch me, will I turn into gold?"

Sigrun stopped and considered it; she had never turned a human into gold before. "I don't know. I have never turned a living being to gold before."

He nodded, and the matter was forgotten as he swept her away to tell his father the news that they were to marry. All embraced Sigrun, for they could see the goodness she radiated.

It was a whirlwind of activity, the engagement, the wedding, and then the wedding night. As a gift, Alarik had found a priest to bless some silver, silk gloves. They controlled her gift so she could finally touch things with both hands; it was wonderful to be able to reach for her husband and not have to worry. She finally learnt the pleasure that touch could bring.

Sigrun was in the chapel, praying. In under a year, she had gone from being sold to a cruel man to finding the love of her life. Her hand moved to her stomach;

she had fallen pregnant on her wedding night, and now there was new life growing inside of her.

She heard shouts and heavy running footsteps. One of the guards burst into the chapel, looking frantically for her. "My Lady, please you must come with me. There is danger here, the King..." He stopped and glanced away.

She held her stomach protectively. "The King, what?"

The guard looked at her with tears in his eyes. "The King is dead, my Lady."

She felt like someone had taken all the air from the room. "Dead. How can he be dead?"

The guard reached for her and gently pulled her behind him as they left the chapel. "The Prince.. No the new King will explain." He drew his sword and looked each way for enemies; though he found none, they moved as fast as they could to the Royal Suite where Alarik was waiting for them.

His face lit up with relief when he saw her, and he roughly embraced her, his shoulders shuddering. "My father..."

She reached up and smoothed his hair. "I know. How?"

He pulled away and crossed to the table in the middle of the room. He threaded his hands through his hair and breathed, "It was an assassin. He took the dart that was meant for me." Grief tore through his voice and, unnoticed by him, tears ran unchecked. "The assassin meant for me to die, and instead they got my father. I was running late from the stables. I had a council meeting with the local minor lords, and father went in my stead. That... that was when the assassin struck."

Sigrun felt the baby kick and rubbed her belly. Tears pricked her eyes and she let herself feel the grief for a moment.

"Did you get the assassin?" She asked suddenly, the walls of the Royal Suite closing in on her.

Alarik nodded.

"Yes. We have him and I will make him tell me who hired him."

There was a knock on the door. Three sharp raps followed by a long rap. Alarik nodded to the guard and Commander of the Guard, Junker Gerhard Von-Rymand, walked into the room.

He was a tall man with greying hair. He snapped to attention and held his helmet under his arm. "Your Majesty. The castle is secure, the assassin is in the dungeon now, and we have placed the King in the chapel."

Alarik looked overwhelmed at the thought of being King. Sigrun took his hand and together they held on to each other for dear life.

Events took on a life of their own after that. The funeral of the old King and the coronation of the new one was a combined affair. All Junkers were required to attend and pledge fealty to the new King and Queen, and Sigrun was stunned to learn how many Lords and Ladies there were in Hessen.

Envoys from Europe arrived and expressed their condolences while watching like predators. It was after one such Envoy from Britain that Sigrun felt fear for the first time in a year. The next Junker to be called was none other than Junker Risteard Von-Hislenad.

He strode up the throne way and bowed low. "Your Majesty, please accept my sympathies for the loss of your father, our great King." Alarik nodded, his face kept smooth by experience. Sigrun held herself still while he spoke, and when Von-Hislenad took in her delicate state, he shot her a look of hatred and envy. "Congratulations on your marriage your Majesties. You must be thanking God for the day she fell into your hands, My Lord."

Alarik stiffened at the Junker's words. "I don't know what you mean, Junker, but I am indeed grateful my wife came into my life when she did." He made a small gesture to the Master of Ceremonies to continue. "Now, My Lord, I look forward to seeing you in the council chamber at another point. We must keep going now."

Risteard Von-Hislenad bowed again and spoke his fealty then backed away the required ten steps before striding off.

Sigrun started to shake as she remembered the look on Risteard's face. She had embarrassed him and she knew he would make her pay somehow. She was intensely thankful for the silk gloves she wore, for her hands had started tingling again and a great pressure was building up inside.

Hours later, in the privacy of her room, she laid hands on any object she could to relieve the pressure. Soon all that wasn't too valuable was solid gold and thrown about the place.

When Alarik entered he was stunned to find his queen asleep on the chair and gold everywhere. He gathered her up in his arms and gently placed her on the bed, covering her with a bed sheet. Then he set to getting rid of the gold from her room so no one would suspect her.

It was a few days later that the winds of war reached their shores. Alarik was called by treaty to help defend the neighboring Principality. The couple spent the time they had left curled up together and making plans. He told her stories of the times he had with his father in the forest, of the small hunting lodge that must still be there deep in the Royal Forest. They talked about the birth of the babe and how she was to send a messenger the moment it was born. They talked until Sigrun fell asleep in his arms.

In the morning, he was gone.

Sigrun wandered the halls of the castle, lonely and slightly scared. Her baby was due any time now and she had no close friends, no family. She found herself drawn to the chapel. It defined sacredness, and Sigrun always felt at peace when she was there. She prayed for her husband to be safe, she prayed her baby would be healthy. She prayed till the first contraction hit and pain consumed her.

Soon, she was surrounded by midwives and was poked and prodded. Stripped of her clothes apart from her shift and gloves, Sigrun was told to walk, told to sit, told when to push. It was one of the worst pains she had ever experienced, and she bit down on a strap of leather and grunted at every contraction; each time she thought she had a handle on it, along came another one, and it started all over again. Sweat soaked her body while she breathed through the latest round of tightening. Her damp hair had been tied back with a cord, and one of the midwives made her lie down on the bed.

She poked her head in between Sigrun's legs and looked up excited. "Not long now, Your Majesty. Soon you will have a baby to hold. Now I want you to start pushing when I say."

Sigrun nodded even though she was exhausted.

"Now push!" Sigrun bore down and pushed until she was told to stop.

"Excellent, now get ready." Sigrun waited.

"Push." She bore down for longer this time, until finally, ten minutes later after one last mighty push, a squeal was heard and the women cheered as one.

As a bloody baby was placed on her chest, sobs burst out of the exhausted woman and she tenderly stroked her child's head. Its eyes opened and, seeing they were such a clear green, she laughed. Sheer exhaustion prevented her from lifting the baby to determine its sex, so she turned to one of the midwives and asked, "Is it a boy or a girl?"

The midwife smiled in delight. "Congratulations, your Majesty, it is a healthy little boy. We have an Heir!"

Sigrun smiled; Alarik would be happy. She would write to him as soon as she could to let him know. The women bustled about, taking the child to clean and bundle him. Soon, both mother and son were clean, doctored, and resting in the Queen's bed. Sigrun had never felt this way about anything one or anything before. An intense love filled her entire being for this little human. He was perfectly formed, chubby in all the right places. A shock of hair graced his head, and he watched her even as they struggled with the feeding.

"I will protect you with everything I have." The boy burped and fell asleep, safe against his mother's breast.

The news spread quickly and Sigrun was grateful for her confinement period. She wrote letters of thanks and accepted invitations for when confinement was over. The first letter she wrote was to King Alarik, informing him of the birth of their healthy boy, sending it out with the fastest messenger.

The messenger was instructed to make haste, but when he passed an inn near the city of Frankenburg, he decided to have one round of ale and a bit of a gamble. Unbeknownst to him, while he had passed out, his satchel had been searched and letter exchanged with a forgery. He continued his journey and found the King in his encampment. "My King, I bring news!"

King Alarik looked up, his face filled with hope. The messenger gave the King his letter and was confused when his face crumpled and sadness filled his eyes. Surely the King should have been happy at the announcement of a healthy boy heir.

"Sit, eat, and sleep. I would have you take back my reply urgently on the morrow." The King took his leave and wrote out a long letter to his loving wife, whom he missed each day.

On the journey back, the messenger stopped at the same inn to drink and gamble. Once again, letters were switched and the messenger, still none the wiser, went on to the castle.

Sigrun, her face glowing and her body plump from feeding her son, reached eagerly for a letter but the messenger only had a letter for the Commander of the Guard, Junker Gerhard Von-Rymand.

The man's face paled and he took a small step back.

"What is it? What does my husband say?" Sigrun demanded.

Von-Rymand cleared his throat a few times, his eyes filled with sadness and anger. "Nothing to worry about, your Majesty, it is just about matters of state. Now I must go about my duties."

He bowed to the young Queen and made his way to the chapel and railed against the King who would order his own wife and child's killing. What had happened to the King he loved?

Gerhard Von-Rymand sat in the back pew. He hadn't been in here for an age; he had given up on God when his wife died. What was he to do? He had to send the Queen away for her own safety. He bowed his head and felt a presence lay their hand over his. He quickly looked up and into the eyes of an angel.

The timeless beauty that graced these creatures struck everyone voiceless the first time they saw them.

The angel smiled and said, "Your plan is a good one. I will help you. Go, kill a doe, and cut out the tongue and eyes and place them into a box. This keeps to the message. Tell the Queen that the King has ordered her away for her own safety, and she will know where to go. Do not tell her what the message said."

Von-Rymand nodded, relieved he wouldn't have to kill the young woman he had grown to respect.

The next morning, the General told the Queen that she was being moved to the forest for the time being. There had been threats against her and the child, and he would send for her the moment it was safe. Sigrun felt he was hiding something from her but didn't press it.

She commanded her maids to make sure to pack the chest by the bed. The chest was special: to the ordinary onlooker it was filled with wooden coins, but to her, it was a godsend. When the need to release her skills came upon her, she reached for a coin and released it into that. She now had a personal fortune hidden away for just this occasion of need.

Sigrun gathered her son and stood looking about her rooms. For some reason, she felt it would be a long time before she came back.

"Your Majesty. We are ready to go," her maid called from the doorway.

She nodded and followed the woman to where the carriage waited for them. The journey to the forest was long and a touch boring. All she could see were the trees and dirt of the forest floor. Sigrun loved being out here, though. She remembered the stories her husband had told her about his adventures in this place.

When they suddenly stopped, her maid poked her head out the window—and then quickly pulled it back in, white as a sheet.

"What is the matter? What is out there?" Sigrun demanded, worried for her child. What if it were brigands?

The maid shook her head and with glassy eyes told her, "There's an angel in the road, your Majesty."

Sigrun's head flew up; she gathered her sleeping son and, ignoring the calling of her maid, was out the carriage and onto the road.

The angel was the same one who had brought her to her husband's kingdom. "Well met, Queen Sigrun. If you want to live, you must listen carefully. You must take your son and walk till you have to stop. There will be a cottage there, which will be your new home until the King returns from war. You will not let anyone come into the cottage, and no one apart from your son will enter unless they say the password, which, if you come closer, I shall tell you..."

Sigrun stepped so close to the angel she was touching him. He bent down and whispered words into her ear. She leapt back shocked at what he had said.

The angel smiled, "We have a sense of humor, too. Now, your belongings have been brought to the cottage. Say farewell to your people and go." The angel then flicked out his massive wings and launched himself upwards. And then he was gone.

Her maid begged her to come back to the palace but Sigrun heeded the angel's word. She whispered a brief 'thank you' to her maid as they embraced, and then she curtsied to Junker Gerhard Von-Rymand. He swept both her and her son in a embrace that surprised them both.

As Sigrun and her son walked, she talked and sang. They walked until the sky grew dark and it started to get cold. Animal noises started to scare her, and when she felt she couldn't walk any further, she all but bumped into a cottage.

The grey stone walls were almost as thick as the castle's walls, the windows wide yet clear. A small garden was all she could see in the growing darkness, so she and her son went inside.

Just like the angel said all her belongings were in place and ready for use. She placed her son into his bassinet and stripped off her sweat- and dirt-streaked clothes. Filling a small basin of water, she washed quickly and changed into new clothes. Next, she washed her son, and soon both of them were clean and ready to eat. Sigrun found the evening meal already prepared on the fire when she arrived. The cottage looked like the one her husband had described in great detail. She felt closer to him now than she had in months, and she hoped he would come for her soon.

The war lasted two years, but it was finally over and he was going home. King Alarik was alarmed. He had not had any letters for two years from the Queen. In fact, no one mentioned her in his presence at all. Letters came from Junker Von-Rymand about the running of his country, the state of the finances, and the comings and goings of the other Junkers, but never any from Sigrun. Today he would see his wife and son, and then she could tell him why she had stopped writing.

Von-Rymand was not looking forward to seeing his King. How could he look him in the eyes with the same respect he had before. The King had asked him to do a despicable act and, while he dodged the act itself, the fact he had been asked rankled him. Horns sounded at the gates and the cheers started. Kassel welcomed its King home in style.

Von-Rymand stood at the top of the steps of the palace and bowed to his King. Alarik looked older, his face worn. He had been tested and had won. He could see him looking around, searching for somebody. He stepped forward and bowed, "Your Majesty, welcome home."

Alarik frowned and demanded, "Where are my wife and child?"

Von-Rymand paled and gestured for silence. "Come with me, your Majesty, there are affairs of state that need your attention."

The King was very confused and worried. What wasn't he tell him?

"Commander—" the King started but was cut off abruptly.

"Not here, Your Majesty. Come with me."

Alarik followed Von-Rymand through the castle till they reached a room that

Alarik knew to be Von-Ryman's personal quarters. The Commander ushered the King in and then just glared at him.

Alarik took a step back and looked around wondering why he was being treated like he had done something wrong. He was exhausted to the bone, and his greatest wish was to finally meet his son. "What is the meaning of this Junker? Where are my wife and child?"

Von-Rymand turned and walked to his desk. He fumbled with it for a moment until his fingers grazed the hidden switch. A draw popped open and he reached in and pulled out a box. He strode back to the King and thrust it into his hands.

"Here is what you seek, my King."

Alarik looked down confused. A horrid smell was emanating from the carved box. He flicked the clasp and gasped, dropping the box. The King pulled his sword and went for the throat of his once most-trusted adviser. An emaciated eye had rolled out of the box—staring at them with its withered gaze.

"What have you done?" Alarik felt rage consume him, that couldn't be his wife's eyeball. He would not accept that.

Von-Rymand's throat convulsively swallowed, he backed up against the wall as best as he could to get away from the sword pressed tightly to his throat. "I only followed your orders, My King. You ordered the Queen and your son dead after his birth."

The news speared through Alarik and he pressed harder, drawing blood, which trickled down the man's throat. "I have never ordered my family dead. You lie!"

Tears welled up unnoticed, and that was what convinced Von-Rymand his King was telling the truth.

"My King, wait! Please wait. I fear there has been a deception here. I can prove it," he pleaded, trying to get through the King's grief and rage. His pleas proved effective, as the King withdrew his sword and removed his arm. The Commander took gasping breaths and steadied himself against the wall for a moment.

"Proof? What proof have you of these terrible lies?" Alarik spat, his eyes still crazy.

Von-Rymand quickly went to the same hidden drawer and withdrew sheets of paper, letters that the king had written and he had saved. He silently handed them to his Lord and waited.

Alarik quickly read them and frowned. He dropped his sword and gripped the last page; his face turned white, and he slowly sank to his knees. "I did not write these. I swear to you, these were not my instructions."

The Commander told him about how the Queen had given birth to a healthy boy and that they had been doing fine until he had received those letters. The King started to sob and Von-Rymand quickly told him. "My King. Please, still your grief. Now that I know you did not order the deaths of your family, I can now safely unburden myself. The Queen still lives; the child as well. I disobeyed your letters and hid them away."

The King's head snapped up and he repeated, "The Queen still lives? The Queen and my child are alive?"

The Commander nodded. "I couldn't kill them, My King. I just couldn't do it. I killed a hart and put its eyes and tongue in the box, thinking you had gone mad."

Alarik jumped to his feet. He grabbed Von-Rymand and hugged him hard. "God bless your honorable heart. You will never want for anything, Junker. Where did you hide them?"

The Junker's heart finally lifted after two years. "In the Royal Forest, My King." Alarik started to run off when the Commander called to him, "I never told her, my King. She thinks you ordered her to safety."

Alarik pressed his fist to his heart in thanks and ran down the hall. He burst out of the castle doors and yelled for his horse. He had a wife and child to find.

The angel followed the King and knew it was time to let him know who was behind the contrivances of these events. He waited until the King had stopped for water then showed himself.

Alarik had been sitting quietly, waiting for his horse to finish drinking so he could continue his search. It had been two days since he had returned home, and he still couldn't find his family. He was staring at nothing and then light filled the clearing—and when he could see again, an angel stood there in front of him.

"Your Majesty. It is time you learned the truth. Many things have happened to you over the years and it is all because of one man. The good is that you met your wife; the bad is that you lost your father, were deceived with wrong letters, and you nearly lost your family. He has chased your wife for many years now, thinking that he could get his hands on her gift, but in the end decided to have her killed. If he couldn't have her then no one would."

The King stood up and asked, "Who did this? How can I get my family back? I have been praying to God so hard to help me find them."

The angel nodded, "He has heard your prayers and your wife's prayers. He is fond of her and holds her in high esteem and has decided to grant you both your wishes. If you follow this path for two more days you will come across a small cottage. Your family will be there. Do not deviate from the path.

"As to whom your enemy is, it is none of than the Junker Risteard Von-Hislenad. He was behind the assassination of your father, which was meant for you, and all else that followed."

The King sank to his knees once more in the last two days and wept tears of joy. "Thank you, thank you, my Lord angel."

The angel came closer and waved his thanks away. "Do not thank me, your Majesty, thank God. When you come to the cottage make sure you utter these words..." he whispered into the King's ear words that made him gasp with shock.

The angel grinned with mirth; he loved having fun with the mortals. "Now go."

The King nodded and jumped into the saddle and rode the path the angel pointed out and he knew he wouldn't ever get off the path until he found his family.

It had been two years since she had been sent into hiding. Sigrun was tired of waiting. Her son was now walking and starting to form sentences. She prayed everyday that the war was over and she could take her son home.

"Mama, noise," her son said as he toddled over to her and pulled her skirt.

Sigrun stopped cleaning and listened to what her son was trying to tell her. In her daydreams, she hadn't noticed knocking on the door. She dropped her cloth in fear and excitement. Was that him? Was it finally time to come home? She ran through the cottage and pressed herself against the door breathing heavily, remembering the angel's warning not to open the door.

"OPEN THE DOOR!" A male voice shouted; it was deeply familiar.

Sigrun's heart quickened as she shouted back through the door, "I cannot open the door; first, say the words!"

There was a whoop of joy from outside then the voice shouted, "OPEN THE GODDAMN DOOR!"

Sigrun reached for the door handle, which suddenly appeared, and flung the door open.

There he stood. The object of her dreams for two years. A little older and less carefree ,but it was Alarik, her love. They stood there, staring at each other, then rushed into the other's arms at the same time.

Alarik kissed her all over her face and she started crying and thanking God and his angels.

She still wore her gloves, the silk smooth against his skin, cooling and heating at the same time.

They were lost in each other until a small voice called out, "Mama?"

Breaking apart, Sigrun took Alarik's hand and pulled him in. "Come meet your son."

The council was assembled and the Junkers were waiting for their King to arrive. Everyone wanted to know why they had been summoned to court. They didn't have long to wait, however, before the doors flung open and a herald proclaimed, "His Majesty, King Alarik and Her Majesty Queen Sigrun."

The murmur died down as the royal couple strode into the council room.

Sigrun scanned the Junkers' eyes and found confirmation in what her husband had told her. Risteard Von-Hislenad's face was white with suppressed rage at her survival. His hands gripped the table and his eyes moved about seeking an exit.

King Alarik motioned to his guard and more men came into the room keeping guard at different sections throughout the room.

An outcry arose as armed soldiers glared at all the Lords.

"Your Majesty, what is the meaning of this?" one brave Lord asked in indignation.

The King looked over the Lords from his place on the dais, making sure to catch the eyes of everyone.

"My Junkers, we have a traitor in our midst. Someone in this very room assassinated my father, tried to kill the Queen and my son, and tried to blacken my name with murder."

At once, voices rose and exclamations were to be heard throughout the room.

The King Held up his hand and the talking stopped. "We know who the traitor is, and now we want everyone to know who he is, too."

Junker Von-Kislle stood up. "Who is it?"

Alarik motioned towards Sigrun. "My Queen will point him out, as he has done the most harm to her."

All eyes flashed towards Sigrun and she calmly pointed to Risteard Von-Hislenad.

Von-Hislenad stood up, his face now red, and spat, "What? You would trust the word of this miller's daughter over the word of a Junker? What nonsense?"

The man standing next to him turned around and backhanded him. Von-Hislenad twisted as he felt to the floor. "That is our Queen you are speaking of."

Von-Hislenad got up; spit hung from his chin and blood streamed down his cheek.

The King stood up and told the Lords. "I trust the word of God, whom through his messengers alerted me to the actions of Risteard Von-Hislenad. Now, Guards, apprehend him and take him to the dungeon. I shall decide his fate later."

The guards all descended on Risteard Von-Hislenad and dragged him out kicking and screaming, his perfect hair all messed up.

Turning back to his Lords, the King smiled.

"Now that that is out of the way, we have also gathered here to proclaim a holiday for the return of our Queen and the birth of our son. Celebrate and be merry."

A cheer went up and everyone praised the Good King and Queen of Hessen.

In the dungeons, a shadow walked. No one saw her and, even if they did, no one would care. This was the first time she had been here, and it was going to be the last. She knew she had to do something to punish that man for his actions. Killing him would be a blessing. She knew he wouldn't fear that. God had spoken to her and told her that while he was a God of peace, he was also the God of retribution. Finding the right cell, she stopped and considered what she was planning. Taking a breath, Sigrun opened the door, revealing Von-Hislenad upon the raised, stone that served as a bed.

He stood up when he saw her, and his face twisted with hate. "YOU! You stupid whore! If only you had done what you were told, I wouldn't be here now." He sneered at her lack of reaction. "I cut off your father's hands you know. Then I burned the mill down." He came closer to her not noticing that she wasn't wearing her gloves. "But, you want to know the best part? You want to know what I did to your mother?"

Sigrun reached out before he could tell her and touched the bare skin on his face with her right hand. A surge went through her, echoing her pain and loss, amplifying her skill.

One touch and that was it. The gold started at his face and turned everything to gold, including his clothes. The slow spread scared her, but it was for the best. He screamed and screamed yet the gold still kept coming. Then it reached his jaw, and the screaming stopped. Soon, there was no human part left and only a statue of gold in the cell.

Sigrun looked closely at the statue and was satisfied. Justice had been served, and now she and Alarik could live happily ever after.

TARRAN JONES works at Collins Booksellers Edwardstown. She lives in Adelaide, Australia with her partner and young daughter. Tarran has been in the book industry selling other people's books for over 10 years and thought it was about time she started thinking about her own. She has finished her first novel *Stones of Power* and is now writing the second. Tarran has previously written articles, reviews and blog posts for her bookstore's blog and has written a great many short stories and one unpublished novella. She has had three short stories published online and was a finalist in the Australian Literature Review short story competition for one of her works. She loves writing all kinds of spec fiction and thinks that it fires up the imagination. Gardening is one of Tarran's passions and when she isn't writing she can be found out in the vegetable garden talking to the plants.

LINKS

https://twitter.com/CastleBookE

Tall

by Jason Kimble

ELSIE knew what she was looking for, but when you got right down to it, she figured she might as well be that tumbleweed stumbling along across her path: she should give up and wander about forever, knowing what she wanted but, without any sort of aim, never getting it. She sipped at the dregs of her water skin. Not much left there; what remained stopped refreshing quite a long time ago.

Wasn't like there was much choice, though. Either she tracked down Oakley, or there likely as not wouldn't be a home to which she could return. Elsie hooked the water skin back onto her belt, flipped her long, black braid behind her again, and set foot to the path. When there weren't any more choices, even the bad ones were better than sitting on a rock and drying up under the miserable sun.

At least there was the fruit. Elsie took a big bite out of one of the green apples she'd stocked up on at the last tree. By the time she finished, her hand was sticky with juice, but her stomach was done fighting to eat its way out from inside her. Elsie dug into the core until she'd grabbed all the seeds. The empty core she dropped by the roadside. The seeds she balled up in her fist, then threw them hard as she could, yelling "Jonny grow!"

Even if Elsie could get away with skipping the Seeder rite (Lord knew there wasn't another soul around here), it seemed lazy and ungracious, and Elsie'd been raised to better than that. Say what you wanted about the Seeders, when a soul was wandering about trying not to fall over starving, and dead tired like Elsie, running across a random fruit tree made you happy to put up with a few preachy folk in tin pot caps. And if saying a couple silly words and tossing seeds made them satisfied, well, there were worse prices a person might have to pay for a meal.

Could always be worse. Pacos' Fall was only a score or so miles north. Nothing grew there. Heck, it was one of the few places where even Seeder trees couldn't take root. So, hot and tired and thirsty as she might be, Elsie still reckoned this path was better than none. The sun was finally setting; the heat would be gone with it. 'Course, night brought a whole 'nother set of problems. Elsie licked fruit juice from her fingers—noticing how all the sun had made her skin even darker and redder than normal—then picked up her pace and hoped she could find some good cover for the night.

Elsie gasped herself awake when the half-moon was straight overhead. Her harsh breath burned in her nose, heart thumped away in her ears, drowning out the cicadas. Why, she couldn't tell you. She pulled her knees up to her chest and breathed easy. Eventually. By the time she could smell the jasmine, it wasn't just cicadas making noise. She thought at first it must be some kind of goat, but there wasn't no denying what it really sounded like.

There was a baby crying.

Elsie stood up from the blanket. Way her blood was racing, she didn't need a cover to keep warm right about now. She brushed off her skirt, just to get a second to pull herself together, catch the last bit of her breath trying to run off without her. Sure enough, there was the baby, crawling out of the tall grass. When he saw her, he quieted right up. She knew little babies didn't smile, but she could swear this one did. Like he knew her. He looked at her with those bright eyes and flashed an even bigger toothy grin.

Elsie wanted to reach down and grab back that blanket again, but she knew there wasn't that kind of time. Whether newborns smiled or not, she'd never seen a one had teeth to do any smiling.

She tried to smile again, to keep it docile and calm, but it already knew. The baby's smile fell into a mean, angry frown, then it started crying again, kicking and carrying on. Elsie backed away, never once taking her eyes off it. She heard a sound like branches breaking in a million pieces, smelled horseflesh mixed in with the jasmine. Watched that baby stand itself up, growing wider, darker, longer.

The body skinnied up, but all over with wiry muscle. Legs grew scales, feet curled to talons. Fingers grew together, wings sprouted. And its face grew out into a snout like a dog or a—no, closest thing Elsie could think of was a horse. But no horse she ever tended had eyes so bloodshot, and she was sure there wasn't a horse alive with the razor teeth she saw when it opened its mouth to shriek like the devil.

Then she finally had the good sense to run.

She couldn't feel her legs at first, didn't catch her feet pounding the ground. It was like she was flying, only she wasn't. But the leed chasing her was. Just as the nerves in her legs caught up to her—the muscles in her thighs burning—she felt the brush of extra wind at her back. Elsie dove. Tall grass sliced at her hands, a rock dug into her left knee. Talons clacked just behind her ears and the leed shrieked again when it missed.

Elsie whipped her head up, catching the back of the leed swooping up. The front horse-hooves pedaled in the wind and it was already turning for another pass. Wasn't nowhere out here to hide. Just a lot of sharp, tall grass and a bunch of rocks not big enough for even a badger to hide behind. Running was a fool's move.

Grabbing the biggest stone in reach, Elsie stood up. The leed was diving again, nostrils flaring wide. Its backend shifted forward, moving the talons front for tearing her to bits—but that meant it had to spread its wings, slow down. Just enough to give a girl the chance to take aim.

The rock thunked square center of the leed's horse head, and the monster fell short. Elsie ran left while the hooves and claws scrambled for footing. It fell sideways, one wing flapping up like a hooked bluegill tail.

Elsie barely had time to pick up a second rock, though, before the leed had itself righted. Moonlight streaked on its face, and not a hint of scratch. Something whirled behind its eyes. She could have sworn the baby's voice was back, giggling. It lowered its front feet to the ground, stomping the earth, shaking its head. Elsie's legs tensed, though she knew there wasn't nowhere to run. Still, she tensed, and spied the leed doing the same, muscles in its shoulders lifting the horse legs even as they spread out the wings.

The leap, when it came, was a beaut. Front legs bent and shoved off like they were spring-loaded. Bird legs pushed forward, claws dug in the ground for better traction. And the wings: one huge flap of them seemed to catch up all the air there was. Sure, it was hard-bent to eat her up, but Elsie couldn't help but notice how so many parts that shouldn't ever be put together worked like it was the most natural thing in the world.

Thankfully, that wasn't the last thing Elsie thought. Instead, she got to wonder how that leap suddenly stopped in mid-air, the leed thrown wild like an invisible hand smacked it aside. It took an extra second to register the echo of the gunshot and the whiff of powder in the air.

This time, the leed was bleeding when it righted itself. Small rivers of moonlit red split and met on the way down from the front right shoulder to the hoof. The leed stood on its bird legs, staring at the wound for a titch, then growling as it looked across Elsie.

"Hurts, yeah? You want more, you just come right ahead."

Elsie turned to see the woman who spoke. Her hair was unkempt and frazzled, her clothes smeared with dirt, frayed at the edges. But her ebony skin shone at her cheeks, and her eyes were clear, sighting along the length of her rifle, no shake or shiver but a dead lock on the beastie. The leed shuffled to the left, toward Elsie, but the rifle followed, and the leed knew it. It growled again, but all that did was draw a crooked-tooth grin from the woman.

A gust of wind wanted to knock Elsie off her pins as the leed took off. She ducked on instinct, but it wheeled around and flew off the other way.

"That's it!" the woman called after it. "You head back East where you belong, damnation. We've had enough of your kind!"

One last shriek quivered through the tall grass, then it was just Elsie and her savior. The woman leaned the gun barrel against her shoulder and Elsie smiled, ignoring the aches all over her body.

"Here I was looking for you, and you went and found me," Elsie said. She walked up, hand forward to shake, adding "Thank you so much. I can't believe it: Oakley here and in person."

Oakley laughed, a cackle that ran just as many shivers down Elsie's spine as the crying from the leed had. The girl's hand fell at the sound, and she stopped short, staring, until the cackle finally subsided and Oakley cocked her head.

"Nothing doing, girl. Oakley's been dead and gone for damn near a Vanwink."

With that, not-Oakley turned and headed off. She walked with a limp, favored her right leg, but she moved fast, no doubt about it. She left Elsie standing in the night air, jasmine and horseflesh and gunpowder scents mixed and stinging her nose.

"Hey," Elsie called, her body deciding maybe it was a good idea not to stand still, better idea not to be alone out here. "Wait for me!"

"You gonna ask, or you gonna just stare at it the rest of your life?" not-Oakley said. They'd been walking near an hour in silence. No sign of the leed. Not that Elsie would have noticed, her eyes wandering back to look at the club foot every few minutes. That is, when she wasn't looking at the gun.

"Wasn't an accident," the woman responded without Elsie managing to speak. "Born this way. Got the foot same time I got the hair and the skin and all the other parts."

"Does it … is there pain?" Elsie managed, weakly.

"Walk enough, any foot's gonna pain you," was all the answer the woman was willing to give. She smiled without looking to Elsie. "So, now that you're talking, you got a name, or maybe I should just call you leedbait?"

Elsie flushed.

"Elsie, ma'am. Elsie Winston."

Now the woman looked, though she didn't slow. Elsie had a cramp in one leg, but she tried not to limp for fear it might look like she was mocking the club foot.

"That the name you were born with?"

The flush deepened, and Elsie's eyes fell to the ground.

"I ain't got no Injun name, if that's what you're asking, ma'am," she muttered.

Not-Oakley harrumphed, then said, "I was ready to ask you if maybe you were a half-blood, but I ain't never known a self-respecting Nuwuvi would let another call her Injun, let alone call herself one. Adopted, then?"

"Yes'm."

"Sue," not-Oakley said. "You keep calling me ma'am, and I'm gonna wither up here and blow away. Name's Sue—Slue-foot, if you're the right folk."

Elsie stopped walking. It took a few long, limpy steps for Sue to notice. Then she stopped and turned around, cocked her head and waved the girl on.

"We ain't got time for waiting around in the middle of the night, girl."

"But…" Elsie started walking again, but she kept having to check the ground for her footing; she felt a little light-headed. "But you're dead."

A quick bark of a laugh. "You should pay more attention, girl. Oakley's dead. I'm alive as it gets. Aim to keep it that way, too. This way."

Slue-foot Sue pointed to a Seeder grove in sight now. They should be safe there; wasn't much malice could last long in a blessed spot like that.

"I know the story, though," Elsie insisted. "Everyone knows the story. Slue-foot Sue died. Pacs are always singing the song, 'bout how Pacos Bill had to do her in himself to keep her from suffering and—"

"—and who do you suppose told the 'Pacs'?" Sue asked, sneering at the last word.

"I … well, I suppose Pacos Bill would have, wouldn't he?"

"There you go, then," Sue returned, as if that was all the answer Elsie needed.

Elsie opened her mouth to respond, then closed it. They walked on in silence a ways—'cept for the cicada buzz, which got louder as they closed in on the grove. Elsie opened her mouth again, and again she couldn't make words turn up for the event. Sue let out a heavy breath, then stomped her foot, turning on Elsie. She walked right up, though Elsie's height meant Sue had to crane her neck to look her in the eye.

"Big as you are, way you threw that rock at the leed, I could have sworn you had more gumption than this."

Elsie took a step back. Sue closed the gap again.

"Look at you, full up with questions and can't bring yourself to ask a single one."

Shaking her head, Sue made a brisk pace toward the grove again. Wasn't much longer before they were there. A dozen fruit trees surrounded by a brush fence. Sue hopped it like it wasn't there. Elsie, a good head and a half taller though she was, caught her knee on the post and toppled to the dirt when she tried to do the same. Least it was good Seeder loam, not hard like the rest of the dirt around here. Still, she'd rather taste some of the apples off the nearest tree than the soil they were growing in. As Elsie tried to rub the grit from her mouth, she looked up to where Sue stood above her, offering a hand up. She took it, and the older woman yanked her to her feet quick and sure.

"Well, you ain't gonna ask questions, then I will. Why were you out here baiting leeds looking for Oakley?"

Sue patted Elsie on the arm, then brushed herself off again and headed deeper into the grove. The moon was starting to set, and Elsie figured the dew would be following shortly. She jogged to catch up.

"My town, we're set up in the shadow of the Big Bones. Keep clear of them most of the time, but a body can't help to notice ox ribs the size of a redwood, you know? Scary when I was little, but I got so I'd look to those bones and feel safe. Town founders was sent by Bunyan himself, paid them to tend to the mess and keep the ground sacred and the like. You oughta feel safe, giant on your side, right?"

Sue let up. She leaned her rifle against a tree, reached up and snagged an apple where it hung low. She sat next to the rifle as she bit into the pale green fruit, nodding for Elsie to take the tree opposite.

"But then a few months ago, couple Pacs hit town. That wasn't nothing new in itself. They're rowdy, sure, but like everybody else, our town pays them right and they keep wrangling the twisters, and that's a kind of scary but safe, too.

"Only this time, they got it in their head to go have themselves a good time at the Big Bones. Got there same time as a couple of giants out on pilgrimage. There was...well, neither side went home with as many as they came with, let's say."

"But someone went home on each side?" Elsie could tell by her tone that Sue got the gist. "Means they'll be coming back, then, both of them."

"Just a few of each was likely to have torn up half the town," the girl kept on. "Was some kind of miracle only a dozen townsfolk was busted up real bad. Those two come back, each one full force? Ain't gonna be a town left, and those ox bones gonna have a lot more littler bones to keep them company."

Sue swallowed the mouthful of apple she had.

"So you need Oakley's gun...?"

"It's all we could think of," Elsie said, wanting like nothing else not to be so frantic. "We ain't fighters, none of us, but my folks, they thought: Oakley's gun don't miss. Someone with that, well, you could keep the strays off the town, let the fight do what it wants and maybe walk out of it alive."

Sue frowned, finishing off the apple. As she dug the seeds out of the core, she asked, "So the white folk who raised you decided they'd send a girl out alone into wasteland chasing after a gun for them."

Elsie's face burned, but she forced herself to speak. "They went to the town, and they thought, well, no one there had blazed a trail since we was founded, and we had giant footprints to follow. But I had savage blood, might keep me going longer than civilized folk."

Calling out the Seeder blessing, Sue tossed her handful of seeds into the darkness.

"They tell you that a lot, did they? About your savage blood?"

Elsie looked down at the ground. She didn't have to answer.

"You ever even met one of these savages you're supposed to be from?"

Now the girl stared at Sue, heartbeat crashing in her ears. "Just thinking about it's like to scare a body to death," she whispered.

Sue tossed the empty apple core to the ground, licking juice from her hands. "Horse pucky," she said. "Ain't nothing more savage about them—and probably a lot more civilized—than there is about the kind of folk that sends a girl to save their yellow butts for them. World ain't changed a bit since I left it, has it?"

Elsie opened her mouth, then stopped. She bit her lip, curiosity and manners having it out in her head. Sue just raised an eyebrow and waited.

"Well?" Sue finally prompted.

"When you left...?" Elsie tried again, but seemed like speech had gone fishing for the day.

Sue snorted, saying, "I know I'm all rough on the edges, but a lady likes to be asked before she tells her tale, you know."

Sue smiled, then started walking again. Two long strides to catch up, and Elsie found her voice.

"I guess I just don't even know where to start. You're just nothing like what I would have thought."

"You thought I was dead. Pretty easy to beat that being alive, I should think," Sue said.

"I mean, besides that. All the stories, and not a one of them said anything about your foot, and nothing whatever about you being a negro, I'm sure of that."

"Pacos Bill can wrangle a twister if he wants to. Ought to figure he's got what it takes to wrestle news to the ground before it spreads that he went and got hitched to a lame negro woman on account of losing a bet."

"He lost a—?"

"They still tell about the fish?"

"The giant catfish you wrangled?" Elsie said. "They say that's when Bill first saw you, riding it down the river, how he knew he had to be with—"

Sue laughed, harsh and loud. Elsie could see where they were headed now: a little log cabin, out here in the middle of nowhere, hid up behind the bushy Seeder grove. Sue hobbled her way to the door, and didn't talk again until they were inside, fire lit while the two women sat at Sue's small table.

"Here's the right of it," Sue finally said, "and unlike that polecat, Bill, I'll even tell you the parts that make me look bad. See, Bill weren't smitten with me, not by a long shot. No, but I took one look at him breaking Widowmaker, and I knew he was my match."

Sue smiled, almost wistful. "Didn't matter what we looked like, we both had it, that fire lets you bend the world the way you need it to be. Same fire that got me sure as tarnation I was gonna land me Pacos Bill and we was gonna be the roughest, toughest couple the world ever did see."

Elsie found herself warming, but didn't catch on she was smiling herself until Sue looked at her, broke things off to start cleaning Oakley's gun.

"When I told Bill that, he laughed in my face. Said wasn't no row you could hoe would make him marry a..." Sue swallowed instead of finishing the sentence, shook her head and managed a pained little smile.

"I wasn't a girl took no, though, and I knew Bill couldn't turn himself down a challenge, so that's what I done. I said 'Bill, you pick any critter you can find, and I can wrangle it, good as you can. Better. And if I can't, I'll be on my way, but if I can, you and me, we're getting hitched.'

"And that's how I got on that giant fish, and sure as shootin', I wrangled that critter faster'n him, just while his good old boys were coming around the bend, and then there wasn't nothing but the ceremony, was there? Well, the ceremony, then the possum-manure groom trying to kill his bride on their honeymoon, then saying he done it for her own good."

Elsie didn't know what to say, though the fact that Sue kept her attention on the rifle helped.

"There's an extra blanket in the chest by the fire," Sue said. "You're welcome to stay the night. Wouldn't do to save you from a leed just to have you eaten up by something else the same night."

The tall girl bit her lip, nodded, and dug out the blanket. In the quiet with the fire snapping, Elsie wondered just why she was here. Would this make her worth something, or would it just be one more "that'll do" from her folks until the next time a body needed someone to take the blame for something gone wrong?

"Well," Elsie said softly the next morning as she finished off the eggs Sue had made her, "if you gave me Oakley's gun, it might hurt the Pacs, and that hurts Bill, right?"

"And helps someone else," Sue said, sitting across the table from Elsie. "How far you come to get this, girl?"

"I...a long way."

"Alone."

"Yes'm."

"A whole town full of folk who filled your head with garbage about what's in your blood. Ain't nothing in your blood, or mine, that ain't in theirs."

Sue gave another snort. "No, that ain't right. 'Cause all of them are cowering in their little houses waiting for the savage to bring 'em back a gun and save 'em all, even though they treated her like she weren't worth the money took to clothe her."

Elsie opened her mouth, closed it again.

"Am I wrong?"

Elsie didn't speak. She thought about the road here, the heat in the day and cold in the night, and the hunger and the dangers like the leed. And there it was, right there, what she'd come looking for, only, did those folk back home deserve it?

"You want to save those folk, do you?" Sue said, gun held out, smug look on her face. Knew she'd made her point. Elsie couldn't say she hadn't. World Elsie knew didn't cotton to her kind—to either of their kind—and she'd spent her whole life learning to keep a clean nose and a shut mouth. Why save folk that would treat a child like that? Raise a body to think she was born a monster? Elsie wasn't no leed.

And maybe that's why she reached out and took the gun. Couldn't help but notice that, for a titch, Sue looked just a mite surprised.

"You've got the right of a lot of things," Elsie said, cradling the rifle in one arm, "but you don't know everything. You can't, not holed up like this, away from the world."

"World's done nothing but hurt me," Sue said, fists on her hips. "You can't tell me it's done better by you."

"Didn't say it did," Elsie answered, turning toward the door.

"You'll up and save them what done you so wrong?"

"Didn't say that, neither," Elsie replied, not looking back. "But what I ain't doing is letting the world alone just because it thinks it's better than me."

Elsie had walked a giant's step before Sue called from the doorway.

"Then why take Oakley's rifle? What are you gonna do, girl?"

Elsie turned around and smiled.

"Don't you worry none, Sue. You'll hear tell of it. You ought to know better'n most: sometimes, no matter how much they don't want to, the story's too good for folk not to tell."

Maybe she was just wishing it, but Elsie thought she saw pride flashing in Sue's eyes for a moment. Then the woman pushed it down, just nodded. "I know those stories get stretched in the telling."

"All the better," Elsie said. "Ain't a good enough story if you know the whole of it, if it's always the same, 'cause then you'd never need to hear it again, would you?"

Elsie nodded back to Sue and, as she turned away for a last time, said, "And I want 'em telling mine for a good while yet."

JASON KIMBLE escaped the arctic climes of Michigan winters for welcoming, sultry Florida. That is, if by "welcoming" you mean "full of retirees who ooze a sense of entitlement," and by "sultry" you mean "grotesquely humid and prone to hurricanes." But it's definitely Florida. Plus: no snow to shovel.

LINKS

http://processwonk.wordpress.com
https://twitter.com/jkasonetc

Princess in Peril

by Shari L. Klase

A DRIENNE huddled tightly in her shell. It enclosed her like iron bars. Anybody looking at Adrienne's enclosure would think it more of a palace when it was, in fact, a castle, but any fortress of safety no matter how large can seem a prison if one is confined to it—even if it is one of your own making.

So Adrienne's was. She was a person destined for suitors. Her kingdom was slowly becoming bankrupt, and gold was desperately needed to sustain it. However, the only way to obtain gold was for her to marry an eligible, rich suitor. Adrienne wanted to follow her heart and marry a man of her own choosing, but alas, that choice was forbidden.

Her kingdom was once rich when ruled by her wise and benevolent father, but is often the case, her father married again, after Adrienne's mother died, to a woman who cared only for the King's riches. Shortly after they married, the King died of a mysterious illness. And when he passed, Adrienne lost her only friend in the palace. Her stepmother made her life miserable by insisting she serve and obey her every whim.

Her stepmother was a sorceress. The Queen tried to hide her enchantments from her subjects to avoid condemnation for witchcraft. She wanted only what could bring herself wealth and happiness but lacked the power of controlling Adrienne's will. She hated Adrienne for her obstinacy. After all, how bad was a loveless marriage? She had entered hers the same and was no worse off for it.

Adrienne tried escaping twice, but she was apprehended and brought back each time. On the third try, she was locked up inside a tower, never to see the light of day until she wed. Her stepmother hired a selfish servant girl to watch over Adrienne until the fated day. So Adrienne hid inside her shell, her eyes wet with tears. No one could see her tears or dared to care because the kingdom was so much more important than the desires of one girl.

Her wedding day dawned clear and bright, but Adrienne was determined not to comply with her stepmother's wishes. She refused to allow the servant girl, Tilly, to even dress her in her elaborate bridal costume. The servant girl was ugly and jealous of Adrienne. She wished with all her heart she could be in her shoes and marry the prince that was preordained for Adrienne.

"You spoiled, selfish, royal rat!" Tilly cried out as Adrienne pulled away and tore a rent in the lovely dress she endeavored to foist over Adrienne's head. "When your mother hears of this, you will be sorry."

"She is not my mother," Adrienne replied. "She is a witch."

"I wish I possessed a witchy mother who would give me a handsome husband and a rich kingdom to rule," Tilly scowled at Adrienne. "Anyway, you have torn the dress and it must be mended. Perhaps, the Queen can talk some sense into you." At that, Tilly stomped out of the tower and locked the door securely behind her.

That would not stop Adrienne from making a last ditch effort to escape her cruel nuptials. She ran to the tower window. Though it was so far down, ivy did creep up the tower walls and she would rather plummet to her death than marry someone she did not love. She hoisted herself out the window and grabbed onto the ivy. She slunk down carefully, the ivy ripping into her tender flesh and leaving a blood stained trail behind her. When she was halfway down, the ivy tore from the walls and she flew into the air and would have toppled to her death; only her stepmother spied her and seeing her plunge, used her powers to transform Adrienne into a bird.

"You wish to fly away. Then, perhaps, you will be better served as a canary," she said mockingly.

"I will fly away and be happy," the canary said joyfully.

"No, you will never be that." She plucked an orange from a nearby tree in her grove and held it in front of the canary. "Into its depths you will hide as you hid in the tower. Yet, surrounded by its sweetness, you will never have a sip of its contents. Perhaps then, you will become more compliant."

Immediately, Adrienne was transported into the center of the orange, where she flapped helplessly at her citrus cage.

"What will you do for a bride?" Tilly asked the Queen, for she had seen the events that passed and was longing to fill Adrienne's place. "If I had been that ungrateful girl, I would have gone to my bridal bed rejoicing."

The Queen looked at the ugly Tilly and frowned. "Yet, what bridegroom would ever smile at your homely face? Well, no matter. You have served me well and deserve a reward. There is no Adrienne here now, so you shall be Adrienne. She waved a hand and Tilly's face became tan and beautiful just like her former mistress. "Now, go and get yourself properly adorned for the wedding," she commanded.

Tilly left happily to obey.

The Queen stroked her chin thoughtfully. "Unfortunately, this spell will not last for when the true Adrienne is released, the false one will turn back into an ugly cow. The kingdom will surely not profit when that happens. Yet, perhaps, a few days trapped will make the real Adrienne more submissive to my wishes."

She placed Adrienne back on the orange tree and left her to her misery. For extra insurance the orange grove was enclosed with an iron fence and locked gate. Inside the enclosure, she placed a snarling dog to guard her prisoner, always one to take precautions.

Meanwhile, the other half of the pair intended for the bridal ceremony, Prince Desire, was just as reluctant to tie the knot as Adrienne. Desire's father, Lord Rondeaux, had grown tired of watching his son drag his feet on the way to the altar. Many girls found Desire—who was as sleek and delicious as Rondeaux was rotund and unappealing—irresistible.

Unfortunately, the prince thought all the girls of his kingdom were boring with their peaches-and-cream complexions and shallow personalities. They didn't think of anything but dresses, dances, and holding parasols over their heads to seal their pasty faces. His fortune was far more alluring to them than any other aspect. When he talked with any of them, they simply said things like "Is that so?" or "very nice" followed by "Is there to be a ball?" or "Is that your carriage?"

"If only I could find a girl who is browned by the sun and cares for the kingdom more than its wealth. She wouldn't care if the 'd' in Desire stood for debt," he sighed. But he didn't really think such a girl existed.

A few days before the intended nuptials, a crate of oranges was sent to Lord Rondeaux from the Witch Queen as a gift. She knew his appetite was immense and he was always longing for new experiences for his palate. Because of this, his weight ballooned so that he had to be hauled about in a wheelchair, which was back-breaking work for his servants. When the oranges arrived, he clapped his hands in glee. He bit into the sweet, succulent fruit and thought it heavenly.

Thinking that his son might be more inclined to wed the princess of the land where such sumptuous fruit flourished, he eagerly summoned Desire to share the oranges with him.

"Taste, my son, and see what sweetness you will experience when you marry into this family."

Desire peeled back the rough orange skin, the color exactly to his liking, and bit into the juicy, sweet meat of the orange. It was unlike anything he sampled before.

"Sweet and tangy," he said to Lord Rondeaux, who was himself devouring oranges. "You say they grow these where my intended bride lives?"

Lord Rondeaux nodded. "I hear the girls are as delectable as the fruit."

"I don't care about other girls, Father, only about the one I am to marry. I am going to bed."

"Sweet dreams," Lord Rondeaux said, orange juice dripping down his chin.

That night Desire dreamt of an enchanted land of orange trees. He plucked one of the fruit and began to peel it but the moment the skin was pierced, a lovely bronze skinned girl appeared.

"Please give me a drink," she pleaded. Desire turned to fill his cask with water from a spring, but when he turned again, in the girl's place was a yellow canary, which flew speedily away. He awoke from his dream with troubled thoughts. Who was the girl? Whomever she was, Desire decided he would marry no one else.

Desire was sure the land of oranges held the secret to finding the girl from his dreams. He would go as his father wished. He would meet the Queen and the Princess—if only to view the orange groves for himself, where the young girl in his dream must surely be.

The next day, he set off on his white steed for the land of orange trees. When he arrived there, the Queen greeted him. Desire recognized in her the same craftiness that the girls of his kingdom displayed when they wished to trap him into marriage.

"It is an honor to meet you, Prince Desire. You must meet my daughter, Adrienne."

"Certainly I shall meet her," he said, suppressing a yawn, "If only I can have another of your delicious oranges while I wait for you to bring her."

"Oranges? Oranges, you say?" she said in alarm, for she immediately ascertained that the Prince might pluck the other Adrienne. Then her jig would be up.

She stroked her chin again. Prince Desire noticed one ugly hair protruding from the chin and grimaced. "Of course you may have oranges but ours are the best in the land and therefore protected. You would not want to be bitten by our guard dog. I will have Adrienne bring you one herself." The witch thought that this gift would certainly seal the deal for the wedding.

But while the evil queen was on her way to find Tilly and instruct her, Desire was on his way to the orange groves. He did not trust the queen and decided he would find oranges on his own accord. Of course, he found a terrifying guard dog blocking his way to the orange grove, as well as a locked gate. Desire did not let these things deter him. He reached in his pocket and drew out the oat cake he had prepared for his journey. He threw it to the dog and immediately it became as gentle as a lamb. The starving dog had not been fed that day and was so thankful for the food, he licked Desire's hand.

The locked gate proved not to be a problem either. When Desire looked at it, he saw the hinges of the gate were very rusty and easily broken. He pushed it aside and walked within the orange grove where he spied the trees. But there were so many and time was fleeting. He needed to pick quickly as he was sure the queen would be back shortly.

He reached up and grabbed three oranges from the tree and placed them in his pockets. At that moment, the Queen arrived and was very angry to see Prince Desire already at the fruit.

"Dog, Dog!" she yelled. "Seize him and hold him for me."

"No," said the dog. "You have not fed me all day and he has been kind to me."

The prince ran for the gate.

"Gate! Gate!" she yelled. "Stop him from leaving,"

"No," the gate answered back. "I won't. You have let me grow rusty, and so I have been broken."

The prince collected his horse and rode away as fast as he could, for he now could see that he was in danger from the Queen.

But after a long gallop he was thirsty and he had to stop. There was no water anywhere. He thought longingly of the oranges in his pocket and removed one from its depths. He did not know whether to wish for a girl or a drink. When he peeled it, there was no girl inside, only an orange. Still, the juicy fruit refreshed him.

Now revived, Desire thought of his dream and this time more sincerely wished for a girl in the orange. Unfortunately, when he unmasked it, there was no girl, only an orange. The first time he was just as satisfied with the fruit, but now he was unhappy with the result. He examined the third fruit and suddenly found it distasteful. If he should peel it and find only orange, it would be the end of all his hopes and dreams. He began to think himself foolish and headed back to the Queen's castle. Perhaps the dream only meant that he was to find the girl in the kingdom where the oranges grew—maybe he was *always* meant to marry the Princess Adrienne.

"I'm sorry if I frightened you," said the Queen upon his return. "I only wanted to tell you that your father had arrived for the wedding, and the feast was being prepared. When I saw you were already in the oranges, I was afraid you would ruin the surprise. The wedding cake was to be topped with lovely, succulent slices of oranges. We have stripped the trees of every last one for the occasion."

Prince Desire fingered the orange left in his pocket. "I'm sorry, I don't care about the oranges any longer. It was a foolish dream that I had that made me want them. A silly dream about yellow birds and an extraordinary girl, but that's over now. Oranges are just oranges."

"Yellow birds?" the Queen asked. Her face paled. "I don't know about them, but my daughter is an extraordinary girl. Though it is bad luck to see her on your wedding day, perhaps if you do, you will see that she is a dream come true. Allow me to summon her."

Desire sighed. "Yes, do summon her. I have had enough of fantasies. I am ready for reality."

But to his surprise, the girl brought before him was his dream girl. Of course, Desire had no way of knowing that Tilly was an imposter in Adrienne's form. He grabbed her hands and pulled her to him.

"May I walk with you? I can't believe that you are real."

Tilly blushed. "I am as real as you want me to be."

Desire looked long and hard at her. "I read a book once about a fairy princess. You are like that princess in the story."

Tilly laughed. "I wouldn't know about that. I never read books."

"Oh," Desire replied disappointedly. "I thought you would. My castle is full of books I would like to share with you."

"Is your castle very large?" Tilly brightened.

Desire studied her. "Yes, I suppose it is. Sometimes, I would like to leave it though and just have adventures."

Tilly laughed. "Isn't living in a rich palace adventure enough for you? I would just spend my days relaxing in luxury." She sighed in anticipation.

Desire sighed as well. "I suppose it would be adventure enough having you for a bride."

Tilly laughed nervously. "I guess I should prepare for our wedding now. I promise you I will be a beautiful ornament for your lovely castle."

Desire startled at her words. "You shall be much more than an ornament to me, dear heart. You will be loved and cherished."

Tilly tittered. "Of course, I only meant that a prince who is a god deserves a goddess by his side."

"I am no god, Adrienne. You will soon see that."

Tilly shrugged. "Someday you will be a King. That's the next best thing."

As Desire was escorted to his room to make preparations, he was deep in thought. Adrienne was not at all as he expected. *Well, that is what comes from weaving delightful visions in your head,* he thought. Adrienne was, after all, just like his dreams in appearance. He sat down sadly beside a handsome mahogany desk, and then realized it was fake. It was a replica. It looked real, though. He poured some water from a pitcher into a glass, but then sat it down. The water seemed uninviting. It was then he remembered the last orange.

He removed the orange from his pocket and sat it upon the table. It was so brilliant it seemed an eternal flame to him. Although he said he didn't care for oranges anymore, this one was different. He could feel the unique quality of it. So he opened it with his fingertips. To his surprise, out popped a canary that hovered over him in desperation.

"Please give me a drink," the canary squeaked. Without a moment's hesitation, Desire raised his glass of water to the canary's beak. It dipped its fluffy head in and swallowed. Desire could see the water cascading down its throat and then suddenly it was not a canary. It was the lovely Adrienne. Yet, how could it be?

"But I just spoke to you and you left to get ready for our wedding," Desire said.

Tears poured from Adrienne's eyes. "It could not be me, sir, who was to marry you, for I will only marry for love. I escaped from my evil stepmother's clutches just so I would not have to marry a Prince Desire from another kingdom who was very rich and would surely save our kingdom. But I could never marry for money."

"You couldn't, Adrienne? You seem so different than the other you I am to marry. Quick! Tell me three things you want more than anything in the world."

"That's easy," Adrienne responded quickly. "To marry for love, to rid the kingdom of my evil stepmother, and to make every day an adventure."

Desire laughed. "I knew it. You are exactly as I dreamed you would be. Dear Adrienne, if you choose to marry me, and only if it is your choice, I will love you with all my heart, deliver you and your kingdom from your stepmother who has held you captive in an orange, and I will make each day of your life a chance for the most delightful happenings you could ever imagine."

Adrienne's heart skipped a beat. "Even though I am pledged to Desire, you are my true desire."

"Yes, Adrienne, and you are mine. Come now, I must make my promise good."

When Adrienne and Desire returned to the wedding hall, instead of another beautiful Adrienne there was an ugly toad named Tilly, croaking her displeasure at any and all who would listen.

"You are a frogmouth," The Queen said, waving her hand, and Tilly turned into a Frogmouth Owl.

Then her eyes turned to Adrienne. "I thought I turned you into a scrumptious cake." Then she saw the truth of the matter as Desire was holding the hand of Adrienne. "Oh, it is of no consequence," she squealed. "I see everything has turned out for the best. You have seen the error of your ways."

"No, I believe we have both seen the error of your ways, you old crow." The next moment the evil Queen was no longer human, but Corvus. For you see, when Desire had lifted the enchantment from Adrienne, he gained some of her captor's powers. And it seemed to him a crow much better suited the Queen.

Adrienne clapped her hands in delight. Desire's father, Lord Rondeaux, was much astounded at all these events that had occurred, but the delicious orange cakes made up for all his discomfort. He was, of course, happy that Desire had finally chosen a bride. Since all the wedding party was present, Desire and Adrienne were wed.

Like two birds of a feather, they flocked together—happily ever after.

S HARI L. KLASE lives in a town on the beautiful Susquehanna River with her artist husband and fellow writer daughter. She also shares her life with an incorrigible corgi named Lucy, who is both inspiration and aggravation in her writing life. She has written over 50 published stories. She loves fairytales because they reinforce the idea of youth in all of us no matter what age we are.

Blood & Water

by Alethea Kontis

L OVE. Love is the reason for many a wonderful and horrible thing. Love was the reason I lived, there in the Deep, in the warm embrace of the ocean where Mother Earth's loins spread and gave birth to the world. Her soul was my soul.

Love is the reason she came to me in the darkness, that brave sea maiden. I remember the taste of her bravery, the euphoric sweetness of her fear. It came to me on wisps of current past the scattered glows of the predators.

The other predators.

Her chest contracted and I felt the sound waves cross the water, heard them with an organ so long unused I had thought it dead.

Help me, she said. I *love him.*

The white stalks of the bloodworms curled about her tail. We had a common purpose, the worms and I. We were both barnacles seeking the same fix, clinging desperately to the soul of the world. Their crimson tips brushed her stomach, her breasts. They could feel it in her, feel her soul in the blood that coursed through her veins. I felt it, too. I yearned for it. A quiet memory waved in the tide.

Patience.

My answer was slow, deliberate. *How much do you love him, little anemone?*

More than life itself, she answered.

She had said the words.

I had not asked her to bring the memories, the pain. There is no time in the Deep, only darkness. I could but guess at how much had passed since those words had been uttered this far down. Until that moment, I had never been sure if the magic would come to me. Those words were the catalyst, the spark that lit the flame.

Flame. Another ancient memory.

The empty vessel that was my body emptied even further. I held my hands out to her breast, and there was light.

I resisted the urge to shut my inner eyelids to it and reveled in the light's painful beauty. It shone beneath her flawless skin like a small sun, bringing me colors...perceptions I had never dared hope to experience again. Slivers of illumination escaped through her gills and glittered down the abalone-lustered scales of her fins. Her hair blossomed in a golden cloud around her perfect face. And her eyes...her eyes were the blue of a sky I had not seen for a very, very long time.

She tilted her head back in surrender and the ball of light floated out of her and into my fingers, thin, white and red-tipped, much as the worms themselves. I cupped her brilliant soul in my palms and felt its power gush through me. So long. So long I had waited for this escape. I had stopped wondering what answer I would give if I should ever hear the words again, ever summon the magic. When the vessel was full, when my dead heart beat again, would I remember? Would I feel remorse? Would I have the strength of will to save her, to turn her away?

You will see him, I told her.

She smiled at me over the pure flame of her soul.

I was a coward.

I pressed her soul into my breast. The moment the light filled me I became her. I could see my body through her eyes—translucent white skin marred by jagged gills, blood-red hair tossed up by the smoky vents and tangling about the worms, black eyes wide, lips parted in ecstasy.

I could see him in the back of her mind, the object of her affection. He was tall and angular, with sealskin hair. There had been a storm and a wreck, and she had saved him. She had dragged him onto a beach and fallen in love with him as she waited for him to open his eyes. She had run her fingers through his hair, touched his face, traced the lines of the crest upon his clothes. He was handsome and different and beautiful. When he awoke, he took her hand in his and smiled with all his heart. And when he kissed her, she knew she would never be able to live a life without him in it.

In that small moment, as the glow of her soul dimmed into me, she told herself it was worth it.

Once the transformation began, the pain pushed all other thoughts out of her head. Water left her as suddenly as her soul had left her, her gills closing up after it. The pressure that filled her chest made her eyes want to pop out. She clamped her mouth shut, instinct telling her that she could no longer breathe her native water. She beat furiously with her tail, fleeing for the surface.

Halfway there, the other pain began. It started at the ends of her fin and spread upwards, like bathing in an oyster garden. The sharpness bit into her, skinning her, slicing her to her very core. Paralyzed, she let her momentum and the pressure in her chest pull her closer to the sky. Part of her hoped she could trust the magic enough to get her there. Part of her didn't care. It wanted to die, and knew it could not.

That price had already been paid.

Her head burst above the waves and she opened her mouth, letting the rest of the water in her escape. Her first full breath of the insubstantial air was like a lungful of jellyfish. She coughed, her upper half now as much in agony as her lower half, not wanting to take that next breath and knowing that she had to.

She lay there on the undulating bed that was once her home and let it heal her. She stared up at the sky until it didn't hurt so much to breathe, until her eyes adjusted, until rough hands plucked her out of the sea.

She was dragged across the deck of a ship much like the one from which she had rescued her lover, right before it had been crushed between the rocks and the sea. The man who had pulled her up clasped her tightly to him. He was covered in hair, more hair than she had ever seen in her life, and in the strangest places. It did not reach the top of his head, but spread down his face and neck and onto his chest. Perhaps it liked this upper world as little as she did and sought a safer, darker haven beneath his clothes. She reached out a hand to touch it, and he spoke to her. The sounds were too high, too light, too short, too loud. She did not understand them. His breath smelled of sardines. She ran a finger through the hair on his face, and he dropped her.

Misery shot through her and she collapsed on the deck. Her hair spilled around her…and her legs. She stared at her new skin. It looked so calm and innocent, but every nerve screamed beneath it. Another man stood before her now, wearing more clothes than the hairy man and shiny things on his ears and around his neck. His bellow was deeper than the first man's but still as coarse and profane, and still foreign to her. He crouched down before her and brushed her hair back from her face. He cooed at her. She touched the bright thing around his neck that twinkled the sun at her, and he grinned. His teeth were flat. She wasn't threatened. Braver now, she pulled at the necklace. He let her slide it over his head and put it around her own neck.

He picked her up and carried her to a place that hid her from the sky and set her somewhere softer than the deck. She liked this place and this man who now worshipped her. He had given her a gift, and now he would take care of her. If only there was a way she could tell him why she was there. She was sure he would help her. Perhaps he could see into her heart and just know.

The man removed his shirt, and she relaxed even more. He wanted to put her at ease. By looking like her, he would make her feel like she belonged. He took off the rest of his clothes and came up beside her. He patted her head, ran his hands down her hair. He touched her breasts, her belly and her legs. Still sensitive, she brushed his hand away. He put it back. She tried to push it away again, but he was stronger.

She frowned. He smiled all those flat teeth at her once more. She wondered if she might have been mistaken. He moaned, parted her knees and entered her.

The misery she had felt before was nothing compared to this anguish. She inhaled the excruciating air and screamed a hoarse cry. She clawed at him, pushed at his weight on top of her, but she could not move him. Agony ripped her body apart again. A tingling sensation washed over her and the light in her eyes began to dim. Somewhere in that darkness, through the pain, she could feel his heartbeat. The emptiness in her cried out. He had something she needed.

She reached up, pulled him to her, and sank her pointed teeth deep into the skin of his neck. She drank him down, consuming his soul, filling the barren places inside her. He collapsed on top of her and still she drank, until there was nothing left.

The door burst open and the hairy man entered. He pulled the naked man off of her. He could tell what the man had done from the blood between her legs. He could tell what she had done from the blood she now licked from her lips.

"Siren," he whispered.

She gasped. In her brain there was an avalanche.

Words flooded her, images and thoughts, smells and sounds. Knowledge. She cried out again and slapped her palms to her head. She had taken the man's soul, and his life right along with it. She watched as the shafts of her golden hair turned deep red, filled with the captain's blood.

The first mate had named her. He knew what she was. She was death, the shark, the thing to fear. She lured men to their graves with her beauty.

In one swift motion, he pulled the knife from his belt. She did not flinch as he approached her. There was nothing left to fear.

The knife swept down and split the captain's throat open, hiding the teethmarks in the cut. He stared deep into her eyes as he pulled a large ruby ring off the dead man's finger and put it on his own. The knife, streaked with what little crimson was left in the captain's body, he brandished at the crowd of men gathered at the door.

"Eddie Lawless, what's goin' on?" the man in front asked. The men behind him whispered low, words like "magic" and "evil" and "witch" catching in her ears.

"It's Lawson, Cooky," the hairy man responded. "Cap'n Lawson. An' don't ye forget it."

"Yessir," the men mumbled. "Yessir, Cap'n."

"Leave me," Lawson ordered.

"But sir, what about Cap'n—"

"*I* am the cap'n," he told them. "Ye can collect the carcass later. Leave me now." He slammed the door in their faces.

The mattress shifted under his weight as he sat down across from her. She did not want to look at him, concentrating instead on the ends of her new hair and the line across the dead man's throat.

Lawson shoved the body onto the floor. "Siren."

She looked up.

"So. Ye can understand me then."

She nodded once.

"Good." He pulled the sheet down and wiped his knife blade with it. "Understand this. I know what ye are, what ye need, and what ye do. If ye do exactly as I tell ye, I won't kill ye."

If she had known how to laugh, she would have. It was unsettling. She knew what laughter was, what caused it and why someone did it, but she didn't have the slightest idea of how to make her body perform such a feat. It was the same with the words—she could understand them, but she couldn't get her tongue around them and speak back. She would have laughed at the thought of this man killing her, for she would have welcomed death. But there was one task she meant to accomplish before that happened. She had to find her lover.

She nodded her head once more.

"Excellent." He left the bed and went to open a trunk on the other side of the room. He rummaged through it for a moment, and then tossed a bundle of burgundy material into her lap. She stared at it, marveling in the slight difference between it and the color of her hair. She reached out and stroked its softness, drawing patterns on it with her finger.

His chuckle brought her out of her state. "Ye 'ave no idea what to do with it, do ye?" He took her by the hand and gently eased her off the bed. "Come on, stand up."

She placed one foot flat on the floor, then the other. Then she pushed up with all her might, locking her knees and propelling herself forward into him.

He caught her before she hit the floor. "Woah. Easy. Ye 'ave to get yer sea legs." He helped her balance enough to stay upright. Surprisingly her feet held her without too much trouble.

"Now," he said, grabbing the bundle off the bed, "ye're lucky I 'ave a daughter an' I'm used to doin' this." He spun her around so that she faced the wall. "Six years ago I only knew 'ow to *undress* a woman." He pulled her hands up above her head and eased the material down around her. He moved her hair to one side so he could button up the back.

"There." He turned her back around. "It's a bit large an' it'll probably be a tad warm. But it'll keep the sun off ye, and the…my…men away from temptation." He looked her up and down. "Not that they'll need much warnin', mind. But ye get enough rum into a man…well…stranger things 'ave 'appened."

He looked down at the former captain's body. "Ye won't need to…eat…again for a while then?"

She shook her head.

"Right. Best if ye only do it when I tell ye." He shoved the knife back into his belt.

Her eyes widened.

"Oh, don't worry," he chuckled. "Ye're aboard a pirate ship, darlin'. If there's one thing we've always got more than our share of, it's blood."

He wasn't wrong.

They encountered a ship three days later. There were blasts from cannons spread amidst the cries of men. She lost her footing when the ship lurched sideways, hooks pulling the losing ship close enough so that men might cross over. She peeked through the windows at the smoke of the guns, swords clashing as the blood flew.

Lawson came back to her room when the battle had died down. He opened the door and threw a man down at her feet. His clothes were ripped and his face was a bloody mess. Gray eyes looked up at her from the red-stained face and filled with terror.

"No…oh, God, no," were the last words he spoke.

His fear was intoxicating.

She closed her eyes when she was finished and let the magic wash over her. It wasn't just the blood she craved; it was everything. She needed the senses and the feelings, the emotions and the pain, the good and the bad. She needed his life—his soul.

Rejuvenated, she tossed her hair back and peered up at Lawson. He cupped her cheek and wiped a spot of blood away from the corner of her mouth. "There's my girl." He threw open the door and kicked the man's body over the threshold. "There's yer cap'n, men," he bellowed. "Seems 'e got into a spot of trouble. Any of ye want the same trouble, just cross me."

Crews were mixed and booty was swapped, and then they were off in search of the next victim.

The second ship they burned. It was spectacular. She ran to the railing and held her hand out to the beautiful, living thing that danced on the sea as it consumed sails and timbers and bodies alike. She had seen candles and lamps, but this was a beast, wild and hot and bright as the sun. Hands grabbed at her clothes to keep her from falling over the rail, and they pinned her down when the magazine finally exploded, taking the rest of that ship's crew with it.

On the third one, she found him.

The battle this time was a long one, and by the time Lawson brought her the captain of the other ship, he was half dead. She drank him anyway. And somewhere in the memories of this man was the someone for whom she had searched.

She gasped when his face came to her. She drew back, her teeth disengaging from her meal, blood running down her chin and staining her dress. This man knew her lover. Not well, but he knew him. She tried to make sense of the jumble of images that flowed through her, but nothing connected. She searched his body for a sign, a hint, something. She found it on the smallest ring he wore, a gold band stamped with the crest she had traced over and over on the beach that day.

When Lawson returned, she pointed at herself and then held up the ring. He smiled and patted her on the head. "O' course ye can keep it, darlin'. Ye can 'ave all the trinkets yer little 'eart desires."

He didn't understand. How would she make him understand? She slid the ring over her red-tipped thumb. She would save it until she thought of a way.

The fourth ship was a long time coming.

She spent most of that time at the bow of the ship. The crew didn't grumble much about having a woman on deck. Most of them apparently didn't consider her a woman. Lawson made it plain that he enjoyed having her there. Word got around about Bloody Captain Lawson and the Siren. They struck fear in the hearts of men and made quite a profit as a result, so if anyone had disagreements, no one made mention of them.

Lawson called her their figurehead. It was an apt description, based on what she had seen on the prows of other ships. She would lean against the rail, arms spread, red hair trailing behind her in the breeze. She liked letting the wind slip through her fingers. It reminded her of home. The currents of air were not that different from the currents of water. Men did not have the freedom of movement that her kind enjoyed, but the principles were the same. They walked among it, breathed it in, let it give them life. It brought sounds and smells to them. They did not see it or think to taste it, but it was always there in them, touching them, surrounding them.

She stood there, day after day, until the salt encrusted her lips and her hair was a burnished orange. What little red appeared in the tips of her fingers had been burned there by the sun. The men avoided her and prayed hard for another ship. They trod lightly around the captain. No one wanted to be the Siren's next meal.

Lawson finally bade her return to the stateroom, and she was too weak to disobey. The table was covered in maps and charts. She walked past them on the way to the bed and glanced down at the area Lawson was plotting. A symbol caught her eye, and she jumped back. She waved at Lawson. She pointed to herself, and to the ring around her thumb. She pointed to herself, and to the same symbol down on the map.

"There?" he asked her. "Ye want to go there? Why?"

She could not answer, so she just kept pointing to herself and the map.

"That's 'ome," Lawson told her, "where Molly is. I promised never to go back until I 'ad a ship full o' riches. She deserves no less." He shook his head. "No, darlin', we can't go there. Not yet."

Frustrated, she closed her eyes. Disjointed thoughts—flashes—skipped through her mind. She tried to remember the man with the ring, tried to bring his soul to the surface. But it had been so long, and she was so weary…and there was a port…

Her eyes snapped open. She moved her finger on the map to an island just off the coast of the country bearing her lover's symbol. She pointed at Lawson, and then stamped her finger back down on the map.

"There? What's there?"

She threw her hands up in exasperation and scanned the room. She held up the medallion of her necklace to him.

"Gold?"

She nodded and kept searching. She found his knife on the table, picked it up, and then shook her head.

"Swords?"

She shook her head again.

"This?" He removed the pistol from his belt and held it out to her. She nodded emphatically.

He cocked his head and grinned. "Siren, if ye're right about this, I'll take ye anywhere in the world." He strode out of the room and hollered to his first mate. "Hard to port, matey!"

"Cap'n?" the first mate asked.

Lawson hooked his thumbs in his belt. "We're goin' 'ome."

The greatest tale of Bloody Lawson and the Siren was the Massacre at Windy Port. Legend had it that their ship, cloaked in dark magic, slipped by the watchmen unnoticed. Once docked, the crew cut a gruesome swath through the town, led by Lawson and his Sea Witch. Lawson brandished a rapier in one hand, a pistol in the other. The Siren, dressed in fine burgundy velvet, marched through town before him, seducing men to their grisly deaths. Her eyes were as black and cold as a shark's, her hair a mass of ebony fire waving about her. They left none living in their wake, took what they wanted, and stole back into the night as invisibly as they had arrived.

Like most legends, not a word of it was true.

They sailed into Windy Port under a royal flag they had appropriated from a previous hunt. They docked without incident, the crew scattering to the winds to pick up intelligence, hefty bar tabs, and the occasional whore.

The moment Lawson set her down on the dock, she fell. The hollowness inside her throbbed. She could not believe anything could have been so still as land. There was no life in it. The air was not strong enough to keep it fluid. It was rock. Still, empty, dead rock. She was but a shell, a humble reconstruction of the world upon which man walked every single day. How did they survive without a connection? She hugged her stomach, doubled up and gagged, only emptiness escaping her dry heaves.

"You okay, honey? Take it easy. It'll pass soon."

The words spoken to her had a cadence she had never heard before, and it surprised her so much she didn't understand them at first. The hands that pulled her hair back away from her face were small and delicate. The woman had on a black dress. Her hair was pinned up on her head and decorated with shiny black beads. She smelled...soft and nice. And she was gentle when she accepted the Siren's embrace.

"It's all right," the woman said as she patted her back. "Everything's going to be all right."

She didn't scream when pointed teeth pierced her flesh.

Everything was going to be just fine.

Suddenly conscious of her appearance, she pulled her dress over her head and began tearing at the woman's clothes. Lawson knelt beside her and motioned for his men to surround them so as not to draw attention to the scene. "Discovered vanity, 'ave we?" he chuckled as he helped her undress the woman's corpse. Once she had changed, the men weighted the body and rolled it into the ocean.

Lawson helped her stand. He tossed a dark cloak about her and covered her hair with its hood. She was glad he didn't force her to wear shoes—it was hard enough enduring this much separation from the water. She didn't know how much more she would be able to bear.

The inn they went to almost pushed her sanity over the edge from sensory overload. The room was filled with people of all shaped and sizes. There were smells from the food, the ale, the dogs in front of the fire, the fire itself. Men and women talked and shouted and joked and laughed. A scrawny youth crawled up beside the dogs at one point and sang for his supper. She was mesmerized. These were so different from the songs of the water, the flash of fish in the currents, the mating of whales in the deep. Some were slow and soft; some were fast and loud. And when the rest of the room joined in, she clapped her hands in merriment.

The crew dropped in one by one to report and consult with Lawson throughout the night. There were nods and low whispers. She watched as papers were signed and money changed hands. Thus Bloody Lawson conquered Windy Port, without ever leaving his seat. When the festivities ended, he paid for his meal, tipped heavily, and left, dragging his cloaked companion behind him. It was the sailors and merchants that returned to their vessels the next morning and found them empty or missing who took their anger out on the citizens of the port. Lawson and his crew were miles away before the massacre even began. Bloody Lawson and the Siren were never heard from again.

Several months later, Edward Malcolm opened a waterfront inn in the capital city named The Sea Lass. He purchased the house next door as well. It had a master suite and a nursery and a very large kitchen that could be used to supplement the inn's in case of overflow. One of the rooms in the house had a door with seven locks. They were installed the day before Molly's return from school.

Molly's homecoming was a grand event. Lawson, now called Edward, had covered every flat surface in the house with sweets and cakes and flowers. He had hired a seamstress to take Molly's measurements for a whole new wardrobe, the only one that didn't seem overly preoccupied with the Prince's upcoming wedding. Paper-wrapped packages of all sizes littered the largest of the tables. A doll and a rose waited on the chair for his princess.

The Siren sat on a stool in the corner, cut off from the sun and the earth, the water and the wind. She waned as she watched the miniature, cherub-faced human run through the door to embrace her father. Her mop of dark brown curls disappeared in her father's coat as she hugged him, right before he picked her up and twirled her around the room. There was something about this strange apparition, this child, and she could not decide what it was.

Molly giggled as she snuggled her doll. She reached out to the rose.

"Be careful," her father warned her.

"Yes, Papa," she said smartly. "I will watch for the pricklies and the thornies." She buried her nose in the crimson petals and took a deep breath. When she opened her eyes, Molly saw the Siren there in the shadows.

The child set her doll down carefully on the table. "Who is she, Papa?" Molly whispered.

"She's..." he started, twisting the ruby ring on his finger. "I saved 'er," he said finally.

"She's so pretty," Molly said. The child came around the table and held the flower out to her. "She's just like the flower."

"Yes," he said. "Just like the rose, Molly. She's got pricklies and thornies, too. You have to be careful around her."

Molly took another step forward, still offering the flower. The Siren took it and grinned, being careful not to show any teeth. Before her father could stop her, Molly launched herself into the Siren's arms.

The child's skin was softer than the woman's at the pier. Her hair smelled of sugar and...something...indescribable. She took another deep breath. There was life within this little bundle, so much life she all but vibrated with it.

Edward wrenched her away. He took her by the arms and held her tightly. He sank down to his knees, so that he could address Molly eye to eye.

"Don't ye *ever* go near 'er again," he said sternly.

"But Papa, she's so sad," Molly cried.

"She is dangerous," he admonished. "Just be a good girl and do as yer papa says."

Molly bowed her head. "Yes, Papa."

"We'll even call 'er Rose, okay? So ye don't forget." Edward chucked her under the chin. "Now, what are ye gonna name yer dolly?"

Molly's eyes brightened again and she rushed back to the table for her doll.

The Siren sunk her nose into the flower and inhaled sugar and sweetness while she watched the child open the rest of her gifts.

That night, as he escorted her to her room, he said to her, "Ye touch my daughter, I'll kill ye." Then he shut the door and turned seven keys in seven locks.

Each day after that was much the same. She was not allowed to leave the house, and the third time Edward caught her staring out the windows, he forbade her that, too. Each night he would take her to her room and give her the same warning about his daughter before turning the seven keys of her prison.

She would sit on her bed and stare into the darkness, wondering what she had done wrong. Had she not given him the riches he desired? Had she not paved the way for him to return home to be with his daughter? She had made him happy— why should she suffer as a result?

She edged closer to the window and watched the moon move across the sky. Somewhere not far, the reflection of that same light was skipping across the waves. Somehow, she would escape from this prison. Someday, seven locks would not hold her.

Every few nights he would bring her someone, long after Molly was asleep. He would wake before the dawn and take the body away. She learned all she could from these poor souls, but it was never enough. They were whores or cheats or liars, people whose absence in some way benefited Edward and whose minds were such a jumble of unreliable information she could never discern anything that could help her.

She waited. She waited while he scolded her every night. She waited as he shoved each of the seven bolts home. She waited as he fed her, sparingly, enough to survive. She waited for him to get comfortable, to slip, to let something get by him.

Like the snitch.

Edward bent over and the unconscious man fell from over his shoulder and onto the bed before her. "Small, but 'e's all ye'll get, understand?"

She opened her mouth, throat contracting. "Yeth," she managed to say.

"Good. 'Cause if ye touch my daughter, I'll kill ye." He shut the door. She counted slowly to seven before pulling the man into her lap and feasting.

Her heart pounded with a foreign pulse.

He was there.

Her lover.

He was everywhere inside this man's head. He sat at the head of a table, talking sternly to a group of older men dressed in black. He sat in a large chair at the end of a hallway. He rode a horse down the path through the garden and along the beach. He rode in a carriage beside a beautiful, golden-haired maid and people threw flowers in the street before them.

He was the Prince.

And he was getting married in a week.

Edward fell ill the next day. He did not come to let her out of her cell. The first two days of isolation weren't bad. The third day, the snitch's body began to smell. The fourth day, she tried to feed off it again and gagged. There had not been much in him to begin with, and whatever was left in him now was gelled and rancid. The fifth day, she began to shake. She pounded on the door and the walls and the window until the skin of her fists shed. The sixth day, she began to scream. It came out of her as a long, keening wail. It echoed her hunger, her desperation, her emptiness. Her voice gave out as the sun rose on the seventh day, his wedding day.

She spent the hours curled up against the door, hoping to hear something. Any sign of movement at all would have been welcomed. She played with the ends of her faded hair, teasing them in and out between her toes. The shadows moved, lengthened, and eventually, the sun's light died. Her hopes went right along with it. She placed her palm flat on the door beside her head.

It was warm.

She closed her eyes and could feel the energy radiating from the other side. She could hear small, shallow breaths. She could taste sugar on the air.

Molly.

She knocked two times on the door.

"Rose?" the tiny voice called hesitantly.

She knocked two times again.

"Daddy's sick and he had to go away." Skirts rustled against the floorboards. "I'm lonely. Are you lonely?"

Two knocks.

"Do you want to play with my dolly?"

She spread her fingers against the door. "Yeth," she croaked.

The warmth faded, and there were sounds of a heavy chair being dragged across the floor. One, two, three, four, five, six, seven keys were all slowly turned in their locks. The chair was pushed aside, and the door opened.

Molly flew into her arms, the momentum pushing her back onto the bed in her weakened state. She cradled the frightened child in her arms, felt the porcelain head of her dolly poking into her side. She soaked up the child's energy, willing it into her empty body. She bent her head and smelled the sweetness of her. She nuzzled her nose in the softness of her, like burrowing into the petals of a newly-opened flower.

She shouldn't. She knew she shouldn't, but he had caused her so much pain, and she had nothing left to lose.

Molly screamed and fought, but every bit of her gave the Siren the strength to hold her down, to fill the abyss inside her with this soul of pure innocence. It was so beautiful. The sensations did not wait until she was finished. They exploded into her mind every second. There was fear—yes, sweet fear—but then came sadness and betrayal. There was happiness and laugher, anger and tears, but most importantly, she finally realized the *whys*. She knew why a person felt joy and why they felt pain. She learned the elation of seeing something for the very first time, and the despair in losing it.

Loss.

She knew now what she had been dealing out all this time. There was no way she could have ever known the impact of death without knowing what it was like to live a life. The weight of all the souls she had consumed pressed heavily upon her. She learned consequences. She realized that the things she did affected people other than the person she was killing. She understood that all the pain she had felt before was nothing to the pain these people would feel for the rest of their lives. She felt regret, and love.

Love.

It spread through her. Unconditional love tickled her down to the red tips of her fingers and toes. Love was trust. Love was faith. Love was believing in the impossible. The rainbow of Molly's soul filled her with love until the last drop. She held Molly's limp body in her arms...and she laughed.

She laughed and laughed, her voice echoing through the dark, vacant house. She laughed until she cried, tears flowing unchecked down her cheeks. She cried for Molly, for all of them. She cried for all the things she had done. She cried for herself, for everything she had lost, for nothing.

Or was it nothing?

She had to hurry. She had to leave this place and never come back. She gently laid Molly's body out on the bed and curled her arm around her dolly. She smoothed back the dark curls and kissed her forehead. She covered herself in the black cloak and fled into the night.

She was glad again to be in the air and running over the earth, despite what little support they gave her. She followed her heart and the dim memories of the snitch straight to the castle gates.

She strode up to the guards there and threw her hood back. Those that knew of her let her pass; those that didn't quickly learned.

The myriad halls and stairs and rooms made the castle a giant labyrinth, but she knew where she was going. Up and up and up...to the balcony suites of the Prince's bedchamber. She did not stop until she was at the foot of his bed, staring down at his sleeping body. She wanted to shake him awake, wanted to explain everything to him, wanted to scream her love for him to the rafters.

But she couldn't.

If he awoke now, he would know what she had become. He would see the evil inside of her, the mark of it in her hair and on her skin. She had saved his life, true, but how many others had she taken on her path back to him? With love came regret. She knew what she had to do. She knew that the only thing she had to offer him now was her absence. If she could just touch him one more time...she reached out a hand to him and stopped herself.

No.

It would not stop at a touch, she knew that from what had happened with Molly. She could never be with him, truly be with him, because eventually she would consume him. His soul was not bright enough for her to survive alone outside it, nor was it strong enough to sustain him once she had consumed it. If she stayed beside him, it would mean his death.

She was a monster.

She forced her hand back to herself and placed it over her heart. She hoped that it spoke enough in the silence for him to hear it, to feel how much she loved him. If it had been water and not air between them, she knew he would have felt it.

He stirred and opened his eyes.

She gave herself one moment, one tiny, blessed moment of looking into his eyes before she turned and ran.

She tripped down the stairs and cut her feet on the stones. The cloak caught on something and she unfastened it. She was sure that soon they would come for her. They would hunt her like the beast she was. She tasted the tears that streamed down her face and knew there was only one refuge.

The cold beach sand kissed her feet like a prayer. The salty spray mixed with her tears, chasing them away. The first tiny wave reached up and licked her toes. Waves rumbled in a cadence she had almost forgotten how to translate.

Come, they pulled.

Home, they crashed.

She took small steps forward. The sand slipped out from beneath her if she stayed too long. The force of the waves pushed her backwards in opposition to the call she felt.

Come, they pulled.

She stumbled, and the tide ripped her sideways along the beach. Gasping, she managed to regain her footing and continue walking out to sea. The current grabbed at her clothes, and she tore them off. The tips of her hair mingled with the foam. Flotsam swirled around her waist.

Home, they crashed.

She walked until the undertow took her and dragged her out to sea.

I lost her sometime before that, back when the moon shone off her white skin and blood red hair. But I didn't have to live inside her anymore to know where she was headed.

She would grab the first sharp object she found—maybe a crab's claw or a clam's shell—and rip gills into herself so that the water could flow through her again. The first one might have been straight, but the rest would be ragged and flawed. She would make her way to the Deep, her body drawn to the neverending call of the soul of the world. She would make a home there among the bloodworms and the warm vents and the other predators.

She would take her love and regret with her. She would heal in the balm of the ocean, away from the complexities of mortal life. She would tell herself that if the day came, if the words were spoken and the magic came to her, she would turn them away. She would not let evil back into the world. The suffering would end with her. She would stew in the self-affliction until it became a dim memory, tucked away in the recesses of her mind like sight and sound, air and fire. Time would fade her lover's face, his name into nothing, and then time itself would melt into darkness. She would ebb and flow and never die.

And when that day did come, ages and ages from now, she would choose the light. She would choose the escape. She would let the evil out one last time just to feel it all again, to live.

As I had.

Strong arms wrapped around me, brushing my satin bedclothes against the small jagged scars on either side of my chest. I leaned back against him, feeling his heartbeat through his chest.

"I just had the strangest dream," he said. I felt his deep voice rumble through the skin of my back. "You came to me while I lay in bed, only your hair was red and your skin was different. You stared at me like you wanted to say something, and then you ran. You looked so...sad."

He turned me around to face him. "The day you saved me was the happiest day of my life. And this day should be the happiest day of yours. Don't be sad."

I smiled and shook my head.

"Good." He kissed me then, long and slow and deep. He hugged me tightly before pulling away. "Come back to bed?"

"Yeth," I whispered, the words still foreign to my tongue. He kissed me once more and left me. I looked out over the moonlit water once more and said my goodbyes before following him, my prince, my soulmate, my love.

Love.

It was the reason I lived.

ALETHEA KONTIS is a princess, a fairy godmother, and a geek. She's also a New York Times bestselling author. She's known for screwing up the alphabet, scolding vampire hunters, and ranting about fairy tales on YouTube.

Her published works include: *The Wonderland Alphabet* (with Janet K. Lee), *Diary of a Mad Scientist Garden Gnome* (with Janet K. Lee), the AlphaOops series (with Bob Kolar), the Woodcutter Sisters fairytale series, the Sand Point romance novel series, and *The Dark-Hunter Companion* (with Sherrilyn Kenyon). Her short fiction, essays, and poetry have appeared in a myriad of anthologies and magazines.

Her YA fairytale novel, *Enchanted*, won the Gelett Burgess Children's Book Award in 2012, was nominated for the Audie Award in 2013, and was selected for World Book Night in 2014. Both *Enchanted* and its sequel, *Hero*, were nominated for the Andre Norton Award.

Born in Burlington, Vermont, Alethea currently lives and writes in Florida, on the Space Coast. She makes the best baklava you've ever tasted and sleeps with a teddy bear named Charlie.

LINKS

http://www.aletheakontis.com
https://twitter.com/aletheakontis

Steadfast

by Hannah Lesniak

T HE Toymaker fastened me atop a glass mirror. That was perfectly fine at
the time. I was of the Old Regime. We were not made to move, but instead
created to bear beauty in our form and figure. The Toymaker breathed life
into us all, and, in deeming us worthy, gave us to children to make them joyous. But
the Old Regime has passed away, leaving only fragments behind. I am the last
fragment in my house.

I am the only so-called Toy to stand resolute. I can see and hear and sometimes
breathe a word or two from my china lips, but never can I move my form. I see the
other Toys, modern with bright paint and some with buttons and gadgets and
Toymaker knows what else. I watch them converse and roam around the nursery
every night when the Little People and Big People are asleep and cannot witness their
revelry. But I can never join them. Even if I could move, I am attached to my
mirror.

I suppose that is punishment enough for being beautiful—my slender, pastel-
painted china body, stuck en pointe, one arm gracefully stretched toward the room,
the other above my head. My neck is bent to gaze into my mirror and see the world
reflected within and without. I have existed for so long that my mirror can no longer
prick my curiosity in showing me places and people outside the house. Even when
my mirror does not reveal the secrets of the outside world, I tire of gazing upon myself.
Stuck and stiff for so long, I have come to despise my reflection. How I would give
anything to move and look out the window across the room. But I can only see a

shadow, a reflection of what is there. And the Toys around me, their substance lacks.

Especially Jack.

The arrogance that rolls off of him is akin to swine eager to show off new muck. He was one of the first to be made in the New Regime and he never lets anyone forget. The Toymaker made the New Regime with parts that move, music playful to the ear, and, on the whole, not easily broken. He made them with everything that I am not. All together, they are far superior Toys for Little Jimmy and his elder sister Little Elaine. And I am beholden to most of them. Blonde Doll, whose waist is small— even smaller than mine—visits me sometimes, and I enjoy her boisterous chatter and gossip. Racecars rush around the room at night, but are ever so polite as to not get into anyone's way. Plush, furry ones wrestle on the rug and the Dolls cuddle with them when they are worn out. They brought me joy in the early days of the New Regime, but now I watch them with envy. Jack, however, sees himself above them all.

He sees himself as one of two Regimes. Last of the Old and First of the New. But me, I am the Last. He comes to me every night to sing my praises and mark me as his own. Of course, the only tune he knows is that of his own box, and I became weary of it after our first meeting. Little Jimmy winds his box and sings some nonsense about a monkey and a weasel and a bush. Little Jimmy's particular song is still better than the drivel that Jack contrives. I never waste my Toymaker breath on Jack. This is probably not the best tactic, as he has taken it as leave to do little else but call on me every evening. I pay him no attention.

The first time Jack came to my balcony, I was intrigued. Here was a Toy whose magical gift was animation in form and not just in spirit. He must be doubly blessed. I glanced down at my mirror. How would my magic mirror portray him if he got close enough? He sprung, and his box landed next to me.

♫ "Way up on a balcony here
I find you all alone.
Would I like to visit you,
Girl! To me unknown." ♫

My eyes shot up. Words, singing words at that, fell from his mouth like so many copper pennies from a rich man's purse, startled me. Was there so much more Toymaker's breath in him? Had I grown so old as to have lost all of mine? Was he triply blessed?

♫ "I'm quite a good companion here
Never shall I annoy
What do you say, pretty girl?
Jack! At your employ." ♫

The bells on his jester's cap tinkled as he gave me a bow. Then he took my outstretched hand and kissed it.

♫ "Take my hand. I'll adulate you,

Make it my sole duty.
You'll have no despair again.
Name! What's yours, beauty?" ♫

He looked at me expectedly, his fat rubbery fingers grasping my small china ones.

How was he able to move about so, voice himself, and wave his blessings around as if it was nothing?

His face inched closer to mine, a heavy drawl lingering upon his words:
♫ "Why have you gone silently now.
What could be the reason?
That's how all the maidens are:
Blush! Show your treason." ♫

I cast my eyes downward towards my glass. His form was certainly there. His springy body, wrapped in velvet and topped with a gossamer ruff beneath his chin, was housed inside a bright red box with yellow polka dots. His nose jutted out of his almost human face, taking up most of it. His smile took up the rest of him.

But then my mirror peeled away the veil of appearances and living beneath Jack's material was—nothing. A coiling blackness lingered, like the first fruits of a dream not to be remembered after the dawning. I had never seen anything like it.

♫ "Come now, beauty. What do you say?
All I need's a signal.
Show me your eyes, fancy girl.
Come! You shall mingle." ♫

I stared at his essence in the mirror. How could Toymaker create such a being? Toys were filled with wonder, hope, and sparkling like gleams in the eyes of children. Where was this Toy's gleam? He had Toymaker's breath and animation, but no essence. For all of his blessings, this Toy was cursed. And he was about to curse me with his presence.

♫ "Never have I acquainted one
Who cannot speak her name.
You are quite odd, maybe deaf.
Yes! You'll be my dame." ♫

He devoured me with his dark plastic eyes. His gaze flickered across my china form, the blackness of his false eyes gorging on my visage. Watching him from the corner of my vision, I saw his smile widen. I dropped my eyes to my mirror: a sea of ink and fog.

♫ "Ah, perhaps you can't even talk,
That would be an outrage.
That's okay I'll declare all.
Girl! You, I'll engage." ♫

He jabbered on and I beheld an abyss slinking out of my mirror I wished him gone.

Jack's tune haunts me even when he's not speaking. Sometimes my own thoughts fit its pattern; had I a heart, the rhythm of it would surely be discordant with each china beat of it...

♫ "He comes to me every night.
His twisted song, he cries.
Darkness lurks upon the notes.
Evil! Ballad of lies." ♫

Big Johnny teaches Little Jimmy how to stoke a fire this morning. Little Jimmy is only eight, and a rude little one, if ever I saw. And I have seen many. He throws Toys around without a care and often abuses them.

I am blessed to be in the Toy house on the stand, forbidden to touch because I am what they call an Antique. Little Susan, who is Big Susan now, often tickles me with a bunch of feathers. I long for the chance to be held, even if for a moment. When she was Little Susan, she would stare at me in wonder and Big Laura would let her take me down to play.

My mirror would gleam with their shimmer and spark, carnations dancing in fields of starlight. As time passes, these lights of People dim and stutter. I have never understood what causes their lights to die. Perhaps it is simply the passing of their lives, like Toymaker's breath passing through Toys. All I know is that the light in Toys reflects the light of People. At least it once did.

This New Regime casts shadows, pale and flickering, like the firelight from the fireplace next to my house. Toys used to shine inside, like the silver liquid that Big Johnny and Little Jimmy are melting over the fire. We used to bubble with joy like that liquid. We swirled and shimmered, bursting with children's laughter. Children would pour themselves into us, like Big Johnny and little Jimmy are pouring the liquid into boxes.

People are quite interesting in their habits. I watch them in the room, coming and going, bringing and taking, living and leaving. The passage of time takes them where it may, while I linger here in a constant cycle of remembrance and forgetting. With a jester of a Toy to keep me company. Perhaps one day I'll shatter.

Big Johnny and Little Jimmy take the boxes apart at the table in the middle of the room. If they leave what they are working on, Toys will be able to see what it is.

Then Jack will come and drone to me about it. Every now and again, something new will come into the room, sometimes a Toy of the New Regime, sometimes tools of People. Other times, Toys or furniture gets taken or moved around. Such events are monumental. Toys watch during the day and gossip at night. Blond Doll will dance over to my house and babble to me after Jack leaves. We watch him bounce around the room from Toy to Toy, checking and inspecting, poking and controlling. I only know what the other Toys think about him through Blonde Doll. He was the first before me. While the others will not visit me, I watch them in my mirror and see their fear billow and smoke alongside their slight respect for Jack. Me, they ignore, the diamond in the castle tower. I have never met any of the others except through my mirror. I watch them and wonder when I'll leave. Immortality leaves much to be desired, especially when nothing is as it once was.

Big Johnny and Little Jimmy work at the table. The light in the room dims as the slow setting of the sun slips past the windows. Jack will come when the clock strikes midnight and profane my china with rubber, my ears with wasted Toymaker's breath, and my mirror with his empty presence.

My melancholy and age makes me Time's fool. I am so near my end. I have to be. Shattering is desirable with my life behind me. Granted, I could just breathe my life away, give away my last Toymaker's breath to the air, but I have lived my life in immobility, in calm poised reverence. Shattering would be so much more preferable, exciting. Shattering would mark my life not a complete waste.

Figures on the table catch my eye. What are they?

Beautiful.

The word comes from my mirror, awe-filled and silver-toned. Yet the glass shows only me. Did I drop that word? Surely not. I would not waste what little I have left on a meaningless word.

Beautiful.

The word comes again. Perhaps my mirror has learned to imitate Jack's falsehoods. I am no longer beautiful. I am ancient. I am stiff. I have nothing but my mirror to show me the truth of others and the outside world. I no longer ask it to show me the world outside. No longer am I disillusioned that I may move myself beyond the balcony and see the world beyond the reflection of my mirror. What is the point of looking at places I will never see? I shall remain, watch the Toys in the room, and wait for the day I shatter.

Beautiful.

Why are you making that noise, Mirror?

My mirror shows me a row of soldiers, freshly reddened with dye. They hold their muskets and look straight forward, chests puffed out. The row behind them is identical, but one on the last row—he is different. His paint drips down his leg. His other leg does not exist, but he still stands at attention. Only one leg, a defect. Little Jimmy would not give attention to such a Toy. Why would Toymaker create such a soldier? Where could these soldiers—?

I glance up into the darkened room to the figures on the table. Three rows of figures. Could it be? I look back at my mirror. The defected soldier stares back at me.

Beautiful.

His soul flutters behind his painted eyes and I recognize him. He is not defective or unmoving. He is just like me. Toymaker has blessed me with one of the Old Regime. I pray he will never move from my sight. But with my mirror I will always be able to see him. So near to me is he. I glance to the table. But yet it is not near enough.

In my mirror his form bursts in soul sparkles. A starlit, evening breeze blows about him and I feel warm. My mirror wants to wrap me up and keep me safe, caressing me like a...oh, wait.

Beautiful, he tells me. He speaks to me through my mirror, caressing me with his soul. If only I could step through and stand close to him. I would touch his arm and breathe my last word to him so he would know.

The clock chimes.

Quick as snuffed flame smoke, Jack is on the table next to the small troop. Leave them be, leave them be. The soldier's gaze never leaves me. Jack jumps in his box around the soldiers and they march in time. They follow Jack off the table and other Toys come out to meet them. All but my soldier, resolute in my sight. My companion of a forgotten era.

Jack sees all.

I see him stop. Look at my soldier and then at me on my balcony. Back at my soldier. He jumps over and tips my soldier over with a rubber fingertip. He falls with a ping and does not move. The other Toys stare. Within seconds they scatter, carrying themselves away from a cursed Toy.

Ow, my soldier tells me.

I wish they could see him as I can, filled with light, a blessed being who thinks and feels like I do. He is sky-lit, star-blessed, an eternity unto himself, within himself, as am I.

But they only see his one leg, his immobility, his muteness. His alienness in a modern era. They can understand me, ancient beyond remembrance; but him, born of the New Regime, they view as cursed.

On the table, my soldier remains. Jack leads the brethren soldiers around the room marching in time with his inane song.

Lovely. Warmth radiates from my mirror. My soldier's inner glow mesmerizes me. I wonder...

Jack jumps onto my balcony.

♫ "Well, we have some newcomers here,

Sure they'll like their station.

I'll set them up guardsmen style.

Safe! Our new nation." ♫

I will not even glance his way tonight. I focus on my soldier at the table. He gazes at me.

Beautiful.

♫ "How about your opinion, dear?

How would you like safety?

The only one allowed in:

Me! Your fine prince-y." ♫

He jumps around me, blocking the view of my soldier. I drop my gaze and find him in my mirror.

I feel Jack hesitate, looking at me. He turns his box toward the table.

♫ "Shame upon the demented one.

He can't fill the rankings.

Look at him lie sullenly.

Die! That I'm banking." ♫

Intense heat firecrackers from my mirror...or is from within myself?

Out of the corner of my vision, I see him contemplate the table. He hums his ditty, thinking. Reflected in my mirror, Jack's black smoke hues scarlet, raining red in a self-contained thunderstorm. I do not have to wait long for it to burst.

♫ "How can you stare contentedly

Upon one so broken?

Don't look at the useless sap.

Me! I'm your token." ♫

Never, never, never. I switch from Jack to my soldier in my mirror. Sparkles fill the glass and I hear his chorus of *Beautiful.* Never have I, in turn, witnessed such beauty as I have in him. The fields and skies of the foreign lands my mirror has shown me cannot compare. He breathes galaxies and headwinds, creating his own universe inside himself, reflected in my mirror. His essence radiates the sands of every shore, glimmering in his own sun. A cooling, forest evergreen, hidden within his white clouds of wonder permeates him. Forever have I existed and never have I come across his equal, New Regime or Old.

Jack sucks in air and puffs outrage.

♫ "If I were to decimate him,

Your love I would contain.

That's how I'll cajole you.

You! My own domain." ♫

My eyes jerk up. He wouldn't. He couldn't. Our People would notice if anything happened to us, including my soldier. Jack lies. His swirling storm in my mirror reaches for me. Lightning bolts shock my soul, marking me. It sullies my gown and cracks into my glass. Go away, go away.

I glare at Jack and he leers at me. He wouldn't do anything to my soldier, would he?

I spend the rest of the evening and most of the morning watching my soldier on the table. Likewise, he gazes at me, sending warmth and sunshine through my mirror and the occasional *Beautiful*. If my glass cheeks could hold heat, they would be aflame.

The Toys return to their positions before our People awaken, but Jack still shoots looks between me and my soldier as if he could disconnect us with his black plastic eyes.

Little Jimmy and Little Elaine play throughout the morning, she with the Blonde Doll and her friends and he with my soldier and his brothers. He likes to play by the window across the room. He is forever attempting to get outside, unlike his sister who prefers to stay indoors. He lines up my soldier and his brothers on the window sill, marching them to and fro.

A voice calls from the next room and the children go to the door to listen.

Within moments, Jack springs up, bounces to the sill and pushes my soldier out the window.

He falls in increments, stages of black and red until there is none left of him. The frames of colored light which have been violently pushed out of my sight. I am stuck to this bloody mirror.

Jack disappears to his position before the children come back into the room. Little Jimmy looks at the soldiers, noticing that mine is missing and sticks his head out of the window.

He points and says something to Little Elaine.

I scour my mirror. There he is: stuck upside down by his musket between two stones in the street. *I'm right here. Can you feel me?*

Yes, Beautiful.

Curses upon my china body. I am physically incapable of helping anyone. Frustration bubbles in me like lava.

In my mirror, I see little Jimmy and Little Elaine near my soldier, but they do not see him. They do not search for long either. Next thing I know they are back inside, acting as if nothing is the matter. As if my soldier had never been pushed out the window away from me.

I watch my soldier as he endures the rain falling in large drops like tears I am incapable of creating within myself. I silently curse Jack. He did this. How dare he! It is one thing to break the rule of immobility in the presence of People, but to physically act against another Toy was betrayal at its worst. The other Toys would not stand for such action. Surely they will rise against Jack in defiance.

The rain ceases and my soldier heaves an internal sigh through my mirror.

Feet come into view in my mirror beside my soldier. I hear a surprised exclamation and a dirty hand scoops up my soldier. Put him down!

Two street boys inspect him and laugh. I see them point at his half leg. I feel a scarlet blush through the mirror. Their disrespect makes my china boil. I could just shatter. The boys laugh again and run along the gutter in the street. They kneel and fashion a boat out of old paper. They move my soldier, marching him to and fro until he is in their paper contraption. One of the boys holds the boat aloft and ceremoniously drops it into the gutter. My heart sinks to my stomach with it. My soldier holds still as the boat sways in the gutter water. The boys run alongside, shouting and clapping.

The water rushes faster and faster, leaving the boys behind, but not me. Oh, soldier, I'm here. I'm right here. I feel his longing for me, his dread as the boat heaves up and down then spirals in the darkness of the gutter beneath the street, beneath the very earth. In the inky depths I can barely see him, only his inner glow, which has begun to fade. Don't give up!

I can barely watch, but I cannot look away. The boat dissipates beneath him. No! You must go on. You must! Do not leave me further!

The swirling depths swallow him and the remains of the boat, and my mirror follows him no farther than the dimming light that sinks further and further away from me.

He's gone. I can no longer see him. I cannot feel his warmth.

Not knowing him would have better. I chastise myself as I look up from my mirror.

The room has become dark. It's almost time for the clock to strike midnight. Not knowing him would not have been better. I would still be here on my balcony. Still immobile. Still surrounded by moving New Regime Toys. Still longing. Now I understand what I have wanted, what I still want: to shatter. To have my last Toymaker's breath leave me. I want my light to extinguish. I want to not feel.

I feel too much.

Cursed old paper. Cursed boys. Damned Jack.

The clock strikes.

Jack jumps up onto my balcony, puffed up. His reflection oozes black gunk as if it was he, not my soldier, who just sunk into the sewer.

♫ "It's done now; we're liberated.

I have you for myself.

You'll ne'er see that soldier 'gain.

Free! Upon our shelf." ♫

I almost waste my last breath on him. I want to curse him. I want to lash out. To shred his jingling cap into a thousand pieces. To melt his rubber face until he is a puddle of the slime he really is. But my soldier would have been better than me.

His short time was pure. His shine was not tainted as mine must be. His essence wasn't black like Jack's. Perhaps I could be like him—steadfast and true.

Jack restlessly hops in front of me, his frustrated nervousness evident.

♫ "What is so wrong with you tonight.

You're more than just quiet.

It's the way you steadfast stand.

Speak! Girl, oh fie it." ♫

With that he jumps from my balcony.

I stand unwavering on my mirror and watched the Toys go about the evening quivering in fear. They stay out of Jack's way, hoping that they will not get pushed out of a window as well.

Shouts of joy and wonder draw me from myself the next day. The People had gathered in the room around Little Jimmy looking in wonder and laughing. What could be the reason for such joy?

Beautiful?

My heart leaps. My soldier?

I search my mirror for him and there he is: in the center of the room in the hands of Little Jimmy, paint peeling and beaten but holding himself upright and proud. He is the reason the People have gathered. I can think of no better.

How? I wonder at him.

A sense of relief fills my mirror, flecked with bewilderment and confusion. My soldier sends me a picture of darkness, of swirling nausea. Jostlement follows and blinding light as a knife comes into view along with a face. Lifted up, I see a kitchen, a fish cut upon a table, and—rushing along to the present—this very room.

Beautiful.

My soldier rests on the table, gazing at me from across the room. Never again shall he be taken from my sight. Never.

Suddenly, Little Jimmy bursts into the room, scoops up my soldier and throws him into the flames of the hearth, jostling my table and balcony in the process.

I tip on my mirror as my insides scream and splinter.

Little Jimmy runs out of the room and a cackling fills the air. Jack hops towards my balcony. His face drowns in his smile that is fixed upon me. Hop, hop, hop.

His final hop gives my balcony a wobble and I tumble over the edge into the flames below.

My soldier, my soldier. I am here.

I see him next to me in the flames. I see the flames curl around him, lick the paint from his chest to reveal his silver heart. My form crackles with the flames but I pay them no heed. My life is bound with his, our silver souls shall entwine.

I feel him struggle to speak, but I speak for us both with my last Toymaker's breath as the flames melt and burn us. "I love you."

As the flames dance a ballet of death around me and my soldier, I hear Jack's evil song one last time:

♫ "My dear, you have abandoned me.
Dare you leave your lover.
Flames are high and shining now:
Burn! The Tin Soldier." ♫

HANNAH LESNIAK is a believer of fairies, spirits, and truth. She knows that the truth can be bitter, but that tea can make anything better. She is a supporter of libraries and continues to make her way through the ranks to become a librarian (currently in the position of squire/circulation). She received her BA in English from Madonna University and is currently working on her Master's in Library and Information Science at Wayne State University.

She has been interested in *The Steadfast Tin Soldier* since she saw a narrated cartoon on the mysterious holiday compilation VHS found in her basement. To this day, she still has no idea from whence it appeared. That particular story had a happy ending, as did the Disney version in *Fantasia 2000*. When she read the original story, the ending haunted her, like death and beauty haunt us all, and led her to write *Steadfast*.

LINKS

http://www.beardedscribe.com/hmlesniak/

Foretoken

by Wayne Ligon

PRIVATE Ethan Little startled awake. His bed-pod reacted, giving off a dim cool light. His workpad woke up and showed the time and his appointments for the day. He lay there, slowly picking at gritty eyes until he could breathe normally.

"You are awake at 2:15 AM in your cycle. Incident scan indicates a possible nightmare. Do you wish to schedule a therapist?" his bedpod softly purred.

Ethan shook his head and slid from the soft surface of the pod. "I'm fine," he muttered. He made fists with his hands until they stopped shaking.

"This is the third sleep disturbance in as many nights. The pattern is suggestive."

I am not getting into another argument with my bed, Ethan thought as he stepped into the shower. Sometimes water helped calm him, but not this time.

The same dream over three nights didn't mean it was genuine prophecy, he told himself. The psi-guard was still divided about whether foretelling was actually possible, but the arguments for it seemed compelling and this was not the first time his dreams had come true.

He bowed his head and let the water rush over his lean form. He tried not to think about the strain he was putting on the recycling system. Even having a shower was an extravagance aboard a space station, but the psi-guard had the best of everything.

He could still see it: the blackness of night shattering and cracking open, the stars burning holes in the firmament. The sky itself had caught on fire.

Before it fell.

He sank to the floor, retching. A yellow alert sounded. He felt himself lifted from the shower, the touch of a dispenser, and then darkness.

It was 5 AM before he woke again. He was in a medical bedpod, Mitchell holding his hand lightly. He managed a weak smile at his Control and tightened his fingers. Mitchell blinked as Ethan woke, his gaze shifting to virtual screens, then back to Ethan. He smiled his gentle smile and Ethan felt a sensation of warmth flood through him. He liked Mitchell. He was the best Control he'd been assigned.

"You had another incident," Mitchell said softly. The small infirmary was dim and quiet as usual, making Mitchell's carefully neutral voice sound like an accusation.

"Did not," Ethan said as he shook his head. "I'm fine, I…" Ethan sat up and Mitchell moved to the edge of the bed, enfolding him in strong arms. Ethan closed his eyes and settled against the taller man. He hugged him back. The fingers of one hand brushed the back of Mitchell's neck, the flesh-to-flesh contact letting him feel flashes of comfort and security. He let that steady him as Mitchell stroked his short, spiky hair.

"Scans say otherwise," Mitchell said carefully. "It wasn't a bad one, but I still have to report it."

Ethan sighed and closed his eyes. Mitchell was his friend—more than his friend—but he was also his Control. Every psi-guard group had a Control, a trained medical tech to monitor their mental health.

"Psi-actives don't go mad. They haven't for…what, decades?"

"I didn't say you were going mad. Your bedpod recorded an incident of possible instability. There's a huge difference. I'm sure if you have a talk with your Senior, that will be enough and we can close the whole thing."

"I could—" Ethan began. Mitchell kissed his neck and parted, giving Ethan a firm pat on the shoulder.

"Good. You have an appointment in forty minutes."

Ethan sank into the soft chair opposite Sarah, his Senior in the Guard. Her office consisted of a simple ring of comfortable chairs designed to put her guests at ease, something that also greatly facilitated scanning their thoughts. He could feel the distant, soft song of her power, expertly controlled. He often felt ashamed around her because he broadcast so easily despite her taking valuable time to work with him personally.

"Senior, I had an incident," he said.

"Can you think of anything that could have triggered it?" Sarah smiled and sipped her tea, her pale grey eyes never leaving Ethan's features.

Ethan shook his head. "I haven't been down to Cambrissa for almost a month. My contact here is monitored. There have been no conflicts."

"Recurring nightmares can be warning signs, but usually they're simply mental housecleaning. Still, we have to take this very seriously. I think I need to experience what you experienced."

Ethan hesitated to use the mnemonic trick that would allow perfect recollection, but a glance at his Senior's grey eyes weakened his resolve. "It's terrible. I don't...I don't want to incite another incident..." he said, and swallowed hard.

Her chair glided over to almost touch his and she offered her hand. Her bare hand. Ethan swallowed. Touching someone like Mitchell made contact much easier. Touching another psi would mean no barriers at all. Instinctively, his hand twitched back, but this was Sarah—his Senior—and she knew what she was doing. He laid his fingers on hers.

I will be there with you, he felt the Senior say, as her thoughts sifted into his. He took a deep breath and fell into the State of Memory. He felt Sarah 'beside' him as she effortlessly sank into the meditative state.

The sky was speckled with stars, the stars you would see from the surface of the planet, Cambrissa, below them. Cambrissa was a young system, much nearer the core than Old Earth, so the sky blazed with light. Against all odds, the old Terran Empire colony had blossomed into a stable world with a hundred million inhabitants who had just begun to re-discover spaceflight when the Expeditionary Force found them a generation ago. Ethan loved the gentle Cambrissans, who had developed unique systems of government, economics, and peacekeeping. They loved stargazing, and stellar themes featured very prominently in the artwork of most of their cultures.

In his dream, though, the stars betrayed the Cambrissans as they slowly detached from the darkness and fell, turning into mountains of fire as they did. He felt the death cries of thousands, mounting into a tidal wave of pain and fear, their final horror like a spike hammered into his mind.

Sarah screamed as she pulled away from the apocalyptic vision. She sprawled on the floor near Ethan, who was twitching with the effort to disengage from the State of Memory. Shivering, she merged with his thoughts again to lead him out and up to the waking world once more. "Private Little! Ethan! Speak to me!"

The door slid open. Paulson, Raye, and Harris—the balance of the station's psi-guard—stumbled in. Most were out of breath, having sprinted from various parts of the station, goaded by Sarah's telepathic cry. Paulson, the oldest, went immediately to Sarah's side. Raye moved to help Ethan. Harris, their newest member after Ethan, couldn't enter the room; he gripped the door frame, fighting to shield himself from the storms of raw emotion.

A medical team, led by Mitchell and Uria, the other Control, was on the scene within minutes. Ethan opened his eyes and the other psi-guard gently separated him from Sarah, who was still wide-eyed from the vision. The two Controls tapped into the medical data streams from the pod's implants, reading each member's stress levels. Ethan swallowed as he met Uria's steely gaze. She handled him with heavily-gloved hands, smoothing sensors into place on his skin. They lit up with information, which she noted with a grunt.

"Logging a level three instability incident," she said calmly into the air, knowing the station would hear her words. "Subjects: Little, Ethan and Mukhopadhyay, Sarah. Primary caregivers on site. Stand down from yellow alert."

Raye looked up in surprise, her wide, dark eyes even wider than usual. Ethan felt a flush of embarrassment. His stupid dream had put the entire station on alert, and now both he and his Senior had a significant black mark on their records. He couldn't look Sarah in the eyes, but he felt her gentle contact.

Don't worry, Ethan. This is nothing. I'll speak to Commander Fox. He has the authorization to alter your record, and he will once I explain the circumstances.

"Uria, are you certain that was necessary?" Mitchell said in a low harsh voice that only Ethan was close enough to hear.

The woman shrugged. Her voice was equally soft, but her tone suggested she didn't much care what Mitchell thought. "They coded, and I'm following procedure. You've gotten too close to these people, Mitch. You've forgotten what a danger they can be."

Mitchell cut his eyes to Ethan, then pulled Uria out of hearing range. They argued quietly while surveying the data streaming from Sarah and Ethan.

Ethan forced himself to look at Sarah. She was already looking calm and composed again.

"Don't apologize," she said kindly. She stood and went to consult with the Controls while the rest of the med team finished their scans. Ethan couldn't read her expression from this angle, but he saw Mitchell look to the ground and Uria's expression harden. Then both the Controls left with the med team.

Once the room was clear, Sarah rearranged the chairs and gestured for everyone to sit, Harris finally entered the room fully and sat on the edge of his chair, eyeing Sarah and Ethan warily.

"What happened?" Raye said. "I got flashes of fire and fear; I thought the station was on fire."

Ethan has been having nightmares, Sarah began, and Ethan opened himself to a degree of contact with his fellows. He felt their surprise and concern, and they in turn felt his fear and shame. Harris twitched back from the contact until Sarah and Paulson reached out to him telepathically and calmed him.

Ethan has convinced me. He has seen the future to some degree, but the incident is so couched in symbolism that it may be undecipherable.

"These things are not unknown," the Senior started verbally, only for Paulson to interrupt her.

"Mystic nonsense. The future does not exist in the same way the past does.

Hundreds of years after telepathy and ESP have been codified and mapped, and this kind of crap is why people still treat us like fortunetellers!"

Ethan has a strong gift, Sarah said, *as strong as mine in most ways.*

But you've never had a prophetic vision? Raye said.

No, I have not; nothing that could be confirmed. But the records are clear that such a thing is possible. My talents are in long-distance and multi-channel communication. Harris is a strong empath. Ethan's official specialty is truthtelling, but his true strengths may lie elsewhere.

Paulson shook his head. "I'll look at the official record, but I'm unconvinced as of now."

Sarah looked at Raye. "You're the strongest shielder I've ever met. Can you protect the others if I show you Ethan's memory? We can't have another incident report so soon. In fact, I'll filter the entire incident through me just to be certain."

"I can," Raye said without hesitation.

Sarah reached over to touch Ethan's neck, and he felt himself pulled back into the dream. He tried his best to steel himself against the fear, and he was grateful that Raye's shielding also helped with that. Vaguely he heard startled gasps from the others, even as he watched the sky break apart and fall, fall...

He opened his eyes when he felt Raye's shield fade away. Harris was gripping his seat, Raye had tears streaming down her face, and Paulson sat with his face in his hands. "I'm sorry to subject you to that," Ethan muttered.

Paulson looked up and took a deep breath. "I will concede that the strength of his vision merits some concern. It may be spillover from the fantasies of a terrorist or madman, both of which fall under our mandate to preserve the Unity."

Finally, Raye said it: "We must notify Commander Fox. If some kind of disaster is about to befall Cambrissa, then he needs to know about it at once."

"I concur," Sarah said, and the others nodded.

Fox stood with Ethan in front of the massive window, the pale brown and blue of Cambrissa below them. White clouds speckled the northern hemisphere, where the inhabitants would be celebrating an old good-harvest holiday. Ethan cut his eyes to the middle-aged man beside him. The conference with Fox had lasted for hours, until they finally took a break. The others were back in the conference room, but Fox had requested to speak to him privately.

"I was instrumental in having you assigned here, you know?" Fox said, looking down at the planet.

Ethan pressed his palms against the window and lowered his head at the news. "I was never told. Why?"

"Because you have the foretelling gift, and that is a rare thing indeed. Yes, the higher-ups know that it is a real thing but it carries a terrible price in increased instability. Most people who have it commit suicide before they enter their teens, but it developed very slowly in you. Despite the high potential incident rate, there was tremendous competition for your services which I won." Fox adjusted his shirt cuffs. "I thought the known benefit outweighed any potential problem, and you were a bright and compassionate young man in any case. I hoped you might see or foresee a way out of our current situation here. Unfortunately for everyone concerned, that has proven to not be the case—and we're out of time."

Ethan looked at Fox. "I'm sorry, sir, I don't understand."

Fox smiled tightly. "The Cambrissans are everything we are not. Isolated for thousands of years on a hostile world that was never meant to be anything more than a fueling weigh-station, they thrived and built a culture unique in human history. Oh, they have their problems and differences, but most people who come here consider the place a paradise. I understand you're particularly appreciative of their art. Many people are.

"The Cambrissans are a problem, though. The Terran Unity has kept the peace for so long because we are unified in deed, thought, and motive. The Expeditionary Force attunes re-discovered colonies so they can rejoin the body of humanity. Most of the colonies we find are small and primitive, the people barely eking out a living on an alien world that was never meant to house them permanently. The old Empire let people just settle wherever. That policy was perhaps admirable in its time, but because of it, most of the Imperial colonies failed when the government collapsed and trade collapsed with it. What a terrible waste. Millions upon millions died."

Fox turned away from the window and sat back down in his chair. Ethan dutifully took a place opposite him.

"I know the normal re-education procedures won't work with the Cambrissans; there are simply too many of them," Ethan said. "There's no way we can acclimate a hundred million people to Unity culture. Is that the problem you were speaking of, sir?"

Fox smiled. "Yes, that is the problem. Efforts to acclimatize the Cambrissans have been stalled for decades. I was sent here to solve this problem, and we'll be solving it this afternoon."

"What have you done?" Ethan said softly.

"You know their hearts and minds like no one else, Ethan. Your truthtelling talent at last made it clear the Cambrissans would never be able to adapt to the Unity. In fact, studies have shown that they could actually act as a psychological poison and destroy the Unity we've spent centuries building. Their way of thinking is simply so different from ours that the only way to bring them into the fold is to wipe the slate and start over."

Ethan stood up out of his chair. Mitchell was there to push him back into it. The man must have entered while Fox was talking.

Fox frowned and looked at his desk. "We've maneuvered an asteroid into position. In about six hours, it will strike the main continent. It will actually fragment as it enters the atmosphere, devastating their main belt of cities. Climate disruption and infrastructure collapse will take care of most of the rest of the populace. They're very dependent on those cities."

Ethan felt Mitchell's hand on his shoulder, firm and comforting. He reached, grabbed the man's wrist. His skin.

The others of his pod sat at the commander's conference table, their heads slumped, chests still.

"You'll kill everyone..." Ethan managed to gasp. He tried to stand but Mitchell's grip held him down.

Fox shook his head. "No, only most; the worst-case scenario calls for a death toll of eighty-three to eighty-six percent, though most models place it at seventy-six. Their culture will collapse and they will fall into barbarism, their ideals and philosophies wiped away in the scramble for survival. A couple of generations from now, we will re-appear and bring them into the fold."

Ethan could feel the truth of his words. This wasn't some sort of weird cruel joke. And Sarah and the others were dead.

It was like he was paralyzed. He felt Mitchell's fingertips brush his cheek. *I'm sure you can hear me,* he felt. *We had to do it. The outcry from so many deaths would drive you all into madness, even with Raye's talent—and an insane telepath would kill everyone on the station.*

Ethan blinked back tears as he looked up at Mitchell. *Why not just relocate us until it was over?*

Mitchell sighed. *Your talent,* he replied. *It's just too dangerous to the Unity, especially with the possibility the others might have gleaned the secret from your mind. Until now, it was just speculation that you might be a foreteller, but with this confirmation...?*

Ethan closed his eyes and put his hand over Mitchell's. *Will you make it quick?*

Of course, I will. I love you. You won't even know when it happens.

Mitchell helped Ethan to his feet and guided him out. "We're going to go look at the stars, Commander, if that's OK?"

"Of course, Mitchell. And Private Little?"

Ethan held back the tears—Commander Fox didn't deserve to see his pain—and turned to face his sentencer. "Yes?"

"Thank you for your service to the Unity."

WAYNE LIGON lives in Montgomery, Alabama, with the requisite cat and far, far too many books and comics. Between regular roleplaying sessions and Meetup groups related to sci-fi and horror, he somehow has time for a job. He's currently working on a novel of far future America.

Ashes of East End

by RS McCoy

A lace-gloved hand dove into the narrow space between corset and chest, retrieved the aged, brass pistol hidden inside, and pulled it up to point straight at Doc Turner's monacled eye. "Do you believe me now?"

"Alright, alright. I believe you!" he gasped out under frayed nerves, pushing away the barrel anywhere else.

"Serves you right. I may be a girl, but I'm a capable girl," Ashton teased him. She extended the handle to him and let him place it on the work table, laughing that a man could be so afraid of his own invention. Doc had assembled the brass weapon from cogs and bits over the last few months. It was a one-of-a-kind piece.

"That's entirely the reason you're standing here, my dear. No one else can pull this off." Doc referred to the highly-anticipated job they had been planning for months. Today's dress rehearsal was the final preparation. He moved about her, pulling on her sleeve to straighten it out.

"Who else could you have picked? Who else could pretend to be a lady?" Her mirrored reflection showed a crisp, white shirt over the top of a boned corset, a royal blue skirt spread wide below.

"No one, really. In their defense, none of them was raised to be a lady either."

"I thought we agreed not to mention that. Are we done?" Without waiting for a response, she peeled the delicate white lace off her hands, forgetting the gemstone rings and tossing them to the floor.

"Now that's no way to treat those fine things. You've spent months collecting that finery. It'd be a waste to ruin it now." At the thought of all the jobs she'd taken to find each piece, Ashton slowed her hurried strokes and conceded to take better care. The rings alone were worth more than she'd earned all last year.

"Sorry, Doc." A freed hand flipped through her mane of russet tendrils, a nervous tic from her childhood. Eager fingers pulled at the high collar tucked into the rim of her shirt.

"Don't be sorry. You'll be great if you don't let your nerves get the best of you."

"I'm not nervous," she protested futilely. Doc was her closest and oldest friend; he knew her far better than that.

"You are, too, and you'd be a fool if you weren't."

"I can handle myself." To prove it, she reached behind and began to loose the ribbon that tied the corset ever so tightly around her ribs.

"Of course you can, angel. But bobbies have been out in force these last few weeks. No one's ever done this before. At least, no one's ever succeeded before."

"That's why it's going to work," Ashton fired back, muffled under the pile of fine fabrics she worked to get over her head. "Why do they call 'em bobbies, anyway? Do they bob in the water when they get pushed in?"

Doc's wrinkled and pocked cheeks broke into a wide smile. "No, child. Robert Peel developed the Queen's police force in London, so they named them after him."

"Then they should call 'em the peelers instead," Ashton teased.

"I'm sure they take suggestions from the likes of us."

Doc may have been brilliant and Ashton may have been beautiful, but both knew their fates were determined by their profession as thieves. Doc never stole anything for himself, but he made it possible for the lovely young woman to accomplish jobs far beyond the caliber of most in East End, a perfect working pair. While she knew few others would have ever made the same choice, she never regretted her life in the slums of London. In her own way, she had made a place for herself.

Back in her loose-legged pants and overlarge men's shirt, Ashton felt like herself. "I've got some errands to run before tonight. See you at six?"

"That's the plan. Tell Mae I say hello."

Ashton cocked her easy smile as she bent for her shoulder bag and hoisted it onto its eponymous position. Its contents were her most valued possessions, worth more than all the stolen rings combined. In all her years in East End, she had never been remotely tempted to sell them for a meal.

A quiet squeak emerged from the folds of the leather sack as the delicate nose of her constant companion poked out in greeting. In response, Ashton flattened her hand next to the tiny body and encouraged him to make the familiar climb to his usual perch in the pocket of her jacket.

"Shall we visit the park first, Augustine?" she asked absently as she patted his little mouse head, her feet already making their way.

Ashton rarely experienced the calm of early morning; the pickings were too good as drunks stumbled home late at night. In the afternoons, women wandered the same paths through the streets of downtown, as if they wanted to be easy targets.

On her way to the park, the fiery young woman slid into a back alley and knocked on the rear door of the small restaurant, just like always.

"You're early," the gruff man offered as he opened the door with his elbow. Despite his words, he wore a warm smile and held out a package wrapped in brown paper and string. It was a little smaller than usual, but Ashton knew that was probably a good thing.

"Got a big job tonight. Thanks, Harv." She reached up to kiss his scruffy cheek as she took the package in her hand.

"Something special today. Give her my best, would ya?" As he spoke, he reached up to place a bit of bread into her jacket pocket for Augustine.

"As always," she said, already starting back down the alley.

"Be safe, love!" he shouted after her, waiting for her customary wave.

As she emerged from the alley, Ashton tucked the package into her satchel for safekeeping. It wouldn't do to be caught with such a treasure. Even she wasn't completely safe on the street.

Before the park, she had one more stop at Duncan's. The walk between Harvey's home-style restaurant and Duncan's store was only a few blocks, but she relished the kick of the morning breeze through her hair all the same.

"What ya got for me today, lass?" Duncan's bald head, heavy wrinkles, and wiry beard were intimidating to some of the children in East End, but she knew better.

"Hey pops. How's this?" From the folds of her bag, Ashton produced an aged silver brooch with a modest pink pearl in the center.

"What's the story on this one?" The shop-owner spun the item in his hands as he asked.

"The usual. Woman with so many things pinned to her, she doesn't notice when one goes missing."

"You plucked this right off her chest?" he asked, incredulous.

"Sure. They never notice. Besides, I'm far too interesting in conversation for them to worry about being robbed." Ashton offered him a wink.

"Anyone ever tell ya you're too good for us?" Duncan slid open the drawer just below the counter and placed the brooch at the front. Turning to the back counter, he opened a small, metal box and retrieved a few paper bills.

"Pops, this is too much," she insisted, separating the papers out on the counter and placing several of them in a pile. "Here."

"That's precisely the right amount. I know you'll give it to someone who needs it."

Ashton leaned over the counter and waited for him to produce his rough cheek for a kiss. "Thanks, pops," she added quietly.

"Go on, now. You've got a big day. And keep clear o' the bobbies." Duncan's deep voice boomed behind the young woman as she slipped through the door and back into the cool of morning.

The paper bills began to burn a hole in her pocket and sent her to the north side with haste. There was one more stop to make before Mae's, and the day was quickly starting to waste away.

Walking along the streets of East End, her boots sank deeper into the permanently muddy streets, signaling her imminent arrival at the only place that felt like home. Mossy stones stretched up until they looked as if they might pierce the clouds, or at least it had looked that way to her eight-year-old self. Now, it was a sad, faded structure that held little hint of the vibrancy inside. She had scarcely turned onto the lane before she heard her name shouted by a hoard of little voices.

"Ash! Ash!" Over and over again and louder and louder until tiny arms clutched tightly around her waist.

"You get bigger by the day, I swear!" she greeted them, an enormous smile consuming her sweet face. Children continued to pour out the doors of the home, but the dozen squeezed in around her prevented her moving any closer to it.

"Did you bring us anything? Today isn't Monday! Madam Grace is going to be so surprised!" Little chants and shouts continued so Ashton could barely hear them all, so intermingled as they were.

"Come on. Let's go in before Madam finds out you're out here in the mud." Patting their backs and tousling their shaggy hair, she attempted to get them headed inside.

"She already knows," came the familiar voice of the stern yet somehow motherly caretaker of the home. Catching sight of her, most of the children dropped their heads and started back toward the large wooden door.

"Good morning, Madam," Ashton offered with a strong embrace when she reached the stoop.

"I've told you a hundred times. You're not a ward anymore. Why can't you call me Grace?"

Ashton laughed it off as she always did; she had no intention of ever calling her anything else. Madam Grace had saved her life when she took in the eight-year-old Ashley Carver, and she wasn't about to forget it. "How are the kids?"

The two women walked into the large stone building with arms locked.

"As well as can be expected, thanks to the regular contributions from a certain criminal." Despite the barb at Ashton's selected profession outside the law, both women knew it kept food on the table for the thirty- four children at the home. It was all they had, so the usually straight-laced Madam Grace was willing to look the other way.

"Speaking of my crimes, here's enough for the rest of the week." Ashton pulled out all but two of the bills and slid them into the narrow pocket on the front of the Madam's skirts.

"This is more than enough. Besides, you already covered this week when you came on Monday. What brings you here on a Saturday?"

"I've got a job tonight, a big one. And if you have enough, then start getting these kids some haircuts. They look like wild dogs."

Madam Grace couldn't help but laugh out as she was unaccustomed to doing; the stress of managing the home for orphans took a great toll on her. "They do look like dogs, don't they?" she said in spite of herself.

"Yes, especially this one." Ashton grabbed the shoulders of the nearest boy, a feisty six year old named Thom. She brought his shoulder to her side and began roughing up his already moppy waves.

"You're one to talk, Ash!" Thom reached up to tug on one of the tight, red curls that haloed her face, pulling it straight and nearly doubling its length.

"Hey, I like my curls," she said with a smile, kissing the boy on his head and attempting to smooth over the damage as he moved off to play with his friends.

Nearly two hours later, Ashton finally began to move toward the door. No matter how she tried, she couldn't leave before visiting with every child and making sure they were well fostered. They loved when she visited, and she wasn't about to leave them disappointed. It was her favorite part of the week.

"What's this big job tonight?" the madam asked when they were alone again on the steps.

Ashton failed to come up with an answer right away; Madam Grace usually held tight to her don't-ask policy.

"Oh, uh, just moving to the other side of town. Just to try it out, really." She was suddenly uncomfortable giving details of her crime to the woman she respected so much.

"Either way, we expect you on Monday. Don't keep us waiting."

Ashton knew it was the woman's way of sharing her worry. After seeing so many children come and go, Madam Grace could hardly be blamed for keeping her emotions to herself.

With a tight hug, Ashton moved down the steps and back down the lane. She had a long way to go before getting back to Doc's.

"Ashley Carver, you be here on Monday." Madam Grace knew the rules as well as anyone. To use the girl's full name meant she was serious—really serious.

The name caused Ashton to stop in her tracks and assess the irony. It was the second time someone had mentioned her past that day. Chills crept down her arms until she had to shake out her hands and start toward Mae's with clouded eyes.

Augustine nestled into the warmth of her jacket as she crossed her arms in the breeze. As sun cascaded through the gaps between clouds, the day was turning out to be a mild one, but she huddled in tight and moved down the streets all the same.

Arriving at the narrow door on the back side of the old building, Ashton knocked twice before entering, just as she always did.

"You're awfully early today, duchess," Mae shouted from upstairs.

"I just couldn't wait to see you," Ashton shouted back, removing her tattered scarf and hanging it on the hook by the door. "Harv and Doc send their best."

She pulled the paper-bound bundle out of her bag and, finding a large portion of steak, she set it on a skewer over the fire to warm. Ashton made her way up the stairs and saw her old friend as she always was: sitting in her worn floral chair and looking out the window.

"Anything new today?" Mae asked.

"Got a big job tonight. Could you do my hair?"

"Get my things and come sit."

Ashton collected the small basked with combs, pins and spray bottles Mae would need to tame the tempest.

"So, what's this big job?"

If there was anyone in the world with whom Ashton could share a secret, it would be Mae. The woman had arthritis so bad in her feet she hadn't left the room in years, and her only son died long ago. Only Ashton came to visit. Mae just didn't have anyone to share secrets.

"Remember how I told you I've been collecting pieces?"

"The finest ones?" The older woman sprayed a minty water onto the mountain of wild curls and began to pull at it gently with a comb before pinning it down in just the right spot.

"Right. Tonight I'm going to dress up like a lady and go to the south side."

"That sounds wonderful," Mae said as she clearly drifted off into imagination. "I wish I could see you done up like the duchess you are."

"Everyone keeps reminding me today. It's like everyone has it on their mind." Augustine crawled from her pocket to scurry down her arm and curl up in the palm of her hand.

"Well, in truth, you are a duchess."

"You know I'm not. At least, not anymore. I gave that up a long time ago."

"Don't you think your father would take you back in a heartbeat?"

"No. I don't. Penelope is the woman in his life now."

"A wife and daughter are two very different things, as I've mentioned a dozen times already." A pin dug into Ashton's head a little too hard.

"But, Mae, he made his choice. He married her, brought her to live with us. And don't get me started on those horrid daughters. What was I supposed to do? Wash dishes and do their laundry all day?"

"I know, child. I know. But you're a woman now. And no one could say you can't handle yourself. I think if you went back it would be very different than before. Look down, dear," she added as she started on the back.

"I have no reason to go back now. I have everything I need right here."

"You wouldn't have to steal."

"I like my job. Besides, it's better than being a tart."

"Very true, duchess."

"You should see the outfit Doc put together. Big billowy blue skirts over a lace petticoat, just like the ladies wear. The leather corset is so tight my waist almost disappears. I stole a lovely white shirt to go over it and a high collar, too."

"And what about all those rings you told me about?"

"I'll wear the emerald one and the pearl. Oh, and the pearl necklace. I tried it all on this morning. Only my hair gave me away."

"Not for long. I'll be done shortly." Then she added, "Do you think anyone will recognize you?"

"I can't imagine. It's been so long."

"What kind of shoes are you going to wear, duchess?"

"Leather boots." It had been the source of debate for Doc and her for weeks; but, in the end, Ashton

made the call. If she had to cut and run, the boots could save her life. Besides, no one could see them under the pile of fabric she would be wearing.

"Boots?" The tone of her voice left no doubt about the contortion on her face.

"Yes, boots. You sound like Doc. They lace all the way up to the knee and they have a bit of a heel, but I can move in them and that's all that matters."

"Fine, wear your boots. They'll be too busy looking at your hair anyway. There you are, duchess. Go have a look." Augustine clambered back up into his usual pocket as she stood.

Mae was far too poor to afford anything as nice as a mirror, but Ashton had found one for her years ago. Stepping into the modest glass, even the spots couldn't mar the otherwise stunning reflection.

Wisps of blood-orange hair dipped down along the sides of her face while the bulk was pulled and tucked into an impressively-smooth-yet-intricate bun behind her. "You're a master, Mae!" Ashton squealed at the vision.

The older woman leaned back in her chair and basked in the glow of her masterpiece. "It is lovely, isn't it?"

"Hungry? Harv sent you a nice, big steak."

"What time do you have to leave?"

"I've got to be back at Doc's by six. What time is it now?"

"Five."

"Shit!"

"Duchess! You better learn to mind your mouth before you get to the south side. They'll turn you over to the bobbies for sure."

"Sorry, Mae. Let me grab your supper before I go." Ashton flew down the wobbly steps before

throwing the steak on one of Mae's plates.

"See you tomorrow," she said too fast as she turned toward the door.

"Can I get a knife, duchess?" Ashton turned to see the woman sitting idly with a steak on a plate and

not a utensil in sight.

"Right." A second flight down the stairs and back up produced a knife and fork before Ashton set to leave.

"Don't you run all the way to Doc's, you hear? You'll mess up that lovely hair of yours."

"Sure thing, Mae," she lied. "Alright, I'm really leaving. See you tomorrow."

"Be safe, duchess."

Ashton was out the door and moving fast, cursing herself for losing track of time. She ran more than

half the distance to Doc's shop before she realized she would make it, slowing to a brisk walk. Several rebellious locks already pulled loose and she spent several minutes attempting to push them back into place.

"There you are, child. I was beginning to think you'd changed your mind." Doc stood at the door, hands wringing in anticipation for the evening.

"Got held up at Mae's," Ashton admitted as she slid into the narrow shop and headed straight for the back.

"I can see why. She's a pure genius, that woman. Ready?"

"As ready as I can be, I suppose." Sliding behind the thin, fabric screen, Ashton peeled off the soiled clothes that let her blend in with the common folk of East End. Doc had provided a basin of warm water for her to get cleaned up; just that bit of warmth and comfort made her feel more like a lady than she cared to admit.

Over the knee-high leather boots, Ashton slid on the white cotton stockings that attached to the slim black garters around her thighs. Cotton drawers slipped over her shoulders followed by a knee-length chemise of crisp white. Then came the sienna brown, leather corset, structured with whale bone and embroidered with filigrees. She could only pull it on to a point before she had to come about the screen for assistance.

"Let me know when it's tight enough," Doc said, clearly discomforted by the whole idea of the corset. "Keep going, much tighter."

"You won't be able to breathe if I go any tighter."

"Sure I will. Put your back into it." Ashton would never forget the pain of her first corset. One of her father's servants had pulled it so tight the young girl wondered if she'd ever breathe again. For the first time since the event, she was happy for the memory; now, she knew what to expect and how tight it needed to be.

When he could pull no more, Doc tied the strings and tucked them under the leather. "How you'll ever make it the whole night with that on, I'll never know." Doc's face was red, a bead of sweat forming from his few minutes of exertion.

"It's not so bad. Now, let me finish." Disappearing behind the partition, she stepped into the crinoline that would support the mountain of ultramarine fabric, hoisting it up around her slender hips and fastening it at the back. Over the steel cage, she pulled on a camisole, two petticoats, and—finally—the dress, with crisp, white lace appliqué circling the hem and matching high collar.

Emerging from the changing area, Ashton couldn't meet Doc's eyes. His drawn-in breath immediately exposed the genuine nature of her disguise. When she saw the tears forming, she knew they had done it.

"Bless you, child," was all he could manage.

"What do you think?" Despite the disingenuous nature of her clothing, she wasn't sure how to feel about being in finery again. She was a blue-blood pretending to be a common thief pretending to be a blue-blood; the entire situation made her mind swirl.

"No one could suspect a thing. Here you are." Doc handed her the lace gloves and a handful of rings and other pieces. " And I think you should wear this—"

To the girl's surprise, her oldest friend crouched to rustle through her worn rucksack, pulling out one of the items that rarely left it.

"Here," he said as he stretched out his hand to give it to her. In shock, she let it fall into her tingling hand, turning it over until she could see the large sapphire surrounded by silver petals: a sunflower. The stone still shimmered despite its years in the inner pocket of her bag.

A stern, "No," was all she could manage. It was completely out of the question.

"Ash, listen." He held his hands in front of him as if that would somehow protect him from her immediate disproval.

"No, put it back." She reached out a firm hand and brought her level gaze to his.

"It could save you."

A breath crept out of her chest as her hand fell into the folds of her dress. "What?"

"If someone should realize that you are not what you seem, then your title will be the only thing to
save you from the bobbies."

"And this ring proves I am my father's daughter." She could see the sense of it, but that didn't change
the esteem of the piece in her mind. The ring was so personally valuable she had never thought to actually wear it.

"Exactly," Doc said just above a whisper.

Hesitantly, she slid the cool metal over her lace-gloved finger and marveled in how it fit. She hadn't put it on since she'd left her father's house a decade ago. Before that, her mother's ring had been far too loose on her adolescent hand.

"If all goes well, child, you won't need it."

Ashton could only nod, the silver weighing down her hand.

"You know the plan?"

Mention of their much-anticipated job brought her back to reality a bit. "'Course. Take the train to the south side, go to the party. Get out by midnight and make the last train to East End."

"Don't forget the train. If you miss it, you'll be trapped there all night. The bobbies'll make quick work of you."

"I can handle it."

"As it is, there's only ten minutes before the seven o'clock starts boarding. Better get going."

"Thanks, Doc. See you at the station?"

"At twenty after, just as we planned."

The short walk out of Doc's shop was rather tumultuous, courtesy of the narrow aisle of mismatched items and housewares. More than one piece of merchandise clattered to the floor as her sizeable skirts moved past. When finally she was out the door, Doc handed her the small clutch with a beaded wristlet before she started silently for the train station a few blocks away.

Ashton was immediately satisfied in her decision to wear the leather boots over some delicate heel. The mud seemed to reach out to pull at her dress and boots causing the short walk to feel like an eon. By the time she arrived at the station platform, what felt like pounds of mud clung to the leather.

"Need a hand, doll?"

Turning toward the voice, Ashton found Regina Thomas, one of the most notorious prostitutes in London.

"Oh, hi, Regina. I'll be alright."

"Nonsense. You can't go to the biggest party of the year with mud on your shoes. Though you should probably have picked something a little nicer." Despite her words, Regina winked as her face lit up with a warm smile.

Donning only a simple, form-fitting red dress, the lithe woman bent down and used an embroidered handcloth to wipe away as much mud as she could before depositing it in the nearest waste bin.

"Don't you need that?" Ashton asked, suddenly guilty to cost Regina her expensive cloth. The bellow of the train horn sounded in the distance.

"I'll get another from the Commissioner tonight. He likes to give gifts."

Ashton hadn't even considered a familiar face at the party, but if it had to be anyone, Regina was as good company as any. If anything, she was an asset with her experience and knowledge of the upper class.

"What brings you to this side of the world?" Ashton asked, suddenly remembering the woman preferred the finer life offered by her profession.

"Visiting my mother. She refuses to leave that house. I've told her time and again I would get her an apartment on the south side."

"You must be doing well, then." Both women know how profitable prostitution could be—and how risky.

"I've found a narrow group of men I like to spend time with. They pay a premium to get more of me."

While it was a path Ashton herself would never choose, she could understand the appeal of it. Spending some time with a man who cared about you didn't seem so awful. In fact, she was a little envious; it had been a while since anyone had held her interest that way.

The ominous black steel of the train engine barreled into the station, screeching its wheels against the track and pouring steam out of every cranny. Only a handful of people emerged from the cars; those in East End hadn't the money for a ticket while those in the south side had no reason to venture to the slums. Regina and Ashton boarded a nearly empty train.

"You're doing well," the dark-haired woman offered, her sultry voice as smooth as the velvet valences and red leather seats.

Ashton navigated the girth of her skirt down the row and sat next to the window. "What do you mean?"

"Your first time on the train and you still board the first class car. I half-expected you in the third class car. I'm impressed."

"Oh, thanks, I guess." She didn't have the heart to tell Regina that she'd never thought to go to the lower class car.

The two women let the twenty-minute ride pass with only the clacking of wheels against the tracks. When finally the train slowed into the south side station, Regina helped Ashton navigate down the steps and onto the platform with her large dress.

"I wish I didn't have to wear this giant dress," Ashton uttered as she looked longingly at the curve- cupping fabric the other woman wore.

"Yes, you do. It marks you as one of them," Regina spoke matter-of-factly. When Ashton neglected to respond, she asked, "How do you know the Lady Astley?"

"We ran into each other at a market and became fast friends." Ashton had repeated the line in her head so many times it easily fell out of her mouth.

"How do you really know her?"

"She was a mark. We did talk, but she didn't know I slid a ring off her finger after I admired the one next to it."

Regina threw her head back and revealed a slender neck as she laughed heartily. "Oh, yes, you'll be just fine, doll. They won't know what hit 'em!"

The two women walked arm-in-arm until Lord and Lady Astley's urban apartment came into view. Already, several well-dressed couples clustered around the base of the steps, chatting happily before going in. Ashton buried the lump in her throat and prepared for an unforgettable night.

"Ah, there you are. Regina, the Lord Godard would like to make your acquaintance." A heavy-set man smiled wide under a thick, curling mustache, but Regina didn't match his enthusiasm. She squeezed Ashton's arm just slightly before pulling away and walking to meet the man.

"A pleasure, Lord Godard." Regina lifted an elegant hand and let the younger man kiss it fervently. "May I introduce the Lady?"

Ashton all but panicked when she realized Regina could say her true name. "Lady Ashton Howell," she said quickly as she crossed the few feet that separated her from the group.

"Well, aren't you lovely, dear! I haven't seen hair that color in ages." The mustachioed man reached out to kiss her hand before explaining, "I am Lord Astley. Hannah mentioned you would be coming tonight, but she didn't say a word about your beauty."

"A pleasure, Lord Astley." Ashton offered what little curtsy she could manage in the heavy dress and stole a quick glance to the suddenly reserved Regina.

"Come inside, Lady Howell. Hannah will be cross if she learns I've kept you on the stoop all night." He laughed so that his whole chest shook beneath the fine silk shirt and black jacket. The gold pocket watch threatened to bounce right out of its place before he used a chubby finger to push it back.

The interior of the home was far more lavish than could be expected from the exterior. Bright light beamed from enormous chandeliers above the stairs and in the rooms to the right and left, bathing the exquisite dresses of the guests. A dark marble hand rail wound up the spinning stair case that was dotted with gossiping young women and eagle-eyed old men.

"You have a lovely home, Lord Astley," the nervous Ashton said honestly.

"I'm glad you like it, dear. I hope you'll be visiting us often."

Ashton would have laughed out loud at the statement if she hadn't been so overwhelmed at her surroundings. Gold and silver, diamonds, and rubies all glittered from every neckline and delicate wrist. Lord Astley's home was the largest congregation of wealth in the city, and now she had the pickings all to herself. Already she began to make a mental list of who wore which pieces, and what was worth a second look.

"Astley, you old dog. Who's this fine young thing?" Ashton's escort turned abruptly to face the youngest man they had seen so far. His dark mustache turned up at the ends like so many others, but his hazel eyes caught hers instantly.

"Robert, this is the Lady Howell." Lord Astley slid a hand along the corset at Ashton's back and pulled her into his side, a clear claim on the new territory.

The man's brown leather vest and white silk shirt were far plainer than the garish exorbitance of the other guests, but he didn't seem to be intimidated. "Howell? I don't recall the name."

Ashton had rehearsed her story so many times, the lie felt more comfortable than anything else. "My mother's been at our estate in Ockley since my father died. She sent me to the city to get acquainted."

"And we are all so thankful she has." Robert reached out for Ashton's hand and planted a warm kiss upon it, a move that caught the breath in her chest. "May I have this dance?"

Ashton felt herself nod slowly a moment before the young Robert escorted her away from their eager host and toward the room directly across the hall. An older woman with a ribbon in her hair sat and strummed a brass harp alongside a pair of violinists and a cellist, bathing the room in vibrant music. Pairs bowed and ducked in perfect rhythm as Ashton stared in horror.

While she had loved dancing and music as a child, life in East End hardly cultivated the sort of style that she would be expected to demonstrate in the next few minutes. Memories of dance lessons with her father flashed through her mind as she observed the spinning couples and attempted to find the pattern in their movements. Thankfully, the song was rather long and allowed her enough time to get a feel for it.

The brief lull that signaled the next song arrived as Robert ushered her into the midst of the group. He found his place along the line of men as she settled in among the women. The delicate notes from the violinists played in unison for a moment before the bouncing tones of the harp joined them. Just as Ashton let the timing of the music catch her, the line of men took a large step forward; she found Robert standing just inches from her so that his tie nearly brushed her nose.

Alarmed as she was by his presence, she failed to step back with the line of ladies; for a half-second, she was the lone woman out of place. Robert smiled wide at her lapse.

Several times the lines moved forward or back in an elegant sort of jousting, men pursuing the women and the women pushing back. Robert continued to take large steps to bring his chest close to hers when the opportunity presented. One time, she felt him bend his head down toward her ear, but she shot back with the women just in time. Ashton wasn't sure if she wanted to know if he would speak to her or kiss her.

"You are a fine dancer, Lady Howell," Robert said as he linked his arm with hers and turned them around the neighboring couple for the finale.

"And you are quite an arrogant dancer, Sir Robert." She hoped her barb would help her to feel less helpless in his presence. Robert only laughed heartily and washed away any hope of overcoming his charm.

"You have a talent for honesty," he continued through his smile. "You're not like the other ladies attending tonight."

Ashton had no response that would wound him enough, and thankfully the music died just in time to save her from it. Robert bent at the waist and bowed formally along with the rest of the men. She couldn't help but notice how his brown leather vest and white silk shirt suited him.

"Alright now, Robert. Let's not occupy too much of the lady's time." A thick-fingered hand arrived on her upper arm and she turned to see Lord Astley looking riled. Both men understood clearly that Lord Astley wanted Robert far away from her.

"I hope to see more of you soon, Lady Howell." Suddenly given the choice, Ashton would have rather stayed with Robert. He might have pushed her buttons and left her speechless, but at least he wasn't some fat, old womanizer. With the prospect of leaving Robert's company for Lord Astley, she realized what a mistake it had been.

"And you as well, Sir Robert." For the first time since entering Lord Astley's home, she didn't tell a lie. The grubby hand pulled her away with one long look back.

"You've yet to be received by my wife, Lady Howell," he explained as they walked. She felt more like a child than a guest, but it was too early to start offending the host.

They only made it a few more feet across the expansive room before Lord Astley stopped to address an older woman with wise eyes and a terse expression. "Lady Howell, may I present the Madam Astley. Mother, this is Lady Howell."

"Good evening, ma'am," Ashton offered with another dutiful curtsy.

"A pleasure, Lady Howell. Luke, go and get the girl some wine. And two for me since you're going." Lord Astley mumbled something about being in his own house but sauntered off all the same.

"Don't let that old bag get his hands on you. He has a taste for women who are too good for him."

"I can handle myself." Ashton fought the urge to let her lace-gloved hand dance across the area of her corset that hid the handmade brass pistol.

"Of course you can, dear. Now get on to that handsome young man over there. That's the sort you need to get to know, not some fat old pig. Go on." Madam Astley nodded so that Ashton had to turn behind her, but when she did, the pleasant-faced Robert stood waiting.

"Lady Howell?" His hand extended in front of him, lingering until she planted hers into it. With hands clutching together gently, Robert pulled her across the room and back into the open entryway filled with guests.

"Where are we going?" she asked, though she knew the answer didn't really matter. She was too intrigued to argue.

"You'll see." Turning toward the stairs, the young man helped her squeeze between the other ladies standing along the rail until they emerged at the top. Rooms spread out in all directions, equally filled with guests as far as Ashton could tell. Robert made a sharp turn and headed for a tall door that she hadn't noticed at first.

The coolness of the falling night struck her as they stepped onto the balcony, Robert shutting the door behind them.

"Madam Astley warned me against her son. Perhaps it's you I should have been warned against." Even as she said the words, the man exuded only calm composure.

"You have nothing to fear from me, Lady Howell. Now, I can't say the same for thieves and prostitutes."

Ashton felt her heart sinking heavily, sliding down her chest and landing firmly in her gut. Her mind raced, searching for some way the man could have known about her, about Regina, in such a short time. She'd barely been there half an hour and hadn't made a single move yet.

It was then that she realized he couldn't know; at that moment, she was innocent of crime. "You would punish a thief or a prostitute?"

"They break the law—so, yes, I would."

"Even if they break the law to feed themselves or their families?"

Robert's lips parted to say something before he slammed them shut and looked at her. A smile crept across his cheeks. "You know, you're the first person to ever give me pause."

"There are thousands that starve in this city, thousands who would work if there were jobs to be had. The city makes them criminals."

"That's a fair point, Lady Howell. How have you come to care so much for the destitute?"

Ashton realized she had deviated too far from her story; she would have to improvise.

"The poverty of London is famous across the country. Everyone knows how terrible things are here."

"And yet your mother still chose to send you?"

"Yes." She knew it was weak, that it was the hole in the web of lies she wove, but there was nothing
else to do.

"And I'm still glad she did." Though Robert moved just an inch closer, the mood changed dramatically.

No longer surrounded by the blur of other dancers, she couldn't deny his proximity. Ashton was aware of how she stood, how her hair flitted in the breeze, how close he was.

"You aren't angry?" she found herself asking.

"And why would I be angry?"

"Because proper women should speak their minds so freely."

"You needn't bother about such things. I'm hardly a man that cares for the rules of society."

"Just the rules according to the law," Ashton teased, but the words were sincere.

Robert laughed and took another step closer until he could rest his hand lightly against the white silk that covered her upper arm. A gentle thumb stroked absently as she struggled to let even breaths in and out.

"You're shaking. I'm sorry I brought you out here. It's far too cold." Robert moved to pull her off the rail and back toward the large door, but she pulled against him.

"I'm not cold, really. I'm glad you brought me out here." As frustrating as she found his position on law, there was no denying the effect he had.

Instead of returning to her side, Robert stepped so close he sank into the fabric of her skirts. A strong hand appeared behind her neck to pull her into him. Lips pressed together until they opened and tongues roved wildly, a kiss like she'd never had before.

Locked together as they were, neither noticed the door opening until Lord Astley's deep voice bellowed, "There you are! I've been looking for you high and low, dear."

Ashton's heels returned to the floor of the balcony and realized she'd been standing on her toes. "Lord Astley," Robert replied rather quietly.

The heavy set man appeared beside her and ushered her back into the chaos on the apartment. She didn't even have a chance to respond before she was inside and moving fast with a firm hand behind her. "Come along, dear. Hannah's just in the drawing room. This way." Across the hall and through the next room, Lord Astley opened a door that led to a darkened room.

Ashton couldn't decide why a wife would spend the evening in her drawing room when she hosted a party in her own home, but too late did she realize her mistake. No sooner did they enter the room than she found herself pushed harshly against the wall.

The wide belly of Lord Astley pinned her onto the cream and cerulean striped wallpaper while his hands reached behind her to try to remove the metal cage that blocked his access. When she had enough space, she dipped the lace glove down the front of her corset and pulled up the brass pistol.

Without reservation or hesitation, she aimed the barrel between his eyes and pressed into his flesh until he began to back away from her. "Now Lord Astley, that's no way to treat a lady."

"You're no lady, no more than Regina is the queen." At once, she understood. He had thought her a prostitute when she arrived at Regina's side.

"If you touch me again, I'll happily shoot you." Ashton extended her thumb and pulled back the hammer for effect. Lord Astley only nodded.

She didn't look back as she walked out the narrow door and back into the crowd. To her surprise, Robert waited for her at the top of the stairs.

"Are you all right?"

"Yes, of course." While she wanted to slam into his chest and let his strong arms wrap around her, he had engaged her under false pretenses. She wasn't a lady and she certainly wasn't a tart. It hit her like a blow to the stomach.

"You look like you need to sit down."

"I'll be fine." Just as she turned to return down the stairs, Lord Astley managed to squeeze himself around the bannister, quickly descending.

"Can we go back to the balcony?" he asked low enough so only she could hear.

"No, we cannot."

"Have I offended you, Lady Howell? I know I was forward, but I thought—" When his voice trailed off, she wondered if she had made a mistake, but the memory of Lord Astley's grotesque belly pressed against her was too horrible to wash away. She wouldn't let it happen again.

"No, Sir Robert, you have not, but I must be going." Doc would be supremely disappointed in the emptiness of her handbag, but it wasn't worth further risk.

"Robert!" The deep voice of Lord Astley shouted from somewhere on the first floor. The young man gave Ashton a last glance before moving down the stairs with speed.

Intent on going home, Ashton began to make her way down, careful to plant each foot firmly on a step before moving on to the next. She heard the commotion before she reached the middle landing.

Regina stood in the doorway next to Robert, who held her arm tightly, her face showing none of the discomfort she must have felt.

"What's going on here?" Careless of the steps, Ashton flew to the bottom floor and arrived at Regina's side as Lord Astley barked at her.

"How dare you come to my house? You're not a lady. You're no more than a common tart. Get her out of my sight!"

"Let her go!" Ashton pleaded, but they scarcely seemed to notice her.

She let her hands fly out until they struck Robert's chest and arms, anything to get him to release her friend. Lord Astley was behind her in an instant along with another man. It took both of them to hold her back amidst flailing arms and kicking feet.

"I'll get her down to the precinct, Lord Astley, but I'll need you to make an official statement." Robert replied to his demands, failing to make eye contact with the frantic Ashton.

"Just get her out of my house. I'll not have the likes of her here."

Robert moved to push Regina through the door and down the steps, but Ashton couldn't let it happen. She was only guilty of walking Ashton to the party, but she would pay with her life. Once the bobbies got a hold of her, they would never let her leave.

"No! Let her go! It's not her fault!" Amidst the ripping pain, Ashton managed to pull her arm free and push against the men just enough to knock the smaller man to the ground. Only Lord Astley's large size protected him from the blows of her elbow.

Robert handed Regina to a nearby party guest and turned to face Ashton. "Lord Astley, release her." He made no attempt to hide the venom. A moment later, he came in close and asked her quietly, "Lady Howell, do you know this woman?"

"She's—" Ashton started.

"No, I don't know her. I met her only a few hours ago," Regina interrupted loudly.

Satisfied, the suddenly solemn young man pulled Regina to the bottom of the stairs and turned to start the four block walk to the south side precinct with his suspect in tow. Their silhouettes soon faded from the porch lights into the dimness of the streets amidst the sudden tolling of a distant bell.

"I'm so sorry about all this, Lady Howell. I promised you an evening of grand enjoyment." Ashton regained her composure a moment later and found the Lady Astley behind her. "Are you alright, dear? You look positively ill. I assure you we don't usually have such street trash at our parties. Come inside and have some wine. It's already midnight, and we have an evening to make up for."

The single word rang out amongst the others: Midnight.

"I'm sorry, Lady Astley. I have to go." She plunged down the stairs as fast as her skirt would allow and started down the street at a light jog. She knew she'd never make the train, but she had to try.

A full block from the south side station, Ashton caught sight of the steel beast barreling down the tracks and surrounded by a cloud of steam. She had missed it by a long shot. Sparing only a moment for self- pity, she quickly turned to the right and began the long walk to East End.

The train ride there had lasted less than twenty minutes, but the walk home was longer than two hours. Ashton was immediately grateful for her boots and the little bit of speed they allowed her. When, at last, she arrived at Doc's shop, she found the single light of the back room still lit. She lifted her hand to the glass and tapped lightly.

Doc's absurd white hair looked even more frayed than usual as he moved to unlock the door. "Are you trying to kill me?"

"I'm fine. I just missed the train." She knew it was a massive understatement but was in no mood to get into it. "Can you get me out of this thing?"

Already she moved to the back room without waiting for an answer. "Your skirts are ruined. Look at all this."

Looking back, she had left a wide swatch of mud everywhere she walked. "Sorry, Doc. I'll help you clean it in the morning."

It was a simple matter to release the few ties that held on the crinoline and corset. Once those were

loosened, the rest could be peeled away layer by layer. She set the rings and gloves onto the narrow table. At last, she could slip into her familiar clothes. They may have been rags, but at least she didn't have to pretend to be someone else in them.

Ashton collapsed into the small cot Doc had left out for her, but despite the hour—and all that had transpired—she couldn't sleep. Hazel eyes bored into her in the dark. Belly fat pressed her against expensive wallpaper. Her hands felt light without the bulk of jewelry.

Shooting up from the cot with a start, Ashton blindly felt her way to the narrow table, examining each piece with deft fingers. Over and over again, she traced them carefully, searching for the piece she was suddenly sure wasn't there.

Doc arrived from his upstairs apartment with a candle in hand. "What's going on?"

"I can't find my ring. It's not here." It was all she could do to sink to the floor in defeat.

"Your mother's ring? Do you know where it could be?"

Lord Astley's apartment. The train station. Anywhere between the south side and East End.

"It's gone," she uttered through a sigh before standing and going back to the cot. She'd managed to turn the biggest job of her life into a total disaster.

Augustine scurried from the darkness and nestled into the pillow just below her jaw, a tiny beacon of comfort after a terrible experience.

As had rarely happened since she started her new life, Ashton let the tears fall easily. She had liked Robert. She had thought he liked her as well, but now it seemed like a cruel trick. Lord Astley thought her a prostitute and tried to take it from her. Regina would pay the price for her foolishness. It was too much to get through in one night.

Morning light crept in through the storefront glass. Ashton felt more like she'd been hit by a train than anything. Sharp pain radiated through her head causing an immediate wince.

"Coffee?"

"Definitely." A warm mug appeared in her hand. She had to sit up to sip at it slowly, relishing the taste of the bit of milk Doc had added.

"You must have gotten into some real trouble last night. What happened?" Doc leaned up against his work table littered with gears and parts, waiting for the tale.

"I messed up everything."

"I'll say. There are posters with your picture. They're offering quite a reward for information about Lady Howell."

"Posters? Already?" A moment later she added, "I didn't take anything."

"I figured as much. That handbag is far too light."

"What do they want with me then?"

"I'm afraid only you know the answer to that, angel. Tell me what happened." He sipped at his steaming coffee and waited.

Recognizing he would hear the tale no matter how long it took, Ashton told him everything, including Regina and Lord Astley. She only left out the kiss on the balcony; it was hardly her proudest moment.

"You pulled a gun on Lord Astley?"

"He attacked me."

"I believe you, but I think that explains the posters. If they think you're from the streets, they won't hesitate to persecute you for the crime. I think you'll be staying here for a while." Satisfied with her information, Doc moved back to his workbench and set his strange magnifying goggles over his head and set to work.

"You think it's not safe to leave?" Ashton set the empty mug on the floor next to the cot.

"I know so, angel. At least, not for a while."

He was right, she knew, but that didn't make it easier. She thrived in East End. She had a role here, and it wouldn't feel good to let that go.

Ashton kept herself busy cleaning the muddy floors for the rest of the morning and most of the afternoon. Doc brought her some bread and stew from his apartment, but otherwise left her alone after the store closed. She never left the small back room.

The next day was Monday, and Ashton had little intention of staying put. Madam Grace would pitch a fit if she didn't show, and she was more than capable of getting across town without being seen. Before Doc came down to open the store, she pulled a hooded cloak from his rack and slipped out, her ragged bag over her shoulder.

In the fog of early morning, the streets were quiet. Posters with her face dotted every post and storefront. Even with her memorable hair hidden from sight, she kept her eyes in all directions. Only once did her heart race at the sight of a pair of men approaching, but they turned down the next street without incident.

Half in disbelief that she had made the trip so quietly, Ashton turned onto the lane leading up to the home. Already, Madam Grace stood on the steps waiting for her with a disapproving glare.

While she wanted little more than to rush into the arms of the woman who raised her, she dreaded the woman's response when she learned of all Ashton had done. This time, she would leave nothing out.

Ashton kept her eyes on the muddy lane until she heard Madam Grace's voice, the distance too great to make out the words. A single upward glance produced a horrifying image: a dozen blue-clad bobbies poured out onto the steps and flew down the lane.

Her hand flew up to pinch the fabric just above Augustine's pocket as she turned and broke into a full run. A pair of stone-faced bobbies turned to block the lone entrance. She was trapped between them and the tall, steel fence. She ran to scale it in a last ditch effort, but merciless hands quickly pulled her back down and threw her hard into the ground.

"Get off me!" She knew the words fell on deaf ears, but she had little intention of going quietly. A moment later, a gap between bodies revealed the children of the home pressed up against every window and lining the steps. She wouldn't let their last memory of her be so pathetic. She clenched her teeth as they pulled her to her feet and lifted her into a steam-powered buggy with a bobby on either side.

Vibrations radiated up through the seat and threatened to bounce her off the back. Only the brass handcuffs chained to the floor and the stone arm of an officer kept her in place. Whey they flew right by the East End precinct and turned south, she knew she was in real trouble.

The early morning streets were nearly empty as they drove quickly. A few minutes later, the elegant trim and arched doorways of the well-off replaced the torn and tattered buildings of the slums. The steam car pulled directly in front of the stairs of the south side precinct before she was unchained and all but carried inside. The bobbies didn't set her down until she reached a room with nothing but a wooden table and a pair of chairs.

When she was seated in the plain, maple chair and her chains secured to it, the bobbies shut the door. A young man with the sparse beginnings of a mustache stood behind an older man with fully-grey hair. It was the older one who spoke first. "Let's start with your name. I think we can all agree you're not Lady Howell."

"What does it matter?" she spat. "You're going to send me to the gallows no matter who I am."

"Just tell us your name." The officer absently scrawled words on paper as if he'd had the conversation a thousand times.

"No." Seeing as how she wasn't going to leave the building alive, she didn't plan on making it easy for them.

"How long have you been a prostitute?"

"I have never been a prostitute."

"Then how long have you been a thief?"

"I'm not a thief, either." It was a bold-faced lie, but it was all she had left. She would deny it all until she believed it as well as they did.

Without a moment's hesitation, the older man stood, his chair screeching loudly against the floor. At the sudden sound, Augustine bolted from the safety of her pocket and clambered up to nestle against the collar of her jacket.

"A rat!" the younger officer shouted before taking a swing. Augustine hit the wall behind her and plummeted to the tile floor. Ashton stood to step between the officer and his target, but the chain prevented the movement.

"Get away from him!" she screamed to ill effect. Heavy boots fell along with the tears. Augustine was faster than the officer, but he was running out of room as he scrambled into the corner.

"Leverton, what is going on here?" Ashton turned in shock to see Robert standing in the doorway. "I was to be notified the moment she arrived."

"There's a rat, sir." The young officer continued to slam his regulation boots into the tile.

"He's a mouse," Ashton said as fresh tears emerged. "He's my friend."

"You heard her, Leverton. Unlock the chain."

At his instruction, Leverton looked up with pause. "But—"

"I said, unlock the chain." Robert spoke slowly, as if the officer were simple. As he waited for his direction to be followed, he stood expressionless.

With the chain released and lying across the floor, Ashton dashed to the corner to collect Augustine in her cupped hands still bound by brass manacles.

"Leave us," Robert said quietly without taking his eyes from the young woman crouched in the corner.

The door shut soon after and left the two alone in the bare room. "I'm sorry for that. I meant to be the one to question you. Please, have a seat." As he spoke, he pulled out the opposing chair and sank into it.

"I don't have anything to say." She remained in the corner of the room with the tiny mouse in her hands.

"Would you tell me your name? Your real name?"

"Ashton," she said before she'd really thought it through.

"Ashton," he repeated before adding, "I like it. It suits you."

"What do you want from me?" she asked as she rose and sat across from him, wiping the last of her tears on the shoulder of her jacket.

"I'd like to learn a little about you."

"I'm not a prostitute."

"No, I don't believe you are." His calm told her he spoke truthfully, but she couldn't decide why she should be there if he already knew it.

"What are you going to do with Regina?"

"She'll be put to the gallows, as the law requires."

"But she didn't do anything! I'm the one who pulled the pistol on Lord Astley. It was me who made him angry." The words tumbled out before she could draw them back.

"You pulled a pistol on Lord Astley?" He stared at her in disbelief until he was consumed with laughter. "Frankly, that's quite impressive. I'd have liked to see his face," he uttered before giving in again.

"I thought that's why I was here," Ashton said more to herself than the officer.

At mention of his purpose, Robert sobered. "First, I need to know where you got this." He produced the sapphire sunflower and set it delicately on the table between them.

Ashton set Augustine in her pocket and picked up the ring she was sure she'd never see again.

"Did you steal it?" he asked.

"No."

"Don't lie to me."

"I'm not lying. It's mine. It was my mother's."

"Then you haven't been honest with me." Enthralled by the piece as she was, she didn't notice him stand and pull open the door. Moving to one side, he called out, "Bring him in."

Nothing could have prepared Ashton for the moment Augustine Carver walked into the room. His fine, brown suit was darker than his grey-streaked hair. He looked much older than she remembered.

"Ashley?" he asked barely above a whisper, his eyes already filling with emotion.

"I go by Ashton now," she replied with an icy chill. She had no sympathy for the man who traded her in for a new family.

"I'll leave you two for a moment," Robert said as he walked into the hall.

"You don't need to leave. This won't be long."

The stoic officer looked a bit surprised, but he came back all the same.

"I've been looking for you for ten years. They told me you never left the city."

"No, I've been here. You must not have looked very hard." In truth, Madam Grace was known for taking in lost children. He could have easily found her—if he had wanted it.

"It's true, I could have been a better father, especially after your mother died." Then he added, "Penelope left me last year."

"And now you're alone? You can't really think I'll go home with you like this never happened."

"I had hoped—" Her father wrung his hands awaiting her response.

Ashton turned to Robert. "We're done here. Get on with whatever punishment you have for me."

"I'm sorry, Duke Carver. We have a few more things to discuss if you'd like to wait at the front." Ashton's father only nodded slowly before he left. Robert closed the door behind him.

"You're really Ashley Carver, the Duchess?" he asked when they were alone again.

"Weren't you listening? I don't go by that name anymore."

"I'm sorry you had to go through that. I told him you probably weren't interested in seeing him if you'd worked so hard to stay hidden, but he insisted. I think after he saw the ring, he wanted to see you for himself."

"You showed it to him?" she asked incredulous.

"I showed it to a lot of people. I wanted to see you again." Ashley could only stare at the tired woodgrain of the tabletop, too furious to contemplate a response to his ridiculous statement. When she remained silent, he added, "You'd really renounce your title and live on the streets?"

"I already have. Does that bother you? First you think I'm a prostitute and kiss me on the balcony. Then you think I'm a duchess in need of rescue. Turns out, I'm just a common thief." She knew her words weren't fair, that they would hurt him, but she was too angry to care.

As if his strength had left him, Robert put his back against the door and kept his eyes on his shoes. Finally, he said, "I never thought you were a prostitute and I like that you're not a duchess. And you're anything but common, Ashton."

She looked up from the table to see if his face offered any more than his perplexing words, but she only found a gaze that bored into her.

"What do you want from me?" she asked quietly.

"Two things, actually. First, I'd like you to help me reform the city."

"Reform?" Ashton repeated the word as if it were the wrong one.

"Tell me how you would solve the problems that plague London."

"Create jobs—real, honest jobs. Those who have enough money won't need to steal to eat. You'll nearly eliminate crime in a single stroke. And stop putting criminals to death. It's despicable to kill someone for making a living the only way they can."

"You mean Regina."

"Everyone I know would be put to death if they were arrested for ever committing a crime. It's just not reasonable. No one can be perfectly lawful their entire life."

Robert smiled as if it were the answer he'd expected from her. "I think that's a very good start. I'd like it if we could get started immediately."

"And what's the second thing?"

"I'd like for you to marry me." He let heavy hands fall to his side as if the words had taken everything to get out.

"What?" she asked, certain she'd misheard him.

"Ashton, will you marry me?"

"You're serious?" She was aware of the shock that covered her face, but she couldn't hide the impact of his words.

In answer, Robert walked around the table and pulled her to her feet. No sooner was she up than he leaned in and pressed his lips to hers. A jolt sped through her, washing away any ideas of pulling away. Without the steel cage in the way, Ashton let her hips sink against his. Strong hands slid down her back to pull her in that much closer.

Before her breath left her entirely, she pulled back and whispered, "Yes."

"Yes, what?" he asked, his thought returning from a daze.

"Yes, I'll marry you."

It was by far the most absurd and illogical thing she'd ever done, but that didn't leave her a single doubt. She leaned up to kiss him through his enormous smile. Any man who could kiss her like that was a man worth keeping.

R S MCCOY didn't ever plan on being a writer. With a career teaching high school science, writing is the last thing she expected. But life never goes the way you think it will. While battling cancer, she picked up her laptop and let the words flow out. One year later, her first published fantasy novel was released on Amazon followed by her second novel six months later. She is a wife, mother of two, a scientist, baker, gardener, and life-long science fiction and fantasy addict.

LINKS

http://www.rsmccoyauthor.com
http://www.facebook.com/AuthorRSMcCoy
https://twitter.com/RSMcCoy1

Fire & Ash

by Joshua Allen Mercier

There were two witches in a wood; one was evil, one was good.
A cloak of red, a cloak of black, like the fire and the ash.

THE cold, autumn gusts ripped across Salem's port, stirring the angry waters, stirring the angry spectators gathered before the gallows—gallows which had not, until this day, been used since the Trials several years back. Men, women, and children—all bore hateful eyes and twisted faces. All bore a deep-seeded fear of the woman before them; they watched and seethed, anger building like fire fed by the winds, waiting for answers, for closure, for justice—for the devil's death.

Constance Archer stared at the sea of faces; she despised all of them, save two—two faces that weren't supposed to be there. Her daughters, Rhiannon and Rowan, hid in the small grove of trees, but she could still see their watery, green eyes piercing through the shadows, their stares stabbing their fear and pain and confusion into her. They weren't supposed to see her like this. With the gag still tightly secured about her mouth, however, her muffled pleas for them to leave went unheard.

Where was their grandmother?

Constance's fiery locks were drenched with tears. Her heart ached. For them, for herself, for her husband, Jacob. She shouldn't have let the rage overtake her; she knew that now, now that it was too late.

"For the crimes of witchcraft, how do you plea?"

Even though the thick rope around her neck made it difficult to escape it—to forget—the reverend's voice jolted her back to reality.

"Not guilty," Constance replied through the gag, unsure if her plea was understood.

"Executioner, please remove the gag from the accused."

The reverend's statement was cold. They had known each other since they were children, but he was but a stranger now as he stood before her. He was once so compassionate, so caring—what had changed?

The executioner approached Constance with apprehension; she soon understood why. Despite the black hood covering his face, his scent—sweet, woody, musky, like freshly-sawn wood mixed with perfume and sweat—immediately revealed his identity: William Black. He removed the gag with haste and stepped across the gallows with a speed she hadn't witnessed him have in years.

How fitting that the town adulterer would be the one to hang her. She wondered who the woman had been, the one whose scent lingered on his clothing and skin. Surely it wasn't his wife, Catherine.

It couldn't be.

She had killed her, in a way, the memory of the act flooding back to her nearly causing her to faint. Seems Catherine and her husband didn't understand the meaning of marriage; then again, neither did Jacob (apparently). Catching him with Catherine was the most heart-breaking of all.

Wyatt Thatcher cleared his throat. "Mrs. Archer—your plea, now that we can hear you."

Constance stared at her old friend, pain and tears welling in her eyes. "Not guilty."

"If not for witchcraft, how do you account for the brutal way you murdered Catherine Black? Surely, you were possessed," countered Reverend Thatcher.

"I didn't murder Catherine Black. As I told you all before, she was attacked by a beast." She wasn't lying, but she wasn't telling the whole truth. The truth wouldn't save her, and she couldn't have her daughters hearing it. They weren't supposed to be here, but calling attention to them now would only make matters worse.

"You're the beast!" a woman's voice sounded from the throng.

"Witch!" said another, followed by her husband's jibe, "You're Satan's whore!"

Reverend Thatcher held his hand to the crowd; without a word, they fell silent. It wasn't their first execution; it probably wouldn't be their last. His attention turned to the defendant, but his eyes remained downcast, staring at the rough wood of the gallows as if it were the most interesting sight he had ever beheld.

Constance knew why Wyatt Thatcher wouldn't look at her, knew he couldn't show a hint of weakness or compassion for her lest he be hanged, too, for sympathizing with the Devil. Satan was in Salem Village that day—no doubt about that. But it wasn't Constance or Reverend Thatcher. The Devil stood in the crowd, reflected in the eyes of every spectator. His hunger bellowed in their calls, their taunts, their glares, and it wouldn't be satisfied until her limp, lifeless body waved in the autumn winds like a banner for their tainted justice, a flag of their blood-stained victory over evil.

Wyatt's hardness broke, even if for just a second, Constance the only witness to the silent tear soaking its fleshy path across his regretful face. "And please explain to us why you were covered in her blood."

"I've told you all this before, Wyatt..." Using the reverend's first name stirred a wave of gasps from the crowd, forcing her to pause. "I carried Catherine into my house to try to stop her bleeding, to prevent her death."

That was a lie; it was what she wanted everyone to believe, but it had been all for naught. It had only sealed her fate.

"And what of your husband's disappearance?" An icy gust of wind blew through Constance's locks of red hair; with it, Thatcher's own coldness returned. "Did you use witchcraft to dispose of his body?"

"My husband was attacked, too, his body dragged into the orchard by the beast."

That was a lie, too. She couldn't tell them the truth—that she had, in a fit of rage after seeing Jacob and Catherine naked in the orchard, cursed her husband's appetite for flesh. The curse had gone horribly wrong...

Horribly, horribly wrong. It turned him into a beast—a huge wolf—a beast whose appetite wasn't satiated with Catherine's flesh, a beast whose appetite would never be satiated. Teeth gnashing, his last kiss was one of death, tearing Catherine's face into an unrecognizable state. The bare breasts to which he had only seconds earlier been so attentive stood like bloody mountains, a deep-red valley between them where her heart had once been.

...Besides, they wouldn't believe her if she had told them the truth.

"If anyone here can speak on behalf of Constance Archer's innocence, please step forward."

Constance searched the now-silent crowd, which stood as still as trees in a forest. Whispers, like the rustle of autumn's fiery leaves, were all that escaped them.

"For the murder of Catherine Black, for the murder of Jacob Archer, and for the crimes of witchcraft, Mrs. Archer, you are found guilty of all charges and sentenced to death by hanging. Do you have any final words or confessions?"

A fire brewed within her; anger, pain, confusion, and regret consumed her—but mostly anger. Her eyes gleamed like emerald glass, tears obscuring her vision. "May the beast that wanders the orchard feed on your children and your children's children!"

The threat was an empty one. She had killed Jacob, too, after he killed Catherine in his beastly hunger, his body consumed by fire and reduced to ash. But they didn't know that.

"Executioner!" Wyatt called out. "Pull the lever."

There were screams and cries when the door of the gallows fell open, but the crowd stayed to watch nonetheless, at least until they were sure the witch was truly dead.

Rowan and Rhiannon waited until everyone had cleared from the gallows before they emerged from the small grove of elm and oak. Rowan buried her face into Rhiannon's shawl—she couldn't look. But Rhiannon stared up at her mother, a small light of life still flickering in her bulging eyes. She watched until it sputtered out, then turned away from the gallows without a word.

Ten years had passed since Constance Archer's life dangled at the end of the hangman's rope at the town gallows, but her name and reputation as a witch hadn't died with her. Despite its invalidity, neither had her curse—at least not the fear of it.

Everyone avoided the orchard; even with the intoxicating scent enticing them, no one dared step within a hundred feet of its fruit-laden trees. Constance's words—like thick smoke—hung heavily in the air, choking, poisoning, haunting the inhabitants of Salem village much like their fear of the craft. Even those who lived on the other side of it would avoid the road cutting through its eastern edge, opting for the longer road circling its western side.

Almost everyone.

Hazel Bishop's cottage sat nestled against its southern edge. In the evening dusk, it was a backdrop of black dotted with red, the tree branches like strangely twisted demon hands soaked in blood. Her grey eyes narrowed, searching the trees for any sign of her granddaughters.

"Rowan...Rhiannon..." Hazel called across the yard into the shadows of the orchard, "dinner will be ready soon!"

Rowan was reaching for a particularly plump apple, her feet nearly slipping on the branch when she heard her name. She arched her neck a bit and cupped her hands on either side of her lips. "Coming, Grandmother!"

She glanced first at the orange sky, quickly greying with the falling daylight, then at the all-but-black ground below. Rhiannon wasn't in sight, but with Edward Winthrop escorting them into the orchard earlier that day, Rowan knew she wouldn't see much of her sister.

With a soft thud, Rowan landed gracefully upon the orchard floor, prized picking in hand, and gathered her belongings. Her basket overwhelmed with apples and a few mushrooms, her quiver and bow upon her shoulder, and the three hares she managed to snag tied to a stick, she bit the apple in her hand and began the search for her elusive twin sister.

A soft giggling gave away Rhiannon's hiding spot.

"C'mon, Rhi. Grandmother's calling us for dinner." Despite the darkness, Rowan's eyes still managed to catch an unintended glance at her sister's bare breast, Rhiannon's pale skin reflecting what little light existed within the orchard's depths. The paleness of her own face flushed slightly. "You should get home, Edward. I don't know how Rhiannon would occupy her time if the beast got you."

"There's no beast, Ro, and you know it," Rhiannon said, clearly unimpressed. "Now help me with my dress."

"Why should I help you? Have Edward do it—he had no issues removing it, he should at least help you put it back on."

"I can't figure out the buttons," Edward said sheepishly.

Rowan chuckled to herself. "Then how did you get it off her?"

"With much difficulty, honestly," he replied softly.

"This is Rhiannon we're talking about, Edward," Rowan said with another soft chuckle. "I doubt there was much difficulty in removing her clothes."

"Rowan Archer! You did not just call me easy!" Rhiannon protested. "Take it back, or I'll..."

"Or you'll what? Tell Grandmother that I had to help you put on your dress because your boyfriend couldn't figure out the buttons?" Even if they couldn't see it through the ever-darkening orchard, Rowan's smile spread from ear to ear.

"He's not my boyfriend!" Rhiannon exclaimed, her temper getting ahead of her thoughts and her tongue.

"I'm not?" Edward asked, slightly heart-broken.

"No..." Rhiannon paused, trying to think of a way to both remedy Edward's pain and cause Rowan some at the same time. "Edward's my fiancé."

"I a..." Edward's words were cut short with the sound of a kick; with a bruised shin and ego, he added, "That's right. Rhi and I are going to be married."

"It isn't your wedding night yet—so get dressed. Grandmother's gonna holler for us again soon."

Rhiannon stepped from beyond a close thicket of trees, still fidgeting with her buttons with one hand and holding Edward's with the other. "Goodnight, Edward."

Edward kissed her softly and released her hand; before turning and heading through the orchard to his family's farm, he replied, "Goodnight, Rhi. Goodnight, Ro."

"Goodnight, Mr. Winthrop," Rowan replied with a sarcastic curtsy, which appeared even more sarcastic given the fact that she was wearing a pair of her father's trousers. "'Ware of the beast on your way home!"

As they made their way to their grandmother's cottage, Rowan remained silent until she was sure Edward would be unable to hear them. "You're not really getting married, are you?"

"I might."

"Does Edward know about your secret love for Asher Black?" Rowan pressed.

"I do not secretly love Asher Black!" defended Rhiannon. "Asher Black is a homely boy; Edward is far more handsome."

It was far from the truth. William 'Asher' Black was the most handsome young man in all of Salem Village. Years of working in the sawmill with his father had burdened him with a lean, muscular frame. That alone was enough to cause some of the young girls—even some older woman—to swoon, but it was his piercing black eyes that hypnotized the lot.

"Don't lie to me, Rhi. I've seen the way you look at him, the longing in your eyes," Rowan countered. "You don't even have that longing in your eyes when you look at Edward."

Rhiannon grabbed Rowan's arm forcefully, nearly knocking the basket of apples from her grasp. "The only way I look at Asher Black is with disgust. His parents are the reason we are without ours! His mother lured our father from our mother— she's the true witch, if you ask me! And his father was the one who pulled the lever at the gallows on the morning of Mother's hanging!"

It was true, mostly. Although he wore the black hood to hide his identity on that fateful morning, William Black made it no secret that he was the one to hang Constance Archer, often—in drunken slurs—boasting of being Salem's Savior for saving the village from the worst witch of all.

Despite sharing his given name, Asher was nothing like his father; Rhiannon, most of all, knew it. Asher was polite and respectful and, since his father's death two years back, the honest and hardworking proprietor of Salem's mill.

Rowan knew the real reason Rhiannon, despite her attraction, hadn't pursued Asher instead of Edward, but as her sister's grip increasingly tightened on her arm, she knew better to hold her tongue.

Tendrils of smoke, smelling heavily of venison and potatoes, curled from the chimney of their grandmother's cottage. The two large windows at the front cast light onto the fieldstone path leading from the gate to the short set of stairs that ascended to the threshold.

"I was getting worried," Hazel greeted them when they finally approached, the cottage's red door swinging open and flooding warm light into the darkness. "Those orchards are full of dangerous predators."

Hazel glanced at Rhiannon's disheveled appearance and added, "Including the two-legged variety."

Rowan laughed to herself at her grandmother's wit, handing her the hares and diverting her attention away from her sister. "Don't worry, Grandmother, if there were a beast out there, I'd have already tracked it down and killed it. We'd be eating it—instead of the other way around."

"I don't doubt you could, my dear, but it's not the beast that has me worried. There are wolves in these parts—real ones that pose real danger, and often hunt in packs," Hazel answered. "You two still need to be careful out there in that orchard."

"You'd think, with us being witches an all, we'd have no reason to worry," Rhiannon said smartly. She knew the subject still struck a bitter chord with her grandmother. "Perhaps if you teach us the craft..."

Deep lines—deeper than the ones time had already forged—cut across Hazel's forehead. With her lips pursed and her eyes narrowed, she declared, "You know full well that there's no such thing as witchcraft!"

It was a lie, but only Rhiannon knew it.

Hazel Bishop was, at one time, the most sought-after witch in all of Salem. She was the best of the best, and she once had her own coven. All of that changed with the Trials, but it didn't stop her from practicing the craft, nor did it stop her from teaching her daughter. It was with her daughter's death, however, that she swore she'd never practice again—and she hadn't.

"Of course not," Rowan placated. "She's just playing, that's all."

The deep lines in Hazel's forehead diminished, leaving only the usual ones in their place. "The food is going to get cold. I've already set the table for dinner, so quickly wash up."

"Yes, Grandmother," the twins said in near unison.

When she was sure her Grandmother was out of earshot, Rowan nudged her sister. "It's a good thing you didn't tell her about your upcoming marriage, eh?"

"Shut it, Ro."

"I'm sure you'll make an excellent wife, Mrs. Winthrop," insisted Rowan as she feigned marching along the braided runner between the door and the kitchen as if in matrimonial procession.

Rhiannon grabbed Rowan's arm as she had before in the orchard. "I said shut it!"

Rowan's eyes narrowed, but she didn't say another word.

Rhiannon woke to her twin sister's scream. She watched confusedly as Rowan frantically grasped about her neck, as if trying to remove the hands of an invisible assailant. "What's wrong, Ro?"

Gasping for air and still fighting an unseen force, Rowan managed, "Rope."

Rhiannon leapt from her bed and crossed the distance to her sister's bed in a flash, barely touching the rough floor enough to feel its icy chill. She felt around her sister's neck but found no rope. "There's nothing, Ro. It was probably just a nightmare."

Rowan's breathing steadied following a series of short coughs. "It was real, Rhi. I could feel the rope around my neck, could feel it tighten. I was being hanged—just like Mother."

"There's no rope," Rhiannon affirmed. "You're probably just remembering Mother's death."

"I can't believe you talked me into going to the gallows that day," Rowan replied. "I hated seeing her like that, hated hearing everyone's hatred and fear."

Rhiannon's compassion for her mother wasn't as great as her sister's. She had seen too much to know her mother was more sinner than saint, to know that she deserved—at least partially—the punishment given to her. If anything, Rhiannon resented her mother almost as much as she resented her grandmother. Both kept far too many secrets from the girls, the biggest being majick.

Rhiannon's eyes gleamed with a strange fire as she turned to Rowan. "Ro," she began, "haven't you ever wondered about majick, about our gifts, about the secrets grandmother refuses to share?"

"Not really. They're just stories—rumors, even. Grandmother is not a witch, Mother wasn't one, and neither are we."

Rhiannon knew better, knew far more than her sister did. Truth be known, they had both witnessed enough majick in their youth, before their mother's death; Rowan must have blocked out the memories, shoved any thoughts of their mother that tainted her perfect image into the deepest recesses of her mind.

But Rhiannon remembered.

"What if I could prove it to you, Ro?" Rhiannon plied. "Would you be open to majick?"

"If majick truly existed, and you could find some way to prove its existence, then sure—I'd have to believe, no?"

Grabbing her robe from the back of their door, Rhiannon crept down the short hallway into the cabin's living quarters. She was thankful for the soft glow flickering from the fireplace, shadow and light dancing off the pine walls and time-polished floors, lighting the way. The hearth bore only a few dying flames, just more than embers, so Rhiannon knew her grandmother had gone to bed hours before. Still, she crept quietly, ever careful of the floorboards that would betray her with their screeching cries of disturbance.

Her grandmother may have stopped practicing the craft, but Rhiannon knew all too well the secret compartment in which all of her paraphernalia was kept. It was truly a clever compartment: a false bottom drawer in the built-in shelves that lined the short, half-wall separating the kitchen from the rest of the living quarters. In it, a myriad of candles, boxes, and jars all concealed the one item for which she searched.

The Grimoire was heavy, crafted of a strange animal skin Rhiannon couldn't place—scaly, as if reptilian, yet soft at the same time, like brushed suede. The cover resisted at first; Rhiannon could have sworn the loud noise emitted from the book when she finally managed to open it was a moan—very human, not at all the sound a book should make. Deciding it best to peruse its pages when silence wasn't such a necessity, Rhiannon replaced the boxes and trinkets that once covered the book and tiptoed back to her bedroom.

Though they were twins and were mirrors of each other in appearance, she and Rowan shared no personality trait, save one. Rowan's curiosity had kept her awake, just as Rhiannon expected it would. "That proof enough for you?"

Rowan's green eyes sparked as if lit by fire, yet there was no flame present in the room. Only the soft glow of the moon cascaded from the window, the shaft of it falling squarely on Rowan's quilt where the Grimoire now rested. "What is it?"

"It's a spellbook," Rhiannon said. "I told you—we're witches. It's our birthright."

"Where did you get this?" A tinge of fear resonated upon Rowan's usual velvety voice, but she couldn't hide the excitement that flickered in her eyes, at least not from Rhiannon. "Why haven't you shown me this before now?"

"You weren't ready," Rhiannon proclaimed. "But you are now, and tomorrow we shall spend the day in the orchard studying it from cover to cover."

"What about Grandmother?" Rowan countered. "Won't she discover the missing grim..."

Rhiannon cut Rowan short. "The Grimoire is the furthest thing from Grandmother's mind; she's probably completely blocked it from her memory—much like you have."

Rhiannon skimmed the Grimoire, whose pages were filled with languages and symbols she didn't recognize, until she landed on one with a drawing of a cloaked figure more resemblant of a raven than a human. The name under the picture—Morrigan—wasn't one that Rhiannon recognized, but the words on the pages that followed were in English. "Ro—get over here!...Rowan!"

"Coming!" Rowan called as she emerged from the trees lining the clearing's western edge. "It's not like I'll likely catch anything now with all your carrying on!"

"Hush. I found something."

Rowan stared down at the picture. "What is it? It looks scary. And grotesque."

"It is," admitted Rhiannon, "but we're summoning it anyway."

"Summoning it? You want that thing here? With us?" Rowan's usual calmness had dissipated, replaced by apprehension and absolute fear. "I...I, uh, I don't think that's a good idea, Rhi—"

"It's the only spell in here I can read," Rhiannon interrupted. "Besides, you don't believe in majick anyway."

"Well, I, uh...if it truly exists, like you say it does, I don't want to see this..." Rowan lingered on the last word as she pointed at the figure, "Morrigan."

Rhiannon skimmed the words on the adjacent page. "Morrigan is the Great Queen, goddess of strife, of spirits, and sovereign of the dead."

"I've heard enough," Rowan said. "Doesn't sound like we should tempt fate."

"Stop being a coward!" Rhiannon exploded.

It certainly wasn't the first time her sister had raised her voice to her, but Rowan sensed a strangeness in Rhiannon's tone; a darkness that had always lingered under the surface was now palpable in the tension between them.

"I'm sorry, Ro, I didn't mean to..." Rhiannon's apology fell silent as she struggled to find her words. She played on her sister's weakness. "If this Morrigan is the goddess of the dead, perhaps she can help us talk to Mother."

Excitement stirred in Rowan's eyes. "Do you really think so?"

"I don't see why not," Rhiannon replied, half-lying. Surely a goddess of the dead could call forth a spirit—even if that wasn't Rhiannon's intention in summoning her. "Feel like gathering some kindling? It says we need a fire to perform the spell."

"Are you sure about this?" Rowan asked, but Rhiannon's returned look was all she needed for an answer.

As Rowan disappeared back into the depths of the orchard in search of small branches for a fire, Rhiannon gathered some grasses from the clearing, making sure they were dry enough to ignite with ease.

On the next page, instructions on preparation for the spell were listed in detail, including a stellate diagram, which Rhiannon studied for some time before searching the clearing for rocks in order to recreate the design upon the ground. Her search in the grasses only procured a few stones, and so, remembering a short rock wall, she ventured east into the forest with her sister's basket in tow. By the time Rowan had returned with enough wood to start and maintain a fire, Rhiannon had nearly completed the pentagram shape with the stones from the wall.

"What is all this?" Rowan asked as she dumped the load of wood at her feet.

"It's the diagram in Grimoire; it's needed for the spell," Rhiannon replied curtly. Without looking up from the task, she pointed to the east side of the clearing. "Now go gather some more rocks from the wall over there. It's almost done."

When the diagram was finished, Rhiannon stood in the crotch of two of the points—Rowan at the tip of the point opposite her—and admired the work. "Now we wait."

"Wait? For what?"

"Nightfall...for witching hour."

Rowan's brow furrowed. "We shouldn't worry Grandmother. We should come back when she's fast asleep."

Rowan expected an outburst from her sister—even a scathing glare—but was surprised when Rhiannon's eyes lightened and the corners of her mouth curled upward into a smile.

At least momentarily. "That was the plan, half-wit."

Rowan checked on her Grandmother twice, assuring that she was truly asleep. "She's snoring. One of her deepest in a long while," she said plainly as she re-entered the bedroom she shared with her sister. Part of her wished she had lied to Rhiannon, that she had delayed their departure, but a sense of excitement for the spell had settled in since their return home. She still feared the creature pictured in the Grimoire, but the allure of majick—the promise of possible power in a world that seemed to hold none for someone of her status—was compelling.

"Good. We have only an hour or so before the witching hour is over, so we must walk quickly."

The orchard loomed over them as they retraced their path back toward the clearing; towers of twisting branches laden with autumn's fruit blocked the pallid light of the moon. Were it not for the sole lantern swinging rhythmically in Rhiannon's grasp, the path would have been impossible to find.

"Place a candle at each of the star's points," Rhiannon commanded once they reached the clearing. "I'll light the central fire."

Rowan did as told, placing a candle at each of the points as she walked the perimeter of the pentagram. She watched her sister pour a bit of lantern fuel on the pile of grass and wood in the center; all at once it was ablaze.

"Shall I light the candles?" Rowan asked.

"There's no need. When the time comes, they'll light of their own accord," Rhiannon explained. "Let me see your hand."

"My hand?"

"Yes. We need to make a blood sacrifice. It'll just be a prick." Rhiannon pulled a knife from the folds of her dress and pricked the tip of her index finger. "See?"

Rowan held out her hand and winced long before Rhiannon stuck her with the blade; hearing the screams emanating from Rowan's mouth upon being cut, one would have thought she was being tortured and murdered.

"Oh, stop it! It wasn't that bad, you big baby," Rhiannon protested. She retrieved a leaf from ground and let it gather some of her blood before holding it under Rowan's fingertip to do the same. When she felt it was painted with enough red, she threw the leaf into the fire.

Upon their sacrifice, the candles sprung to flame in progression until each flickered wildly in the growing breeze around them.

"Come hold my hand and recite this passage with me."

Rowan joined her sister—who held the Grimoire open to the incantation—at the northern point of the star. She let Rhiannon take the lead on the recitation, but soon the gaps in their words faded until they spoke in perfect unison:

"Guardians of the Shadowlands, hear and guide our plea;
When the witching hour rings true, bring Morrigan for us to see.
Other souls who hear our calls are not welcome in this place;
Only she who is known as Morrigan may enter our sacred space."

Three times the twins repeated the incantation, as directed by the Grimoire, but nothing happened. What seemed like minutes passed by in silence before Rowan exhaled the breath she had been holding in anticipation for the appearance of the creature drawn on the page of the book before them.

"Shhh!" Rhiannon said as she drew her blood-stained finger to her lips and scowled at her sister.

"Nothing happened, Rhi. Face it—we're not witches."

The wind began to howl around them, the force of it extinguishing the candles placed about the perimeter, and the flames at the center danced wickedly.

"Oh, but you are, my dearies."

The sisters stopped their bickering and quickly turned to the increasing blaze in the center, the source of the voice. A hooded figure now stood within the fire, its black cloak unaffected by the flames.

"Who are you?" Rowan asked stupidly.

The feather-lined cowl of the black cloak hid the figure's face completely—only darkness and shadow lingering beneath it. A chill of fear and excitement stirred within Rhiannon.

No answer came from the depths of the hood. Only the sound of the crackling fire filled the silence.

Despite its stupidity, Rhiannon reiterated her sister's query, "Who are you?"

"I think it's the Devil," Rowan said softly. "I told you we shouldn't have done this."

"You also said that majick didn't exist." Rhiannon's jaw tightened as the words slid past her grating teeth. "This witch stands before you as proof, proof that we are also the witches we are rumored to be."

A sinister laugh—a cackle of sorts—resonated from within the cloak. *"It was you who called us. Clearly you know who we are."*

"Us?" Rowan asked, confused by the singular entity that stood before them.

A strange sound—the innocent laughter of a child mixed with primordial darkness—resonated from under the hood. The sinister cackle became louder and deeper, splitting into two separate tones. The figure shifted with the flames, solidified, and then stepped from the fire to stand before the twins. Two voices in perfect unison spoke, *"We are older than the craft, the Devil, and the Earth upon which you stand. The only witches here, dearhearts, are the two of you. There is only one reason for you to summon us, one reason why the Grimoire revealed only this spell to you. You know nothing of the world from which you come, The Other. We are here to grant you that knowledge."*

"The Other?" Rowan echoed.

"Of course. The Shadowlands, Land of Shadow and Majick," answered the first. *"It is the land of your people, from where your mother..."*

"Your mother's mother..." continued the second.

"And all their mothers before that descend," concluded the first.

"It is our birthplace," they said, again as one, *"the loins of light and darkness from which we were born."*

"You can teach us majick?" Rhiannon asked, her eyes widening and her heartbeat quickening, excitement replacing fear.

"Grandmother would forbid it," Rowan answered shakily.

"Poor, poor Rowan. Always the obedient one," said the first.

"How did you know her name?" Rhiannon asked taking a slow-but-steady step backward, her excitement quickly dissipating.

"We know all, my dear Rhiannon," answered the dual voices, the two oddly blended as one. *"We have no ears..."*

"But we hear every whisper," said the second.

"And every outcry," the first concluded.

"We have no eyes..." the two voices joined once again.

"But we can see all the darkness," said the first.

"And all the light," said the second.

"We have no mouth and only tongues of flame," said the two.

"But we can speak of truth," said the second.

"And we can speak of lies," countered the first.

"Are you good or evil?" Rowan demanded.

"She is evil," said the second.

"She is good," said the other.

Then together, as if one, *"We are neither and we are both. We are light and darkness, night and day, life and death, fortune and strife... We are Morrigan, two souls in one vessel, twins born of fire and ash."*

"Without her..." one voice said.

"She doesn't exist," said the second. *"And without her..."*

"She is nothing," said the first.

"We need to leave," Rowan pleaded to her sister.

"Come with us, to The Other, The Shadowlands, stay with us a while and we'll show you the majick your grandmother has forbade you to know."

"We will not go!" Rowan proclaimed.

"One voice," said the first.

"*Answering for two,*" said the other.

Then both, "*How oddly familiar. And what of your decision, Rhiannon?*"

"I want to know majick—like Mother—but I will not go with you," Rhiannon admitted. "There must be another way."

The second, softer voice laughed, a childlike innocence mingling among the tones, "*There is a way.*"

"*But there is but one,*" finished the first, followed by a haunting cackle.

"And what is that?" Rowan demanded.

"*Come closer and we'll show you,*" said both.

"*Yes, do please...*" said the second.

"*Come closer,*" the first continued.

What had once been a roaring blaze had now died to embers and sputtering flames, weak tongues stuttering, limply licking their prey. Morrigan turned to look at the dwindling fire with unseen eyes then turned back to Rowan and Rhiannon. Ivory fingers, once concealed, protruded from the feather-cuffed sleeve of the cloak, stark white against the folds of ebony. She placed the tips of her left thumb and middle finger together; with a loud snap, the fire roared back to life.

Rhiannon's lips curled in admiration. She took a step forward. And then another.

"Rhiannon, no!" Rowan protested, grabbing her sister's arm. "It's a trick."

"*I'm a trickster, that's true enough,*" said the first.

"*But I am not,*" said the second. "*I assure you there is no trick.*"

Rhiannon took two more steps closer to the fire, closer to the cloaked figure who spoke promises of majick; Rowan followed hesitantly but remained two steps behind her sister.

"*Closer, lovelies,*" Morrigan hissed, "*so that you may hold our hands.*"

The fire roared a little fiercer with each step that Rhiannon took...one, two, three...closer, until she was nearly touching Morrigan's emaciated, outstretched hands; her own fire within roared a little fiercer, too, longing for the majick she was never taught, never allowed to use.

"*Come, Rowan,*" said the second.

"*Come, Rhiannon,*" said the first.

Then both, "*Join us, and we will show you majick.*"

Rhiannon reached for Morrigan's right hand while Rowan, though hesitant, reached for her left. As soon as their hands touched Morrigan's icy, pale skin, the fire in the center of the star blazed about them, the ash and smoke suffocating Rhiannon and the flame and embers searing Rowan's skin.

Rowan and Rhiannon screamed, their opened mouths soon filling with fire and ash respectively, and their screams extinguished.

"*You must learn to control it,*" the dual voices of Morrigan said.

"*Command the fire,*" said the second.

"*Manipulate the ash,*" said the first. "*Embrace its energy...*"

"And with it, its majick," finished the second.

"And with it, all majick," added the first.

Rhiannon coughed, spewing the smoke and ash; it swirled in tendrils about her head, her arms, her chest, until shrouding her like the darkness over the night sky. What was once ethereal and soot was now solid, a hooded cloak of black now in its place.

Rowan struggled to tame the fire that engulfed her. Its heat was stifling, sweat beading on her porcelain skin, but it did not burn her.

"Embrace it, my dear," said the second. *"Become one with the flames."*

Rowan's eyes narrowed and her face hardened in concentration. Her eyes rolled back, showing only white, and darted back and forth violently. The fire that danced along Rowan's body soon turned to blood-red velvet, a crimson cloak to rival Rhiannon's.

Morrigan, whose cold hands still firmly gripped the sisters', tightened her grasp even more. She pulled them closer, toward the fire that had since been replaced. *"Come, my sweets, to The Other."*

"You said we didn't have to go," Rowan protested, struggling to free herself from Morrigan's corpse-like hands.

"You said there was another way," added Rhiannon.

Morrigan pulled harder, standing, drawing them closer to the fire.

Rowan dug her heels into the sod and grunted, "Let go!"

"We will not. Not until you show us your majick."

"Let go!" Rhiannon echoed, but it was no use.

The two sisters looked at one another, an idea stirring; the majick coursed through them, giving them strength, but they didn't fight the force of Morrigan. With a mischievous look upon her face, Rhiannon shouted, "Now!"

With their newfound strength, the twins—instead of pulling—pushed Morrigan into the fire, the momentum launching her into the flames.

The fire sputtered and died out.

"Allow me," Rowan said, smiling. She held her hand, palm facing up, and blew across its surface, flames instantly dancing to life at her fingertips. They waltzed across the air and into the makeshift hearth, and the fire roared once more.

The flames danced upon Morrigan's ebony cloak, but it did not burn. It turned crimson, like Rowan's, and then Morrigan vanished completely, her dual-toned, cackling laughter mixed with the crackling of the wood, as if one.

With no sign of the Morrigan amongst the fire and ash, Rowan and Rhiannon called each back, summoning the elements into their enchanted cloaks. They doused the embers and retrieved their belongings, then headed back to the cottage.

"Should we have destroyed the pentagram?" Rowan asked, eliciting a genuine smile from her sister's face.

"Don't worry, Ro, no one is going to see it," Rhiannon answered. "Everyone still fears the orchard."

Asher Black never ventured into the orchard. He wasn't fearful of it, like most, and he never believed in such nonsense as Constance Archer's curse or the beast rumored to haunt it. And yet, the unequivocal darkness lingering within the grove of twisted branches kept him out just the same.

Except today.

A voice called to him. Not directly, but it called to him nevertheless. He had followed the melodic notes, which had drifted to Salem's mill like a birdsong along the breeze, to the orchard's edge where he now stood. The voice wasn't one he recognized, but the song was familiar, a haunting folksong about the orchard from whence it came. His grandmother had sang it to him on several occasions; so had his mother, before her death. The haunting lyrics were unmistakable, the melody sung as sweetly as he had ever heard it despite the dark nature. He knew the song was dribble, a ploy by the church to maintain their Puritan rule over Salem, and a failed attempt to keep the budding youth from picking the proverbial apple.

As he entered the wood, he sang along with the hidden voice, the words crisp and hardened in his memory:

> *The Grim be a creature wicked and strange*
> *He rises from the darkness to change*
> *Into a man, more evil than good,*
> *Its home? It is in Salem Wood.*
>
> *When he be man, he takes a wife,*
> *When he be beast, he takes her life.*
> *Ladies, beware of the Devil's brood,*
> *A beast who comes from Salem Wood.*
>
> *His love they willingly accept,*
> *But after they have loved and slept,*
> *Who is the beast that drinks their blood?*
> *'Tis the Grim from Salem Wood.*
>
> *From south o' the wood, a maiden came*
> *A target for his charm, his bane.*
> *Eager for love, though no fool's lass,*
> *She knew the secret of the craft.*

Just before the last verse was sung, Asher spotted a clearing in the orchard and the source of the beautiful singing. Rowan Archer sat on a felled tree; she continued to sing as she turned to see him, and he sang the words with her just the same:

And so, while the Grim kissed the dame,
She summoned the ash, she conjured a flame;
She had majick power, it was in her blood,
To slay the beast from Salem Wood.

"You have a beautiful voice," Asher offered as he approached. "I followed it through the orchard."

Rowan's cheeks turned as red as her cloak. "Thank you. Yours isn't half bad either."

"I'm Asher." His hand extended in front of him in greeting, though she didn't take it.

"I know," she said, instantly regretting her words. Not wanting to sound as desperate as her words indicated, she quickly added, "Your father was the executioner who killed my mother," regretting those words, too.

"And your mother was hanged for killing mine." The words weren't as cold as they should have been, more truth than taunt.

"My grandmother would tan my hide if she knew I was even speaking to you; she forbade it."

Asher smiled. He had seen Rowan many times in the village, but there was something different about her, something radiant, something fiery in her voice and her eyes. He always secretly longed for her, but now he wanted her even more. "Then I guess we shouldn't tell her."

"I'm Rowan." Her cheeks flushed again as their hands touched, his skin sending ripples of fire down her spine. She'd never led on that she, too, secretly pined for Asher just as Rhiannon did, and Rhiannon was never the wiser.

He smiled again, a devilish grin that elicited more fire under the surface of Rowan's skin. "I know."

"I should go," she said, "my sister will be looking for me any moment."

It was no secret—not even to Asher—that Rhiannon liked him. "Yes. Your sister's presence would be most unfortunate."

Rowan couldn't help but chuckle.

"May I see you again?" Asher asked. "When your sister's presence isn't a possibility, that is."

"Rhiannon will be occupied by Edward Winthrop tomorrow until late evening," Rowan stated. "They're to be married, you know, come spring."

"Does she love him?"

"She loves the attention he gives her," Rowan offered with a bit of laughter. "But I am unsure that Rhiannon is capable of love."

"Harsh."

"Yes, perhaps, but not untruthful." Not wanting to linger on the subject of her twin sister, Rowan diverted the conversation. "Shall we meet here tomorrow?"

"I will be here around four o'clock."

"Promise?"

Asher's black eyes seemed to sparkle, most likely from the reflection of the waning sun, but they hypnotized Rowan just the same. He stepped closer to her and she could sense the electricity in the air between them. *Had he secretly longed for her as she longed for him all this time?*

His lips were inches from hers, though the invisible fire that lingered upon her own was as if they were already touching.

He stepped closer and whispered, "Let's seal it with a kiss, shall we?"

As if to answer, Rowan closed her eyes and awaited the touch of his lips—lips that occupied more thoughts than she cared to admit. When she opened her eyes again, Asher was gone. *Had this, too, been a dream?* If it weren't for the undeniable scent of sawn wood that still lingered upon the air, she would have thought so.

Later that evening, Asher stared into the lantern on the table before him and watched the dancing flame. It reminded him of Rowan—but, then again, what didn't? Even before his father's death, Asher had felt so alone, so empty. But thoughts of Rowan Archer filled that void, completed him. He had seen her several times in town, but had never dared utter a word to her for fear of the unsolicited wrath she would have to endure from her sister.

But all that had changed. She loved him, too!

He walked dreamily to bed—perhaps all of it was but a dream—as if drunk, but the only intoxicant his lips had ever touched were Rowan Archer's lips. He could still taste them, sweet and sugary like a late-harvest apple, its ivory flesh cloaked in crimson.

Rhiannon lowered her cowl to hide her eyes as she ducked behind a building. Edward couldn't see her, couldn't know that she was following him. She wondered where he could be going at this hour—they were to be married just three days hence—but with the next turn he took, Rhiannon knew his destination: Rebekah Goldthwaite's farm.

She hadn't wanted to believe the gossip—the other girls had always been jealous of her relationship with Edward—but the details of the rumors and the discrepancies in his recent whereabouts was what had her skulking behind him in secret and darkness.

The Goldthwaite farm shone like a beacon in the blanket of night, a flickering candle still blazing from every window despite the hour. A smile flooded over Edward's lips, the same smile that once illuminated his face whenever he was with Rhiannon. Her temper threatened to consume her like a fire burning inside the depths of her stomach, threatening to expel from her mouth in a hot and seething flow of emotion. She moved forward with him, toward the house, but when the light nearly heralded her presence, she ducked into the shadows of a huge elm nearby. She couldn't be caught—but she needed proof.

Rhiannon had beckoned to her father as she followed him through the orchard, but the rustling leaves drowned out her calls and the wind carried her voice away from his ears. He didn't know she had followed him, didn't know she saw him kissing a woman other than her mother. Now, as she hid behind an apple tree at the edge of the clearing, she realized she wasn't the only one to follow her father.

Rhiannon ducked in the shadows of the orchard—undiscovered, undetected— and stared across the clearing at her mother's green eyes, which now flickered with tempestuous anger. She couldn't hear the words spoken, couldn't hear the curse expelled from her mother's tongue, but she saw the effects.

Her father's body—naked, thrusting, rapt with lust for the naked woman lying underneath of him—seized, his limbs twitching and neck twisting to inhuman lengths. He threw his head back, not caused by the throws of passion but in a savage howl, a voice more monster than man. His hands, which remained on the ground as he held himself over the woman, transformed into beastly paws—complete with razor-sharp claws. The hair that covered what used to be his hands began sprouting from his wrists, his arms, moving upward until his entire body was wrapped in a suit of blackish-brown fur.

It was only a legend. Stories. Tales meant to ward children from venturing into the Orchard unaccompanied. But as Rhiannon cowered in the shadows, she couldn't deny the very real creature in the clearing between her mother and herself. A grim. The Grim.

He howled again; whatever remnant of a man lingered behind the first howl was completely absent this time. The naked woman lying under him screamed in horror. Rhiannon did the same, so startled by the woman's piercing notes.

The Grim's eyes were now fixated on the woman, who writhed and wrenched in an attempt to escape. Fruitless. The first snap of the beast's jaws landed on her neck; the screams stopped then—even Rhiannon's. She froze in fear as she watched the blood pool in the grass around the woman's lifeless body, watched the repeated gnashing of teeth now stained red with life.

When the beast tore the heart from the woman's chest, Rhiannon couldn't hold

back her screams; despite her own hands over her mouth, the notes still eked out
between tiny fingers. Her mother hadn't heard it, but the beast had. With the still-
beating heart in clenched teeth and blood dripping from gaping jowls, the beast
turned his attention to the shadows, to Rhiannon.

It launched itself toward the clearing's edge, its eyes piercing the darkness to stare
deeply into Rhiannon's. She wasn't sure why, but as it leapt toward the trees, she
closed them. When no teeth fell upon her neck, when she wasn't devoured as she
expected, she re-opened them to see a pile of ash before her, still smoldering within a
ring of fire upon the ground.

Rhiannon wiped a tear from her face. The memory had crept in unexpectedly, but why? She still stood in the shadows of the elm, but with a quick glance at the moon's position in the sky, she could tell much time had passed.

Stepping from the shadows, she re-entered the little path to the front door of Rebekah's farmhouse. Though the candles were nearly spent, they were still lit, a sign the occupants of the house were too pre-occupied with other affairs to bother with snuffing them.

Fueled by anger and the pain that still lingered from the memory of her father's death, she placed a hand on the knob. The door opened much more quietly than the door to Grandmother's cottage; for this, she was thankful. From the foyer, she could hear commotion above, and she ascended the stairs on the tips of her toes.

It wasn't in vain, either, as the two making the commotion hadn't heard her enter. The white of Edward's ass bobbed up and down as if he were a ship at the docks, except it wasn't to her bollard his mooring was tethered. She watched them, amused, bewildered, heartbroken, and scorned. "So this is how you spend your time when I'm not by your side?"

Her voice was calm, calculated, much more than it should have been.

"Rhi—" Edward began in earnest, but there was no recovery or denial from what her eyes had just seen—what they were still seeing as both he and Rebekah covered themselves frantically.

"And you!" she shouted, jabbing her finger in the air toward Rebekah's sweaty, disheveled face. "I should have known never to trust the daughter of a whore!"

"My mother was no whore!" Rebekah defended. She should have stopped there, but she didn't. "But I'd rather be the daughter of a whore than the daughter of a witch!"

"Silly, silly girl," Rhiannon replied with unusual restraint. "Were you not all bosom and partially brain, you would realize just how asinine that statement truly is. A whore's only power lies between her legs, whereas a witch's power is found within the entirety of her body. It's in her blood, her tears, even in the words she speaks."

"So you are a witch?" Edward asked. An axe, shed or no shed, he never was.

Rhiannon's eyes flamed, restraint no longer a possibility. Drawing her hand back momentarily, the one whose finger still pointed with intent, she extended it once more. This time, however, her cloak of black rose from her body in tendrils of smoke—which, too, reached out, following where her finger aimed. With not so much as a thought and but a quick snap of her wrist, Rhiannon wrapped the tendrils around Rebekah's pretty little neck. "Just so you know, Rebekah, they hanged the whores of Salem alongside the witches."

Another quick flick of her wrist, and the sound of Rebekah's neck as it broke echoed in the darkness of the room, a smile betraying the tears that lingered in Rhiannon's eyes.

"NO!" Edward shouted.

"Poor, poor Edward," Rhiannon said tauntingly. She looked at his body, everything exposed, no longer covered as he cradled Rebekah's lifeless one. She loved him—still—but she'd never trust him. "I guess the two of you were meant for one another, for now your lover is as limp as your prick."

He didn't reply, save the tears that poured from his eyes, his attention never drifting from the woman to whom he still hopelessly clung.

Rhiannon lifted her hand and drew her lips close to her palm, blowing as Rowan had done those many, many months ago when they first acquired their cloaks. Black tendrils curled from her fingertips, filling the room with darkness and smoke. She walked toward the door, looking back one last time at her fiancé. "Where there's smoke, there's fire; and where there's fire, there's ash."

Her descent down the steps wasn't nearly as cautious as her ascent had been, and the quietness of the door mattered not as she flew over its threshold in haste. When she had reached the same elm, she turned back toward the house.

Smoke curled from the chimneys and open door. She could hear sobbing amidst the choking, but she cared not. As she had promised, the smoke soon turned to fire, the flames consuming the interior of the farmhouse in a matter of minutes. She finally understood her mother and the vision she had before entering the house; the illusion she had had of her perfect father existed no more, and his indiscretion had been brought to light with Edward's.

She heard the townspeople on the path, drawn by the smoke and fire, making their way toward the property. She wouldn't be humiliated! She would not suffer as her mother had suffered, would not be put on display and mocked. Before she could see them, and as agonizingly as she could, she cried out to the townspeople, "Help!" She coughed, an act, before calling out again. "Please, help us!"

Her power served her well. Ash now covered her face as if she, too, had been in the fire and had escaped; the tears—which came a little too easily, she admitted, vowing this night would be the last time she'd cry—streaked the black soot on her face for effect.

Her eyes narrowed as Reverend Thatcher came into view. She hadn't expected, hadn't wanted, to see him. She should have realized, with his property the closest to the Goldthwaite's, he would be the first to arrive.

But she quickly recovered her feign...

"Oh, Reverend! Please! Edward is still in there! He—" she paused to sob, whether an act or in earnest even she could not say, "—we went in to make sure no one was inside. He searched the upper floor and I searched the lower; when I found it empty, he told me to go outside.

"The whole place was filled with smoke and was so hot, Reverend," she said as she stared sharply into his worried eyes and played on his profession. "It was as if I were glimpsing Hell."

He wrapped his arms around her tightly, as if to protect her from the Infernal fires. "Oh, Rhiannon, my dear. It will surely be the only glimpse of it you'll ever get, my child, a sweet girl like yourself..."

She hated his touch; she hated him. He'd let her mother die; he'd let her hang. She wanted to kill him on the spot, snap his neck like he had ordered for her mother's fate, like she had just done to Rebekah, but she had to endure his arms around her if she wanted to play the part of the damsel. She couldn't kill him—at least not today.

"HELP!" a voice called from within.

"He's still alive!" Rhiannon exclaimed. *How could he still be alive?* She thought as her eyes narrowed once more. "Someone PLEASE! Help my Edward!"

Solomon Cole, the largest man in Salem and the kindest, dashed past Rhiannon and Reverend Thatcher and through the ring of fire that was now the threshold. If anyone in Salem could save Edward Winthrop from a fiery death, it'd be Solomon—and as much as Rhiannon adored gentle Solomon, Edward couldn't live. He'd talk, and Rhiannon couldn't have that.

Reaching deep within, she summoned the full strength of her power. The rest of the village had arrived to help, but it was too late. With a thunderous clamor and expulsion of soot and smoke, the Goldthwaite's farmhouse collapsed upon itself...as burning houses often do. Rhiannon only needed to give it a bit of a push—it's not like it wouldn't have happened on its own.

"EDWARD!!" she screamed, fleeing the Reverend's hold toward the pile of fiery rubble, and dropped to her knees in a dramatic ploy. She allowed herself to cry once more; this time it was no act. She cried for her mother—not Edward— something she had never allowed herself to do that day at the gallows or any day since. She understood, finally, and she knew all she had to do to avenge her.

When Rhiannon reached the clearing, she didn't expect to see Asher Black; she stopped dead in her tracks and remained in the shadows. Her eyes were deceiving her, that was her initial thought, but upon hearing his voice—deep and soft and unforgettable—she knew her eyes revealed only truth.

Seeing him would have been a welcomed sight; seeing him standing so close to her sister, Rowan, however, was not. Even the two of them standing there would have been forgivable, but when she saw them kiss, saw the look of longing in Asher's eyes just prior, it was all she could do to keep herself from screaming, from bolting from the shadows and reducing Rowan to a pile of ash. She could have—she wanted to—but she stood and waited.

She didn't care if Rowan loved him—she loved him first. She would get a kiss from Asher Black, even if it were the last thing she did.

Asher Black stared at his reflection in the looking glass; much had changed since he had last looked into it many years before. All the pain and loneliness he had felt over the years following his parents' deaths—especially his mother's—was still echoed in his sunken cheekbones and the lines etched upon his face, but his black eyes now held a fiery sparkle and his once-pale skin now glowed with the same warmth.

He smiled, the memory of two afternoons before creeping into the foreground of his mind. It still seemed like a dream...

Asher stood in the shadows of the trees around the clearing, the butterflies in his stomach threatening to escape him. What he wanted more than anything stood in the center of the clearing.

"I didn't think you were coming, love," Rowan said when she saw him finally approach.

"I..uh—" he paused as he searched his coat pocket, "—I had a little trouble finding this." As he spoke the last word, he fell to one knee at Rowan's feet and withdrew his hand from his pocket, presenting her with his find. The ruby stone in the center of the setting shone brightly, seeming to emanate its own light, and the circlet of diamonds surrounding the ruby reflected the titian glow of the afternoon sun and made them appear like a ring of fire. "Rowan Archer...will you—"

"Yes!" Rowan exclaimed before he could finish. "Yes, I'll marry you!"

Asher stood while simultaneously sliding the ring on Rowan's finger, then he pulled her into a tight embrace. "We can get married on Monday, if you'd like."

"Monday? But that's only two days from now!" Rowan cried in a mix of excitement and disbelief. "How—and where—will I find a dress in such short notice?"

"Did your grandmother not keep your mother's?"

"Even if she did," Rowan began, "I cannot ask. Grandmother forbade either of us to befriend you."

"I'm so glad you listened," Asher said with a wide smile, which incited laughter from both of them. "You can wear my mother's dress, if you'd like."

"That'll work just fine," replied Rowan. "As long as we're married, I care not whose dress I wear."

At that, Asher kissed her. It was the type of kiss that enflamed the very soul, that sparked the fire between two people to burn for a lifetime.

Rowan tiptoed from the bedroom and out of her grandmother's cottage. Even though tonight was the last she'd spend in either, she didn't bother packing anything except the clothes she was wearing and her basket, which held the Grimoire and everything else she would need.

She stared at the ring on her finger, a detail both Rhiannon and her grandmother seemed to overlook during the two days since she received it. She thought about removing it, just while in their presence, but when neither made mention of it, she decided to wear it proudly and answer any questions they may have should they even arise. And they hadn't.

Even though Puritans didn't have traditional wedding ceremonies, Rowan had read one described in the Grimoire and decided right then she wanted her marriage to happen just like it. Besides, she didn't exactly consider herself Puritan any longer. She hadn't attended church in months, despite protests from her grandmother. The majick had changed her, opened her eyes to the world she was forbidden to know, opened her heart to a man she was forbidden to love.

Forbidden or not, however, Rowan was not letting go of Asher. He had made her life complete, something she always believed Rhiannon—her other *half*—did until Asher. Truth be told, however, half is all she ever was...half of a set of twins so identical and yet so different that she never truly had an identity of her own.

As she walked into the clearing where Asher stood, the moonlight gleaming off his wide smile and watery eyes, she realized that she was about to become another half, but deep down she knew what mattered most is that the man whose name she was about to take was sharing more than that. His heart was hers—completely—as was hers, his. The love that he gave her filled the emptiness she seemed to have felt since the death of her mother, filled the void of the companionship she should have received from her sister but had not.

"Are you ready?" she asked through a wide smile.

Asher smiled and nodded. "It's a good thing Reverend Thatcher isn't here to witness your Devil worship," he added with a playful chuckle.

"It's not Devil worship," Rowan clarified despite knowing Asher was joking with her. "Do you have the rings?"

Asher dug deeply in his right pocket and withdrew two gold bands. "Yep."

"Where'd you get them?" Rowan asked.

"They're from the old world... Belonged to my grandmother and grandfather, much like—" he grabbed her hand, kissing it, "—this ruby ring here."

"They're perfect, Asher." She kissed him gently and took the rings from him, placing them upon a small stone. She opened the Grimoire and searched for the right page, Asher staring intently at the strange object the entire time.

"So that's it, eh?" he asked. "It looks scary."

Rowan hadn't planned to tell him about being a witch, but when he showed up early for one of their meetings and stumbled upon her manipulating a fireball in the air with her bare hands, she had no other choice. "It's not as scary as it looks—honest."

"I'm only scared of losing you... You know, like your..." he said, unable to finish his sentence.

"Okay, found it!" she said excitedly. "And that's not going to happen." She turned to him, her expression more serious and grabbed a leaf from the ground. "Now give me your finger."

As Asher willingly gave his finger to his bride-to-be, Rowan withdrew a small knife from the basket and pricked the tip of it. Before he could react, she held his finger over the ring intended for her finger and let a few drops spill onto the gold, then held it over the leaf and let a few more fall. She did the same with her own finger, first to his ring and then to the leaf.

Rowan closed her eyes and focused her mind on the rings in front of them. With no words uttered from her mouth, the gold began to glow and turned red-hot within seconds. Fire danced around the rings when Rowan opened her eyes again, and then sputtered out. "I think we're ready."

Rowan handed the rings to Asher, grabbing his free hand with one of hers and the basket and leaf with the other, and led him to the center of the clearing where the pentagram—though covered by the tall grass—remained; a shaft of moonlight fell directly upon the center of the henge.

She removed five candles from her basket and instructed him to place them at the points while she went to the center pyre and invoked a flame in her palm as easy as breath. When all the candles were placed, she tossed the leaf onto the now-roaring flames.

As before with Rhiannon on the night they received their cloaks—and many nights following—the candles at the points came to life.

From her basket, Rowan withdrew a length of white ribbon, strung it through both rings, and began to tie it. As she tightened the knot, she faced East and spoke: "Blessed be this union with the gifts from the East. Communication of the heart, body, and mind; the knowledge of growth found only in the sharing of silence; a fresh beginning with the rising of each Sun."

Another pass through the rings and another knot as she faced South: "Blessed be this union with the gifts from the South. Warmth of hearth and home, the heat of the heart's passion, the heat created by both, to lighten the darkest of times."

Rowan turned to the West as she tied another knot about the rings: "Blessed be this union with the gifts of the West: the deep commitments of the lake, the swift excitement of the river, the refreshing cleansing of the rain, and the all-encompassing passion of the sea.

"Blessed be this union with the gifts of the North. Firm foundation on which to build, fertility of the fields to enrich your lives, a stable home to which you may always return." As she said the last, as she had with all the others, Rowan faced the direction she invoked and tied the last knot about the rings—now completely bound in white silk.

Again, no words escaped her mouth as she laid them back onto the stone, but within moments, it burst into flames and disappeared.

"Wh—Where did the rings go?" Asher asked, completely dumbfounded and slightly worried for the loss.

"You'll see," she all but whispered. "Now give me your hand."

Without hesitation, Asher held his hand to her, but he could not hold his tongue, "You're not going to stab it or anything, are you?"

"You'll see," she whispered again with a slight chuckle; and still, his hand remained. She placed her hand over his and wove her fingers between, curling them slightly under and squeezing ever so slightly. With a sharp breath, a ribbon of fire shot from her mouth and wrapped itself around their hands. When Asher looked down, surprised the fire had not burned him, he saw but a white, silk ribbon binding their hands; upon his fourth finger was a band of gold, and upon hers was one to match.

"You may kiss your bride," she said softly, to which he graciously obliged.

He lifted her so that her legs wrapped about his waist. "Let's go home... Mrs. Black."

Wyatt Thatcher took another copious drink of brandy, warming the chuckle that escaped his throat. He swallowed another sip, ingesting it alongside the irony. A drinking reverend was an oxymoron—he had spent his clergyhood devoted to stopping such gluttony, among other imperfections he possessed; now, however, it was his only solace from the guilt.

Eleven years had passed since the gallows took the life of one of Salem's residents; after hearing the crack of her neck and her last breath expelled, and seeing her beautiful eyes fade and her bladder empty itself in a shameful stream onto the ground below, Reverend Thatcher vowed that Constance's life would be the last to grow limp at the end of a noose.

He had always known Catherine to be a witch; he protected her just the same, even after she broke his heart by marrying his best friend, Jacob Archer. But when the town called for a trial after Jacob's death, there was no way to protect her from the blood they demanded for the crime.

Guilt. His final judgement; his eternal prison. There was no escape—only brandy. With another swallow, the tears freed themselves from their determined hold they had had on his eyes.

He stared intently at the drawing of Constance, an image that was echoed about him on the walls, the shelves, even the ceiling and parts of the floor—all drawings of a madman, it would seem, only he was but a heart-broken fool.

A single tear managed to find its way through the forest of whiskers that covered his face, straight onto his latest sketch. The charcoal smeared under its deluge, and the image that haunted his dreams—his every waking moment—now stared back at him. Constance's eyes were now black as ash and bulged from their sockets, and her lips ran with blood—his blood, which now painted the sheet of paper in staccattoed splashes.

A glance at his snifter, and the source of the blood, the sting in his lip upon the discovery, was revealed. A chip in the rim, now highlighted like crimson fire, mocked his sin. He turned the glass and spilled all but a drop into his mouth, which he saved to wet a handkerchief to nurse his wounded lip.

Swill from the glass dribbled onto the paper below, starting at the top corner and tracing a line across Constance's neck, and when he finished tending the wound on his lip, the unhealed one within his heart tore deeper and wider. The stain was so resemblant of the rope that had hanged her, Wyatt cried out from the memory.

The snifter soared across the room, striking the opposite wall in an angry chorus of shrill and shriek. Consumed by pain, haunted by guilt, his mind swimming with brandy and bereavement, Wyatt ran about the room like a demon unleashed, tearing at all the images of Constance until they whipped about him like a whirling dervish.

"So you do feel guilt," said a voice from the shadows.

Thatcher froze and cried out once more, this time from shock. "Who goes there?"

"The judger of your sins," answered the voice, closer this time, "how do you plea?"

"That voice," Thatcher said, ignoring the taunt out of recognition of a voice he hadn't heard in quite some time. "Constance, is that you?"

No answer came, but something in the shadows shifted closer.

"I'm sorry, Constance," the reverend pleaded into the darkness. "I tried protecting you as long as I could, but I couldn't risk being hanged myself—please understand."

Still, only silence save the phantom creak of a floorboard.

"Constance, I loved you—I still do," he continued. "I wanted to save you, I truly did, but I couldn't..."

Something shifted closer yet, so close that Thatcher could hear its breathing.

"Please understand," Thatcher pleaded once more.

"There's nothing to understand," the voice called from the shadows. "You said nothing! You let her die!"

"Her?" Thatcher asked. His submissive, pleading expression turned instantly to one of confusion.

A figure cloaked in black—blacker than the shadows from which it emerged—stepped forward. Tendrils of smoke and ash, like those from an extinguished wick, radiated from the figure almost intelligently. "You killed my mother—" said the figure, "—where's the love in that?"

Thatcher's confusion burst like a levy, the floodwaters of realization pulling him under. "Rhiannon? What are you doing here?"

"Question is, Reverend, what are you doing here?" Rhiannon's voice was throaty, burdened by pain, threatening to crack—much like her.

"I don't follow..."

"How are you still alive? With all the people who've died at your command, how is it that none of their family has sought revenge?"

"We live in a Puritanical society, Rhiannon." Thatcher's tone was not dissimilar to his tone on Sunday mornings. "People just don't go around killing each other."

A cackle roared from under the black cowl. "Says the man who killed my mother. Says the man who currently has more blood on his hands than anyone else in Salem Village...for now."

Rhiannon held out her hand, palm facing up, and blew across it as she slowly spun in a circle. Dozens of candles that line shelves and tables about the room sparked to life. She wanted him to see her—to see her power—even if momentarily.

A surprised gasp escaped Wyatt, his watery eyes now illuminated by the newly-born flames.

"What?" Rhiannon said with a smile. "You thought the craft would die with my mother?

"When I saw my mother hanging from the gallows that day, I was glad. I had watched her slaughter my father, never understanding her reasons, foolishly naïve of my father's true nature. I was blind of it until just recently..." Rhiannon announced as the flames about the room extinguished. Tendrils of ash curling from her cloak were unnoticed by Thatcher. Masked by the darkness and obscured by shadow, they now made their way through the air and encircled the reverend's body. "Fire will eventually die, but ash will always remain. We are all made of ash, and to ash we all shall return."

With her last words, her cloak rose above her, hovered momentarily, and then darted through the darkness and completely enswathed Thatcher in a fuliginous pall.

Thatcher fought with all his might to find a way out of the majick that bound him, but the more he fought and writhed on the floor, the tighter the cloak constricted him. His last breath was that of ash, which filled his lungs until they collapsed.

The ash withdrew from his body and returned to its cloak form around its owner, who had already turned away, headed for the door.

Whispers of Reverend Thatcher drinking himself to death didn't arrive until Sunday. When he didn't show for service that morning, a few of the townsmen found his body. Six days of decomposition had left his body nearly unrecognizable; fortunately, it also deterred anyone from suspecting foul play and the story of him drowning his sorrows—and his spirit—with brandy all the more believable.

"Who knew he was so obsessed with Salem's wicked witch? They said that there were hundreds of drawings of Constance Archer all over his cabin!" Mary Cromwell exclaimed to the gaggle of girls that surrounded her.

"I heard that he even hanged himself with the rope that was used to hang the old hag," replied Verity Lewis, which elicited a series of squeals from the others.

Rhiannon glared at them as they walked by, though they were too busy gossiping to even notice her standing there. Just before Hannah Cromwell passed her, Rhiannon stuck out her foot, sending Hannah face first onto the gravel path.

"Watch where you're going—" Mary shouted at Rhiannon, running to her younger sister's aid, adding, "—witch!"

Rhiannon snapped back around, her cloak twirling about her like a pillar of smoke. Her eyes flashed like green lightning. "What'd you say?"

"N-no-nothing," Verity stammered; "she didn't say anything."

"That's what I thought." The corners of Rhiannon's lips curled mischievously. "I thought I was going to have drag all of you to the orchard and send the beast after you."

Two days later, the Cromwell sisters and their friend, Verity, went missing. A search party found them a day after that. Their bodies had been mangled. Hannah's face was completely gone, as if some wild animal had chewed it off; they found Verity's head several yards away from where the rest of her body lay; and there were so many pieces of Mary strewn about— each leg had been torn from the body, an arm here, a finger there, an eye hanging from a branch in one tree and the other hanging from another—that the search party was sure they left most of her behind.

"If you're looking for Rowan," Asher said as he placed another board onto the pallet, "she's gone into town."

"I'm not looking for Rowan," Rhiannon replied. She stepped closer and placed her hand on his arm, gently caressing his skin until she reached his shoulder. "I came to see you."

"You've seen me," Asher replied, forcibly removing her hand from his shoulder, "and now you can leave."

"Not until I get what I came for," she said with a grin.

Asher wiped the sweat from his brow and moved to the other side of the stack of boards, away from Rhiannon. "And what is that?"

"A kiss."

"You've wasted your time. And you're wasting mine now, too, so please—just go."

"What's the matter, Asher? Don't think one kiss would suffice?" she asked cheekily. "Afraid of following too closely in Mommy's footsteps?"

Asher reached across the stack of boards to slap Rhiannon across the face, but his hand froze mid-swing.

"It looks like you take after dear old Daddy, too... Didn't he always strike your mother?" Rhiannon taunted. "Oh well, no matter. Now that you can't move, I'll get that kiss anyway. You'll see what you've been missing by choosing my sister over me. I guarantee you that you'll want more, and you'll come crawling into my arms, just like your whore of a mother crawled into my father's."

As she slowly made her way around the pallet, Asher's face twisted as he fought against the majick holding him. "You're nothing like your sister, twins or not." He opened his mouth to say more, but found his tongue, too, was now immoveable.

"You're right—I'm better!" she agreed. She was inches from him now, her face so close their lips were almost touching, but she didn't kiss him. She ran her finger along his neck, the sweat slick on his skin, and down to his chest. His muscles twitched under her touch, and she continued her roust by sliding her hand down his abdomen and past the waist of his pants, wrapping her fingers around his manhood. "Well... It appears not *all* of you is paralyzed."

Without removing her hand from his pants, she leaned in and kissed him. And screamed.

Her lips felt as if they were covered in liquid fire. She screamed again, this time at Asher, "You knew this would happen, didn't you?"

He still couldn't speak, but the confusion on his face spoke volumes.

"She thinks she's clever, does she? Thinks she's smarter than me?" Rhiannon fumed. "I'll show her who's the smarter of us! If I can't have you, neither can she!"

As Rhiannon raised her hand, Asher winced again, sure that she was planning on killing him. He was surprised that he could move at all, but he closed his eyes tightly and hoped the death would be quick.

When he reopened them, he found himself closer to the ground, and as he looked closer, he realized he was on all fours. His whole body ached as it contorted, especially his face and nose—which was now a fur-covered snout.

Panic set in as he watched his fingers sprout sharp claws, and then panic turned to rage.

He lunged at Rhiannon, but in an instant, she had disappeared in a billow of black smoke.

"I know it was you," her grandmother said to her as she walked through the door.

Rhiannon was caught off guard by the sight of her grandmother, even more so by her cryptic accusation. "You...what was me?"

"The Grimoire. I know you took it."

"Yes, I did," Rhiannon admitted, "which proves you have lied to us all this time! You could have taught us—mother could have taught us, too—but you both cowered in the shadows when the Trials came."

"We didn't cower," Hazel defended. "We were trying to protect you and Rowan from a life of persecution. So many of our kind died, so many innocent people, too. Ignorance of the craft was your only protection."

"Knowledge of it, on the other hand, would have been protection enough," Rhiannon refuted. "Instead, Rowan and I were forced to—with the help of Morrigan—teach ourselves."

Hazel's expression quickly changed from scolding to scared. "You released Morrigan?"

"We summoned her, if that's what you mean."

"She's a trickster; that wasn't a summoning spell, despite what it said—it was a releasing spell, and now she's running loose somewhere in this realm."

"Don't worry, Grandmother," Rhiannon bolstered, "Rowan and I burned her in the fire."

"Silly, silly girl," Hazel tsk-tsked. "Morrigan is of fire and ash—you cannot burn her! You probably made her stronger, in fact. Now—" Hazel held out her open palms, "—the Grimoire, please, so we can banish her back to her the Shadowlands."

"I don't have it—I think Rowan took it. Besides, I don't need it anymore." Rhiannon and Rowan had agreed to keep their enchanted cloaks a secret from their grandmother, but since she already admitted to taking the Grimoire, Rhiannon decided that revealing the extent of her new powers to Hazel would be all right. With a slow twirl, Rhiannon closed her eyes and summoned the ash and smoke and darkness. Wisps of soot and shadow flew toward her and coalesced into a stunning, black velvet cloak. "I have *this* now."

"Rhiannon," Hazel said softly, "this...this is where Morrigan is hiding. She is your source of majick, not your true gift. Your cloak is one half of the whole, and I am guessing Rowan has the other half. We must destroy it; by destroying yours, the other cannot continue to exist."

"You're just jealous! That's the real reason you wish to destroy it!"

Hazel held up her hand and Rhiannon was paralyzed—just like Rhiannon had done to Asher. When her grandmother started speaking in tongues, a language Rhiannon couldn't understand, the cloak writhed upon Rhiannon's body and started to lift away altogether.

"No!" Rhiannon screamed; her tongue still worked, for now. Despite her body being immobilized, she fought against her grandmother's spell; soon, the wisps returned once more. "You're not destroying it!"

Asher was no longer human, except his mind; though his reasons for finding Rhiannon held some intelligence, his desire to find her was purely animalistic. He wanted revenge, wanted her blood. He ran through the orchard, rather fast due to the speed of using all of his limbs, sure that he'd find Rhiannon at her grandmother's house. When he got there, he wasn't disappointed.

Neither Rhiannon nor Hazel had heard him enter the cottage; neither one had seen his glowing red eyes, nor had they smelled the musky smell of damp fur mixed with that of freshly-sawn wood. They were so occupied with fighting one another, they didn't see him leap at Rhiannon, nor his flight through the air just over Rhiannon as she ducked a blow.

Asher hadn't seen it either—the animal in him had shut him off, hungry for red vengeance—and when he landed hard against a body, which collapsed backwards under his weight, his jaws and teeth quickly went to work on shredding the flesh underneath him.

"No!" he heard Rhiannon cry out. "Grandmother!"

When Asher opened his eyes, Hazel's face stared back at him. The human in him came to, fast to realize his folly. As much as he longed to attack Rhiannon, to pay her back for turning him into the beast he now was, he couldn't stand the sight of the blood pooling from the gaping wound on Hazel's neck—and he fled as fast as he had entered, nearly colliding with Rowan on his way to the orchard.

Asher had been missing for hours, and as much as she hated to ask her sister for help, Rowan was worried about her husband.

The light from her grandmother's cottage was only slightly visible against the afternoon sky, but something large and blackish-brown was barreling toward her as she made her way out of the orchard and across the yard. As she drew closer, its outline was blurred against the flammeous edges of the setting sun.

It nearly ran straight into her, close enough for her to catch a glimpse of something she was told only existed in legend, in stories: a Grim. *A Grim!* Panic flooded her and she screeched louder than a barn owl as it passed, so shrill it curdled even her own blood.

But the beast shot past her, stopping only momentarily from the shock of her scream.

Another scream sounded from within the cottage—Rhiannon!—and though she hesitated to turn her back on the beast, she ran impossibly fast toward the gaping threshold.

Rhiannon was covered in blood—if it were hers, Rowan couldn't be sure. "Are you all right? What happened?"

"The Beast!" Rhiannon cried out. "It k-ki-killed Grandmother!"

When Rowan looked down, she finally saw the source of all the blood. Breath left her lungs so swiftly she was sure someone had struck her square in the chest; her knees buckled, unable to handle the weight with which she was now burdened, and she fell straight to the floor.

She awoke, slightly dazed, and had it not been for Rhiannon's blood-soaked clothes, it would have taken her sometime to regain her composure. Upon the sight, however, she shot straight up and headed toward her old bedroom.

"Where are you going?" Rhiannon asked to the back of Rowan's head. Either Rowan hadn't heard her question or she didn't care. With her quiver over her shoulder and her bow in hand, she walked straight past Rhiannon without a word and into the growing darkness outside. "Wait!"

Rowan followed the same path the Grim had taken as it passed her, the unmarked but well-worn path to the clearing. As she entered the pitch-blackness of the orchard, she summoned her fiery cloak to light the way.

Trying to swallow it whole, Asher tried to push his feral side to the depths of his stomach. When he reached the clearing, he paused to catch his breath, his thoughts.

He wondered if he would be stuck in his current form forever, if the spell that Rhiannon cast was temporary, if Rowan would be able to reverse the spell, or—more importantly—if she'd even recognize him if given the chance.

A scarlet light approached from the same path he had taken. He knew it had to be Rowan, her enchanted cloak unmistakable. It billowed behind her like wildfire with the same fierceness as the expression on her face. She was upset—why wouldn't she be? He had slain her grandmother, the part of him that wasn't him at all.

Not knowing what else to do, he cried out—a pitiful, sad howl that echoed about the clearing as if it had been a deep valley.

Rowan approached the clearing with caution. She could see the Grim standing there, on two legs nonetheless, could see the inquisitive way he looked at her with those black eyes. They reminded her of Asher, and her heart pained with worry.

Had Asher, too, fallen victim to the Grim?

As if echoing the pain inside of her, the beast called out, its cry lonesome and heart-wrenching. It could have killed her already, had it wanted to, but it just stood there watching her. Still, she pulled an arrow from her quiver and, keeping the bow lowered, nocked it onto the taut sinew.

As she drew closer to it, wanting to make sure the shot—if she needed to make it—would be as accurate as possible given the waning sunlight, she could smell the mill—her home. *Yet the wind blew in the direction opposite.*

"Rowan!" Rhiannon's voice called out from behind, the startling break in silence nearly releasing the soul from her body. "Where are you?"

Rowan didn't answer for fear of startling the Grim. She knew her sister was close enough that she'd soon discover them in the clearing, so close, actually, that the Grim began to sniff the air, ears alert. *Why had it not attacked her?*

As Rhiannon entered the clearing, the last few rays of sunlight fell upon her cloak, the contrast of black and crimson like dying embers of a fire. "Rowan! The beast!" she screamed out, as if Rowan had not already seen the creature mere yards from her. "Get back here before he attacks you!"

"Shh!" Rowan said, turning slightly and holding a finger to her lips. "If he wanted me dead, I'd already be lying in a pool of red."

The beast gave a low growl, its hair standing on end, agitated with the additional company. It lowered itself back to four legs, its back now arched in warning.

"Get back here, Rowan!" Rhiannon demanded. Rowan was oddly unthreatened by the beast, but because of his current state, she backed away toward her sister. "Kill it, Rowan! Kill *him*!"

The Grim growled louder, more fervently, and its razor-sharp teeth were bared with the snarl of its lip.

"Shoot it!" Rhiannon demanded.

At that, the Grim bolted toward Rhiannon, throwing Rowan to the ground at it charged past, whose bow soared through the air unbridled and whose quiver landed against the ground with a crack. Soon, Rhiannon was running about the clearing, the Grim upon her heels and inching closer.

When Rowan finally found her bow and recovered an arrow from the tall grass, she steadied her aim upon the moving target, the difficulty increasing alongside the darkness. When the Grim managed to overpower Rhiannon, Rowan took her shot just as its jaws were about to snap.

The arrow landed perfectly, striking the Grim in the back and eliciting a howl more pitiful than the first she had heard. A scream mixed with it—her own—and she fell to the ground. Her heart felt as though it were torn in two, felt as though it were pierced with the arrow she just released upon the Grim. The ring upon her finger, too, grew hot and singed her skin.

Asher stared down at Rhiannon, the one responsible for his cursed appearance, and as much as he wanted to clench his teeth upon her neck and rip out her throat, the pain was too much, his increasing weakness too great. He could feel the arrow in his chest, feel the blood leaving his body, so he took the last of his strength to wrench it from the wound. He howled out in pain again, the loudest howl yet. As he rolled to the side, he stared at his wife, who hobbled to her sister's side; she held her chest as he held his, yet she had no wound.

"Are you okay, Rhi," he heard Rowan say as she helped Rhiannon stand.

Who cares, he thought.

He wondered how his wife could look at Rhiannon and not see the monster inside, yet she couldn't look at him without seeing a beast, couldn't see her husband past the fur and the fangs.

Rhiannon didn't answer Rowan's question, instead asking one of her own. "Is he dead?"

"The Grim?" Rowan asked. Asher could hear the confusion in her voice—*did she realize who HE was?* "I think so... There's a lot of blood."

"Good!" Rhiannon said. "Let's go home."

"Home?" Rowan stared at her sister. "My home is with Asher, and he's missing—I must find him."

I'm right here, Love! If only his tongue could form the words.

"I was going to tell you sooner..." he heard Rhiannon say. "He's cheating on you, just like Father cheated on Mother, just like Edward cheated on me. I've seen him around town with Abigail Danvers."

LIAR! A rumble escaped Asher's slumped body.

"Asher is not a cheater!" Rowan argued. "He is gentle and loving and doting and has bound himself to me—in marriage and in majick."

"I wonder if Abigail says the same thing," Rhiannon snapped.

Asher could see her frustration, the same frustration—anger—he felt. He wanted her dead, just as she had wanted him dead. He should have tore out her throat when he had had the chance, then she couldn't spread the awful, slanderous lies that spewed from her tongue.

Asher could see Rowan's frustration, too, and her pain—*she didn't believe her sister...did she?* A tear rolled from Rowan's cheek unchecked. He couldn't just watch anymore, couldn't have her fabricate more falsities—with everything that was left in him, he launched himself at Rhiannon once again.

Rowan screamed out when the Grim barreled toward Rhiannon. The creature was again on top of her sister, who lay speechless, the air knocked from her lungs upon hitting the ground—and then her voice returned in full force. Rowan watched as her sister's larynx was torn from her neck mid-scream, a fountain of red barely visible from the half-moon sky.

She wanted to scream out again, but in the silence that now settled upon the clearing, she dared not draw any attention to herself. She stifled her voice behind her hand as the Grim inched closer to her, his black eyes burning into her like coal.

Rowan watched in disbelief as the fur on the Grim began to fall away, revealing a man's naked body underneath. "Asher!" She started to run to him, but hesitated. "You're the Grim?"

Asher looked over at Rhiannon, whose body lay lifeless. "I'm sorry for killing your grandmother. Rhiannon was the intended target." He hung his head, unable to look at his wife, unable to see the pain he had caused. "But there's a lot you may not realize about your sister."

Rowan's tongue wouldn't cooperate; she stared blankly even as he told her what had transpired at the mill, not quite able to process.

"...When I wouldn't kiss her willingly, she transformed me," he explained with struggled breaths.

"You're still hurt—" realizing she had caused the wound, she added, "I'm sorry."

She raised her hand to the wound on his chest, placing it against his skin. He winced at first, but then heat dulled the pain; when she pulled her hand away, the faint outline of a hole is all that remained.

Asher pulled her close and kissed her like it'd be their last. "Let's go home."

"Just one last thing..." Rowan said as she stood. She walked to where Rhiannon's body lay upon the grass and stared into her sister's lifeless, green eyes. Summoning a flame in her palm, she blew forcefully until Rhiannon's entire body was engulfed in fire. "Burn, bitch!"

As she went to turn away, a black cloud of smoke rose from the pyre and hit her like a solid wall. She fell backward, still pressed by the ash cloud. All at once, the wall funneled into her open mouth like an unstopped drain until all the ash was inside of her.

"Are you okay?" Asher asked, grabbing her hand.

Rowan coughed then stood. A sound, similar to the laughter of a small child, escaped Rowan's throat when she opened her mouth to answer. "We're fine."

Redcap Charlie

by Robert D. Moores

A long time ago, it was considered not only normal but positively fashionable to talk about such things as fairies, elves, and goblins as if they were an everyday part of life. Every time something went missing, every time something was inexplicably accomplished, every time a baby was born uglier than his (purported) father, there was believed to be a special sort of agent at work. There were not many people at that time who would fault you if, looking aghast at the ugly face of your deformed newborn child, you cried out that you were the victim of a changeling. This was a perfectly acceptable complaint back then, and odds were good that everyone not only believed and sympathized with you, but had even seen the likes of a changeling before.

In those days, lots of little miracles seemed to happen, and even the terrible stories of that era seem somehow more attractive to us today than the tales of our modern woes. So much so, in fact, that to this day there is a place in our hearts for fairytales, which can be warmed by nothing else.

But such stories were not considered stories back then. They were rather considered anecdotes, snippets of experience from the countryside taken quite seriously, just as if they really were happening.

And why should the simple people of this bygone era have taken such silly fantasies so seriously? Precisely because they weren't fantasies at all. In fact, though liars and embellishers ever have lied and embellished, the truth is that most of the fairytales that have been so lovingly preserved from that time were all based in some point of fact—they really happened, and are only outrageous insomuch as the details have been stretched and plied, no differently than they are stretched and plied in the telling of any tale down through the ages.

And who am I to state such an extraordinary thing? Naturally, you want to know. After all, here are two hundred and more years of rigorous scientific study quite sturdily debunking every fairytale we ever put forward in our unenlightened youth, and this man today comes to tell us that all of it is wrong? On what authority shall we forget the processes of science that have given us space satellites, rovers on Mars, smartphones, the internet, MRIs, and endless other observable marvels just to go back to believing in unobservable fairies and goblins?

It's a fair question, to be sure, and yet I can offer you only the most unsatisfactory answer possible. I am, in fact, nobody. I am utterly forgettable in the chronicles of human history. You would not know me by name, nor by any accomplishment, nor by any discovery of mine; I am literally unknown to you, and can't possibly deign to appeal to you on the grounds that some previous extraordinary claim of mine was in fact vindicated.

And can it be, that a perfect nobody has really come forward to say that fairies and goblins are real, despite all the assurances of well-known scholars to the contrary? It can! It is! But how, and why? What gives such a nobody the confidence to swear with certainty that happenings some two hundred and more years past were not fiction, but did in fact take place?

What if I told you that I was there? That my own two eyes have witnessed the goings on of centuries past, and that I can say, with utter certainty, not only that goblins did back then steal the infants of human beings and replace them with their own, but also that they sometimes do it still today?

I am an eyewitness to this and many other fairytales besides. And the irony of it, the sheer brilliance of the whole situation, is precisely that I am nobody. What danger is there in sharing secrets with a man to whom nobody listens? Especially when for two hundred years you have been actively obfuscating your secrets under the most ingenious camouflage ever conceived: rational reality?

But for what it's worth, here and now I am making an effort to forewarn you that the unseen world shall not remain unseen much longer. Perhaps you'll deign to hear me out, and in so doing perhaps you'll see for yourself that my words are too close to the mark and too finely detailed to be mere fiction. And if not? Well if not, then at any rate you'll see for yourself soon enough.

There are within the Realm certain grumblings, not entirely unfounded, frankly, that the fairy folk were unfairly driven out from under the sun by what has turned out to be the rather unexpected and radical conquest of the whole Earth by human beings.

Some of the Folk are more displeased with it than some others, of course, but none of them has, at this point, failed to grumble at least once. Humans have changed everything for the Folk. Humans have hunted, captured, coveted, lynched, enslaved, and killed every sort of fairy who ever crossed our paths. Small wonder, really, that they chose to disappear when at last it became apparent that we were destined to be the most collectively successful species on Earth.

But on that long ago day when the two Courts of the Folk came to the agreement that they should make themselves scarce for a time, cease all their interactions with us, and simply observe our behavior, there was not a perfect consensus. Far from it, in fact.

You may or may not be familiar with the two Courts of which I speak. In case you aren't, I suppose I should begin there. It explains a lot, actually.

The Folk of the Realm belong generally to two groups. The Seelie Court is happy and wants to make others happy. To them belong the fairies, brownies, elves, and many other fair and beautiful creatures. They are the very definition of joy. In fact, their name is the origin of our word *silly*. And on the other hand is the Unseelie Court, who is unhappy and wants to make others unhappy. To them belong goblins, trolls, gremlins, and many other malevolent (and often ugly) creatures. They know nothing of joy, but positively live for making misfortune for humans, and they are usually associated with bad luck or grim tidings.

As you can probably imagine, the Seelie Court and the Unseelie Court don't often agree in any meaningful way. They are rather like human conservatives and liberals, or the religious and atheists. They are fundamentally and essentially incompatible.

It was the Seelie Court who first proposed that the Folk should disappear. Convincing the Unseelie Court was a mammoth achievement, but there was plenty of dissent. In fact, dissent in the Unseelie Court is more rule than exception. It's a wonder they ever agree about anything at all.

Eventually, though, it was agreed that humans would destroy the entire Realm if ever they found it. Even the Unseelie were being harassed by then (it was the middle of the 1300s by our reckoning), and so the time was ripe for a truce between the Courts.

Hundreds of years later, however, the simmering discontent of the Unseelie Court has begun to boil. They are living up to that famous old ballad of theirs (except of course it isn't famous to you at all, as you've probably never heard it):

"For all the coals you count in Hell,
Unseelie Court cannot sit still!
For all the grief in which we drown,
Unseelie Court will not lie down!"

Restlessness and chaos are the hallmarks of the Unseelie, you see. Staying hidden isn't something that they do well. They're experts at it for short periods of time, as any mischief-maker necessarily is, but given centuries...

Suffice to say that it's the Unseelie Court who is grumbling the most. And it's the same Court who can control themselves the least.

Now I should clarify that both the Seelie and Unseelie Courts have continued to make occasional appearances on Earth, though much more discreetly than in centuries past. But the Unseelie Court has been more prone to wander by far, and so most fairytales of the current era, if they were known, would be of the most miserable sort, such as the one I will relay to you shortly.

It is of utmost importance, you see, that you learn the ways and habits of the Folk before many of them arrive. You must know how to spot them—and how to treat them if you do. There are many Folk in both Courts who are slow to forgive an insult, and the truth is that neither the Seelie nor the Unseelie would be trivial enemies if pressed to be enemies at all.

But before I begin to educate you, my friends, in the finer points of fairy etiquette, there remains one more bit of background I suppose I must share. It simply can't be helped. You won't believe a word I say until you know exactly how I came to be in possession of the knowledge I am promising to share.

As I said, you won't recognize my name, I'm simply nobody in the scheme of human history. To prove it, let me tell you the name that I was born with: they called me, so it's said, Joseph Clewelly. I suppose it was my original fate to be a young Joey, and then a grownup Joe, although looking at my own face I have a hard time making either name fit. Joseph, perhaps... But at any rate, what does that matter now?

It doesn't. I remember the name clearly enough for some reason (I learned of it from my, shall we say, 'adoptive parents'), but I couldn't have been called by it more than five times in my whole life. To be Joseph Clewelly ultimately was not my destiny.

The name I have been known by for most of my life is Gantry. It was given to me by my adoptive parents when they 'acquired' me.

The day after I was born, you see, I was stolen from my cradle by none other than goblins of the Unseelie Court. I am, in fact, known in the Realm as a changeling. A quite ugly goblin—perhaps the original Gantry—was left a changeling on Earth in my place.

I was brought to the Realm and raised as a member of the Unseelie Court until I was about five or six years old, at which time it seems my goblin parents were somehow able to determine that I was not fit to be a child of goblins. I can't even imagine what that means, but the reality is that I was abandoned by them and never saw them again. I hardly remember them.

A discarded changeling is referred to as 'dropped' or 'a drop' among the Folk. That's me. Gantry the Drop.

Drops occupy a rather unique position in life. After all, we are essentially forgotten remnants of two different worlds, familiar with both but unloved by either. And being unloved, you surely realize, propagates a number of disadvantages for a child.

But.

It also creates certain advantages, too, and I am one of those very few and very lucky drops who happened to understand this early and make use of it often.

Because I am human by birth, for example, I have no trouble blending in on Earth. I've traveled quite a lot of Europe and North America, in fact. Maybe some of you have even crossed my path, who knows?

And on the other hand, because I was raised in the Realm, homeless and without roots to keep me still, I can wander the lands of the Folk just as easily. Not an elf or troll in the whole Realm would bat an eye. Human changelings are a common enough sight, and we understand the customs and habits of the Folk because, in our way, we are Folk ourselves.

For short periods of time, nobody in either world can see the slightest thing strange about me. Because of this, I make sure to spend only short periods of time in any one place. I must confess, I am not really unlike the Unseelie who guided my first few years of life: restless, alone, always a bit unhappy.

But you know, I am not really all that malevolent. I've considered the possibility that this was why my goblin Ma and Da didn't want me; perhaps I was disgraceful in the eyes of the Unseelie Court because I possess a capacity for happiness which they do not.

At any rate, I've done some wandering. And what you need to know is that I have wandered not only over distances but over ages as well. You see, there are quite clever portals laid out all around you. A long time ago, you took to calling them fairy circles. You've quite disproven their magical origins, and now know that they're nothing more than mushrooms growing in a preordained pattern according to very predictable rules of biology and physics. And, of course, you're entirely right. In a way.

Fairy circles have a peculiar property about them. If you have been to the place and time where one leads, you can use it. If not, then of course it's nothing but an interesting formation of mushrooms. This, in essence, means that you have to be escorted through a circle for the first time by someone who has used it before, and this is just one of the clever tricks that the Folk have used to hide under the noses of humans for centuries.

But changelings, like myself, have a starting point. We have been on both sides of at least one circle, which gives us a pass back and forth between both worlds. And because we blend in well enough on either side, we often take to traveling.

There are rules and limitations on how fairy circles work, but I could never justly share them with the human world; it would be the undoing of the Realm. The last thing I will say about them is that they are not necessarily restricted to a single point in time. Time, or so I've heard, is not the cut and dry sort of chain it appears to be. You can travel fairy circles through time, if you know how they're connected, although there are some things that aren't possible.

Everywhere that there has ever been a fairy, there has been a fairy circle nearby. This is important for you to know. It's the answer to the golden question, you see. How have I acquired firsthand accounts of the many fairytales I have to share? I have been there! Even if the story took place five hundred years ago, I have been there!

And so at last you are ready to hear a new sort of fairytale. As promised, it will be a cautionary tale, a tale you would do well to have in mind at all times, for sooner than you think there will be more just like it.

For the sake of an old tradition, let's begin it with...

Once upon a time, in a small town in New England, an old homeless man used to sit mumbling to himself at a bus stop in the middle of town.

Without much study, it was clear the man had been a vagabond for a good many years. He was old, squat, broad shouldered, and broad bellied, with deep creases the length of his whole face. His hair was long, gray, and hopelessly tangled. His clothes were a mismatched confetti of rags he had collected and layered upon himself to keep out the increasing chill of autumn; like his whole person, they were crusted over with filth. His teeth, what few he had, were yellowed and broken, as were his fingernails.

This old vagabond had blown into town from no one knew where, but had become a familiar sight in short order. He wore a knitted red cap that was a distinctive sight in the area, and he was always sitting at the same bus stop, all day every day, without ever getting on a bus that anyone could recall. If on any given day you happened to mention the old man with the red hat to any local, that local would know exactly whom you meant with no further explanation necessary.

After a month or so of the vagabond's presence in town, people took to calling him Redcap Charlie. No one was sure where the name started, and in fact no one had any reason to believe his real name was even Charlie, but the name stuck at once and began to go around.

It quickly became common among the children, who were just settling back into their school routines, to use the name Redcap Charlie in virtually any kind of insult their little minds could dredge up. Such was the general opinion of him around town, that the children would taunt each other with remarks like, "You smell worse than Redcap Charlie!"

One child was even picked on by her peers because she made the grievous error of being seen talking to Redcap Charlie, although the truth of it was that he had been mumbling something she didn't understand just as she was walking by, and she had only stopped because she didn't know if he was talking to her or not. But, of course, none of the other kids would listen long enough to let her explain, and she became known all over school as Redcap Charlie's best friend.

Now this poor little girl, eight years old and in the third grade at the time, unfortunately was not new to the role of misfit. Her name, so far as we are concerned, can be Janie so that we have something to call her, and Janie was no stranger to insults. This was mostly because she was poor and unclean, always the first to be sent home with head lice, always the first to catch every cold, always wearing the same clothes more than one day per week, and—worst of all—always smiling and trying to be friendly even though nobody liked her.

Despite being an all-around misfit, Janie happened to be a kind girl all the way down deep where true kindness originates. This is especially remarkable because most misfits tend to develop a form of defiance that doesn't translate into kindness at all. But something in Janie's little heart didn't want her to be defiant, it wanted her to be harmonious and accepting. Perhaps this is simply because those were the things she most wanted for herself, and she was lucky enough—even at the age of eight—to realize that if something were worth wanting for oneself, it must certainly be worth giving to others.

At any rate, Janie didn't understand why it should be that talking to Redcap Charlie was automatically a bad thing, since no one really even knew if he was a bad man in the first place. She smiled and laughed at herself along with the others whenever they teased her about it, but she was inwardly befuddled by their disapproval.

With this and other thoughts weighing heavily on her little mind, it so happened that Janie found herself walking past old Redcap Charlie again one day, and again he started mumbling in a way so incoherent but so seemingly insistent that she couldn't quite figure out if he was talking to her.

And since, whatever he was saying, it sounded so important the way that he was saying it, she disregarded all the teasing she'd been subjected to for talking to him the first time, and she stopped to listen to him again.

Seeing that she had stopped to pay attention, Redcap Charlie gave the little girl a terrifically big grin, his nasty broken teeth displayed rather like the sharp fangs of a childhood nightmare. His tiny eyes were compressed into narrow slots of darkness, and a strangely cunning light gleamed in them.

"Um," said little Janie hesitantly. "Were you talking to me?"

Redcap Charlie cackled in the back of his throat, still wearing his rather monstrous looking grin. He then proceeded to issue a stream of noise that strongly resembled words, but not one of them made a bit of sense to Janie.

"Oh," she said, not wanting to let on that she didn't understand. Then, feeling that she should at least try to make some polite conversation since she had started something it would have been rude to walk away from, she asked him, "Are you waiting for a bus?"

To this, however, Redcap Charlie not only offered no reply but gave no acknowledgement that he was even listening. Instead, his lips and jaw worked back and forth as if he were chewing on something, and his beady eyes stared off into the distance.

Janie knew not what to make of this, but thought it would be rude to interrupt the old man's preoccupied staring, so she held her tongue.

Seeing that talking to Redcap Charlie was not at all as easy as it ought to have been, she was just about to excuse herself and go on about her day when another, quite different voice spoke to her from the sidelines.

"He never gets on the bus," offered a pleasant-sounding man's voice.

Turning around, Janie found that a well-dressed, middle-aged man had been sitting on a nearby bench while she had been trying to make nice with the vagabond and had heard her question.

"Oh," she answered him uncertainly.

"In fact," the well-dressed man added, "I've heard that it's bad luck if you see Redcap Charlie get on the bus."

Here, Redcap Charlie twisted his big ugly head upon his neck, looking crookedly at the man on the bench. With a twinkle in his eye, he let out a low, nasty sounding cackle that also rather resembled a persistent smoker's cough: "Hech-hech-hech-hech, heccch!"

Janie appeared more than a little bothered by the sickly sound of his cackle, and even took an unconscious step away from him.

Looking at the more pleasant man, she wondered, "How can it be bad luck for someone to get on the bus?"

The well-dressed man shrugged his complete agreement with her. "I'm not saying it's true, just that I've heard it. I hear that he only gets on the bus when something really bad happens."

"So... if I see him get on the bus, will something happen to me?"

"Hmm. Haven't heard one way or the other about that," said the man. "What do you say, Charlie? Anything bad going to happen to this nice little girl if she sees you get on the bus?"

"Hrrrrm. Hech-hech, heccch!" Redcap Charlie replied, looking directly at the well-dressed man who was asking.

The well-dressed man, after nodding thoughtfully, turned his attention back to Janie, and then informed her, "He laughs at the very thought of it. Maybe it's just a silly rumor."

He gave her the kind of exaggerated smile and theatrical shrug of his shoulders that a man uses who is accustomed to dealing with children and knows how to be one of them.

"But...if he's a bad man, he would tell me no anyway," she pointed out, casting him a brief, suspicious glance.

"Sure," said the man. "So it really comes down to what you believe. And maybe safety. Maybe you should always believe the thing that's safest to believe. Then if you're wrong, it doesn't matter; you were just being extra safe. Right?"

"Okay," she said, appearing both enlightened and confused at once.

But such, of course, is the nature of enlightenment, after all.

"Speaking of safety," he went on, "you must have heard that you shouldn't talk to strangers without your mom or dad."

She looked positively anguished as she thought back on all the reams of advice that her mother (who, by the way, was a raging drug addict and well-known tramp) must have offered her in the last eight years, trying to find that particular gem.

"I guess so," she offered, apparently not finding it.

"It's really good advice," he insisted.

"What's your name?" she asked him.

"My name? I'm Mr. Gantry. I'm a teacher, but not in this area. But... you know that I'm really still a stranger, right? And so is Mr. Charlie here. You should be careful."

Now this particular town was a small one but also a bustling one, and as it was mid-afternoon, its compact epicenter did not fail to continue its bustling all the while that Janie, Mr. Gantry, and Redcap Charlie were getting to know each other. People passed by in a calm but steady trickle of cars, pedestrians, bikers, and what-have-you, mostly going about their business with minimal interest in the bus stop trio.

But bus stops are a public commodity, and as such they have a tendency to aggregate a diverse crowd throughout the day. It happened during their conversation that two other people arrived, both young boys around sixteen or seventeen, who weren't overly keen on such enlightenment as strangers could offer—they, of course, possessed enough of it already themselves.

Their contribution to the conversation was no less impassioned, however, for their lack of interest. It began with one of them, a smoothly-shaved lad who didn't know that the visor of his hat was meant to be centered on his forehead to shield his eyes from the sun, saying, "Holy shit, Redcap Charlie had a fuckin' baby!"

He kindly illustrated his point for those listeners too slow to pick it up on their own by turning a disgusted face upon Janie, whose nose was running a bit and whose hair could have used some brushing.

Janie, who had already taken plenty of grief for being Redcap Charlie's BFF, immediately understood that she had been insulted. Having no interest in facing the affront head on, she glanced at Mr. Gantry and said, "Okay, bye."

With that, she hurried away.

Crooked Hat was not happy to let her go quietly, however. "Hey, your dad says he'll be home around ten!" he called cleverly after her.

Crooked Hat's friend, whom we'll call Shorts-With-Sweatshirt, shook his head at Crooked Hat in a mixture of disbelief and admiration. He must have been the less creative of the two; he had nothing of his own to add.

Seeing that Janie was not going to acknowledge the extreme wit he had demonstrated in her honor, Crooked Hat glanced at Mr. Gantry. Mr. Gantry had already turned his attention to his smartphone, it seemed, and was not even looking at the boys. This left Redcap Charlie, who was not only looking the boys over but even let loose another of his unpleasant, choking cackles: "Hech-hech-hech, heccch!"

"Dude, you fuckin' stink!" Crooked Hat told him. "You smell like a dead asshole."

To his credit, he was actually fairly close to the mark. The stinking cloud that clung to Redcap Charlie's general person resembled death indeed.

This made the old man cackle even harder for some reason. He even had the audacity to direct his merry cacophony right at Crooked Hat, who groaned and covered his nose.

"Get the fuck out of here!" Crooked Hat demanded through the palm of his hand.

"He doesn't even ride the fuckin' bus," Shorts-With-Sweatshirt pointed out.

"Yeah! Get out of here and stop stinking the place up for people who actually fuckin' use it!"

This must have amused Redcap Charlie mightily, for his cackling took on a new and higher pitch: "Heeee-heeee-heeee! Hech-hech-hech!" He even brought one enormous hand up from his lap and gave his knee a hearty slap.

Crooked Hat and Shorts-With-Sweatshirt, seeing that old Charlie was not to be perturbed (and possibly didn't understand a word they were saying), decided then to relocate a bit closer to Mr. Gantry's bench, which is to say farther away from the vagabond.

"Dude," Crooked Hat sputtered at Mr. Gantry, who still had not so much as glanced at him, "how can you sit near this nasty guy?"

Mr. Gantry, who was calmly scrolling through news headlines on his phone, peeked up at the boy momentarily. "I've learned to share the world with all kinds," he said sensibly.

"Somebody needs to share a bar of fuckin' soap with him."

"That's a terrific plan," Mr. Gantry agreed, giving up on his phone and tucking it into the side pocket of his light fall jacket. "He lives right back there, I believe. Drop a bar off for him."

Charlie, still cackling lightly, met Mr. Gantry's eyes for the second time as Gantry was gesturing toward a rundown and currently unoccupied store building behind the bus stop.

"Shit," Crooked Hat balked at the man. "If he smells this bad, what's his house smell like?"

"I've never been," Mr. Gantry said with a shrug. "But I'm guessing you aren't really planning to make a donation anyway, am I right? Look. Bus is here."

"Holy shit. Finally!" Crooked Hat squawked, rushing forward to meet the town bus as it approached.

Mr. Gantry, too, rose from his seat to board the bus. Before doing so, however, he took a step toward Redcap Charlie. Reaching out to tug one corner of Charlie's signature red cap down over his eye as if playfully familiar with the old vagabond, he leaned low and quietly told him, "Just in time, eh? I'll send them your way. But play nice. Everyone can repent."

Redcap Charlie cackled with gratitude. "Hech-hech-hech!"

Mr. Gantry then turned to the bus, rubbing together the fingers with which he had touched the old man's hat. A reddish brown smudge had appeared on the tips.

That night, Crooked Hat and Shorts-With-Sweatshirt came up with the most capital idea to prank Redcap Charlie: they decided to find the old skunk where he slept and spray him head to toe with deodorant. Acting on intelligence they had gathered from Mr. Gantry and were able to confirm with other sources, they made their way to the old abandoned store behind the bus stop in the dark of night, flashlights and spray cans at the ready.

But imagine their surprise when their flashlights found a person, indeed, sitting comfortably upon a counter in the darkness of the old store, and it was not Redcap Charlie at all but Mr. Gantry himself, wearing a careworn overcoat and matching dress hat that were as out of place a thing as could possibly get in such a dilapidated old haunt.

"Somehow I knew you'd do this," the man said as they found him.

"…fuckin' jumped the fuck outta me," Crooked Hat sputtered. "What are you a fuckin' cop?"

"Not at all," Mr. Gantry said with a reassuring smile that probably didn't look very reassuring given the timing. "In fact, I'm not even going to call them. I'm just going to ask you not to do what you're thinking of doing. One of you can still walk away."

At that moment, there came a familiar cackle from the darkness behind Mr. Gantry: "Hech-hech-hech, heccch!"

It made both of the boys jump visibly.

"Yup," said Shorts-With-Sweatshirt, "I'm leaving. Fuck this."

He didn't wait for his friend's approval, but disappeared right back out the door through which he had come.

"Well, that's a pisser for you," Mr. Gantry told Crooked Hat. "You can't both get away."

"You ain't scary," Crooked Hat assured him with a remarkably steady voice. There was even a touch of laughter about it.

"That's okay," the man said. "I'm not much of a threat. I'm even boring, all-in-all. But Redcap Charlie... oh man, he's a different story."

"What's he gonna do, choke me with his breath?"

"No. There's no blood in that. I don't know exactly what he'll do, but usually he either decapitates or opens the guts with his cane. It's sharp on the end, like a—I don't know, like a sword, I guess. They used to carry pikes, but those don't really blend in these days."

This somewhat rambling answer was punctuated by another loud cackle from Charlie, who was still hiding in the darkness.

"You're trying to scare me."

"Well. Yes."

"Whatever. You know what, I'm just going to leave. It's dumb to waste deodorant on a fuckin' hobo anyway. But you don't fuckin' scare me."

"Buddy. Listen. You're not going anywhere. You can't outrun a redcap. And he can't let both of you go. His cap is almost dry. You should have been nicer. Like the little girl you were making fun of, she even tried to talk to him. She has a nice, bright future, and you... you're just dead, you fucking brat."

At this point it may be true that Crooked Hat was a little freaked out, but to his credit he turned away from Mr. Gantry as calm as you please and started to walk away.

Unfortunately, he ran straight into Redcap Charlie, who had appeared just behind him while Gantry was talking.

And Redcap Charlie was quite amused; he laughed and laughed his ugly, death-wheedle of a laugh.

Crooked Hat had time to let out a sharp cry of surprise, but it was cut short. Not much was visible as his flashlight went sailing away into the dark storefront. There was a gurgle, a pause, a great thud, and Redcap Charlie cackling his ugly head off. It was over as quickly as it started.

Mr. Gantry retrieved the flashlight and brought it to the scene to observe, owing mainly to a morbid curiosity. The boy was lying in two pieces on the floor of the old building, cut apart at an angle from one side of his neck to the opposite armpit. A thick pool of blood already occupied most of the space between the two pieces.

Redcap Charlie had doffed his cap and was sweeping it back and forth in the puddle.

"The poor bastard," said Gantry.

"Him?" balked Charlie. "I was almost done for! One more day, I bet. One more day!"

"You had at least a week," Gantry scoffed. "But that's not even the point. You were well within the rules. I just feel sorry for humans. We're a strange breed."

"Inconsistent," Charlie agreed. "That's your problem. You can't pick a way and stay with it."

"In our defense, we don't live to be a thousand, traditionally."

"Psh!" Charlie laughed, slapping his quite moist cap back on his yellowing head. "A goblin is a goblin from day one. Humans. They don't know what they are. And they stay that way."

"There's some truth in that," Gantry agreed. "But come on. I'll help you clean up. Police will be here mighty soon, I bet. I'd stay off the bus this time."

"Redcap Charlie always rides the bus!" Charlie cackled, sounding far healthier than he had just minutes before.

Gantry nodded, appearing not at all surprised by this answer. "You're getting too liberal with the rules, Charlie."

"For all the coals you count in hell," he recited, pleased with himself, "Unseelie Court cannot sit still!"

"It's not a joke. You'll start a war. That's what humans do."

"I've been around for a few wars, kiddo. They're not half bad, truth be told."

Now a good fairytale generally comes with at least a little closure, although in this particular endeavor I want you to be assured that I bring you more beginning than ending. But in keeping with tradition, here's a bit of help with some loose ends.

The clever reader will have observed that I myself played a bit part in this tale, but even the most observant can't know the extent of it. Thanks to the peculiarities of fairy circles and the nature of time, I was present for this occasion no fewer than four distinct times. How did the ugly vagabond at the bus stop acquire the nickname of Redcap Charlie? A fellow just passing through happened to coin the term at a convenience store. That fellow was me. What inspired Crooked Hat and Shorts-With-Sweatshirt to pay a visit to old Charlie with cans of deodorant? Some kids around town heard someone talking about something similar, and the idea percolated for a few days, until someone else reminded Crooked Hat that he had heard it. Both someones were me.

And Janie? What has Janie got to do with it all? That part we'll take up later.

But I was quite taken with her, and sooner or later I'll tell you all about it.

But what was it all for? What's the meaning of it all? Have I set out to share this tale only to leave you with the feeling that I, myself, am a bloodthirsty murderer of children, orchestrating their deaths anonymously with my knowledge of the Realm?

You know, I really didn't like Crooked Hat, and I'm not sorry. Humans have a funny filter that doesn't allow them to say what they really feel. I never acquired the art of filtration, I suppose. My poor, misguided mouth simply says what it means.

I didn't like Crooked Hat at all.

But the truth is, I didn't want him to die any more than I wanted him to live. It was Charlie who needed his blood.

Redcap goblins are one of the most fearsome of all the Folk. Their caps are dyed with the blood of their human victims. They can't go long without killing: if their caps dry, they die. This creates an understandable problem for them, as they can't very well avoid humans and kill them at the same time.

It was therefore agreed that redcap goblins are permitted to spend as much time on Earth as necessary to keep themselves alive. But there are rules. And one of the biggest is that they can't kill just anyone.

None of the Folk are very tolerant of an insult. That was what killed Crooked Hat. Insult a redcap goblin and the Folk almost unanimously agree that your death is a just one. After all, they have to kill someone. Why not the disrespectful ones?

Friends! The Unseelie Court is getting restless! They've hidden for centuries in the Realm, and what's worse they've been subjected to rules! Nothing is more grueling to the Unseelie than century upon century of rules!

Mark my words. They will come. Some bring joy, and others bring despair, but the Folk are coming back to Earth. And the Unseelie, wretched chaotic things that they are, are only too eager to have their way again. For now you have but one recourse, and that's to make them play by the rules of the Realm. Here is the first of them, the very most important one, perhaps. Never insult the Folk.

But playing along isn't going to be easy. The Folk have learned to hide. Even the murderous redcaps know that a certain geographical distribution is all it takes to hide large scale mass murder right under your noses. And how do they find victims? By being ugly. By being strange. By positively begging you to hurl your insults upon them! And your only hope is to be stronger than their bait.

My friends, this much you must believe. Insult a redcap goblin, and you will not live happily ever after!

ROBERT D. MOORES is a semi-professional photographer at Hidden Aspect Photography, part-time humanist blogger at Basic Humanity, occasional dabbler in the all-but-dead art of poetry, aspiring fiction writer with a philosophical bent, and a full-time husband and father. His love for literature and art as a means of communicating the universal human condition has remained constant in an ever-evolving life.

LINKS

http://www.hiddenaspectphotography.com
https://twitter.com/HAPPhoto

A Prophecy Untamed

by Diana Murdock

"I cannot wait to be Mrs. Tyler Conway. It's a shame we have to wait."
Ashley snuggled contently within the confines of her fiancé's arms, basking
in the sun's first rays that splashed across their bed. She angled her hand
back and forth, catching the morning light on the diamond engagement ring.

"I want to be with you forever," she said.

Tyler wrapped his arms around her and pulled her close. "That's the general
idea," he crooned.

"Hey, you know, I've been thinking," Ashley said. "I'd like to have a themed
wedding."

Tyler rolled his eyes. "I guess this is where I step back, right? Get out of the way
of the bride and wedding plans."

"Hey," she said, sliding out of his grip. "This is serious stuff. Women dream of
this day since they are little girls." She sat up, eager to talk. "So what ideas do you
have?"

"Why don't you tell me what you've decided," he said.

"But—"

Tyler gently put a finger to her lips.

"We both know you've already made up your mind, Ashley. But I appreciate
you at least pretending you want my opinion."

"But I'm not pretending."

"It's okay," he said, laughing. "Whatever you want, I'm okay with. I love you."

"Oh, baby, I love you, too. Okay... So here's what I was thinking. Celtic. You know, kilts and everything."

Tyler's brows shot up. "That should be interesting, and it'll be fun for you." He wrapped a few strands of her long, red hair around his finger. "Let you get back to your Irish roots."

"I know, right? I'm going to see Grandma after work today. She's got to have some great ideas."

Tyler laced his fingers with hers. "Whatever makes you happy, babe. I'm behind you one-hundred percent."

Ashley pushed open the front door of the quaint, grandmotherly-looking house that always smelled of freshly-baked cookies.

"Good morning, Grandma!"

Family photos lined the walls and faces of children and grandchildren smiled from their frames along the mantle. Coziness simmered from the doilies and knitted blankets draped over the tables and sofa. A large knitting basket, one Ashley had never actually seen her grandmother touch, overflowed with skeins of yarn and unfinished projects. It was a good cover-up, Ashley thought for the hundredth time since finding out about her grandmother's passion for anything paranormal. It was a well-kept secret that her grandmother, Evelyn, spent hours reading about unexplained phenomenon, extraterrestrial, or the spirit world, and Ashley had come to share her passion.

"In the kitchen, Ashley!" Evelyn called out.

Ashley rounded the corner just as her grandmother pulled a tray of cookies from the oven.

"Yum. My favorite." Ashley grabbed a cookie and perched on a stool.

"So what's up, Grandma? How was the tribal retreat?"

Her grandmother stopped cutting the vegetables and peered at Ashley over her glasses. "You're bursting at the seams, sweetie. You didn't come here for small talk, so spill."

"Ha! You're right, as usual. Okay, so I was thinking about planning the wedding around a Celtic theme."

"I think that's a wonderful idea," Evelyn said. "Let me know if you want my help."

"I definitely want your help, but for now I thought you might know some stories that would inspire me."

Evelyn wagged the knife at her. "Oh, you be wanting me to be telling you tales of the Clan Napier, do ye now?" Evelyn said in her best Irish voice.

"I say it'd be a fine time for a tale." Ashley mimicked.

Evelyn resumed chopping, lost in thought. Finally, she put down the knife and wiped her hands on her apron.

"I know of one. You remind me of the girl in the tale. Gorgeous red hair, just like yours. So full of life. Very beautiful... from what the stories say."

"What was her name?" Ashley asked.

"Deirdre."

"Deirdre," Ashley said slowly. "Deirdre. What a pretty name. So tell me the story." She grabbed another cookie and settled in.

Evelyn laughed. "With your flair for drama, this should intrigue you. I'll tell you what I know, but it's not much. I'm still discovering it for myself."

"Well maybe we can do some research on it." Ashley said.

"Not this one. The story isn't yet complete."

"What do you mean?"

Evelyn shook her head. "Never mind. Anyway, many centuries ago, a beautiful child was born. The Druids foretold that she would cause the death of many of their men. This alarmed her father, so in counsel with the king, it was decided to send the child away until she was of age. Then she would marry the king. So for eighteen years, a wise old woman, named Leabharcham, raised Deirdre deep in the woods. Now, Deirdre didn't want to marry the king because for many weeks she'd been dreaming of another man. When she told Leabharcham about her dream, she immediately recognized the man who Deirdre described. It was Naoise, one of the king's guard. Deirdre begged the old woman to arrange for them to meet."

"And did she?" Ashley asked.

Evelyn shrugged. "I don't know, but I do know that Leabharcham seriously thought about it because she didn't like to see Deirdre so sad. But, she also knew it would be pointless for them to meet because her marriage to the king was already arranged."

"Oh, wow," Ashley sighed. "What a romantic story." She rested her chin in her hand and stared out the window. "To have no choice at all who to spend the rest of your life with is so tragic."

Ashley's own love story with Tyler wasn't so dramatic, but it was love at first sight. They had met right after college at a restaurant where they both worked, Tyler as a waiter, and Ashley as a hostess; she'd always make it a point to fill up his section first. It took a few weeks before he caught on and finally took notice of her. They'd been together ever since.

"So if you need help with the decorations or your dress, let me know." Her grandmother waved her hand in front of Ashley's face when she didn't respond. "Hello?"

"What? Oh, yeah. Dresses. Okay. That's next on the list."

Ashley leaned over the counter and kissed Evelyn.

"Thanks, Grandma. I'll call you."

"Isn't that a great story, Ty?"

"But you don't even know how it turns out." Tyler slid under the bedcovers next to her.

"Yeah, but it's just the thought of what might happen that's so romantic."

He laughed. "Something right out of your romance books."

Ashley yawned. "It sure is. I wonder if they fell in love at first sight."

Tyler's hand slid around her waist. "If she's anything like you, I doubt he'd have any choice but to fall in love with her." His grip tightened.

Ashley smiled. It'd been this way their entire relationship. Easy, comfortable. As if they'd known each other forever. She rolled over to face him. What if Deirdre and Naoise had fallen in love? What would've happened? In those days, there wouldn't have been much choice, especially if the king had had his mind set on marrying Deirdre. What would she do if she was Deirdre and she fell in love with Naoise? Ashley squeezed Tyler's hand. That was easy. She'd run away with him.

Tyler reached above and turned out the lights. "Good night, babe. Sweet dreams."

She sighed and let the sound of Tyler's breathing soothe her into sleep.

Ashley stood in the shadow of the trees that bordered a lush meadow. Lavender stalks and swaying poppies splashed vibrant shades of purple and gold in between the tall leaves of grass.

She shifted her weight against the mix of broken twigs and dried leaves that poked at the soles of her feet. Brisk morning air held her where she stood, as if waiting for the earth to take its first breath of the day before letting her move.

A short distance away, a small hut claimed its space in the meadow. A well-tended garden thrived on one side, overflowing with herbs and vegetables. On the other side, three well-fed chickens and one rooster clucked about, scratching the dirt. The walls of the hut were worn and the windows appeared clouded from years of protecting those who lived inside.

A woman with fiery red hair appeared in the window. Even through the tired pane, Ashley could see the anticipation in the woman's eyes.

"That must be Deirdre..." Ashley whispered. She raised her hand to get her attention, but Deirdre had moved from the window, appearing moments later, stepping out the front door. Deirdre stood into the sunbeams that blanketed the meadow, eagerness pulling at the corners of her mouth. She tipped her face to the sun and her smile grew brighter.

Behind her, an old woman nudged Deirdre aside and closed the door behind them. Only two steps from the door, the old woman stopped. Her eyes squinted against the sun and into the trees surrounding the house.

"Come, Leabharcham. Let us hurry." Deirdre tugged at the old woman's sleeve.

She cast one more look around, then reluctantly followed Deirdre across the meadow.

"Grandma?" Ashley sat up quickly, her breath catching in her throat, her eyes blinking to adjust to the dark bedroom. Pressing her nails into the mattress assured her she was truly in her bed and not in a cold, damp forest.

"Hey, baby. It's okay. It's okay." Tyler reached over and rubbed her back.

She turned into him, burying her face in his chest.

"Oh my God, Tyler. It felt like I was there. Deirdre and the old lady were at their house in the forest."

"You mean the woman in the Irish story?" Tyler yawned.

"Yeah. It had to have been her."

"Then why did you call for Evelyn?"

Ashley rested back against her pillow. "Well, that's the strange part. The old lady looked just like Grandma. She looked around, like she thought someone was watching them. She had that same frown that Grandma gets when she is trying to figure something out."

"That is strange." Tyler said.

"I swear it was like watching the story unfold right where Grandma left off."

Tyler yawned again. "Maybe your imagination just got the better of you."

"Maybe," Ashley said, "but it was so real."

Tyler snuggled closer. "I love you, Ashley. I'm here for you."

"Thank you," she whispered.

Though Tyler was good about listening to her, he could never understand. He didn't want to understand. Despite the warmth of Tyler's skin against hers, a chill shimmied down her spine. She'd have to ask her grandmother what she knew, because that was no ordinary dream.

"Grandma?"

Ashley checked all the rooms before spotting her grandmother through the kitchen window, cutting flowers.

"You were there!" Ashley blurted as she pushed open the back screen door. "I know it!"

"Ashley! You startled me!" Evelyn put down her clippers and basket of roses. Where was I?"

"I know it sounds strange, but I dreamed of Deirdre. She and the old woman were headed toward the forest. Grandma, the old lady looked just like you!"

Evelyn's smile dropped and her face paled.

"Oh, no. I didn't mean to say you were old..." Ashley said.

"No, that's not it." Evelyn put down her basket. "What exactly happened?"

"I told you. Deirdre and—"

Evelyn put up her hand. "How did you have this dream?"

"I don't know," Ashley shrugged. "I guess I was just thinking about Deirdre."

"You sure it wasn't your imagination?"

Ashley shook her head. "Why are you dismissing this as imagination? I thought—of all people—you would understand. I mean we talk about this stuff all the time. This felt so real."

"I'm sorry. I don't mean to be so insensitive about this. You just caught me off guard."

A sigh escaped Ashley's lips. "So you do understand. That's a relief."

Evelyn looked at her watch. "Oh, look at the time. I'll be late for my bridge game. Would you put these roses in a vase before you leave? And please lock up, will you, dear?"

Evelyn gathered her basket and shears, and shoved them into Ashley's hands.

"Okay." Ashley said. "Hey, Grandma. Is everything okay?"

Evelyn paused at the door. "I'm just concerned you might get caught up in this tale of Deirdre. Try to clear your mind when you go to bed tonight. I've got to go now. Bye, dear."

Evelyn closed the door firmly behind her.

"Hey, baby." Tyler wrapped his arms around Ashley. "Are you okay?"

She stopped washing the dishes and leaned back against his chest.

"Yeah." Ashley sighed. "I'm just tired. Last night is catching up with me, I think. Grandma acted really strange when I told her about my dream. Not at all what I expected."

"Really? Evelyn?"

"Yeah. She suggested it was my imagination, too."

"I'd think she would've given you some explanation."

"I did, too." She finished the dishes and gave the towel to Tyler. "I'm going to bed."

"What about our movie date?"

She turned to him. "I probably wouldn't be the best company. Can we make it tomorrow night?"

His shoulders slumped. He didn't say anything for a few moments.

Ashley felt instant regret. She hated to disappoint him, but she was worn out.

"Sure, Ash. We can do it tomorrow."

"If I get to sleep now," Ashley stood on tiptoe and pressed her lips to his, "I'll feel better for tomorrow night," she said.

"I hope so. Sleep well."

Once under the blankets, Ashley tucked them tightly beneath her chin, intent on falling asleep and staying asleep. Her body sunk deeper into the bed as she squeezed her eyes tight. An image of Deirdre bled into the periphery of her mind and the same chill, the same tingling sensation she felt the night before, pulsed through her body.

Darkness behind her eyes melted into gray fog that slowly gave way to reveal an endless field. Sharp pebbles and blades of grass poked the bottom of Ashley's feet. She shifted uncomfortably, wishing she'd worn shoes in her dream. She squinted against the bright sunlight that warmed the flowers nestled in the field of grass. Ash sniffed the air. Their combined fragrances bested the fragrance of her grandmother's prized rose garden. She plucked a poppy and held it to her nose. Definitely better, somehow less diluted than at home.

Not far from where she stood, Deirdre and the old woman made their way across the tall grass toward an expanse of trees, where columns of light anchored the sun to the forest floor.

A charge of energy crackled through the air and the old woman rubbed her arms in response.

Ashley's heart beat faster. She shadowed them as close as she dared, straining to hear their conversation, but it seemed as though Deirdre was determined to get to where she was going and her caretaker had no chance to talk her out of it.

Wait a minute, Ashley thought. *Why am I so worried that they hear me?*

"Deirdre?" she called out.

Deirdre and Leabharcham stopped and quickly looked behind them.

Ashley crouched low, hoping the swaying shafts of grass would hide her. She covered her mouth, stifling a giggle.

"Who calls my name?" Deirdre asked.

"It is I, Naoise." A male voice called out from the shadows of the trees.

"Huh?" Ashley stood, unable to contain her curiosity.

They all looked toward the trees.

Tall, muscular, and handsome, the man who consumed Deirdre's dreams stepped into the meadow and confidently strode toward Deirdre.

A sigh escaped Ashley's lips. He was the most beautiful man she had ever seen—high cheekbones, startling blue eyes set against sun-bronzed skin. His thick, wavy hair cascaded down just below his shoulders, catching the sunlight as if to spotlight the magnificence of the moment.

Naoise, oblivious to the old woman, stepped close and pulled Deirdre into his embrace. The moment was completely and utterly perfect. Two souls who didn't know they needed each other, united on the chance of a dream.

Ashley lost herself in the fairytale of this blooming romance, and clapped her hands in excitement, then froze, horrified by her intrusion.

All three glanced warily through the trees behind Naoise, then their gazes swept the meadow, breaking the magic and infusing the moment with fear and suspicion. Naoise and the old lady moved protectively around Deirdre, looking for the source of the noise.

Deirdre's eyes narrowed and locked eyes with Ashley.

Ashley hid again.

The old lady noticed Deirdre's intensity and looked in Ashley's direction.

"What is it that you see, child?" Leabharcham asked.

"Ahh, geez," Ashley muttered. "Way to go. Hurry and wake up. Wake up. Wake up. Wake up."

The air cushioned her body and buffered her mind in a soft fog. The grass under her feet melted away into the tangled mess of her bed sheets. She bolted upright with a gasp.

"Ashley! What the hell?"

She blinked against the darkness. She couldn't make out his face, but she could feel Tyler's concern and confusion.

"I'm sorry," she whispered, reaching out and feeling for his hand. A mix of dread and fascination pooled in her stomach. It was starting to feel more and more as if she were part of the tale that Evelyn started.

"Are you okay? You're shivering." Tyler sat up, wrapping his arms around her.

"I was dreaming again. I was there. This time they *saw* me."

"That doesn't seem too odd for a dream." He stifled a yawn. "What's really bothering you about this?"

"I don't know. Something seems so otherworldly about it. I'm not trying to dream about her, but I feel like I'm being drawn in."

"Maybe we should change the theme of the wedding," he muttered, "then maybe this will go away," he said.

"I think it's too late for that."

He leaned back to look at her. "You sound worried, which now makes me worried."

"Let's just forget about this," she said. "I'm just being silly. Let's get back to sleep."

"Grandma?"

She had questions. The past two mornings she had woken feeling as if she hadn't slept at all. Something pulled her from her exhausted body into a place so foreign—yet so familiar—and she had no control over it. She needed answers.

Evelyn walked out of the bedroom wrapping her robe around her. "Just in time. I believe the water is ready for tea." She motioned for Ashley to follow her to the kitchen. She took two mugs from the cupboard and placed them on the counter.

"You had a dream about Deirdre again."

"How did you know?"

Evelyn smiled. "You really have to ask? Your face is covered in worry lines." Evelyn gestured for Ashley to sit. "Time for a lesson about parallel universes. You've been a fly on the wall in Deirdre's life. Well, a noisy fly, anyway."

"What? But she lived forever ago."

"Actually she lives *now*—in a parallel universe."

Alarms went off in Ashley's mind, but what her grandmother was implying sent a bone chilling resonance through her heart. She wasn't sure if the flutter she felt was excitement or fear.

"You said yourself how real it felt," Evelyn said.

"Yeah, but—"

"And Deirdre heard you clap."

Ashley's jaw dropped. "How did you know?"

Evelyn put tea bags into the mugs and poured hot water over them. "I heard you."

"You heard me? How…" Ashley's brow wrinkled in confusion.

"Because I was in the forest, too."

Ashley leaned hard against the kitchen counter. "I don't understand. How are you in my dream?"

"I didn't want to say anything until I was certain, but now I am." Evelyn took a carton of cream out of the refrigerator. "Would you like cream in your tea?"

"What? Um, yeah. That's fine. What are you certain about?"

"You're not having a dream. You're seeing yourself. Deirdre is you in a parallel universe." Evelyn poured the cream and put a mug in front of Ashley. "Everything happens simultaneously," she said. "Past lives, future lives, present lives." She sighed at Ashley's incredulous expression. "I don't mean to frighten or confuse you. I suspected you were capable of passing through the barriers. It runs in our family. We're spiritually connected to our other selves."

"And the old woman? That's you in a past life?"

"In a *present* life. A life that is happening now." She laughed. "When you're old, like me, it seems everyone's life is more exciting than our own."

Ashley sat back in her chair, forgetting about her tea.

"This is so crazy. So I'm Deirdre? I'm living two lives that take place hundreds of years apart?"

"Or, she could be you." Evelyn said, "Actually it's a consciousness that split off into a different reality."

Ashley's jaw went slack. "You're totally serious about this."

"Very serious, and it's not your place to interfere." Evelyn jabbed her finger onto the counter for emphasis. "No matter what."

Ashley sat straighter, her eyes wide with excitement. Of all the things Evelyn and she had talked about, this was definitely not one of them.

"Can I talk to her?"

Her grandmother nodded. "We can talk to our other selves . That's how we gain knowledge that will help us in this life. I talk to Leabharcham all the time. I've even told her about you, though I think she has a hard time dealing with all this." Evelyn laughed. "The other me isn't quite as progressive."

"Wow," Ashley whispered. "How cool is that?"

Evelyn grabbed Ashley's hand.

"Now, child. Don't start getting ideas. The laws of nature are very precise. Deirdre's timeline is her own, just as yours is yours. And keep in mind as you travel to other lives, you leave yourself vulnerable, just like leaving your front door unlocked."

"But you said she is *me*. So…"

"No!" Evelyn tightened her grip. "You're not hearing me. Do *not* interfere."

Ashley sighed. "Okay, so tell me again, Grandma. You heard me clap or did

Leabharcham tell you?"

"I was behind you, watching. I guess I've been caught up in the outcome of this drama as well."

"Why didn't you say anything to me?"

"Because," Evelyn said, "if I had, you probably wouldn't have been able to keep quiet. And you found out that sound travels."

Ashley hung her head. "I know. I messed up. I'm sorry."

"The rules are simple, Ashley. Don't interfere."

"Grandma wasn't kidding, Tyler."

Tyler sighed and turned down the television.

"Ash, you've been on that computer all week. Come sit with me." He patted the cushion bedside him.

She turned in her chair, rolling the kinks out of her neck and shoulders.

"I know. I know. There's just so much to learn." She pointed to the list of search engine results. "I had no idea any of this was possible." She got up and joined him on the couch, snuggling close.

"Maybe it's not," he said.

"Of course it is. How can you explain the times I get glimpses of a forest or passing shadows when I dream? Last night I was on some kind of island. I smelled the seaweed on the beach. I heard the surf. It's not my imagination."

He clicked off the TV and tossed the remote on the coffee table with a sigh.

"Tyler, I can't believe you're being so close-minded about this."

He turned to her and pressed his forehead to hers. "Maybe I wouldn't be so close-minded if I didn't feel like this was taking over."

"You're jealous?"

"I'm feeling disconnected. When was the last time we had dinner together or went to bed at the same time?" His lips found hers and playfully pulled on her bottom lip. "Come to bed now," he whispered. "With me."

"Aww, baby." She wrapped her arms around his neck. "I'll join you in a little bit."

"Seriously, Ash?" He sighed and stood abruptly. "Fine."

Ashley pulled him back. "I promise to make this up to you."

He gazed at her upturned face, his jaw tightening with indecision. "I'm going to hold you to that." He gave her a mischievous grin. "One kiss for every minute you aren't in bed with me," he said as he tapped his watch. "I'm keeping track."

"Hmm. Maybe I'll stay away longer. After all, I have a lifetime to pay off the debt."

Tyler grinned. "So very true. Goodnight, baby."

He raised his hand in a wave as he disappeared down the hall.

"Who might you be?" Deirdre's lilting Irish brogue carried on the ocean breeze.

Though Ashley had been waiting months for this moment, the sound of Deirdre's voice startled her. Deirdre and Naoise had fled the kingdom and traveled all over Ireland, hoping to find refuge, but no one would help them. Ashley had watched, frustrated along with Deirdre, until they made their home on an island off the coast of Scotland.

Ashley had been staying close to the shore of the island, keeping her distance, remembering what her grandmother had said about not interfering, but since Deirdre sought her out, she couldn't pass up this chance to talk with her other self.

Ashley turned to face her.

Deirdre stood tall, her arms crossed, her jaw set. The dark green overdress covering her white chemise set a striking contrast to her brilliant red hair. Waves of vermillion that fell past her waist, framed a flawless complexion. She looked so radiant, so…angry.

Ashley stepped back. "My name is Ashley. I'm sorry if I'm intruding."

"What're ye doin' here? Where did ye come from?" Deirdre asked.

Ashley had wanted to speak to her for so long, but now that she stood face-to-face with her other self, she was at a loss for any words, let alone explain how she got there. Ashley glanced at her sweat pants and old sorority t-shirt and realized how she must look.

"Umm, I'm not from around here," Ashley said.

"Aye. That much I can see." Deirdre pressed her lips together.

"I mean…" Ashley didn't know where to start.

Deirdre broke in. "Why ye are spying on me? I'd assumed the king had sent ye, but your garments," she indicated Ashley's pajamas, "that would have been most unusual."

"Yeah, well, I don't seem to have much control over how I dress when I visit here."

Deirdre looked across the ocean. "Where is your ship? Or do ye live among the trees?"

Ashley took a deep breath. "I live in a place called California."

"Cal-if-ornia?" Deirdre said it slowly. "That'd be where Evelyn is from, if I am not mistaken."

"You know her?"

"Leabharcham has mentioned a woman, though I have not seen her. She told a story of another world. I believed this Evelyn was someone Leabharcham's aging mind had woven."

They stared at each other for a few moments in silence.

Deirdre's arms fell to her sides, dropping her guard. "I suppose I should be frightened, but am not. Honestly I'm happy you are here. It can be a bit lonely, being the only woman about this island."

"What about the old woman? I haven't seen her."

"Leabharcham? Oh, no. She isn't here. When Naoise and I decided to be together, Leabharcham spoke against it so soundly that our only choice was to find a place far way. So here we stand on this island."

Ashley's heart ached for the woman who stood before her. To be so far from a life she knew, just to be together with the one she loved, was a difficult sacrifice.

What little smile had played on Deirdre's lips slid away, and a shadow of sorrow settled into her eyes.

"Are you happy, Deirdre?" Ashley asked.

Deirdre looked to the ocean, her eyes scanning the horizon as if to see her home.

"Aye, mostly. Naoise is a bit restless at times. I know he misses the homeland, but our love binds us together through the difficult times."

Ashley placed her hand to her heart, hoping to smother the ache that pulled at its strings. Tyler was home alone, knowing she dreamed, yet he stayed very supportive and rarely asked her questions about her nights. Not that she had any answers for him. Lately, though, his hugs were tighter and lasted longer. And his kisses…. He kissed her as if it were the last time.

"What about ye?" Deirdre interrupted her thoughts. "Is yer life so dreary that ye spend so many hours here?"

"Oh, no. Not at all," Ashley said. At first being there, watching Deirdre, was out of her control. Something kept pulling her into this life. Her grandmother couldn't explain why that was happening, but as time passed and the more Ashley found out about Deirdre and her plight, she found herself wanting to be here, to watch what decision her other self would make. She should be spending her time enjoying the moments wrapped in Tyler's arms. He was to her as Naoise was to Deirdre. Ashley often wondered, if she and Deirdre were one in the same, what of Naoise and Tyler?

"Do you have a lover?" Deirdre asked.

Ashley nodded. "His name is Tyler. In fact, we're to be married soon. I just need to make the final arrangements like the caterer, the reception hall—"

"Caterer? Hall?"

"Oh, you'd love it, Deirdre. I've chosen a Celtic theme. Tyler is going to wear a kilt and I'm going to wear a beautiful gown, like yours."

"That sounds lovely." For a moment Deirdre's face clouded with regret, but quickly brightened again. "I would be liking to see that." She motioned for Ashley to sit beside her. "Tell me of this California."

Ashley settled beside Deirdre and described cars, movies, online dating, the Internet, her wedding plans, and in a few hours the bond between them grew strong.

"I wish you could see it," Ashley said.

"As do I. How can I be getting to such a far away world?"

"But that's the beauty of it, Deirdre." Ashley tapped her temple. "It's all up here. You can put yourself there by picturing me in your mind, pretending you are there and then you kind of melt into it."

Deirdre's brow rose and her gaze once again sought out the ocean. "Mind travel. So Leabharcham did speak the truth."

"It's more like soul travel," Ashley said.

"But you are here." Deirdre reached out to touch Ashley's arm, but her hand passed through. She sucked in her breath.

Ashley's jaw dropped. "I didn't even think about that. I can feel everything—" she passed her hand through Deirdre, "—except you. That makes perfect sense. We can't be in the same place at the same time. Not physically anyway."

Creases marred Deirdre's smooth forehead. "Are ye perhaps sick of mind, Ashley? A fever perhaps?"

Ashley laughed. "I suppose it does seem unbelievable, but Evelyn and I are proof. Grandma told Leabharcham about it."

"Och! Leabharcham is one who would rather not be knowing about such things," she sighed. "Whether ye speak the truth or not, yer world seems to be a wonderful place."

Ashley shrugged. "In some ways, it is, but we also have lost touch with ourselves. Technology. Information in a second. Food ready in minutes. Shopping online. Convenient, yes, but we lose a lot in the rush to have it all. Simple can be nice."

"Aye, the simple life is less... complicated, but yer life... sounds marvelous. Oh, Ashley. Ye have given me hope." Deirdre squeezed Ashley's hand—or would have if she could. "Will ye still visit me when I leave this island?"

"You're leaving?"

"Aye," Deirdre said. She brushed her skirt smooth, her lips pressed into a tight line.

"Where are you going?" Regret and panic dug at Ashley's heart.

"To the palace. The king has summoned for us."

Ashley gasped. "How did he find you?"

"He has spies everywhere. I am not surprised." Deirdre stood and brushed herself off. "It was only a matter of time. The message said all is forgiven and that we will be welcomed home." Deirdre sniffed and wiped her eyes. "But I be thinking it is but a trap."

"What does Naoise say? He won't go back, will he?"

"He believes the king. Though he loves me, he does still have his loyalty to the king's guard."

Ashley started to reach for Deirdre's hands, but stopped. "So don't go back. Stay here."

"Oh, no. I could not imagine me life without him. Could ye watch yer Tyler walk away?"

That thought wouldn't even have been considered. From their first date, Ashley knew she'd follow him anywhere.

"Maybe enough time has passed that the king will change his mind about marrying you?"

"Perhaps." Deirdre attempted a weak smile, but faltered. "I must go now before Naoise worries. Go be with yer Tyler and wish me well."

"I wish you only the best. Oh, I wish I could give you a hug." Ashley crossed her arms.

"Are you certain ye can find me?"

"I'm certain," Ashley said. "We're connected. Better than sisters. Just think of me and I'll find you."

"Thank you, Ashley," Deirdre said. "I don't know how I can thank ye for helping."

"Grandma! You'll never believe it!"

Evelyn looked up from her book. "Oh, Ashley. I've been wanting to talk with you. Leabharcham told me the king sent for Deirdre."

"Yes! Can you believe that? She doesn't want to go Personally, I don't think—"

"You didn't put any ideas into her head, did you?"

"No. No." Ashley waved away the thought. "Did you know that Deirdre knows about you and where you live? She thought Leabharcham was crazy."

"Really? Leabharcham told her? She seemed so frightened by the idea, that I didn't say much more about parallel universes."

"I don't think either are convinced of it." Ashley sat next to Evelyn. "Grandma, I'm worried. What if it's a trap?"

Evelyn took her glasses off. "The message? It could very well be. No one knows for sure."

"We can't let that happen. We have to convince—"

"Ashley!" Evelyn shut her book with a snap. "Did you not understand what I told you about interfering? It's not our place."

"But I don't want anything bad to happen to them. If Tyler and I were walking into a dangerous situation, I'd appreciate some advice."

"It's not our decision. So, now. Changing the subject. Will you and Tyler come over for dinner tonight?"

How in the world was she supposed to let it go so easily? Deirdre wasn't just anyone, Ashley thought. She wasn't some figment of her imagination. Deirdre was flesh and blood. She was *her*. How could she let her make a decision that might be the wrong one?

"No, I don't think I'm up for dinner. I'd like to spend some time with Tyler." She got up and kissed her grandmother. "I love you."

It felt good to connect with Tyler again, Ashley thought. She hoped the special dinner she planned would close the gap between them. She had been so preoccupied with Deirdre that she'd lost sight of how important Tyler was to her. Tonight was going to be their night.

"Oh!" Ashley dropped the bag of lettuce. "Deirdre!"

Deirdre stood at the door, her smile and eyes growing wide as she took in the cheeriness of the kitchen fixtures.

"I did not know what to expect, but certainly not this!" Like a child, Deirdre touched and poked around, marveling at the textures and buttons.

"My God!" Ashley said. "I can't believe you're here! How long have you...? Oh, it doesn't matter. This is so great! Come on! Let me show you around."

Ashley gestured for Deirdre to follow her, and pointed out the refrigerator, running water, and television before heading to the bathroom. She was just about to show Deirdre the Jacuzzi tub when the front door slammed shut.

"Ashley?"

Ashley startled. "Oh! Tyler is home! You've got to meet him!"

"Ashley," Deirdre's smile faded along with her body.

"No! No! Don't go!" Ashley's hands flailed through the air in front of her, trying to hold onto Deirdre.

Tyler rushed in.

"Ashley! What's wrong? Honey?" He grabbed her by the arms and held her to his chest.

She blinked in confusion. "Where is she? Where is Deirdre?"

"Come on, babe." He picked her up and walked to the bedroom.

"She was here, Tyler. She was here."

"You're scaring me, Ash."

"Deirdre was here. I was showing her around. You must have startled her and she lost her concentration."

"Come on. Let's get you to bed." He sat her on the edge of the bed and pulled down the covers. "There you go." He gently pushed her back against the pillow and tucked the covers around her. "Nice and warm. Can I get you anything?"

"I'm serious, Tyler. Why don't you believe me?"

The lines around his eyes, usually so soft, were taut with worry. He stroked her cheek. "I guess it's a little hard to imagine something I can't see," he said, trailing his fingers across her cheeks. "You've been so distant lately. I was telling your grandmother the other day—"

"Oh, no." She pressed her hands over her face. "You've been talking with Grandma?"

"Shhh. It'll be all right. You just rest. I'll be in the living room."

"In just a few more weeks, I'll be able to call you Mrs. Conway," Tyler said.

Ashley handed him a traveling coffee mug. "Here's to our honeymoon in Italy." They lifted their mugs in cheer.

The way things had been going, Ashley knew if she kept insisting on the Irish theme, there was a good chance the wedding memories would be tainted. Together they decided the ceremony would be traditional with a trip to Italy instead of Ireland. Not exactly what she wanted, but she would do it for him.

"I think the wedding plans are turning out real nicely," Tyler said. "You're doing a fantastic job with everything."

Ashley put her cup down and wrapped her arms around him.

"Thanks for hanging in there with me."

"Hey, I love you. I'd do anything for you. But... I'd better go or I'll be late."

He kissed her goodbye and after grabbing his laptop, headed out the door.

As long as she lived, she knew she'd never get tired of hearing him say that he loved her. She couldn't wait to be married.

Ashley put the breakfast plates in the dishwasher.

A thump and a quiet curse from the living room broke her thoughts.

"Tyler? What did you forget?"

Curious, she put down the bowl and peeked around the corner.

A veiled blur of a woman slid through the hall toward her bedroom.

"No!" Ashley's shock came out a strangled gasp. *It can't be. Why is she here?*

Ashley rushed to her room and looked around.

"Deirdre? Deirdre?"

The air around her chilled her skin and the fleeting essence of salt water filled her senses. Apparently she hadn't pushed thoughts of Deirdre's life far enough away from her mind and the emotions came flooding back.

She's on a ship. Ashley thought. *She's going back to the king.*

Ashley paced the room. A pang of guilt grew in her stomach. She'd promised

Deirdre she would find her again, to help her through her journey, but she also told Tyler she would let it go. The guilt, though, quickly blossomed into dread.

"Please let her be okay. Please let the king be forgiving." She paced the room a few more times before giving up. "Oh, who am I kidding? It's a trap. They disobeyed the freakin' king. How else would it turn out? He's not going to let this go that easily."

Ashley pressed her hands to her head, struggling to let the thoughts go.

"She knows what she's doing. It's her life, and I've got to get to work. I need to forget this whole thing."

A sob welled in her throat. Ashley took a deep breath and swallowed it down.

"Coffee. More coffee." She headed to the kitchen then quickly turned toward the bedroom. "Shower. Keep moving. Get to work." Tears spill over and trickled down her face. "Turn back, Deirdre. Please turn back."

Ashley threw open the closet doors and quickly rifled through her clothes.

"What to wear, what to wear..." So many choices. Choices Deirdre may never have again.

"Okay, Ashley, just call Grandma and get it over with," she said.

She grabbed her cell from the bedside table then quickly put it down.

"No. No. No. Step away from the phone. Let it go, Ash. She'll only tell you not to get involved anyway."

She headed to the shower, determined to get through the morning. She caught her reflection in the bathroom mirror. Her skin was taut against her cheekbones, her hair badly in need of a trim.

"This is nuts." Ashley covered her face and shook her head. "I've got to stop."

She'd almost neglected her life because of Deirdre, and it definitely showed. Enough was enough. Almost.

She grabbed her phone and this time let her call go through to her grandmother.

"Hi, Grandma."

"Ashley, is everything all right? Why aren't you at work?"

"Grandma, I think she's going back to the palace."

Evelyn gave no response except for a heavy sigh.

"Grandma?"

"I know, Ashley. The king is expecting her soon."

Ashley's heart sank.

"Leave it be," her grandmother said. "I know it's difficult."

"But she loves Naoise. All she wanted was to be with the man she loves."

"We can't save anyone once they're on their path. It's all a learning process."

"What if she could stay here with me? Bring her to California."

"You can't do that. You know as well as I do that you can't have two of yourselves physically in the same time and space. It's just not the way it works. Ashley, you and Tyler have so much to focus on and a future of choices to make." She sighed again. "I'm so sorry I brought this whole thing up. I only wanted for you to be entertained by a story."

"No, Grandma. I'm sorry. I've made a mess of things. It's just that knowing she's probably going to get in trouble makes me a little anxious."

"We don't know that for sure." Evelyn said.

"I know," Ashley whispered. It was difficult not to think about it. The harder she tried to push the thoughts away, the harder they pushed back.

"Go enjoy your day, sweetie," Evelyn said. "You have a wonderful life ahead of you. Don't waste it."

"Okay, Grandma. I love you."

"I love you, too."

Ashley hung up and tossed the phone on the bed, determined not to get caught up in Deirdre's life.

She shoved her fingers through her hair. Hell, who was she kidding? She knew there was no way she could let it go.

The dark seemed to be getting darker as the night wore on. Ashley definitely wasn't going to sleep. Different scenarios played out in her mind. Best case was that the king forgave them and let them be together. Worst case was that he punished them, and in between those possibilities there was a myriad of choices that the king could make.

"But there's only one outcome I want her to have," Ashley whispered. "The same as mine."

She gently laced her fingers with Tyler's and listened to his gentle, rhythmic breathing. She felt so secure and grounded with him. She closed her eyes and focused on their life together, how they met, and all the plans they had made for their life as husband and wife. A condo close to the ocean, traveling a bit before having children. Maybe making their home in San Francisco.

Thousands of pulsing lights vibrated around her, electrifying the air and tickling her skin. A bubble of pressure squeezed her body, threatening to smother her. At last, it released her, pitching her face down onto the cold and dirty stone floor of the palace.

Heavy and determined footsteps echoed across the walls.

Ashley lifted her gaze to see a royal guard moving quickly toward the king, who sat before a food-laden table.

"Your Highness." The guard bowed low. "They've arrived."

The king took a delicate bite of venison, savoring the moment. No one in the room said a word as he chewed the meat painfully slow. When at long last he swallowed his food, he glanced at the guard as if he had just noticed him. "Why, show them in, of course. Do not make them wait."

The guard bowed again, turned and signaled to the other guards who stood at the doors.

Deirdre, Naoise, and his brothers—all stripped of their weapons—walked in slowly, eyeing the guards and people who stood against the walls. They bowed low.

The king's face showed no emotion at all as he looked down upon Deirdre and Naoise. His hand raised ever so slightly and with a flick of his wrist, the large wooden doors behind them closed with a terminal thud. His gaze skimmed the brothers, disappointment muting his eyes, then fell to Deirdre, the lines around his eyes and mouth turning sharp.

"Who will kill these traitors for me?" the king's voice echoed off the stone walls.

Deirdre slipped her hand into Naoise's as they both looked around nervously.

Movement from behind a pillar across the hall caught Ashley's attention. A knight, black armor snugly covering his broad shoulders, sprinted toward Naoise's brothers, his massive sword raised.

"Behind you!" Ashley screamed, but if anyone heard her, her warning was lost in the confusion, save for one person.

"No, Ashley!"

Ashley turned to the voice.

Evelyn stood against the wall, hand to her heart, the demand etched deeply into her frown.

Ashley turned back around, scanning the faces that fixated on the attack—brows raised, mouths rounded with surprise, mingled with cold hearts relishing in the bloodshed through narrowed eyes and smug smiles.

In seconds, the knight had run his sword through the closest brother and pushed him aside, raising his bloody weapon high, ready for the next strike. The remaining two stood shoulder to shoulder, a barrier protecting Deirdre and Naoise.

The knight showed no hesitation. He plowed into one, ramming the hilt into the side of his head, watching him collapse. The last brother lunged, wrapping his arms around the knight's waist, momentarily taking him off balance.

Despite his size, the knight was quick and with a fluid movement, brought his sword underneath the brother's chest and cut him through, until his arms released their hold.

When the last of the brothers fell, all eyes locked upon Deirdre and Naoise, who stood, eyes squeezed shut, as if bracing for the blow.

Without thought, Ashley sprinted to their side and faltered only steps away, for the vibrancy of Deirdre's hair dimmed and the strong lines of Naoise's features blurred. In unison their bodies lost definition, and Ashley watched as they became transparent, wispy imitations of who they were, and with a palpable crackle, they disappeared.

"What the..?" Ashley grasped the air where they had fearfully stood only moments before. "Deirdre!"

She spun around, eyes wildly searching the room.

The knight stopped, searching along with Ashley, then a ruthless grin spread across his face, and he shifted his sword to other hand.

Ashley followed his menacing gaze.

"What? No!" Ashley screamed.

Tyler, in only his t-shirt and boxers, stood in Naoise's place, blinking quickly, lost in his surprise.

"Tyler! Watch out!" Ashley rushed toward the knight, latching onto his arm, but that did little to stop the gap between him and Tyler from closing.

Tyler focused on Ashley, confusion clouding his face.

The knight glanced at Ashley, a snarl curling his lip. "Be gone with ye, lass."

"But you're making a mistake! He didn't do anything!"

The knight shoved his shoulder into Ashley, freeing his arm. He raised his sword high over his shoulder and brought it down across Tyler's chest.

Tyler crumpled in a heap at the knight's feet, blood spilling from the wound and pooling around him.

Ashley's screams filled the room, unnoticed by those who stood in the great hall. She rushed the knight, pummeling his chest with her fists. "You killed him!" She suddenly stopped, stepping back, her mouth covering her shock. "I touched you..."

The knight's scowl grew deeper. He pushed her away, sending her sprawling to the floor, then wiped his blade across his sleeve.

Ashley's sobs convulsed her body. "No, no. This can't be happening." On shaking arms and legs, she crawled to Tyler's side. Sitting beside him, she cradled his head in her lap, brushing his hair back from his face.

"This feels so real, just like you said." He coughed, flicking tiny drops of blood across his lips.

Ashley quickly wiped it way, as if that could erase the horror before her.

"That feels real, too. I can't wait to wake up." Tyler's laugh turned into a groan. "This is a dream, isn't it?"

His face blurred through her tears. "Yeah, baby. It's a dream. A really bad dream." Ashley pressed her hand over the deepest part of the wound, hoping to staunch the bleeding.

"This really hurts, Ash." His breaths came out in labored, raspy burst. "Are your dreams—" he grimaced over another cough, "—always like this?"

"Ashley." Evelyn kneeled next to Ashley. "I'm so sorry."

Ashley hardly recognized the woman before her. Usually so brave, so stoic, Evelyn's eyes were red and puffy, tears streaming down her face. Her shoulders slumped as if a heavy weight were suddenly placed upon them. Ashley had no sympathy for her.

"Sorry? You're sorry? You started this!"

"Evelyn?" Tyler strained to see her. "You're in my dream, too?" He rested his head back and sucked in a breath. "All your talk about that Irish story has me dreaming about it, too." He squeezed Ashley's hand. His eyes rolled back before refocusing on Ashley. "I think I'm waking up because I don't feel the pain anymore."

"Look what you've done, Grandma." She wiped away the sheen that beaded upon Tyler's brow. "No, Ty. No. Don't go. Stay with me, baby." Ashley tightened her grip on his hand.

"It's okay," he said. Tomorrow we'll do something fun. This is just a dream. A pretty lousy dream, though."

He sucked in a stuttering breath that stalled in his throat. His body relaxed, and the breath slipped out for the last time.

"Tyler?" Ashley gasped. "Tyler!"

The torrent of tears broke free. She wanted to crawl inside his body and fix whatever was broken. How could this have gone so terribly wrong? She looked up, but Evelyn was gone. "Get back here!" Ashley screamed at the space where Evelyn had stood. "Do you hear me? Don't leave us!"

Her chest heaved with grief and panic. *Such a bad, bad, bad dream.* Spent of her will, she lay across Tyler's chest, willing herself to go wherever he was—but nothing was happening. His lifeless eyes stared at her from across the expanse of whatever dimension he had vanished. She couldn't live without him, and now she was trapped in this place she had tried so desperately to forget. *Why couldn't she have just let go?*

Now, she decided, was as good a time as any. Without Tyler—especially in this place—there remained no reason for her to hold on. Her thoughts reached out for something—everything—anything to release her from this world. She spotted a smooth chunk of marble not too far from Tyler's arm, the crumbled statue above its likely source. Without further thought, she sat up and grabbed it, bringing it forcefully to her temple...once, twice, three times...until she fell upon the floor beside her fiancé. She didn't feel any pain, but she could feel herself slipping away. "'Til death do us part..." she whispered, the metallic taste of blood filling her mouth, painting her words red.

The king's brow furrowed as he looked around at the bodies. He signaled to the guards. "Go find them. They could not have gone far."

The soft glow of the moonlight spilled through the window, splashing across the rumpled bed covers. Deirdre and Naoise lay together, legs entwined, holding each other tight.

"This will take much getting used to, Naoise. But trust me. Ashley told me that where we are now, this California, is a safe place. We'll never have to see the king again."

DIANA MURDOCK, from a very young age, has always dabbled with stories and poems and shared them only with family and friends. It wasn't until she had a very powerful and dream, a dream that became her first novel, that she took her writing seriously. With many stories now lining up, waiting to be written, Diana is committed to penning each and every one. To add more variety, she's adapted the first in her trilogy into a screenplay and is a partner in an independent film production company. A single mother of two boys, she'll take on the world, one story at a time.

LINKS

http://www.dianamurdock.com
http://www.facebook.com/pages/Diana-Murdock-Author/114706771907294
https://twitter.com/Diana_Murdock

The Wolf's Gambit

by Nick Nafpliotis

"**B**RANDON, you old dog!"

Sultan hadn't heard anyone call him by his first name in years. The Wolf, however, had known him long before he went legit. He was also one of the only people who might be able to help him stay that way.

"Good to see you, Wolf," Sultan replied as the two embraced. "Sorry it's been so long. I wasn't even sure if it'd be safe for me to come..."

"You stow that thought this instant, old man," The Wolf interrupted, his yellow eyes momentarily glowing brighter. "We may be on different sides of the coin now, but that doesn't mean you have to worry about me acting like a jealous ex-girlfriend. If someone tries to wipe you, I promise that it'll never be me."

"Somehow, I find that both terrifying and reassuring," Sultan said while shaking his head. "But still, I get the feeling that everyone looks at me like some type of traitor."

"And anyone who says they wouldn't have taken that job themselves is a liar," The Wolf shot back. "We're all in this to make money; a private gig for the Tarnath family is about as good as it gets. No one from the old crew who was worth a damn expected you to try and keep running with us. Can't draw a huge paycheck like that with a foot still in the black market, right?"

"I guess not," Sultan said with a shrug. "But don't think that means I forgot about everyone. Have you heard from any of them lately?"

"They're all scattered about these days," The Wolf replied wistfully. "Price and

Bennett are with a new group that smuggles meat past the Outerlands. Wiz is still modding and running weapons for anybody that'll pay him. That psycho, Nivelles, is working freelance by himself now, taking contracts that no sane person would even consider."

"Did he ever get over his thing about rats?" Sultan asked with a grin.

"Hell no!" The Wolf exclaimed with a laugh. "I think the main reason Nivelles went solo was because of that time we put one in his weapons cache. I swear...that loon would try to go toe to toe with a hundred man strike force, but put a mouse within ten meters of him and he completely loses his shit. Remember that time he pissed his pants during an op when a mouse went across his foot?"

The two men shared the joyous laughter that only nostalgia and shared experiences can bring. For the briefest of moments, Sultan felt like he was thirty years old again, scraping by on odd smuggling and pirate jobs while having the time of his life.

"I really miss you guys," he said after a long sigh. "The money's great, but the job isn't anywhere near as exciting as the stuff we used to get into. With the exception of Nivelles, I'll always consider you and the others to be my real crew."

"That's another big reason that none of us hold any ill will towards ya," The Wolf replied with a warm smile. "Those Tarnaths have you leading a damn private army, but it somehow never seems to catch any of us. Don't think for a second that we didn't notice or appreciate that."

"That's actually why I'm here," Sultan replied, suddenly finding it difficult to maintain eye contact. "I overheard the Tarnaths talking the other night; turns out I'm getting canned at the end of the month."

The smile that had been stretched across The Wolf's face since he'd greeted him dropped into a horrifying sneer. It was a look that Sultan had seen plenty of times before, but it still caused his blood to chill. The Wolf was well known as a ruthless kidnapper and assassin, but the smoldering expression that formed on his face when something displeased him had been what really earned him his nickname.

"What the hell do you mean they're canning you?" he asked as his yellow eyes began to narrow. "You've been serving at those rich assholes' beck and call for twenty years now. Did you do something to piss them off...or better yet, did you screw the wife?"

"I wish," Sultan sighed. "They said I was 'too old' to be part of their security force now that they had a son. I guess they're hoping to replace me with someone your age who's got the same genetic skill set."

"Well, if you came here worrying about me taking your job, you can put your mind at ease," The Wolf replied. "I know what I got makes things a bit different; never held it against you for finding work that paid what you deserved."

"I know," Sultan said while putting a hand on his old friend's shoulder. "But that 'special something' you got...and our history together...it's why I'm here now. I need your help, Wolf."

"Brandon, you know I'm there for you," The Wolf replied while clasping his friend's arm. "You trained me, provided for me, and made sure I was safe. Now you let me continue to earn a living. Ain't no shame in asking me to lend you a hand…and I think I know just how to do it."

Sultan hated babysitting assignments. He'd much rather be in the middle of a fight with his team or investigating a potential breach. Unfortunately, working security for the Tarnaths meant that you occasionally had to guard them during their excursions to the park.

Tonight, however, there were two factors making him feel far tenser than he'd normally be during this type of assignment. For starters, the Tarnaths' three-year-old son, Robbie, was with him. The kid was nice enough, but he could also be an unholy terror to supervise. Sultan was pretty sure that targeting a mini-drone in a driving rain storm was easier than locking down the boy's location some days.

The main thing that had him on edge, however, was that The Wolf would be arriving at any moment. His old partner would've been a formidable adversary without the genetic enhancements, but his ability to teleport short distances (along with having the wits to properly make use of it) made him seem unstoppable. Watching The Wolf work had sent chills up his spine back when they were on the same crew. He wasn't sure at all, though, how it would feel to pretend to be against him while the rest of the team really was. He trusted his old friend not to get to shot, but he was still wary about the prospect of one of his men getting killed.

"Whatever you do, please do not wipe anyone on my team," he'd half-pleaded, half-commanded while making their final preparations.

"Geez, Brandon, maybe you are getting too old for this," The Wolf replied with a friendly shove. "You must be going senile if you can't remember the twenty times I already told you I'd be careful.

"I know," Sultan replied with a nod, "but you can also kill far more easily than most. Most folks with your abilities can't rein it in."

"And as you probably know all too well, I ain't most folks, old man," The Wolf replied with a wry smile, his yellow eyes glowing brightly in the night sky. "I haven't stayed alive this long by being stupid. This'll work out. I promise."

Sultan was finally beginning come around on the idea of trust his friend when a voice came blaring through his earpiece.

"CONTACT RIGHT!"

He knew that was The Wolf, starting the entire chain of the events exactly the way he said he would. Sultan now had to play his part, making sure that the men pursued without being able to engage. Fortunately, catching The Wolf was a monumental task for even the best trained and equipped private forces.

"IT'S A PORTER!" another voice rasped into Sultan's ear.

"Keep your shit together and calm the hell down," Sultan barked through his receiver. "Fan out in a staggered perimeter. Use the Tarnaths' current location as the center and watch your fire."

Sultan's team quickly got into position, their movements fluid from hours of drilling and practice. Despite the presence of an enemy that could disappear and reappear at will, no one had fired yet. Everyone was waiting to gauge the time and distance the teleporter needed for each jump before engaging.

"This is why those pretentious pricks shouldn't fire me," Sultan thought as he peered through his weapon's scope. "I may be old and ordinary, but still I know how to make a unit work together."

From approximately a hundred meters away, the sound of The Wolf's teleporting ripped through the air like the back fire from a high powered pistol. Every pop was followed by Sultan's team tensing and raising their guns in unison.

"I'm calculating a twenty-meter port radius for this guy," a younger sounding voice said quietly through everyone's earpieces.

"Twenty-two, but close enough, kid," Sultan thought as the loud pops continued to circle their perimeter.

"You know what would be nice right now?" the same young man's voice continued. "If we had someone on our team with a tactical gene mod."

"Oh, but we do," another voice chimed in. "Doakes could turn into a monkey and start flinging shit at him."

"Shut the hell up, you assholes," Doakes shot back over the murmur of nervous chuckling.

Sultan was glad his team was loose, even if their banter was at Doakes expense. He felt bad for the kid; it's not like Doakes was the only person who'd had an unsuccessful gene mod operation. The high probability of death or failure was the main reason that most people in their line of work still wouldn't even consider it. Doakes was pretty lucky that his mod hadn't resulted in a painful death or an out-of-control mutation.

Unfortunately, the operation altered his genes just enough so that he could temporarily change into large versions of mammals which shared a large portion of their DNA with humans. It had made for some pretty impressive party tricks, but ended up having absolutely no tactical use.

The animals Doakes could change into weren't even humanoid versions of their species, either. In fact, their enlarged size (combined with the unfamiliar muscle and skeletal structures) made him slower and clumsier than a blind house cat. The forms could also only be held for a maximum of two minutes before the pain forced him to change back. All of this combined to make the gene mod operation an obscenely expensive mistake…which put him on the receiving end of constant derision from his teammates.

"Hey Doakes," a female voice whispered. "Do you ever change into a dog just so you can lick your own balls?"

"Alright, that's enough!" Sultan barked into his com. "Unless this guy's showing off, we're going to have an engagement pretty soon. Stay..."

Before Sultan could finish, he heard one of his men screaming. That alone was enough to give him a start, but the man's cries weren't coming from the perimeter. They were coming from above.

A second later, the screaming team member came crashing down at his feet. The Wolf, who had apparently learned to extend his porting range much further than twenty-two meters, was picking up another one of Sultan's troops and dropping her from the sky when the gunfire started.

"Hold your fire, damn it!" he screamed into his com as the air popped all around him.

As a third troop fell out of the sky, Sultan caught a glimpse of The Wolf, pistols firing in both hands. Before he blinked out of existence again, five rounds hit five different targets, all of whom grunted and fell to the ground.

"Wolf, what the hell are you doing?" Sultan screamed, no longer caring about blowing his cover.

These were his people. He knew that they wouldn't stand a chance against his old crew member, but he'd also expected The Wolf to show a large degree of restraint. Now, however, his team was being dropped out of the sky or shot. This wasn't worth his job.

"HE'S GOT ROBBIE!" a female voice barked through into his earpiece. "Hostage proto..."

The Wolf appeared in front of the soldier, whipped the crying boy to one side, and quickly emptied three rounds into her left leg. After another loud pop, he was gone again.

After realizing that he was the only one left standing, Sultan broke into a sprint towards the tree line. In front of him, pops rang out through the forest in the direction that The Wolf had told him to go. The tree branches scratched against his face as he closed the distance between himself and the porter. After running until his lungs burned, he came to a small clearing two kilometers away from the open park space where the conflict had started. There stood The Wolf, wearing a huge grin on his face while holding an unconscious Robbie in his arms.

"What the hell do you think you're doing?" Sultan panted while taking a cautious step forward.

"Relax, he's not dead...and neither are your troops," The Wolf replied as his eyes glowed in the shadows. "I made sure that they were all wounded enough not to give chase. No one will die. I also injected this kid with a sedative because he wouldn't shut up. Maybe you should bring some back to the Tarnaths; they might give you a raise."

"That was anything but a non-intrusive snatch-and-grab!" Sultan yelled, his voice and anger coming back to him. "You could have killed somebody out there, including the boy!"

"But I didn't," he replied with a wry smile. "You know me better than that, Brandon. I don't ever miss my target. And besides, how the heck did you think I was going to incapacitate the rest of your team while you retrieved the package? Harsh language?"

Sultan knew he was right. Getting the boy had been the easy part for The Wolf; making sure no one else knew about their plan was the hard one. Now, however, Robbie and his team would not bear witness to the exchange.

"This still might look suspicious," Sultan said softly while regretting his previous outburst.

"Before I leave, fire your gun into the air a few times," The Wolf replied as he handed over the child. "Make sure you shoot in multiple directions and hit a couple trees. It'll look like you were trying to hit a porter. Also, take this."

The Wolf pulled out a knife and cut into his arm. Yellow blood seeped out of his skin, which he took and spattered onto Sultan's body armor.

"You should feel honored," he said with a grin that doubled as a painful grimace. "No one ever gets a hit on me. Now go; take that boy back to his family and get your job back from them, too."

Dinner that night was the best Sultan had eaten in years, which was really something considering his impressive salary. Once he'd shown up with Robbie, Mrs. Tarnath had insisted that they have him over for dinner so that he could be thanked properly. Mr. Tarnath wasn't too thrilled about the idea of one of his underlings dining at their table, but his wife wouldn't hear otherwise.

"He saved our boy," she'd whispered, not realizing that his com receiver could pick up everything being said. "I don't care if that's what you pay him to do. Robbie could very well have been kidnapped or dead right now if it wasn't for that man, so we're having him eat with us at our table. End. Of. Discussion."

But as good as the food was, Sultan found the ambiance to be more than a little unsettling. He enjoyed eating with his troops, listening to them tell stories while giving each other a hard time. Now he sat with two WASPs at a luxurious table, their conversations never moving past surface courtesy and feigned interest.

Once dinner was mercifully over, the Tarnaths gave him the rest of the night off. The police, who had swarmed and covered the residence, weren't nearly as good as his team. Unfortunately, his troops were all in the hospital recovering from various injuries. Sultan went to see them, played the good sport while they ribbed him over eating with the lords of the castle, and then set off to the coordinates transmitted through an encrypted file to his tablet.

"So, did you cross screwing Mrs. Tarnath off the old bucket list?" The Wolf asked while fidgeting with the bandage on his arm.

"C'mon, Wolf…" Sultan responded with an exasperated sigh. "They just had me inside their house for dinner. That's it.

"You forgot to pick up some boner pills, didn't you?" The Wolf replied.

Sultan would have normally laughed, but he was wary of The Wolf's reasons for calling on him like this. A part of him had known all along never to expect anyone to take such a risk for free, even if he were an old friend. Now, as The Wolf's yellow eyes glowed at him from across the table, he knew the terms of payment were about to be laid bare.

"So now that you've locked up some job security with the missus," The Wolf began after sipping his coffee, "are you still gonna let me and the rest of our prestigious alumni continue operating in peace…or are you gonna make me feel like a sheep that's been duped by a wolf wearing its prettiest dress?"

"Nothing changes," Sultan replied firmly. "And if tonight proved anything, it's that we couldn't catch you even if we wanted to."

"Probably not," The Wolf replied with a smug grin stretching across his face. "But as far as the whole 'nothing changes' thing goes, there is one thing that could benefit from some flexibility on your part."

"Oh, great!" Sultan said while slamming his hands down on the table. "Here it comes: The part where you tell me to kidnap Mrs. Tarnath for you or make some other outrageous demand that I can't possibly allow to happen."

"No, nothing like that…unless there's some way you could make the Mrs. Tarnath thing happen."

"No," Sultan responded without a trace of humor in his voice.

"Fine," The Wolf said with a resigned sigh. "What I need isn't nearly that craven…or difficult. I recently took a contract with someone who has quite an affinity for cars, all of which can be found in Mr. Tarnath's garage. If I port in and out and only use a small crew, it should take me no more than ten minutes to get all ten of them."

"You've got to be kidding me," Sultan shot back. "I'm okay if you 'steal' from the Tarnaths when it involves their businesses and ships, but I can't actually let you steal something from their home. That man would fire me on the spot. And besides, those are items inside his house. You shouldn't be trying to take that sort of thing from anyone."

"Now's not a real good time to develop a moral compass, Brandon," The Wolf hissed. "You just let me put their boy in danger to save your own skin."

"Wolf, you know I can't let you do this," Sultan replied while shaking his head. "Just because I've got leeway with the Tarnaths now doesn't mean I can let something that big slide by me. I'd get canned for sure."

"Fine," The Wolf replied as his namesake expression spread across his face.

"Then I guess I'll just have to make you realize what happens when washed up smugglers don't honor good deeds done by their friends."

Sultan instinctively reached towards his holster, but The Wolf only giggled a bit as he languidly got up from their table.

"Relax, Brandon. I promised that if you ever got wiped, I wouldn't be the one who did it. I intend to keep that promise...and still kick your ungrateful ass into next week. Good luck keeping your job after this shit storm."

Sultan waited for The Wolf to walk out the door before running out to his car and driving as fast as he could back to the Tarnath residence.

"Mr. and Mrs. Tarnath, I need you both to go to the safe room," Sultan said as calmly as he could after passing through the police barricade.

"What the hell's going on, Sultan?" Mr. Tarnath replied with a scowl.

"The abductor from before is probably going to attempt an assault on your residence. The rest of my team won't be there to help take him down this time," Sultan said as he ushered the family downstairs.

"Your team got their asses handed to them out at the park," Mr. Tarnath snarled. "We have the police here now, they..."

"The police won't be able to do jack shit against this guy," Sultan interrupted.

He glanced over at a nearby officer and gave a helpless shrug. What he'd just said wasn't very kind, but it was also the truth. Law enforcement hadn't caught up with the changing weapon landscape like the black market had.

"I thought you wounded him!" Mr. Tarnath shouted over protests from his wife. "Why would a wounded criminal come here to..."

Sultan slammed the door shut before the question was finished. He could talk his way out of the particulars later. Right now, there was the small matter of how he would take on The Wolf (who wouldn't be holding back this time) by himself. The man said he wouldn't be the one to kill him, but he also always made good on his threats...and he rarely took long to do so. That meant that some form of reckoning was surely coming his way.

After Sultan got upstairs to the gun tower, he began scanning in all directions. When nothing showed up for over three kilometers, he started to think that maybe The Wolf had maybe cooled off and reconsidered. That hope was shattered by an enormous radar reading moving at a high rate of speed in his direction. After it got into view, Sultan couldn't believe what he was seeing.

"You have got to be shitting me," he whispered.

A Warthog-class mech was running at full tilt towards the front of the Tarnath residence. The arms on the bipedal exosuit were swinging back and forth as its legs pounded into the ground. Sultan couldn't see who was behind the center mounted canopy, but he knew it wasn't The Wolf. The porter was popping in and out the air directly in front of the colossal robot, disappearing right before it reached him each time.

"Hey there, ya old dog," a voice crackled through his ear piece. "Figured since I put all your troops in the hospital, this line would be a nice and secure place for us to talk."

Sultan didn't say anything. He wasn't surprised that The Wolf had cracked his network's encryption, but he had absolutely no idea what to make of the metal monstrosity that was rapidly bearing down on him.

"Remember that 'psycho' Nivelles?" The Wolf asked between ports. "Well, it turns out that he's still local, just as crazy as before, and more than willing to take on an insane contract...only now he's got himself a cool new toy."

Before Sultan could try and make contact with the police stationed outside the house, two rockets blasted from less than a kilometer away. The orange and red streaks shot straight into the armored tanks at the front of the perimeter, leaving piles of burning metal and panicked screams in the wake. Another streak went up into the sky and connected with a helicopter, causing it to crash back down to Earth on the other side of the house.

"...and that should have them officially bugging out, I think," The Wolf said with a satisfied chuckle.

Sure enough, the police started backing up and fleeing towards the city. Sultan didn't normally feel bad about the authorities getting wiped, but these guys didn't even know why they were being attacked or what to do about it. A call to the National Guard would have been made after the first blast, but the fight would be over long before they arrived.

"You know, Brandon," The Wolf continued, "when I first got this job, I was really conflicted about it. I didn't want to have to cause you any trouble. So when you showed up with hat in hand asking me for a favor, I figured that the perfect solution had just dropped into my lap. You'd let me in, I'd get the merchandise, and no one gets hurt. But then you had to go and get all loyal to the guy who writes your paychecks."

Sultan was listening, but still had no idea how to respond. The Warthog had now reached the front yard, its guns spinning and spitting bullets at any of the remaining authorities who'd dared to stay and fight. Turning his gun down towards the ground below, Sultan began his own stream of fire, which harmlessly pinged off the mech's exterior. It looked up in his direction and raised an arm, a blue light beginning to glow through the rounded open above its hand. Sultan had just enough time to dive back down the stairs before the tower was obliterated above him.

"Looks like you've still got some moves, old man!" The Wolf said shouted after a maniacal laugh.

Sultan struggled to get back up, his body aching from the fall as well as the debris that had toppled down on him. As he got up, he noticed a man taking cover in the corner of the upstairs entryway. He'd first thought it was a police officer who'd turned tail and ran like the rest. Upon closer inspection, however, he noticed that it was someone who he knew.

"Doakes?" Sultan asked as he rushed over to him. "What the hell are you doing back here?"

"I didn't get shot, sir," he replied. "Just got dropped from pretty high up. Knocked me out. Doctors said I should stay out of active engagement for a while, but I could come get my things out of my locker. Looks like made it here in time for one heck of a party."

As Sultan looked at Doakes, an idea hit him so hard that he almost lost his balance.

"Doakes!" he shouted, the sudden exuberance in his voice confusing the man standing before him. "I think I know how to stop this...and you're the only one who can pull it off."

"Permission to speak freely, sir?" Doakes asked as they crawled along the floor to the front of the house.

"Go ahead," Sultan whispered back.

"This is humiliating."

"I can definitely understand how you'd see it that way," Sultan said while putting a hand on his shoulder. "But it's better than being dead. Now stay down and let me get this rolling. When I call for you, come out and do your thing."

Sultan took out a blue flare, the signal for a parlay request, and shot it through a broken window. He then turned his com back on and prayed that The Wolf would honor it.

"Well, well, well..." The Wolf said with a smile so wide it could be heard on the other end of the line. "I guess I'll hear what you have to say, especially if it's something along the lines of 'Sorry for being an ungrateful asshole.' You ready to do right by me, old man?"

"I STILL GET PAID OR I KILL HIM ANYWAY!" Nivelles shouted into his receiver.

"Yes, Nivey, it'll all be taken care of," The Wolf sighed, letting a hint of exasperation creep into his otherwise gleeful tone. "Now, Brandon, come on out here and say something that'll put everyone in a better mood."

"Oh, I was just going to ask your little minion there if he remembered the time he pissed his pants during an op when a cute little mouse ran across his shoe," the Sultan responded with a derisive snort.

Nivelles yelled something unintelligible into his receiver, causing both The Wolf and Sultan to flinch while grabbing at their ears. Before either one of them had time to recover, the Warthog was charging full speed ahead towards the house.

"Do it now, Doakes!" Sultan screamed over the clanging of the mech's rapidly approaching feet.

Doakes popped out from behind the shredded front door, his entire body shaking as if he were in the grip of a massive seizure. As the Warthog continued barreling forward, however, Doakes' skin suddenly became covered in grey fur. A long, pink tail sprouted out of his backside just as he was turning around to face the robot with a newly elongated snout and beady, red eyes.

The scream that emitted from Nivelles this time was so loud and anguished that it almost didn't sound human. The Warthog jerked upright for a split second before its legs became tangled, launching the entire thing forward like some type of intoxicated giant. After crashing to the ground, the mech slid for a few meters before grinding to a halt. Nivelles' screams never stopped.

Sultan stood and stared, first at his team member in the form of a giant rat, then at the colossal machine laying on the front yard in front of him. An eerie silence fell over the scene before it was broken by The Wolf cackling hysterically.

"HOLY SHIT! THAT WAS BRILLIANT!" he howled. "I got to see the whole thing from up here in a tree and it was glorious."

"I bet the inside of his cabin smells like piss and shit, too," Sultan replied, smiling despite the anger and fear still swirling inside him. "So it looks like you're going have to find another way to make me 'learn my lesson' or man up and do it yourself."

"Bah!" The Wolf said between fits of laughter. "I got my money's worth after that spectacle. Nivelles' fee can be earned back in a week...or at least half of it can. You alright with half price for failing to complete your job due to being a total spaz, Nivey?"

"Whatever, man! I'll take it!" Nivelles shouted back through the com. "Just don't make me have to get near that thing again...and get us out of here now!"

"I think I've caused enough of a headache for you over this one," The Wolf continued while ignoring his partner's pleas. "I'll drop this job if you don't hold sending Nivey after you against me."

"What are you going to do about your contract," Sultan asked. "Most employers aren't too keen on letting people dump them for sentimental reasons."

"I'll figure something out," The Wolf responded as he ported to pick up Neville and disappeared again. "It's not like he could kill me if he wanted to, and he'll need my services again."

Sultan looked around at the ruined house. Mr. Tarnath would be royally pissed and he'd have to explain and trust Doakes with his secret. The Wolf had left him with a gigantic mess to clean up. But he had a job...for now, at least.

"Fine, go on your way, Wolf," he said gruffly. "Wish you'd had such a good sense of humor about things before unleashing hell on me."

"Maybe I'll learn to control my temper, one day," he replied with a sigh. "And it seems I could still learn a thing or two from you. Maybe the old dog can teach me a few tricks sometime."

Sultan smiled in spite of himself. He looked over at Doakes, who had turned back into his human form and was just getting up off the floor.

"What the heck was that all about?" he asked while putting his shirt back on.

"It's a long, strange story..." Sultan began as the two headed back downstairs to unlock the safe room.

NICK NAFPLIOTIS is a music teacher and writer from Charleston, South Carolina. During the day, he instructs students from the ages of 11-14 on how to play band instruments. At night, he writes about weird crime, bizarre history, pop culture, and humorous classroom experiences on his blog. He is also a television, novel, and comic book reviewer for *Adventures in Poor Taste*.

LINKS

http://www.ramblingbeachcat.com
http://www.adventuresinpoortaste.com

https://twitter.com/NickNafster79

Swan Song

by Elizabeth J. Norton

Moscow, October 1945

L UC leaned wearily against the wall of the crumbling hotel, breathing in the
fresh night air. Inside, it was crowded and noisy, the air so thick with the
smell of illness and unwashed bodies that he could taste it. The camps had
been liberated, but now there was another war to be fought. As if fighting the Nazis
hadn't been hard enough, now there were thousands—no, tens of thousands—of
refugees pouring into Moscow from the newly-liberated camps. The sight of them—
emaciated, haunted, clothes hanging from wasted bodies—nauseated him. And
everywhere he turned, there were more. One of them had to be Lydia. He didn't
think he could live with himself if he didn't find her.

He'd been in the hotel for hours, looking for her, hoping to see her somewhere
among the masses. Many of the refugees were unrecognizable after their time in the
camps, needing to be identified through handwriting samples, but Luc knew that no
matter what horrors Lydia had faced since that last night, her eyes would be the same.
No matter what had happened to her, she would still be beautiful to him.

He lit a cigarette, hoping to prolong the time before he would be needed back
inside, and allowed thoughts of her to fill his mind and chase away the horrors for a
moment. He remembered how she'd looked when last he saw her, elegant in a red
dress as he walked her to the theater for her last dance. Her dance bag slung over one

shoulder, she moved with a grace honed by years on stage. They had talked only a little, each lost in their own preparations for the evening ahead—her mind on *Swan Lake*, his on the explosives that would keep the soldiers away from her for one more performance. Hers was like silk in his rough hand, and when he'd kissed her goodbye at the stage door, stray dark curls escaping from her bun had tickled his neck.

Approaching footsteps snapped him out of his reverie, putting him instantly on alert. The flickering streetlight was too dim for him to make out more than a silhouette, but battle instincts kicked in and he dropped the cigarette, crushing it to dust beneath his heel.

"Since when do you waste a good smoke?"

"You should know not to sneak up on me like that, Alek."

"I was hardly sneaking. Came out to find you, actually. You've been gone for well over an hour."

Guilt bubbled up in Luc's chest. He truly hadn't meant to be gone so long, and standing here daydreaming helped no one. "Sorry."

"Not a worry, really. Things are slowing down for the night. Besides, you're not the only one who needed a break. Finding you was just a convenient excuse."

They stood in silence for a while as Alek lit his own cigarette. The night wind sent a chill down Luc's spine and he turned up the collar of his coat. In doing so, his hand brushed his cheek and came away wet. He reached up covertly to wipe away the rest of the moisture, but Alek knew him too well.

"Hell, isn't it? Seeing them, I mean."

Luc opened his mouth to reply, but couldn't seem to get the words out around a sudden thickness in his throat. He stared straight ahead, blinking rapidly to clear the blurriness in his vision. Finally, he was able to reply. "Worse than we ever imagined. And so many of them."

"Yes, this place has more than it can handle. There are more new arrivals coming in tomorrow, and those are going to be sent to the Bolshoi Theater for processing."

The mention of the theater made a longing fist clutch around Luc's heart. The Bolshoi had been the center point of his and Lydia's courtship. Before the war, he'd spent hours there, watching her dance, had walked her home on countless evenings, and it was the last place he had seen her. Now, it could be the place where they were reunited. It felt like destiny, and his mood lightened a bit. "I should get back. I only meant to take a quick break."

Alek took one last drag on his cigarette before dropping and extinguishing it. "I'm headed home, Luc. You should go home, too. Things are quieting down for the night. Besides, when did you sleep last? You'll be no use to anyone if you wear yourself out."

"You fuss like an old maid, Alek. But if you're sure they don't need me, I'll head home."

"I'm positive. Go home. Sleep. And tomorrow, we can go to the Bolshoi. They're going to need all the help they can get."

The night was getting cold, but Luc still took the long route, in no rush to reach the emptiness of his apartment. Still, it was all too soon that he was climbing the back stairs, his key scraping in the lock. Opening the door brought an instant assault of memories, equal parts wonderful and excruciating. Lydia had been gone for three years now, but her presence was still everywhere.

He bent to pick up the single letter from the mail slot, and cold fury bubbled up inside him. He didn't even have to look at the return address—it was unmistakably addressed in Nik's hand. *Nik. Nik was a traitor and a coward. How was it fair that Luc had lost everything and Nik had survived the war?* Tears threatened again, and he squeezed his eyes shut tight against them. Crying would do no one any good. With a sigh, he went into the living room, opened the grate of the stove, and watched the letter curl into ashes.

He had lived here alone since the night of the raid, but couldn't get used to the fact that the place was now his and his alone. Moving toward his bedroom, he tiptoed down the hall, pausing at Anastasia's room to crack the door open to check on his sleeping daughter, and felt a small stab of pain as empty darkness greeted him. *Of course she wasn't there.*

Finally reaching his room, he checked to make sure that the curtains were closed, then crossed to the closet. Standing on tiptoe to reach the high shelf, his fingers fumbled for a moment until they found what they sought in the darkest corner— Lydia's dance bag.

Luc's fingers closed around the case and he pulled it down deftly. Made of black leather with a brass clasp and a shoulder strap, it was innocuous enough to have escaped notice (and pillaging) during the raid on the Bolshoi. Alek had retrieved it for him a few days after the raid, and Luc had opened it only once since; it contained only a hairbrush, a vial of perfume with just a few drops left in it, a stub of a lipstick, and a pair of pointe shoes. Now, with hope flaring in his heart, he opened it again, sank to the floor, and let the memories wash over him.

October 1938

He was never going to forgive Alek. It was Saturday night and the club was crowded and noisy with college students enjoying their weekend. Up on the stage, a band played the latest swing music from America, and while Luc was definitely enjoying the music, he could just as easily have found something similar on the radio. Try as he might, Luc never seemed to fit in at social gatherings, and tonight was no exception. Alek had dragged him out, then immediately found a dancing partner in an attractive blonde. And so Luc was, as usual, sitting alone at a table, smoking a cigarette, nursing a drink, wanting to be anywhere but here. He checked his watch, wondering how much longer he would have to sit there before he could slip away.

Ten more minutes, he thought. *Ten more minutes, and I'll be out of this place.* Inwardly, he sighed, lamenting that he'd never had his best friend's easy personality around other people. Alek could walk into a room and make new friends within five minutes. Everyone wanted to be Alek's friend. Luc, on the other hand, never seemed to know what to say to anyone, especially girls. He was handsome enough, he supposed, because girls would sometimes approach and flirt with him, but he never knew how to keep a conversation going. Sometimes he came to the club with Alek just to watch the people, but he hadn't wanted to come tonight. Still, Alek had insisted.

Finally, ten minutes passed. Luc drained the last of his drink, stubbed out his cigarette in the ashtray, and scanned the room for Alek and his girl of the moment. Spotting them in a corner, he stood and began to make his way through the crowd to say goodbye. As he tried to politely elbow his way through the crowd, he stumbled, knocking into someone. Blushing furiously, he mumbled apologies, expecting a rebuff, but the stranger merely steadied him with a soft, firm grip.

"Are you all right?" asked a soft, lilting voice, and Luc finally made eye contact—with the prettiest girl he had ever seen. She was as tall as he was, with eyes the color of smoke, fringed with long lashes. Her dark auburn hair cascaded over her shoulders in soft waves, and her skin was creamy white, a delicate silver chain with a tiny pendant showing above the slightly daring neckline of a dark blue dress with a curly embroidery trim.

"Are you all right?" she asked again, snapping him out of his reverie. He realized he'd been staring and immediately cast his eyes to the floor.

"Fine. Thanks. I'm sorry." Once again, he seemed to have lost his ability to speak in sentences. He straightened his shoulders and started to pull away, but she didn't let go of his arm.

"The best way to apologize to a girl is to buy her a drink, you know."

Luc wished fervently that the floor would open up and swallow him. All he really wanted was to go home and read. He had no idea how to talk to this girl who flirted so easily and seemed to have stolen his ability to speak, but he had almost knocked her over. *What would Alek do?* He supposed it would be gentlemanly to buy her a drink. "I suppose I did spill yours. What were you drinking?"

"Lime and soda." She took his arm, and together they walked to the bar. She smiled at him, showing perfect white teeth. "Now, will you sit with me while I drink it?"

"Um... okay." *What was he thinking? This was a really bad idea.* Miraculously, the table Luc had abandoned a few minutes earlier was still open, and he remembered to pull out her chair before taking his own. His mother would have been proud. *Of course, she'd be prouder if he could think of something to say,* he thought.

"My name's Lydia. What's yours?"

"Luc. Nice to meet you, Lydia."

"Luc. A short name for a man of few words. I like it. And tell me, Luc, where is it that you'd rather be tonight?"

"Is it that obvious? I'm sorry—I came with a friend and he's much better than me at this sort of thing."

"It's all right." She sipped her drink. "I came with a friend, too, but I'm mostly here for the music."

He grinned. "Me, too. I love swing. Could do without the crowd, though. And..." he paused. "Never mind. I'm babbling."

"No, what else? Please tell me."

"I've got an exam on Monday. I should be studying."

"You're at the University, then?"

"Yes, studying engineering. And you?"

"No...I'd have loved to study literature, but I'm sort of...tied to the family business."

She didn't elaborate, and he decided not to pry. He couldn't believe how easy it was to talk to Lydia, and they spent some time discussing their favorite books. She liked poetry; he favored the Revolutionary writers. All his thoughts of leaving faded away. They ordered another round of drinks and the conversation continued.

"Luc!" Alek suddenly appeared at their table, without a girl for the first time all night, eyes bright with excitement and perhaps one drink too many. "I thought you'd gone home! And who's your friend?"

"Alek, this is Lydia. Lydia—my best friend, Alek." They shook hands.

"Pleasure to meet you, Lydia. You must be pretty special to keep Luc away from his books all night."

Luc could feel his face turning red to the roots of his blond hair, and he hoped that the semidarkness of the club hid his embarrassment. *Why did Alek always have to play the ladies' man? And just when he and Lydia were having such a nice conversation, too.* He was about to give Alek a piece of his mind when his friend continued. "Anyway, Luc, it's time to go home. The club's about to close."

Luc's embarrassment quickly changed to astonishment. He'd been so engrossed in his conversation with Lydia that he hadn't even noticed the passage of time. Pushing aside his empty glass, he rose to help Lydia with her coat.

"It was great meeting you, Luc," she said as they made their way to the door. "Will you be here next Saturday night?"

"I don't know yet. I only come when Alek makes me, usually."

"Alek, make sure he's here next week, same time, won't you? We didn't get to dance." With those words, she disappeared into the night. As Luc walked home, he felt as though stars had suddenly burst into view in his soul, and for the rest of the weekend, his exam studies were sometimes sidetracked by thoughts of the grey-eyed beauty from the club.

Moscow, October 1945

The chiming of a distant church bell interrupted Luc's memories. He was leaning against the closet door with Lydia's bag in his lap, his legs cramped from hours of sitting still. Standing carefully and supporting himself against the wall as blood began to flow back into his legs, he eased the bag back into its special compartment and closed it. With any luck, soon he could return it to its rightful owner.

It was late and he knew he should try to sleep, but he dreaded the dreams that would come if he closed his eyes—the nightmares that had plagued him since the raid on the Bolshoi, which had only worsened when he began looking for Lydia in the masses of refugees. With a sigh, he lifted the curtain aside from the window to look outside. The sky was just beginning to change from the first grey-blue light of dawn to light pink shot through with gold. He'd been daydreaming all night.

There was still time to catch a couple hours of sleep before he and Alek usually met up to go to the refugee centers, and Alek would fuss interminably if he knew Luc hadn't slept a wink. Luc lay down on top of the covers, but there was no getting comfortable enough to nap. He felt twitchy and restless, his mind abuzz with memories and the hope of finding Lydia, alive and safe in the very place where they had been separated. It was only a few minutes before he abandoned the bed again. After a quick shower and shave, he changed into fresh clothes. Pulling on his jacket and shoes, he left his apartment, arriving two hours early at his and Alek's usual meeting place, settling on a park bench to watch the city come to life around him. The morning sky was clear, a light breeze coming off the Volga with just a tiny hint of an autumn chill. Moscow had suffered badly during the war, but now there were signs of life slowly returning to normal, businesses reopening and damage being repaired along the riverfront. The emotional toll of the war years would take longer to repair.

If Alek noticed that Luc was even more tired than usual that morning, he didn't mention it. They bantered as usual during the first part of the walk to the Bolshoi Theater, but then Alek turned suddenly serious.

"Luc…are you sure about this?"

"Sure about what?"

"About going to the Bolshoi. There are other places where help is needed. You don't have to…"

Luc cut him off in a flash of anger. "And then what? Be trapped in my house with my memories all day? Are you saying I'm not up to the job? Do you want to imprison me like that because I…" He broke off, unable to say the words. *Because I failed. Because I wasn't careful enough, and it cost me everything.*

Alek recoiled as if Luc had punched him. "Of course not! It's just that I know—I know it's hard on you, seeing the survivors. Other people might not notice, but I've known you too long. If you need to take a day off, there's no shame in it."

"Oh, for God's sake, Alek. You really are a mother hen. Look, I appreciate your concern, but I don't need a day off." He felt a twinge of shame for the hard edge in his voice; Alek knew him better than anyone, and was probably right to be concerned. "But," he added, "maybe we could leave a little earlier today and get a drink afterward?"

"You actually want to go out? That's a change. Of course we can get a drink tonight."

Luc hoped he had allayed some of Alek's concern about his health, but he knew better than to think he had dissolved it completely. Whatever the case, they had reached the theater, and there was no more time for conversation. The Bolshoi was already crowded with refugees and relief workers.

Nothing had prepared Luc for his visceral reaction to seeing the inside of the Bolshoi again. He hadn't been back since the night of the raid, and the sight hit him like a punch to the gut. Everything had changed outside. The whole world had changed. But the theater seemed untouched. It looked exactly as he remembered it, and for a moment, the memory of his panic and fear at realizing Lydia had been taken threatened to overwhelm him. He shoved the memory away, throwing himself into the work to keep it at bay.

January 1, 1939

Luc slept late on New Year's Day, and woke with a smile on his face. New Year's Eve was the biggest holiday in the Russian calendar, and as usual, he had gone to Red Square to watch the fireworks, but this year was different. Three months had passed since their first encounter at the club, and Lydia had quickly become his best friend—after Alek, of course. Their relationship had started slowly, first with dancing at the swing club on Saturday nights, then afternoon coffee in quiet cafés. Soon they were seeing each other nearly every day. It was amazing how much they had in common. He wanted to ask her properly for a date, but wasn't sure how to go about doing so.

The fireworks in Red Square were the epicenter of the New Year celebration in Moscow, and he nearly always went with Alek. This year, he and Lydia had mutually agreed to meet up there about a week before the holiday, and so he looked forward to it more than usual. He hummed to himself as he got ready, dressing in black pants, a white shirt, and a pale blue cable-knitted sweater. He was ready and waiting when Alek knocked on the door.

"Wow, Luc," Alek teased gently as they walked through the snowy night toward the celebration. "Look at you, all dressed up. This Lydia must be really special."

"She is," Luc agreed, surprised that he wasn't as embarrassed as he always was when the subject of girls came up.

"You're in love with her."

"We're friends. That's all."

"I think you could be more than friends, if you asked her."

"Hmm…maybe."

"No, really. You could be. I've seen the way you two look at each other. Why not ask? You see each other every day anyway. She's just waiting for you to ask."

"You think?"

"I don't think. I *know*."

Luc still wasn't sure, but Alek's confidence somehow bolstered his own. Lydia was waiting for them, sitting on the edge of the fountain, and greeted them with her usual brilliant smile and a wave. After a quick and polite hello, Alek disappeared into the crowd, saying he'd see them later, and Luc found himself alone with Lydia. She inched over on the edge of the fountain to allow him to sit next to her, then slid her hand into his. Even through both of their gloves, it felt soft and warm to him.

"Enjoying your school break?" she asked.

"Yes, very much. I've been reading a lot. Did you have a rehearsal today?"

"No, though I practiced for a couple hours on my own. The theater is closed for the rest of this week, but next week we start rehearsals for *The Sleeping Beauty*. I'll be dancing the part of Aurora."

He remembered now that she had auditioned for the role the week before. "Congratulations! You must have done really well in your audition."

"Yes, I must have…but…maybe it's all in the shoes." She added the last part so quietly he almost didn't hear.

"What do you mean, all in the shoes?"

"That's rather a long story. I'll tell you sometime. But Luc, will you come see me dance on opening night?"

"You know I will."

They lapsed into comfortable silence, and he absentmindedly stroked her hand with his thumb as he studied her profile: neck gracefully arched—like a swan's, back held straight, porcelain cheeks flushed with the cold, and auburn hair swept up into a bun above the collar of her coat. The softly-falling snowflakes tangled in her hair, sparkling like stars. Around them, as the hour grew later, the sky darkened and the square grew more crowded with revelers. He gazed across the square at the onion domes of St. Basil's Cathedral and wondered, not for the first time, if he should just ask her out. After all, Alek did it all the time.

Next to him, he felt Lydia shiver a little, and it broke the spell. "You all right?" he asked.

"I'm fine. Just a little cold."

"Here." He opened his coat, slipped one arm free, and draped half around her, pulling her close. She snuggled in and laid her head on his shoulder. "Better?"

"Lovely, thanks."

"We don't have to stay. Do you want me to walk you home?"

"No, I want to stay here with you. You could walk me home later, though."

There was just the slightest hint of flirting in her statement, overlaid with her gentle teasing and...was it longing? He took a chance, leaning over to whisper in her ear. "Lydia...will you please be my sweetheart?"

She didn't answer, but turned her head to meet his lips and kissed him, slowly at first, soft and sweet, then harder, communicating a thousand yeses without saying a word. At that moment, the clock struck midnight and fireworks boomed overhead. Luc hardly noticed. Whatever those fireworks looked like, the true beauty of the night was encapsulated in the girl next to him and the firecrackers going off in his own heart.

November 30, 1939

Lydia stayed an extra hour after rehearsal ended to make sure she was properly cooled down, hoping to keep her muscles from stiffening too much. Her hip and thigh were already bruised and throbbed dully from her fall that afternoon, but not half as much as her pride. To have fallen on such a basic move was nearly unthinkable. More troubling, though, were the whispers behind her back. Jewish filth? Lydia had never set foot in a synagogue. If she had any religion at all, it was music and dance...and Luc. Walking toward the café where they had arranged to meet, she tried to work out how much she could tell him about her day. He was too perceptive for her to say nothing; he'd notice something was wrong. Everything was stacking up on her mind—the taunts, the fall, Tetya Svetlana's letter... The weight of it all made it hard to put one foot in front of the other in the dying afternoon light.

The sight of Luc, head bent over the newspaper, lightened her heart. In spite of everything, she couldn't help smiling. He was still the best thing that ever happened to her. He looked up from the paper and smiled at her, but his eyes looked troubled.

"How was dance?" he asked as she pulled out the chair across from him.

Up close, Luc looked worn and haggard, as if the weight of Mother Russia rested on his shoulders. As much as she longed to tell her husband all her troubles, she couldn't. Not here. Her throat constricted, and she had to fight to keep her voice from breaking, but she managed to answer, "Fine, thanks. What's in the paper?"

"Border negotiations with Finland. Not going well, I'm afraid. It worries me."

A waiter came over, and they ordered coffee. It arrived, and Lydia wrapped her hands around the steaming cup, but the thickness in her throat refused to go away and she knew she wouldn't be able to swallow it. Unbidden, a single tear trailed down her cheek, splashing onto the table next to her cup before she could stop it.

Looking alarmed, Luc reached across the table and took her hand, fiddling with her wedding ring. "What is it, *solnychka*? What's happened?"

She shook her head. "Nothing. Really."

"But you wouldn't cry over nothing. Please tell me."

She wanted to curl up in his arms, cry her heart out against his chest. *Not here. Not now.* "I heard...at dance today...I heard Natalia and the other girls saying I shouldn't be allowed on stage."

"They're jealous of you! And why wouldn't you be allowed to dance?"

"Because I'm Jewish. Natalia's father sympathizes with Hitler, and I had three Jewish grandparents. Under the Third Reich, that makes me Jewish by law."

"But surely they wouldn't stop you from dancing just for that."

"I don't know. But I also had a letter from my aunt in Poland. She said the Jews there have been made to register and had terrible restrictions put on them. They have to wear armbands now, yellow stars, so everyone knows who and what they are." Fresh tears filled her eyes, trailing down her cheeks before she could stop them. "Why would they do that?"

"I don't know, *zvezda moya*. I don't understand it."

"I'm scared." She couldn't keep her voice from breaking any longer.

"Do you want to go home?"

"I don't want to cut our date short, but..."

"There will be other dates. Come on, let's go home." She stood and gathered her bag while he shoved a few rubles under his saucer to pay for their drinks.

Neither of them said much as they walked the few blocks home. Lydia's mind kept replaying the horrible moments of the day in succession. Were it not for Luc's hand securely holding her own, she was certain she'd fly to pieces at the slightest provocation. The afternoon sunlight had faded, and there was something menacing in the twilight, like a beast waiting to pounce. As they reached their front door, they heard shouting in the street. She turned toward the sound, but Luc laid a protective hand on her shoulder.

"Go inside. I'm going to see what the commotion's about."

"No, I'm coming with you."

Together, they ran toward the shouting and up to a group of young men gathered on the street corner.

"What's happened?" Luc asked, and Lydia could hear the apprehension in his voice.

"The Soviet Union has invaded Finland. We're at war."

Lydia's knees buckled and she crumpled against Luc, sobbing into his chest. She lost herself to the fear and shock radiating through her body, only dimly aware of Luc talking to her, half-carrying her inside and forcing her fingers closed around a mug. She sipped mechanically—tea, hot and heavily sweetened—and the sweetness seemed to bring her back to herself. A few more swallows, and the world came into sharper focus. She was seated at the kitchen table, and Luc, across from her, looked as worried as she had ever seen him.

Self-consciously, Lydia scrubbed the last of the tears from her face with the back of her hand. "Sorry," she mumbled.

"Don't apologize. Are you all right?"

She nodded, then shook her head. "I'm afraid."

He grabbed her hand and squeezed it. "I think maybe we should all be afraid."

Tears threatened again, but Lydia closed her eyes against them. Her head was already throbbing, and further crying would make it worse. Luc released her hand, came over, and put his arms around her. His warm, solid presence was comforting, and she melted into his arms, laying her cheek against the soft cotton of his shirt. He stroked her hair, hand radiating heat into her scalp.

"Feels good…" she murmured.

"You're freezing," he responded, and she realized it was true—she was shivering. "We need to get you warm before you catch your death. Do you want me to run you a bath?"

His tone was low and gentle, as though he were trying to comfort a wounded animal. It rankled, and she mentally cursed her childishness. "Thanks, but I can do it."

When she emerged from the bath, Luc was in his favorite chair, a book in his lap, but the book was closed and he appeared to be lost in thought. Instead of taking her usual place in the other chair, she curled up at his feet, knees to her chest, and rested her head on his lap.

"Better?" he asked.

"A little."

"I'm glad. Are you sure you're comfortable there?"

"Yes. I just want to be close to you. You make me feel safe." She sighed. "I can't help but worry."

"Me neither, but try not to think about it right now, all right? Whatever happens, we'll face it together. You won't be alone."

"I don't ever want to be alone. Only ever wanted to be with you, since we met."

"I was in love with you, too, from the first time I saw you, when I spilled your drink and made a fool of myself."

Lydia grinned in spite of herself. "It was a lucky chance meeting, wasn't it? Thank God Alek dragged you out that night."

Now they were both smiling at the shared memory. "The next week, he dragged me out again," Luc remembered. "I was terrified, but we danced to Glenn Miller. It was the best night of my life."

"You were so awkward then. I thought you'd never ask me out!" She frowned, coming back to the present. "I'd give anything to go back to that night."

He was quiet for a moment, then asked, "Lydia, would you dance with me now?"

"What, here?"

"Yes. Here. Right now." He stood up and went over to the turntable and stack of records. After a minute, the opening bars of Louis Armstrong's "Sweet as a Song" began to play. Then he came back to her and offered his hand. "May I have this dance?"

Nothing could take Lydia's mind off her troubles like dance, ballet or otherwise. Together they danced around their living room, and when the song ended, he pulled her into a long embrace.

Lydia kissed him, grateful to feel somewhat normal again, pleasantly drowsy but no longer weighed down. This was her Luc: always knowing exactly the right thing to make her feel better. Face buried in his neck, she breathed in the scent of him— books, coffee, cigarette smoke, and just a hint of his after-shave lotion—and stifled a yawn.

"Are you tired, *solnychka*?"

"Not so tired. I love dancing with you."

"It's been a long day. You should rest."

Lydia knew he was right, but all her earlier worries were starting to crowd back in now, and the thought of trying to sleep terrified her. "But you'll be staying up. I've kept you from your schoolwork."

"Yes, but you can get the bed warm for me. Come." He swept her into his arms, carried her to the bedroom, laid her gently on the bed and tucked the covers under her chin. "Get some sleep, love." He kissed her forehead, and she watched him turn to leave, silhouetted in the light from the hallway.

"Luc, please stay with me. I don't want to be alone."

There was a pause, then the light in the hall went out and his footsteps returned. He didn't say anything, but she heard the familiar sounds of him preparing for bed in the darkness, then his warm weight slid in beside her and he held her close. "The fact that there's a war on really puts things into perspective," he whispered.

She didn't respond, but curled into him, grateful for his presence. He made the night seem less sinister, but she still couldn't sleep. The hitch in his breathing told her he wasn't sleeping, either, and he seemed to be holding her more tightly than necessary, as though she might disappear if he let go. They neither spoke nor slept, but as the hours passed, they inched closer together, skin resting on skin until they lay as one. Only then, as the moon sank in the sky outside the window and the stars winked out, did Lydia fall into a light, dreamless sleep.

January 26, 1940

Luc paced in Nik's kitchen, smoking a cigarette. The door was bolted, the curtains and blackout shades drawn, and the only light came from a small bulb over the sink. From the outside, he hoped, the apartment looked like he was gone for the evening. He checked his watch: 8:35 PM. Fifteen minutes until Alek would arrive with Lydia. Not for the first time, he wished that his work schedule would allow him to escort her to Nik's himself, but Alek was the next best thing.

He wished with all his heart that he could just stop reading the newspapers; there wasn't a lot of news to be had in Russia that wasn't Nazi propaganda these days. But the Nazi lies were sometimes wrapped around a shred of truth. That truth, he confirmed and supplemented with a steady diet of BBC news picked up on the secret radio stashed in Nik's closet. In truth, though, the newspapers weren't worth much now, except as rolling material for cigarettes.

He paused in his pacing, listened for their approaching footsteps, and checked his watch again—8:58. They should be here by now. Had they been caught? Hitler's forces were currently nowhere near Moscow, but the police were still out in force, and curfew was 9:00 in the evening. He finished his cigarette and itched to light another, but forced himself not to; his supply was running low.

"Pacing and smoking again," Nik said, coming into the kitchen. "Can you do one without the other?"

Luc gave him a Look. "They're late."

"They'll be here. You need to calm down."

"It's almost curfew. If they get caught..." he was interrupted by knocking on the door. Alek and Lydia had arrived. Luc hastily let them in, then bolted the door behind them.

"What took you so long?" he hissed through clenched teeth. "We were worried!"

"Well, Luc was worried, like he always is," Nik put in. "I knew you'd get here."

"We got stopped. A policeman checked our papers on the way."

The four had been heading toward the back bedroom and the radio, but Luc stopped in his tracks. "My god."

Lydia grabbed his wrist to keep him moving. "It's okay. We're here. We'll tell you about it later, but if we don't hurry, we're going to miss the news."

When they reached the bedroom, Nik turned on the overhead light briefly as he retrieved the radio from a secret compartment in the closet and tuned it, keeping the volume low. Static crackled through the speakers, followed by gibberish, fuzzy voices, and finally the signal cleared. He switched off the light and they huddled in the darkness, listening.

The news wasn't good. Britain was being pounded by Blitzkrieg every night; children were being evacuated to the countryside. Meanwhile, Hitler's forces were coming ever closer to Moscow.

When the broadcast was over, Nik flipped off the radio and they sat in silence for a few minutes. Luc couldn't see his friends' faces in the dark, but he could bet that Alek's jaw would be tightly set, while Nik would have his left hand clenched into a fist on his knee, and Lydia's brow would be furrowed. "Tell me about the police," he said. "What happened to you on your way here?"

There was a pause, then Lydia spoke. "It was nothing, Luc. The officer checked our papers, gave us a warning about being out past curfew, and let us go. I had my bag over my shoulder, so he couldn't see my star."

"They don't warn, Lydia. You of all people should know."

"Please, Luc. Don't start…Don't…"

He could feel the edge of her anger and knew it wasn't really directed at him, but Alek cut her off, gently but firmly. "I'm sorry, Lydia, but Luc is right about this. It's already dangerous with the few German troops that are around now. It will get much worse if the main German forces actually make it this far."

"We'll just have to be more careful, that's all. Resistance groups are already popping up all over, and we've agreed since the beginning that if Hitler came to Moscow, we'd fight back. That's what I want. To fight back, together."

"That's all very well," Alek responded. "But I think we should have some sort of contingency plan."

"Okay," Lydia said. "But a contingency plan means I only have to use it as a very last resort, agreed?"

Luc could hear the stubbornness in her voice. Whatever the plan, he knew that if it had to be implemented, she would need to be dragged into it kicking and screaming. Since her breakdown the night of the Finnish invasion, she seemed to have grown a second skin made of pure iron. He admired her all the more for it. "It would make me feel better knowing we have at least some idea of how to keep you safe."

"You two are so overprotective!" she complained. "Okay, we'll make a contingency plan. If the Nazis reach Moscow and it gets too dangerous for me, I'll go into hiding."

"Hide where?" Luc wanted to know.

"Or I'll stow away on a boat and go to America. There are good ballet companies in New York." In spite of the bleak situation, he could hear a hint of fun in her voice.

"Lydia! Please take this seriously!"

"I am taking it seriously!"

"We can't decide the logistics now," Alek cut in reasonably. "But it's good to know that you're willing to hide if you have to, Lydia."

"Besides, I'm not going to run and hide just because there are patrols in the streets," Lydia said, sounding defiant now. "I'm going to put up a hell of a fight first."

"We all will," Luc promised. He reached for her hand in the dark and squeezed it.

September 16, 1941

Luc was ready and waiting when Alek's signal knock came on the door. He let his friend in, bolted the door behind him, and didn't even wait for Alek to remove his coat before asking, "Did you get it?"

"'Course I did. It's in the public archive. All I had to do was tell them I needed the blueprints for an assignment. Easy as cake."

"Anyone see you coming?"

"No. God, Luc, please stop fussing. Where's Nik?"

"Not coming. He had a late study session. Lydia's at dance and Anastasia's sleeping."

"It feels strange to do this without them, but you're the expert."

"All right then, let's see it." They spread the blueprints out on Luc's kitchen table and he studied them, drumming his fingers. "As bridges go in this town, this one's good."

"But can you do it?"

"Is there any other way?"

"Not really. We'd need a dozen snipers and hardware for all of them, and if this isn't just a diversionary tactic, then it's a suicide mission."

"Then I can do it." Luc did some quick calculations in his head, then scratched it out in a school notebook to check his work. "Yes, I can do it. I'll go out tomorrow in the daylight and scope it out for sure, but...twelve small charges. We'll place them like such—" he indicated on the blueprints "—and put them on a long fuse. I'll light the fuse and run after the first two explosions."

"I want to go with you as your backup."

"Alek, there's no one I trust more in the world, but you've got a more important job that night. You and Nik are Lydia's backup." Not for the first time, Luc wished he could be in two places at once. He trusted Alek with his life—Lydia's and Anastasia's, too—but he couldn't help worrying.

Alek seemed to sense his thoughts. "We'll get them out." He paused and lit a cigarette. "Try not to worry too much."

Luc shook his head. "I really don't have time to worry. This diversion is huge and if something, one little tiny thing, goes wrong... Hitler will be here in two weeks. We have to be ready for him."

"Last night of *Swan Lake*, right?"

"Yes. With any luck, the Nazis will find themselves delayed and this will be nothing more than some early New Year fireworks."

"We're giving Lydia her last dance."

"Yes, and Alek? If I don't make it back, you get them the hell out of there, you understand?"

"Don't talk like that's even a possibility. You're going to be there for your girl's curtain call."

"I'm not trying to be pessimistic. It's not her last dance, either. When this war's over, she's going to dance again. -But you'd better get going; it's almost curfew."

October 2, 1941; 6:30 PM

The wind had picked up by the time Luc returned home, and clouds were rolling in. Casting a glance skyward, he spared a second to hope that rain would hold off until tomorrow, but just as quickly banished the thought from his mind. There would be time enough for worrying later. He slipped inside, resisting the urge to call out in case Anastasia was still napping.

He found Lydia in their bedroom, dressed for dance, perched on the edge of the bed and staring intently at the pointe shoes she held in her lap. She startled a bit at the sound of his footsteps, then smiled up at him.

"Ready?" she asked.

"Ready as I'll ever be. You?"

She made a noncommittal noise in her throat and patted the mattress beside her. "Sit with me for a minute, won't you? I have something to tell you."

"Of course." As he sat, she took a deep breath, seemingly trying to compose herself. "It's going to be fine, *solnychka*. Don't be afraid."

"I'm not afraid," she said quietly. "But if something happens to me..." He opened his mouth to reassure her again, and she shook her head vehemently, moving the shoes from her lap to his. "If anything happens to me, Luc, you need to keep these for Anastasia."

"But you'll be wearing them," he pointed out, utterly confused.

"No. I've been breaking in a new pair."

"Why?"

"Because...well...there's a family legend. These pointe shoes are special. They were my mother's. She started dancing when she was very young, and she was very, very talented. She became a dancer at the Romanov court and was a special favorite of Tsaritsa Alexandra. Sometimes, she would be called to entertain Tsarevich Alexei when he was ill. She also served as the assistant to the Grand Duchesses' dance instructor.

"Once, during a performance, the Tsarevich got very sick suddenly. The dancers were sent away, but Tsaritsa Alexandra asked my mother to stay with her and pray for the Tsarevich. In fact, Tsarevich Alexei was desperately sick, and Rasputin was called in to give him his last rites. He survived but was bedridden for some time, and my mother danced to entertain him until he was well.

"Tsaritsa Alexandra was convinced that her son had been healed by the combination of Rasputin's prayers and my mother's dancing. She gave my mother a special pair of pointe shoes, white silk, and the legend says that she had Rasputin put a charm on them so that they would never wear out, and whoever wore them would be talented beyond measure. According to the legend, the talent and the shoes should be passed down from mother to daughter for as long as there were dancers to wear them.

"My mother stayed at the court for some time, but as the Bolsheviks rose to power, she met my father and decided to leave the Romanovs to raise her family. She brought the shoes with her, along with the legend. Even years after she left the court, my mother still held high regard for Tsaritsa Alexandra, and she gave me the shoes on my sixteenth birthday. I've worn them ever since."

"So why stop now?"

There was a long pause as she searched for the right words. "It's my last dance." She paused, then started again. "I don't know if the legend is true or not, but if anything happens to me, I want you to save the shoes for Anastasia. I want her to have the same legacy I had."

"But it isn't your last dance. You're just going away until it's safe. You'll be back."

"I hope you're right. But that's only part of it. I don't know if the shoes are actually magical, although they've certainly had an unnaturally long life. Tonight I'll go without them, so the audience will see my true talent—for my own satisfaction."

Carefully, he set the shoes beside him on the bed and pulled her into an embrace. "I'll keep them. But you'll be here to tell our daughter that story when the time is right. I'm going to keep you safe, my beautiful black swan."

In response, she tucked her head against his chest, leaning up to press a soft kiss on his neck. "I trust you. And I'm not afraid."

October 2, 1941; 10:24 PM
Jewish or not, filth or not, Lydia was positively radiant when she danced. And

as much as Nik didn't want to admit it, he was questioning himself. Watching her perform from his perch in the wings, his lap heavy with the weight of Anastasia and his heart heavy with the weight of regret, he dreaded the moment he knew would come. Any other night, he would have been rapt as the performance reached its climax, but not tonight—tonight, he was thinking.

Two years earlier, Nik had been on the verge of graduating secondary school at the top of his class. He should have gone on to college in Berlin, studied engineering, found a wife and a job...but all of it changed when a car accident took his parents and siblings while he had been at a Hitler Youth meeting. After that, everything had seemed pointless. Uncle von Bock had become his guardian, and been determined to mold his nephew into the perfect Aryan image. And Nik had followed blindly. Somewhere along the line, he had lost his humanity and became nothing more than a pawn in the Reich's sick, twisted game. Now, that sickened him.

Nik's coming to Moscow had been Uncle von Bock's idea. He'd said it would give him a fresh start and new friends, away from his past. But Uncle never did anything without an ulterior motive, and what he had really wanted was to place Nik in a position to infiltrate any Resistance movement that popped up in Moscow. And as luck would have it, Nik's best friends had been at the heart of that movement. He had passed information back to his uncle. He hadn't regretted his choices—until now.

How could the beautiful Black Swan—his best friend's wife—how could she be filth? He had lost his parents—how could he inflict that pain on the little girl in his lap? Absentmindedly, he stroked Anastasia's dark curls. *Maybe Luc would be successful. Maybe he already had been. Maybe he was worrying for nothing.* His thoughts spun desperately as the ballet reached its climax, the chorus of ten swans and two leads at center stage and the music swelling. *There had to be something he could do—he just needed to think.* And then he heard the sounds he had been expecting and dreading all night: Marching boots. Voices shouting in German. The deed was done. It was too late.

October 2, 1941; 10:58 PM

Alek was running blind. He had bolted from his seat in the wings the minute he heard the voices, but Lydia was too far away to grab and for whatever reason, the Nazis had come straight for her. He had watched in horror as she was shoved against a wall and held at gunpoint and had thought of a thousand stupid plans to rescue her. But then, like a coward, he had turned and run. Through the wings, out the stage door, and out into the street in whatever direction his legs chose to carry him—he only knew he needed to get out of the Bolshoi as fast as he could.

October 2, 1941; 11:00 PM

Chaos. Everything was chaos. People were screaming. Anastasia squirmed in Nik's lap, whimpering.

"Shh, little one," he murmured. "Stay with me. It's all right." But the girl was panicking, and she managed to get out of his grasp, running to her mother. He took a step after her, but then Uncle von Bock was at his side, as approving as Nik had ever seen him.

"You've done well." His smile was cold. "But why are you going after the whelp? She's nothing, Niklaus. Filth."

"She's innocent. She's just a little girl!"

"I've left you too long and you've forgotten yourself. She's a Jew. Scum. Just like her whore of a mother." He pulled out a pistol, leveling it at Lydia, who had been shoved against the wall.

"They didn't do anything wrong!" He tried to run after Anastasia again, but his uncle grasped him firmly, holding him back.

"I raised you better than this, Niklaus. Don't disappoint me." He pressed the gun into Nik's hand. "Now remember who you are. Shoot the whelp."

No. He would not be a pawn. He had made a mistake, and now it was time to make amends. He jerked free of his guardian's grasp, adrenaline and hatred like fire in his veins. "Of course, Uncle. The filth doesn't deserve to live." And without further thought, he leveled the pistol on his uncle's heart and pulled the trigger. Without looking back, Nik ploughed through the crowd, grabbed Anastasia, and ran.

October 2, 1941; 11:14 PM

It was dark now, pouring rain. The glare of streetlights on puddles provided scant lighting, and unseeing, Alek tripped and fell headlong, crashing facedown into the street, but something broke his fall. Winded, it took a moment for Alek to realize that the object he'd tripped over was...a body. He scrambled off, looked down, and his heart sank as recognition dawned.

"Luc? Luc!" No response. Luc lay unconscious in the street in a puddle, blood staining his jacket and the front of his shirt. Quickly, Alek knelt at his side and ripped the shirt open to assess the damage. Blood flowed freely from a wound in Luc's abdomen, and Alek tore off his own jacket, balling it up to put pressure on the wound. Luc's eyes fluttered open then and he groaned in pain.

"Can't...breathe."

"Don't talk. Just stay still. We're going to get you help."

"They're here..." Luc gasped and coughed, and blood spattered his lips and Alek's hands.

"I know. Stay with me. Don't you dare die on me."

Alek's mind worked furiously. It was raining harder now, and Luc was still bleeding heavily, and God alone knew how long he'd been lying there before Alek had tripped over him. Gunshots rang out, and he instinctively threw himself across his friend. They had to get off the street, but where could they go? Luc's apartment was too far. The hospital was further. The shots died down, and after a minute he crawled off of Luc, whose eyes were still open.

"Luc, I need you to tell me what happened at the bridge. It's important."

"Charges...didn't..." He fell unconscious again.

That was all Alek needed to know. If the charges hadn't worked, then either they had been sabotaged or someone had tipped off the Nazis. And where the hell was Nik? Luc was still bleeding, and Alek knew time was running out. He thought briefly of the safe house to which he had been going to deliver Lydia, but if someone had tipped off the Nazis, there was a good chance that the safe house wouldn't be safe any longer. There was another, he knew, run by a man who went by the name of Viktor, two miles southeast of the Bolshoi in the workers' district. He had only a rough idea of where it was located, but it was probably their best chance. Alek had never been religious, but his mother prayed regularly to the icons in her bedroom. Visualizing the icons, Alek breathed what was possibly the first fervent prayer of his life, picked up Luc as carefully as he could, and took off in what he hoped was the direction of the man called Viktor and relative safety.

October 2, 1941; 11:28 PM

Alek slumped on a sofa in the safe house, fighting despair. He had no idea how much time had passed since they had reached safety. After half-running through the streets carrying Luc, he had all but collapsed himself. His knees had given way in front of an unassuming house, and from there, he remembered close to nothing, only a blur of light and noise and then silence. None of his thoughts made sense, but his mind was still racing and his pulse still pounded. The room was warm, but he shivered uncontrollably. How had everything gone so wrong? Lydia was gone, and on the other side of the wall, Luc was unconscious, fighting for his life.

"Soldier, you hurt?" The voice seemed to come from very far away and he struggled to respond.

"I...I don't..."

Sudden gunshots rang out in the street, and he startled, realizing his hands and clothes were covered with blood. His mind filled with the image of Luc lying in the street, blood and rain pooling under him. The room spun and his stomach lurched.

"Take it easy, Soldier. It's just shock. Put your head down. Deep breaths." Someone forced his head between his legs, and he closed his eyes until the world steadied.

Feeling more stable, he raised his head and opened his eyes. The room seemed impossibly bright. The owner of the voice, a man in his fifties, stocky and blonde with green eyes and a two-day stubble of beard, pressed a glass into his hand.

"Drink it," he commanded, and Alek obeyed. Surprisingly, it was clear water, not spirits.

"You haven't got anything stronger?"

"In a little while, to help you sleep. You're going to have to lie low here until your buddy can travel."

"How is Luc?"

"Damned lucky to be alive. He took three bullets. Two glanced off his ribs; the other buried itself in his gut but missed everything vital. The ribs are broken and he lost a lot of blood, but he'll be fine. As I said, he's damned lucky. What's your name?"

"Aleksandr, but everyone calls me Alek. Can I see him? I don't want him waking up alone."

"Nice to meet you, Alek. You can call me Viktor. Your friend's heavily sedated and he's going to be out for several more hours. You should clean up and sleep first, then you can sit with him."

"Please. I'm not tired. I need to be with Luc. He can't wake up alone."

Viktor held firm. "You ran halfway across the city through gunfire, carrying a friend who was too injured to be anything but dead weight. Trust me, you get a hot shower and some clean clothes and you'll want to do nothing but sleep for a week. Your muscles will hurt like hell, too, once the shock wears off."

"But..."

"I promise you, your friend's out cold and he'll stay that way for hours, if not a whole day. You've got plenty of time to clean up and catch a bit of sleep before he wakes up. Besides, how do you think he'd react if he woke up with you next to him, covered with blood?"

The relief Alek had felt when he was told Luc would heal was fading fast, replaced by dread. He'd have to tell Luc that Lydia had been taken. Somehow the dread drove the fight from him, and he nodded. Immediately he wished he hadn't as another wave of dizziness swept over him.

"Good man. Now put your head down again and stay here for a minute while I get you some fresh clothes. There are fresh towels in the bathroom, there." Viktor pointed. "While you're cleaning up, I'll make up a bed for you."

Locked in the bathroom, Alek stripped off his blood-soaked shirt and scrubbed himself ruthlessly under the hot water until his skin was raw. The weight of all that had transpired that night hit him all over again, making his breath come in sobbing gasps. If tears mingled with the hot water on his face, he neither knew nor cared. When the water ran cold, he stepped from the shower and wrapped himself in a towel, avoiding his own gaze in the mirror. Dressed in the clothes Viktor had laid out for him, Alek left the bathroom and returned to the sofa he'd vacated earlier.

October 3, 1941; 1:28 PM
Alek was stretched out on the sofa, staring at the clean white ceiling. He realized he must have slept, but for how long, he wasn't sure. Someone had covered him with a blanket.

Viktor stood over him, holding a steaming mug. "You feeling better?"

Alek sat up and pushed the blanket off. His muscles screamed in protest and he winced. "Maybe. What time is it?"

"Half past one in the afternoon. You've slept quite a few hours." He held out the mug. "Coffee? It's the real thing—been saving it for awhile now."

"Yes, please." He took the cup and sipped. It was, as Viktor had said, the real thing, strong and sweet. "How is Luc?"

"Still sedated. Running a bit of a fever, but his pulse is good and there's no other sign of infection, so it's likely from shock and blood loss. We'll keep an eye on it, but as I said a few hours ago, he is incredibly lucky."

Alek stared into his cup, blinking moisture from his eyes. "That's good news. It is."

"You sound like you're trying to convince yourself."

"It's just...I'm a coward. That's all."

"You carried your friend halfway across the city through gunfire while he bled out in your arms. Hardly cowardly, Aleksandr."

"No. There were four in our circuit. Me, Luc, our friend Nik, and Luc's wife, Lydia. Lydia's a prima ballerina at the Bolshoi. She's Jewish. She worked with our circuit until a week or so ago, then we heard the Nazis were advancing and it got too dangerous. She was going into hiding." Now that he was talking, he couldn't make himself stop. The incriminating words poured out, tumbling over each other.

"I was with her, and Nik, at the Bolshoi. I don't know what happened exactly, but the Nazis...they came to the theater. They took Lydia...I don't know where."

"She's probably on her way to the camps."

"We had this plan—Luc was going to destroy a bridge to buy Lydia some time for one last dance."

"An army of four—four *amateurs*—destroying a huge bridge. Your friend in there must be a genius."

"Top of his engineering class. You can't tear our Luc away from his books. Well, Lydia could...can."

"Did anyone else know about your plan? Anyone at all?"

Alek shook his head. "We didn't tell anyone. And we only ever discussed it in Nik's apartment. It's unlikely we were overheard."

"I read the newspaper while you were sleeping, and there's nothing about the bridge, so it's likely that part of the plan failed. If you're sure no one else knew... How well did you know this Nik?"

"Not particularly well; he only transferred into the University this year, and..." He trailed off as the implication of Viktor's question hit home. "Christ. You think he was a collaborator?"

"It's possible. But even if he was, how does that make you a coward?"

"I'm a coward because I know I'm going to have to tell my best friend that his wife and daughter are gone. And I'm afraid he'll hate me for it."

Viktor sighed. "I'm not saying it will be easy, but if Luc is any kind of friend, then he's not going to hold any of this against you. It's a war, and terrible things happen in wars. You could have died saving Lydia, or both of you could have been taken."

"Instead, they're gone, and Luc's..."

"Luc is going to be fine, and he has you to thank for that. You saved his life. He'll take their loss hard, but he'll heal. I promise. You can go and sit with him now, if you'd like."

Slowly, Alek nodded. "I'd like that. I don't want him waking up alone."

October 1945

The last of the gear was packed up. The Bolshoi's brief life as a refugee-processing center had come to a close. Luc had seen and personally spoken to countless individuals, and all anyone knew of Lydia was that she was designated *Nacht und Nebel*—Night and Fog. No longer useful to the Nazis, she had been made to disappear, like just another face in a crowd of millions. All of his efforts seemed to have been in vain. He couldn't protect her on the final night of *Swan Lake*, and he couldn't find her now. Alone in the darkness of the Bolshoi, Luc perched on the edge of the stage and placed Lydia's pointe shoes beside him. Overcome with sorrow for Lydia and for all who had been lost, he buried his face in his hands and cried. Sobs racked his body, as though years of grief were suddenly clamoring to escape all at once, and he made no effort to stop them.

Finally acknowledging his loss, he allowed himself to drown in it for a while. Lydia was gone—perhaps in part because of Luc's failure—and the pain of that knowledge seemed unbearable. There would be no more shared afternoons in the café, no more kisses under the stars. He would never again see her dance at center stage of the Bolshoi, and she would never reclaim her magical shoes. Part of him wanted to believe they truly were—and his thoughts stirred with the what ifs... What if she had been wearing them that night, what if their magic could have protected her, what if she were here—right now—with him? Tomorrow, he would need to find a way to go on without her, but right now, it seemed utterly impossible.

He had no idea how long he'd been wallowing in his grief in the darkness of the theater, but suddenly, Luc felt a hand on his shoulder. A slight chill ran down his spine, just a tingle, not unpleasant. In spite of the chill, warmth enveloped him, almost as if someone had put an arm around him. Through his tears, he saw the outline of the shoes lift in the dark to perfect pointe as they took on an eerie, ethereal glow. *No. Surely his eyes were deceiving him. He was tired, so tired. Too much grief. Too many sleepless nights.* He wiped his eyes with his sleeve and shook his head to clear it. Then, inexplicably, the opening theme of *Swan Lake* filled the air and the shoes, still en pointe, began to move.

In that moment, Luc forgot where he was. All the horrors and sadness of the war years simply fell away, and he saw Lydia, beautiful and graceful as ever, dancing in her glory to the phantom music coming from the empty orchestra pit. When the final chord faded away, she came to the edge of the stage and sat next to him.

"Lydia..."

"I'm not really here, my love. You have to stop looking for me, Luc."

A sob caught in his throat. "No."

"You've carried this burden too long. It's too heavy. Let it go."

"But I...I can't..."

She reached up as if to caress his cheek, then stopped. "I can't touch you, but listen. It's too late for me. I've had my last dance, but yours is still going on. Go on with it."

"How am I supposed to do that? I failed you, both of you." Her image was blurring, fading into the darkness. "Don't leave me, Lydia, please! I'm sorry! Please don't leave!"

"The thing you're looking for is right in front of you, and you've ignored it for weeks. Read the letter. Read it...and forgive."

Her image disappeared and her voice faded to silence, leaving Luc wondering if he hadn't just been hallucinating. Shakily, he stood and rushed home, ignoring the cold and rain. Another envelope, identical to the one he had burned, lay on the doormat. He picked it up, ripped it open, and slumped against the wall, sliding to the floor as he read.

September 1945

Dear Luc,

    I don't know if this letter will reach you, but now that the war is over, I have to try. By now you have spent years wondering and grieving. You deserve closure and peace, and I hope to give you some of both. I won't ask for your forgiveness, because I know I don't deserve it, but I hope I have done right by you, and by Lydia.

    Years ago, I told you that I moved to Moscow from Berlin after my parents were killed, but that was only part of the story. In losing my family, I also lost my humanity. I covered my grief with devotion to the Nazi cause, and living with my uncle only helped foster that. When my whole life was in tatters, my uncle was the one solid thing, and I followed him blindly.

    My uncle was Field Marshal Fedor Von Boch, and the Fuhrer had placed him in charge of the invasion of the USSR. He hoped that by placing me in Moscow, I could infiltrate any Resistance movement that started there and pass him information...and I did. It was I who betrayed you. I loved you and Alek like brothers, and your Anastasia reminded me so much of my baby sister Marta that I had started to remember what it was like to be human. My loyalties were completely torn. I loved you all like family, but I owed so very much to my uncle, it was impossible not to do as he asked me. Doing so was a terrible mistake.

    Anastasia ran to her mother in the chaos of the raid, and Uncle had his sights set on Lydia. He ordered me to shoot your little girl, but I couldn't do it. Instead, I turned the gun on my uncle. Then I dropped the gun, grabbed Anastasia, and ran.

    I knew that you and Alek had planned to meet up at a safe house, but once I had turned sides, it wasn't safe for me to find you and explain—it could have brought my uncle's men straight to you. I knew my only choice was to disappear, and take Anastasia with me. Eventually, we made our way here to Switzerland. She is well, safe, and beautiful—she looks exactly like Lydia. She still calls me Uncle Nik, and I tell her every day what a great man her father is.

It took Luc several tries to read the rest of the letter as it obscured in his vision through a fresh round of tears. His trust in Nik had not been misplaced. Lydia was gone, but Anastasia was alive. *Well, safe, and beautiful.* Wiping the tears from his eyes, he stood and went to his bedroom, retrieving Lydia's dance bag once more from its place on the high shelf. Folding the letter carefully, he tucked it inside before closing the clasp and hugging the bag to his chest. Crossing to the window, he watched the sun rise over Moscow; new hope in burning in his soul as he mentally planned a trip to Switzerland. He had a promise to keep.

Elizabeth J. Norton has been the Teen Librarian the Commerce Township (MI) Community Library since 2007. An avid reader, writer, knitter, coffee addict, and the Assistant Editor (a.k.a. Head Minion) of The Bearded Scribe Press' blog; she also reviews young adult and professional books for *Voice of Youth Advocates Magazine*. She lives in metro Detroit with her cat, Bianca, and too many books.

LINKS

http://www.beardedscribe.com/ejnorton
https://twitter.com/divinelibrarian
http://www.pinterest.com/Lavinia1981

Iron Strong Adalie

by Bobbie Palmer

A
DALIE walked to the stream with her golden ball in her hand as she did most days. It was childish for a young woman, she knew, but it was something her mother had given her before she'd died. She missed her mother so much. The stream was where her mother had always taken her to play as a child. It was always calm and surrounded by beautiful wild flowers. They would play catch and dance to the music in their heads.

It was perfect.

Throwing the ball in the air, she pretended her mother was throwing it back to her. She caught it and threw it right back up. That's when a breeze came, blowing it away from her hand and sending it flying into the stream.

Chasing after it, Adalie was hoping she could reach it before it got too deep in the water, but with one look, she knew she was too late. A tear slid down her face as she said, "I would give all my jewels and satin if someone could just bring back my ball to me."

"You're crying, Princess. What's wrong?" a voice called to her.

She looked around but couldn't find the voice's owner. She had hoped someone was there to get her ball back, but all she saw were the pink and purple flowers surrounding her.

"Princess, what's wrong?" she heard again. Looking down to where she heard the voice, she saw an ugly green frog.

"Oh, it was you talking. I'm crying because my ball fell into the water."

"Stop crying. I can help you, for a price," the frog said.

"You can have anything you want, my clothes, my jewels, my money," she answered desperately.

"I don't want your things, your clothes, your jewels, or even your money. I want your love and for you to accept me as a friend. Let me have dinner with you and eat off of your golden plate and drink from your cup. I also want to sleep on your pillow for three nights. If you promise me that, I'll get your ball."

"Yes, I promise. Now, go get my ball," she said, but in her mind, all she could think was, *The stupid frog—all he does is sit in the water and eat flies. He can't be my friend.*

The frog dove deep into the water and the Princess watched intently, waiting to see if he'd be able to get her ball. When he finally surfaced, he had her ball in his mouth. That meant she was going to have to clean it when she got back to the castle. Gross frog spit and probably a few bug legs. But at the moment, it was okay. She had it back, that's all that mattered.

"My ball," she said with a smile and grabbed it. She stood up, wanting to get it cleaned and home, where there was no chance of it getting lost. She wasn't going to be throwing it near the stream anymore.

"Princess," she heard the frog yell as she ran away from him. "Princess, you promised!"

The next day, Adalie was sitting down to dinner with her father when she heard something. It was a wet sound, like someone walking around in wet boots, but it was too quiet for it to be one of the soldiers. Then there was a faint knocking sound, barely heard over the footsteps of the kitchen staff as they were bringing in the food.

"Princess, open the door so I can dine with you," a voice said.

"Who's that?" the King asked.

"It's no one," she answered and picked up her fork, ready to eat.

"Princess, are you going to break your promise?"

"Let him in," the King said to one of the staff. He turned to his daughter and asked, "What promise is this?"

"I promised that, if he retrieved my ball, he could eat off of my plate and sleep on my pillow," she said dejectedly. The King was horrified. No man was going to sleep on his daughter's pillow. Why would she promise such a thing?

"Thank you, Your Majesty," a voice said. He looked around, but saw no one. "Down here."

The King looked down and saw a talking frog, something he'd never seen before and hoped to never see again. The thing looked disgusting with his slimy, green skin.

He could see why his daughter had broken her promise, but she needed to learn to follow through.

"Adalie, you will allow this frog to eat off of your plate and sleep on your pillow. You made a promise and now you need to keep it," the King said.

"Fine," she answered, and sat in her seat sulking.

There was a wet sound with every step the frog made toward the Princess. The King didn't like that he was making her do this. Who knew what diseases the frog might have? He really hoped she didn't catch anything, but she needed to learn. How was she going to be a good queen if her word meant nothing?

"Can I get some help, please?" the frog asked.

Adalie glanced down and saw the disgusting thing next to her chair and looking up at her. She reached down and picked him up, trying not to get his slime all over her. Gross. She was going to have to clean her hands after touching him.

"Can you please move the plate a little closer?" the frog asked.

She did as he asked and pushed the plate closer to him. Watching him eat made her lose her appetite. He was using his long tongue to eat, not a fork. How was she supposed to eat off of a plate he'd used like that?

"I'm finished and ready for bed. Please, carry me to your bed so we can go to sleep," the frog said.

She began to cry. She didn't want to sleep with a frog. She didn't want his slime in her bed, on her pillow. She didn't want any of this—she had just wanted her ball.

"You asked for his help and he asked very little of you in return. He got your ball, and now you must do as he has asked. That was the deal you made," her father said.

Nodding, she picked up the frog by his leg and carried him to her room. She placed him on her makeup table before changing clothes and climbing into her bed.

"I'm tired and want to sleep. Take me to your pillow or I will yell for your father," the frog said.

Adalie was so angry with him and herself. She couldn't take any more, and she couldn't let that frog sleep in her bed. It was too much. She had to do something.

Standing up, she walked over to the table, picked him up by his leg again, and threw him into the furthest wall. "There! Enjoy your sleep, you disgusting thing!" she yelled before climbing back into bed.

"Thank you," she heard a man say from across the room. Sitting up and turning toward the voice, she found a handsome man in the frog's place. She was shocked. Who was he? "I am Prince Goddard. An evil witch had turned me into a frog."

"Y... You're the frog?" she asked.

"I am, and I want to marry you for all your kindness and for releasing me from the curse."

Her kindness? She hadn't been kind to him. "Okay," she said, not knowing what else to say. A handsome prince wanted to marry her. Who was she to say no?

"Good. Now I'm tired. Let's go to sleep and we can tell your father in the morning," he said with a smile.

Adalie curled up in the blankets and felt the bed dip as Goddard climbed in next to her. She stiffened when he pulled her close, but then she realized this was how her life was going to be, a man sleeping in her bed. Not just a man, though, a handsome prince.

The King was sitting down to breakfast when his daughter and a strange man walked in. "Who is this?" he asked Adalie a little angrily. Why would a man be visiting this early, and why hadn't he been told?

"This is Prince Goddard. He has asked me to marry him," she said with a bright smile. His daughter was smiling? That very rarely happened. But he didn't know this Goddard. He'd never even heard of him. "He was the frog. A witch cursed him and turned him into a frog."

"I see," the King said.

"We want to get married as soon as possible, Your Highness," Goddard said, pulling Adalie close.

"All right. I'll alert the staff and make the announcement."

"Thank you, Father," his daughter said and hugged him.

Her happiness was all that mattered to him. But it did seem odd that last night she didn't want to have anything to do with Goddard, but now she was about to marry him. Something strange was going on, but as she was happy so he was going to let it be.

The wedding went off without a hitch. It was beautiful and Adalie seemed to be so elated. The King had watched the two for the past few weeks as they had prepared for the wedding, and they had looked so happy together. His daughter was in love and he was growing to like Goddard. He seemed like a very nice young man, who he hoped one day would make a great king.

The King decided to travel to the neighboring kingdom to visit a friend. He wanted to give the newlyweds a chance to have some time to themselves. They needed to get to know each other as husband and wife without him hanging around.

As they left the kingdom, a strange sound came from the carriage. It sounded like metal and wood breaking. What in the world was going on? He leaned out the window, trying to see what the source of the noise was, only to see a wheel break off, tipping the carriage to the front and side.

"What's going on?" he yelled, before there was another crack and the carriage crashed into a tree. The King looked up in time to see a branch come through the roof just before imbedding itself in his chest.

Adalie stood in her father's room looking around. The funeral had been a few days before, but she still couldn't believe he was gone. He was such a strong man, capable of taking on anyone, and he had been killed in a carriage accident? How could that have happened? The carriage had been in good condition, her father had them all checked regularly. There was no way something had been wrong with it.

"My Queen," she heard Goddard say behind her.

That was something she wasn't used to being called and something to which she didn't think she'd ever become accustomed. She wasn't supposed to be Queen for a few more years. She wasn't ready for it, she didn't think she ever would be. Her father was supposed to be the one in charge, not her.

Turning around, she saw Goddard smiling at her from the door. "There is a man here asking to speak with you. He said he's having some trouble in town."

"Can you take care of it, please? I don't feel up to it yet," she said with a small smile. She hated to put this on him, he didn't know the people, but if he was going to be King, he needed to start somewhere. She hoped the people would listen to him and trust him.

"I will. Is there anything else I can do for you?" he asked.

"No, thank you," she answered. Goddard had been great through all of this. He'd been at her side the entire time, trying to comfort her and just be there. She didn't know how she would have survived this without him.

He nodded and left her alone to her father's things. She knew she needed to start packing things up. These were the royal chambers. It was supposed to be Goddard's and her room, but she didn't have it in her to sleep in her father's bed yet.

"My Queen, may I speak with you?" one of the maids asked.

"Of course," she said, and directed the young woman into the room to sit down. Adalie had been staying in her father's chambers, trying to get up the strength to pack it up. It had been a month since her father had passed and it was time. He wasn't coming back, and she needed to step up to the role of being Queen.

"The King, he... He..." the maid said before bursting into tears.

"What's wrong? You can tell me," she said, running her hand up and down the maid's back, trying to soothe her.

"The King, he k... Killed my brother."

"What?"

"I'm sorry, My Queen, this isn't your problem. I just... I didn't know who else to turn to," she said, trying to stand up.

"No, tell me what happened."

"My brother. He was protesting the King's demand that we pay twice the amount of tax. The King came to our home and had him hanged on a tree outside of our house," she sobbed.

"You will stay here at the castle for now. I'm going to go have a little chat with my husband," Adalie said, standing up.

"No, Your Highness, you can't. I know you've been in mourning and haven't seen it, but your husband is dangerous. I don't want you to get hurt. You're all we have," the maid said.

"What do you mean? How is he dangerous?" she asked. There were things going on and she needed to know what they were, but whatever they were, they didn't sound good.

"I'll show you," she said, and pulled out a plain cloak and dress from the dressing cabinet for the Queen to wear.

Adalie was a little confused. She had no problem going into town, but why couldn't the maid just tell her? If things were as bad as she was making them out to be, shouldn't they be trying to fix them as soon as they could?

"You'll understand more once you see," the maid explained as she handed her the dress.

Adalie was on her horse, riding next to the maid. This was the first time in a very long time that she'd been to the village without an escort, and she didn't like it. The feeling she was getting from the people was just wrong. They were unhappy and looked underfed. Some looked sickly. They needed food and a doctor. But she had a feeling that that wasn't what the maid wanted to show her.

Going to the other edge of town, she immediately smelled something burning. This wasn't good. Nothing should be burning.

"This is my cousin's house. His family's now staying with me until they can rebuild," the maid said as they came up to a house that was charred wood and ash.

"What happened?" Adalie asked.

"They weren't able to pay the entire tax."

"This isn't right."

"Down the road there are three more houses like this. They weren't as lucky as my cousin," she said sadly.

"This...? Goddard did this?" she asked.

"I'm sorry, Your Highness. You needed to know," the maid said quietly.

"I'm glad you showed me. We'll figure out something," she said, and moved her horse to go back to the castle. She needed to think of something to help these people, she just didn't know what. She wished her father were there to help.

Walking through the castle doors, Adalie went in search of her husband. On the ride back, her anger grew until she was furious. How could he do that? They were innocent people! The job of the King was to lead and protect people, not starve and kill them. If she had known this was how the people were living, she would gladly have given all her food to those who were starving and her clothes to the ones who were freezing.

"Ah, there you are. I was looking everywhere for you," Goddard said with a smile when he saw her.

"How could you do this?" she asked.

"What are you talking about?"

"I'm talking about the state of my kingdom. I've known these people my entire life. They are my friends, and you are killing them!" she yelled at him. Adalie had always been a somewhat passive person, but seeing everything her family had worked to build destroyed was something for which she wouldn't stand.

Before she could move or react, Goddard slapped her across the face. "How dare you talk to me like that? Do you have any idea who I am?" he yelled at her.

"You are my husband. You might be the King, but I am the Queen, and I will not allow you to do this to my home and my people," she said, holding her ground.

Within an instant, Adalie couldn't breathe. It was as if all the air had been sucked out of her lungs.

"You will go back into mourning and not leave your room. If you step out of the castle again, you will suffer much more than you are now—and so will your kingdom," Goddard said.

She nodded as best she could before the feeling was gone. She was able to breathe again. That was when she made a decision and went to her father's chambers, which were now her own. She was going to move everything out of the room she shared with her husband, and she was going to stand tall and be the Queen her kingdom needed. She was going to get it back.

"I need you to bring the loyal staff members here," she said to the maid who had lost her brother.

"Are you sure?" the maid asked.

"Yes. This is not what my father wanted. He wanted our kingdom to be peaceful and safe. This is not what my family stands for, and I'm going to fight until it's back to what it used to be."

"All right, we'll meet here tonight, after everyone goes to bed."

Adalie nodded, and was then left to her own thoughts and plans. She didn't know how she'd missed it. How had she not seen that he had magic? He was her husband—how had she not known what kind of man he was? How could she have let this happen to her kingdom?

The only thing she could think of was her father's death. She didn't know how to run a kingdom without him. She didn't know how to do anything without him. Was that why he died? Did Goddard know she wouldn't be able to function with her father gone? Did he kill him?

That thought had her sitting straight up. He could have killed her father. She had thought it was an accident, but it had seemed strange. How else could that carriage have fallen apart like that? With magic, it was possible. She felt like such an idiot for not knowing and for letting this happen. How had she not seen it sooner?

Everyone was assembled in Adalie's room, waiting to see what she was going to say, and what her plan was. The only problem was she didn't have one. How do you take on someone with magic? How was she going to save her kingdom? How could she ever be a good queen if she didn't know how to save it?

"My Queen, this is everyone," the maid said.

Adalie looked around and saw over half the staff standing around her room. How would she be able to help all these people? "Thank you for coming," she said with a weak smile. "I'm sorry for what has happened. I didn't know. It's not an excuse, but it's the truth."

"What are we going to do?" one of the cooks asked.

"I... I don't know. He's too strong."

"We need to kill him. It's the only way to make sure he's gone," a stableman said.

"I can't do it. He's too strong. Earlier, he almost killed me without laying a hand on me," she said, touching her throat and remembering the fear she'd felt.

"My Queen, there is no other way. He has too much power. It's the only way to defeat him," the man said.

She nodded. She would do anything for her kingdom, but could she kill him? She was probably the only one who could get close enough. The question was, would she survive it?

"Here," one of the guards said. Adalie looked down and saw a knife in his hand. "You will need a weapon. Make sure you aim for his heart or throat. If not, he might survive and kill you."

"All right," she said, taking a deep breath and reaching for the knife. It was heavier than she'd thought it would be.

"Good night, My Queen," he said, bowing to her.

Adalie watched as everyone left. Staring at the knife, she wondered if she could do it, if she really could kill someone. She had to, though. She needed to save everyone. Tonight. She would do it tonight. No one would question her going into her old chambers, and it was late; Goddard was probably asleep.

Adalie closed her eyes and pictured her father, how strong he had been and how he would have done this without hesitation. Then she pictured the home she'd seen that was burned to the ground and the people who were starving. She could do this.

Gripping the knife tightly and hiding it in her skirt, Adalie made her way to her old bedroom. She was surprised when she didn't see a guard outside the room. Her father had always had someone posted there. Assassination attempts weren't unheard of. Maybe her husband wasn't aware of that, or thought he didn't need a guard because of how powerful he was. Either way, it was something for which she was very happy.

Adalie pushed the door open and saw Goddard asleep in bed. *Good.* She wanted this to be easy and with no fighting. She didn't believe in stabbing someone who was defenseless, but Goddard was hurting too many people. He was evil and needed to be killed. But he wasn't really defenseless if he had magic.

She stood over him, the knife gripped in her hand and held high above her head. Adalie wanted to make sure she had the strength behind the blow to kill him. She hesitated for a moment. She had to kill him, but she'd never killed anyone before. Could she do it?

Goddard turned over with a big smile on his face, then he noticed the knife held in her hand. That smile—that was made her swing her arm down and plunge the knife into his heart. It was the smile he'd used when he'd taken the air from her. It was proof he wasn't defenseless and that he planned to kill her. In that one moment, she knew she was right to do this and would feel no guilt over it.

Adalie walked out into the courtyard, hoping to find the guard who had given her his knife. She wanted him to have it back. He might need it.

"My Queen?" someone said.

"Can you find Rune for me, please?" she asked.

"It's cold out. Let me get you inside and I'll send him to your chambers," he said kindly. She nodded and let him lead her to her father's chambers. "Wait here and I'll get him."

Sitting down, she stared at the knife covered with blood, and at the blood that stained her dress. She'd done it. She'd freed her kingdom from him. They were safe now.

"My Queen?" she heard Rune say.

"I wanted to give this back to you," she said, holding his knife out to him.

"Are you okay?" he asked, noticing all the blood.

"I'm fine. You might want to have someone take care of Goddard, though."

"I will. Let me get someone who can help you get cleaned up," he said, and she watched him step outside and speak to someone. "Okay, Goddard is being taken care of and one of the maids is being fetched."

"Can you help me, please?" she asked. She didn't care about anyone seeing her. She wanted out of the dress and to clean the blood from her skin. It was starting to get sticky.

He looked like he was about to say something, but just nodded then walked over to her, helping her get the bloody dress off.

"Rune," Adalie said as she sat in the garden.

"Yes?" he said.

"You have been with me almost every second since Goddard. Why?" she asked.

"Because I want to make sure you're okay," he answered, not looking at her.

"I'm okay, but it has to be more than that. You only leave me to sleep, and only then when you have two men watching over me. Why?"

"Because you're the Queen."

"No, I know there's more to it than that."

"Because I care about you," he answered quietly.

"I thought so. Then if you care about me, why not become my king?" she asked.

"I..."

"Rune, you helped me through something unimaginable. You held me when I cried and you made me laugh when I needed it. And I care about you, too," she said just as quietly as he had.

"Do you mean it?" he asked, moving to sit next to her.

"I do. I want you to be my king," she said with a smile. Rune smiled and kissed her. "Is that a yes?"

"It's a yes," he whispered against her lips before kissing her again.

It hadn't been a quick love; it had been a quiet one that had grown over the previous months. Adalie had gotten to know Rune and knew he was a good man. He would fill her father's role with a kind heart and offer the healing they needed.

BOBBIE PALMER writes both paranormal and thriller novels. She loves reading just about anything, and when she's not writing, she has her nose stuck in a book. She loves to cook and hang out with her nephews and two cats. She is very involved in the writing community, hosting a writer's breakfast once a month, and is the Municipal Liaison for NaNoWriMo. Currently she has two books out, *The Baltimore Butcher*, and *Lucy's Wolverine*.

LINKS

http://bobbiepalmer.yolasite.com
http://www.facebook.com/pages/Bobbie-Palmer/304444518542
https://twitter.com/bobbie_palmer

Wish Witch

by William Petersen

TOM awoke abruptly with a pounding headache, a blinding sunbeam attacking his clinched eyelids, and his tongue stuck to the roof of his mouth. "Aarrrr," he declared feebly while ungraciously stumbling to his feet, eyes still tightly shut. After positioning his back towards the assault of sunlight, he gingerly opened his eyes and, without having to look at his phone, knew that there were several missed calls, rude texts, and voicemail messages from his boss. He was late...again.

"I hate this crap," he stated flatly to his tiny, cluttered bedroom. Rushing to zip up his pants and look around for his boots, he snatched up his phone and pulled up the contact for the cab service; they knew him well since his second DWI. Not having a license was bad enough, but paying for a cab ride every day, a couple times a day, ate up nearly half of his net income. The dispatcher commented that he must be running late today as he rolled his eyes and tried to put together the pieces of the previous night's drinking binge.

"I don't *think* I did anything stupid," he thought while pulling up the number for Anderson's Tree and Landscaping, his employer of nearly five years. Five years was an employment record for Tom; most of his jobs never lasted the first year. The office secretary answered with the standard greeting, and Tom announced himself and immediately heard the pleasant tone change to one of impatience and annoyance.

"They're at the job site already; you're seriously late, again, and Chuck is really mad. You better call him before you show up," she informed him.

"Great...thanks," he hung up without formality and dialed Chuck's number.

Chuck Anderson, the company owner's son, was the foreman, office manager, and everyone's direct supervisor. He was also a micromanaging, lazy jerk, prone to eruptions and tantrums that would make a two-year-old uncomfortable. Tom was relieved when Chuck did not answer his phone.

The cab driver was smart enough to realize that he was not in the mood for conversation and gratefully remained silent for the entire ride. When they arrived at the job site, the work was well underway, the sounds of lawn care equipment and chainsaws running enthusiastically composed a roaring noise when he stepped out of the cab. Paying the driver and saying goodbye, he caught sight of Chuck near the end of the wood chipper, standing in his normal spot. Chuck stood near the back of the chipper all day and told other people how to push branches into the machine—sometimes grabbing them himself when in a bad mood, rudely and with exaggerated movements, for visual effect and further humiliation of the workers.

He headed straight towards the big man, noting with some disgust that he was again wearing a snap-up, flannel shirt with its sleeves cut off at the armpits, and it was open and flapping in the wind, revealing his enormous beer gut. He looked totally ridiculous. Chuck worked outdoors all year round and had the tan to prove it; sporting dark brown arms from the shoulders down, a tan-and-protruding belly, a nearly-white chest, and a leathery, red face. It was a lot to take in the first time, particularly when it was all in motion.

Chuck spotted Tom in his peripheral vision and did a double-take, then immediately yelled at the man feeding limbs into the chipper, motioning at him to keep working. Chuck stormed over to him and surprised him by not yelling right away, "This is the second time this week. This is a big job, and if you don't want to get paid, then keep your lazy butt at home. As a matter of fact, take your butt back home now. You're not working today. You can't get to the office on time to get a ride, and you can't get to work on your own, so stay home today. We don't need you here."

And with that, he turned and walked off, shaking his head and muttering profanities under his breath. Tom looked around hopefully, but the cab was gone. He turned and yelled back at Chuck, "Can I get some reimbursement for the cab fare at least?" broadcasting it a little louder than he had intended.

Chuck stopped in his tracks and jerked off his ball cap, slammed it to the ground and began marching towards him. His mouth was very animated, though Tom couldn't hear what sounds were coming out, due to the cacophony of power tools and machinery in operation. One of Tom's favorite coworkers came running into view and intercepted Chuck before he got any closer, trying hard to keep the big man focused on him and not Tom.

"Alright, alright...I'm leaving," Tom yelled back, then turned to walk to the other side of the street—where he wouldn't be so temped to rattle Chuck's cage—to call another cab.

Ryan, the coworker who had intervened on his behalf, walked up to where Tom was now waiting for his cab and offered, "Well, at least you get another day off."

"Yeah, but I really need the money more than I need a day off, especially since I just spent twenty bucks on the ride here...for nothing. Screw it...I'm going to the bar," Tom replied. Shifting his line of sight to take in the repulsive view of Chuck working. Tom noticed, and not for the first time, that Chuck's flapping shirt was dangling precariously close to the entrance of the wood chipper.

Ryan, following his stare, repeated his predictable comment, "One of these days, that shirt is going to get caught in there, and he's going to get chewed up by that thing."

"I hope that fat jerk does get sucked in there. Then we could work in peace everyday and not have to put up with his crap anymore," it was more of the morning sun on his head, baking his hangover, that inspired his words than anything else. Still, it shocked Ryan all the same, even though he had heard Tom say it before.

"Dang bro, that's pretty brutal. You do need a drink. I gotta get back to work though, because I don't know anyone here that will stop Chuck from kicking *my* butt," he said with a grin.

"Take care, buddy, and don't work too hard...I'll toss one back for you," Tom called after him, spotting his cab turning onto the road a few blocks away.

Tom forgot about everything else and momentarily got lost in the cab's radio. In this part of town, the cabbies didn't know him as well, and this driver was one he had never seen before. He had gotten in and handed her a twenty, then inquired if she knew where Jimmy's Place was in Park Charles. She nodded into her rear-view mirror and took the cash, and even though she had large, dark glasses on, Tom could see she was grinning. He disregarded it and sat listening as AC/DC's "Highway to Hell" played on the cab's cheap stereo. He managed to nod off for a few minutes along the way and woke up from the motion of the car stopping and leaning him forward. As soon as his eyes adjusted and he could see out of the window, he was rewarded with the familiar site of Jimmy's Place, the bar's name written on the green canopy above the front door.

He opened the door but paused with one leg out, looking back to the driver's reflection in the mirror. She was just staring back at him, a faint outline of her eyes just visible through her sunglasses, not saying a word. He felt uncomfortable and got out of the car, walked to the front door and, as he reached out to open it, he heard, "Have a good time," in a soft and sensual voice come from behind him.

Tom turned to see the cabbie had removed her glasses and ball cap—and she was hot. She couldn't have been more than thirty, if that, but exuded an air of natural beauty. Even from his present distance, he could see she was not made up at all, and there was something about her eyes. Tom looked back into the bar through the glass pane on the door, then turned back to her and said, "I wish I knew how..." rather pathetically.

"Careful what you wish for..." she said, grinning.

"Hmmm, I'll do that, thanks," he absently replied as he opened the door, ringing the bell on the other side. He knew she was way out of his league; there was no point in wasting the time or effort on that scene. Tom looked around and was immediately greeted with several loud salutations and raised glasses. He smiled and thought to himself, *"Now these people are more my speed."*

Settling into his favorite bar stool at the end, Tom ordered a draft beer, three shots of rail bourbon, and pulled out a cigarette in anticipation of his drinks. The shots warmed his belly and face, and he greedily downed all three in turn, chasing them with swigs of beer. Jess and Sharon—two dedicated, divorcée barflies that were at Jimmy's seven days a week, rain or shine—were heard before they were seen. Once again, they were ranting and raving about some ghost show or paranormal movie, believing whatever they heard about the subjects and repeating it as gospel, regardless of factual basis.

He nodded and raised his glass to them, both smiled and waved back in turn, and he could see that the television above their table was tuned to one of the many ghost-hunting shows over which they relentlessly obsessed. Unconsciously rolling his eyes, Tom returned to his drinking. He noticed that he was getting fairly buzzed right away and decided he should slow down a bit. It was still morning, and he had not eaten anything yet. He picked up a menu from the bar and began looking for something good to chow down on for brunch.

"What's good?" a female voice almost whispered from behind him, startling him a little.

"Umm, beer..." Tom offered, with a goofy smile and a raise of his glass.

"Sounds good to me," she said as she grabbed her own pitcher of beer off of the bar—which took Tom by surprise, as he didn't notice it there just a moment ago—and filled a glass that had apparently been in her hand already. The attractive woman looked to be about thirty or just under, with dark hair and green eyes, and she was wearing a black top and brown skirt with black hose. She was smoking hot.

She looked a lot like the cab driver from earlier, and this really piqued his interest. Tom was taken aback for a moment, not able to think of anything to say and suddenly wished he wasn't as drunk as he felt. She slammed her beer without taking a breath and then leaned over and kissed him passionately, breaking away as slowly as she could, not opening her eyes until their lips were no longer touching. When she did open her eyes, Tom saw the greenest irises he had ever witnessed, accented by the darkest pupils he'd ever seen, temporarily giving him the sensation of being looked *through*—not looked at.

"Be right back," she said with a coy smile.

Tom watched her walk away with great interest, not able to take his eyes off of her rear end, and only looked up when Sharon's shrill, intoxicated voice snatched away his focus. "What's wrong with you, man? Why are you acting so weird today, and why are you in here this early? Shouldn't you be at work?"

"Yeah, yeah. I'm off today, so I figured I'd come here and grace you with my presence again. I know you missed me," he said with grin.

"Well, quit being weird, you're freaking Jess out and cracking me up," she said as she wrapped an arm around his shoulder. Her offensive and overpowering perfume wafted right into his face, then thankfully, she patted his arm and went back to her paranormal nonsense.

The front door burst open, causing the bell on the top to rattle violently and the commotion drew everyone's attention to the front of the bar. Kyle, Tom's roommate was standing in the doorway, panting and obviously winded. Tom nodded in his direction and smiled, thinking to himself: *Poor guy must not have had money for a cab. Looks like he ran the whole way here... Must have been really thirsty."* He started to laugh at the mental picture forming, when Kyle jerked him around in his seat and nearly pulled him right out of his stool. He looked around the bar nervously, then pulled Tom closer to him and began to whisper frantically.

"Have you looked at the television since you've been here?" Kyle asked, wide-eyed.

"Not really, wh..." his inquiry was cut short as he saw a picture of his boss, Chuck, on the screen just above where he was sitting. He couldn't hear what was being said, but the next image spoke volumes. A large, blue tarp covered a piece of machinery, which Tom recognized instantly from the angled, box-metal shaft protruding from one end of the tarp. It was the wood chipper. Even through the grainy aerial views shown on the newscast, and with a tarp tied down around it, the blood pools at each end of the machine told the story. Tom felt a chill dance its way up his spine and come to rest at the base of his skull.

"Tom, it was Chuck. That's *Chuck's* blood all over the place there. He got run through the chipper." Kyle's eyes were huge in their sockets, and they were darting back and forth.

Tom looked back up to see his own face on the television and suddenly felt light-headed and ready to vomit. He looked questioningly at Kyle.

"Dude, you made some kind of comment at work today, something about him falling into the chipper. A lot of people heard you man, and," now almost a whisper, "the cops came by the house looking for you. That's why I ran down here."

This was not making Tom feel any better.

"Bro, there's more," Kyle said, trying to prepare him for the blow, "They asked about Lisa, too. They wouldn't tell my why or anything, but I thought you should know. I told them to look for you in the city, but it won't be long before they catch up with you."

The color drained from Tom's face and his lips were nearly blue. Kyle thought he might be having a heart attack and started to ask him about it when the door to the bar burst open yet again. This time, it was two uniformed police officers and two detectives in plain clothes.

"Tommy Boy!" one of the detectives shouted gleefully. "How you doing man? It's alright everybody," the detective announced, while simultaneously pulling his badge—which hung on a chain around his neck—out of his shirt. "We just need to ask Tom-Tom here a few questions. You can go back to your fun, we'll be out of here in a jiffy."

Tom didn't move; like a deer caught in blinding headlights, he was frozen. The officers and detectives moved into positions around him and asked him to slowly stand up. One of the uniformed officers frisked him and picked up his phone as the detective held onto to his elbow. As he walked unsteadily towards the door, he heard first giggling, then outright laughing. Turning back to see what was so funny, he saw his hot girl at the very back of the bar, now laughing hysterically and pointing right at him, though no one else seemed to notice, as he was led out the door and out of sight.

Tom didn't say a word until he was at the police station and only then began answering questions after he realized he was not being booked for anything—yet.

"So you took a cab to Jimmy's Place, but why is there no dispatch record of your ride, and we know there's no receipt, since you told us that you paid with cash," a detective asked him, who he now knew as Detective Whitfield (though he had already forgotten the other detective's name).

"I don't know. Why don't you ask Ryan?" Tom countered, for how many times now he couldn't remember. "I was talking to him right before I left."

"Yes, but he had his back to you when you supposedly got into the cab. He never actually *saw* you get in or leave," Whitfield reminded him.

They had covered the aspects of Chuck's death over and over, and Tom repeatedly tried to reinforce the theory that his shirt had simply gotten caught in the machinery. He could not, however, explain away the set of shoe prints at the crime scene that were unaccounted for at the present moment. Fortunately, the prints didn't match any of his shoes or boots. While Tom and Whitfield were engaging in their back and forth, other detectives had been preparing the next line of questioning.

A detective entered the room from behind him, and Tom wholly expected the guy to snatch him up, put him in cuffs, and then haul him off to a cell. Instead, the detective placed a brown file folder on the desk in front of Whitfield and left the room without speaking. "So," Whitfield began, opening the file and looking intently at the contents of the folder, "lets talk about Lisa."

"I'd rather not," Tom stated automatically and just a little too quickly.

"Too bad, she's dead, Tom. She was choked to death in the stairwell of her apartment last night. We estimate the time of death to be around midnight," Whitfield informed him. "Where were you around that time, Tommy Boy?"

They could read his body language, and while he tried to mask it, the trained eyes of the detectives saw that he was clearly saddened and shocked by the news, lending credibility to his innocence. "Stop calling me that, I was at home in bed. I left the bar before midnight and went straight home," Tom declared.

"Funny, no one saw you or can verify your whereabouts. That makes it hard to sell your story there, pal," Whitefield explained, "and the girl you talked about... No one else saw her, but more than a couple people did see you talking to *yourself* several times."

"Look, I don't what to say. I didn't have anything to do with either of these killings, and with all the science and CSI crap you cops have, you should know that by now," Tom was getting annoyed, he had been there for hours now and was tired, hungry, and still slightly hung-over. He also wanted to find out more about what happened to Lisa.

"Didn't she leave you for another woman? An aerobics instructor, wasn't it? We have here some transcriptions of text messages and voice mail messages left by you, which were used to obtain the restraining order against you previously," Whitefield said as he pulled several sheets of paper out of the folder and placed them in front of Tom.

Several lines of each page were highlighted with yellow marker, drawing his eye directly to them: "...I wish you would choke... I hope you choke to death...I wish you would choke and die..." he read on and all the old, painful memories came rushing back. Tom's head dropped as the familiar emotions came rushing back just as fresh as they had been at that point in time.

"Look, Tom, we know it was a tough break-up, and we're trying to help you here, but we wouldn't be doing our jobs if we didn't look into this. Come on, man, you said those *exact* words—about two people—and now both of those people are dead. Not just dead, but dead in the exact same way you were heard publicly wishing they would die. We need you to help us explain this so we can let you get back to your life and we can get those responsible," the detective provided.

This went on for hours, but in the end, there simply wasn't enough evidence to hold him. After a short break, the detectives returned and Whitfield informed him of the situation. "We're gonna cut you loose, Tom, for now. We're not done, though, because we are still investigating this, and when I find that one thing that links you back to either one of these crimes, we'll be talking again," he stated matter-of-factly.

Tom was escorted out of the station as whispers and scowls worked their ways through the clusters of people he passed. Once out of the front door, he started walking as fast as he could, without drawing attention to himself. He just wanted to get home, get drunk, and forget this day ever happened. He looked down at his phone to see the time but its charge was gone, it was at that point that he realized it was now nighttime. Tucking his head down as close to his chest as possible, Tom picked up his pace a bit and headed towards home.

Tom reached his apartment complex without incident and promptly retrieved the half-full, gallon bottle of vodka from behind his television set and took a long, hard pull from it. The day had taken its toll on him, and he was mentally and physically exhausted.

He awoke sometime in the morning from nightmares involving ground up bodies and a blue-faced, black-lipped Lisa lying in a dark stairwell, along with the familiar dry mouth and disorientation of a person who has woken up still slightly drunk. Tom sat up and gingerly rubbed his head and face as he tried to shake off the remnants of the dream, while beginning the process of getting his eyes open and acclimating to the harsh realities of consciousness, mainly the bright lights and sounds that accentuated his pounding head.

Even before he could get his eyes open, Tom felt his stomach rumbling and remembered that he hadn't eaten anything since the day before yesterday. Knowing full well that there would be no work today—and if there was, he wouldn't be welcomed to any work site after yesterday—he decided to take the rest of the day to think and clear his head.

"Kyle?" Tom called as he exited his bedroom, pulling a t-shirt over his head and lighting a cigarette. He noticed right away that Kyle's bedroom door was slightly ajar and peeked inside, realizing that he hadn't been home at all. Kyle was a smooth operator when it came to the ladies, and he spent more time sleeping at their places than at his own apartment. He would often disappear for several days, only to turn up at the bar with a new, temporary trophy on his arm.

Kyle was on disability and didn't work at all. He was diagnosed as HIV positive three years ago and was basically riding the government gravy train until he either drank himself to death or the virus progressed and eventually killed him. Tom often resented him for his free ride. Even though he would pay for it sooner or later, it still irked him that Kyle could sit on his butt and live however he wanted to, funded by the government, just because he made it with an infected tramp and was now infected himself. Tom also knew that Kyle's frequent sex partners had no clue of his condition, and that Kyle was indeed spreading the gift that kept on giving. Or as Tom liked to call it when Kyle was not present, *The Blind Ninja*, also known as full-blown AIDS.

"Your loss..." Tom stated to the empty apartment, "I was gonna take you out to lunch, and I was even going to pay."

He left the apartment and walked the half-mile to the tiny strip mall by his apartment complex, thinking about the previous day's events. The detectives had explained to him the details of Lisa's murder, right down to the fact that there were no signs of a struggle, which was odd, since choking someone to death takes time and effort; the victim does not die right away and fights for air, driven by survival instinct. Lisa's body lay exactly where the incident started; her attacker grabbed her neck with such force that the bones and windpipe were crushed immediately, and she died within a few seconds. Even so, the killer held on for some time, ensuring she had indeed expired.

Taken together, all of the evidence pointed to a physically strong person who had to know Lisa in order to get close enough for a frontal attack without provoking any suspicion from her. The killing was clearly personal, as no money way taken and nothing was disturbed—other than her neck. It all pointed conveniently to him. However, the only physical evidence, the marks around her neck, showed that the perpetrator had small hands and fingers, like a woman's. This, and the fact that the shoe prints at Chuck's murder scene didn't match any of his own and were a much smaller size altogether, were the only reasons he was not sitting in a jail cell right now.

Tom pushed the thoughts to the back of his mind as he stepped into the Chinese buffet. The smell of sweet and spicy medleys filled his nasal cavity and brought a large, genuine smile to his face, the first natural one in quite a while. He grabbed a plate and began stacking food on it, in a hurry to get back to his table and chow down. He ate enthusiastically and quickly, trying to make up for nearly forty-eight hours without any sustenance, until he noticed that he was being watched.

A small and very petite girl was standing just behind the buffet tables, near the entrance to the restrooms, staring and smiling at him. She was obviously one of the owner's or employee's daughters, clearly of Asian descent, and looking a lot like the waitress who sat him. He turned his attention back to his food, but his eyes were again drawn back to the little China doll. She was still staring and smiling. Tom finished his mouthful of breaded shrimp and dabbed at his face with a napkin, then offered a friendly smile back to the little girl.

The smile immediately ran away from the girl's face, and she became solemn as a statue. Her now piercing dark eyes were a far cry from the endearing, twinkling orbs they had been. As if she had seen something in him when he smiled, the girl continued to stand and stare, to the point that it made Tom uncomfortable, and he looked back down to his plate. When he looked back up, she was gone. He had lost his appetite by this point and scouted around for the little girl as he gathered his things, paid, and left as quickly as he could. Outside, he asked himself out loud, "What the Hell is going on with me?" but no answers came.

He tried to keep his thoughts at bay as he walked back home. Tom walked around the general area surrounding his apartment complex for a while before heading back inside and caught sight of Louie, the complex's live-in manager and landlord, heading in his general direction. Tom hurried to get inside and shut the door before he was spotted, but the call of, "Hey, Tom!" from behind stopped him in mid-stride, just as he was about the slam the door shut.

He knew better than to just go in. Louie would knock and call to him loudly until he opened up; it was better to get it over with now. Turning to find the squat, bald, and smelly man just a few feet away, Tom said, "Hey, Louie, I'll have my part of the rent this Friday. Sorry it's late again, but I'll make sure to include the late fee, too," thinking the whole time of how everyone knew he pocketed repair money, security deposits and, of course, late fees. The worst part was, his uncle, the owner of the property, also knew and didn't seem to care.

His hopes of a quick interaction were dashed when Louie replied with, "It's not that," then elaborated: "Several of the other tenants have been to see me over the last two days about what is going on with you. People aren't comfortable with you living here, and they are threatening to leave unless you do. So, I'm going to have to ask you to move out right away. You can keep your last month's rent, if it will help speed up the process, but I need you out of here as soon as possible. I know we've had our issues in the past, but this is strictly business; I can't lose dozens of tenants because they think a killer is living next door."

Louie turned and walked off in the direction of his own apartment, as Tom stood in his doorway with his mouth open for several minutes. When he came back to reality, he slammed the door and plopped himself down on the couch, absently turning on the television in the living room.

"It figures," Tom said to the empty apartment, while one of the many supernatural shows Kyle watched came to life on the television screen. He was instantly reminded of why he hated the whole business of paranormal anything. He felt that the entire show, all of the shows for that matter, could be summed up in a couple of simple phrases: "Ooh, did you hear that? Ooh, did you feel that?" And his personal favorite: cold spots.

"Oh, wow," Tom mocked, "I found a cold spot on the floor of a basement, it *must* be a ghost. What else could cause cold spots in a basement, in winter?" He laughed heartily. "Superstitious morons..." he muttered under his breath as he shut off the show and began to pace around the tiny apartment. "What am I going to do now?" he asked the empty dwelling.

Tom knew that he couldn't afford to live anywhere else. His complex was one of the cheapest in the entire county and the only one that was willing to take a chance on his terrible credit history. His mind slipped back into an old, familiar thought pattern. There were losers and winners, that's just the way it was, and one could never change that. The losers stayed losers because the winners kept them down, in one way or another, and kept themselves in that elevated state by standing on the hunched backs of the losers. The cycle never ended. It was like being cursed.

Suddenly feeling the cramped confines of the apartment closing in on him, Tom realized he was heading towards another bout of depression and The Blame Game. Tom's familiar and disturbing routine consisted of getting sloppy drunk, then whining and ranting about all of the reasons he was not in a better situation, which always amounted to other people keeping him down. From his former boss to that fat ball of a landlord, they were all conspiring to keep him in the gutter—and, as far as he could tell, it was working.

"I gotta get out of here," Tom surmised, and bolted out the front door without closing it all the way, then pulled out his phone to call a cab as he strode off towards the road. The next thing he realized, he was outside of Jimmy's Place, looking out from the cab window and wondering how he would be received, that is, if he could muster enough courage to go inside. After what seemed like an eternity of wavering on his decision, he finally committed himself and started to get out of the cab.

"Keep it running, would you?" he asked the driver, then, as he walked toward the entrance, added, "I may be right back…"

As soon as he entered, the sparse crowd inside stopped moving and talking, almost in unison, to look toward the front door. The bell was still jingling when Jim himself started speaking rather loudly, "Oh no…no way, man, you can't be in here. You've gotta go right now, Tom…and you can't come back. "

While there were no actual bouncers working during the day, there were several patrons who were more than willing to help with removing unwanted company at a moment's notice, and one in particular, Paul, also known as Rooster, didn't like Tom in the first place. Rooster stood up eagerly, but before the drama could unfold, Tom turned around and walked right back out the door. He walked to the cab, and he stood looking at his reflection in the mirror for a moment when he heard the bell on the bar door ring. Tom expected to see Rooster & Friends barging out for the fight they had wanted for some time, but he was pleasantly surprised to see Jess and Sharon instead.

"Oh, God, Tom…we're so sorry. Everybody is real worked up about the last few days, and it's just not a good time for you to be here right now," Sharon professed.

"Tell me about it," he sarcastically replied.

"Look, Tom, we've known you for a while, and we know you didn't have anything to do with any of this. It will all come out in the end. Then everything will be cool, and you can come back and hang with us again. Here's my number. Call me and let me know what's going on, and I'll keep you posted on what's up here. And Tom…stay sober for a while. You need a clear head until this all blows over."

Tom smiled and took the napkin with Sharon's number on it. She and Jess both hugged him in turn, and he got in the cab. He looked at the bar as it receded to the point that he could no longer crane his neck to keep it in view, and he had a sinking feeling that he would never step foot in there again.

Back at his apartment, Tom let the depression and vodka take him away, finishing the bottle and, after alternating screaming and crying fits, passing out in the middle of the living room on the floor with no shirt. The noise would have normally prompted neighbors to call the police, but they were all too scared of him now. A crashing sound ripped him from his drunken slumber as the front door of the apartment flew right off of its hinges and landed right on top of him. While he struggled to grasp what was happening, hands grabbed at him from several directions and the room filled with the urgent cries of, "Show me your hands! Hands…now! Show me your hands!"

Tom was jostled and dragged about, finally coming to rest against the wall, hands cuffed behind his back, as more than a dozen police offers and crime scene technicians began to pour over every inch of the apartment. He looked up to see Detective Whitfield standing in the doorway. "I told you I'd be back for you," Whitfield smugly commented, then to one of the technicians, "We'll need him processed, too. Go with him back to the station."

At the police station, after taking his clothes, checking his body for trace evidence, and providing him with a paper jumpsuit, Tom was led into a familiar interrogation room, where he waited for what seemed like days.

When the monotony was finally broken, Whitfield entered, although without his normal entourage. "We've got something to talk about, Tom," Whitfield said flatly. "It seems as though you've got yourself tied to another killing. James Callier, you know him as Jimmy, the owner and bartender at Jimmy's Place, was beaten to death behind the bar while taking out the trash at the end of the night."

Tom felt himself slide from nervousness to shock. He and Jimmy had argued a lot, sure, but nothing more than that. He was escorted out from time to time for being obnoxious or just too drunk to stand up, though nothing physical ever came to pass. He actually liked Jimmy, most of the time.

"You went there yesterday and he threw you out, which is to be expected, but what I want to know is, why in the world would you go there? Of all the places in this town, after the last few days, why *there*?" the detective questioned.

"I just wanted a drink and to see some familiar faces, that's all. I didn't have anywhere else to go," Tom offered in his defense.

"And then what, you got mad when he told you to leave, waited for closing time and beat his head in?" Whitfield persisted.

"No, I..." Tom tried to respond but was cut off by the detective.

"Your landlord is dead, too, buddy boy. We found him on the way to your place. We stopped to get the key first, so we wouldn't have to bust in, and there he was. *Someone...* Snapped his neck for him, just grabbed his chin and a handful of hair and twisted. Twisted so hard, in fact, that his head turned almost three-hundred degrees, tearing the skin open on one side," the detective revealed. "What happened to your hands, Tom?" Whitfield asked.

"Like I'm sure your technicians told you already, I punched a few holes in the walls last night. I was pretty drunk." Tom countered. He looked down and saw both of his hands swollen and puffy; the right one had two small cuts on the middle knuckle. They hurt, too, and now that he was paying attention to them, he realized that they both hurt pretty bad. His head was swimming, so rather than say anything incriminating, he opted to keep his mouth shut.

"That's real convenient for you, isn't it? I'm sure you think you're pretty smart. You all do, but let me tell you, no matter how good you think you are covering your tracks, we are going to get you. And if anyone helped you, we'll get them, too. There is always some evidence, and while I wish I had it right now so I could lock you away, I know that, sooner or later, we *will* find it."

"Careful what you wish for detective," Tom heard himself say.

Whitfield shrugged it off. "We're waiting on DNA confirmation, but the cases against you are pretty strong already. More than one of your neighbors stated hearing an extended—and quite disturbing—tirade coming from your place last night." He removed a notepad from his inner jacket pocket and read from it directly: "...I wish someone would catch you out back and beat your head in..." He continued, "...I hope someone snaps your fat neck..."

"These are just a few of the phrases corroborated by neighbors and one person just walking his dog. You also mentioned names—Jimmy and Louie, to be precise. So, are you ready to tell me what's going on here?" the detective asked, almost sympathetically.

"I...I don't know," Tom more exhaled the words than spoke them as he slumped down in his chair.

Whitfield's impatience was growing and it showed. He stood and, without looking directly at Tom added: "Kyle's missing, too... Hasn't been seen in two days. We tried to find him for questioning."

Before Tom could slip any further into shock, the interrogation room door burst open and a young, suit-laden man stormed in with a uniformed officer close behind.

"Are you questioning my client without legal counsel present detective?" the young man, apparently a lawyer, demanded to know. "Surely you wouldn't jeopardize such an important case by not playing by the rules, would you? Have you formally charged my client?"

"*Your client?*" Tom thought.

"I'm having the release paperwork processed right now, and my client will be leaving with me. In the meantime, I'd appreciate some time alone to consult with him privately, if you don't mind," added the confident young counselor.

Tom was quite impressed, even more so when the detective glared at them momentarily and then left the room. The young man in the suit sat down, and while he had a visitors badge, it had no name on it. However, Tom quickly stopped caring who he was, realizing that he may be his only way out of this mess.

"Don't say anything to anyone, keep your mouth shut and try to act confused," he paused and looked at Tom briefly. "Looks like you got that one down already."

Much to his surprise, Tom and his new best friend were escorted through the back hallways and locked doors of the station to emerge in the lobby. The lobby was empty, but once out the front doors of the station, Tom saw several news vans parked up and down both sides of the street, though no reporters or news crews were visible.

"They're all in the press room, waiting for updates, which is why we came for you now. You're quite the celebrity as of late," the lawyer-type offered when he noticed Tom staring at the caravan of mobile news vehicles.

"*Did he say* we?" Tom asked himself. Before he could answer, he was being hurried into a waiting cab where they both sat in silence for the remainder of the ride, only occasionally stealing sideways glances at each other.

The cab stopped at a cheap motel a few miles outside of town. Tom and his escort got out and, after paying the driver, the lawyer-man directed him towards the far end of the long, single-story rectangular building. As they passed by each identical door, Tom wondered what waited for him here; he was far too drained, mentally and physically, to be afraid or even anxious. He was just curious now.

Lawyer-man knocked, and the door opened to reveal another young man that could have been lawyer-man's older brother, and movement behind him drew his attention to the girl sitting on one of the two beds in the room. Tom was gently guided in, and the girl stood up to greet him.

"I'm Catherine, I'm here to help," she said.

She was not exactly unattractive, but she definitely needed to spruce up a bit. Wearing a black sweater and dark gray skirt with black stockings, accentuated by her straight, jet black hair, presented an underwhelming first impression. However, Tom reminded himself that he wasn't here for a date and brought his thoughts back to the moment.

"Help me what?" Tom wanted to know.

"You know what. Can you explain what is going on around you right now?" she inquired, though the blank expression on her face never changed. She seemed sad to him. Tom looked around the room, and he saw books open on both beds and the small, round table in the corner of the room. Individual sheets of paper and notepads were interspersed throughout the room as well, further confusing him and raising his ire.

"What do you want, and why am I here?" Tom asked, the annoyance noticeable in his voice.

"Do you believe in God, Tom?" she asked, catching him totally off guard.

"Not really," he replied.

"What about evil, do you believe in that?" she asked.

"Sure...it's a real thing, just look at the news," Tom asserted sarcastically.

"Then keep that in mind, because I think that something evil is..." she paused, "...interested in you."

"What are you *talking* about?" he felt his ears getting warm.

"I have reasons to believe that some kind of presence, if you want to call it that, is at work here. I've seen this before. If I'm right, more people are going to turn up dead, and their deaths will be linked to you. Ready to talk now?"

Tom's anger was giving way to confusion again, he sat down at the table and started glancing at the open books and notes in front of him. As she talked, Tom only heard bits and pieces, because he was distracted by the subject matter. Demons, ghosts, witches and warlocks. Devils and angels. It was all of the crap that drove him completely insane.

He looked up abruptly, Catherine was going on about serial killers, how most throughout history either never get caught at all or when they were caught, the person was unbelievable as a killer or simply admitted to other killings that were yet unsolved. How many were written off as copy-cat killers and wannabe killers? What if some of those cases were somehow related to his? What if some of those cases were not actually solved? What if the suspects were simply admitting to murders to get them to stop?

He interrupted her, "Are you saying that you think I'm cursed or something? What is this mumbo-jumbo crap?" He picked up the book closest to him, pointing to the paragraph he had just scanned about the history of genies and other wish-granting entities. "Do you seriously think a genie—*a genie!*—is following me around and killing people that annoy me?"

The question stopped him cold. In his head, several connections were made in rapid succession, each one causing his mind to swim even more than it was already. He thought hard for a moment, thinking back to recent comments he had made and those he had been told about. A chill ran up his spine. He turned and fumbled with the door knob until he got it open, walking out and into the night without closing the door or looking back. Tom stood in the parking lot of the motel for a while, trying to combat the realizations that were forming in his head.

"I don't believe in this crap," he said out loud to the night air.

His shoulders slumped as he turned around and walked back towards the open door. It was a rectangle of light amidst the surrounding darkness, and the darkness was creeping in.

"So what are you saying? I need some answers here," Tom said as soon as the door was closed.

"I don't really know. I'm trying to understand it, but these are just theories," she admitted, though elaborated further:

"Evil is a real thing, we've all seen it in one form or another. I've tried to connect this with legends and myths, even looking into notorious rulers throughout history, and there are many parallels between some of them and what we are seeing here. Deaths surrounding a common person that are neither justified or properly explained and those that seemed to be part of coups or the work of serial killers. But all too often, the killings just stop, with the true killer never being discovered. Most experts believe those situations mean that the killer has most likely expired. But what if the person *did* expire, just not of natural causes?

"What if you could intend harm on others, without actually touching them? Not like psychic powers, but more like the deed was done for you. What if when you asked for harm to come to someone, and if you were really serious and asked enough times, *something* heard you?" A guilty look passed over her face, and then: "I know how it sounds, but try to keep an open mind for a minute. How long have you been getting drunk and yelling out what you wanted to happen to those people. And it happened, in the very same way you asked for it to happen, each time. How do you explain that? The evidence doesn't point to you at all, and you would have a pile of it against you by now if you were involved." She nodded towards lawyer-man, "...we would know."

"What makes you so sure about any of this?" Tom asked.

She looked at the floor for several minutes before responding, then whispered, "I've seen it happening to someone else." Regaining her composure, she went on, "I think it always ends with seven people dying, but the 'requester' doesn't get off free. If there are any truths to the myths and legends, there is always a price to pay for the one making these—*requests*."

"And what *is* that price?" Tom wanted to know.

"I don't know that either, but if the current situation is any indication, it won't be pleasant," she replied.

"So what can I do?" Tom asked.

"Be careful what you wish for..." slipped quietly from her mouth.

Catherine stood and collected a book bag that Tom at first thought was just a drab purse to go with the rest of her drab outfit, and in that moment he saw an underlying beauty in her that came on strong and relentlessly. On the cue of her movements, both of her companions stood and left the room ahead of her. "You stay here and read up. I hear you have no place to go at the moment. Maybe you can find a clue I've missed. We're staying in another room...and Tom, don't get drunk. You're going to need all of your wits," she told him.

He was already moving towards her and hadn't heard a thing she had said. He was taken over by adrenaline-fueled lust and tried to lean forward to kiss her, but she snapped her head back as if recoiling from a striking snake.

"We can't do that Tom, ever. We *are* connected, but not in that way. Look around you, there's something serious going on here, and we're running out of time," she said, then turned and closed the door.

A moment of panic overcame him as he had no idea of what room they were in or if they were actually staying at the same motel. In a mad rush, he started to run out the door and try to catch them before they were out of sight when he noticed the piece of paper taped to the door. "Room 127" the note read, obviously in a woman's handwriting. He opened the door and smiled, relieved to see the number "115" on his door.

Tom closed the door and grabbed the book referring to the legends of genies from the table, kicked off his shoes. And stretched out on the bed to peruse the information with an enlightened—but not completely open—mind. The more he read, the more he realized the blatant differences between the ancient forms of the myths and the modern versions. The original stories had been watered down over the ages, to the point of being fairytales instead of what they really were, which were serious warnings. And just as Catherine had mentioned, the recipient of whatever wishes, needs, or deeds granted always paid dearly in the end, often with a similar fate to those which they had wished harm upon. Another thing that stood out to him throughout all of the texts was the fact that in the older, original legends, no good wishes or deeds were performed; only acts of violence and destruction were mentioned.

The room suddenly got cold as he gazed at the sticky note affixed to the page he was scanning, 'No good deeds?' and 'Careful what you wish for...' were both written upon the note and underlined several times.

Tom managed to drift off into a fitful sleep after some time spent watching infomercials on the motel television. He dreamed of swimming in a whiskey tumbler, trying desperately to get purchase on a shard of ice lurking at the edge, away from the towering cubes that would surely crush him. Just as he gained a secured hold on the ice shard, freezing and shivering so bad that the motion radiated ripples outward in a crude outline of the shard, a huge and piercingly high-pitched crash nearly split his eardrums. The sound was deafening and was accompanied by a massive wave of bourbon and water, clearly distinguished by the layered color differences; the darker bourbon pushed up from below the clearer water as the wave neared and grew in size. The impact was massive, though somehow he managed to hold onto his ice shard, albeit with one arm, as the other was repeatedly smashed between the ice shard to which he clung and the wall of the tumbler. The arm was now useless.

Dangling helplessly and slowly slipping off the chunk of ice that was his lifeline, he looked up to see a familiar and very attractive girl with jet-black hair and bright green eyes, raising the toothpick up and out of the glass, which to him was the size of a telephone pole that was sharpened at both ends. She was coming in for another stab. She smiled, and the giant skewer descended directly above him as he tried to suck in as much of the liquid surrounding him as possible to numb himself. He closed his eyes and felt cold on his face and body as the massive stake pierced him through and dragged him below the surface. There was no pain, only cold, and as he looked up through the murky liquid and giant ice cubes, he could clearly see the woman grinning.

Tom woke up in a pool of sweat and out of breath, shivering, yet hot at the same time.

"Screw this crap!" he said to the empty room and got dressed, dialing the familiar cab number in the process. Tom stood outside the door of the room, not wanting to look at the books and notes any longer, and when the cab arrived he ran out to meet it. Tossing a twenty to the driver, he pointed east, away from Park Charles towards the city and said, "The nearest bar," while climbing into the back seat.

The cab dropped off Tom at a strip club just outside of the city, where he found a quiet corner to down several shots of bourbon and work on a pitcher of beer. About halfway through the pitcher and four shots later, an attractive woman with platinum blond hair and piercing green eyes came up and asked to join him.

Looking around his general area, suspecting a joke of some kind, he reluctantly gave in and motioned for her to sit. There was no conversation, not even an exchange of names. Tom watched her intently as she downed two shots, taken by her beauty and vividly green eyes. Without a word, she leaned over and kissed him passionately, and he could smell and taste the sweet hint of bourbon on her. Within a few minutes, the two of them were making out like unbridled teenagers in the back of a car after prom.

The drunker he became, the more of the evening he lost to blackouts. He didn't realize at the time that, one by one, similar looking women replaced one other at his little party and then disappeared in turn. He woke up in the parking lot wedged between two cars with a beer bottle in his right hand, signifying to him that the odds of him having been kicked out and escorted to the parking lot were slim. Satisfied with his assessment, Tom used the door handles and mirrors of the cars to climb himself up into a semi-standing position. He unzipped his jeans and began to urinate, while tipping the bottle of beer up to take a long, hard pull from it. Letting out a huge belch, he zipped his pants and started the process of climbing back down the cars and getting back to his nap when a soft, female voice came from behind him.

"Hey, partner.." the voice called from what seemed like miles away, "...wanna go inside and grab a couple of drinks with me?" she offered, then added, "You look like you need it, and my ride left me to go party with some strippers. What do you say?"

He was lost, but she was so pretty—sandy blonde hair and dark, glassy-green eyes, a beacon of beauty and vibrant sensuality punching through the murky cloud that now surrounded him. She was also dressed like a slutty cowgirl, complete with a red-and-white checkered shirt (tied in a knot at the midriff) and cowboy hat and boots; it was hard for a man in his position—that is, drunk and horny—to ignore an offer like that.

She extended her hand and he saw himself take it in his own as the beer bottle hit the ground and broke into pieces, covering his shoes in beer and bits of glass, though neither looked down.

He stared intently at her as they approached the entrance, where he paused before they got within reach of the outer doors. "I just need to make a quick call, I'll meet you inside," he handed the beauty a twenty and added, "get us a pitcher and some shots to get us started."

She cheerfully smiled and nodded, parading through the double doors like she was in some kind of music video. Tom absently wondered what her soundtrack was. He turned his attention back to the doorman that was looking at him in puzzlement. Tom suspected he was wondering what that hot chick was doing with *him*.

The motel picked up and he asked for Catherine's room. Before she could ask what was going on he interjected, "What did you mean by seeing it happening to someone else?"

A long silence followed. "It's happening to someone I know," she finally replied.

"How many so far?" he asked in a voice that had just a hint of fear in it.

"Seven," she said immediately.

"What happened then?" Tom needed to know.

"I don't know. It's me, Tom. It's happening to me. I used to be married to a very rich man, and I had a life that you probably couldn't imagine. To make a long story short, I was a spoiled, vindictive brat that lashed out at everyone sooner or later and brought drama wherever I went. I said terrible things to people and wished terrible things on people, but then, one day, some of those things started happening to the very people I had wished them on. It was more than coincidence, and I knew right away. I've spent nearly every dime I have on trying to figure out what this is and why it is happening to me, but you are the closest thing to proof or an answer that I've come across."

She carried on, "I don't know what comes next. I guess I hoped that we could figure that out before, well, before anything else happened."

"Was it a woman?" Tom asked quietly, turning back around to face the entrance of the club again. "Was it a woman that came to you?"

After a moment, her voice came through the phone, "No, he's a man...and he looks a lot like you."

Tom stood in silence and didn't notice that the call had dropped until the loud beeping forced him to pull the phone away. He looked around, wide-eyed and scared, when he caught sight of something familiar out of the corner of his eye. He looked back to see the little Chinese girl from the restaurant standing in the parking lot, about five spaces back, staring in his direction. He squinted to be sure of what he was seeing and saw her mouth move, but couldn't hear anything; she was too far away and the noise of the club was drowning out nearly all other sounds. He squinted again and strained to hear what she was saying. The little girl pointed at him, and at that moment, Tom could see her lips forming the words. He no longer needed sound to know what she was saying.

"Careful what you wish for..."

Tom froze in place, heart racing, as he looked back towards the club entrance momentarily. He thought of what was waiting inside for him, and when he looked back, the little girl was gone. Tom shoved his phone in his pocket and stormed back into the club, scanning until he spotted the cowboy hat. She was sitting patiently at the bar, with an empty seat next to her, two shots and a pitcher of beer with glasses at the ready.

Tom grabbed her arm, spun her around in the chair, and began yelling, "Why are you doing this to me? Who are you? *What*...are you? What in the hell is going on?"

She grabbed him by the throat with a strength that surprised a yelp out of him. He was slammed onto the floor and immediately overwhelmed by the pair of burning black eyes that stared into his own with an ancient evil that absorbed all light, reflecting nothing, with only glowing, silvery-green rings as irises. "Careful...

What... You... Wish... For..." she said through clenched teeth, now pointed and serrated, accenting each word with a squeeze of her clawed hand.

Tom clinched his eyes shut and grabbed her throat with all his strength, screaming, "I wish you were dead, I wish you would burn and die! I Wish You Were Dead! I Wish *You* Would Die! Now!"

A piercing scream overwhelmed all other sounds as her pupils suddenly turned a dark red and the green irises disappeared altogether. As he watched from his unenviable vantage point, he followed the wailing, flailing creature that ran through the club and over the pool tables with such speed and force that the billiard balls flung from beneath her feet and across the club at frightening speeds. No one seemed to be distracted by the ruckus as the banshee threw herself through the plate glass window, flying off into the night, shrieking.

Tom stumbled to his feet while massaging his throat and staring at the broken window. He followed his first instinct and headed for the door, not turning around or making eye contact with anyone along the way. Once outside, he started walking towards a gas station just past the end of the parking lot and called the motel again. The clerk answered, and he asked for room 127, but this time the clerk kept mumbling nervously, asking him to wait a moment.

"This is Detective Whitfield with the Park Charles police department, who is this?" the phone emanated.

Tom hung up and stopped in a grassy area that separated the club parking lot from the gas station lot, he dropped his phone and squatted on his haunches with his hands covering his face, knowing exactly what that meant for him: Catherine was now gone, too. He heard sirens, a lot of them, in the distance. The sirens got louder and louder and he could see the flashing lights, even with his hands over his closed eyes. Screeching tires preempted the announcements of, "Get down, get down! Get on the ground now!"

And down he went.

He could hear the muted conversations of other inmates and immediately caught snippets of them discussing him:

"Crazy bastard...that's what he is...serial killer or not, put him in with me and see who leaves in a bag."

"No way, man...there's something weird about that dude. I've heard that he doesn't leave behind any evidence, and when he does, it's explainable and they can't pin anything on him—yet. My girl watches the paranormal shows and hangs out in chat rooms online talking about that mumbo-jumbo, and she says they all think he is some kind of demon that kills with his mind or something like that. The cops just think that he is having someone else do the work, but they can't find any evidence at all to put a real case on him."

A distant clang announced company on the cell block, and the jingling of keys and chains confirmed that officers were coming to take one of them somewhere. He knew long before they got there that they were coming for him, what he didn't expect, was five officers and a full complement of restraints, which included leg shackles and the notorious black box, locked into place at the merger of the two cuffs to further restrict mobility. Not a sound came from the other cells, and as he shuffled unsteadily down the long, poorly-lit walkway, the other inmates just stared as he kept his gaze firmly on his own feet.

Another interrogation room, but this time the inquisitors looked much different, somehow more official and in more expensive suits, complete with laminated identification badges on which he noticed the letters FBI. His insides went cold and he wondered.. "*What now?*"

Of the four agents on the other side of the rectangular table, only one stood. A tall man with salt and pepper hair cropped close to the head, broad shoulders, and blue eyes, who introduced himself as Special Agent Martin. The agent extended a large hand to grasp one of Tom's own, but as he leaned forward and pressed up on the balls of his feet to shake, the officers behind him grabbed him immediately and held him in place.

"It's alright guys, he's not going to try anything funny, are you?" Agent Martin stated with a warm, fatherly smile that was both disarming and authoritative.

"Couldn't even if I wanted to," Tom replied, glancing down at his many restraints. The officers helped him get into his chair and then all but two left the room, standing silently in opposite corners behind him.

"Can we get you anything to drink?"

"A beer and a cigarette would be great.."

Agent Martin laughed heartily, "How about a nice hot cup of coffee instead?"

"I'll take what I can get."

After a few loud slurps of his coffee, Agent Martin said, "Okay, I'm going to get right to the point here. A lot of really smart people think you are a fledgling serial killer and that we should treat you as such and lock you away forever. I, on the other hand, am not convinced yet. So...what we're going to do is get to the bottom of this, one way or the other, right here, today.

"I'm going to ask you some questions, and if you try to jack me around in any way, I'll drop you into a dark, wet holding cell deep in the rectum of the Federal penal system and let the psychiatrists and psychologists have at you for the next twenty years or so. The only thing that is keeping that from happening at this moment in time is me...so don't jack me around. Okay?"

Tom thought briefly and replied, "Sure, but if we're really getting to the point here, then don't jack me around either. The only reason you're here is that there is no real evidence against me, and we all know it. That's the only reason you haven't dropped me into that cell yet, and it's the only reason you're trying to be so polite. So let's cut the crap and get this over with...I need to get drunk...I've had a rough couple of days, you know?"

"Yes, yes, I do know. And you're right, sort of. We don't have a lot of strong evidence, yet, but the circumstantial evidence is piling up on you, buddy—and sometimes that is all it takes. We have more than enough justification to detain you indefinitely right now, if for nothing more than the general safety of the public. People keep dying around you, pal, and not of natural causes.

"Did you know that Rooster from the bar is dead? Someone beat the crap out him and shoved a cue stick up his anus until it punched through his insides. Now that's exactly, to the word, how you publicly stated that you wished he would die. And I know that you know Catherine is dead. We have a record of you calling her before and after she was strangled to death in her motel room," Martin added.

"We found Kyle today, face-down in a ditch with a knife wound in his kidney, and no money or credit cards in his wallet. Did you wish that on him?" Martin pressed.

"I'm sure I did," Tom said quietly.

"Sharon from the bar is missing. Did you know that? Did you wish anything on her?"

Tom sat there, motionless and emotionless, staring off into space.

Agent Martin exploded, "I just told that two more people you know are dead and another is missing, and you didn't even bat an eye! What is going on here?" He screamed the last part, slamming his hands onto the table for emphasis.

"It's over now," Tom mumbled, "I got her...it's over now."

After being shown the security camera footage from the strip club and seeing himself partying alone, yelling at no one and rolling on the floor by himself, looking like he was having a seizure, he let it all out. He provided every detail he could remember from the first meeting in the bar to the strip club. Eventually, Agent Martin, looking haggard and ruffled, gave up and let him go, but ordered around-the-clock surveillance on him. Tom called a cab and went straight to the nearest bar, ordering seven shots of Jack Daniels and a pitcher of beer—a shot for each dead person weighing on his conscience.

His rapidly-intoxicating mind could not suppress the chain reaction of thoughts slamming together in his head, so he ordered more shots and tried to drown them. Jimmy, Catherine, Louie, Lisa, Chuck, Kyle, and even Rooster...their faces swam in his subconscious and all cast accusing stares that were perceptible through their lifeless, milky-white and bulging eyes. All except for Chuck, he was just a lump of shredded meat. Tom suspected Sharon's face would join them soon.

He sensed the presence before he heard anything and turned his gaze to the glass of beer in front of him, locking on and focusing intently on it, not wanting to see what he knew was there.

"Hey there, Tommy Boy, how's it hangin'?" the sweet, soft voice said to the right side of his head. "You really didn't think that would work...did you? You can't kill us..."

At this, his head snapped up and he locked eyes with her.

She was grinning. "Yes, I said *us*... We are eternal, Tommy Boy. We've always been and always will be."

She produced a frosty glass, from where he had no idea, and poured herself a beer, then took the seat next to him. Something in the background caught his attention and he took several squinting moments to make the connection. It was the two 'lawyers' at the back of the bar. They were obviously watching him closely and trying to be nonchalant to the point of being obvious. Glancing around further, he noticed two other men at a table near the end of the bar, recognizing one of them as an agent from the morning's inquisition at the city jail.

I'm quite the popular person these days, he thought sarcastically. "So...what now?" he asked her, once again staring intently through his glass of beer, his cigarette burning lazily in an ashtray, trailing smoke across his view.

"Nothing," she said, then slammed the entire glass of beer and got up, turned as if to walk away, then stopped with her back to his. "I'm done with you...time to move on. You got your seven wishes and you killed seven people. You wanted them dead, in very detailed ways. You said so yourself, out loud, seven times for each one...and *I* heard you. Now you have what you wished for.."

"So that's it; it's over now?"

"For you, it is."

"Again...what now?"

She had somehow moved back beside him without making a sound, whispering into his ear, her warm breath moving across the side of his head, "A lot of people have wished harm on you, too, Tommy Boy, especially in light of recent developments. We'll see each other again soon..."

And then she was gone.

The agents and 'lawyers' watched as the crazy-looking, disheveled man at the bar finally stopped talking to himself, his shoulders visibly slumping, and ordered seven more shots, loudly declaring with obvious cynicism to his glass of beer, "Careful what you wish for!"

FAIRYTALE, FOLKLORE, & MYTH. REIMAGINED & REMASTERED.

WILLIAM PETERSEN is a Missouri native and life-long resident, an avid outdoor enthusiast, and constant writer. Born in the 1970s, William's career has taken him from website design and promotion, music promotion and advertising to commercial non-fiction writing. Early in the new century, William began writing fiction for his own entertainment, which eventually led to the consideration of publication.

William's writing is heavily influenced by the natural world, as well as the ever-changing course and endless possibilities of the human race. William has written three books, with a fourth in the works, along with seven short stories that explore the darker side of *What If?* William's first published story, an urban fantasy novella entitled *Mythical*, was guided and edited by none other than best-selling author Piers Anthony.

LINKS

http://theinwardspiral.wordpress.com
https://twitter.com/WideWorldOfWill

WILLIAM PETERSEN | 499

Brenna and the Spaceman

by Rebekah Phillips

THE knock at the door came on a Thursday in the midst of a thunderstorm. My father was lying on the beaten-up couch, sleeping, the fumes of his shirt making my youngest sister dizzy. Mom was singing quietly as she made supper with the help of myself and two of my other sisters, trying not to wake dad.

For a moment, we thought that the knock was just a strange quirk of the thunder. Little Alyssa covered her ears and howled, and Nikki demanded an encore by pounding a wooden spoon against a metal pan she had stolen from the sink.

Hazel, who was born two years after me, neatly took the pan away from Nikki and then looked at me. "I think," she said, "we might actually have a visitor."

"Don't be stupid," I started to say, "who would be out in this weather?"

But the pounding had started again, and this time, a human voice punctuated it. "Is anyone home?"

It was clearly a male speaking, even though his words were half blown away by the wind. I raised my eyebrows and looked at my mother, who wiped her hands on a towel and went to open the door.

Standing there in the door was a pathetic little man, soaked and shivering, his lips nearly as blue as his eyes. Hazel gasped beside me and poked me in the side. "Brenna," she whispered, "Brenna. Look."

That's when I noticed he was wearing a spaceman's uniform, black as the empty space between planets. I looked at Hazel sharply as she stepped closer to him.

I didn't like knowing that a spaceman was in town. They usually meant trouble. My mother could remember a time when nobody liked the earthbound military—the Navy and the Marines and the like—but that resentment is long gone. The earthbound protected us from threats we did know about, or, at least, knew a *little* about; the spacemen handled problems none of us could ever begin to understand. Sure, they did good things like divert asteroids so they didn't plummet straight into the Earth and mess up our already destroyed atmosphere, and they mined other planets so we could import fresh water. But who knows what else they did up there in the sky, their space station shining almost as brightly as the moon?

"Hazel, get this man a blanket," Mom said sharply, and Hazel left, barely masking her irritation at being asked to leave the spaceman's presence. Mom ushered the shivering man inside, and sat him down at the table. "Would you like to stay for supper? It isn't much, but it will be warm."

"I c-can't stay," the spaceman said, shivering violently. Hazel dashed back into the room with the blanket from our bed and she threw it, roughly, over his shoulders. I scowled. Of course, she would have to give him *our* blanket. Now I would have to sleep under a damp cover. "I was s-sent on ur-urgent b-business."

Mom's eyes flicked to me, and then back at the man. My stomach twisted. Urgent business? What type of urgent business could a spaceman have here, in the middle of nowhere?

Hazel sat down at the man's side. "I'm sure it can wait until you've had something to eat," she said.

The man shook his head. "No. The mission is clear. I can't waste any time." He clutched my blanket around his shoulders and looked desperately at my mother. "Is this the house of Brenna Wilkes?"

Hazel froze and glared at me hatefully before peeling away from the spaceman and stalking towards the kitchen counter. Mom's eyes glazed over, and I watched her mouth harden into a sharp line. "No," she snapped, coming to life again in an instant.

I held my breath and tried to look as if I, too, had never heard of a Brenna Wilkes. Hazel was looking at me, her lips just parted; the truth was not sitting easily on her tongue. All over the house, I could see the lie on my sibling's faces, and the spaceman saw it, too. He watched as everyone looked directly at me, and then his own brown eyes swung towards me, pleading with me silently.

And, without knowing why, I said, "I have been called by that name."

Relief poured into his face and brightened his cheeks. He half-stood, still clutching my blanket to him, and reached out a hand towards me. "Brenna," he breathed.

On the couch, my father awoke with a start.

The spaceman turned towards my father sharply, watching with the rest of us as my father fell off of the couch and then stood. I could tell already he was in the throes of a vicious hangover. His lips were pulled back in a snarl and his eyes were mean and bloodshot. "Water," he demanded in a raspy voice, and Allison ran to get him a cup.

He drank the entire glass, and then made Allison refill it again and again. His eyes were still unfocused, and his left hand was twitching. When he had had three cups without stopping he dropped the cup on the ground and wiped his mouth with the back of his hand. Then, surveying the room, he saw the spaceman standing there. "What is he doing here?" he growled.

The spaceman stepped towards my father. "I've come for Brenna Wilkes," he said. "And, if you give her to me, I will make you wealthier than you have ever imagined."

For a moment, my father stared at him, and then he started to laugh. "You want to marry her? Is that it? You'll regret spending any dowry on her, I promise you that."

The spaceman flushed all the way to the tips of his ears, and I kept my eyes on the threadbare carpet and hid my fists behind my back. "I'm not going to marry her."

"Then what do you want her for?" Dad had stopped laughing and was rubbing his head now. Too much thought was required to solve this riddle. If *I* didn't even know what was going on, there was no way my dad could understand.

"I'm not allowed to say. It's official military business," the spaceman replied then turned towards me.

"I won't go," I said immediately. "I'm needed here."

"Your family will be compensated." He stepped towards me, the eager, puppyish look firmly back on his face. He was incredibly young; I had not realized that before. He was probably only a few years older than myself. "We are prepared to offer you wealth beyond what you've ever imagined. Your family will want for nothing."

I looked at my mother and at my sisters and brothers, who looked up at me with big eyes, confused and worried. "I won't. I *can't*."

"Wealthier than I have ever imagined," my father said softly to himself, looking around the room.

My father was a farmer, trying desperately to grow grapes in our vineyard, apples in our orchard, and corn in the many acres that surrounded our small house. When I was young, he also owned cows and hogs, but poverty had taken them from us. We had eaten or sold them long ago.

I do not know if it was because the earth beneath our feet was tired after years of abuse, or whether it was because my father was useless as a farmer, but we had never been able to do more than just eke out an existence for ourselves. And every year or two my mother had another child, bearing the burden as gracefully as she could. My father, on the other hand, took to drinking. In his way, he could forget the fact that his seed had multiplied in unlooked for ways, and now the truth of it wandered the barren fields barefoot in dirty, ragged clothes. He could forget that the crops we had planted had failed for three years now, and that the house we were living in was run-down and ugly, and that many nights his oldest children went to bed hungry so that the youngest could have a small portion.

It did not surprise me to see that his bleary eyes looked around and saw the chipped paint, the scratched table, and the smelly and worn couch, and feel an itch in his fingers. He could have the world. And what was the cost of this unheard of luxury? Only his eldest daughter. The consequences could be hanged. If he never saw me again, at least my absence would not be in vain; he could grow fat with food and drink, surrounded by beautiful things.

He turned to look at me and said, "You should go."

My mother sat down heavily at the table, passing a hand over her stomach. "I'm needed here," I said firmly, crossing over to her and putting my arms around her thin shoulders. Her hand covered mine, and she looked at me gratefully.

"I would go," Hazel said longingly.

The spaceman shook his head. "It must be Brenna," he said.

If I went, we would be compensated. Wealth beyond anything I had ever imagined. Hazel could go to school on that money. Alyssa wouldn't have to wear clothes that had been altered and re-altered so many times there was no saving them, and Nikki could buy the flute she wanted so much. My mother might be able to grow round with something besides new life.

Perhaps I would do more good if I left. At least I would have the small satisfaction of knowing I had been sold for great wealth, and not for a paltry amount. I wondered if that was something I could brag about: "Yeah, I sold myself for unimaginable wealth."

"You've heard what she has to say," my mother said firmly. "Her answer is no."

"I see," the spaceman said. His shoulder slumped heavily, and the light went out of his eyes. "Thank you for your time." He turned and left, closing the door softly behind him. Hazel moved over to the sink and started to wash the dishes, banging the pans and sloshing soapy water everywhere. She was frowning fiercely, and looked like she might cry.

"Wealthier than I have ever imagined," my father said.

I looked around the house. More clearly than I had in years, I saw how the roof sagged, and the mold in the corner, and the leak that was just beginning to sprout over the couch. I saw how Alyssa's cheekbones protruded, and that Nikki's pants now resembled something closer to capris. "Wait!" I shouted, and I pulled my hand from my mother's. "Wait for me, please! Wait!"

"Brenna," my mother said, astonished. I bent down and kissed her roughly.

"I have to," I said, feeling hot tears prick at my eyes. "I would never forgive myself if I had the opportunity to make all of your lives better and I didn't do it. Don't you see?"

I opened the door and went outside, hearing my father stumble after me. The storm buffeted me, the rain freezing my skin. It was almost impossible to see. I ran blindly, calling, "Wait—I will come with you!" I stumbled across the yard until a pair of hands grabbed mine and pulled me close, and a flashlight lit up the night.

The spaceman stood beside a small, two-person shuttle. His eyes lit up when he saw me. "You're coming," he said, not even noticing my father, who was somehow making his half-drunken self teeter across the yard. "He will be so glad."

I blinked. "He?" I repeated, but my father interrupted.

"Here she is," he said, putting an arm around me. "And now—I believe you promised money."

I slunk out from under his arm. He hadn't even said good-bye and he was already demanding payment. The spaceman nodded, his face blank, and he pulled a clear bank card out of his pocket, with an account number taped on the face of it. Father snatched it out of his hands, crowed, and vanished back inside. This behavior did not surprise me, but the twang of pain I felt did. I would probably never see him again, and he had not even given me a glance.

"I'm glad you're coming," the spaceman told me. He opened the shuttle door and helped me inside. I had never been inside a shuttle before, and found the cramped space awkward. It reminded me very much of being tucked inside of a large egg. I managed to slip into my seat, but could not figure out how the belt worked. The spaceman leaned over me, apologizing frequently, and helped me buckle in, crossing thick belts across my chest and over my stomach.

I kept my eyes on the ground as we took off. I wanted to fix the way it looked in my mind—the way the house seemed lit from within, the leaves of our tree blowing in the wind, the smoking chimney of the house next door. My nails dug half-moon prints into my palms, and I forced myself breathe evenly.

"Are you afraid?" the spaceman asked me.

I looked away from the ground, now a muddy mess of dark green and black rivers. The shuttle rocketed faster than any craft I had ever been in, and already we were probably halfway out of the atmosphere. We were in the heavens now, breaking through the cloud cover to the stars. Home was behind me, invisible to my eyes, and there was no going back. "No," I said. "I am not afraid."

His name was Tim. He guided the shuttle to the stars silently, guiding me to the large space station that swallowed the whole universe. I gasped. It had to be as big as the moon. He navigated around dozens of other shuttles, all going to unknown destinations, and finally slowed by a giant spaceship docked at the station.

It looked brand-new; it shone so brightly I almost thought it was a star. "Beautiful, isn't she?" Tim asked quietly, his voice full of reverential wonder. "Her name is the *Ursus Maritimus*. It's Latin for—"

"White bear," I breathed.

This I knew, at least. In school I had done dozens of projects on the polar bear. Nearly extinct, I had fallen in love with the animal the first time I saw a picture of its inky black eyes in my biology textbook.

"Sea bear, actually," Tim corrected me. "But—polar bear, colloquially."

The spaceship was magnificent. I could see the name, painted in white, towards the head of the ship. In fact, the ship reminded me a little of a bear; the shape took on the contours of a bear's ears and sloping shoulders. It was impossible to pin down, but it did not seem an accident that the ship had been given the name *Ursus Maritimus*. A hatch opened in the side, and the shuttle gently flew inside and stopped on the floor.

The inside of the ship was stunning: Gleaming with cleanliness, everything white and silver, with giant windows in every room so everywhere I went I could see the stars beyond. The sight of them made me gasp. They were so much more abundant, so much more beautiful, here. Tim nudged me to keep me going.

He led me down a maze of hallways. He walked quickly, and I had to trot to keep up. We ran up and down stairs until I was too out of breath to even ask where we were going. Finally we arrived in front of a set of silver doors. Tim stopped, smiled, and held the door open for me. I looked at him hesitantly before I went through.

The room to which he had led me was the bridge. The captain's chair was empty, gazing silently out of the large window towards the universe beyond. Dozens of lights were flickering on the dashboard. Bending over, I saw a stream of words running across a screen: *oxygenation levels steady, heating systems at seventy percent, ship currently docked.* What concerned me, however, was the one word at the top of the screen that did *not* move: Autopilot.

"General Ellison will be here in a moment," Tim said, turning to go. "She'll explain everything."

"No need to wait," I heard a woman's voice say. "I'm here now."

Tim snapped to attention beside me. I turned around to see a frightening woman. Her nose was long and pointed, with a wart at the tip. But it was her eyes that worried me; they dared me to defy her, and warned of the consequences of doing so. She smiled coldly at the two of us. "Thank you, Timothy," she said. "That is all. You may go."

Tim all but bolted out of the door, leaving me with the scary troll of a woman. I crossed my arms unthinkingly, and then, wondering if it made me look scared, forced myself to let them hang at my side. General Ellison took me in, circling me as if I were no more than a piece of meat.

"So," the general said, "you're Brenna. You certainly don't look like much."

Ouch. That smarted.

"We had this ship specially made," she said, turning towards me. "Unfortunately, it is not complete. And there were...conditions." She scowled, and her nose twitched.

"Conditions," I repeated carefully.

"Even generals are subject to certain rules," she said. "Unfortunately."

I forced myself to take a step forward. "Just tell me what I can do to help, and I'll do it."

Standing so close to her, I realized we were the same height. General Ellison must have realized this at the same time I did, because her nostrils flared with anger.

"Everything will become clear to you shortly."

"You're not going to tell me?" I asked. General Ellison only smiled mockingly.

"Tell me, Brenna," she said, spitting my name out like a seed, "are you afraid?"

"No," I said, more bravely than I felt.

"Well," she said, "you will be."

She turned and walked away, leaving me alone in the room. I stood there for a moment, shocked. The room seemed a great deal emptier without her vibrant presence. Rubbing my hands over my arms—it was chilly in space—I turned towards the dashboard, hoping to make some sense of what was going on. Motion caught my eye. I could see Tim's shuttle flying out in space, heading towards the space station.

That was when I realized the space ship was moving. The ship had started gliding forward so smoothly I had not noticed. We couldn't be going very fast. I frowned and bent over the dashboard, looking for coordinates—anything.

A strange muffled sound, almost like a cry, reached my ears. I frowned again. It was clear to me, from following Tim around, that no one else was on the ship. Frightened that something was going wrong with the ship so soon after it had started towards its unknown destination, I turned around, hoping to find a manual to decode the flashing lights and came face to face with a polar bear.

He stood at least a head taller than I did, and he crept towards me on paws that couldn't hide their sharp, black nails. He moaned in the back of his throat and then bent his head towards me, so his nose was only a few inches from my face. I thought I would smell his breath, made up of rancid, rotting meat, but when I finally forced myself to take a breath all I could smell was fresh winter snow.

For several long seconds we stood there, nose-to-nose, with me hardly daring to breathe. His eyes watched me carefully, and they looked almost human—but I had to be imagining that spark of intelligence in them. I had to be imagining all of this. An hour ago I was surrounded by my family, listening to the rain fall on the roof and, in some cases, falling onto the floor of my house. And I had traded all of that in to be eaten by a polar bear.

I regretted every homework assignment I had done on polar bears in school. I regretted leaving home. I closed my eyes, and waited to feel his teeth on my throat.

Then the white bear said, "Brenna."

My name sounded funny in his mouth, more like a low rumble made up only of vowels. His head bobbed from side to side angrily, and I stepped back, certain that this talking bear was about to succumb to his nature and maul my face. But he lifted his head and managed to say, "Follow me, please," before slowly ambling out of the bridge.

I put a shaking hand to my face, checking to make sure it was still there. I was intact; the bear hadn't touched me. But it had talked. The bear had talked to me. Bears didn't talk. Apes could use sign language; parrots could mimic human language; dolphins had a language of their own. But polar bears, speaking English as if it made sense to them—saying my *name*? Without thinking, I charged after the polar bear, all thoughts of mauling forgotten.

He pawed at a door and opened it to reveal a kitchen, the first truly warm room I had encountered. Already on a table was a full meal: Fish, veal, potatoes, vegetables. "We didn't know what you would like." He nodded at the table.

"I don't believe it," I said.

"Sit," the bear said, and I sat. He was too big to argue with. "Eat."

My stomach rumbled, and I obeyed. I loaded my plate with food and started to eat.

"Where is everyone?" I asked as calmly as I could. I could not be the only human on this ship. A spaceship of this size was not made for a girl and a polar bear, and the way General Ellison talked about it, this ship was destined for great things. If the spacemen wanted to mess around with polar bears in space, that was their prerogative, but I still didn't see what a poor farm girl had to do with any of it.

"There is no one else." He blinked and shook his head again. I wondered if he could possibly have fleas, or something that would make him shake his head like that.

"What do you mean, no one else?"

He didn't answer—assuming, correctly, that the statement spoke for itself—and looked at my plate. "Eat."

Obligingly, I stuffed a forkful of something in my mouth. "There have to be other people on board," I said. "It's impossible for a ship this size to run on autopilot with a girl and a talking polar bear!"

If it was possible, there was a touch of humor in the bear's voice. "Not."

"It is!" I insisted. "What is the point of this? Why am I here with a talking polar bear? And speaking of excellent questions—how can you talk?"

"I cannot tell you," the polar bear said. "Now eat your dinner."

I crossed my arms. "I won't eat another bite until you tell me why I'm here."

"Then you will go hungry." He stood and walked to the door. "There is only one rule, Brenna Wilkes," he said, turning back so I could see his strange black eyes. "And, so long as you keep this one rule, all shall be well. Many strange things will happen on this journey, but you must ask no questions. The more questions you ask, the worse it shall be. Do you understand this?"

I stared at him. "No."

He sighed deeply, rumbling in his chest. "It will be made clear with time," he said. "Just be patient, and ask me no questions."

And he loped out of the room, out into the endless maze of hallways of the spaceship named for the talking polar bear.

When I finished eating, I went back out into the hallway and saw the polar bear waiting there for me. He led me silently to my room, and I didn't try to press the silence. All I wanted to know was what my family was doing now. Were they all up late, pressed against a large fire, plotting how to spend the money when the sun rose in the morning? I pressed my hand against my eyes, keeping the tears there from falling. *Things will look better in the morning*, I told myself. Surely everything would become clear after a night of sleep.

I had to stand in the door for a long moment before my tired eyes managed to convey to my brain that it was a bed I saw. And such a magnificent bed, too. The covers were thick and a deep, emerald green, with at least five pillows sitting up waiting for a head to support. There was also a large wooden chest and a desk. I went to the chest and found it was full of clothing, all of it in my size.

"Good night," the polar bear said, but when I turned around, he was gone. I returned to the chest full of clothing and dug out a nightgown and slipped into the adjoining bathroom, which was as big as my cottage back home. I quickly changed and then turned the light off—and couldn't see a thing.

Shocked, I cried out, and then flipped the light switch back on. I had not realized that space would be so *dark*—even the far-off stars hadn't filled the room with any light. Shivering and chastising myself, a hardy farm girl, for screaming about something as silly as the dark, I left the light on and then crawled into bed, resolving that I would leave it on just for tonight.

Sleep was slow to come. I was tired, but it seemed impossible to fall asleep with the light on. Getting up to turn it off, though, felt impossible. I felt glued to the bed, unwilling to face the mind-numbing dark again. I managed to fall into a heavy doze, eventually, something that vaguely resembled sleep.

I woke with a start early in the morning—or, at least, it felt like it. There was no clock to tell me what time it was, and no moon to measure the progress of the night. For a moment, I lay in bed, feeling my heart race, wondering what it was that had woken me. That was when I realized that the light in my room had gone off, and it was pitch black.

The light was probably timed to go off when it didn't sense motion—that, or the polar bear had come to check on me and turned it off himself. The image of the polar bear trying to flick a switch with his giant paws made me smile. I turned over in bed, trying to tell myself that this mystery was a *good* thing. I couldn't baby myself about the dark like this; I needed to grow up and face it. As I rolled over, I slid slightly towards the center of the bed. Something was pressing the bed on the right side down—no. Not something. *Someone.*

Someone was in bed with me.

My first thought, oddly, was exhilaration: The white bear had been lying! I was not the only human on this ship! My second, fittingly, was terror.

But, I reasoned, he—I assumed it was a he, because he smelt of soap and grass and man-musk—had not tried to touch me, and he hadn't even awoken me when he came in. I reached out to touch his shoulder and wake him up, but something stopped me. There was a barrier there, and my hand jerked away, my fingertips tingling. I frowned. He had to be wearing a charged electrical field.

The United Nations had decreed charged electrical fields inhumane, but I knew that they were still used secretly by the military as a torture device and occasionally worn by police officers when they escorted dangerous criminals. I could not touch the man in the bed, but he could touch me—and if he did, it would burn.

What could the spacemen want with a near-empty spaceship, a farmgirl, a talking polar bear, and a man with a charged electrical field surrounding him? The questions stacked, one on top of the other, just like a Jenga tower with no solution. There was no one to ask. The man in my bed was barred from me, and the polar bear had made no secret about his disdain for questions.

In the morning, I would ask the polar bear if there was another room—for a ship this size, there had to be another that was suited to me. But the stranger's presence was comforting, especially in the terrible darkness of space. Closing my eyes, I fell into a much deeper sleep than the one before, and woke the next morning to a still-dark room, the man who had spent the night with me was gone.

Perhaps I had dreamt the whole thing. I sat up and stretched, then made the bed, just as I did every day at home. As I bent over to straighten one of the pillows, I smelled the scent of grass and soap and man again. There had been someone in my bed last night.

I got up and went in search of the breakfast room again, hoping that today my questions would be answered and that last night would be explained to me. When I arrived in the mess, though, nothing had changed. The polar bear was lying down on the floor, and he lifted his head when he saw me. "Good morning," he said. "Did you sleep well?"

He asked it so innocently I wondered if he could possibly know about my nighttime visitor. He had seemed so convinced yesterday about the two of us being the only creatures on board the ship. "No, not really," I said, going for a half-truth. "I'm not used to such dark nights."

His black eyes regarded me carefully. "Are you afraid of the dark?"

"No," I spluttered, indignant. But then I remembered how my heart had stopped in terror when I first turned out the light. "At least—I never was before."

"You will get used to it," the bear told me solemnly.

"How do you know?" I asked, forgetting, briefly, the edict against my asking questions of any sort. His eyes darkened, and—for an instant—I thought I saw the animal in him. Then I blinked, and it was gone. Except for the gooseflesh on my arms, the look might never have been there at all.

"Space is always alarming at first," he told me. "But the adaptability of humans is astounding."

He laughed—or, I thought he did. It sounded like marbles were clacking in his throat. I sat down at the table and rubbed my thumb over the side of the plate. "I was wondering if I could get a new room."

The bear looked down at his paws. "There are no other rooms."

"But on a ship this big—"

"You must stay where you are," he said. He stood, and his eyes stared me down urgently. "We put you there for a reason, Brenna."

"But—" He turned to go, and I swallowed my questions. He was my only company on this ship, the stranger in my bed aside. "Don't go," I said.

The bear hovered for a moment, one paw in the air, and then he sat again on the floor.

"You never told me," I said, as casually as I could, "what your name was."

The polar bear's ear twitched as he thought, and he considered my carefully-posed question. "You may call me Bear," he said.

That was victory enough.

The day came when I had discovered every room in the spaceship. I was tired. Bored. I was tired of having questions with no answers, and I was bored with this ship. I took to spending my days in bed, and, if I ever left it, lounging in the captain's bridge, watching the stars and pretending they were getting closer.

Bear started to notice. He would watch me without saying anything, and at dinner, if he tried to make me talk, I answered in one-word syllables. "Are you unwell?" he finally asked as I dozed in the captain's chair, watching random lights flash and blink at me.

I considered him. Sometime in the weeks I had been aboard the spaceship, Bear had become a familiar figure to me. I no longer jumped when I saw him, or looked around for a place to hide when I heard his footfalls. He looked as if he might have been concerned—emotions were hard to read in his eyes. The more powerfully he felt something, the more I thought I could see it reflected in his black eyes.

"Is it true," I asked, not caring that it was a question, "that a polar bear's skin is black, underneath the white fur?"

He blew air through his nose and pawed at the ground. "Brenna. Answer me. Are you unwell?"

"And what's with the questions?" I continued. "I can't ask any, but you can ask as many as you like?" Bear's head was close to the ground, and he was growling, but I ignored him. "It's *natural* to ask questions, Bear. You know what *isn't* natural? Talking polar bears. Refusing to answer questions. Locking a girl up in a spaceship with the assurance that her family will become wealthy. Locking a girl up in a spaceship *with a talking polar bear*."

I spun around in the captain's chair, giddy with my pent-up questions. Bear was still growling, and his eyes looked like a light had been turned off. I didn't care. I was drunk on my bravery. "So what's the deal, Bear? Why this giant ship—*Ursus Maritimus*—aptly named for you? Why the human crew of one? *Why is there a man in my bed every night?*"

Bear moaned, and then turned and left. I laughed, almost delighted, and spun around and around again in my chair. Then I began to feel sorry for him. I had learned first-hand that my questions seemed to only cause him pain, and there I was, purposefully throwing question after question at him.

"I'm not sorry, though," I said to myself, and then, louder, "I'm not sorry! It's all true!"

Just because it was true, though, did it make things right? I worried my lower lip and at last stood. I would go and apologize to Bear. I would tell him the truth: That I was not unwell as much as homesick and bored.

I left the captain's room and started to creep around tentatively. I did not know if Bear had a room to which he would return; in my search of the ship, I hadn't found anything that stood out to be as completely belonging to Bear. In fact, I hadn't given much thought to what Bear did when he wasn't around me. He seemed to disappear and reappear, and I had never questioned it. *An odd thing not to notice, Miss Curiosity*, I thought sourly.

Bear was pacing back and forth, his head weaving like a snake's, by the ship's pool. When I saw him, I halted, stunned. I remembered vaguely that this was typical bear behavior; in every zoo I had ever visited, I had been told that bears in captivity paced endlessly. Zookeepers still didn't know why they did it. Caged myself, I wondered if I might understand what he was going through.

"Bear," I whispered, crouching low. "Bear. Talk to me."

Bear moaned, but he didn't meet my gaze. He continued to pace back and forth next to the pool. For a moment, I watched him and his watery reflection creep back and forth. What scared me most was that I could no longer recognize anything human in him, as I had been able to before—the humor in his eyes when I told a joke, the way he almost seemed to smile when he was amused, the way he had of rubbing his front feet together when he was nervous or embarrassed.

I closed my eyes and thought for a long moment. Then I opened my eyes and started to talk.

"The reason I asked about if you had black skin underneath," I said awkwardly, slow to warm up to my story, "is because there was a polar bear in a story I once read. It was about a man who sold his birthright. He was half-black and half-white, in a time when black people didn't have the same rights as white people. He had no name, just like you, but some people called him the ex-colored man. And the ex-colored man wanted to be a musician."

Slowly, I recounted the story, about the man who wanted to play the blues, chronicling Negro folk songs and proving to the world that black Americans had a culture. He attempted college but had his money stolen and had to fend for himself. He integrated with the Cubans, learning to speak Spanish, but his real test was when he moved to New York City to pass as a white man. He wouldn't have managed it but for the help of a millionaire benefactor.

"The millionaire fell in love with him," I said, "and took him around the world. But before they had even made it to Europe, the man saw an iceberg. It glowed brightly, like it were a million different colors, and he looked and looked for a polar bear, believing that on every iceberg there would be a polar bear. But he could not find a polar bear."

Bear roused himself, just a tad. He had stopped pacing as I told the story, although his head continued to sway alarmingly. "Why?" he asked, his voice as rough and bear-like as I had ever heard it.

"Because he was the polar bear," I said. "Metaphorically, I mean. He gave up his black self to become a white man, and marry a white woman, and have white children. And while he loved his wife and children, he regretted giving up his identity every day. Especially after his wife died."

His head stopped swaying as he considered this. "So it wasn't worth it."

I paused. "I'm not sure what you mean."

"The man. He struggled for so long to one end but chose the easy road. And it wasn't worth it."

I kicked off my shoes and slipped my feet in the water, watching the way the lights overhead reflected on its surface. "No," I said. "I don't think giving yourself up is ever worth it."

Bear looked at me thoughtfully. Then he looked at the pool and dived in. The splash he made soaked me, and I spluttered indignantly. "Bear!" I shouted when he broke the surface. Water dripped from his fur. Soaked, he looked thinner. Not at all as scary as I had taken him to be the first time I had seen him.

He showed his teeth in what—had he been human—would have been a smirk. "Come in," he said. "The water's fine!" And he went under again, using his giant paws to propel him back and forth.

I laughed; I couldn't help it. Then I slid off of the lip of the pool, submerging myself until Bear and I rested almost nose-to-nose under the water. I blew a stream of bubbles his way and he took off, looking behind him to see if I would follow. I raced after him, knowing that a mere human could not hope to beat a polar bear, but trying to anyway.

It was then that I knew Bear would be no help to me in discovering who my stranger was. I would have to discover who he was, and the mystery of the *Ursus Maritimus*, myself.

That night, before I went to bed, I slipped away from Bear and snuck onto the front deck. There, hidden in the emergency panel, was a flashlight and a few candles. Breathing a sigh of relief, I pocked both items, along with a small pack of matches. Flashlights didn't always work with electrical fields; too much electricity distorted the flashlight's own inner workings, rendering it useless. Candles, archaic and obsolete as they might have been, worked best when dealing with high voltage.

I lay awake and refused to let myself sleep. When I found myself starting to doze off, I reminded myself that I wasn't just doing this to get answers for myself—I was hoping to rescue the stranger as well.

I do not remember when the stranger entered the room. There was no sound at all. I lay there, wide awake, I am certain, and then felt the mattress dip on my left. The stranger was in bed with me. Exultant, I tried to breathe evenly, and trick the stranger into thinking I was asleep. I waited for an agonizingly long time, until I was sure he was asleep, and then I leaned over and reached for my pilfered items.

Thinking that it wouldn't hurt, I tried the flashlight first. For a moment, it looked like it would light up. The bulb in the center glowed faintly, pulsed once, and then died. I stifled a sigh. It had been worth a shot. At least I had the candles, even though their light would be hesitant, and nowhere near as good as the flashlight's beam would have been.

Striking a match, I held the flame towards the candle, but it refused to catch. Instead, it slipped down the thin matchstick and bit me on my fingers. "Ow!" I cried, sucking on my fingers. The stranger beside me stirred, but didn't wake. I tried again, but this time the matchstick refused to light at all, no matter how many times I tried.

I pulled out a third matchstick and lit it easily, the brightness of it blinding me. It caught the wick on the candle easily and, within moments, was shining in the room. I could see the green velvet sheets and the soft green carpet. Turning, I cast the little light onto the sleeping figure beside me. He was turned away from me, so all I could see was his dark skin. Slowly getting out of bed, shielding the flame with my hand, I crept towards his side of the bed, so I could see his face.

He was beautiful. His skin was a rich brown, like mahogany, like the soft feathers on a robin. I wondered if he might be as soft as a bird's wing. As if to contrast his skin, he wore a white shirt. It only served to make him darker. Without thinking, I leaned closer, wanting to take in every detail of his face—the curve of his nose, the set of his eyes, the part of his lips. I got too close. Forgetting that candles are made of wax, that they are not the same as a flashlight, I foolishly let a single drop of candle wax fall onto his shoulder.

He was awake in an instant, and I stumbled back. His eyes pierced through me. "You," I gasped, recognizing the black eyes instantly. They were Bear's eyes.

"I thought you would have known better," he hissed. Without the bear's thick tongue impeding his language, I almost didn't understand him. There was also a slight accent in his words I couldn't place. "The more we run to the stars the more we forget the old ways. I thought that you, a poor man's daughter, would know what was at stake here!"

"I don't understand." Slowly, I tried to stand up, and Bear rose, too. He was tall, taller than me, and broad; he invoked too much of Bear even in his human form, and all I could do was cower against the wall, hating myself for it.

"General Ellison will be pleased," he continued bitterly, running a hand over his head. "She hoped this would fail from the start. She hates rules, and being boxed in; this only happened because of General Nolan."

"You're not making any sense!" I cried, forcing myself to stand tall. His black eyes flicked back to me, and I nearly stumbled again.

"I'm not? You wanted answers, Brenna—so listen! Ellison wants her own glorious army. And what better army than one made of creatures with the rationale of man but the raw strength of an animal? I volunteered, unthinkingly—cursed to this experiment of how long a man can live in a bear's body without being strangled by it."

"But something went wrong."

"Yes. This creature she made of me, with her serums and her genetic manipulation, all of the plasmids that entered into my body and warped it—it's illegal. Humans are still proud, too proud, to admit that we are animals, too. We want to believe that we have reached perfection, that we don't need animal traits to better ourselves. But Ellison saw potential. She thought that with the brute force of a bear and the mind of a man—a docile mind, trapped in a bear's brain, easily succumbing to suggestions—she could have her powerful, receptive army. Ellison broke law with me, and when Nolan found out, he was livid. So he took me away. He's an old man, Nolan, fond of the ancient tales. He believes in morality, that no one is against the law. But he also believes in Ellison. She was his student, many years ago, and if not for him, she might never have come as far as she did—not because he eased the way, but because to have even a single person on your side gives you confidence. He said that I had a year and a day for the bacteria inside of me to run its course and slowly return me to normal. To that end, he would give me a single companion of his choice, to give me the confidence he had given Ellison—but that companion must never find out until the year and the day have passed. If that companion did find out, I would be returned to Ellison, to continue on wandering space as this half-man, half-bear, her victory prize."

"Why me?" I asked. "There's nothing special about me, Bear; why would General Nolan pick me as your companion?"

"He likes to give people chances, Brenna. Like you, Nolan was raised on a farm, and he would have stayed there, if someone hadn't taken a chance on him."

"There are a million girls like me to choose from."

"I could scour the entire universe and never find anyone at all like you," Bear corrected. "Does it matter how or why he picked you, Brenna? All that matters is that he did, and, for a short while at least, I knew you."

I looked at him, his face serious and pale. My beautiful Bear had to go back to that horrible general with the long nose, and it was my fault. I thought again of the nameless man who had sold his birthright to live as a white man; a black bear shrouded in white fur. What mess of pottage could ever make a man like this choose to give up his humanity? Love had prompted the ex-colored man, but I could not believe love motivated Bear to sacrifice himself.

A strange noise filled the ship then, one I did not recognize. Bear looked up and stepped away from me. "What's going on?" I asked, filled with the feeling that the most important information was still being withheld from me. "Bear, answer me!"

"She's come for me," he said dully. "She did not think this enterprise likely to succeed. She has been following us in her own ship the entire trip, just waiting for this to happen."

"Bear," I whispered, "I'm so sorry."

"There's nothing to be done now," he said. "I have to go with her."

"Exactly," said a pleased voice. I spun around and saw General Ellison stride into the room. She was exactly as I remembered her: Tall, with a vicious, self-pleased smirk beneath her large nose. In her hand, she carried a small electromagnetic device, which she put to Bear's neck, dismantling the charge around him. "I ought to thank you, Anna dear——"

"Brenna," I interrupted.

She waved an arm dismissively and turned towards the door. Bear looked at me hopelessly. Ellison half-turned, putting a possessive hand on his shoulder, steering him away from me.

"Bear!" I cried, running after him.

"There's nothing you can do, Brenna," he whispered softly, reaching out and gently tucking a lock of my hair behind my ear. "Goodbye."

Ellison dragged him from the room. I was furious to discover that tears were streaming down my cheeks. Rubbing at them with a fist, I took a deep breath.

"I'm sorry, Brenna."

This time I looked up and saw Tim, woebegone and sorry-looking. I thought he looked thinner than he had the last time I had seen him. "Tim?" I gasped. He seemed like a ghost from a life I didn't believe in anymore.

"I'm to take you to an escape pod and help you get home," Tim said. He shrugged helplessly, not meeting my eyes.

I let Tim take me to one of the escape pods. As we walked, I saw spacemen crawling all over the once-empty halls. "General Ellison is taking the ship back over," Tim explained. "It's hers now."

I could care less about the ship. It had been a luxurious prison anyway. I only cared about Bear.

Tim secured a pod for us, and helped me inside. It was small and claustrophobic and hummed dangerously. It sounded as if it might fall apart at any moment. I wiped at tears with the back of my hand and tried to focus on the white-hot anger coursing through me. All I could hear, over and over, was Bear, telling me there was nothing I could do. I could not believe that. I could not stand idly by and let him be used by that horrible woman.

I lifted my head, focusing on all of the dials that lay before me. I understood absolutely none of them. I had been content to let the *Ursus Maritimus* continue on autopilot, and had never questioned how the ship ran. "Tim," I said, as he strapped himself in beside me. "How do you drive this thing?"

It was actually ridiculously easy to fly a space pod. While the *Ursus Maritimus* turned back to Earth, to be properly fitted for a spaceman crew, Ellison's ship, the *Ice Maiden*, took a different route. I followed it, piloting past space debris.

"This is actually fun," I said, turning to Tim, who looked very green. I had tied him to his seat, his arms strapped uselessly at his sides, once I felt I had gotten the hang of flying the pod.

"We're just going to follow her?" he asked pathetically.

"Whatever it takes," I said firmly. "I have to get aboard that ship, Tim."

He shook his head. Then he sighed and said, "There is a way on board. We might be able to make it work."

I looked at him out of the corner of my eye. He might have been young, and scared, but he was still a spaceman. "Can I trust you to help?"

He licked his lips and stared ahead of us at the *Ice Maiden*. "Your sister has been sending you letters, care of the space station. I wrote back to tell her there was no way of getting them to you. Then she wrote back. So I wrote her back."

I looked at him out of the corner of my eye and saw him shrug. There was a slight blush on his cheeks, and I wondered how many times they had been writing each other. Well, I thought, Hazel could do worse than Tim. At least *her* boyfriend wasn't a half-polar bear controlled by a long-nosed power-hungry spaceman general.

"Fly towards that light," Tim instructed. "On my signal, you're going to go straight through as fast as you can. No stopping."

The light was actually a discharge platform, for trash to be burnt and then released into space. I maneuvered the pod with some difficulty to get as close as I could without being charred—and waited until the light went out.

"Now," Tim said.

I hit the accelerator and flew into the little tunnel.

The passage was warm, and fumes penetrated into the pod, smelling of skunk and woodsmoke and burnt plastic. Sweat beaded along my spine and on my upper lip. Tim looked awful. His green pallor had gone more of a purple, and he was breathing in ragged shifts, as if he really might throw up.

"Don't bail on me now, Tim," I said.

"Wouldn't...dream of it," he breathed.

The tunnel let out in the trash room. No one was in there except for a few mindless drones, their metallic joints clicking as they moved. I parked the pod and jumped out, cutting Tim loose. I dragged him out of the trash room, past the robots, into an empty hallway. I thought about leaving him behind, but knew someone would come along sooner or later, and even though he had just gotten me safely inside of the ship, I wasn't sure I could trust him not to blab to someone. He would have to come with me.

"Where would she have put Bear?" I asked Tim.

Tim blinked at me. "Bear" was just a moniker, I remembered; now that he was restored to his human self, he would go by his real name again.

"She would keep him close by," he finally said.

"Then where would she be?" I could hear footsteps. I ducked down a dark tunnel, pulling Tim in close after me. The idiot opened his mouth to answer, but I clapped a hand over his mouth until the footsteps had gone. "Well?"

"The bridge," he said quietly.

"Lead the way."

We slunk around corners, keeping, I hoped, to the unused routes. Eventually, though, Tim straightened up, tugged his spaceman hat low over his eyes, and said, "Follow my lead."

He had taken me to the main hallway. Spacemen and women walked briskly, each with the fear of God in their faces—placed there, no doubt, by Ellison. Tim nodded briefly at them, and they did the same to him. I kept my eyes on the ground and didn't look anyone straight in the face. By walking quickly and staying close to Tim, I hoped no one would pay me too much attention.

Tim stopped in front of a large door at last. "Here you are," he said. His face was pale, and he looked like he might be sick again. I put a gentle hand on his shoulder.

"Thank you," I said. He shrugged and readjusted the hat so it covered even more of his face. "If you want to run, go ahead," I said.

"What good would it do now?" Tim said.

At least he was logical. I pulled my shoulders back and stepped towards the door, and it slid open to admit me. Standing in the room was General Ellison and an older man in uniform I didn't recognize. Beside me, Tim gasped, but I ignored him.

"General Ellison," I said, grateful that my voice was loud and strong, "I've come to make a bargain with you."

She turned from the spaceman and scowled at me. The old man raised an eyebrow and crossed his arms.

"I thought you were taking her back to Earth," Ellison snapped. Tim flushed and ducked his head.

"I kidnapped him," I said brightly. "I'm a *very* talented girl, General."

The old man laughed, and Tim leaned towards me and tugged on my sleeve. "Brenna," he whispered. I shook him off.

"I can see," Ellison said dryly. Her scowl deepened and her nose twitched. Out of the corner of my eye, I saw the captain's chair slowly swaying. Someone was inside of it, listening to every word.

"What kind of a bargain?" the man asked. He was tilting his head now, but there was a smile on his face that seemed to say, *I'm glad you're here.*

"Brenna," Tim whispered again, "That's General Nolan."

The captain's chair swayed slightly again. Ellison's eyes flicked to the chair and then back to me. I stood with my mouth open, the words dead in my throat. That man, whose blue eyes twinkled, was General Nolan? I had been expecting someone colder—someone who could look at Ellison and be proud of her lawlessness and cruelty.

"She doesn't have a bargain," Ellison said. She barked once, in a crude imitation of laughter. "Anna acts before she thinks."

"Brenna," I whispered.

"Go home, Brianna. Go back to your filthy little family. Although, I hope they're not so filthy anymore. We spent quite a lot of money to bring you here." She looked at General Nolan, who shook his head.

"Not so fast, Rachel," he said. "I want to hear the girl's bargain."

"Why not?" Ellison said. "Go on, then. Make my life more interesting."

Tim shifted behind me, and I swallowed. General Ellison stepped towards me, and I took a step back. She grinned, like a predator would once she had gotten hold of her prey. Her teeth were white, white, white. I thought I could see myself reflected in them.

Then I remembered: Bear's shirt, so white it made him look like the night sky.

"I stained Bear's shirt with candle wax," I said. "If you can clean his shirt with only your hands, you'll have proven that you deserve him. However, if I can clean his shirt, and you can't, I get to take him home with me—and," I continued, with a sudden burst of inspiration, "you must promise to never continue your experiments, even if you find someone willing."

Her grin seemed frozen in place. "Do you think I crawled my way up to become general of the spacemen—the spacemen, you hear, not the space*women*—by being a washerwoman? That I would hang the future of all of the spacemen on the whim of a young girl?"

General Nolan laughed delightedly. "Listen to her! She has spunk, Rachel. Just like I expected. We take your bet, Brenna."

"Sir," Ellison objected, "I absolutely will not wash a shirt to prove to a stupid girl just how silly she is."

For the first time, I saw the light in General Nolan's eyes die, and his expression hardened. "I gave you your chance at redemption, General. And now I say that you give this girl one, too. Bhaer! Come here."

And, from the captain's chair, came my Bear. He was dressed in a spaceman's uniform now, but he had his nightshirt balled up in his fist and presented it to Ellison. He did not look at me, or even at her, but kept his eyes on the ground.

"Bear," I whispered, but he would not look at me.

General Ellison took the shirt and shook it out, searching for the tallow stain. With her fingers she tried to pick at it, and then she rubbed, but the warmth in her fingers made the wax supple, and the stain became worse. "What the—!" she cried, rubbing at it even harder. But the stain just worked itself into the cloth and glared at her with a yellow eye.

"You've had a fair chance," Bear said suddenly, snatching it away from her. "You've only made it worse. Anyone could see that."

Nolan laughed and nodded. "Yes. Let's see what Brenna can do."

"I'm going to need some warm water and a bit of iron," I said. Ellison laughed and crossed her arms.

"Go and get it," she said to Tim, who fled. "Water and iron? You think that will fix it?" she scoffed. It did not bother me. I had grown up on a farm where we were too poor to even own a washer and dryer. I had grown used to washing my clothes and my siblings' by hand. I had handled worse stains than candle wax before.

"The fate of the world has hung on the tip of a needle before," General Nolan murmured. "Wait and see what happens, Rachel."

Tim returned with a small tub full of water and a bit of worked metal, which was better than nothing for a washboard. I thanked him, and settled down on the ground, dipping the shirt in the water and scrubbing. For a moment nothing happened, and Ellison cried out in victory, "You see!"

But the warm water did its magic, and the wax started to lift. I scrubbed for a little longer, and then lifted the shirt from the water, as white as fresh snow.

"That's impossible!" Ellison cried.

"You see she's won," Bear growled. He strode across the room to me and put an arm over my shoulder. "And you must honor your promise. If I ever hear of another poor man-turned-animal I shall rip you apart myself."

General Ellison's mouth worked soundlessly. "You can't speak to me like that," she managed to say. "Bhaer, don't you understand...?"

"No!" Bear said. "I do not belong to you anymore. I am through with you and the spacemen."

"General," Ellison cried, turning to General Nolan, who shrugged.

"You lost this one, Rachel. There is nothing you or I can do about it. Better luck next time."

She stared at him for a long moment and then turned to me. "*You*," she roared, but Bear stepped in front of me.

"Try to touch her," he said. "I've spent too long in a bear's mind. I could maul you as easily as I breathe."

I watched her breathe, her chest rising and falling drastically, her face bright red. Then, with a cry of rage, she turned and strode away.

General Nolan turned to me and touched his hat with his fingers. "An admirable job, Brenna," he said. "I'd be glad to see you join the spacemen. You could go far. Farther, I think, than even General Ellison."

"No, thanks," I said. "I'd rather go home, where I belong."

He smiled. "If you're sure. But if you change your mind..."

"I'll look you up," I promised.

General Nolan turned and left. He still seemed like an affable man, but I could see now how thin his lips were, and how calculating his eyes were. I shivered and drew closer to Bear, who radiated heat.

"You did it," Tim breathed.

Bear looked at me for the first time and smiled. "Yes she did," he agreed. And he pulled me into his arms and kissed me.

"You never told me your real name," I whispered to him.

He laughed. I loved his laugh; I could feel it rumbling deep inside of him. "It's Bhaer," he said. "Alexander Bhaer. You had it right all along." He let me go, and turned towards the exit.

"We should go," he continued. "I won't feel safe until I am back on Earth."

"Yes," I agreed, my fingers entwined with his. "Let's go home."

R EBEKAH PHILLIPS has always loved fairytales, and her favorite has
been *East O' the Sun, West O' the Moon*, ever since she discovered it in one
of her mother's storybooks. Inspired by the notion of a woman saving her
true love rather than the other way around, she spent most of her childhood fighting
for knights—some real, some imaginary—in distress. Grown up now, Rebekah
works as an editor and is a teaching assistant at an Ohio university, where she
specializes in reminding her students that periods are a non-optional part of sentences.

Polyphonic Dream Machine

by Asa Powers

P INN tried to make his new body as small as possible, curling up in a damp corner beside a dumpster. He wished the curtain of shadow covering the alley would swallow him up, hide him away. The wail of the seeker drones poured out into the murky night air, bouncing off the high, dilapidated walls of the surrounding buildings; it made it seem as though their sirens came from all directions. The pale light of the moon was shut out all around him, replaced with the flashing red and blue lights that spun frantically atop the torpedo-like bodies of his hunters as they glided through the air. Pinn was finally free from his prison, and he couldn't even enjoy it.

The notion came to him that this may be a good time to cry, but he wasn't quite sure, since he'd never had the chance before, at least that he could recall. A hand, cold and metal, touched the side of his face. It was his hand, his new hand. He couldn't feel his face; a synthetic body lacked some of the senses, but at the same time, an odd sensation came over him; it was his hand, but it almost felt like either he was touching someone else or someone else was touching him, someone so far apart from the sickly boy he had been only hours before.

That morning started out like any other, trapped in his own mind, in a useless body, as he had been since he was very young. Pinn said, or rather thought, *good morning ceiling*, just as he did every morning—followed shortly by, *good morning father*. His grey eyes, the only part of him he could control, moved slowly to the old man at his bedside. His father, Maestro, was ready as usual with the morning injections that kept Pinn's atrophied confines alive for another day.

"I've got a surprise for you, Pinn. Today is the day!" Maestro said, emptying the third syringe into the IV. He rubbed the sleep from his tired eyes and adjusted a pair of glasses that always seemed just a size too small for the old man's wide, expressive face. A crack in one of the lenses made his eyes look off-kilter. "Miss Pixxi should be along any moment."

With the breakfast cocktail administered, Maestro gently lifted Pinn's withered form from the bed and placed him in his wheelchair. Pinn's left arm swayed at the side of the chair, like a brittle leaf in a gentle breeze, until his father placed it in his lap. Maestro wheeled him into their living room, a room already tiny made even more cramped and cluttered with parts and materials from the old man's in-home business as an outfitter. He worked in fitting people with cybernetic enhancements and learned pretty quickly—and much to his despair—that all of his skills as an outfitter couldn't overcome the inability of Pinn's broken body to handle the stress of procedures so intrusive. The internal ventilator unit he had implanted to monitor and maintain Pinn's breathing had nearly killed the boy during recovery due to the resulting infection. He dared not attempt any further enhancements.

The near constant attention Maestro usually paid to Pinn was today aimed at the front door. And with every passing moment the old man's pacing gradually increased with his anticipation.

"Miss Pixxi is a savant in her field; you've got nothing to worry about!" Maestro said as he poured himself a cup of coffee. Pinn wasn't sure if his father was saying that for him or to reassure himself, maybe both. His father seemed to know nothing but worry. The dim grey sky of the morning bled into the black blanket of afternoon smoke from Factory Row. Maestro cracked open the front door to take a peak outside, and the heavy sounds of machinery working away poured into the ramshackle cottage-converted-to-workshop. "Where is that girl? She best not back out now. She owes me!"

A silver arm reached out to Pinn. A woman in grimy blue coveralls with cropped blonde hair was beckoning him to follower her. It took his new mind, however superior to the old, a moment to process who she was.

"Pixxi, why are they chasing me?" Pinn asked, not daring to move an inch from his spot beside the dumpster.

"I'll explain in a minute. Right now, we've got to get you off the street. Follow me, and keep quiet!" Pixxi directed him to a nearby open manhole and motioned quickly for him to descend. Once they were beneath the streets and the cover secured, she spoke up again, "It's really the worst time to say this, but you're lucky in a way. You aren't tagged. If you were, it wouldn't matter where you ran, the drones would find you. We should be ok down here for now."

"Pixxi, what's going on? Where's my father?"

"Maestro was taken by the Department of Transhuman Affairs for questioning."

"Why? He didn't do anything wrong!"

"Kid, I hate to tell you this, but its better you know now. You're an echo. As far as the DTA is concerned, your father is an accomplice to several serious crimes."

An echo. Pinn only knew of them from the stations his father would leave on for background noise as he worked. Some were entertainers, others slaves or laborers. Those that did none of those things were hunted for sport. Pinn was confused as to how he could possibly be an echo. Come to think of it, he didn't actually know what qualified someone as an echo.

"You do know what an echo is, boy?" She looked back towards him briefly, but didn't slow her pace.

"I've seen the games on the Capital Station, so many of them get destroyed during the games. They're criminals right?"

"Bah, that's what I thought, you don't know. You just know what the stations want you to know. Well, it's not your fault. No one likes to talk about it. We don't have a lot of time, but it's only right you know fully the position you're in, so I'll give you the short version. While I was placing you in your new body, there was a surge in the system that knocked out the connection for a moment. If at any time the process is interrupted during a Conversion when a person's consciousness is being transferred to an artificial body, even in cases like yours where the transfer still finishes, that person is considered legally dead."

Pinn emitted a synthesized gasp from the tiny speaker holes over his new mouth. It was very strange to hear the sound of breathing in sharply yet not feel the air on the back of his throat.

"Don't worry, I don't think people that end up like you are dead, and I'm not the only one. That's a definition established by a bunch of self-righteous bureaucrats who insist that the 'spark' or 'essence' of a person is lost when things go pear-shaped. Thanks to these scumbags, legally, an echo has no rights. They are considered a copy and nothing more, so they are rounded up, offered either destruction or slavery, and used as entertainment. They call you echoes to mock what they think you've lost. If they had their way, Conversion would be illegal entirely!" Her voice bounced off the cavernous walls as she spit out the end of her rant. She held her silver arm up, as if checking a watch, and tapped on the forearm which brought up a little holo-display of the street above them represented in simple lines and bright colors. "The little blimp bastards don't seem to be on our trail. Oh—before I forget, this should come in handy if we get separated."

For a brief moment, Pinn's vision hazed around the edges and he heard the slight sound of static. The split-second event disoriented him and he stumbled, kicking up stale water around his ankles. "What was that?"

"I uploaded a map of the city to your brain. Nifty, huh?"

"Um, thanks." It felt awkward outwardly expressing emotions to another person. Happiness, sadness—these things felt fuzzy, half-formed. Up until now, all that he was had been within his mind. He loved his father, but had never been able to express it. It seemed his old body hadn't been the only thing to atrophy. For now, all he could do was respond with whatever felt right at the time, like groping around in a dark room with a wall full of nearly identical switches, trying to find the one that turns on the light.

"Hel-o. Th— o— is –MN—" A garbled voice whispered in the vents of the boy's ears.

"Did you hear that?"

"Hear what? Listen, I think I know what our next move is. I figure if we can get ahold of a tag, we can get you across the border into less zealous territory."

"I guess it was nothing. Never mind. You mentioned that before, what is a tag?" Pinn couldn't help asking so many questions; in fact, the urge to ask the questions piling up inside him about the world outside his home was nearly equal with the worry about his current situation.

"Converts are tagged with an ID once the process is complete. Even if you retain your spark, they still want to keep track of you. In your case, we ran before the system could tag you. An untagged echo is considered extremely dangerous, so the sooner we can get you one the better. I know some people who may be able to set us up with a forgery. They aren't exactly saints, but we don't have much choice."

"Pixxi, why go to all this trouble for me? You put yourself at risk."

The young woman shot her florescent eyes at him, enhancements that shown in brilliant glowing rings of blue in the dim light of the underground. "Hey, they're looking for me, too. Besides, I owe the old man," she said, tapping her cybernetic silver hand on her thigh. The light ting of metal on metal between the thin layer of her grease-smeared clothing carried softly around them. "I owe him everything."

The sign above the double doors blinked and sputtered the club's name in a soft purple light. It would go from reading "Fuoco's" to a mess of jumbled pixels and back. Sharp, obnoxious house music blared from open windows out into the street. The inside was a large open area, complete with a stage, dance floor, and bar. Tables were filled with patrons made loud and unruly with booze. Pixxi and Pinn were headed for the far back corner where her questionable contacts were awaiting them.

Two Converts, a man and woman, stood alone in the smoky haze of revelry. The man was slim, almost elegant in appearance and dressed in a tailored suit and long coat with a cane in his left hand. The woman next to him looked more ragged, feral, but beautiful. She was leaning on a barstool, wearing a low cut evening dress which stopped just above the knee, exposing her polished black and white metal skin.

"Mr. Hobble, Mrs. Syteless, thanks for meeting us on such short notice."

"Anything for you, Pixxi dear," said the man called Mr. Hobble. The only parts of his artificial nature, his head and hands, were red and white in color.

"So, this is the guy who needs a tag?" asked Mrs. Syteless, leaving the stool to inspect Pinn. She set her bright yellow eyes on him, vertical slits narrowing as she focused.

"I never said who it was for," said Pixxi.

"Don't take us for fools; he's an echo, isn't he? An echo without a tag."

Pixxi moved to speak, not nearly as cordial as before, but Mr. Hobble cut in. "Mrs. Syteless, that wasn't very nice. Please, let's all do our best to keep our heads about us, shall we? Miss Pixxi and her companion are here to do business." Mr. Hobble took his turn giving Pinn's new body a closer look. The holes where Mr. Hobble's eyes and mouth should have been were lit up from the inside with a burning orange light, like a jack-o'-lantern; it was a feature that made it hard to read both his attention and intentions. "This is quite an interesting vessel, Miss Pixxi, where did you find it?"

"Same place as usual, the scrapyards."

"A steal to be sure. You've a good eye."

"I'm Pinn, it's nice to meet you." An introduction is all the boy could muster. Pinn felt worlds out of place in such a setting. If Pixxi hadn't been there, he'd be lost for words and heading for the nearest exit to safe, familiar conversations with Mr. Ceiling or his father.

"Oh, so you're just a boy in there—and so well mannered. How sad. I don't envy your fate. Where are your parents?" The woman asked, brushing a clawed hand down his cheek.

"My father was taken—"

"Pinn, don't say anymore."

"Pixxi, you wound me, I thought we were friends?" The two women looked at one another and the atmosphere around them changed. It was as though they were sizing each other up, each waiting for the other to strike first. "Well, perhaps I should leave. I'm sure Mr. Hobble can handle the transaction on his own," said Mrs. Syteless, who then disappeared into the writhing crowd.

"Good idea." Pixxi cracked the knuckles of her human hand.

Mr. Hobble looked silently in the direction his partner went and then turned back to Pixxi. "Now that the pleasantries are out of the way, we can get down to business. Follow me please. We'll need a little more privacy."

The three of them moved back through the crowd to a hallway on the other side of the club, next to the stage. Pinn stayed in the middle, with Pixxi bringing up the rear. He felt safer that way. Pinn wondered if they'd be able to get a tag for him. What if they did, but it didn't pass as genuine? He thought of father and realized he'd never been apart from him for this long. The boy suddenly felt lost, alone, being among so many people only made him feel worse. He didn't belong here. An urge stronger than anything he'd ever felt before rose up within him, and for a moment he wanted nothing more than to run back home and crawl under his covers.

Mr. Hobble held his hand to his ear for a moment. "Pinn, you'd like to find your father, wouldn't you?"

"Yes, more than anything." They were about halfway down the hall and away from the screaming patrons, much to Pinn's relief.

"Well, my partner may have a lead. She just informed me that she looked into your case file."

"You can tell me were father is?"

"We can do you one better, we shall bring him to you—for a price of course."

"Pixxi, did you hear that? They can rescue father!"

Pinn turned back in his excitement and saw only the other end of the hall. The music and cheering had coalesced into a muffled hum by now. He froze in panic; his only friend was nowhere to be seen.

"Don't be alarmed. Miss Pixxi has left you in our care. We are to rescue your father and provide you with a tag."

"But—so suddenly, she didn't even say goodbye. Are you sure she meant to leave me?"

"Quite. She didn't have the heart to bid a fond farewell, dear boy. Now come, we've a price to discuss," Mr. Hobble said as they reached a metal door flanked by two large men at the end of the hallway.

"Well, ok."

Something about the situation just didn't feel right, but Pinn couldn't risk losing a chance to get his father back, and Mr. Hobble seemed nice enough, nicer than that rude woman he worked with. No matter how much he wanted to run. He couldn't. Not now. Pixxi was gone and once again Pinn was in the dark, trying to find the right switch to light his way.

"Hello. Th-- one -s G3--1. He i- --ing." The incomprehensible voice that came from seemingly nowhere once again spoke to him. No one else gave any indication that they had heard it, so Pinn kept quiet. Better that he not give them reason to think he's crazy. Mr. Hobble whispered something to one of the men and he opened the door. On the other side was a broad man with a great beard, sitting at a desk and surrounded by monitors.

"Master Fouco, I've got a most intriguing find for you. Pinn, this is Game Master Fouco. You are familiar with the games?"

"Another echo, eh?" Fouco leaned over his desk, his chair moaning under his weight. He put on a set of glasses with several different lenses and looked Pinn up and down a few times. "Well, this one isn't your average, generic piece of junk. Who are you? Let me see your tag."

At the mention of a tag, Mr. Hobble suddenly lost his cool, gentlemanly demeanor, wringing his cane between his hands before he spoke. "Sir, there's the rub, he hasn't got one yet."

Fuoco's face grew sharp and fierce and he threw the glasses onto his desk with enough force to crack some of the lenses. He stood up from his chair and the floorboards trembled. "Why do you waste my time with this? The last time I acquired an echo with one of your cheap forgeries, the DTA almost destroyed my whole operation! An entire season's worth of gladiators seized! You remember what it cost you then, don't you, Mr. Hobble?"

The angry giant swung a thick finger to the far wall where the mounted head of a dapper fellow hung with a sly grin on his face.

"Yes, and I am eternally grateful for the second chance you've given me, which is why I thought it prudent to show you before I implanted the tag. As I suspected, you can tell this echo is truly a rare find. Master Fouco, our methods in crafting tags have improved a great deal since then. I assure you—"

Fouco slammed one of his massive hands on the desk and rubbed at his temple with the other. "This is it, Hobble. This is your last chance. If this causes me any kind of trouble, any at all; you'll lose your other head. Got it?"

Mr. Hobble slipped comfortably back into his suave façade and turned to Pinn. "Well, my boy, looks like we've got a deal. I'll see about your tag while these gentlemen show to you a place you can rest for the evening."

Pinn felt completely numb to the awkward and somewhat frightening scene that just took place between the two men. Fouco was a Game Master? Did he intend to put Pinn in the games? Mr. Hobble had shooed him away with the guards before he could ask any questions. Questions about the deal he'd apparently made, about the tag, about father. If not for those last two, the boy would already be out the door.

"Hello. This one is G3MN-1. Relinquish control." The voice only Pinn could here came in clear this time. It was stiff and deathly calm.

That voice again. What is it? Pinn thought, reluctantly following the guards.

"This vessel houses G3MN-1, as it does you. Now, relinquish control if you wish to live."

Can you hear my thoughts? I don't understand.

"You are being lied to. The one called Hobble has sold you into slavery and eventual destruction. Relax your will and give this one momentary control."

Pinn stopped and realized without hesitation that the voice was telling the truth. He wasn't sure how or why he felt that way. It was almost instinctual, like trusting a truth spoken by yourself. The voice was connected to him, it was part of him. Pinn imagined himself back in his old body, lifeless and brittle, unable to move. He let himself sink deeper and deeper into that familiar prison; embracing it like an old security blanket. There he dreamt.

He heard yelling and gun fire, but all the sounds were nearly smothered out, as though Pinn were underwater. He opened his human eyes to a hallway where one man was lying motionless on the ground and another was pointing a gun at him. Well, not *at him* exactly. It was more like a scene were playing out on a screen while Pinn watched from the perspective of the camera.

A mechanical arm came into the frame with a blade of white hot plasma protruding from the forearm. The burning weapon was giving off smoke from its initial taste of flesh. The armed man began backing away, shouting frantically, not a word coming in clear. Then, an explosion from the end of the hallway behind the man made the walls quake.

A Convert in a suit and long coat ran out of a door, away from the explosion and past the armed man who also began to run. When the two drew close to the camera, the bladed arm slashed quick as lightning as they passed. The fleeing Convert was soon followed by two women, who appeared to fly through the door— or rather, a woman in blue, whose legs were partially bound, was slamming a Convert woman with yellow eyes into the wall of the hallway. She then proceeded to drag the Convert woman along the length of the wall using the force of the fire coming from her feet to push her forward at a violent speed, splintering wood with the other woman's face and upper body as she went.

The mechanical arm withdrew its weapon when the woman in blue looked at the camera. She dropped the limp body of the Convert woman whose artificial eyes were destroyed along with much of her face. She began yelling and the camera. The same words over and over. Each time they became a little clearer until finally the surface of the dream was broken.

"Pinn, run!"

Pinn awoke mid stride, running through a field of junk and scrap metal. The sudden change in surroundings since falling asleep in the hallway surprised him and he tripped over his own heavy foot, falling end over end until coming to a stop against the remains of a rusted-out vehicle of some sort. With a grunt, he sat himself upright and leaned against it. Then he realized he was holding something in his left hand, an elegant red and yellow arm still wearing the sleeve of a suit and jacket. He dropped it and shied away in shock. "Mr. Hobbles arm? Why am I carrying his arm?"

"It contains a tag. You needed one, correct?" replied the voice no one else seemed to hear.

"Well, that's true, but did you have to cut off Mr. Hobble's arm? He didn't seem so bad."

"It is the top priority of this one to assist the subject and ensure the survival of this vessel."

"Is it? Well I really hope he didn't know anything about father."

"As I said, the one called Hobble was lying. He did not know where your father is."

"How did you know?"

"It was obvious from the tone and brevity of his words; the increase of his heart rate as he spoke."

"Why didn't you say anything earlier?"

"This one could not. This one was damaged when this unit was dumped in the scrapyards. The map the one called Pixxi provided you with, in the moment she transferred the map to you, this one commandeered the stream and calculated the most efficient route within the system to the archives that held the data necessary for repairs. It took time to complete repairs."

"G3M—can I just call you Jim?"

"That will be acceptable."

"Jim, what are you exactly, and where are we?" Pinn looked to his left and right; the sea of trash seemed endless. Large industrial buildings billowed black smoke into the air on the rust-colored horizon.

"This one is the onboard A.I. for the Dhalst Mk II Anti-Personnel Vessel. The primary purpose of this A.I. is to assist the transferred subject during combat operations. This one concluded that the scrapyards would be a low risk area to retreat to until contact with the one called Pixxi is re-established."

"So someone dumped a battle vessel in the trash? I mean, this is where Pixxi found you. That doesn't make a lot of sense."

"The creators of this vessel did not dump it. As indicated by recent transmissions, the Mk II APV was stolen by persons unknown. The creators want it back."

"You can hear what they're saying?"

"Correct. This one is aware of their movements and transmissions. Much of their traffic has gone dark however. It is likely that unauthorized access to their archives to retrieve the repair files alerted them to this one's ability to monitor them. This one has also maintained silence so they cannot track it. They will seek this one out at any cost. They seek you as well."

"You mean the DTA?"

Before Jim could answer, a familiar voice filled Pinn's ears. "Son? I miss you. I can't find you. Where are you?"

"Father!"

"Do not listen. He has been set as bait. They are not transmitting directly; this one has made that impossible. This is broadcasting city-wide, a sign of desperation."

"Son, please come home."

Pinn found the right switch in the dark room and a burning light fed his anger. How dare they use Father in such a way! It was intolerable, inexcusable!

"Do not go to him."

Maestro began to cry. His father usually only cried when he thought he was out of earshot of Pinn, but if nothing else, the boy learned to be observant. He could tell his father's bad days from his good ones. Maestro would storm into the room wearing his ever-cheerful mask, but that mask had developed cracks over time, cracks that exposed red, puffy eyes, stuffy noses, and sometimes the faint glint of dried tears on his rosy cheeks. The last time he'd actually seen Maestro cry was after that single implant had nearly killed Pinn.

His father's cries dredged up old feelings. There was a time when Pinn hated himself for making his father so unhappy, for making everyday a struggle with life and death. In his darkest of moods, he thought it may be better if he just died; Maestro could be free, but he could do nothing to alleviate the pain he caused. He could do nothing but stare at the door frame while his father wept silently on the other side.

Pinn shot to his feet. He spun around and began beating on the junked out vehicle again and again. The metal shell gave as though made of paper under his blows. One of the blades in his arms sprang out and he plunged it into a large safe nearby. When he pulled back, some of the molten metal splashed onto his foot.

"Right blade, retract." The blade listened to the A.I.'s command instantly.

"I don't care if it's a trap. This body is a weapon? Then we'll use it. We'll save father. We have to!"

"This is highly inadvisable. The Mk II APV only operates at optimal levels when both subject and A.I. are well trained to work as one. You have not had adequate time to learn. Victory is not certain. If captured, you will be purged from this vessel."

"Then you'll have to help me so that doesn't happen. It's your job right? We're going."

Under the cover of night, Pinn entered the house. It looked just as it always did, but so much smaller. It was a tiny cottage already, but now it was like a dollhouse. He felt like a giant, his head nearly scraping against the ceiling. He navigated carefully through the living room, avoiding clutter like hot coals so as to not make a sound. His old wheelchair lay in the doorway to his room. It must have gotten knocked over in the chaos after they ran. He picked it up in one hand and it felt so alien to him. This rickety, poorly made thing used to be his legs. He moved it aside and entered his room. His father was waiting for him, sitting in his chair by the bed.

There was a thin metal strip along one side of his head with a small green light on either end.

"Son, welcome home. Welcome home. I'm sorry."

"Father—what's on his head Jim?" Pinn wanted to run and hug his father, but he was afraid he would break him. He'd never noticed before just how old and frail his father was. He'd always remembered him as a much taller man of great strength.

"It's an implant that influences a subject's words and actions through powerful suggestion. It's primarily used for interrogations or enslavement. The implant also puts out a homing signal so their position is known to their masters at all times."

"They're here. I'm so sorry." Maestro's eyes began to well up. He reached for his son with a withered hand.

"Pinn, you must relinquish control, now."

Spotlights invaded from every window and the hum of tri-rotored assault choppers surrounded the house.

"I want to help this time. I need to learn, right? How about you lead and I follow?"

"If that is what you wish."

"Echo, you will submit. There's nowhere to run. Cooperate, and no one gets hurt!" the command blared from a speaker overhead.

Pinn gently took his father's hand in his own, which was almost big enough to engulf the old man's forearm. "Father, you stay here. Jim and I are going to rescue you."

Pinn emerged from the house and saw the three DTA assault choppers, their lights fixed on him. Several lines fell from the hovering behemoths and black figures slid down as one group. They immediately began to encircle the boy. Their silhouettes resembled Pinn's in general shape, but when they stepped into the light, their black, rounded armor made them look like beetles. Pinn's unpainted, off-white surface made for poor camouflage in the dark by comparison.

"Battlefield assessment: As predicted, they send in Mk I APVs. These intermediate models bridge the gap between manned combat suits and the Mk II APV. They are inferior to this model, as they require a human subject to physically interface with the vessel's A.I. to achieve Direct Fluid Communication. They have the advantage in numbers, but they carry no ranged weapons. They do not wish to severely damage this prototype," Jim said.

Three of the soldiers on either side of Pinn shot out cables from their shoulders that wrapped around his arms. Three more entangled him around the neck and each group began to pull down in an effort to force Pinn to the ground.

"We will begin combat. Verbally issuing instructions is inefficient; we will communicate through thought at a speed many times faster than human speech. Do you understand Pinn? This is the groundwork for working as one."

"I got it." Pinn opened himself to the A.I. rather than submitting to it as he did before; and instead of watching from behind a screen, he became the machine behind the camera. He could hear the whir of servos, he could see the processes maintaining the vessel and he became intimately aware of every bolt and wire that made up his body, every scrap of data that raced through his consciousness.

Pinn twisted his arms around the cables, grabbing hold of them; he released a powerful electric shock that brought his attackers to their knees. With the cables falling away, he stood up straight and extended both plasma blades from his arms.

"All forces advance. Engage in melee, but do not destroy the target. Try and ground him," said the voice overhead.

The soldiers each revealed their own blades, made of metal rather than plasma. Pinn knew why; he knew because Jim knew. The extra room required for the human subject did not allow for plasma weapons. It also meant they were physically weaker than a vessel driven by pure mechanical force.

Pinn grabbed the arm of the first attacker to swing at him and tossed him aside. Another landed a hit on his back, an arc of sparks chasing after his blade. Pinn turned, answering with his own blade, cutting through both the weapon and arm of the soldier who flinched and backed away, clutching his stump. The cauterized wound was bloodless but still gruesome. The image rattled Pinn's concentration and he hesitated. His connection with Jim was threatening to shatter.

"Pinn, calm yourself. They wish to dispose of you and your father. It is either them or you. Remember that."

The boy pushed any doubt from his mind and focused on a single task, to keep his father safe. Soldiers on one side of him again used their cables on one of his arms while soldiers on the other side tackled him to the ground. Pinn had regained his composure a moment too late. Flat on the ground, his heavy form was cumbersome. The soldiers scrambled like ants trying to subdue a larger, stronger foe. It was getting harder to move by the second as they began to wrap him up in their cables.

Two small ports, one on each of Pinn's shoulders, opened up and a swarm of dart-like projectiles flew from them. They looked like a sort of nightmarish robotic insect with drills for mouths, hooked prongs for legs and clear glass abdomens filled with a gaseous substance. They flew around the attackers like hornets whose nest had been disturbed, searching for targets. They began latching onto the helmets of the soldiers, drilling through the armor. The first one to make it through to the vulnerable human inside released the gas from its abdomen, incapacitating him in moments. An instant later, the rest of the soldiers were down as well. The dart swarm lay motionless, their payload spent. Pinn wrestled with the hastily-tied cables; the ones that didn't come lose, he snapped. He stood up and looked towards the copters.

"What are you waiting for? Send it in dammit!" The voice overhead was getting flustered.

The other two copters moved forward, carrying something immense between them, suspended by wires that Pinn hadn't noticed before—a huge machine of some kind, bigger than his house.

"This, too, was anticipated, but only in a worst case scenario. That is a Krieger 88 Mobile Fortress, a heavy-class bipedal tank. Victory is unlikely."

As the two copters lowered the tank to the ground, Pinn was positive he heard a woman screaming. A moment later, an explosion destroyed a rotor on one of the hovering machines. The craft pitched forward, dropping the tank which also pulled down the other copter and the two collided, crashing in a fiery, twisted heap on top of the tank.

"What the hell was that?" asked the voice from the remaining copter.

Pinn caught a glimpse of a blue streak flying by the final copter. He watched as she dropped a bomb into one of the craft's rear rotors. The explosion sent it plunging to the ground like the other two.

"It seems Pixxi received the encrypted message this one sent about your suicidal plan."

Pixxi did a celebratory loop in the air before landing in front of them, the rockets in her feet slowing her decent until she landed softly.

"Kid, the crap you just pulled was really stupid, but I'd be lying if I didn't say that was the most fun I've had in a while." She smacked his shoulder with her silver hand. Pinn, unable to contain himself, picked her up, giving her a hug that was perhaps a little too tight. "Hey, ease up, my ribs are still made of bone."

"Oh, sorry." He put her down.

"So where's the old man? We need to get out of here, now; reinforcements will be here any minute."

"I'm here." Maestro was at the front door, leaning on the frame. He looked exhausted."

"This was all my fault. I'm so sorry old man."

"No," began Jim. "The surge that interrupted the transfer of Pinn's mind was a countermeasure devised by the creators. Should this vessel ever be lost, unauthorized use of it would trigger the failure and alert them to its location. You were not at fault, Pixxi. Your skill allowed the transfer to complete, saving Pinn in the process."

"Toying with people's lives just to get their weapon back—" Pixxi shook her head, unable to finish venting the extent of her outrage.

"We have to help Father," said Pinn.

"Right now, you two have to get as far away from here as possible, and I need to get him as far away from you as possible as long as this implant is active." Pixxi took ahold of Maestro and launched herself into the air. "Don't worry, he'll be fine! We'll make contact once this junk is out of his head and things calm down. You two need to get going!"

It would be two weeks; two long, agonizing weeks until Pinn received a message from Pixxi. In those two weeks, the boy held onto hope by a thread, and each day that ended without mention of a flying woman in blue being captured meant she and Father were safe. Pinn thought for certain that, if the worst did happen, it would be mentioned; the DTA would have loved to make an example of her.

The message was short, but clear: The implant had been removed with the help of some shifty acquaintances, people more reliable than Mr. Hobble and Mrs. Syteless at least. The four of them were to cross the border in two separate groups. Pinn and Jim would go first.

The line was unbearably long. Pinn felt alone and exposed standing out in the open regardless of how many people stood in the lines on either side of him.

"I really hope this works," Pinn said under his breath.

"The tag has been successfully installed. Victory is likely."

"Not everything is a battle Jim."

"No, but most events have either positive or negative outcomes. Do they not?"

Pinn's anxiety dug the pit in his stomach a little deeper whenever the red light flashed and a harsh, electronic beep blared, signaling another person in line being scanned for ID. Before he knew it, his turn had come. The wait suddenly felt far too short. The border guard had his scanning device at the ready, waiting for him to step forward. When Pinn didn't move right away, people began to stare. The guard looked up at him and the boy couldn't move.

"Hold out your arm, sir. This will only take a moment."

Pinn forced himself forward and held out his arm, straight and stiff. The guard ran his scanner over the tag. Sound and light sprang from all sides.

ASA POWERS grew up in a musical family in the Ozarks. Initially interested in illustration, he fell in love with writing in high school. Apart from writing fiction, he enjoys singing and playing his ukulele. He is currently pursuing his Master's in English.

The Leatherworker's Deal

by Joe Powers

I T was a small, unspectacular shop in the middle of a half-empty strip mall near the edge of town. More than a bit run down, it reflected the neighborhood it represented. The clientele was specialized and the product was high end. The sign above the door boldly proclaimed it as the *Underworld Leather Shop*, and in fine print below, *Oscar and Russell Goddard, proprietors*.

While that was technically true, it was Oscar, a burly, bearded man with full sleeve tattoos, who really ran the show. It was his handiwork—boots, jackets, vests, et cetera—on display around the shop, and his business savvy that kept them afloat. Russell, tall and thin but muscular, also heavily-tattooed with a shaven head and goatee, had a good rapport with customers but no head for numbers and was more than happy to leave that aspect of the business up to his big brother.

When business was good it was very good, for the Goddard brothers had a reputation for quality items at only slightly inflated prices. When business took a turn for the worse, however, it turned drastically. This was through no fault of the brothers, but simply the state of the economy within which they existed. In short, times were hard, and small family-owned businesses like theirs were feeling the crunch across the board.

It was in light of this set of circumstances that Russell stood in the back office across the desk from his brother early one Monday morning. Oscar sat rigidly in his chair, which Russell knew usually meant bad news. His default position was reclined far back with his feet propped on the edge of the desk; he only sat up for serious business.

"Listen man, I've been going over the books, and it's not good," Oscar said. "We've been running in the red for months. I've been covering the spread out of my own pocket, but the well has just about run dry. I've got us covered the rest of the month, but after that—unless things turn around drastically—we're busted."

"So what's that mean? We're gonna close the shop?"

"I dunno what else to tell ya, kid," he answered. "Outlet stores selling cheap knockoffs, the economy bein' what it is, we're just not moving the merchandise these days. I don't want to shut it down, and it might not have to be forever—maybe just a little while until things start to bounce back. But for now, I think..."

"I could pull a couple of jobs," Russell interrupted. "I know a guy who's looking for some muscle on a night deposits hit."

Oscar shook his shaggy head in disgust. "You wanna go back inside?" he asked. "They catch you again, especially on an armed robbery charge, you're lookin' at a long stretch, Russ. Hell, they might not let you out this time."

Russell threw his hands in the air, exasperated. "Well, what then? We're busted, Oscar. We've got what, three weeks, until what will probably be our last weekend in business? Less than a month until you're out of money, and we're both out of a job? We make nice stuff out of leather, we ride bikes, and that's about it. What else we gonna do?"

The morning passed slowly for the brothers, the air filled with apprehension and uncertainty. Twice Oscar had to talk Russell out of calling up old associates and signing on for duty in questionable enterprises. Things were on the verge of escalating in the midst of one particularly heated exchange, which started when Russell accused his brother of using the circumstances as an opportunity to venture forth on his own. It was untrue and hurtful; no brothers were ever any closer than the Goddards—and Russell knew it.

Oscar raised a finger and opened his mouth to reply when the bell over the front door jingled. The two looked up and the tension between them melted away instantly as a wiry, leather-clad man of about sixty-five barged into the shop. He sported a patch over one eye, but the other one gleamed with delight and a broad smile spread across his face. He held his arms wide in greeting. "Well, well," he said in a gravelly rumble, "the gang's all here."

"G'day Cutter," greeted Oscar with a smile of his own, wrapping the smaller man in a bear hug.

Russell came around the counter and clapped the man on the back. "What brings you out this way, old man?"

"Just thought I'd drop in and see how my boys're doin'," Cutter replied, looking around the shop. "How's business?"

"Oh, you know, same old thing," Oscar said. "Another day, another dollar."

"Tough times is how we're doin'," Russell chimed in, ignoring his brother's black look. "We're damn near out of business, and no sign of the cavalry on the horizon."

Cutter's eyebrows shot up in surprise. "That bad?" he asked.

"Aw, you know how it is," Oscar put in. "Everybody wants somethin' for nothin' these days. The way the world's goin'." He took a step toward the office. "Never mind that. You want a beer? How long you in town for?"

Cutter ignored his elder son's attempt to downplay his situation. He rubbed his stubbly chin thoughtfully, lost in thought. His mannerisms changed, and when he spoke again he seemed to choose his words carefully. "I might know someone who could help," he said. "How much time we got to work with here?"

"We can maybe hang on 'til the end of the month, not much more," Oscar replied dejectedly. "Whatever you've got in your bag of tricks, bring it on, old man. I'm wide open to suggestions here."

"Never mind, you just leave everything to me," he said, waving his hands dismissively. "You boys go on now, take a run down to the tavern and have a couple of cold ones on ol' Cutter. Go for a ride in the hills; do whatever. Just stay out o' here until tomorrow." He leveled his sons with a stare. "I mean it, whatever you do, do not come back here today."

Oscar shrugged. "Fine by me," he said. "It ain't like we're busy here anyway. I'll try anything at this point. C'mon Russ, we've got our orders." Each shook hands with their father, extracted a promise to get together to catch up on old times soon, and headed out the door. Cutter stood at the window, arms crossed, and watched them pull away. When he was certain they were gone, he took out his cellphone, made a short call, and wandered into the back office to wait.

The brothers arrived at the shop the next morning, having overcome their curiosity and dutifully steered clear of the premises all night per their instructions. As he slid his key into the lock on the front door, Oscar absently noted it was locked and assumed whatever scheme their father was cooking up was still in the works. They walked inside and immediately noticed a strange pungent odor permeating the room instead of the familiar leather smell. A fine, cloudy mist covered much of the floor, swirling around their feet but dissipating within minutes of their arrival. They took this in with interest, never having witnessed such before, and silently pondered what it could mean. Neither of these things, however, as unusual as they were, held their attention like the new display sitting atop the workbench.

Before leaving the previous day, Oscar had cut and laid out the pieces for a pair of boots on his workbench. From where he stood, he could see all of his prep work was now missing. Instead, on the counter near the front of the store, was a finished pair of boots. Etched into them was a design so intricate and detailed as to be almost lifelike. Immaculately placed studs and fringes completed the package. Not a stitch or seam could be detected, so flawless was the work. Oscar was stunned beyond words. He obviously hadn't made the boots, his brother was incapable of such elaborate work, and he knew there was nobody else who could have made them. Even if somebody had, it seemed unlikely they could have done so in such a short time, with such precision. Simply put, they were perfect.

The brothers looked at each other, silently running through a litany of questions for which neither had any answers. That Cutter had taken steps to help out was obvious, but beyond that, they were unable to fathom what had taken place in the little shop during their absence.

The rumble of motorcycles filled the air, and three large bikes eased off the highway into the parking lot outside. As they pulled up in front of the shop, Oscar spotted the patches on their jackets and recognized them as members of the local chapter of a prominent motorcycle club. The trio sauntered inside the store, looking around at the various and sundry items on display. Though he didn't know these three personally, Oscar was acquainted with various members of the myriad of clubs in the area; their presence was nothing out of the ordinary. "Mornin', fellas. Help you with anything?" he asked.

One of the men grunted something unintelligible to the effect that they were just looking and continued their seemingly disinterested browsing. Probably just killing time on a run, Oscar thought, and went back to what he was doing.

"Hey, all right. Now this is what I'm talking about, right here." One of the bikers was admiring the mysterious new boots, turning one of them over in his hands and smiling appreciatively at the fine craftsmanship. He held it up and nodded toward Oscar. "You make these, brother? I'm impressed."

By the greatest of luck the boots fit the biker perfectly, as though they'd been made for him specifically. A brief round of negotiations ensued that concluded with the man happily paying Oscar nearly triple the value of the boots. The other two men placed orders for boots of their own, and bought a couple of other items on their way out. Oscar stood dumbfounded, clutching a thick stack of bills in his hand, scarcely able to believe what had just taken place.

The pattern quickly became a familiar one, with the brothers laying out the materials for one or more items just before closing the shop for the night and dutifully staying away until the following morning. Each day brought the same sort of surprise discovery: boots, jackets, saddlebags, and numerous other items—all beautifully crafted and all spoken for and sold within hours. Word was getting around that Underworld Leather was the premier place to find unique, high quality, eye-catching pieces, and business picked up considerably virtually overnight. By the time the end of the month rolled around, the shop was prospering beyond the brothers' wildest dreams, and all thoughts of going under were long forgotten.

"I said, what did you do?" Oscar had to raise his voice to be heard over the racket that raged around Cutter in whatever unknown location he was. It had taken him nearly a week to track down his father, and he struggled to keep his patience as he tried to get answers to the many questions he had.

"Look, you boys needed some help. I got you some," Cutter coyly answered. "A friend of mine owed me a favor, a guy who had a couple of old world leatherworkers at his disposal. He sent them in, they're working for you now. End of story."

"That doesn't make any sense, Dad," Oscar countered. "Why haven't we ever seen them? How do they get in and out of the shop? What..."

"You know all you need to know about it," Cutter interrupted. "Now you listen to me, Oscar. Under no circumstances can you go in there and watch them work, you got it? You need to just leave them alone to do their thing, and you'll have them for as long as you need them. Or aren't they earning you enough?"

"The money's great, Dad. We're back on our feet and then some. I just don't get what the big secret is. What does your buddy have over these guys to keep them working for free every single night?"

Cutter paused. "Think of them like Santa's little elves, son," he said. "They work hard for no pay, with no goal in life other than to please their master. That's the best I can give you right now. Just enjoy the gift, and keep quiet about it."

Oscar tried to press for more details, but his father wouldn't be swayed.

"I gotta go, Oscar. Remember what I told you." The line went dead, and Oscar was left with more questions than when he'd started.

One day—about a month into their newfound prosperity—Russell strolled into the office with a bag in his hand and a concerned look on his face.

"I've been thinking," he said. "We've been working the elves pretty hard. Why don't we give them the night off?"

Oscar looked up from his paperwork, eyebrows raised. "They're not actually elves, Russ, I hope you understand that. That was just... never mind." He leaned back in his chair, stretched, and propped his feet on the desk. "Anyway, I don't think it works like that. They come in unbidden, they do their thing, and they go away. Night after night, it's the same routine. Besides, I don't think they observe the same holidays as we do."

Russell ignored the weak attempt at humor, his brows knit in mild frustration. "I just thought it might be nice to cut them a break, since they've turned our lives back around and all," he said.

"Look, the bottom line is, these guys are amazing workers," Oscar said. "Their craftsmanship is up there with the best I've ever seen. Maybe the best ever seen by anyone. And we've got a monopoly on their services. The last thing I want to do is rock the boat and risk wrecking this great thing we've got going."

"Well, anyway, check this out," said Russell, grinning as he proudly held up the bag. He reached inside and withdrew a small wristband, intricately tooled and inlaid with gleaming studs. There were three more in the pouch, which he laid in a row on the counter.

Oscar was impressed. Russell had obviously been practicing, and his efforts showed in the results. "You made these? Damn, awesome work, little brother." He turned one over carefully in his hands, admiring his brother's handiwork. "But how come they're so small?"

"They're for the little guys," Russell replied. "All they've done for us, I figured it was the least we could do for them."

Oscar stared levelly at Russell, trying to comprehend how his brother could believe the mysterious nocturnal workers were literally elves. A slight frown creased his features. "You know Russ, I'm not sure we're supposed to know about them," he said. "I mean, they sneak in here at night, do their thing, and bail out before anyone shows up in the morning. They go out of their way to come and go unseen, unacknowledged. Don't you think they might be... I dunno, scared off or offended or something if they know we're onto them?"

"Ah, what's the harm? They've made us a fortune, they deserve a little recognition. I won't confront them or anything. Look, I'll just leave them on the bench here. If they don't like them, I'll put them out front. Someone will want 'em for their kid or something, maybe."

The brothers entered the store the next morning in good spirits. Russell was struggling to tell his brother a story about an encounter the previous night, but was laughing so hard he could barely get the words out. Oscar, as amused by the telling as the story itself, was so weak from laughter he could barely stand. They stumbled through the door, leaning on whatever was nearby to balance themselves, and made their way toward the back. The night may have been over, but the celebration was still well underway, and Oscar always kept a bottle stashed in his desk drawer. He made to go in and fetch it but stopped in the doorway when his brother gripped his arm suddenly. Russell was no longer laughing; he stared straight ahead and bore a look that combined wonderment and fear.

Two creatures, about the size of small dogs, were perched on the workbench, resting on their haunches. Their skin was a dull gray and covered with tiny scales. They had long arms with delicate fingers ending in wicked claws. Large, round eyes—like those of a cat—and wide, crocodilian mouths, filled with tiny, needle-like teeth. They gave off a slight musty odor, like rotting fruit. Each of the lizard-like beings clutched one of Russell's crafted bracers in one clawed hand.

"Gentlemen," one of the creatures spoke in an unexpectedly deep, clear voice. For some reason, Russell was reminded of James Earl Jones, and had to stifle a chuckle.

"What... who are you?" Oscar managed. "What are you doing in my shop?" The pieces began to fall into place, and he knew the answer almost before the words were out of his mouth.

"You know very well what we're doing here, Oscar," the thing answered. It raised its arms in an exaggerated gesture of officiousness. "We're creating masterpieces on your behalf, for which you are claiming full credit and selling at inflated prices."

"Those two old bastards summoned us here to serve you," the other creature spat. "It's disheartening, really, when a mortal holds sway over those of our kind. Still, it's impressive when one has the power to call those of our kind forth. As humans go, one of them does have some amount of power. However, there is always a catch, a loophole, which you fools have managed to find."

Oscar could hardly believe what he was seeing—he'd heard stories of demons and summoning since he was a kid, but had never believed any of it to be real. And yet, there in his shop, standing before him, were two otherworldly beings, brought and held against their will.

"What kind of loophole?" he asked. "What do you mean, we've found it? What are you talking about?"

"The wristbands your brother crafted and gave to us," the demon said. "By giving us such a gift, you treated us not as slaves, but as equals. Therefore, we are no longer bound to this place nor are we forced to perform our previous duties."

"You've freed us from our servitude, for which we are most grateful," purred the second demon, its voice dripping with sarcasm. "However, now that we're no longer confined to this cramped space and are free to do as we please, it's time to get back to doing what we do best." At that, the two demonic beings leapt down from their perch, landing soundlessly on the floor in front of the stunned brothers.

Nobody was around to hear the sounds of violence, the bangs and crashes or the screams from inside the store. Nor did anyone question the closed sign that appeared in the window over the next several days. Freed from their entrapment, and both witnesses to their presence exterminated, the diabolical pair spent the rest of the day gathering their strength before setting out on the next leg of their journey.

Cutter felt around the cluttered nightstand, cursing quietly as he knocked over bottles and food containers. The female form lying beside him didn't stir despite the ringing phone, which he located at length. "What?" he slurred as he fumbled with the keypad.

"They're coming, Cutter," came a frantic voice that sounded anything but sleepy.

The old biker rubbed the cobwebs from his eyes, trying to place the voice. "Who's coming? That you, Foley? The hell are you talkin' about?"

"They got loose, I'm tellin' ya," the voice insisted. "I dunno how, but the spell's broken, and they're gonna try to get us, sure as Hell."

Cutter lay back and closed his eyes. Sure as Hell indeed, he thought. He suddenly felt very old and tired.

FAIRYTALE, FOLKLORE, & MYTH. REIMAGINED & REMASTERED.

JOE POWERS is a horror writer with a fondness for literary sleight-of-hand. He loves the idea of prompting a strong emotional reaction using no more than words and his slightly off-center imagination, and delights in taking the reader on journeys to previously unexplored regions. He occasionally dabbles in genres that follow safer, more conventional routes, but the path he loves most is the twisted, winding one that leads through those dark, shadowy corners of the mind, where unseen things creep and slither and nothing is ever entirely as it seems. His stories have appeared in *Twisted Tails VII: Irreverence* (Double Dragon Publishing), *Twisted Tails VIII: Para-Abnormal* (DDP), and *Hard Luck* (Burnt Offerings Books).

LINKS

http://www.joepowersauthor.com
https://twitter.com/Joe_SoWhatElse

JOE POWERS | 545

The Scales of Rumpelstiltskin

by Brian Rathbone

T HE scales were magical, they said; this, everyone knew.

Hamlin Barr approached the shop with trepidation. Magic was invisible, undetectable, a mystery for those wiser than he. And yet, here he found himself, faced with the one magic everyone knew existed. Most had the good sense to stay away from the scale smith's shop, which made Hamlin wonder again how the man fed his family. These mysteries were likely to remain as they were, misunderstood and tickling Hamlin's senses, telling him he was making a terrible mistake.

Duty. It was a difficult word on the best of days, but there were times it was downright deadly. He'd been fortunate over the years. The king had asked little of him, save to guard his royal person. Threats were distant and the real risk rested on those charged with defending the countryside from marauders. It was not even those dangers that brought him here, though. What drove him was far more pervasive: greed. Like a plague, it infected the people but left no visible trace save the glint Hamlin had come to recognize in their eyes. Understanding and detecting the lust for coin was one thing; knowing when one was being taken advantage of was entirely another.

Taking a deep breath, Hamlin Barr grabbed the door to Medin the scale smith's shop. Expansive windows provided a view of the many varied scales hanging from nails driven into the timber rafters. More filled cabinets and shelves, most looking older than the kingdom itself. There was no semblance of order. Copper scales, green with age, hung next to wooden scales amidst those of ceramic and bone. Ornate pieces flanked plainer scales not unlike the ones used in shops across the kingdom. Hamlin found himself wondering if all the scales were magical, or if it was only a few. How was he to know the difference, he asked himself.

"You don't," came a voice from the back of the shop.

"Excuse me," Hamlin said once he'd recovered from the shock. Despite having been trained to be observant, he hadn't seen the man enter. Had he been there the entire time?

"You don't know what you want," said Medin the scale smith. "It's written in your eyes."

"The king," Hamlin said, hesitantly, not liking the way Medin looked at him, as if reading his every thought. He then cleared his throat. "His Majesty, the king, wishes one of your finest magical scales."

Anger sent blood to Hamlin's cheeks when the old man laughed. "You don't really believe these pieces of metal and wood are truly magic, do you?"

Hamlin didn't know what he believed, but he knew what the king believed. "Those are dangerous words, friend."

Medin waved away the statement. "I mean no insult. I'm but a simple man plying my wares to those who value quality work. Magic, it would seem, is in the eye of the witness. I claim no mystical powers, and yet they are nonetheless assigned to me."

"So you refuse the king's request?"

"Refuse?" the scale smith said, his voice betraying at least a hint of concern, which showed the man had at least some sense. "No. I would comply if I could, but I cannot. As I've said, the scales are not magical. If I were to sell you scales under that pretense, then I would be deceiving my liege. I've no wish to do so. You may take all the scales you wish, but of magic you'll find none."

"The king will not take this refusal kindly," Hamlin said, hoping to talk sense into the man quickly so he could be gone from this place. He was not a superstitious man, but something about Medin and his shop unnerved him.

"What's the matter, Papa?" asked another from the back of the shop, and Hamlin cursed himself again for inattentiveness. This time it was a young woman who'd snuck up on him; such mistakes could quickly turn deadly. Looking the girl over, he committed details to memory, as his training dictated. On the ring finger of her right hand, she wore a simple silver ring, around her neck a pendant of colored glass, far from the trappings of the wealthy but more than could be afforded by the poor.

"Now there, Lisa," the shopkeeper said, "don't you worry. Everything will be as it should."

Hamlin wasn't certain he agreed.

"This, good sir, is my daughter, Lisa,'" the shopkeeper said. "She's the only magic in my life." The girl remained where she was, running a wooden comb through her hair, as if out of habit. "You see her, taking the straw that grows from her head and spinning it into gold? This is the only magic we possess, and I doubt it will suit the king."

"A girl who spins straw into gold, you say," King Nebed ruminated, looking intrigued.

That hadn't been what Hamlin had said exactly, but as usual, the king heard what he wanted to hear and not what his trusted guardsman actually said. "Golden hair, Your Highness. The man claimed no magic at all. He said the scales were nothing more than ordinary implements."

"Magical scales might deter those who would cheat me, but a girl who could spin straw into gold? Now that would be something entirely different," the king said. "Bring the girl to me."

Hamlin knew better than to argue. The walk back into town was spent in heavy contemplation. His years serving Nebed had given him insight into the man's thoughts, and this situation did not bode well. Nebed was a kind and gentle man, save when he thought he was being deceived. Too many people had the king's ear, and too many of those told tales beyond belief. For Hamlin, the key was to know the difference between truth and fable, and somehow help King Nebed see which were which. When he arrived at the scale smith's shop, the feeling of unease returned. Hamlin had children of his own and had no desire to do what had been asked of him, but it was his sworn duty. Still, that gave him no solace as he pulled open the shop door. The tinkling of brass bells announced his presence, and Hamlin looked around for Medin, not wanting to be caught again unaware.

It was small satisfaction when the man and his daughter emerged from the back. The scale smith looked at him with knowing eyes. The young woman carried a small burlap sack; at the opening could be seen white and blue frills of a dress not unlike the one she wore. Though nearly of marrying age, it was clear the girl wished to remain her father's little girl. The way she looked at him, the way she dressed, and even the way she spoke—all would have been more suited to a girl perhaps half her age.

"Everything will be as it should, my dear," Medin said. "Now go and show the king you are loyal and kind. I know he'll come to see the truth."

Hamlin was about to ask how the scale smith could know he'd come for the girl, but chills raised his flesh and stayed his tongue. If the girl was ready to come with him, there was no need for words.

"Come," Lisa said, taking Hamlin's hand, and he couldn't help but feel as if he were the one in true danger instead of the girl. She exuded the calm that eluded

Hamlin in that moment. His knees trembled, and he left the shop before his courage completely fled.

"The king's a good man," Hamlin said before they reached the palace. "He'll come to see the truth."

"You're a good man, too," Lisa said, and Hamlin had to wonder if it were true. What kind of man took a girl from her father and delivered her to a king who expected her to do magic? A better man would have found the words to convince the king to leave them be, to find some other way to combat the greed festering in the kingdom. Surely, this would do no good. Feeling like a failure, Hamlin led Lisa to the room that had been prepared for her.

High in a towering minaret, a solitary cell waited. Within were only a spinning wheel and a small pile of golden straw. Seeing these objects made Hamlin feel sick. What was the girl supposed to do with them? The king believed the girl possessed magic, and when she didn't produce... Hamlin tried not to think about it. Lisa entered the room without a word. She looked at Hamlin; kindness and compassion in her eyes, as if she were the one leaving him to die.

"Do not worry, Hamlin Barr," she said.

Those words did little to lessen his guilt.

"Bring her," the king said.

Hamlin walked the halls and climbed the spiral stair lining the tower with deliberate slowness. His mind whirled as he tried to find the words to convince his king this was folly. To his utter amazement, he found Lisa within the tower alone, the pile of straw gone.

"What..?" he started to ask, but the girl simply held out a handful of golden strands, each glittering in the sunlight which poured through the solitary window. "But...how?"

The girl did not answer immediately. She smiled first, a shy smile holding no mirth. "Everything will be as it should."

Hamlin could find no words. Not knowing what else to do, he brought the girl to his king, his mind reeling. When they arrived, the king watched with keen eyes, his smile growing when he saw the gleaming strands the girl held in her right hand.

"I told you there was magic, Hamlin!" the king exclaimed upon seeing the gold.

Wordlessly, Lisa handed the gold strands to her king. He marveled at them. Hamlin, too, stared. Never had he seen gold in such a form. Even the greatest craftsmen, he knew, would have taken weeks to produce such fine filaments; if they could have done it at all. How the girl had produced them he could not fathom. She hadn't brought the strands with her—he'd been intentionally observant, committing the details to memory. It was then he noticed her ring was missing. The girl met his eyes, as if knowing his thoughts. She simply nodded in acknowledgment. What did it mean?

"More," the king said. "Tomorrow, bring me more."

No longer knowing what to think, Hamlin led Lisa back to the tower, the words 'Everything will be as it should' ringing in his mind.

Hamlin had to wonder who was the greediest among them when the king ordered twice as much straw brought to the tower. His steps were been driven by conscience this time, and he once again found himself standing before the scale smith's shop. He was still trying to figure out why he'd come when he reached the door. Part of him wanted to apologize for taking Lisa, no matter how accepting the smith had been. Another part wanted to throttle the man for not revealing the true nature of his daughter's magic. They had both made him look like a fool, but this was not the true source of his anger. Darker forces were at work; he could feel them. Some unknown danger threatened his king, and it was his sworn duty to both identify and neutralize that threat. Grabbing the door handle, anticipating the light tinkle of brass bells when he entered, Hamlin prepared himself to get the truth out of the old man. When he yanked on the handle, though, the door was locked.

Cursing, Hamlin returned to the palace, promising himself he would return every day until he found the man and learned the truth. His legs did not want to climb the spiral stair to find the girl with or without gold. Neither outcome suited him, since either would result in more questions he'd likely be unable to answer.

As always, duty drove him forward. Days such as this made him question that duty, question his loyalty to his king, but such were the thoughts of dead men. When he opened the door to Lisa's chamber, now guarded at all times, Hamlin was not shocked to see the straw gone. Within, Lisa stood awaiting him, long strands of gold in both hands. The girl's neckline drew his attention. It was not lust or covetousness that lured his eyes, but the absence of something. The glass pendant she'd been wearing upon her arrival was gone. He was about to ask what had happened to it when she walked from the room. Moving quickly to catch up, Hamlin had to admire the girl's spirit and her memory. Without fear or hesitation, she walked the corridors leading back to the king's chambers.

Part of Hamlin felt a sense of alarm that the girl had so quickly learned her way around the palace; a place specifically designed to confuse visitors and prevent direct access to the king. Still, he had to admire her skills of observation and retention.

"I do believe I'm falling in love with this girl!" the king exclaimed when they arrived at his apartments. The man Hamlin was sworn to protect looked at the girl just as greedily as he looked at the gold she held out to him. She said nothing, and Hamlin supposed those who could spin gold from straw had little need of words. "More," the king said after examining the gold. "I want more."

A cold feeling filled Hamlin's gut.

"Do this for me, tonight,' the king said to Lisa, who did not meet his eyes, 'and I'll marry you on the morrow."

When Hamlin returned Lisa to the tower, his already growing concern for her and his king became overwhelming. Within the tower there was now only enough room for the spinning wheel and a single person. The rest of the space was filled with golden straw stacked all the way to the vaulted ceilings. In days past, Hamlin would not have given such piles more than a passing glance, but now he saw them as gleaming piles of the most precious metal, and he couldn't help but want some for himself. There was so much, how would anyone miss just a little? These thoughts frightened Hamlin more than anything else. Greed, he now knew, was an infectious disease and all of them were susceptible.

Feeling like the lowest of the low, Hamlin Barr left Lisa to her wheel, secretly hoping she or the king would see fit to share the wealth.

Sitting amid the towering piles of straw, Lisa waited, worried. She'd done as her father had instructed, but now she had nothing left to offer, nothing to give. When the imp came to the window on flitting wings, just as it had the two nights before, she failed to banish her fear. While the king might marry her if she filled the chamber with gold, she had to ask herself what he would do if she refused—if the imp refused.

With a smirk, the misshapen creature looked at the straw and whistled through pointed teeth. "Truly, our king must defeat the greed that threatens to devour us all." His nasally voice was thick with sarcasm.

Lisa shied away from the small creature's hands, which were covered in greenish skin that seemed too thin. Like colored glass, it provided a distorted image of what lay beneath. The thought of the imp touching her nearly made her retch. Her father had told her this day would come, and she did her best to be strong for him.

"What will you give me?" the imp asked, a wicked gleam in his eyes. "What price shall you pay?"

Lisa said nothing. She had nothing more. Already she'd given the imp her ring and pendant—the only two things of any value she'd brought with her.

"Nothing, she says!" the imp whispered, in spite of the fact that Lisa had not uttered a word. He wore her simple silver ring on a gnarled finger and her pendant of glass around his neck, hanging from the very leather thong that had once graced her slender, pale nape. "There must be something...surely you would not ask me to spin all this into gold without some paltry compensation."

It made no sense to Lisa that the imp would need anything from her. Anyone with the magic to spin straw into gold could buy a mountain of the simple trinkets within Lisa's means. Locked away as she was in this tower, even those simple things were beyond her reach.

"Let it not be said that I am unreasonable," the imp continued. "Let it not be said that I am unkind or that I lack generosity."

Saying nothing, Lisa simply waited.

"If I refuse, you die," the imp said. "The king is a good man, but he is a fool. Greed has crept into his heart and it colors everything he sees. There can be no hope for you and your line without my help."

His words stank of bitter truth, and Lisa cried. How could her father have betrayed her in such a way? How could he have sent her to this place without enough trinkets to satisfy the imp?

"No matter what they say," the imp continued, "I am not without kindness. After all, have I not gotten you this far? Have I not pleased the king?"

He had, indeed, done those things. Lisa did not know where she would be without the imp's help, and yet his assistance had not set her free, it had only deepened her dilemma. "What would you ask of me?"

Hamlin was torn. He wanted his king to have that which he desired. He wanted Lisa to live and be free, but he could see no way for both to be true. The king had said he would marry the girl, but even that could be a form of imprisonment. What kind of life would she have, locked in a tower and forced to convert straw into gold. Hamlin loved his king but also saw what greed did to people. The effects of the disease were already fouling the court. What had started with cheating merchants had grown to infect them all—even him. Now, it seemed too late.

Guards flanked the lower entrance to the tower stairwell as well as the tower cell's upper doorway, and yet Hamlin was still a little surprised to find Lisa there. He was even more surprised to see the chamber filled with gold. He had known she could do it, but the scale of it seemed impossible. Never had the king's treasury held so much gold. In spite of himself, Hamlin felt the nearly insatiable desire to take some—only a small amount. Surely no one would miss just a little.

With a knowing look, Lisa walked from the room, making Hamlin rush to keep up. Again, she led the way without hesitation, naught but a single strand of gold in her hand.

In the firelight, the imp danced, casting distorted shadows on the trees surrounding the clearing. A light wind rustled the leaves, the branches joining the dance. Magic filled the air, glittering and sparkling from sharp nails protruding from slender fingers. Pointed teeth glowed orange, reflecting the firelight as the imp jigged around the flames.

"Tomorrow," the grotesquely deformed creature said to himself, grinning. A gust of wind descended from above and sent embers into the air like fleeting fireflies, there one instant, winking out the next. "Tomorrow," the imp said again, his voice now higher in pitch and hinting at madness. "Tomorrow I'll get what is rightfully mine, or my name isn't Rumplestiltskin!"

Rustling of the trees distracted the imp and pulled him for a moment from his revelry. He looked about with distrustful eyes, his gaze scouring the darkness surrounding the clearing. Seeing nothing in the shadows, the imp resumed his dance. On his right hand glittered a simple silver ring, around his neck a leather thong holding a pendant of colored glass.

"Tomorrow," he said one last time, greed glittering in his beady eyes. When the trees rustled again, he did not look up; if he had, he might have reconsidered.

Within her chambers, Queen Lisa sat, sewing. Though she had more seamstresses at her disposal than anyone in the kingdom, the activity calmed her nerves. Everything would be as it should, she reminded herself. Those words had brought her comfort over the years. Life with the king was good—better than she deserved, but darkness lurked at the back of her mind, preventing true peace. She had not gotten here alone. No more was she asked to spin straw into gold, which was good, since the skill had never truly been hers.

It seemed great irony that she now had more trinkets than any one person could ever need. Years ago, when the need had been greatest, she'd had nothing. Forced to bargain with things she hadn't yet possessed, the value of which she hadn't yet truly realized; she knew a price would be paid. The king did not understand why she required so much more security than he'd ever had for himself, leaving the palace bristling with swords. The hands holding those swords were often slow with boredom, and Lisa did what she could to encourage the master at arms to drill the guard more often. Even that was small comfort and did little to assuage her fears.

When Prince Geddy stormed into the room, knocking over Lisa's sewing kit in his haste to outrun the dragon chasing him, she laughed, the darkness driven back by her son's laughter. Making the dragon costume for the king's faithful hound had been many hours of work, but it had been a labor of love worth every moment and the sore fingers. She had thimbles in quantities no one person would ever need, but she preferred to feel the needle as she worked. Thimbles made her numb, immune to the relaxing effect the needles brought her.

A stiff wind invaded the queen's sitting room and cast precious threads across the carpets covering the carven stone floor. Getting up to pull the shudders before Geddy caught a chill, Lisa stepped on an errant needle and drew a sharp intake of breath. Pain brought clarity and her fears returned full force. Blood stained her finger after she pulled free the needle. Not wanting to soil her pristine linens, she sucked on her finger, the blood leaving an unpleasant metallic aftertaste.

Again the wind blew, reminding Lisa of why she'd gotten up in the first place. Watching the carpet more carefully, she shooed Geddy away from the fallen contents of her sewing kit, not wanting him to find any of her other needles. The air gusted cold and bitter, predicting a harsh winter. Somehow, it smelled of pain and longing, as if foreshadowing what was to come.

She saw him then, sitting on the cold stone sill, his twisted form mostly concealed within coarse robes that moved with the persistent wind. Lisa froze, her heart feeling as if it would stop from the surprise if not fear.

"I've come to gather that which is rightfully mine," the imp said.

"No," Lisa said, unable to keep the word from her lips. Geddy looked up at her, fear in his precious blue eyes—eyes like those of his father. Within an instant, the king's hound fled the room, his dragon's tail between his legs. Geddy made to follow, but the imp gestured with his misshapen hand, and the doors slammed shut. Shouting could be heard now from outside the chamber, as the guard seemed to realize something was amiss. Little good they had done her, Lisa thought, her eyes scanning the room, looking for something she could use to defend herself and her son. It was no use, she decided. What defense was there against magic? There was none. "I have trinkets."

The imp laughed a high-pitched, maniacal laugh that permeated the halls. Men banged on the doors now, trying to get to the queen and prince, but the imp showed the might of his magic, for the door held. "Trinkets? What need have I of trinkets?"

Lisa's thoughts raced, trying to find some words to convince the imp to leave, to go away and never come back, and most certainly to leave her son. The fact that the imp still wore her simple ring and pendant betrayed his words. What need did he have of such things, she asked herself. There was no answer.

"Come to me, my dear boy," the imp said with a feral grin. "Prince Gedric, right? But they call you Geddy. Come."

Clinging to Lisa's robes, Geddy stood with tears in his eyes. Lisa knew when her son was afraid, and at that moment he was absolutely terrified, just as she was. Outside the room, the king could be heard bellowing in rage as he made his way closer. "Tear down the doors," he fumed. "Tear down the palace itself, but get me to my wife and son!"

"Greed does terrible things to a person," the imp said grinning. "It can only be cured by giving the greedy that which they desire most and then taking it away. Now come with me, Geddy my boy. The time has come for us to go."

"There must be something else you want?" Lisa asked. "There must be some other way to repay you. Please. I'll give you anything you want; just leave my son alone."

The king could be heard pounding on the doors with his bare fists, but still the doors held.

"Let it not be said that I am unreasonable," the imp said with a wicked grin. "Let it not be said that I am unkind or that I lack generosity."

Lisa doubted his words but dared to hope, now fingering the indecipherable note her father had delivered the previous day.

"There is one way," the imp said, his grin widening to show pointed yellow teeth. "If you can guess my name, then I will consider your debt paid. If not..." The imp shrugged, licked his lips and stared at Geddy, who cowered deeper within the folds of Lisa's dress.

"Rumplestiltskin," Lisa said, finally understanding the nature of the salvation her father had provided.

Nothing could be heard over the shrieking imp, who cursed the king's line and everyone in the kingdom. His eyes grew wild. "How did you know? You've deceived me. You took advantage of me! You never had any intention of repaying the kindness that saved your life!"

His words were true but brought no remorse. "Get out, Rumplestiltskin! GET OUT!" The queen's words were forceful and brought even the king to silence. No one could save her; only she could save herself.

Howling with rage, the imp did not keep his word. Drawing a curved blade, he advanced on the queen and her child. His smile gone, only hatred and vengeance filled his eyes. "If I cannot have what is rightfully mine, then no one shall!"

"No," Lisa screamed as the imp advanced on Geddy. Her husband resumed his assault on the doors. It mattered not. Cold metal arced toward the prince too quickly for Lisa to do anything to stop it. Gliding across her son's neck, like the caress of her hand, the sharp edge parted flesh.

"Vengeance!" the imp yelled with glee, bouncing up and down as the word escaped his twisted lips.

Prince Geddy, for all his fear and fragility did not fall, though, nor did he cry out. A trickle of blood ran down his tunic, and Lisa reached for him with trembling hands. Beneath the parted flesh, where sinew, muscle, and bone should be, came a gleaming of metal. Like a coat of the finest gold mail, overlapping disks could be seen beneath the young boy's skin.

"No!" the imp screamed, his magic not seeming so powerful then. The doors to the chamber flew open, the king's reddened visage bursting through, his ceremonial sword in hand. With a final glare at Lisa, her son and the king, Rumplestiltskin fled the chamber, his vein-covered wings looking fragile and weak as he took to the sky.

Everything will be as it should. Her father's words brought the queen strength and solace.   Looking at her son, she wiped the tears from his eyes and smiled—having a dragon in the family was not so bad.

The scales were magical, they said; this, everyone knew.

BRIAN RATHBONE was born in the garden part of The Garden State, far from the New Jersey seen in the *Sopranos*. Farm life shaded his perceptions and old-world knowledge seemed to separate him from his peers—or perhaps it was the ever-present smell of horse manure. Though he obtained a certain level of skill working with horses, he somehow knew his life would take a different path.

Corporate America called to him. He imagined it would be better to work in an air-conditioned office than in the fields or on the racetrack. He started in the mailroom and worked every day to learn new skills and advance his position. He got lucky, and some wonderful people gave him the chance to prove his worth, but as Brian climbed higher and higher on the corporate ladder, he came to see that the machine was broken.

He started working from home and finally found the time to write down the story that had been growing in his mind for over a decade. At times, Brian felt like a juggler in motley while he balanced the writing of code and the writing of fiction, but it's all been worthwhile.

LINKS

http://www.brianrathbone.com
https://twitter.com/brianrathbone

The Underbelly of the Pig

by Julianne Snow

FOREVER and a day ago, three young Pigs were sent out into the world to make their own way. Each of them had big plans: an education, a career, finding the loves of their lives, and maybe even a few piglets of their own.

They studied hard, each of them working to make a name for themselves, but as it always happens in each family, there were ones who excelled above the rest.

While Clarence tried his hardest, he dropped out of high school to work at the local Gas 'n Sip on the overnight shift, finding the local no-tell motel the only home he could barely afford. Theodore managed to get a degree in marketing from the local college, ending up in the suburbs with his new wife and a job he deplored. But Phillip really made his own mark on the world of Finance, graduating with an MBA and taking over the largest bank in the city. He'd really made something of himself and had the luxuries to show it. A huge house in the Hills, a garage full of expensive cars, and the bank account to back it all up.

Then the problems started...

"Yeah, I said I'd take care of it, Boss," BB Wulf growled into the phone he held to his furry ear. "Don't worry about it. If I say I'll do something, I'll do it." He listened as the voice on the other end squealed more instructions at him. His dark eyes rolled upward in their sockets; he was tired of the bullshit and even more tired of the job that pitted him against the addictions of the city.

"Got it, Boss, I'll—" the dial tone cut him off. "Fucking Pigs... They're worse than the Sheep!"

Turning over the engine of his suped-up Cadillac, BB rammed it into gear and took off down the street. His destination: a small, seedy motel in the bad part of town. The kind of place you went when you'd dropped lower than rock bottom...

Clarence leaned back as the drug took its hold, spreading through his veins and delivering the pleasure he sought. The numbness was pervasive, taking the edge off all that ailed him. The feeling was glorious.

But it never lasted long enough.

And with each new hit, it cost him more than he had to give. His dealer had fronted him too much already, knowing that if push came to shove the elder Pig would bail his brother out of yet another jam. That didn't stop Clarence from wanting more though—he always craved the next hit even as the current one coursed through his veins. He was a junkie, plain and simple.

The knock on the door was rude. It stole a little bit of his high and brought Clarence back to his desolate reality. He could still feel it, but the intense pleasure was lessened. Man, he was going to need another hit after this.

Climbing to his feet, he kicked away some of the garbage that littered the floor as he made his way to the scarred door. He'd been living in the motel for a few months; it was all he could afford and if times got tough, the hard-nosed Cock at the front desk would accept a few pleasure-filled moments from Clarence in lieu of payment. It was an arrangement he didn't particularly enjoy, but it left him with more money for smack so he greedily accepted it.

Pulling his shirtsleeve down over his pink porcine flesh, he yelled through the door, "Who is it?"

"I've got a little gift for you from the Boss," the heavily timbered voice replied.

Clarence could barely contain the squeal of panic that forced itself up his throat. If the Boss sent a gift to your door, it usually meant a broken leg or two.

"What is it?" he asked, nervous to hear the answer.

"Why don't you let me in and we can talk about it?" Wulf answered, feeling the exasperation build throughout his body. He hated calling in debts, but when the Boss called, you had to get to work. If he didn't, it'd be his ass on the line.

"Yeah right, asshole," came the brazen response from the other side of the door. "Not by the hair on my fucking chin!"

It was the last straw. "Look, Clarence, either you let me in, or I'll have no choice but to take out my Huffington and blow your fucking door in."

Placing his hand on the holster on his left hip, BB growled through the door, trying to keep his temper contained. The last thing he needed was the cops showing up and interrupting the little party he was about to have. That certainly wouldn't go over well with the Boss.

"Fuck you!" came the voice from deep inside the apartment.

BB took a deep breath and pulled out his trusty sidearm—his Huffington .45 complete with a silencer—and gave the Pig one last chance, "Open the door, Clarence!"

There was no answer. No telltale click of the lock, no voice responding back. Nothing but silence.

Raising his gun, BB aimed for the lock and pulled off a round. The slug went through the cheap lock, the momentum pushing the door out of its strike plate and open slightly. As easy as blowing down a house made of straw. Using the gun to push the door the rest of the way open, BB was met with an empty room. Clarence had fled and BB knew the Boss wouldn't be terribly thrilled. The only good news was that Wulf had a pretty good idea where the deadbeat Pig had gone.

"What do you want, Clarence?" Theodore asked through the wooden door.

"I need to come in. Wulf is out to get me and I need a place to lay low for a while. Someplace I know he won't look for me." Clarence gazed over his shoulder at the neatly manicured lawns illuminated by the subtle streetlights, wishing for a moment he'd made more of himself.

Taking a deep breath, Theodore leaned against the inside of the door, resting his fuzzy pink forehead on the cool wooden surface. Whenever his brother was in trouble, he always ran to Theodore, but now that he had a wife and a few piglets on the way, it didn't seem fair that he should have to offer any kind of help.

"Who's at the door, Hun?" Brenda had snuck up behind him, still able to gracefully maneuver despite the fact her belly hung low in gestation.

Jumping at the sudden intrusion, Theodore turned, "It's Clarence. Says he's in trouble again. I was just going to tell him to leave."

"Why? He's your brother. You have to help him," she said, waddling to the door and unlocking it. As if on cue, Clarence turned the knob and the door swung inward. "Hi Clarence, good to see you again."

Clarence swept Brenda up in a big bear hug, looking at his brother's face over her shoulder. He knew Theodore was mad, but family was family and deep down he knew his brother would help him.

"My, my, you're getting big! How many weeks along are you?"

"I've got just about two weeks to go now, Clarence, and then you'll be an uncle!" Her face beamed as she rubbed her swollen stomach. She half-turned to include Theodore, noticing for the first time his tense body and brooding face. "Relax Theo, no one knows he's here. It'll be fine."

The sound of squealing tires interrupted the serenity of the night as headlights turned the corner. No one in their neighborhood drove like that, especially in this hour of the night. It could only mean one thing—Wulf had figured out where Clarence would go.

Slamming the door shut and re-locking it, Theodore swore under his breath. He'd hoped that Brenda wouldn't find out about his debts, but once BB was in the house, there was no way he wouldn't try to collect what he owed the Boss. He hated having deceived her for so long, but it wasn't his fault the stupid horses never ran fast enough.

"What is it, Hun?" Brenda asked, her arms protectively crossed over her swollen middle.

"It's Wulf, isn't it?" Clarence asked, his snout pressed up against the glass pane to the right of the front door. Seeing the furry face illuminated as the door to the Cadillac opened was all the answer he needed.

"Clarence, take Brenda into the kitchen. Let me deal with him. Alone," Theodore said, taking the time to quickly kiss Brenda on her forehead before walking to stand next to the door, his hand resting on the doorknob.

As the pair walked away, a determined knock echoed through the door.

"Who is it?" Theodore asked, knowing full well who stood on its opposite side.

"Theodore, it's BB here. I have a message from the Boss. Why don't you let me come in and we can discuss it like men," Wulf's voice thundered through the oak slab.

"Yeah, that's not going to happen, BB. Why don't you ask the Boss to call me himself?" It never hurt to take a shot, right?

"Theo, man, you know the Boss doesn't make his own calls. C'mon, when have you ever talked to him? You know, as well as I know, he lets everyone else make the deals for him. He's just there to call the collection shots when people get too far behind," BB answered, trying to keep his tone even. "Speaking of getting behind…"

Wulf let the statement dangle in the air between them. Theodore knew he owed more than he could pay in that exact moment, but had hoped he could buy some time. It was beginning to look like the Boss had decided to call in the debt—what would he do when Brenda found out their nest egg was gone?

"You still there, Theo?"

"Yeah."

"Now that I have you listening, why don't you just let me in?" BB continued. "I know Clarence is in there with you, and if you don't resist, no one has to get hurt."

Wulf let the implication fall into place between them. The only person Theodore cared about protecting was Brenda and he'd be damned if he opened the door. "No."

It was simple and direct, and it made BB's blood boil. How dare these fucking Pigs deny him entry? "Don't make me take my Huff out and blow your door in, too!"

Theodore looked over his shoulder toward the kitchen, catching a glimpse of Clarence standing just inside the arch as he listened to the conversation between the henchman and his brother. He barely made out the words his brother mouthed to him.

Let's get the fuck out of here.

Knowing it was his only option, Theodore nodded his head. Leaving the door, he strode into the kitchen, grabbing Brenda's hand in one of his and the car keys in the other.

"Theo?" BB called from the porch. "What's taking so long? Just open the door."

And Theodore did open the door—to the garage—pushing both Brenda and Clarence into the darkened concrete enclosure. He pressed the button on his key fob, releasing the door locks as he closed the kitchen door behind him. Getting into the driver's seat, he told them to keep quiet, knowing he'd have to time their escape perfectly for it to work.

When he heard the front door slam off the drywall, Theodore started the car, rammed it into gear, and reversed out of the garage—thankfully he'd forgotten to close the garage door when he'd gotten home from work earlier that day.

The windshield blossomed with thin cracks as the bullet passed through it, each of them looking up to see Wulf highlighted by the headlamps. Not stopping as he entered the street, Theodore pulled the wheel sharply to the left, and slammed the car into drive. The gears screamed in resistance but obeyed. The Camry peeled off into the night, leaving a frustrated Wulf in its wake.

The Boss wasn't going to like hearing the news that both Clarence and Theodore had escaped into the night. It'd be okay though; eventually Theodore would bring his wife back to the beautiful house he'd made of sticks.

"Phillip, you have to help us!" Theodore pleaded after explaining the predicament in which both he and Clarence now found themselves. Luckily Brenda was resting in one of the rooms upstairs, having her pick of the lavishly appointed bedrooms in her brother-in-law's mansion in the Hills.

"Why?" It was a simple question. Phillip sat behind his large, teak desk in his study, a cigar held firmly between his lips.

Clarence and Theodore shared a look before he answered, "Because you're our brother. Doesn't family mean anything to you?"

The rich Pig laughed heartily, his rotund stomach bouncing with his mirth. "Family? You're going to use the family card with me?"

The three brothers stared at one another as the implication of family swum around them. Abandoned by their mother at a young age, each of them had been given the same chances. It was obvious, looking at the three of them, who had made the most of that chance.

"But..." Clarence sniveled, letting the word drop into silence. The brothers stared at one another until Phillip spoke again.

"The two of you had the same chance I did. The same chance to make something of yourselves. Theo, I can't really fault you—you have a great job, a nice house, and a beautiful wife. But you, Clarence—you work the night shift and can't even afford to pay your rent half the time." He stopped for a moment to consider the pair standing in front of him. "Each time you get into trouble, you come running to me. Clarence, when you can't pay your dealer, who do you ask for money? Me."

Theodore looked at Clarence, seeing the truth of it in his eyes and written on his arms. He took a step away in judgement.

"Oh, don't think for a second you're perfect, little brother. How much have you lost this year alone? How many horses have failed to cross that finish line ahead of all the others?" Phillip said as his black eyes bore down on Theodore.

Theodore couldn't speak; he could feel the tightness in his chest as he heard his failures laid out before him. He felt shame, his head spinning with the knowledge he would have to admit them to Brenda.

"It's over brothers. I won't bail you out any longer. If you can pay, I suggest you get the money together tonight. If you can't, I'd suggest running. But I have a feeling the Boss will find you wherever you go."

Clarence and Theodore's shoulders slumped, each of them selfishly thinking of how they could escape the wrath of the Boss. While they both knew it was pointless to run, it didn't stop either one of them from imagining they could actually get away.

"Ahh, Wulf, so nice of you to finally join us! My brothers here have been telling me all about tonight," Phillip said as he motioned BB into the room. "We'll have to have a talk later about your recovery rate. It's beginning to slip into unacceptable levels."

BB grimaced, knowing he'd have to face the Boss later that evening. "Well, hello there, gentlemen. I see you've finally met the Boss." He let the words sink in for a moment, relishing in the reveal. Noting their confused faces he continued, "Who did you think the Boss was?"

The question went unanswered as he got the nod from the Pig behind the desk. Pulling out his Huff, he lined up his shots in turn, glad to erase the look of betrayal from the face of each brother with a bullet.

"It's a shame really, BB. I did like my brothers," Phillip said as he looked at the bodies now dirtying his marble floor. "But business is business."

"And we must always pay our debts."

J ULIANNE SNOW is the author of the *Days with the Undead* series and *Glimpses of the Undead*. She is the founder of Zombieholics Anonymous and the Co-Founder and Publicist at Sirens Call Publications. Writing in the realms of speculative fiction, Julianne has roots that go deep into horror and is a member of the Horror Writers Association. With pieces of short fiction in various publications, Julianne always has a few surprises up her sleeves. Be sure to check out *The Carnival 13*, a collaborative round-robin novella for charity, released in October 2013, to which she contributed and helped to spearhead.

LINKS

http://dayswiththeundead.com
http://theflipsideofjulianne.wordpress.com
http://zombieholicsanonymous.com
http://www.facebook.com/JulianneSnowAuthor
https://twitter.com/CdnZmbiRytr

Sinobrody 0.9.8

by Tracy Arthur Soldan

HIS mediaspace flashed a priority incoming message alert from Grobowiec. Another candidate had been identified. "I must apologize, Minister Zamojski, but someone thinks they have an item I have to review immediately."

"Of course, Mr. Wojciechowski." An aide materialized at a small gesture from the Minister. "Will you need hardcopy?"

"No, sir, just secure access."

The aide led him from the reception to a small side room lined with bookshelves. An enormous leather chair with a lamp on the side table dominated the space. The aide indicated the second switch on the lamp's base. "Please have a seat, sir. This activates the field, it extends one-and-a-half meters from the chair." The aide paused. "Based on one of your designs, sir."

"Thank you. That will be all."

"Of course, sir." He departed with a distinctly brisk step.

Sinobrody seated himself and switched on the security field, sighing as it initialized. He should be used to how people reacted to him after all these years. He accessed the brief from Grobowiec. Yes, a prime candidate on the surface, and a valuable addition to the company regardless. He loaded the full dossier to his personal network for later review, approved going forward with the offer, switched off the field, and rejoined the reception.

"Ah, Mr. Wojciechowski. That didn't take long."

"It's not quite as immediate as they believed it might be. However, I will be reviewing it in depth later. Which is, I'm afraid, a slightly clumsy segue to the topic we were both looking forward to discussing this evening, sir." It had taken weeks to arrange a backchannel opportunity to discuss the condition of the Vistula Lagoon seawalls.

The Minister eyed him momentarily before acquiescing with a half-smile and nodded towards another side room.

Dear Ms. Sahnoune,

Your academic achievements and publications have been brought to our attention as a candidate for direct recruitment. We are pleased to extend to you a conditional offer of contracted employment with Sinobrody Enterprises at our corporate headquarters in Kantgrad, Kantgrad Republic. If, following discussion, we confirm this offer and you choose to accept it, Sinobrody Enterprises will additionally sponsor you for citizenship in the Kantgrad Republic to satisfy legal requirements.

Please contact Sinobrody Staffing through secure means to discuss the details of this offer. A listing of secure communications providers is included below; you will be reimbursed costs for using one of them. You may alternatively make a physical appointment with any Sinobrody Enterprises branch office. You will need to submit biometric validation to establish your identity and enable a secure communications channel.

Sinobrody Staffing reserves the right to withdraw this conditional offer at will. The conditional offer will be withdrawn at 11:59:59 GMT on February 16, 2091 if not accepted, declined, or withdrawn prior to that time.

Marcin Grobowiec
Director of Special Recruitment
Sinobrody Staffing, a division of Sinobrody Enterprises

The message sat on the screen like a bad joke. Helene didn't think it was a joke at all. The encryption had been stronger than most spammers or even con artists used. Not that there was much to gain from grifting her family. The portable and the peripherals docked to it were the most valuable items in the paired shipping containers that had been converted to the apartment in which they lived. The kitchen contents were worth nearly as much. Squinting at the message, she began building a searchbot.

Helene looked up from the screen as her mother came home a little more than an hour later. She waited until the door was wrestled closed against the wintry blast. The Baltic seemed to funnel weather into Gdansk and straight to their door. "How was work last night?"

Annaliese stood by the door, stripping off layers of clothes. "Good, this time. The floor had decent respirs, and breaks were honest. I wouldn't mind a permanent slot there. Have they gotten back to you about the paper yet?" Annaliese glanced at the screen on the way to the bathroom and stopped. "Ah, yes, them! How did you know it was Sinobrody?"

"I didn't, I was just doing some research on them."

"Thinking of apping for a slot? I know it's hard to get paid publication but you can do much better than a line job. You should be looking for an inside seat."

Helene swiveled the chair around. "It *is* an office position. Contract employment at corporate HQ, not through an agency, if I can pass the interview. I didn't even apply to them. They do that sometimes, you know, offer it to people from immigrant families or legal migrants. They say it's because some of the best talent goes unrecognized only because life stacked the deck against them, and they're trying to find that talent. I've been checking on them."

She studied her daughter's face for several moments. "So what's wrong with them?"

"Nothing I can find. It's part of their corporate philosophy, the same as going beyond minimum industrial safety standards like the factory you worked at last night and subsidizing Medical upgrades for full-time employees. They seem legit." She sighed and looked away. "If I pass the interview and accept it, they'll also sponsor me for Kantgrad citizenship. Kantgrad provides Standard Medical to immediate relatives of citizens who aren't citizens themselves. Sinobrody counts direct contractors the same as employees, and subsidizes Medical level upgrades for full-time employees. I could upgrade everyone to Major Medical..."

"Ah." Annaliese Sahnoune knew immediately what was troubling her. Helene harbored a distrust of large corporations, but her father had died twelve years earlier because medical services were prioritized in most of Europe. Her younger brothers both needed viral regimens to clear their asthma for good, and while Amelie was generally healthy, she needed a metabolic reset to avoid obesity later in life. Neither was covered by Standard but they were included in Major. Annaliese herself hadn't had regular doctor visits since she and Ahmad had emigrated from Algeria in the years following the Baltic War.

Annaliese collected a change of clothes and continued to the bathroom. She knew her daughter well, she would accept it for the citizenship and related benefits regardless of her reservations. Standing in front of her smelling of sweat and solvents wouldn't help her as she struggled to that decision.

Helene kept to the kitchen space as the tomatons assembled the standard furnishings. Beds with storage above and below, dining set, couch and end chairs. The corporate apartment was only about half as spacious as the containers, but having been designed as living space to begin with, it felt much larger. The tomatons rolled quickly and quietly, depositing their personal belongings according to the labels. Twice the botboss asked her what to do with crates with damaged labels. The personalization supplies were last, several crates set on the dining table. The botboss turned to her as the tomatons lined up by the door.

"All right, ma'am. Ready for inspection." He smiled and cut in before she could wave it off. "It's necessary, ma'am. Even if you just do a cursory review." He leaned forward a little, lowering his voice. "It's rules. You should get used to doing what the rules say since you're at HQ now. Even if you don't apply them as strongly as you could. There are people like that who work for Sinobrody, you know? Some of management is supposed to be like that, too." He winked at her, still holding out the pad. After a moment she smiled ruefully and took it from him.

The inspection was more thorough than she had intended, but eventually she signed off on the install and the botboss led the tomatons out the door. Her mother and siblings came in almost as soon as the last tomaton cleared the doorway. Georges, Francois, and Amelie immediately headed for their rooms to begin unpacking. Annaliese joined Helene in the kitchen. They each took a box and began sorting out where to put things and what needed to be disposed of.

Annaliese eventually broke the silence. "You accepted the internship, said everything checks out, we're moving in, but something bothers you."

Helene let out a frustrated sigh. "I don't know! Forty-four others were recruited before us, and they've all gone on to middle management or better, or are on track for it. Seven are in the executive offices now, including Marcin Grobowiec. And the four who declined are no better or worse off than before." She put her hands on the counter and hung her head. "The other five in this year's batch more-or-less think they've won the lottery. Maybe I'm just being a cynical twenty-nothing and looking for a catch that isn't really there."

Annaliese laid a hand on her shoulder. "The world is hard, worse than when I was your age, and there's a lot of catches. But there are still people who look forward, who reach down to help others up. Sometimes the hardest thing to accept is that you're the person to whom they're reaching down." She kissed her daughter's forehead. "Now, what's for dinner?"

They'd placed her in HR. She knew that she was constantly being tested and evaluated almost immediately. Response to the unexpected, discretion, assigning and receiving delegation, office diplomacy, thinking outside the box, ability to request help, ability to request tutoring, ability to accept blame in a way that didn't destroy her credibility. The invitation came at the end of her first month. The event was two weeks away, a formal celebration of Immanuel Kant's birthday. Boilerplate language, contact point if she had questions or any special requests, but not something normally extended to employees below middle management—and even then uncommon. So: socializing, public charm, repartee, handling gossip, perhaps dancing. They were serious about grooming her as potential management.

Helene clicked on the contact link. The window showed a young woman, only a few years older than her. Sevda Ilken, a Special Recruitment alumnus. "Good afternoon, Ms. Sahnoune, how may I be of assistance?"

"Oh, uh…my apologies, I hadn't realized it would be you."

Ilken smiled. "Quite all right, Ms. Sahnoune. It's a large company and only a few of us were recruited the way we were. Did you have any questions regarding the invitation?"

Helene mentally kicked herself into gear. Of course it would be about that, why else would she be calling the Director of Charitable Activities? "It's a formal event, will attendees be expected to arrive as couples?"

"It's not required, strictly."

Not required but a good idea. Ilken's expression was neutral as Helene considered. "I think attending with a companion would be best. Someone established with the company, single, but not necessarily fodder for gossip. Perhaps you could suggest someone?"

Ilken's brisk voice carried a hint of approval. "There are several attendees who are currently unattached. Shall I forward the list to you?"

"Thank you, but would you be able to make the arrangements for me? I'm still pretty new and wouldn't want to give the wrong impression." *Such as approaching someone too far up the corporate ladder, or too low.*

"Certainly. Is there anything else you require of me?"

"Would you be able to recommend where I might pick up an appropriate outfit? I do have things I wouldn't be ashamed to be seen in public with, but…"

"I'll recommend you to the ones I use. Anything else?" Helene shook her head, and Ilken smiled. "I'm looking forward to working with you, Ms. Sahnoune. Perhaps we'll have a few minutes at the celebration?"

Helene inclined her head, *of course*, and the connection closed.

Helene relaxed slightly. She'd made the right moves, or at least avoided making the wrong ones. A new message popped into her inbox, from Ilken, then two more in quick succession. Introductions and recommendations to three designers. That was fast work. Unless they'd been drafted already? Wait, they were all ateliers. A quick query left her aghast at the prices they commanded. She'd barely begun wondering how she could possibly manage when a reply popped up: Was she free tomorrow afternoon for a consultation? A second one came in moments later: Was tomorrow evening too soon to fit into her schedule?

The choice of words clicked into focus as she re-read the introductions. *"Allow me to recommend Ms. Helene Sahnoune to you... please allow a consultation... looking forward to your expertise on display at the Kant Celebration..."* Ilken had strong-armed them into giving her priority.

The understanding of the heights to which she was being catapulted insinuated itself into her awareness. *No, not here, time enough for nerves later.* She responded to the ateliers individually, asked what times might suit their schedules, and, soon enough, had appointments worked out for both. The third responded with apologies for being unable to see her until the following week, which she replied would regretfully be too soon before the event...

Muireann observed from the background, sharing it with Sevda. They agreed Helene had done a satisfactory job and forwarded their assessment to Marcin. Sinobrody would be pleased.

Daniel was career middle management and, at forty-five, more than twice her age, unlikely to move further up than head of Security at some plant, but with almost twenty-five years seniority. He wasn't able to hide his surprise when he picked her up. Halfway to the Celebration, he confessed with red-faced embarrassment he hadn't checked her images when Ilken suggested they attend together. He'd been expecting someone pinch-faced and in her fifties who needed a date for appearances, and certainly not...well, he felt self-conscious at his own appearance now. She took pity on him and gently let him believe that, sorry, I really did need a date but you're not my type, without actually saying it. By the time they arrived, he'd shifted to taking pride in escorting someone who was going to turn heads as soon as they stepped out the car.

Helene settled into the post-toasting routine by following his example. Amble a little ways, chat with an acquaintance, perhaps get into a conversation, and otherwise move on. Acknowledge compliments, reply in kind whether polite, genuine, or barbed. No gossiping just yet, though there would be some opportunities later with a few of the people she'd met so far. Answer a few questions for the media, yes it's a Marklund original, they were quite gracious in my hour of need; the invitation did surprise me, but I couldn't miss this for the world; oh, it's not so different from the mixers when I was a girl…

"Ah, Helene! There you are!"

Sevda Ilken had found her, accompanied by another woman about the same age, fair-skinned with auburn hair in contrast to Ilken's Mediterranean complexion and dark hair, and an almost stereotypically-Nordic thirtyish man, blond and blue-eyed, strapped into a discrete exoframe from mid-chest down.

Muireann Rothe and Marcin Grobowiec; Muireann was VP of IT Infrastructure and yet another direct recruit. Introductions around, some light chat, and Helene had been smoothly separated from Daniel and incorporated in their group.

Marcin turned to her as they found themselves on the edge of a conversation. "So, how are things going for you? Close to two months since you started and I haven't heard any complaints yet." He peered into her eyes. "Be honest, now. How are things?"

Helene paused. How were things going, really? Work was a daily challenge, but they were clearly hoping to move her upchain—sooner rather than later—and it would only get worse. Her siblings were receiving personalized catch-up schooling on top of their treatments. Her mother was taking the vocational courses she'd never been able to afford that would move her off the production line. The company was a true patron, investing much more than her direct costs to ensure she succeeded.

"Well enough. Nothing I can't—haven't been able to—handle." Her eyes searched his, trying to convey that for which she couldn't find the right words. "It doesn't seem real. I keep waiting for the other shoe to fall."

Marcin chuckled. "I felt the same way. Even after the accident that left me in this thing," he patted the brace for his right thigh, "they invested so much in me, not just rehabilitation but getting me back to work. They really are a white hat."

"A what?"

"I'm sorry, I forgot you don't have a mediaspace yet. It's an American metaphor for someone who does the right thing for the right reasons." He touched Muireann's elbow to get her attention. "Didn't we allocate a budget to give key employees mediaspaces?"

She pursed her lips. "Yes, but the recipients were all selected months ago. There won't be any more until the new budget cycle." She eyed Helene down and up with a small smile that didn't quite reach her eyes. "I suspect you'll be earmarked for one of them."

Helene was saved from making a response as the orchestra started up, a short introductory piece letting everyone know the dancing would begin soon. The crowd's Brownian motion increased as people re-sorted themselves socially. Helene searched for Daniel amongst it until Marcin caught her hand and squeezed it twice. She followed his gaze.

She immediately recognized the older man with a full beard and dressed in white tie and tails making his way towards them. Every bit of exposed flesh had a blue tinge to it, even his eyes. It was more pronounced in his hair and nails. Zygmunt Wojciechowski, who had designed the systems that provided active EM shielding small enough to be man-portable and which had eventually helped Kantgrad (then Kaliningrad) win its independence in the Baltic War. The man who called himself Sinobrody after the War—Polish for "Bluebeard"—embraced the coloration and neurological damage the viral bioterror weapon had left him with to show the lie behind it. Founder, President, and CEO of Sinobrody Enterprises, the corporate sponsor for the annual celebration of Kant's birthday. Rumor had it the bioweapon had also damaged his ability to read social cues, though some pre-War accounts suggested he never really could in the first place. He marched straight to them, and the subtle unease so many had reported when meeting him rose up in her.

"Good evening, ladies, Marcin. Muireann, would you join me for the first dance?" There was only a hint of slurring from the paralysis when he spoke.

"Of course, sir." She didn't even try to hide that she'd really rather not.

"Excellent. You must be Helene Sahnoune."

"A pleasure to meet you, sir." He took her offered hand, clicked his heels, and bowed, almost but not quite kissing the back of her hand before releasing it. A gesture from a bygone era that somehow seemed entirely appropriate from him, and did nothing to ease her disquiet. Turning to Marcin he asked, "So, how is she fitting in?"

Marcin straightened, hands clasped behind his back. "Quite well, sir. I was just discussing with Muireann that she doesn't have a mediaspace yet."

Helene's instincts told her to keep silent even as they discussed her as if she wasn't there. *Another test?*

"Of course not; she wouldn't have been able to afford it. You think it'd be a worthwhile investment? She's still on contract."

"I don't think she's going to complete it."

"Oh?" The introductory piece ended and Sinobrody turned to lead Muireann onto the dance floor. Several seconds passed before Marcin slouched and exhaled.

Sevda touched Helene's arm. "He can't pick up social cues subconsciously. He has to think about them, decode them. He's a genius, but he hasn't mastered the knack of only tracking the people who are important when there's a crowd. And the facial paralysis doesn't help, either. You've heard of the 'uncanny valley?' Some people have that reaction to him when he's in a crowd. He can't smile or frown or give you a disgusted look, and he's too busy keeping track of everyone else's cues to use voice tone. He's more personable when it's just a few people. You'll see."

There were only a half-dozen couples on the floor as the first waltz began. When it concluded they split up and brought in new partners; Sinobrody choose Sevda while Muireann brought out a grandfatherly figure. For the third dance he chose someone from the far side of the hall while Sevda selected a senior military officer with a chest full of medals; Muireann left the dance floor entirely. *Wait until you're brought out for a dance, bring someone else out, and then you're free to leave the dance floor if you want.* Even with a few leaving, the dance floor already had about twenty couples circling and spiraling. Helene relaxed, enjoying the atmosphere. It was like a piece of history come alive.

She claimed a pair of champagne flutes from a waiter as the next waltz began, holding one out to Marcin. He looked at her questioningly. "One glass won't hurt."

He conceded with a nod, accepting the flute and turning back towards the dance floor as he sipped. "You're on his radar."

"Oh?"

His face was wholly neutral as he watched the dancers. "I forward dozens of candidates every year, and only a handful are given the opportunity. Occasionally, something piques his interest and he examines them in more detail. You're one of them. Muireann and Sevda caught his attention; I did, too, though that was sheer chance—it was before Special Recruitment was created. So did Jadranka Mrkonjic, Roland Fitussi, Orsino Di Gennaro, and Mirela Demeter."

She knew those names. "All contractors that fast-tracked to senior management. Well, Jadranka is his executive assistant, but she's in on almost everything."

"Yes. No one who's gotten his attention has washed out, though that's always a possibility. There are tremendous perks that come with it, and drawbacks. You'd be working with him closely on an ongoing basis. And with the rest of us." He tossed back the champagne in a single gulp. "There are some people who would just as soon not have anyone else inducted to our little circle."

There it was, the other shoe she had been dreading. *Power politics at the top, and I'm a new contender no matter what I say. But I can't just quit, Georges and Francois need those treatments. Amelie not so much, but the reset...*

He gave a lopsided smile. "Welcome to the club. Ah, here's our patron."

The dance had ended, and Sinobrody had come back to them. He offered a hand to Helene. "May I have the next dance?"

She made herself smile, passing her glass to Marcin as she took his hand. "I was wondering when you would ask." *I know you've got an interest in me.*

As they walked to the dance floor, he asked, "Did you choose your dress yourself?" *How independent-minded are you? How ambitious?*

"I'm sorry? Oh, only as far as accepting Atelier Marklund's recommendation. They offered several options, but this was the one they favored most. I decided to trust their judgment." *I'm not a fool. When an expert recommends something, they're usually right.*

"And how were you able to afford it?" *That didn't answer my question.*

"It's on loan. We're about to repay the favor by being seen. The reporters will focus on you, and note that I was wearing Marklund, that the color complements your, ah, skin tone, and speculate and gossip about how a junior employee was asked to dance by Sinobrody. Which will be good PR and advertising for Atelier Marklund." She looked him in the eye as they took their starting positions. "All of which you already knew. Just as you know I'm uncomfortable around you." *It's a tradeoff. Working for you gives me what I want. I'll keeping doing it as long as what I'm getting is worth it to me.*

Sinobrody gave a small nod. "It suits you."

She couldn't quite make out the subtext, though he seemed to approve, and the orchestra began before either of them could say anything else. He was an excellent dancer, leading her through unfamiliar variations of steps she knew. When the dance was over, they thanked each other, and he walked with her as she headed back to Marcin.

Muireann had returned, breaking off whatever she had been saying to Marcin as Sinobrody spoke without preamble. "Helene needs a mediaspace ahead of schedule. Submit it as a capital expenditure by the President's Office."

Muireann simply nodded, and Sinobrody walked off towards the refreshments.

Helene said, "It looks like we're going to be working together in the near future, Ms. Rothe."

Muireann's expression started to turn sour, changing to a sad smile. She looked down and sighed, speaking towards the floor. "You can't oppose him. He'll plow right over you, and get his way anyway. It's better to just go along. And even when you're right and it's a mistake, he has a way of recovering, of salvaging it so it isn't a total loss. Like how he turned being a bioweapon victim into a defining quality." She looked up, tears glistening in her eyes. "Be careful. He has a way of getting into you, of changing your mind about things."

Marcin caught Helene's arm and kept her from following Muireann as she turned and left. "No, don't. She thought he was in love with her, and when she found out he wasn't…well. She's a consummate professional, but there are some topics you shouldn't bring up with her."

She watched Muireann make her way through the doors. Sevda was chatting animatedly on the far side of the ballroom. Helene laid her hand across his. "Looks like it's just you and me. Would you care to dance?"

"I have a small problem with that." His free hand tapped the exoframe.

"You mean to tell me that thing isn't programmed for just such an eventuality?" She half-led, half-pulled him onto the dance floor.

It was, in fact, quite capable of taking him through a waltz. Afterwards, she found Daniel for the next dance, and then the HR manager who was her supervisor. By then, nearly everyone had been on the dance floor at least once, and the music shifted to tangos and rhumbas. No one who was impolitic to decline asked her to dance, leaving her to socialize for a while. She spotted Sinobrody a few times on the far side of the hall, but her fellow direct recruits were gone for the rest of the evening.

Helene's brow knit as she considered the ramifications of the policy change. Sinobrody wanted her input on the proposal in time for the afternoon meeting. He had a penchant for dropping 'Right Now' special projects on people regardless if they were actually within their job function. Her manager had given up tracking her HR workload after the fifth time he'd done it to Helene. As long as everything was done competently and on time. The mediaspace made it possible to keep up. Barely.

Reduce the minimum full-time paid workweek by two hours, and seven percent of the non-citizen employee base, less than three percent overall, would fall below the weekly hourly threshold for corporate matching of the optional premiums bringing them up to Major Medical. But only twelve percent of eligible employees used the match...what if the threshold was calculated as...

An urgent message flashed at the corner of her perception. She flagged it, it would only take a few more minutes to finish the counterproposal and then she'd see what it was. Another urgent message appeared, then three more almost simultaneously. Another one came in as she was flagging the others, they were from Marcin, Sevda, Orsino, Roland...

Her mediaspace flickered, and a window to Muireann opened by itself. She was already speaking, a trace of Irish accent betraying her stress, "-elene! Sorry for barging in like this, but there's been an accident, a bad one. It's Jadranka."

"How did...what? What happened?"

Jadranka was the closest thing she had to an ally in the elite circle into which she'd been drafted. Almost a mentor, and something that might have been a friend under other circumstances.

"They don't know. She was on her way back from The Hague ahead of Sinobrody. All contact with the plane was lost, everything, even the passengers' devices. It crashed about twenty minutes ago. There aren't any reports of missile launches or explosions." The link split, the new section showing a map with a pulsing red dot southwest of Kantgrad on the strip of land that separated the Baltic Sea from the Vistula Lagoon. "It hit the seawall in Polish territory, about a kilometer before the border. Seawall sensors are reporting a breach."

"A breach. That means—"

"Emergency services are giving the seawall top priority. Everyone's mobilizing as an international disaster response."

If the seawall gave out, the Baltic would flood into the lagoon. Most of Kantgrad was built close to what had been sea level a century ago; if the Lagoon equalized with the Baltic, large portions of the city, and countryside around the Lagoon, would be inundated.

"Which means there's fewer people available to search for survivors."

"Yes." Muireann paused with a pained look. "Helene, I know you and Jadranka got along with each other. I'm sorry."

"But her chances aren't very good." She took a deep breath. "Would you return my mediaspace? I have things to do." It flickered again and she had control once more. "Muireann. Thank you for letting me know right away."

The window closed. Planes had so many failsafes and backups, how had it crashed? How had the passengers' links been lost? Helene slumped back. There was no way to know yet, nothing she could do to affect the situation. She responded to the others' messages, set up alerts and news filters, messaged her family. Word of the emergency was already beginning to spread.

Back to revising the policy.

Sinobrody's message informing her she would be his acting executive assistant and relieving her of her other duties didn't surprise her at all. Marcin's prediction had been accurate: she wasn't a contractor any more.

The mansion perched on top of the ridge was briefly visible before the driver turned right, into the woods that had reclaimed the area after the rising Baltic forced the abandonment of Yantarny in the '60s. The road curved this way and that as they climbed the ridge through trees that were busily recreating a forest that had disappeared more than a century earlier. A final turn and the mansion was ahead, lit by the mid-August, afternoon sun. There was no gate, no wall marking the edge of the estate, but none was needed. The estate was alone out here, and there were enough sensors and electronics throughout the grounds to generate an accurate census of the squirrels that called it home.

The footmen wore modern suit and tie, one opening the car door for her, the other retrieving her overnight bag from the boot and following a few steps behind her. A woman dressed similarly fell in step beside her as the car pulled away. "Your suite is ready. The others have already arrived. Dinner is at seven."

Sinobrody would not be arriving for another hour.

Dinner conversation was about work, as it always was at these inner circle meetings. One of Sinobrody's peculiarities was that discussions had to be spoken when you were present in person, though files could be swapped back and forth. Afterwards, he broke with the usual pattern and brought everyone out to the upper balcony. The Baltic stretched out below them, a black void under a rare, cloudless night, the new moon already gone. The glow from the twin cities, Gdansk and Gdynia, subtly lit the horizon to the southwest.

Sinobrody put his hands on the railing, staring out into the darkness. "This conversation is privileged. Please disable networking and recording."

Helene glanced around. The others were just as surprised as her. It was a few moments before Orsino spoke. "Yes, sir."

His mediaspace dropped off the network, followed by Mirela's and Muireann's before Helene herself disconnected.

After a few moments, Sinobrody nodded, still facing westward. "Jadranka's death put it in focus for me. One person, one life, versus millions if the seawall had broken. We made a mistake during the war, in the other direction. Nuking Moscow to get the Kremlin was more tragic for the loss of the Vavilov Institute than those killed directly. Seventy-three million still suffer from the bioweapons they created there. Three decades of research hasn't solved the telomere booby trap. There isn't much hope they will in the time I have left. If we could do it over again, I would argue against dropping that nuke. So many dead and suffering because those records were lost.

"But I am old, and have earned a little selfishness. Non-viral anagathics are beginning to lose their potency. My remaining years are numbered. Most of my contemporaries are already dead. But I will not give in. An alternate avenue of research has opened, which I will be funding to the exclusion of other options. Effective immediately, my personal funding of research into the Vavilov viruses has ended. Corporate funding will remain untouched." He turned to face them. "It may not produce results, or not soon enough to save me. I'm naming you Trustees for the company. If I die, or become senile, ownership will be divided among you and you will continue to operate it."

Mirela finally broke the stunned silence. "How...how long do you...?"

"Between four and nine years."

Orsino asked, "What's this other research? Surely not another viral treatment!"

"I can't tell you, yet. But it isn't viral."

Helene struggled to wrap her head around what was happening. He was getting desperate, starting to reach out for anything that might save him...but he was planning ahead in case it failed...or was he? Even she had trouble believing how businesslike her voice sounded. "How far along are the contingency plans to hand operations over to us?"

The others rounded on her, exclaiming shock and disbelief.

Sinobrody raised a hand, forestalling further outbursts. "The initial documents were forwarded to Legal this evening, just before we came out here. It'll take at least a month to put them in place."

"And the conditions for when they are activated?"

"When I am declared clinically dead or mentally incompetent."

"Will we be given any additional authority before then?"

"Other than being Trustees, no."

Helene felt their silent rebukes as she pressed on. "Mental competency is decided by the state, and requires a family member or power of attorney to concur. You have no living family. Who are you setting up for that?"

"A unanimous vote of the Trustees."

"Will you have a seat on the Board of Trustees, or a veto, or the ability to keep us from looking into things? You can fire us from our positions, but will you be able to dismiss us as Trustees?"

"No, none of those things."

Helene smiled, she could see the pattern of his plans. "We can't stop you from pursuing this with your own resources. You're formalizing our authority for oversight and input, as Trustees we'll be able to watchdog against you draining the company, but since you're the sole owner, we won't have authority over company activities outside our normal responsibilities as long as you're of sound mind and body. Once it's official, you can't remove us as Trustees. We can't strip control from you for mental defect without the state asking us to do it, and even then we have to be of one mind on it. And if you die, we inherit the company but have to continue working together." She raised an eyebrow, to which he inclined his head, acknowledging her analysis. Helene silently canvassed the others, reading the conflicting emotions on their faces. One by one, they gave assent, first Sevda, followed by the others, Marcin and Roland last.

Helene turned back to Sinobrody. "Do we have the ability to decline?"

"Yes. Although I hope none of you do that. I can get top people at will, but I trust you to run the company the way I would. I didn't choose you all because of your skills and experience, though you've proven yourselves. What you do have is the ability to seize opportunities with clear eyes, recognize necessity, think for yourselves..." He leaned back against the railing and gestured to her. "...and not least, assume control when you have to."

The others were watching her, waiting to see what she would do. No, looking to her for leadership. How had that happened? *While they were still digesting it, I stepped to the fore, overrode their objections, showed them what was really happening.* They would follow her lead, go along with her choice, whichever way it went. Muireann's comment months before rose up: *'You can't oppose him. He'll plow right over you, and get his way anyway.'* They had all done that at some point and paid the penalty. They were gun-shy. So, don't oppose him. He was going to do what he wanted to do, but if she—they—could guide it, modify it, make sure he didn't take everything down with him...

Helene looked around to the others once more. Marcin wore a faint smile. Muireann was tearing up. Orsino's eyes were so wide he almost looked like a manga caricature. Sevda and Mirela were hopeful, Roland resigned...she stood straighter and took a step forward. "We can't say yes or no until we review the docs."

"Of course." Sinobrody pushed off from the railing and stepped closer to Helene. "I think you'll be a fine Chair." Turning, he skirted them and headed towards the door back inside. "The privileged portion of this conversation is done. You may re-enable."

A cascade of messages from the others began the moment she was hooked back into the network. Everyone was trying to figure out the next step. Enough. "Stop it!" The flow of queries and replies dried up as she turned to face the group. Her peers now. "Don't assume anything until we see the docs. And no messaging when we're in person. Sevda, you deal with trustee boards all the time. Check the structure and processes he wants. Muireann, analyze the language for loopholes. Orsino, you're a controller. Once we're set up, you'll be in charge of auditing for unusual cash flows. Marcin—"

Roland broke in, "What will you be doing, then?"

Helene looked him in the eye and met his challenge with a serene smile. "Two things: handling PR, and keeping you all focused and on task."

Muireann spoke up. "Okay, here are copies of the docs. I'll have a preliminary parse tomorrow by noon."

Still holding Roland's gaze, Helene said, "Marcin, we need candidate standards in case one of us is unable to continue as Trustee."

"Right."

Sevda was next. "The structure looks fairly typical, but there's a couple of sections I want to look at more closely."

"Can you have a first pass by midday?"

"Yes, I think so."

"Good. Let's tentatively schedule a meeting for noon. Roland, we have to know where everything is and you're over Holdings. We need you to track down all the investments and properties once we have access."

Several tense seconds passed before, reluctantly, he looked down and nodded.

"Mirela, we need you to..."

Sinobrody monitored their feeds as he made his way back to his personal quarters. They'd played their parts perfectly, and Helene was every bit as superb as Marcin had thought. Very few people as young as her could have taken control of a group that high-powered as swiftly as she had. Yes, she would do very nicely if the procedure were successful.

The media storm in response to the twin announcements of the Board of Trustees and Sinobrody's discontinuing of personal funding research into a cure for Vavilov Syndrome lasted weeks. It was early December before it finally died down.

The whispers about how Helene had "earned" her position as Chair were expected and dealt with. It was harder on her family. Georges choosing to enlist in the Republic army garnered far more attention than he'd wanted, to the point his training base was put off-limits to civilians able to provide live streams. Francois transferred to a private academy attended mostly by the scions of the social elites, who made a show of snubbing him until Sinobrody himself made an unannounced visit. A short, closed-door discussion with the headmaster resulted in several students being called to the headmaster's office over the next two days, and with the ringleaders out of the picture, Francois began to fit in.

Annaliese spawned a meme, of all things, a stern look and arched eyebrow captioned: "Ask me that again. Go on, ask me again." It had originally been aimed at a freelance vlogger, who'd shouted an amazingly rude question at her. Amelie dealt with the tumult the most gracefully despite being the youngest; somehow. Vietnam seized on her likeness, and depictions of "Petite Soeur Amelie"—Buddha-like in her serenity and composure in the face of the most ridiculous and bizarre situations—swept through Indochina and penetrated the global net to a modest degree.

The Board itself settled in and found a working dynamic. Roland—and, to a lesser degree, Mirela—assumed the role of "loyal opposition," regularly finding ways to pick at topics; Sevda and Marcin were their foils most often. Muireann and Orsino kept low profiles. Helene tried to keep out of the actual debates, steering digressions back on topic and keeping everything civil. Publicly they stressed they worked co-operatively; the vague rumors of dissension on the Board were counteracted by suggestions that Helene was a *wunderkind*, efficiently and effectively running the show and earning the others' respect. They did find some irregularities that traced back to senior employees, but nothing on Sinobrody himself.

The private meeting with him at the estate about "potential changes that could affect corporate structure" came out of the blue. She was still his executive assistant, and there were plenty of opportunities for private meetings without going all the way out to there. None of the other Trustees had been invited or knew what it was about, and were as disquieted about what it might be. The obvious speculation was that it related to the "alternative avenue of research" he had found. On the drive out that evening, through the first real blizzard of the winter, the whisper in the back of her head, quiet for so long, had returned.

He was waiting for her in the second floor parlor, staring out a rimed window at the growing fury of the storm. "My apologies for making you come out tonight. It looks like you'll be staying the night. But this is both time- and business-sensitive."

"The alternative research path?"

"Only tangentially." He left the window, crossing to one of the armchairs beside the fireplace and gestured she should take the other. He waited until she sat before forwarding a file. "My latest medical update. I have no more than five years left, possibly as little as three and half." He waited as she scanned through it with growing dismay. "The viral strain I contracted wasn't innocuous aside from the nerve damage and keratin coloration after all. It infected the microglia, over-stimulating them. Which creates more plaques, in turn hastening the formation of neurofibrillary tangles. Standard treatments have been addressing the tangles without knowing the virus's impact, but they're becoming ineffective. There is a nontrivial chance that I will be unable to run the company in less than three years. Dementia within four years is virtually assured. Even should the research prove out, there is a large probability it won't be in time to preserve me...as me."

Helene clamped down on the urge to say something immediately, forcing herself to think through the implications. *This is why the Board was set up in the first place, why did you bring me out here for this without the rest of them?*

Sinobrody watched her silently as she racked her brain.

She could almost imagine him analyzing her microexpressions...he *was* doing that, like he always did. She kept coming back to why none of the other Trustees were invited. As Chair, she didn't have any more operational authority than...wait, that was it. The Chair can bring new topics to the Board, and table discussions and topics. *Potential changes that could affect corporate structure...* She called up the projected readiness of the Board to assume control in the event he was declared mentally unfit. Three years was too soon; four years, the initial minimum estimate, would barely be adequate.

"We won't be ready to take control in less than four years. You want me to present some kind of reorganization plan to the Board, to set up new contingencies with an accelerated time frame."

"Not quite. I have something else in mind. It requires your personal agreement."

What is he getting at? "I'm not sure I understand. I'm limited in what I can do as a Trustee, even as the Chair."

His eyes caught hers, and her stomach sank as he spoke. "There's no feasible way to shift control earlier than currently planned for without destabilizing the company. Instead, a direct successor will be established for when I'm no longer capable of running the company. They will still be subject to Board oversight. I want you to be that person."

Helene blinked. "I, I don't have the qualifications for—a"

He leaned forward, cutting off the rest of her objection. "No, you do not have the work history expected of the head of an established major corporation, and your degree is in Sociology. You're twenty-one, an age when most ambitious young people are getting their first real job. But you do have the skills and talents for it. Anyone who completes a Master's at your age, complete with several published papers, without a fixed home, is undeniably gifted and driven. I'm confident you can do it, and do it well." He paused, but she had nothing to rejoinder with. "Currently the Board must approve the appointment of a designated successor. In a Board vote, you would have to recuse yourself. Roland, Mirela, and Muireann would oppose it, leaving a deadlock."

She had to smile at that, he was absolutely correct. "So how do I become undisputedly next in line? I know you too well, you've got something in mind." Her voice held a hint of challenge.

He held out his hand, palm up. "There is another avenue—inheritance."

Why do I get blindsided by something he does every time I come out here? Helene looked away as she called up Republic inheritance law. She inhaled deeply before replying as her mediaspace sorted and distilled the relevant sections. "I'm too old to legally adopt. Placing me as legal guardian or non-family inheritor conflicts with my Board position, leading back to a Board vote and deadlock. You don't have any living relatives closer than third degree." She saw it then. Disbelieving, her eyes wide, she turned back to him. "Are you suggesting…?"

He nodded once. His hand was still outstretched. "Yes. Marriage. More precisely, registered domestic union."

Helene rose and walked to the window, not seeing the blizzard as her blood thundered in her ears. Less than a year ago, she was a migrant, scratching at the door of academic respectability. The section on domestic unions hovered in her mediaspace. *In the absence of a spouse, first-degree blood relatives (as defined by section V.5.b.vi) or registered legal guardianship, primary partners of registered domestic unions have power of attorney and primary inheritance rights over all assets not specifically bequeathed…*

"Unions are intended for same-gender couples, or relationships with nonstandard gender issues."

She startled as he replied from just behind her, too close for comfort, she hadn't heard him come up. "There is precedent. In 2078, a union was granted to Anzelm Lojewski and Gizela Sutula, specifically to clarify a convoluted inheritance situation. And in 2084, a special union was granted to the Deptula-Makos-Pokrywka-Tworeg polyamorous grouping. That one was complicated, everyone had to name their primary partner, and it wasn't always the expected person." The corner of his mouth twitched upward as she faced him, as close to a smile as he could manage. "But, yes, the intent is for relationships where there is no prospect of natural childbirth. Which also applies here." He sidestepped her and laid a blue-tinged hand on the window, staring out once more.

"There were virtually no prospects of ever reversing…this," he gestured at his face, "…and I cannot condemn another generation to the same defects. I had myself sterilized a few years after the war. The sex drive was eliminated as well. I'm not able to perform, even if someone wanted me to. You do not need to worry about me crawling into your bed in the middle of the night, or any other time."

Helene didn't know how to respond, other than to lay a hand on his shoulder. He reached up and pulled it off, still looking out.

"No, no sympathy. I knew what I was doing." He sighed. "But I do want to leave a legacy. I built the company with a goal in mind, to be a bulwark against the growing tide of dehumanization. To show that we still mean something as people in a world where automation drives most of mankind to the lowest denominator of existence. It's not exaggerating to say there's almost no one else in the world who could have done what I have done. I've spent over a decade searching for someone like that to recruit and haven't found them." He turned away from the window, his back to her. "But I did find someone who could take what I've built and, when I'm gone, preserve it."

Helene swallowed the lump in her throat. "Me."

"You." He walked back to the fireplace and stood in front of it, hands clasped behind his back, still facing away from her. "It's not a love match. It's a business proposition, to ensure the company continues when I'm no longer capable of running it. I'd like your answer within the week, please."

Helene ordered her thoughts as she walked slowly back to her room. She'd found the medical records—he was telling the truth about being voluntarily sterilized. The precedent cases, too. His taking a special interest in a handful of people out of the blue was plausible, if he really was searching for someone who could take over the company and run it the way he wanted. His concern for the company was believable, history was littered with companies that stalled and disintegrated once the founders were gone.

No, she had to be honest with herself, her biggest fear was that he'd made a mistake and she wasn't up to the job. But what if he was right? She kept coming back to how much of himself he'd shared with her, trying to convince her to agree.

'You can't oppose him. He'll plow right over you, and get his way anyway.'

Back in the suite, she picked at the meal she'd ordered before giving up and messaging her mother.

The reply was short: "I taught you to do what is best for yourself first, as long as it doesn't harm anyone else, then do what is best for the greatest number. If that means accepting, then do it; if it means refusing, turn him down."

Helene argued silently with herself for several minutes before gathering her courage and messaging Sinobrody that she tentatively accepted but would like to discuss it further in the morning. He responded in moments, suggesting they talk it over at breakfast. She cleared everything from her mediaspace and lay back on her bed, thinking of how to tell the Board she was accepting his offer. Eventually, she sent a short note to everyone saying they needed to work through a few things in what he'd proposed and would report in full the next day. They acknowledged receipt with varying degrees of impatience as she began drafting the announcement.

The room was blurry at first, until she focused on Sinobrody seated next to her. She felt...strange, both disoriented and clear-headed. It took a moment to register that there were others in the room. Marcin, Sevda, Orsino, Muireann, all the Trustees were gathered around the bed. It wasn't the bedroom of her assigned suite, or any other place she frequented, but it wasn't a hospital. Sinobrody took her hand.

"How do you feel?"

"...odd. Like I have to use a remote to control my body. What happened? Did I have a seizure?"

Sinobrody gently massaged her hand. "No, but you did have a procedure. You've been here for two days now. Don't worry, we let your family know you're fine. What's the last thing you remember?"

Helene shifted to sit a little higher. Why was everyone looking so grave? "I was drafting the announcement. About the union." She glanced around. "Did you...?"

Roland answered, "Yes, we know you accepted his offer."

Sevda was next. "It was the final test."

Mirela: "If you'd declined, the procedure would have gone differently."

Helene shook her head. "Wait, wait. What do you mean 'would have gone differently?' What's this procedure you're all talking about?"

Sinobrody said, "I'm sorry, but we lied to you about the so-called 'alternative research path.' I've been pursuing it for years now. Everyone here but myself has undergone the procedure. You are the final test."

"What procedure?"

Sinobrody patted her hand and turned to the others. Simultaneously they said, "Mind emulation. Synthetic simulation of mental processes. Digital minds."

"What? That's impossible, no one has the capacity to..." She faltered as the way they'd spoken sank in. She looked at each of them in turn, and they nodded, once again in perfect unison. She turned back to Sinobrody. "How...assuming this isn't some horrible dream, how can you map someone's thoughts?"

Sinobrody sounded like a proud father. "Quantum spin hyper-MRI. I have the only hyMRI in private hands here. Once you start, you have to go all the way to the end or you don't get all the interrelations, and you have to move fairly quickly. Finding and refining a way to do it fast enough was the hardest part, really."

"But hyMRIs are banned for medical uses! They destroy tissue as they scan things!"

"Yes, it is a bit hard on the brain. Metabolic suspension helps, but even so speed is essential."

Helene bowed her head as her thoughts raced through the implications. "So you're saying you destroyed my brain in the process of scanning my memories, and now I'm just a program running on a server somewhere."

"Essentially. Your brain is gone, but we replaced it with a custom system powered by your body's organic processes. Chiefly heat exchange. Your emulation is running on a server here, and communicating with the system in your body's head. Your data inputs are your organic senses, just as before, but once you're more familiar with your new capabilities, you'll be able to link directly to the net without needing to use your mediaspace."

Quietly she asked, "Why me? Why did you do this? And why aren't the others good enough? Or were you just using them as trials?" She sensed more than heard or saw the others' interest as he replied. Something important was happening.

"In a way, yes, they were trials, but it goes back to why I needed to perfect it. I *am* dying from the virus. I *will* suffer mental deterioration in the next few years. And I refuse to give in. It is impossible to mechanically transfer mental matrices to a brain, leaving mind emulation as the only viable alternative. I needed to perfect it before I undergo it myself. And, unfortunately, the one thing that cannot be controlled is exactly what needs to be preserved in the process." He made a small motion with his head towards the others. "None of them accepted their new situation, and they had to be edited. They're still mostly themselves, not even their relatives can tell any difference. For an emulation to succeed, you have to have a high degree of pragmatism. You had enough pragmatism to accept my offer in spite of your dislike for me. If you hadn't, we wouldn't be having this discussion in the same way."

"Jadranka, too?"

"Yes. It's a shame that she had to make way for you, and about the others on the plane. But she'll have a new body in a few months. And it did prove to the Poles that they need to maintain the seawall more diligently."

She sat up, staring straight forward and pulling her hand free from his. Muireann happened to be directly ahead of her. "And…what happens if you decide I'm a successful test?"

"I have tissue samples from before the war. It'll take a year to grow a clone free of the virus for me, just as one is being prepared for Jadranka. Once I transition, I'll start over elsewhere. At the moment Surinam looks to be a good place. You'll join me, of course. A tragic terrorist attack will dispose of the old bodies, or a yachting accident." He cupped her chin, turning it so she faced him. "If you're not fond of the idea, you can be edited. Just as they were."

Slowly, she lifted her hand and caressed his cheek. "I…I think that might be for the best. Not the editing. Starting over. I rather like the way I am, and I'm not keen on being changed."

The others turned and filed out of the room as Sinobrody rose. "Good. Very, very good. I've been monitoring you. Roland and Jadranka tried to fool me at first, but I don't see that in you. I'll be back shortly." A constellation of windows materialized around her. "I've enabled full access for you. You should practice, stretch your new boundaries."

He left, and she was alone.

She resisted the urge to heave a sigh of relief. He hadn't figured out she'd been lying to him, hiding her true feelings. It had been the tear trickling down Muireann's cheek that had told her the truth. Sinobrody had edited them to complete compliance, but inside they were still themselves. She reviewed all the conversations she'd had with them, picking out time and again the subtle warnings that she'd missed or misinterpreted.

She had to assume he was still monitoring her and could shut her down at will.

She wasn't sure how she'd managed to fool him, but she couldn't count on it working again if he focused on her. She had to bide her time, wait for the chance to bring him down.

The windows around her shifted as she began exploring what she'd been given access to.

Stars sparkled in the clear February night as the car pulled up outside the mansion. Helene hugged her family as they got out and led them inside. Sinobrody was waiting inside to greet them. Dinner was full of talk about the upcoming wedding. Afterwards, she took them on a tour of the mansion while Sinobrody excused himself.

As she led them down a side corridor, Annaliese remarked, "I don't need to see the servants' quarters. I spent enough time in them when you were younger."

"That's not what's back here, Mother. It's a secret lab." Helene put on a teasing smile and leaned over to stage-whisper, "He's a mad scientist! He's actually more like his namesake than people believe." She winked, and they all laughed. At the end of the hall around a corner was a door without a knob. She sent the code, and the door slid aside.

Sinobrody's voice filled the hallway. "Helene, you know that's a restricted area."

"I'm sorry, dear, but they need to see what you've been up to. If you shut me down, they'll know something's wrong. And you can't edit me while I'm running."

He didn't reply.

Her family was looking around in confusion as she herded them through the doorway. Francois was the first to speak. "Umm, are you sure...?"

"Yes, absolutely. He's been up to some vile things, and it's time to end them. Ah, he's cut my access. But I already know where everything is. Is everyone recording?"

Amelie frowned. "What did you mean, when you were talking about being shut down or edited? That made it sound like you were a program or something."

Helene coded the door closed. He could open it again, but it would delay the staff. She kept them moving as she answered her sister. "Yes, that's right. He's been experimenting with mind emulation for over a decade."

As they passed the room in which she'd woken up, all of their devices beeped as the connections to the outside world dropped. "He's raised a security field. Georges, the door on the left."

The room was lined with servers. "He's dying from the virus and there's no way to reverse it. So he turned to his great skill, EM fields." Helene walked over to the first stack, found the server she wanted, and switched off the power. "He cracked the problem of reading and recording memories, the mind, in digital format." She turned off a second server. "You have to use a hyMRI on the brain." A third server went dark.

Georges blurted out, "How could he do that? You wouldn't be able to read a dead brain."

Helene paused and looked over, her hand on a fourth server's power switch. "You're right. You can't read a dead brain that way." She snapped it off as, one by one, they realized what that meant. "But he needed to test it before he used it on himself. So he found candidates that seemed to match his profile." Snap went another server. "Marcin Grobowiec was the first. Then Sevda Ilken." Snap. "And the rest of the Trustees." Snap. She turned to face them. "Each of them went under the hyMRI, and their bodies were borged with processors instead of brains."

Sinobrody spoke from the door, pointing an old—but very deadly—automatic pistol at her. "Very succinct. How did you trick me?"

Helene tilted her head, appearing to consider. "I honestly don't know. Maybe my pragmatism was strong enough to prevent spikes in the program algorithms." She stepped slowly towards him as the rest of her family crowded to one side of the room, Georges in front. "Or maybe I reached my conclusions and decided without having to think through every step. You do seem to have gotten it right with me, at least. I'm good enough that you missed that I never wanted what you did to me, never accepted it.

"But it doesn't matter. I've shut them down, even Jadranka. Six senior executives collapsing, dead, almost simultaneously. You can't keep the secret from getting out. There will be autopsies. And then they'll come for you. The company will collapse, but it was just a means to an end for you all along."

"But...why? Why destroy it all?"

She was inches from the gun when she stopped. "For the greater good. The technique will get out. They always do. And then others get it. There's no way to keep the lid on it. How many people will be killed? How long before someone with less blinkered vision sees the criminal possibilities? But, most importantly...you killed me. You killed the others," she waved at the servers, "you killed an entire plane of people. Who knows how many others you've killed, all because you didn't see what an inspiration you've been to the world and only saw how you'd been marked as different against your will. All because you were wounded in a war in which YOU CHOSE TO FIGHT!"

She grabbed his gun hand, lifting it until the barrel pointed at her forehead. "You might as well shoot me. Because you've already killed me. You're going to die in a few years anyway, they'll take out your implants and never let you near anything with a processor ever again."

"No." He jerked the gun away from her. "You're only half-right. You've cost me everything. But I'm not vindictive. And I resurrected you. I was wrong, you *were* my equal. However, you're also wrong. I will not suffer." He put the gun to the side of his head pulled the trigger.

Helene stared at his body as Georges pushed past her to check it. She couldn't feel disgust, or pity, or regret. All she knew was that it was nearly over.

Annaliese asked, "Honey? Are you okay?"

Footsteps echoed from the hallway, the staff was coming.

Helene's lips quirked. "No, I'm not okay." Everyone was silent after that until the first of the staff arrived, one of the footmen. "Nobody touch him. Call the police to let them know there's been a suicide. You'll need to leave the premises, he cut my access before raising the field. Also call the Ministry of Security, tell them they *will* want to send a team out here."

The man gulped and left, starting to give instructions to the slower ones just now arriving.

"All right. There's just one more thing to take care of. Make sure the Ministry team understands what's in these systems. Show them your recordings. Francois, a little further down the hall is a cloning lab. There's a half-grown, decerebrate body. Genotyping will match it to Jadranka. And another, about a month old, that will match him. I need you to stand guard there, make sure no one messes with them. Georges, there's a hyMRI with custom programming further down. Don't let anyone touch it. Mother, would you make sure the staff stays on the other side of the security door until the authorities get here?" Helene turned to Amelie as the others left the room, stepping carefully to avoid the grue. "There is more than enough evidence on the servers to make the government want to raze the place to the ground. But don't let them turn on the servers I've already turned off."

Amelie frowned. "Why are you having me do that? Aren't you...?" Helene merely looked at her, and her sister paled. "No. No, you can't do that!"

"Yes, I can. And I will. I'm not a person anymore. I'm just a program."

She reached out to the server stack next to her and turned herself off.

TRACY ARTHUR SOLDAN is a recent transplant from the Pacific Northwest to Roswell, Georgia. He works for a large multinational you've never heard of because its industry is neither sexy nor controversial. He discovered science fiction and fantasy almost as soon as he learned how to read. He was introduced to roleplaying games (RPGs) with Blue Book D&D and has been active in Live-Action Roleplaying (LARPing) for nearly 20 years. He wonders why the Muses waited until he was 48 before deciding to start inflicting him with stories to write. He lives alone, with no pets. Not even a goldfish.

LINKS

https://twitter.com/Archon1995

The Black Stair

by C.L. Stegall

D EVIN Demarco tramped through the forest like an elephant on PCP, knocking aside branches, lashing out at defenseless bushes, and stomping on perfectly innocent flowers. He kicked at a tree and then cursed aloud at the pain he received in payment. He drew back his fist to pummel the affronting oak but halted when the song reached his ears.

He had heard the song somewhere before. In a moment of clarity, he recognized the words, but the melody was different; more lilting and ethereal, contrasting with the song's original soulful sound. *Sittin' on the Dock of the Bay.* This was not Redding's bluesy voice, though. This was easily the most delicate and beautiful voice he had ever heard. The forgotten anger drifted away on the breeze even as the warmth of the tune took its place.

Devin had been through this part of the forest several times before. It was part of the Mark Twain National Forest, yet it was a section rarely visited. Deep undergrowth and thick, closely-set trees left it mostly immune to the harsh presence of man. He scanned the surrounding woods, only to find nothing more than the empty timberland he had expected. So, from where was the voice coming? He closed his eyes and isolated the direction he thought was correct. Devin made his way through the thicket a mile or so southwest of Sugar Creek. This was far enough off the beaten path that there was almost no one ever in the area but him. Hence his comfort level in his outward display of emotion.

He arrived at a smallish clearing that wasn't so much a clearing as a paddock of blossoming sage, which surrounded what looked to be the thickest damned tree he'd ever seen. He realized, then, that it wasn't a tree at all. The singing had led him to a hidden stone tower some thirty feet in height. In the various nooks and crevices of the stones, Virginia creeper had taken solid root over the decades and transformed the tower into what appeared to be a humongous tree. Devin circled the edifice, more than thirty-five feet in circumference. He could locate no entrance to the tower. Indeed, there was but one entrance. A single window. Twenty feet straight up.

The woods were thick for miles surrounding the tower. He could only imagine just how long it had been there. Alongside the tower were the expansive beds of common sage, the lavender-blue of the flowers pointing skyward in all their late-spring glory. The air was filled with the scent of that sage and the occasional hum of bees. A multitude of colorful butterflies lilted about on the warm breeze as if dancing to the tune that wafted from the window above. Devin's eyes lifted to rest upon the window. *What the hell? He* thought to himself.

During a momentary lapse in the song, Devin heard the distinct sounds of someone making their way through the undergrowth nearby. Without thinking, he leapt for cover on the far side of a thick scarlet oak. With the sage growing so heavy here, Devin was able to conceal himself as he sat behind the tree and peered toward the tower, curious as all hell to find out who else knew about this place.

From the far side of the sage field, a woman appeared. She was average height, older, perhaps in her fifties. *Still*, Devin thought, *she's doable.* The woman was quite fit, with long, dark auburn hair pulled back in a loose bun. She carried a small backpack and a messenger bag looped across her shoulder. With distinct purpose, the woman stepped up to the edge of the tower, just beneath the high window.

The woman called out softly, "Let down the Black Stair." She then began whistling a sad, melancholy tune. Devin felt the frown crease his face and wondered what in the hell was going on. The beautiful voice that had emanated from the tower faded away and a face poked out from the window.

Devin held his breath upon seeing the girl in the window. She could very well have been a model on the cover of any high-end women's magazine in the world. She had perfect bone structure and what looked to be a flawless complexion. Dark hair enveloped that gorgeous face until it fell all around her. He forced himself to take a slow breath, as what he observed seemed impossible to grasp. Thick tufts of ebony hair became heavy strands that then came together to form a heavy rope. All of it appeared to be the hair from the young girl in the window. Devin thought he was imagining things, and then he was certain of it when the woman in the sage tucked the end of the hair under her arms, around her back, and began to climb the side of the tower as she was pulled upward by the hair. She disappeared into the window.

Devin stared wide-eyed at the ridiculous display. This was absurd. A hidden tower in the middle of nowhere. Some girl, locked away in the tower with hair that had to have been almost thirty feet long. A woman lifted into the high window of the tower by the same hair. Devin was certain he hadn't smoked any funky weed in at least a week. He didn't drink. So, what gave? For long moments, he wondered what he should do next. The Black Stair? That was what the older woman had called for and then the girl threw down her hair. None of it made any sense. After sitting for almost a half-hour, and hearing no more singing or even seeing any sign of the two people in the tower, Devin decided to mark the spot, carefully retrace his steps, and return tomorrow. After some sleep and some follow-up verification, it would be simpler to know if he was going crazy or not.

It was not until the third day, attempting to relocate the tower, that Devin finally stumbled upon it once again. This was due, in no small part, to the singing he heard once he got close. Using the sound, he found the sage meadow and the tower. He kept his distance at first, uncertain if the older woman was present or not. He took stock and could not for the life of him figure out how he had missed this place during the past two days' attempts. He remembered the spot vividly. In fact, only yesterday, he had come within fifty feet of where he was standing now, only to pass it by as if it had never been there.

Today, it was much later than it had been the first day he'd arrived. The sun was about to set and shadows were enveloping the forest as if the shades in an office room were being brought down. Devin did not miss the office. His father would be pissed that he'd taken as much leave as he had, but after that debacle with Kathryn, he wasn't taking any chances. Distance fed forgetfulness. Hopefully, it would have all blown over by the time he got back.

In the meantime, he sat silent by the huge oak tree and pondered his next moves. He did not have to wait long until he heard that same melancholy tune whistled continuously from high up in the window. Sure enough, in mere moments, he watched the woman with the backpack being lowered by the thick, black ribbons of hair as she whistled the whole way down. Upon being set on the ground, her whistling ceased and she waved to the girl in the high window. Devin was awestruck by the girl. He had rarely seen such a natural beauty. He was lost in thoughts of the girl when he caught sight of the hair flowing back out of the window. It was with quite a shock that he realized he was whistling the same tune the woman had whistled. He halted, taking in a breath at the sudden understanding that the hair presented.

It was the tune.

The tune caused the hair to come down to retrieve the woman and lift her into the window and back down again. He was not crazy. His eyes were not lying to him. Nor were his ears. The tune was now solidified in his mind. A dark smile crept into the corners of his narrow-set lips. A plan formed in his head. It was time to make some preparations and see where this adventure might lead.

The following day, Devin arrived at approximately the same time he had the day before. He would have to wait and see if his timing was correct. He had gone over his plan a dozen times, when he heard the whistling begin. Devin crouched even lower behind the oak and waited for the woman to be lowered to the ground and leave. He waited another half-hour before stepping away from the tree and edging through the sage up to the tower wall.

He had noted that the woman continued the whistling even as she was drawn through the window. In preparation, he decided it was better to be safe than sorry, so he had recorded himself whistling the sad tune into his cell phone's recorder app and now he set it on repeat. There was no telling what he might encounter upon reaching the window. If, that is, this attempt even worked in the first place.

As always, the hair streamed through the window and down the height of the tower. He held his breath a little as the hair encircled his waist, tightening to a firm grip but not cutting off his breath. Gently, he was lifted, walking his way up the tower wall toward the window. The hair was doing all of the work, but he followed the older woman's lead rather than just be dragged up the side of the tower.

"Did you forget something, Aunt Juniper?" The lovely voice could only belong to the girl he'd seen and heard. As he stepped through the window, he saw her, hand over her mouth, stepping backward at the sight of him. In reaction, he held up his hands, palms out. "Who are you?" she asked.

"I'm not here to hurt you," he said. "I promise. I only wanted to meet the girl with the voice." He noticed that, although his presence had shocked her, she had dropped her hands and was simply looking him over, from head to foot and back again.

"You shouldn't be here," she said, her voice even and soft. Her eyes narrowed and she moved her head from one side to the other. "Where is that sound coming from?"

Devin glanced down at his phone and realized he still had the player going. He retrieved it from his pocket and tapped the pause button. The next few seconds were a blur. Even as the final note faded, Devin was gripped tighter than ever by the thick strands of hair, jerked forward, and then slammed up against the inner wall of the tower, his shoes more than two feet off the floor. He saw stars from the force of the actions.

"I said, who *are* you?" the girl asked, strolling closer to him, not an ounce of fear to be seen.

Devin took a moment or two to really take in the vision. The girl was in her late teens, maybe twenty. She had piercing green eyes that were shadowed by the thick, billowing waves of jet-black hair. As far as he could tell, the hair wrapped over her shoulders like a cloak, along the floor, and then up and around him, holding him fast to the wall. Her pale skin and delicate features contrasted against the fearlessness he was witnessing in her eyes.

"My name is Devin," he said. "I just wanted to meet you. I heard you singing the other day. Your voice is just... Oh, it's just beautiful." Her eyes widened and then softened ever so slightly. "I'm sorry," he said. "I didn't mean to frighten you. I didn't know any other way to get up here."

"There is no other way. How did you...?"

"I saw the lady yesterday," he lied. "I heard the whistle and, well, I just tried to mimic it. I wasn't sure what would happen, actually." He kept his voice low and even and added a touch of uncertainty, just for the effect. "I'm not sure why."

"Brave."

"Or, stupid," he added, his eyes falling from hers to the rough concrete floor at her feet. He felt the pressure of the hair loosen, then set him gently on the floor.

"If Aunt Juniper found you in here..." the girl said, leaving the rest to his imagination.

"I only wanted to meet you."

"You should not have even found me." Her statement was one of undeniable truth. It was a simple fact that she believed wholeheartedly. Devin wondered for the millionth time why this girl was locked up here in some hidden tower.

"I don't understand," he said, placing his hands behind him in a show of respect. "What on earth are you doing out here in the middle of nowhere, all alone?"

"I'm not alone," she said, turning to retrieve a chair from the single table on one side of the room. The room was circular, covering the entire breadth of the tower and had a separate, upper level where he noticed the edge of a bed. When she indicated the other chair at the table, Devin eased across the room and took the seat.

"What's your name?" Devin asked.

"Sage."

"Like all the flowers outside," he said.

She nodded as her hair, seemingly of its own accord, slithered back behind her and thickened about her as if it were an ebony cloak.

"That's amazing," he said, his eyes fixed on her vibrant tresses. That earned him a smile. Her face changed, lightened by the shift in features and he saw that she was even more beautiful than he had first believed.

"Have you always been able to sing like that?" he asked. She only nodded, her hands clasped together in her lap, eyes directed at his chest rather than his own eyes. "It is truly an amazing gift." He leaned back in his chair to show his comfort and mimicked her hand position. "How long have you been here?"

Sage hesitated and glanced out the window. Devin waited with great patience as she opened and closed her mouth a few times before deciding to speak. "It's been thirteen years."

Devin, unable to respond to that, held his tongue, hoping for more information. Sage squirmed in her chair, finally settling in and staring at Devin.

"So, how did you find me...Devin?" She spoke his name with something akin to reverence.

"I was just rambling around the forest. I do that on occasion to get away from everything. To find some peace."

"Peace from what?"

"Oh, you know. Parents. Responsibility. People, in general, sometimes. It all gets to be too much. The forest helps me find myself. Lets me think." Devin found himself surprised at his own honesty. Still, it was not without borders, this unwarranted honesty.

"But, there have been others who've wandered through here. Not one of them has ever seen me or my tower."

"Yeah," he said, leaning forward. "What's that all about?"

"Protection."

"You think someone will hurt you? Is someone after you?"

"No," she said, a tiny giggle lilting up from her core. It was so cute, Devin could barely contain himself. "Aunt Juniper takes great care of us. She's taught me, kept me informed, but kept us safely tucked away here. It's better this way."

"Oh, God. Why? You like being out here all by yourself?"

"I do. For the most part." She paused and then cocked her head a little. "What do you do, Devin? Do you have a job?"

"Sort of," he said. It was his turn to stare out the window, into the green distance. "I'm supposed to take over the family business, I suppose. I've recently gotten my business degree, so it won't be long before my father drags me full-bore into the mud."

"I'm sorry. I don't understand." Sage smiled one of those smiles that Devin had seen his mother smile at small children and the help when they were being obtuse. For a moment, he felt familiar heat touch his skin and his knuckles began to whiten. He forced himself to face the fact that this girl had no clue about the real world. Locked away here, she would have no idea of the pressures he faced on a daily basis. She was like some fairytale princess. It was not without some irony that he wondered what his role in this story might truly be.

"Let's just say that I have a lot on my plate. I will soon be required to take my place at my father's side. To be a man and a leader. And, let's just say, I'm not all that ready for such crap." This last elicited a genuine smile, bright and wide, from Sage.

They talked about several subjects over the following hour or two. Finally, Devin noted that he needed to be going. He promised to visit Sage again, if she would want him to. He milked it for all it was worth, all smiles and bows. She admitted she'd like that, and he tapped the play button on his phone. As the whistling permeated the room, Sage's hair drifted toward him, easing him out the window, and down the side of the tower. It was the strangest experience he'd ever had and he wanted desperately to broach the subject with her. Still, Devin was inherently wise in the ways of women. He would need to give this one time. He could do that. He had little doubt that it would be worth it in the end.

Over the next few days, Devin made his evening trips to Sage's tower. His father would want him back by the end of the week, and this left him little time to work his magic. He used all of his charm and wiles on Sage. It was strange that he even noticed himself laughing openly along with her whenever he elicited such from her. He was drawn to her in ways he was not familiar. This, he found, irritated him to no end.

On the fourth day, he decided to go for it and sneaked in a comment at the end of one of her adorable laughs.

"I'm almost ashamed to admit how much I'd like to kiss you, Sage." He spoke with a lower register to his voice, keeping it just above a whisper. He captured her eyes with his and then looked away quickly. He made a little show of fiddling with his fingers.

"I've never kissed anyone," Sage replied just as softly. "Other than a peck on the cheek for Aunt Juniper."

"Oh, I would never presume—" he began.

"I would," she blurted out, then giggled for a second and looked down at her own hands. They were each sitting on their chairs, opposite one another, as they had since the first day he'd entered the tower.

Devin slid his chair forward. The sound of its wooden legs scraping across the stone floor alleviated some of the tension. Both of them smiled as he pulled himself face to face with her. He took her hands and held them, drawing her in with her own curiosity and hormonal drive. This was *his* game. His arena. Here, he was master and commander. He lifted his eyes from her hands to her face and waited for her inevitable gaze. He did not wait long.

She leaned in, her curiosity and building desire now driving her actions. Devin allowed her lips to touch his briefly before placing one of his hands lightly against her cheek. He heard and felt her intake of breath as the significance of her first real kiss threatened to drown her in her own emotion. At just the right instant, he pulled away, watching as her eyes remained closed, lost in that moment.

"Wow," she said with a single heavy breath. Devin knew he had her.

Much of the following day was spent in the arms of the lovely Sage. It took all of his patience and skill to keep his own lust in check. He played his game, drawing her in more and more, releasing her, and then pulling her back in. Kiss after kiss, giggle after breathy giggle. By the end of the day, he knew that tomorrow she would do whatever he wanted, without question.

Devin arrived and remained silent behind the tree as he spied Aunt Juniper being lowered to the soft earth outside the tower. He gave it a few minutes after she left before he stalked up to the tower and whistled the tune he now knew so well.

Moments later, Sage was in his arms. Her lips found his and the scent and warmth of her fed his desire to the point of no return. His movements were slow, practiced. His hand upon her breast drew an instant sigh from her, yet she made no move against him. It was all he could do not to smile during their kissing. She was his now.

With only two days remaining before he would have to return to his father's business, Devin put all of his skills to the test. A word here, a soft and gentle touch there. Several times, he paused and asked, "Are you sure?" His own perceived hesitancy was the straw that broke the camel's back, so to speak. Sage gave in to his every whim and suggestion.

With whispered words of love and longing, he led Sage into womanhood through his deceit and manipulation. She was far more intense than he expected, once they were underway. The girl was innocent but ravenous when it came to the ways of human intimacy. If he were honest with himself, he would have to admit that it shocked him. What was more was the fact that her hair seemed to be participating in its own manner as well. It was strangely exciting, and he caught himself lost in the rapture more than once, despite this being the result of his own influence.

"Why do you stay here, Sage?" he found himself asking. He wasn't certain why he'd even spoken.

"What do you mean?" Her voice was low, breathy. Incredibly sexy.

"I'm certain you could leave if you wished. Yes?"

Sage was quiet, her head lying against his chest, face toward the foot of the simple bed. Everything here was simple. *Except*, Devin thought, *this strange girl herself.*

"It's safer," she said. He waited for some further explanation, yet none came.

"I only have one more day," he said, changing the subject. No sense getting too deeply involved. He was accomplishing exactly what it was he set out to accomplish. End of story. "I've really enjoyed being with you. But, it may be a while before I am able to return." They had spoken at length about his responsibilities to his father. For what it was worth, she seemed to understand.

"That was incredible," Sage said. Her smile shone with vibrancy and life. She had pulled her face up to gaze at him and she ran her fingers through his dark, thick hair. Her own hair had coiled about them and settled into a peaceful rest itself, like a python after a grand meal. Her smile shifted to something more...hungry. She peered into his eyes. "Can we do it again?"

Afterwards, exhausted and satiated, Devin took his leave of her. Too tired to maintain the required tune, the somber whistling emanated from his phone as the Black Stair lowered him to the forest floor.

Devin returned the following day. His last day for a long while. He would enjoy the fruits of his labor for one last time before his necessary departure. With any luck, it could work to his benefit, building in her the desire to wait for him in eager abandon.

His music played; down came the Black Stair. Even as her hair drew him into the room, Devin saw that the situation was suddenly changed. Sage ran to him, wrapping her arms around him in a fierce hug as Aunt Juniper glared at him, hands on her hips, fury in her eyes.

"Idiot," the woman spat. "What have you done?"

"I told her," Sage whispered. "And, I told her that I wanted to leave with you."

Devin held his breath, thoughts whirling about his mind. This had taken an unexpected turn. He had been careless not to check for the woman first. He certainly had not wanted to have Sage want to leave the tower with him. Still, there was something else in the woman's eyes. It struck him as odd, but he couldn't put his finger on it. It was almost as if the fact that he had deflowered this girl was not the main issue at hand.

"I'm sorry, Juniper," he said, bowing his head slightly while attempting to come up with some viable excuse or explanation. Sadly, nothing came to mind. Nothing that sounded worthwhile, anyway.

"She cannot leave with you." The woman had spoken directly to Devin with authority and complete dominance. Although he respected her stance, the effect was a grating on the inside of his skull and he fought to maintain his calm demeanor. Thankfully, Juniper then turned her attention to the girl. "You know you can't. It isn't safe."

"It's different now," Sage said. The way she spoke the words, the weight of the undertone drew Devin's eyes to the girl by his side with the determined stare and thirty feet of hair. "I'm fine. I'm an adult. It is my decision."

"It's dangerous and you know it," Juniper said. She pointed to Devin. "Just allowing him up here is dangerous. The boy is clueless. He has no idea of what he's gotten himself into."

"Shut up!" The words were louder than Devin had expected; more strength poured from those words than it seemed the tiny young lady would have been capable of. Juniper's expression showed that she was shocked as well. Her eyes widened and then narrowed in quick succession.

"What the hell is going on here?" Devin said before he could stop himself. "Why can't she leave if she wants to?" He felt like slapping himself. Why the hell had he said that? He didn't give a shit whether the girl left or not. And, certainly not with him. That was the last thing he wanted.

"Shut up, Devin," the woman ordered.

"How do you know my name?" he said, taking an automatic step forward.

"I know all about you, boy. I have my ways, and you are no different from any other male. Worse even. How many women have you bedded through your lies and manipulation? Dozens? A hundred?"

"Devin?" Sage's voice was so small compared to her previous outburst.

"She doesn't know what she's talking about," Devin said. His arm snaked around Sage's waist and he pulled her close to him. "She just doesn't want us to be together."

"Oh, good God. You *are* a little shit, aren't you, boy?" Juniper crossed her arms and stared at Devin with obvious insolence.

"Shut up, you bitch." Devin regretted the words as soon as they fell from his lips.

"Devin?" Sage turned toward him, his arm still holding her close. "You love me, don't you? You said you love me."

"That boy doesn't even know what the word means," Juniper said. Like a flash of black lightning, thick strands of Sage's hair struck out and flicked at Juniper's crossed arms, leaving a thick welt along the length of one. The woman cried out in pain, grasping her wounded arm.

"What the hell?" Devin said, glaring at the hair as it retreated back to surround both him and Sage.

"She's dangerous! See?" Juniper begged. "He has no idea."

"Seriously," Devin said. "What in the hell is going on here?" He couldn't correlate his suspicion to what he understood to be reality.

"You know this has been for the good of everyone," Juniper said. Her hand was disappearing into the purse hanging loosely at her side. "You and your sister could never survive out there. Things are complicated enough already."

"Wait," Devin said. "What sister?" All of a sudden, he was lost. When Juniper pointed to the length of jet-black tresses encircling them, it took long moments before Devin's thoughts could congeal. "That's not possible."

"Really?" Juniper said. "And, the fact that that same hair lifted and lowered you from this tower is altogether different?"

"I told you, things are different now!" Sage repeated, as if not hearing any of the ongoing conversation.

Several thoughts rippled through Devin's mind, one after the other. His eyes noted Juniper's hand in her purse, possibly going for a gun. He then removed his hand from Sage's back and caressed her hair. He whispered a few words, uncertain if this plan made any sense whatsoever. It took only a second to find out.

"No!" Sage screamed. Her hair was writhing toward Juniper after being told by Devin that the woman was the only thing keeping the three of them from being together. Sage stared at Devin with new eyes and he knew that he had just destroyed everything he had built with her up to this point.

The Black Stair encircled Juniper, who withdrew a large pair of scissors from her purse. The next few moments were but a blur, a flurry of motion, as the Black Stair closed upon Juniper, pulling her arms tight to her side. Juniper was then lifted from the floor and flung with great force directly at the solitary window, her head bouncing off one side, the scissors skittering across the floor to the wall. The sound of her skull cracking was followed by the sharp snap of her twisted neck. Juniper fell to the forest floor like a discarded rag doll, broken and unwanted.

Devin watched as Sage crumpled to the floor in tears, sobs wracking her small frame. The Black Stair, her apparent parasitic twin, wrapped itself around her like a blanket. For long moments, he stood in silence, uncertain of what might come next. A myriad of options flooded his brain. He could try and keep this whole situation in check by professing his love for them both. He could play one against the other, which made a more perverse sense for the outcome he preferred. Whatever decision he would have made, it was too late.

"She didn't mean to," Sage said, her sobs easing. On those words, her speech hesitated slightly, but then it grew steadier. Husky and worn, the girl's voice began to resonate with solidity. "She never meant to kill our mother. She had no idea. She thought it was just hair. If she had not tried to trim it, everything would've been fine."

Devin clamped down on his words, trying to decipher what she meant, to what she was referring. It occurred to him that he finally understood. Sage's mom had tried to cut the little girl's hair and the hair—Sage's absorbed twin sister—fought back, struck back in the only way it knew and that was why Sage was here. It wasn't for her own safety. That was what she meant when she said it wasn't safe out there. She was talking about the danger to others.

"We thought we loved you," Sage said, her eyes finding Devin's. In a flash, he knew he had made too many mistakes—the worst being stepping into this tower in the first place. His legs moved of their own accord, his back brushing up against the stone wall.

"Sage," he said. "Please. I do love you." He didn't believe his own words and Sage did not either.

"So many lies," she said. She stood and faced him, anger replacing the hurt in her eyes. "We've had enough."

Devin reacted, squatting and quickly retrieving the scissors that had fallen from Juniper's hand. He held them out, open wide, pointing at Sage. "I don't want this," he said. "I only wanted you."

"Well, you can't have us," Sage replied. She spread her arms wide and Devin saw that the two sisters were in perfect sync now.

The Black Stair flowed out to either side of him and he danced over thick strands to escape to his right. He waved the scissors about, but he knew in an instant that his only hope was to get to Sage, to take her out. He was no match for the Black Stair. His leg muscles bunched and he leaped, scissors outstretched and aimed for the girl's heart. He made it less than five feet.

In a flash of black silken fury, the Black Stair bound itself around Devin's waist while a cable-thick strand worked itself in the opposite direction around his head and face. Devin did not even have time to try and scream before the two separated at lightning speed, twisting and tearing his head from his body.

Sage collapsed to the floor, again the pain and anger of being betrayed wracking the cries from her anguished soul. The Black Stair gently began to wrap itself about her sister, caressing her, consoling her. Waiting.

When Sage could cry no more, she watched as her hair writhed across the floor to the window, anchoring itself to the hook near the inner edge. It was from this hook that they had lifted and lowered Aunt Juniper innumerable times. Now, it was their turn.

With gentle ease, Sage was lowered to the forest floor and, surrounded by the flowers whose name she bore, prepared herself for the world at hand. The Black Stair manipulated and wove itself into the perfect imitation of a solid black cloak, draped over Sage's head, over her shoulders and down her back. In silence and determination, they set off to find their future.

C.L.

STEGALL, President of Dark Red Press, began writing short stories in his freshman year of high school for extra credit. He continues to write for extra credit to this very day, since one never knows when one will need it.

He is the author of *Weight of Night*, and the adult Urban Fantasy novel, *Blood of Others*. He is also the senior editor for the Dark Red Press novella anthologies *4POCALYPSE* and *4RCHETYPES*. He is an ex-military geek with a penchant for fantasy. This makes him rather dangerous in a literary perspective.

LINKS

http://www.clstegall.com
http://www.darkredpress.com
http://www.facebook.com/CLStegall.Author
https://twitter.com/clstegall

The Dragon's Tinder

by Brian W. Taylor

Some time ago, in a land similar to ours, townsfolk disappeared each evening.
Evil ruled the night. Times were bleak, and people sought a spark...

DINNER, thus far, had been a disaster. The cook hadn't seasoned the mashed potatoes properly, Victoria's father had spilled his wine, and her mother, Lucille, had had seven glasses of wine. Each week her parents found some excuse to fire the chef and the next day a new one took their place. Victoria looked from her mother to father and felt shame burn all the way through to her soul. At seventeen, she understood more about charity and humility than her parents, often spending her money on the city folk—a loaf of bread here, a new pair of shoes there, and a month's rent later her father had been ready to take her purse away. She had gotten so charitable that her father had even forbade her from leaving the mansion, paying university professors to conduct lessons on the property, and going so far as locking Victoria away behind sturdy doors and barred windows.

Despite her father's foul mood, Victoria felt the need to voice her feelings about the arranged marriage. "Can we talk about the wedding, please?"

Reginald slammed a fist into the table and rose to his feet red-faced. "You're marrying Lionel Staunton on your eighteenth birthday, whether you like it or not. I won't have you tarnish this family's good name because you're too nearsighted to see the value of an arranged marriage. Our families have been connected through marriage for generations, going all the way back to the old country. The chain must not be broken."

Victoria pushed away her half-eaten plate of game hen, mashed potatoes, and fresh greens. She sat back and took a deep breath. How many times did she have to say the same thing? "Lionel Staunton is a spoiled playboy who has a new lady toy each week. He doesn't care about me. I'd be surprised if he knew the meaning of love, let alone monogamy. You always say us Ashworths are second to none. Surely that includes me." She kept her tone even, calm. Letting her emotions get the better of her would be her downfall. "I will not soil myself, or the sanctity of marriage, with the likes of him."

Reginald threw his napkin down on the table in disgust. "What is wrong with *your* daughter?" he said to Lucille.

Lucille visibly swayed while slurping down another glass of wine. "At least our daughter knows how to eloquently get her point across." She glared at her husband.

"I can't believe the two of you," Reginald said, letting his exasperation show. "This marriage has been arranged since Victoria was nine years old. We cannot back out now—or ever. The Stauntons are the most influential family in this country and will make our lives a living hell if we even think about calling it off. I will not be forced to scurry around like a rat eating scraps from their table. That'll be the day!"

"Quite right, dear," Lucille added with a snort. A look of concentration on her face, she poked at her plate before grimacing and pushing it away untouched.

Victoria shook her head. She had been fighting this battle for four years now. At first, the thought of marrying a rich and powerful man had intrigued her. Some of the other girls had been jealous of her betrothal. That was before she had gotten to know Lionel a little better. Now she felt like a wounded fawn as a pack of hungry wolves closed in, her father leading the charge. She needed to find a way out, and fast.

"I've lost my appetite," Reginald proclaimed. He clapped his hands and several servants buzzed about the dining hall clearing away the mostly-untouched meals. "Bring more wine," he ordered.

Lucille clapped her approval and waited as a hunched-back servant emerged with a full bottle. "Thank you, Ramona." She swilled the contents of her glass and sniffed before swallowing half the glass in one gulp.

"Leave the bottle," Reginald said after his glass was full.

Ramona placed the bottle on the table and bowed before disappearing through the kitchen doors.

"At least one of the godforsaken servants knows how to do their job properly."

Lucille raised her glass and said, "Here, here." She downed the rest of her wine and put a hand to her mouth. "I'm not feeling very well."

"You've had too much wine, Mother." Victoria rose and walked around the entirely-too-large table and helped her mother to her feet. "Come, I'll help you up to your room."

"Thank you, dear."

Reginald slammed his empty wine glass down. "You *will* marry Lionel. I don't care if I have to lock you in the dungeon for the next month. There will be no further discussions." He didn't bother with the glass and drank directly from the bottle. "Don't force my hand in this."

"Why do you force mine?"

"How dare you!" Reginald stood and threw the half-empty bottle into the fireplace. "You owe everything to the Ashworth name. Everything. A wise woman knows her place in the world and works to keep it with both hands. Perhaps we should have left you languishing in that orphanage, hmm?"

"Oh, I know my place in this world. Believe me when I say I'm meant for more than being a rich man's trophy. You can't make me love him." Victoria pulled her mother up and wrapped an arm around her waist, steadying her.

"Love?" Reginald bellowed. "Seventeen and already you're an expert in love! Let me assure you that love, like anything else, can be learned. Your professors all inform me that learning comes easily for you." He inclined his head and chuckled.

Victoria's cheeks flashed red, but she managed to bite her tongue. It was true; she had an affinity for knowledge. The more she had, the more likely she would never have to depend on men like her father or Lionel Staunton ever again. She'd be free to be who she wanted to be.

"Ramona," Reginald called, apparently finished arguing. After the old crone slipped into the room as silent as an assassin, he said, "Can you please help my wife to her room? Get one of your nephews to help." Reginald grabbed another bottle of wine and poured a tall glass.

Ramona eyed the bottle before nodding and hurrying to Victoria and her mother. Together the three of them struggled out of the dining hall and made it to the grand stairwell when Lucille passed out.

"Wait here," Ramona said. "I'll fetch Sandu."

Victoria leaned against the bannister and waited, her mind bubbling with thought. Her father wasn't fit to govern, or, much less lead anyone. All he ever cared about was his place in society. And money. Dear lord, they had almost three chests full of coin hidden away in an underground vault guarded day and night. Her father had taken Ramona's nephews on as added security after their mother had been found dead ten years prior. He always marveled at how loyal they had grown to be.

Sandu, the eldest brother, hurried toward Lucille and scooped her into his chiseled arms. His eyes, always intense, narrowed on the dining hall door. "Are you okay, my lady?"

Victoria took a step back and nodded. She never felt at ease around Sandu. Maybe it had something to do with him being fifteen years her elder. The twins, Nico and Rica, had always been easy on the eyes but lacked a certain spark of intelligence. It almost seemed like they shared the same brain. Lastly, there was sweet and kind Dorin. For the past nine years, Victoria and Dorin had been inseparable.

His shaggy brown hair and dimpled smile seemed to cast a spell on her. She still remembered the sweetness of their last kiss, shared before he left for the war a little over a year ago.

Victoria smiled. "Yes, I'm fine. Take Mother up to her room, please. I'll be up shortly."

Sandu grunted and started up the carpeted steps.

The door to the dining hall crashed open. Victoria, startled at the noise, stopped halfway up the stairs.

"The nerve of that child, talking to me like a guest in my own home. Cattle. You're all cattle!" Reginald yelled, his words echoing along the stone walls of the castle.

Victoria crouched behind the bannister, listening. Ramona entered from the servant's quarters. Even though Victoria couldn't hear all that was being said, she could tell Ramona was urging Reginald to go to his room by the way she tugged at his arm.

"Take your hands from me, woman. *I'm* the master of this house and I'll do as I please." Reginald yanked his arm free so violently that Ramona nearly fell on her face. "Years of loyal service aside, I'm warning you..."

Victoria leaned closer, concentrating to hear.

"Warning me?" Ramona said. "Have you forgotten the day my sister discovered your true identity, Mr. Ashworth? She urged you to give the child up peacefully. Your pride and sovereignty have always been your weakness. Victoria is leaving with me. I'll see to it that she never marries any Staunton."

Reginald's eyes darkened. "You think I don't know what you are?" His lips parted revealing fangs. He smiled, cold and predatory. "To think she scorns Lionel Staunton but fawns over an orphaned vampire slayer. She'll be turned on her eighteenth birthday like all the other Ashworth women before her."

Victoria put a hand over her mouth. Vampires were stories old crones told children to make them behave. She never believed they were real. Not until witnessing those fangs. Some of the townsfolk told stories of orphans disappearing in the night. Had her father murdered them? So many thoughts rushed through her mind—and all at once. Victoria suddenly understood why she was never allowed any wine. It wasn't really wine.

Ramona pulled something from an apron pocket and threw it at Reginald before running up the stairs. He jumped back narrowly escaping what smelled like a cloud of garlic fumes, choking.

Reginald surged up the steps after her. Rage twisted his mouth into a snarl, saliva dripping from his fangs like a rabid animal. He wrapped his hands around Ramona's neck and squeezed. After a long moment she went limp. He lunged forward, his mouth opening wider, and bit down on the throbbing vein in her neck.

Victoria gasped.

Ramona's eyes snapped open. She clawed frantically at Reginald. Her hooked nose twitched as her life force was drained. Reginald clamped down harder. The sickening sounds of him slurping carried up to Victoria. Reginald's eyes burned with hatred as Ramona fell limply away.

Rica emerged from the dining hall, broom in hand, and stopped mid-step when he saw his aunt lying in a bloody heap. "What have you done?" He snapped the broom in half, holding the makeshift wooden stake high, and charged.

Victoria was unsure what to do. If her father was a vampire than it was logical to assume her mother was, too. Sandu, she feared, was probably dead. She felt faint at the realization her whole life had been a lie but steeled her nerves and hurried down to Ramona, feeling for a pulse. It was weak, but steady.

In a blur of motion Reginald was on Rica before he had time to react. Rica howled as Reginald twisted his arm until it snapped. The jagged broom handle clacked harmlessly away.

"Your mother put up more of a fight than you." With a sharp twist, Reginald snapped Rica's neck and tossed him effortlessly aside.

"Stop!" Victoria yelled.

Reginald turned. "Obedience is the only thing that will save you now."

Nico poured through the servants' quarters door like smoke. He held a finger up to his mouth, creeping along the wall until reaching the discarded broom handle.

"You've always cared too much about the servants. Marry Lionel Staunton as planned or watch as they suffer."

Ramona reached up an arm, tugging at Victoria's dress. "Flee. Now," she whispered.

Nico scurried over to the staircase.

"I've raised you as my own. After you're turned none of this will matter. You'll welcome your new power and feast on those beneath your class," Reginald said, slowly ascending the stairs.

Nico broke into a run raising the broom handle. Reginald turned a moment before the wood penetrated his flesh. He snatched the broom handle from Nico and drove it through his heart. "How do you like it?" he hissed.

Nico's eyes bulged and his mouth hung open, the look of surprise his last. Reginald tossed the body aside and grinned. "They made much better servants than vampire hunters, don't you think?"

A scream from upstairs sliced through the tension. It sounded like a man—probably Sandu—in great pain. The scream trailed off as eerie silence settled over the castle. Victoria realized it was the sound of death.

"I see your mother has finished her meal. She never could feed without playing with her food," Reginald said with a shake of his head.

As Victoria turned to run, an unusually strong hand grabbed her. "You're not going anywhere."

Victoria kicked to no avail. Reginald held fast and even seemed to enjoy her struggles. She took a deep breath and slowly released it, calming her nerves. Just yesterday she sat staring out her window for any sign of Dorin's return; today she found herself caught between two powerful vampire families.

"What do you want with me?"

"Marry Lionel. If you do, Ramona's and Dorin's deaths will be quick and painless. Refuse, and I'll keep them alive in the dungeons, slowly bleeding them until they can't bleed anymore. Their suffering will be legendary."

Victoria's eyes widened at the mention of Dorin.

Reginald pulled Victoria closer. "Give me your word or I'll make you watch as Dorin is bled dry." His smile widened until his fangs were showing.

Dorin had promised to live through the war if only to see her one more time. In that moment, Victoria realized her feelings went deeper than just affection. She loved him, and the thought of his torture tore at her. Then again, the thought of becoming a vampire seemed infinitely worse. Either way, she would lose—her love, or her soul. Probably both.

Victoria shook her head as tears rolled down her cheeks. Through quivering lips she said, "I won't marry Lionel." At least she would stay true to herself and not succumb to desperation. Cooler heads always prevailed. She had to keep fighting. If not for her, then for the citizens under her father's care. There had to be a way of stopping him and she had the best chance.

"Foolish girl. Once you're turned you'll see the error in your choice."

Victoria slapped Reginald, snapping his head sideways, a hand-sized welt covering his cheek. "My heart and mind will always be mine no matter what you do to me."

The rest of the color drained from Reginald's pale face. He grabbed Ramona and slung her over a shoulder. Victoria kicked him between the legs. Reginald laughed before striking her once.

Colors blurred as Victoria's eyes lost focus. She tried to call out to Dorin but was pressed down under a wave of darkness.

Motion, followed by a metallic clang, startled Victoria awake. Her heart dropped when she recognized she was in the dungeons. Ramona moaned from the other side of the cell on a bed of filthy straw. It smelled like the alley behind the tavern, only worse. The high slit in the wall didn't provide much light, but it was better than nothing. Other than the straw, the only thing in the cell was a wooden bucket meant for their waste.

"Ramona," Victoria whispered.

There was no answer.

She crawled over to where her friend lay and gave a gentle nudge.

Ramona's eyes rolled. She moaned. Her pale skin was covered in sweat. Victoria placed the back of a hand against Ramona's head. She was unusually hot. Reginald had bitten her. Ramona was turning.

"Good, you're awake," Ramona rasped. "I don't know how much time I have left so I need you to listen."

Victoria swallowed the feeling of dread. She nodded.

"Sandu, Rika, and Nico are dead. Dorin is due home any day now, and a friend in the guard has gone to intercept him before he arrives. I'm turning. You're going to have to help me with that…when the time comes."

"How long have you known about my parents being vampires?"

Ramona cracked a smile. "I've always known. For generations my family has hunted their kind. We're sensitive to the paranormal. I was born with certain…abilities. This may be difficult for you to believe, but I can raise the dead."

"That's witchcraft!" Victoria said unable to hide her uneasiness.

Ramona waved a hand. "Let me finish. Only wronged souls can be brought back to set things right. In the old country, we call them revenants. They will heed your call after I teach you. The first thing you're going to need," she said, leaning over and pulling something from the straw, "is this antique tinderbox."

Victoria took the tinderbox and ran her fingers over the slightly tarnished tin, marveling at its good condition. The box itself was circular, about five inches in diameter, and appeared like any common candleholder except the bottom opened up to reveal a compartment containing a steel striker, flint, some char cloth, and a two-inch nub of a red candle. The steel striker had been fashioned to look like a dragon—its sleek head and neck curling around one side and a scaled tail on the other. The iron scent of blood wafted up from the tinderbox and a wave of unease washed over Victoria.

"How did you smuggle it in?"

Again, Ramona smiled. "Many of the servants have no love for your parents but have plenty for you. Smuggling this here was easy."

"Teach me how to use it."

"You must light the candle using the contents of the box. Call upon the spirit you wish to invoke by asking them to come forward and cleanse the world of the evil that befell them. A drop of blood must be offered to the Zmeu—dragon—in exchange for life. If the dragon approves, the flame will burn blue. The revenant will rise and seek vengeance."

Victoria swallowed. "The revenants won't come looking for me, will they?"

"Only if their instructions are unclear. Once vengeance is fulfilled they'll return to the afterlife. Remember," Ramona said, her tone darkening, "they seek the blood of those who wronged them. Blood for blood."

Victoria looked at the tinderbox and shuddered. Raising the dead seemed immoral, but she couldn't let her parents get away with what they had done. This was her best chance to rid the world of their kind of evil.

"This tinderbox has passed from woman to woman in my family for generations. I give it to you with one condition." Ramona grabbed Victoria's hand and squeezed. "Promise you'll marry Dorin and pass it along to your daughter. You're all he has left."

Victoria's heart fluttered at the mention of Dorin. There was nothing she wanted more. "I will."

Ramona coughed, her breath ragged. Her body shuddered as the infection spread. Sweat matted her salt and pepper hair to her head. "Please, release me from this curse."

The only thing Victoria could think to use was the wooden bucket. She turned it upside down and stomped on it until the wood cracked. A piece of wood about a foot long splintered off, a suitable stake. Ramona had always been so kind, motherly. She didn't know if she could do it.

"I…can't."

"Yes, you can. Don't let me become one of them."

Victoria placed the wooden stake over Ramona's heart. Tears fell freely as she leaned on it, the wood piercing through to her friend's heart. "Rest now."

Ramona's smile faded. "Thank…you." Her eyelids closed one final time.

Victoria wept as she prepared the tinderbox. At seventeen she hadn't seen many horrible things, let alone committed any horrible acts. Even though she knew Ramona would rather be dead than become a vampire, she wished there had been some other way. This was, after all, her father's fault. The best way of honoring Ramona would be to ensure Reginald didn't get away with it.

She struck the flint with the dragon shaped striker. It appeared as though the dragon's eyes momentarily glowed red. Hadn't they? The char cloth caught and the room went cold. Goosebumps dotted Victoria's flesh. Once the candle was lit, she pricked a finger with a sharpened piece of wood and watched the crimson drop fall toward the wick.

As the blood hit the flame, Victoria did as instructed and called upon the spirits of Sandu, Rica, and Nico. Outside, the sunlight dimmed and it seemed like the world stopped on its axis for a moment. Victoria jumped as the flame flared up a foot and burned the bluest color she had ever seen.

It occurred to Victoria that she didn't know what to do next. Had the ritual worked? Should she blow out the candle?

Just as she thought about blowing out the candle, a frigid breeze rushed through the bars extinguishing the tiny flame. Victoria looked around but saw no one. With shaky hands she replaced the contents of the tinderbox and waited for another sign.

She didn't wait long.

Sounds of struggle floated from under the dungeon door. After a minute it opened and Nico walked through, blood dotting his pallid face. He walked stiffly toward Victoria's cell and unlocked it. Without waiting to see if she followed, he hurried into the hallway.

Victoria hurried after him. "Nico?"

Nico stopped and slowly turned. Victoria's face blanched as she realized his eyes were as black as night—no irises, sclera, or pupils, only darkened pools. There was even a bloody hole in his chest where Reginald had stabbed him. Victoria's mind couldn't find a logical explanation for what her eyes saw. As Nico moved, she stayed at least an arm's length behind, concern stiffening her legs.

Several dead guards littered the hallway. Victoria hiked up her dress, stepping over and around corpses and blood alike. In minutes, they were on the first floor.

Men shouting in the distance could be heard in the direction of the dining hall. Nico walked toward the commotion, pushing the doors open. With a chair in one hand and a broken bottle in the other, Reginald was trying fight off Nico's resurrected twin. Rica, wielding a sword, turned and cut down the remaining guard. His broken neck lolled from side to side as he slashed and stabbed. He swatted the bottle from Reginald's hand as Nico sprinted to his aid. Together the undead twins pinned the vampire down on the table.

"What have you done?" Reginald said to his daughter. "Your mother and I took you from a life of poverty and offered you eternal life. We—I—loved you like my own flesh and blood."

"You don't know what love is," Victoria said flatly.

Reginald struggled but Nico and Rica held fast. "You're both dead. You can't come back. No one comes back."

"I summoned these revenants," Victoria said. "They require vengeance on those who wronged them."

Reginald's eyes widened as a shrill cry echoed from somewhere upstairs. They listened as the sound of footsteps descended, step after step, until Sandu appeared. He walked with purpose over to where Reginald was being held and dropped Lucille's head on the table next to him. Sandu licked at the crimson smear trickling down his chin.

Reginald screamed for help.

None came.

Victoria leaned in close and whispered, "Blood for blood, Reginald."

Nico and Rica fell on the helpless vampire as Victoria turned and walked away. She cringed as the twins bit and gnawed, drinking in their righteous fury. Reginald's cries brought no remorse from the young woman he called his daughter. If anything, she wondered how many victims he had feasted upon throughout the years, how many families he had torn apart. *Never again*, she thought, clutching the tinderbox to her chest.

After the revenants had gone, Victoria and Dorin were wed to the joy of their subjects. With Reginald and Lucille dead, it fell to Victoria to rule in their stead. She adopted a dragon the color of steel as her sigil, its eyes as red as blood. In wayward taverns townsfolk still whisper stories of a mystical tinderbox and the righteous lineage of women who control the fury of the dragon's tinder.

BRIAN W. TAYLOR is a former soldier turned writer with a soft spot for the horror genre, black Labs, and soul patches. He grew up in Rochester, New York watching horror movies with his grandmother before Cancer took her, which naturally led him to seek out horror in literature. It was then that he stumbled upon Dean Koontz and never looked back. He likes his stories grand with authors like Margaret Weis and Tim Lebbon also serving as influences.

When he was younger, Brian believes he saw the ghost of his great aunt. He found out the next day she had passed the night before. He's been a believer ever since. He even messed around with an Ouija board, but will never touch one again. Ever. In his opinion, horror should be intelligent, play off reader's fear of the unknown, and also be based around some kind of truth. He tries to bring those same characteristics to his stories and can't imagine a life without horror.

His short fiction has appeared in several anthologies and he has several short stories still under consideration. Click the links below to check out his titles.

LINKS

http://descentintoslushland.wordpress.com
https://twitter.com/WriteBWT

The Awoken

by Kenechi Udogu

"I would not touch that if I were you!"

Philip's hand sprang back at the note of urgency in the squire's voice. He usually took little notice when people raised their voices at him, having long accepted his inability to instill regal decorum in his subjects. But the boy never yelled at anyone and knew better than to start with the prince, which worried Philip.

The green film covering the wall of trees before them was thick and bubbly, giving an illusion of vegetation from a distance but, on close inspection, it bore no resemble to any organic matter he had ever come across. If the boy had not noticed the veil, they would have carried on riding past what Philip now realized could be the focus of their search.

"I had no intention of touching it." The defensive note to Philip's voice was not deliberate, but it was there nonetheless. He had many weaknesses but stupidity was not one of them.

"I would also step back if I were you." Sir Thomas, the burly knight served by the squire, placed a hand on Philip's lean shoulder, ensuring the prince took his advice.

The group of nearly a dozen men stared at the wall in silence. Philip was not surprised by the sense of relief that hung in the air, tinged with uncertainty of what was behind the veil. He wondered if most of them had truly believed in the mission on which they had embarked several weeks before. He certainly had not. Escaping the confines of the palace was what propelled him towards their mysterious destination.

In fact, if Sir Thomas had suggested heading south on the night his father's sweet wine had rooted the seeds of adventure in Philip's mind, they would have been riding in that direction. But, as the knight's squire refilled their empty goblets, the soft-faced boy had spoken of a princess long abandoned in a castle no man had set eyes upon for decades.

The tale was not new to the prince; it was one of many from his childhood which he had relegated to the back of his mind with other silly cautionary myths shared by the maids who catered for him. However, that night, hearing the story recounted with such gusto by a boy who was clearly too simpleminded to understand the absurdity of any living creature sleeping for so long without sustenance, Philip felt a yearning to do something more than sit on his backside waiting for things to change in his life.

The young prince had always felt uneasy in his third born position in a family of five children. He had never longed for regality or scholarship like his brothers; neither had he been humble enough to aspire to the priesthood like his parents wanted for him. Even his sister showed more enthusiasm for swordsmanship than he did, despite being banned from joining in. He was not exactly the butt of their jokes, but he knew he did not shine in the eyes of his family.

Apart from the appeal of escaping the palace, finding and waking a sleeping princess sounded dignified enough a task to help him break free of the mould in which he had been stuck for the last eighteen years. Even when his parents had laughed at his suggestion, and his siblings had barely hidden their sniggers, he held on to the thought of what he and his companions could encounter on their journey.

The truth was, because he could not allow his mind to suspend disbelief like the squire had done, Philip had never really thought their quest would lead to anything substantial. Not until the moment they stood staring at the veil.

"This is it for certain," the squire, Andrew, announced after a few minutes had passed. As if to assure them of his conviction, he pulled out a worn book from his satchel and thumbed through it, nodding when he stopped at the page he sought.

Philip knew the book held notes on all the research the boy had gathered for the mission. He had been shown a few pages at the start of their journey but the scribbled text confused him and he had chosen to leave the logistics of the expedition to Andrew.

In many ways, Andrew was the real reason they stood there. Although he never mentioned it, the prince was hoping to provide the boy with a taste of the adventure he so clearly wanted. An experience he could brag about to his friends for the rest of his life. The boy had only been in the service of Sir Thomas for a few months and would likely not see a real battlefield since the knight had been told he would never fully recover from an injury he sustained in combat a year ago.

"And to think your father said we would never find it. You should be proud of this achievement, Your Highness." Someone patted Philip on the shoulder.

"We cannot be sure until we get to the other side." Philip's hesitation was brought on by the realization that there could be nothing waiting for them behind the veil. The slimy film was an oddity, but did not mean much on its own. They had stumbled upon a number of peculiarities on their journey, all of which had proven to be unrelated to the princess.

"Have some faith, Your Highness." The squire grinned as he tucked his book away and nodded at the seven henchmen who accompanied them. The king had refused to waste royal guards on what he considered a trivial pursuit but he had not completely denied the prince some aid.

The men advanced and began to hack away at the low hanging branches behind the film. The instant the gelatinous seal broke, a putrid stench filled the air, causing them to lift their hands to their noses to shield their senses from the assault.

"That cannot be good."

Sir Thomas chuckled. "It is only a little stagnation. You would not have lasted long at the battle of Roane. The foul air consumed us five miles before we reached the city and it was less bearable than this. Brace yourself, Philip. You are leading us to resurrect the dead; surely the girl will smell worse."

Philip shrugged. A small part of him still thought there would be no one for them to revive when they got to the castle. That is, if they ever got to it. If in truth the trees had been left to grow for decades with no disturbance, who knew how long it would take to cut through the web of branches, which pushed back, at the swords that struck them?

After about an hour of chopping, a decision was made to leave two men behind with the horses as the rest of the group advanced behind the working men. And when they had not progressed much further after another hour, Philip joined in with the laborious work. He had become accustomed to lending a hand over the course of their journey so no one flinched when his sword swung in sync with the others.

Metal finally clanked against stone, stirring a small cheer from the men. The work took on a different route, this time along the perimeter of the radial wall they had discovered. If the wall had been any lower, they might have attempted scaling it, but they could not see the top from where they stood. When a monstrously sized gate was located, a second cheer was let out. Ramming a hole through the rotting wood proved to be the easiest task they had faced so far.

"Should we be concerned about being so loud?" Philip asked when they spilled out onto the other side of the gate. The deserted road was almost as heavily overgrown as the forest from which they had emerged, but it felt wrong to be callous about their arrival.

"Afraid of awakening the dead too soon?" Sir Thomas joked as he came to stand beside the prince.

Philip noticed the knight's sword had not been returned to its scabbard. Perhaps the disquieting sensation in his chest was not something only he felt. It did not help that the stench had grown worse. Their lungs were filled with enough of it to prevent any retching, but it still hung heavily around them.

"Perhaps we should be." One of the henchmen grunted, pointing out a fading sign nailed to a large stone archway that appeared to lead to the rest of the enclosed kingdom:

THE SOULS OF THE JUST FIND SOLACE IN DEATH,
BUT THE FORSAKEN FIND THEIR JUDGEMENT IN DECAY.

Sir Thomas scoffed. "That was written to scare away folks like us. Stop us from looting the place. Not very likely with such a cryptic message."

"It almost sounds like a prayer." Philip's tone was contemplative as he stared at the sign.

"Pity we did not drag a priest along with us to confirm it. Come on, we better get on with it. The girl might have sensed your royal presence and taken flight." The knight laughed at his gag and a few of the men joined in. He was one of the more vocal unbelievers of the group but had been content to indulge the prince because the quest had been an opportunity to show he was still useful. Not many people took knights seriously if all they could do was guard heirs to the throne at home.

They proceeded through the archway and onto a street flanked by single-story houses, which looked every bit as deserted as the road on which they stood. The castle, their final destination, loomed in the distance. What struck Philip the most was that every inanimate object left outside had been carefully stowed against buildings—carts, saddles, market stalls—almost as if the people had been prepared for whatever tragedy had befallen them. There was also no sign of animal life. Not a single bird or dog carcass in sight. All that consumed the street was wild foliage, which wrapped itself tightly around everything it touched. Something about the scene seized the tongues of the formerly animated pack, and they approached the first house in silence.

Sir Thomas advanced, sword in hand, and tried the doorknob. He had insisted on being the first one forward whenever they faced an unknown, completely ignoring Philip's desire to lead the expedition.

"There is nothing to discuss, Your Highness. I swore an oath to protect you, and that is what I intend to do."

He only addressed Philip by his official title when he wanted to emphasize the difference in their significance to the realm. Despite the seven years of experience he had over the prince, the two had grown close in the time the knight had been bedridden; Philip knew better than to argue with the older, stronger man.

When the door swung open easily, the knight beckoned one of the henchmen to follow him. The team emerged almost immediately, declaring the house empty. It was the same with the second and third. They expected to find no one in the fourth, suspecting that people had fled the kingdom and not stayed back as the stories told, but the front door was locked.

"Perhaps they left behind items of value," Philip reasoned as he noticed Sir Thomas's raised brow.

The knight shrugged and broke the lock that held the door shut.

A strong waft of stale air hit the men, bringing tears to their eyes and an intense round of sneezing. A henchman standing close to the door went visibly weak at the knees.

"It is more likely they were trying to keep something in," Andrew, who had remained beside the prince, said in a low voice.

Philip's stomach churned at the thought. It was not just the boy's words that made him weary, it was the way he said it. When a sullen-faced Sir Thomas emerged and signaled for him to follow, the weight in Philip's stomach solidified. Covering his nose with his sleeve, he crossed the threshold and stopped short at the sight of why the knight had called him in.

Bodies.

There were so many; he could not ascertain the number without getting the men to move the people around. And it did not look like they had been bundled into the room against their will. The bodies were either sitting propped up in chairs, or lying on rolled up bundles of clothing on the floor. The most curious thing about the scene was the yellow film, which cloaked the people; a translucent sheath almost as slimy as the one that covered the trees through which they had come.

"What is this sorcery?" one of the henchmen gasped as he leaned in to inspect the bodies.

Below the film, the people were incredibly well preserved for corpses, which must have been there for many decades.

"It has to be some form of mummification," Sir Thomas offered, ever ready to dispel the thought that anything they came across could be linked to a darker, unknown source.

"Not mummification, Sire. I think they are asleep."

Andrew, who had followed the prince inside, was the only one who seemed completely unperturbed by the scene. He approached one of the sallow bodies, which appeared to belong to a female child, and placed the back of his palm over her nose.

"All of them? How can that be?"

"The legend is true. To ensure the princess was not alone in her slumber, her kingdom was put to rest with her. She must truly be in the castle, awaiting our arrival." The excitement in his voice was raw and a little grating.

This time, even Sir Thomas had no snarky comeback as they took in what the boy had said. Could it really have been true all along? Were there really hundreds, or maybe thousands more bodies locked away in houses, waiting for them to revive one girl?

"Why are there so many in one house? And who locked the door from the outside?"

"Most likely the person who spun the enchantment. We must make sure to lock the door behind us when we leave." Andrew said as he started to withdraw from the room. His departure prompted the others to follow.

"But we broke the lock."

"We will wedge it shut then. These people were kept in for a reason. I believe we should leave everything as we found it, until we are certain we have not disturbed the balance created here by the spell."

Not for the first time, Philip marveled at how readily the lot of them did as the boy suggested. It was possibly because he spoke with such surety when it came to matters relating to the princess and her curse. At the start of their journey, when someone had teased him about his unusual depth of knowledge, he had responded by pulling out the battered book he constantly consulted.

"My father left this to me when he died. His great-great-grandfather claimed to hail from the kingdom of the sleeping princess, so he spent a good amount of time documenting the tale. It felt like a wasted effort because he never had the opportunity to prove or refute his theory but, now we are on the road, I hope I can do that for him."

It was the first time he let the group look through the book. No one understood the scrawls or made much of an effort to try but, following that exchange, they stopped questioning the boy's authority on the subject. He was occasionally ribbed, mostly when alcohol was introduced into their meals, but never outrightly challenged. Nobody wanted to mock the memory of a father he so clearly cherished.

That was what Philip envied; the sense of ownership the boy had about their mission. The power to convince a prince that embarking on such a ludicrous outing was more than just a time-passing adventure.

"Do as he says, wedge it shut."

They avoided all other houses with locked doors. The image of the bodies already deeply engrained in their memories was not one they wanted to supplement. Instead, they went through only unlocked doors to confirm they were vacant.

After a few searches, Philip realized all the occupied houses had timber-shuttered windows, leaving glass-windowed houses empty. It made some sense. Wood would be more difficult to break through if anyone wanted to get into the occupied houses. Or, perhaps, as Andrew had suggested, if anyone wanted to break out. He shook his head, not ready to believe that was the intention of the locked doors.

But why would anyone want to keep an entire sleeping kingdom locked away? To protect them from scavengers and looters? The maddening thought was, if they could not wake the people, they would never find out. Noting a growing look of fear on the faces of his companions, Philip decided it was unwise to say anything about his observations.

Soon the ashlar-faced castle standing at the heart of the settlement came into full view. As the men approached its high walls, the number of locked doors diminished with an increase in glass-windowed houses. They had clearly reached the wealthier abodes of the kingdom. With this reduction came a noticeable ebb in the foulness of the air. In fact, by the time they arrived at the entrance to the castle, the men were taking deep breaths to clear their lungs of the staleness in which they had been submerged.

"Does your book say anything about where she will be?" Sir Thomas asked his squire when they finally arrived at the large timber door that served as the building's entrance.

He was not alone in his eagerness to get the task done. The men crowded around the squire, waiting for some direction.

The boy shook his head, produced the book and flicked through it, his hands visibly quivering for the first time. The prince could feel his own heart beating violently against his ribcage, sharing in the excitement of being so close to achieving their goal.

"Then we must search every room until we find her," the knight declared with a smile. "Come on men, one last hurdle and we will be done with all this. It has been too long since I set eyes upon Lady Eleanor."

Breaking down the fortified door took some effort but the men worked patiently and soon the group was inside the castle. Two men were left outside as the others began their search of the building, taking a wing at a time. By the time they got to the third wing, Philip sensed the men were struggling to contain themselves. He was as equally puzzled as they were by the absence of any living soul in the castle. The building should have contained scores of sleeping servants, awaiting the return of their princess, but every door was unlocked, and every room was empty.

Except for two rooms on the topmost floor.

Even without opening the doors, sighs of relief poured out of the men and Philip found himself beaming at Sir Thomas. She had to be inside one of the rooms, but which one?

They broke the lock on the first door and the knight entered before waving the rest of them in. Heavy drapes prevented much light from seeping into the room but these were quickly drawn to reveal the contents of the space. The room was enormous and so opulently furnished that the years had not done much to tarnish its appeal. The focal point was a large, four-post bed right at the center of the room. It was occupied, but not by a young girl.

"I believe we have discovered the King and Queen."

The monarchs, covered in the same thin film as their subjects, looked only a little dehydrated and very much regal in sleep. Again, Philip wondered where everyone else was. Why would they abandon their king and queen?

They wedged the door shut before progressing to the second room. This was similarly laid out and as lavishly furnished but, as they drew close to the bed, it was obvious something was different. First of all, there was no yellow film in sight. In fact, unlike the rest of the rooms they had entered, there was no speck of dust in the space. It was almost like the bed and everything surrounding it was cloaked in an invisible shield, preventing them from becoming marred.

This time, Philip took the first step towards the body on the bed. He barely had a choice as his legs propelled him towards what had to be one of the most exquisite creatures he had ever set eyes upon. Lustrous dark hair cascaded around the impeccably structured face, which rested on a soft white pillow. Lashes so long, they practically rested on her cheeks; lips so full, it was impossible to look away. Stories about the gift of beauty bestowed on her were evidently true. No one would have guessed the princess had been in a state of slumber for the last century.

As her chest rose and fell gently beneath her burgundy silk nightdress, the prince leaned in a little closer but caught himself just before he touched her.

"What do we do now?" he asked, even though he knew what was expected of him.

"You rouse her, Your Highness. She is to be awoken by a king's son." Andrew spoke gently, almost as if he was afraid of waking the girl himself.

That was all the prompting Philip needed to touch her. Even though he knew she was alive, he was surprised to feel warmth when his hand made contact with her body. His hand rested on her shoulder a little too long before he shook her lightly.

Nothing happened. So he attempted a more vigorous shove.

Still nothing.

"Looks like you might have to kiss her."

This suggestion came from a smirking Sir Thomas. He had stood well away from the bed when they entered, making Philip wonder if he was afraid of being so close to the source of such great sorcery.

"What?"

The knight shrugged, taking a step forward. "Many legends are fulfilled in a similar way—true love's kiss and all."

Philip shuddered. Despite his undeniable attraction to the sleeping girl, he was not sure he was ready to let his lips touch what was, in effect, a corpse.

"Nonsense! I do not know the girl. How can kissing her be true love's kiss?"

"He is right, Your Highness," the squire interjected. "We often read of how it worked for knights and royalty who were faced with not too dissimilar predicaments. It might be the only way."

Philip could not believe they were seriously considering a kiss as a plausible option. He stared in disbelief at the knight and the boy for a few seconds before shaking his head and stepping away from the bed. "Your book did not say we had to wake her that way. Besides, if you think it is such a good idea, you should kiss her."

"Your Highness!"

"If anyone feels anything close to love for her, surely it is you. You are the one who has done all the hard work entailed in finding her."

The boy turned a bright shade of red as his mouth dropped open. It was his turn to stare at the other occupants of the room in confusion.

"He does have a point, Andrew."

Philip was relieved to hear Sir Thomas agree with him for the first time in a long while, but the smile on the knight's face made it clear he still considered the whole scenario a bit of a joke.

"Think of what you are saying," Andrew protested. "I cannot take this privilege away from you. What will people say when they find out I was the one who woke her?"

"If you prefer they never find out, no one in this room will say otherwise. Agreed?"

The men nodded when they realized the prince was serious about letting the boy take his place. Like Sir Thomas, some had tagged along out of sheer curiosity, but most joined the group hoping to get paid handsomely at the end of the expedition. If the prince wanted them to lie to the world about what went on, they were unlikely to object out of principle.

But Andrew shook his head and moved away from the bed, standing even further back than the knight. "I am sorry, Your Highness. I cannot do it. It is not my place to write history. I know we have come a long way for this, but if you do not wake her, none of us should. We do not know what the outcome of breaking her spell will be if someone not of royal blood attempts to rouse her."

Philip sighed and closed his eyes. If one of his brothers had been there in his place, they would have muscled the squire into carrying out the deed. Even his sister might have found a way to convince the boy to do it. But that was not in his nature. If kissing the girl were truly the only way to rouse her, then their journey would be wasted if he refused to do so.

It was only a kiss; a quick brush of his lips against hers. Why was he so afraid of the simple action? All eyes were on him, awaiting his decision. Inquisitive, fear filled, hopeful eyes. He realized he had little choice in the matter. It was too late to walk away.

Taking a deep breath, Philip turned back to the girl and leaned in towards her. A sigh escaped from him before his quivering lips touched her slightly parted own for a second.

"Good God, Philip! Surely you can give it a better go than that!" Sir Thomas barked at the prince, frustrated by the pace of events.

Philip stood up straight, ready to defend his feeble attempt at awakening the princess, when someone yelled, "Look!"

Heavy eyelids fluttered open and blinked a few times as the once sleeping beauty stirred. She was even more stunning with color in her cheeks. Her wide-eyed stare at the sight of them was not unexpected; in fact it was a little surprising that her first reaction was not a bit more hostile. Philip could not imagine how terrified she must have felt, waking up to find half a dozen men in her bedroom.

"What have you done?" Her words came out as a croak but the girl's voice somehow managed to sound melodic.

Those were not the words of gratitude the prince had been expecting to hear but he beamed as he stepped back to give the girl some space. "We are here to save you.

My men and I have traveled a long way to..."

"No, no, you have to fix this! I cannot stay awake."

It was not Philip alone who gaped at the girl after that outburst. Perhaps the girl had slept for too long and her brain needed some time to get used to the idea of the present.

"Why? Surely you did not intend to sleep forever!"

The girl was still too weak to move quickly but she slowly attempted to leave the bed. "It will start again. All that we did will be for naught. Please, we have to make haste."

"What will start again?

As if on cue, piercing screams filled the air. It sounded like hundreds, possibly thousands of voices, joined in unison to create the noise that ripped through the castle and drained all color from the men's faces.

"What in God's name was that?"

"I hoped we would have more time, but it has begun already." The girl had finally found her feet and was beginning to make her way towards the door.

"Wait, you have to explain. Why are you so upset? And what was that awful sound?" Philip stopped her by grabbing her shoulders before she could dash past him. She felt so small and delicate to hold and yet she continued to struggle to get away with a fierceness he could barely control.

"They have been awakened. All of them, including those who fell under the spindle's curse. My parents, I need to find them."

"They are in the next room."

"You have seen them?" the girl gasped, her thrashing easing for a moment. "You unlocked the door to their room? Did you lock it when you left?" She looked truly horrified at the thought of the door being left open.

"Yes, we wedged it shut." Andrew spoke up this time. There was a hint of pride in his voice, probably because he had been the one to suggest locking any doors they opened.

"Good. We must go to them but we must ensure we hear them speak before we enter."

"Forgive my interruption," Sir Thomas made his presence known, "but you make it sound like we have done something gravely wrong by waking you. And from the continued wailing coming from out there, I think you need to tell us more before we leave this room."

The girl's sigh was filled with frustration, but it was clear the men had no intention of letting her go anywhere without some clarification; she stopped her attempts to break free of the prince's hold.

"The forsaken do not speak. That is why we must make sure my parents say words we can understand. Not grunts, not screams—words."

The forsaken. That word had been written on the sign they saw at the entrance; the sign which had momentarily sent a chill through Philip when he read it. It was beginning to sound like there had been a good reason for that feeling. The men looked at each other in silence, fear growing in their chests by the second.

"And who are these forsaken?" Philip asked, glad the girl was finally cooperating.

"Those who have lost the gift of tongue, and so, so much more." Sorrow dripping from her voice, her incredibly long lashes fanned her eyes as a tear slid down her cheek.

For Philip, the sight was more terrifying than anything they had encountered so far.

"You have to be a little bit clearer than that." The tear apparently had little effect on Sir Thomas.

"Please, we need to see them. We need to make sure they are still themselves. Then we can try to rectify what you have done."

Rectify what they had done? They had saved her from a hundred years of sleep, and she was bent on correcting what they had achieved. Nothing she said made any sense.

"Your Highness..."

More screams poured in from outside but they did not sound like they were getting any closer. Philip had a sinking feeling their containment would not last for long. He wondered if they should let the girl see her parents after all.

"Let her pass."

"What?"

"I do not like the sound of those cries. If she thinks she knows how to stop them, we should let her go to her parents."

His companions looked unconvinced but no one stopped the girl when she sprinted out of the room. The men got to her just as she began banging on the door to the room they had vacated earlier.

"Mama, Papa, please answer me," she called out in a barely audible voice as she choked back tears.

For someone who had been so worried about her parents' state of mind, the girl had placed herself right in the path of danger. The door had been barricaded using a high cabinet the men had retrieved from another room, but if someone on the inside wanted to get out, all they had to do was open the door and push really hard. Philip quickly went over and placed himself between the girl and the door.

"Just in case," he said softly when the expression on her face indicated she realized her mistake. Sir Thomas also came up behind her and gently pulled her away so he could stand beside the prince.

"Would you permit me to state how preposterous this all is, Your Highness?" the knight posed as he inched closer to the door, his hand ready on his scabbard.

"You already have, my friend. But I believe we must err on the side of caution for now. At least until we find out what is causing that awful noise and get it to stop."

When there was no response from the other side, the girl inched closer to the door. "They have a spindle with them. It is the only thing that will end the madness that is about to descend on us."

The prince nodded as if he understood what she was talking about. Why would her parents keep a spindle with them? The one thing they had been told would trigger a curse on their daughter was, surely, meant to be kept as far away from her as possible.

"They should be up by now. It has been a while since she woke up," the knight observed, just before the silence from the other side of the door was interrupted by shuffling sounds.

The men pressed closer to the door when another sound was heard. Mumblings, but no words. Followed by more shuffling. And then it came.

"Rose?" A high-pitched voice called out, "My sweet! Is that you?"

"Mama," the girl cried as she rushed towards the door. "Oh Mama, I never thought I would hear your voice again."

A smile could be heard in the warm response. "Nothing will ever keep me away from you, my sweet. Not even the clutches of wickedness. Who is with you? You are not alone."

Rose turned to the men and actually smiled. The action lit up her face, bringing her features together in an even more appealing way. "Those who wish to undo what was done. They meant well but the curse has not been broken." The smile faded from her lips. "The kiss of a prince was not enough to heal what has started. Everyone has been awoken. We must use the spindle."

More movement was heard before the queen's voice came through. "Your father put it away. I have been trying to get him to rise since I woke up. He is awake but all he does is stare into space. Perhaps you can do a better job than I have." Her mother's voice was distant, like she had gone back to the bed.

"Oh no," Rose inhaled, taking a step back, her eyes widening as her hand rose to her trembling lips.

At the same time, Philip started to speak, "Shall we go..."

He barely got the words out before a blood-curdling cry filled the hallway.

"No!" Rose screamed even louder but she remained away from the door, beckoning the men to step back too.

"Your father?" Sir Thomas asked, drawing his sword.

The girl nodded, not bothering to hold back her tears this time. "The curse must have gotten to him," she cried. "I thought its reach would slow down when we were asleep but it must have taken hold in him beforehand."

A gurgling sound was heard followed by a loud thump, much like the sound a body would make when it hit the floor.

"Surely we should help your mother," Philip's sword had also been drawn. He could not understand how she could listen to the muffled grunts coming from behind the door and ask them to remain inactive.

"It is too late," Rose shook her head. "We can do nothing for her; for either of them. But we can still save all those who remain untarnished. We have to get to the spindle."

The events of the last few minutes were too much for Philip to pretend he was okay with things as they stood. If he was to believe what the girl was suggesting, her mother had just died and her father had carried out the act. How could she think of nothing more than getting to the spindle?

"Your Highness, this is madness. I insist we know what is in there before we enter." Sir Thomas did not look like he was going to let the prince ignore his intentions this time.

His insistence was unnecessary. Whatever had happened in the room was enough to weaken the girl into submission. She slumped to the ground and buried her head in her hands as she let herself weep for her loss. The men watched in silence, unsure of what to make of the situation.

When her words finally came, they were ragged. "You know the story of my birth and my curse?"

Philip nodded, glancing nervously at the door when they heard a soft groan. There was not much distance to cross between the bed and the door and he wondered how much time they had for the girl's explanation.

"You were born to your parents after many years of trying to conceive a child. There was a feast in honor of your naming day, but someone was left out."

Rose nodded.

"A certain lady of high standing, the daughter of a disgraced clothing merchant. My parents assured me she had not been intentionally overlooked; they swore the omission was an unfortunate coincidence. It was one for which we have all suffered."

"She attended the event to place a death enchantment on you, but someone was able to ease it into a sleep curse, one that would come to fruition around your sixteenth birthday," the prince continued for her.

The princess looked up at him, her eyes now brimming with tears. "I wish we had let that happen from the start like we were supposed to. What followed was much worse. I was kept away from spindles and my sixteenth birthday came and went with no upset. But shortly after, people began to notice…peculiarities amongst their neighbors. Reports poured in about a large number of the population being unable to sleep. At first we were unsure of the source of the condition and made no connection to my curse. It was only when the days of sleeplessness prolonged that one of my father's sages realized what was happening. The longer I avoided my curse, the more my people degenerated into a state of hopelessness."

She paused and looked away, as if the thought of what followed was too difficult to recount.

"You must go on, Your Highness," Philip prompted, aware of the increased volume of the groans.

Rose must have heard them, too, because she got up and wiped her tears.

"The royal physicians were surprised people did not drop dead from such extended sleep deprivation. They told us the brain could not sustain itself without rejuvenation and they were right. Stories of changes in people of all ages escalated but the first attacks began about a month after my birthday. What we heard was shocking; people being mauled, savagely beaten, or worse."

What could possibly be worse than being mauled or savagely beaten? Philip wondered as he tried not to think of her mother and why she had not let them try to save her.

The girl glanced towards the door, clearly yearning to end her story and retrieve the spindle like she had been begging to do.

"We had waited too long to right the wrong we had done by keeping me awake. Far too many were in transition when it was decided I had to be put to sleep. We must not make that mistake again today."

"You mean you chose to do this to yourself?" This eruption came from Andrew. Even after all she had told them, the boy looked genuinely confused as to why she would have chosen that line of action.

"Of course!" Her response was paired with an equally puzzled expression as to why the boy would think otherwise. "We had no other choice. It was for the good of my people. There had been too much loss..."

It was Sir Thomas's turn to interrupt. "Was any of this in your book, Andrew? Did you bring us out here knowing something this...perverse happened here?" As he spoke, the knight snatched the book in question away from the boy. For a man who claimed not to believe in the mystical, he looked exceedingly concerned.

"I...I..." the boy stuttered, taking a step back, terrified that the knight's next action might bear a bit more violence.

Now even Philip turned to him, eyes narrowed. "It mentioned it? And you did not think it was in our best interest to know?"

"It only briefly mentions a sickness of the mind." By then Andrew looked like he would disintegrate into full-blown sobbing. It was not clear if this was from fear of the rage emanating from his companions or because he was sorry for not picking up on signs of the change in circumstances in the book.

"When the curse took hold, my ancestor was away from the land, which is why he escaped it. By the time he returned, there was no way for him to enter the sealed kingdom. The whole place had been locked in and was heavily overgrown. He must have recounted only what he had heard but would have had no way to know for certain. He claimed the only person who would be granted a way in would be the..."

"Son of a king," Philip finished for him.

The prince was torn between a growing annoyance at the situation in which they now found themselves and his usual sense of empathy towards the boy. How could he have left something so important out of all their discussions? Had he been so desperate to rediscover his ancestral home that he had ignored such a huge indication of danger just to find it? He must have known they would not have embarked on the quest if they knew they would potentially be walking into something more than a waking mission, something that prompted a woken princess to want to return to her former state of unconsciousness.

"Open the door."

"Your Highness!"

"If she is right, we need to get a measure of what she is talking about. We cannot stand here until those people break free of their hold. Her father is the closest example of the condition, and if the spindle really is in there, we might as well try to get it."

The grunts from the room had grown louder as they waited. Whatever it was that was making the noise had reached the door and started to bang on it but made no real effort to try the handle.

Yet.

Philip went to the princess and dared to take her hand. He was a little surprised when she did not pull away. "I am sorry for what we might be forced to do when we open that door."

"Your apology is unnecessary. He was long gone before you woke me." Rose held his gaze for a moment before he let go and nodded at the knight.

The stench was the first thing to hit them once they pushed the cabinet away and flung the door open. It was not as putrid as it had been in the house at the outskirts, but the peculiar thing was it had not been present when they entered the room less than an hour ago.

The second shock was the ferocity in the body that flung itself at Sir Thomas when he took a step into the room. Followed by the animalistic growls that came from the yellow, ragged body of the man who had once been king.

"Use your sword," Sir Thomas yelled at the prince. His own metal had been flung from his hand when the king slammed into him. The knight made an attempt to hold the body away from his but it was proving difficult.

Philip did not hesitate as he sprang into action, thrusting his sword into the king's back and shoving the limp weight off the knight. As he helped his friend up, one of the henchmen entered the room and went over to check on the king. No one had taken any notice of the other body that lay beside the bed, mangled and barely recognizable as the queen. If they had, they might have guarded themselves differently.

"Argh!"

They jumped at the roar that escaped from the henchman. Philip, turning towards the sound, could not believe what his eyes were forced to look upon. The king's body continued to bleed profusely from where the prince had stabbed him and yet his grip on the henchman was firm as he buried his head in the man's chest and yanked his head back multiple times, taking chunks of flesh with him.

"Heaven protect us!" the prince yelled as he took a step back. They watched, horrified, as the king gnawed his way through the man, oblivious to his repulsed audience. Even though all the guts and blood must have blinded him, the mad king kept going.

"No!" It was Rose's cry of disbelief when she entered the room that shook the men out of their stupor, otherwise they might have stood there until the king finished with his victim and turned on them.

Again Philip was the first to react. Running towards the dying man and the mad king, he plunged his sword into the two bodies, pinning them to the floor with a single action. To his amazement, the henchman's body went limp whilst the king continued to claw away under his weight.

"I have never seen anything like this." Sir Thomas joined the prince as the other men poured into the room to stare at the sovereign who would not die.

"You see why we need to find that spindle?" Rose sobbed, clutching her chest as she looked on at her father. "They do not die. None of them do. They only find rest in sleep. We must put them back to sleep now."

But as she spoke, Sir Thomas scoffed, raised his sword and brought it down with a clean sweep, which took the heads off the two bodies. It was only then that the king joined the henchman in stillness.

"Sorcery or not, not many creatures function so well without their heads," the knight explained to the gaping occupants of the room. "That was one of the first lessons the battle field taught me."

With that, he pulled Philip's sword out of the bodies and handed it back to the prince. "Jacob was a good man. He did not deserve to die that way. No one does. We better find that spindle fast, put her to sleep, and get out of here."

"Have some compassion, Thomas," Philip chastised the knight. He looked at Rose to see how she had taken the knight's comment but the girl had gone to cover her mother's body with a blanket. Philip grabbed the rest of the linen from the bed and did the same for her father and the henchman.

"Forgive me for caring more about the lives of my prince and my men than that of a complete stranger," Sir Thomas hissed at the prince as he pulled him to one side. "The girl should bloody well be dead. That is what started this whole mess in the first place. She was supposed to die and she escaped death."

"She can hear you!" Philip whispered sharply in return.

"I do not care." Sir Thomas spat the words out. Watching one of his men being torn apart by a deranged king had rattled him beyond measure.

"Gentle, Thomas, it is not her fault."

"And whose fault is it? Ours? If we kill her, surely all this madness will cease."

"But Sire, what if we kill her and it does not stop the infection?" Andrew approached the men, glancing at the girl who had commenced her search for the large pin once her mother was sheathed. She was pretending not to listen but her eyes widened as she pulled out drawers. "What if their state of mind is only linked to her sleep and not her death? The original curse was altered and so was the sleep curse.

We know nothing other than what we have been told. We cannot know for certain how the connection works."

Sir Thomas glared at his squire, annoyed at the interruption, however well-thought-out it was. "I still say it is worth a shot. If she was supposed to die, her death must be the end to all this."

Philip had not taken his eyes off the girl as his companions spoke. The knight had a point. If the people were linked to the girl so that they slept when she did, it made sense they would die when she did, too. But this was meant to be a rescue mission, not a slaughter. How could he seriously consider driving his sword through the innocent creature before him? Especially when all she truly seemed to want was an end to what had started with her birth.

"Andrew is right. Her parents would have tried everything possible to prevent this. They would not sacrifice their entire kingdom for the sake of one person if they thought her death would resolve this."

"Even if it was for their only child? Think about it Philip…"

"I found it!" The excitement in Rose's voice surged through the room as she waved an old wooden pin in the air. She practically skipped over to show the item to her rescuers. "Soon all this will be over. I have one favor to ask, if you would oblige me."

Philip suppressed a smile and it must have taken all the nerve in the world for Sir Thomas not to roll his eyes.

"We clearly have no time for my parents to receive a proper burial but if your men could move them into…"

She did not get a chance to finish her request because a loud crash came from outside, pulling the inhabitants of the room towards the windows which looked out on to the courtyard.

"It appears we have no time to oblige you with anything," Sir Thomas fumed as they watched an agitated group enter the courtyard and head straight for the two men who had been left outside the castle's main door.

"Get inside, you fools, and bar the door," Philip poked his head out of the window to bark at the startled men. They must have sensed the mayhem that was coming from the rabble because they obeyed without question. The mob hit the door with a deafening thud but it held fast. "Go down and help them hold that door," Philip instructed the others who scurried away with no hesitation.

"Those cannot be the people from the house we entered at the outskirts. It would have taken them much longer to reach the palace." Sir Thomas noted before turning to the girl. "We saw hundreds of locked houses on our way here. Will they all be filled with people like this?"

Rose shook her head, her body trembling slightly as she watched her people continue to throw themselves at the door. "Those unaffected by the curse will also be out there. Before I went to sleep, they were already being separated from the others, but they would not have left their loved ones behind. I can only pray they have the good sense to stay hidden. I have to do this now before more break free and find their way here or into those other houses."

With that, she raised the spindle and would have pricked her finger right then if Andrew had not snatched it away from her.

"Your Highness," the squire implored, raising the spindle above his head so the princess could not reach it. "I do not think we should be here when she does this. If the curse engulfs everyone in the vicinity, we will be stuck here for eternity."

The horror on the faces of the prince and the knight suggested they had not considered that possibility. Despite his earlier anger at the boy for putting them in such unimaginable danger, Philip was grateful he was with them. His quick thinking had certainly done more good than harm. Only the princess looked irritated by the delay to her plans as grunts and groans continued to pour in through the windows.

"We must leave now." Philip took the spindle from the squire and addressed the princess. "You will take us to the exit furthest away from the entrance. I will get the men to fortify the front door before we leave but you must give us some time to leave this place."

The girl eyed the spindle he held loosely before taking one more look out of the window. "We cannot afford to waste any more time."

"Please, Your Highness," Philip supplicated. He gently placed his hand on hers, addressing her in a manner she was more accustomed to, making sure to maintain eye contact. "These men have wives, children. If you do not give us a chance to get away, there will be many in my kingdom who will wonder what became of us. I can see you care for your people and I care for mine, too. I beg of you, give us as much time as you possibly can. It took about an hour for us to get here from the gate but if we run…"

He broke off because he did not know how to finish the sentence. Even if they ran like the hounds of hell were at their shins, would they make it out of the walled in city without encountering other breakaways?

Rose's furrowed brows deepened as her gaze fluttered between the prince, the knight, and his squire. For a moment Philip thought she would continue to insist on using the spindle, but her chest fell when she took a look at the covered bodies they had all managed to ignore. "I cannot condemn you to the fate of my people. Come, we must hurry."

They ran downstairs to help the men pile every piece of heavy furniture they could find against the door—only pausing to retch at the rancid stench coming from the other side—before the princess took them to another door at the opposite end of the building.

"This leads to an enclosed garden. There is a gate at the end of it. Turn right once you leave and you will come upon some houses. Make sure you hurry, please, or this would all be for naught."

The prince gave her hand one final squeeze as he handed her the spindle, wondering if they were doing the right thing by leaving the girl behind with all they had seen. "You can use this time to honor your parents and our friend in a manner befitting the dead," he offered a parting suggestion. It would take her mind off what was going on outside and hopefully give them more time to get to the main gates. "Thank you for doing this, Your Highness."

"Rose," the girl choked back a sob. "I want you to remember me by my name, because it embodies who I am. The girl who turned out to be a thorn in the flesh of all the people she loved."

Philip was surprised when she reached forward and hugged him. If no one else stumbled upon the little kingdom, his body would be the last warmth she would ever feel. With that in mind, he held on to her tightly and planted a kiss on her cheek when they finally drew apart.

"Goodbye, Rose, and good luck."

The prince and his men did not look back once the door was shut. The backyard was overgrown but clear of people, and the gate was easy to find. In no time at all, the small group found themselves on the streets. Now they stood so close to the houses, the screeches and moans they had heard back at the palace were ear-splitting. No one said a word as they stuck close together and tried to retrace their steps to the gates. Despite all the noise, all the doors remained shut. The mob that made it to the palace had most definitely broken out of a house closer to the building.

"Thank heavens!" one of the men exclaimed once they passed the closed door to the house they had previously entered and the stone archway came into sight. No one else dared speak but similar sentiments were expressed in smiles and heavy sighs.

Their pace did not falter; Philip knew they still had to get through the gate before they could breathe easily. They had made it to the entrance but he had no way of knowing if the girl's patience had worn thin. And if the mob at the palace managed to break in, she would have no choice but to use the spindle. The men reached the timber gate and filed out through the hole they had created on their arrival.

It was only when they had shoved the hole shut with rocks they retrieved from around the wall that they let out a unified cheer. Even Philip could not contain himself as he joined in on the celebration. Whatever else happened, they had finally sealed the madness behind the high walls. Making it back to their horses and the men they left behind would only take minutes through the path they had cleared.

"Remind me never ever to embark on another hare-brained adventure," Philip's laugh was throaty and relieved as he embraced his friend, "especially ones involving enchanted princesses."

"You have my word on that, Philip. We still have a little way to go. I have no intention of joining the fair princess and her accursed people in sleep," Sir Thomas patted the prince on the back, but there was a reassuring smile on his face.

His hand had barely left the prince's back when a sickly yellow hand broke free of the undergrowth it had been buried under and grabbed the knight's calf. No one had taken any notice of the guard's body because it had been too well hidden to draw any attention. An emaciated head followed suit, baring remarkably well-preserved teeth, which sank through the fabric of the knight's garment and deep into his flesh. The knight cried out, dropping to his knees as the guard took another chomp.

This time, Philip was too stunned to react. He stood frozen to the spot, watching his truest friend and protector try to fend off more bites from the sallow-skinned body that held him. How could this be happening? They had left the inhabitants of the kingdom behind the stone wall. They were supposed to be safe where they stood.

Philip barely saw the flash of the blade as it came down, making contact with the guard's neck. Andrew had never struck a living creature in his life but he was standing closest to the knight and realized the prince was not going to respond to the threat before them. The squire yanked his small sword out of the man's neck and took one more swipe at him before the head was severed from the body.

"Sire," the boy cried, stooping beside the knight and covering the gaping wound in his calf with his hands. His fingers did little to stop the blood from flowing but he held on tightly. The knight continued to bellow in pain but he also tried to reach around to put pressure on the wound.

"Your Highness, we must hurry," one of the henchmen grabbed the rigid prince and began to drag him towards the cleared path. The brusque physical contact was what stirred Philip back to life.

"No, we must help Thomas," he struggled to get to his friend but two other men joined the first and bundled him away.

"Your father would never forgive us if we returned without you," the men explained, managing to hold on to him despite his protests. They made haste, pulling him through the trees until they emerged at the spot where they had entered the enchanted forest.

Philip burst into tears when he saw the expressions on the faces of the men they had left with the horses. Too much had happened in the last few hours for him to care what they thought of him. How could he have stood there and done nothing when Thomas was attacked? He had saved him back at the palace but that had only been because the knight had told him what to do. What kind of example had he set for the men who had put their lives in peril for him?

"Thomas," he wept, pulling free of the men who held him down and rushing over to hold his friend when the rest of the group burst through the trees. The knight was incredibly pale and drew shallow breaths, but he was conscious. "Please forgive me."

"He has lost a lot of blood," the squire whispered. "But he might live if we return to the last village we passed. There was an apothecary there who sold us some salve."

"Your Highness!" The call came from the henchman who had dragged the prince out.

Turning to observe why the man was drawing their attention, the group watched the green film they had ripped through bubble noisily as the gelatinous substance slowly began to reseal itself.

"Does this mean…"

"I pray that is what it means."

There was no need to define what they all thought.

"Look!" This cry came from the squire and they turned back to the knight just in time to watch an equally thick yellow film engulf the man's wound.

Philip reached down and touched the suspicious coating on the wound. It felt as slimy and revolting as it looked but it had stopped the bleeding. The knight's breathing also eased as he lapsed into sleep. Philip had never feared the thought of sleep in his life like he did at that moment.

"Sorcery?"

"Yes, it looks the same as what covered the people behind the wall." Philip rose, motioning for the men to load the knight on to his steed. "I do not know what it means in the long run, but it might buy us more time to help him."

"What do we do now?"

"We find that apothecary and hope for the best," the prince replied, trying not to think of what the worst could be.

"And what do we tell him when he sees this? What do we tell anyone of our findings here?"

Philip let his head drop into his hands as he fought to prevent more tears. "That they should heed our warning and let the forsaken find solace in sleep." Turning to the squire, he said, "Once we get to the village, you must burn that book of yours and never speak of this place again. Do you understand?"

The squire nodded frantically, needing no further prompting. After all they had gone through because of him, he was surprised the prince was not asking for his head on a stake.

Before he mounted his horse, Philip glanced at his friend, then back at the green film for one last time. He finally understood what people meant when they said there were things far worse than death. Whatever happened to Thomas, even if they lost him to the wound, at least he would not be forgotten for eternity behind a wall of thick brambles and thorns.

Unless…

The knight had fallen asleep just after his wound was sealed. They were supposed to be outside of the curse's grasp but the yellow coating suggested otherwise. If the apothecary managed to get to his wound in time, would they be able to wake him? And if he awoke, were they to expect the rabidity they had witnessed in the others?

The prince shook his head. It made no sense to think that way. No sense at all. But if it came to it, he would not ask the other to take the swipe that would end it all. Thomas would want him to do it.

He owed his friend that much.

KENECHI UDOGU lives in London and enjoys writing fantasy/paranormal fiction and short stories. She is the author of a number of young adult books including *The Other Slipper*, a retelling of the Cinderella story, and *The Mentalist* Series, a set of novels about a young girl with mind-altering abilities. She also hates the cold and hopes to one day figure out how to hibernate in winter.

LINKS

http://caeblogs.wordpress.com
http://www.facebook.com/kenechiudogu
https://twitter.com/kenechiudogu

The World After

by Onser von Fullon

DESPITE the only other passenger's protests, I exited the automobile. I moved quickly to the building so I could get under the thick canvas awning. I wasn't exactly dressed for this weather, but I would rather tolerate a little rain than sit and listen to that stuffy, odorous bureaucrat any longer. I ducked under the awning and entered the decontamination room.

A slight man in a modest envirosuit toweled off the rain.

"You didn't wear your full suit today, sir?"

"No, I've been out of town. I didn't know the weather was going to be so poor this afternoon."

He nodded politely and asked me to wait for the sanitation process to complete. After the spray died down, the attendant grabbed a fresh towel from a case nearby and gently removed the residue. A moment later, he opened the door. I slid down my filtration mask and stepped inside.

This public house was a little too bright after being under storm clouds all morning. They were spending a fortune on fluorescent lighting, but even placed small mirrors around each bulb for good measure. Even in the middle of the afternoon, seating was pretty thin. I only saw a couple open spots at the bar. While music played softly on the speakers, I moved in that direction, bumping as few other patrons as possible. I peeled off my rose-tinted goggles and pulled my leather cap back before sitting.

I was thankful that my father's babysitter wasn't chasing me inside. I needed a little time to myself before returning home. This last venture had been an utter failure and I wasn't sure I could face my father without gathering myself.

I broke off a chip from my gold card and slid it to the barkeep. The man queued my flavor of choice—Spring in the Mountains—and a slot in the bar slid back to reveal the triangular, rubber apparatus. I was barely starting to lose the lingering feeling of my respirator mask when I grabbed the new one and fit it neatly over my nose and mouth.

The oxy shot into my lungs. I let my eyes close as I inhaled deeply and slowly. It was slightly cool, like mountain air before the pollution. Sure, it wasn't the cleanest air I had ever tasted, but it was almost as good as the filtered atmo from home.

When I relaxed a bit, I took a look around the bar. Everyone else wore their fully sealing weather suits. The cheaper ones always looked like gaudy, glittered wetsuits, but the clientele here took pride in their appearance. Their suits were all smooth and evenly colored. Just what you'd expect from patrons of the most expensive oxy bar in Budapest. People that could still afford things nearly went broke proving to everyone else how much money they had.

"What do you miss the most about the old days?"

I hadn't noticed the woman when she sat next to me. She sounded stressed.

"Pardon?"

"Somehow, I always get asked that when I stop at a bar—" She flagged down the bartender and asked for a red wine—a very, very old one—and Sea Foam. "—as if the people I sit beside have a very small list of things to say. So I like to get it out of the way early."

She took a long pull from her mask and the tension visibly left her shoulders.

"Really? That seems awfully pessimistic."

"The oceans have turned to blood. Isn't that a sign of the end times?" She trailed, then looked like she suddenly realized where she was. "Sorry. That's not exactly appropriate oxy bar convo."

I took another pull from my mask while she tried to hide a slight blush in hers. "The Hungarian National Philharmonic Orchestra."

"Ooo, good answer."

"Thank you."

"All right, then. I'll bite. What was so wonderful about the philharmonic orchestra?"

"You mean, other than historical significance and devotion to high art and culture?"

"Sure. In addition to that."

"It was the only time my family sat down together. Now, I still listen to Offenbach and Chopin and the Strausses, but it's not the same."

"On earbuds?"

"Yes. When music is played live, it *becomes* alive. The first time I went, the orchestra played *Orpheus and the Underworld*. It was special. There would be no other time on Earth that exact song would be played that exact way. But off a disk or an MP3—it's never quite the same. Even after I found a recording of *Orpheus* from that night, it felt different. Hollow, perhaps."

"I know what you mean."

"Not to mention, of course, that classical music is better in good company."

She smiled. A little to my surprise, her lips weren't chapped or cracked in the least and—from what I could tell—she still had all her teeth. Even the richest patrons in here likely suffered from some form of vitamin deficiency.

"If that's a come-on, it's terrible."

I laughed. "No come-on. Just a statement of fact."

She looked me over again. "I can't picture you listening to the Strausses."

"But you can picture me listening to Offenbach?"

"It just seems their music catered to die-hard patriots. Like Wagner."

"What do you mean?"

"Like the pretentious ass who rode in on the black coffin." She whispered knowingly, "You know he listens to *Twilight of the Gods* as he counts his bullion at night."

"Black coffin... You mean the limo?" *My limo.*

"What kind of world does *that* person live in, that wasting money on a comfortable transit is more important than developing filtration systems? Or grand-scale purifiers for our oceans."

I shrugged. "Maybe he's already spent his money on those projects."

"And then bought an ostentatious auto with money that could feed a large family for a month?"

To be honest, I didn't know how much the limo had cost. Or what it would take to feed a large Hungarian family for a month. I didn't say anything while the woman puffed from her mask. By the time she was done it felt like the subject had moved on. "And you?"

"Pardon?"

"And what do you miss most about before?"

She sat still for a moment and looked pensive. She was quiet for a while and I started to think that she hadn't heard me. "Hummingbirds."

"Seriously?"

"What, is that not interesting enough?"

"Hey, it's your game. I was just expecting a more...ah...yeah, that's not interesting enough."

"I see. Well, then—" she thought for a moment longer, "—a steaming, foamy cup of white chocolate latté with a shot of Arabica bean espresso. When we could still use filtered water and nonfat milk and full-fat whipped cream. I'd put a sprinkle of chocolate shavings on top, just to make certain that my teeth would rot out."

Try as I might, I couldn't suppress an "Mmm" as my mouth watered.

"You know, that might be the first time I've been honest about that."

"Really?"

"I usually say cleaner air; that's the kind of generic response everyone gives. But I'd sleep outside for a week if it would conjure a latté. The way they were." She sighed heavily with mingled exhaustion and nostalgia.

"Oh, I don't think the cost has to be that high."

While she gave me a look of pure incredulity, I signaled the barkeep and asked for two white chocolate lattés with espresso. The woman put a hand on my arm.

"Oh, no, no, no. You don't have to do that. That must be so expensive—"

"Oh, of course not. I would never spend so much money on someone I've just met."

"Oh..."

"Without learning her name first."

She bit the corner of her mouth to keep back a smile.

"Bianka."

I placed a hand over my heart—it was a little old-fashioned, but habits stick with us for a reason—and genuinely smiled. "Claud."

I turned back to the barkeep. "Nonfat milk, full-fat whipped cream, some chocolate shavings on top. And make sure everything is triple filtered, not the ninety-seven percent drivel I've seen you hand out."

The barkeep cleared his throat and poorly hid the surliness on his face, but he choked most of it down when he took my gold chips.

"It will take a few minutes. I'll have to make sure everything is available in the kitchen."

"Don't take too long. We're thirsty."

When the man left, Bianka stared at me again. "I hope you're not doing this just to impress me."

"Can I help it if coffee sounded like the perfect drink for the moment? It's no World Cup, but you described it so well...I won't be able to get it off my mind until I have some. And besides, the worse the world gets out there—" I nodded to the windows, so heavily shaded that people walking in front of them were little more than a scurrying mass, "—the greater our responsibility to make it better where we can."

"Our responsibility?"

"Our duty."

"I see." She nodded knowingly. "I think I'm putting it together."

"How so?"

"Duty, responsibility, disposable income, a personality that shows you're used to getting what you want... Is your father, by chance, a military man?"

"After a manner."

"A general?"

"No, but he's worked with generals."

"A—what's below general—major, then?"

"No."

"Captain?"

I shook my head.

"Are you going to let me keep guessing?"

I nodded my head.

"Navy? Air Force? No? You *did* say he worked with generals? Is he a politician then?"

I smiled. "Warmer."

She held her hands up in surrender. "I'm done guessing, then."

"Aw, why is that?"

"The last thing I want is to get mixed up with a politician's son."

"Who's doing any mixing?"

"Don't play so innocent."

"There's no need to be defensive. My father's politics don't have anything to do with our friendly chat."

"They always will. I've been down that road before."

"What road is that?"

She started what seemed like a rather eventful story, but stopped and sighed instead. "Sorry, again. It's been a long day."

"No, please. Keep going."

"You sure?"

"But I feel I do need a little clarification on something..."

"What's that?"

"You said it was supposed to get less interesting after that question. I find the opposite to be true. When someone lets their guard down enough to talk about things that they have lost, they tend to open up about all those other little relatable things. The things that draw people together."

"A man with no secrets will have no friends."

"Who said that? Camus?"

"Me."

"Very well. In that spirit, I will tell you a secret—a small secret—in hopes that you will return the trust."

There was a hint of sarcasm when she said, "Oh, please do."

I leaned in close and glanced around in mock suspicion. I lowered my voice conspiratorially. "The limo outside is mine."

Her brow furrowed. "Yours?"

"Well, it is for me. My family owns it."

"Oh...Oh, my. Sorry about the...comment about it."

"Comment? Which comment?"

"The, ah—"

"Pretentious ass one?"

"The—that one, yes."

Our conversation went quiet for a moment.

The bartender brought our drink order—small porcelain cups served on small porcelain dishes, both full of a sweet, heady brew that reeked of caffeine and raw brown sugar. Unprocessed was the craze here. The health nuts had to have their fads, especially when the alternative with paste from a tube. And, of course, the bar could charge quadruple for healthy, low-phosphate, *real* sugar.

When I thought about it, this ticket might feed a large family for a couple weeks or more. Putting things in that context weighed a little harder on my conscience than I expected it would. I knew all my father's speeches about being a beacon of stolidity to the masses, how we had to continue our lifestyles to keep up morale for the country, but they didn't really seem to balance out.

I was roused from my thoughts by Bianka's soft groan. I expected her to be ecstatic, but she stared into her cup, disappointment all over her face.

"What, is it too hot?"

She wiped a silken-gloved finger over her lip where the foam still lingered.

"It's not that." She held the finger under her nose. It wrinkled.

I held my cup under my nose and breathed in the steam.

"Hmm. Hazelnut?"

"That's what I thought." She set the cup down and pushed the saucer away.

I snapped my fingers for the barkeep's attention. "This is hazelnut."

His only answer was a shrug. I was fully ready to demand to see the owner to ask why his staff was so pitifully inattentive to his guests that I was out of my seat when Bianka put a gentle hand on my back.

"Let it go, it's fine."

"An establishment like this should be better staffed, if they want to keep any business."

"I know, it's a debacle and a horror. Will you let it go anyway?"

I nodded and sat again. I tried the coffee myself, but couldn't get the first sip past my lips before a quickly creeping wave of nausea rippled towards my throat.

"My thoughts exactly," she said when she saw my face.

I pushed the porcelain away as well. "Shame. I was looking forward to coffee."

"Especially when you spent—how much was it?"

"I don't know. Three or four chips."

"Ah."

We each took a few pulls of oxy in silence. It wasn't an unpleasant silence, but the rules of conversation must be followed in polite company.

"I believe it's your turn."

"For what?" she asked.

"I told you a secret in confidence. Now it's your turn."

"Ah. Does that really count as a secret?"

"We're the only two people in the building who know."

"Oh. Well, it certainly is, then."

"So, it's only fair."

"All right, since it's *fair*." She thought for a moment. "I may have been slightly misleading earlier."

"Oh, now how is that supposed to build trust?" I gave her my best look of mock suspicion.

She broke a smile. "Just listen. When I said earlier than I've been involved with politicians, there is perhaps a better term to use. A more accurate one."

"Is that so? What is this more accurate term? Robots? Martians?"

"Royalty."

Hmm. Now that was interesting. "I see. Now, when you say involved, do you mean you are part of some obscure duchy or an ancient, lost genial line?"

"No. I mean the pressures of the world we live in, now more than ever, encourage people to fall back on old principles. You know, archaic mindsets."

"That's true."

"And some people function better in those types of archaic environments than others."

"But we do what we must for our people. My father always says that his responsibility is to his family, and his family is all people loyal to the Hungarian Empire. He is their protector, guide, and arbitrator."

"You mean..." she began.

At this point I will admit, I fucking *love* being able to play this card: "He is their king."

I said it low enough that only she could hear, but she glanced around as if expecting someone else to register the confusion she felt. She teetered between belief and disbelief for a moment, her mouth slightly agape. When she realized she was doing so, she compensated by pursing her lips in concentration until— "I don't believe you."

"See? No trust between us whatsoever. Such a shame." I feigned hurt while I stared off at nothing.

"If you're a prince, why don't I recognize you?"

"If you've ever seen my face, it was likely before I was a teenager. Before the...before the world changed, too."

Her brown eyes burrowed into my face, demanding confirmation. "Hmm. Still not convinced. Do you have identification?"

"Not with me."

"That's convenient."

"Not if I'm telling the truth."

"Fine then. I'll give you one chance to prove to me that you are a prince—"

"*The* prince." I stood and faced her. "Prince Claud Aba of the Unified Kingdom of Hungary."

That got some attention.

I bowed deeply before her. If the music weren't playing, you could have heard a pin drop across the room. When I straightened, there was a pleasant shock of blush in her cheeks. Her mouth fell open a bit longer that time. I gave her my most assuring smile. "Are you convinced, yet?"

She hesitated in a moment out of shock—which, I will admit, I enjoyed—but before she could answer, I heard something muttered low beside me.

I turned to the man that made the noise.

"What was that, sir? I didn't hear you."

"I said, some people would think it unwise to announce that," the man said as he stood. His goggles were around his neck, but his shiny, dark green hood still obscured most of his face. He had dark eyes under dark brows and his skin was pocked viciously in places. "And I'm not a *sir*."

"May I have your name then, friend?"

"No."

The tone in his voice was a red flag. I needed to diffuse the tension quickly. "I assure you that I fear nothing from my people. I work to care for them."

The man laughed in my face. His breath reeked of old eggs.

"What *work* have you done? What changes has your family *enacted* since the world turned, huh? How have you made us safer?" As he continued to emphasize, I could smell a hint of vodka.

"My friend, my father has done everything——"

He took a step closer. Now I could smell the synthetic ointment he used to clean his rocky face, a horrid mix of silicone and aloe.

"I am *not* your friend."

He was about to bowl me over with his chest alone when Bianka stood.

"Settle down, boys."

"Stay out of this!" the man roared at her.

"There's nothing to yell about," I started. "We can discuss this like——"

He rounded on me again and grabbed my suit with both hands. His brow furrowed so deeply that his eyes were almost hidden, replaced by flaring nostrils and parted teeth. I blinked back against the spittle that nearly blinded me and Bianka strode forward and put a hand on the man's shoulder. He growled and let me go with one hand so he could push her back—he grabbed her wrist and shoved hard. There was a loud, dull *thunk* as her elbow collided with my face.

I saw white spots, and a line of pain split my vision a second after her elbow bounced off my lips and nose. I staggered back a step and found my eyes watering, but at least I wasn't being clawed at any longer.

"Sit down!" I heard Bianka say harshly, immediately followed by the thud of a large man taking his seat.

Her light steps neared me and by the time her gentle hands were on my arm I could see again. She was a vision of concern. Kind of sweet, in a motherly sort of way. It almost distracted me from how embarrassing the whole ordeal was.

"Are you okay?"

I nodded, not yet trusting my lips to form thanks.

"Here, let me look."

She gently pulled me towards one of the lights. The amplified glare stung a bit and I closed my eyes against it.

"That's too close."

I moved back a step.

"Better?" She put both hands on either end of my jawline and tilted my head around, slowly. I opened an eye when she stepped away to grab one of the cloth napkins from a stack on the bar. She folded it neatly and held it to my nose. "Hold this."

I did.

"The bleeding isn't bad and you didn't split your lip, at least."

"*I* didn't split my lip?"

"I am so, so sorry that happened."

"No real harm done." I looked past her to where the instigator still sat, hunched over the bar and puffing on a mask. As quietly as I could, I added, "Could have been much worse."

Bianka half-smiled and reached for the napkin to check my nose again. The song playing ended and changed. That seemed to be the cue for those watching the show to find something else to do. Things around us went back to normal. We weren't being stared at anymore. I let her look me over a moment longer before I spoke again.

"I suppose this is as good a time as any to ask you to come home with me."

"I—" she started. "That's a little forward, don't you think?"

"Purely as a guest, of course."

"Oh, I couldn't accept. Not after this."

"I'll not hear of it. You should accept *because* of this." I raised an eyebrow. "To prove that there is no bad blood between us." I tossed the soiled napkin into a nearby wastebin.

She hid the smile better in her mouth than in her eyes. She feigned consideration for a moment, then consented. "Very well. I won't have it said a Laczkovich denied the hospitality of the crown."

So she was of royal blood. Interesting.

"I would be honored to be your guest…your Grace."

Suited up again, we stepped into atmo together.

"May I ride with you? The chip in my auto died again, I was waiting inside for a driver."

"You may call and cancel from the limo. Our phones are linked into the local network. You'll ride with us as we'll take care of your vehicle."

"Oh, not if it's any trouble."

"None whatsoever."

My driver, dutiful as always, held the door for us. I gestured toward it.

Bianka hesitated just a moment.

"I should have recognized you, your Grace," Bianka said. "I hope you'll forgive me, but it's more difficult to remember who's who when you're not seeing their faces on the news every day. Like you said, that was some time ago."

"Of course."

Bianka slid her goggles down and slid herself into the limo. I followed suit. I told the driver to take us to the manor and we were off seconds later.

"Oh, now we are ready to return home?" the man across from me quipped.

"And I'm going to have to reprimand my staff for not keeping me apprised of *all* the noblewomen of marriageable age."

"To be honest, I've spent some effort to keep a low profile around the city. I prefer to keep my heritage quiet to avoid...well, exactly what we just encountered."

My adviser made a nasty noise in the back of his throat. "What happened this time, your Grace? Did they serve vodka instead of gin?"

"You'll have to forgive Mr. Zseid. He seems to think that I care more about liquor than my own blood." I tried not to let my tone go too icy, but I didn't try very hard. "No, actually. I announced my station to miss Bianka of House Laczkovich and another patron...was displeased by this revelation."

"Which is why I *insisted* that you not go in such a place. Good God, your nose! He struck you?"

"No need to get upset. It was a simple misunderstanding."

I saw Zseid's blood pressure spike. "If he laid a single finger on the crown prince, I'll have him hanged! Driver! Halt immediately?"

The limo stopped on a dime.

"Did you get the traitor's name?" Zseid was already sweating, despite the filtered air conditioning.

"It was nothing."

"Nothing?" Mr. Zseid picked up his tablet. "Give me his description, this anarchist! I'll have an officer track him down. I'd go back there myself if I were a few years younger."

Bianka stared out a side window, anxious not to incriminate herself.

"I already forgot what he looks like."

The other man sighed wearily. "Your selective memory—"

"Enough." I let him sit quietly for a moment. "If you wish to lecture me, please wait until we no longer have company. I'd hate for Lady Bianka to listen to me remove you from your employment. I imagine seeing a grown man break down in tears would be uncomfortable to watch."

I waited until he lower his eyes. "Driver—take us home, please."

Zseid fumed the rest of the drive, but at least he did so quietly.

Ten minutes to the city limits, another forty to the Aba estate. While the Danube was never really blue, it was now a ruddy brown, colored by overgrowth of algae. Out here, where people no longer lived, the lush land by the Danube had been reduced to little more than a red, smoky wasteland. Sure, the air was bad in the cities, but several high-volume air filters had been installed in Budapest making the air breathable, though any exposure over seconds is recommended to be filtered through a mask.

Lingering out here could be lethal in minutes. People who survived exposure without a filter would be sick for days. There would be a week or so where they would feel better, then the real sickness would strike. Then organ calcification would begin. Other disorders—not the least of which being pulmonary fibrosis or even smoking stool—would wreak havoc on one's health. Even contact with the rain burned bare skin of plant and animal alike, wiping out whole species of living things that couldn't be protected in time.

People who survived the initial climate turn migrated toward cities for work and medical aid. Most of them were forced to stay in polluted areas that wouldn't be cleaned for years. They developed something of a tolerance to phosphorus and could even consume it again in regular foods, but this adaptation came at a cost. People who "adjusted" to the increased levels of phosphorus showed drastically reduced lifespans and drastically increased risk of birth defects in continued generations. Many families lived through the change in the oceans and land just to have their children die in their arms year after year.

The rest of us, those who have yet to suffer this kind of phosphorus poisoning, are called "pure bloods" by some. We developed a heightened aversion to red phosphorous to such an extent that it affected the way we smelled food. Scientists around Europe believe this was another evolutionary defense to environmental change, but it put considerable strain on our dietary needs. Since nearly every type of food contains phosphorus, deficiency was uncommon. Diagnosis and treatment came slowly. It took considerable time and money spent in synthetic supplements and finely regulated phosphorous dosage, but for those who could afford it, proper nutrition was eventually balanced out.

However, the issue of "blood purity" became another rift in our society.

When we needed most to pull together as one nation, one European state, one World, we fell back on old party lines and medieval ruling systems. Father had to reinstate supreme autocracy just to hold Hungary together. He was criticized by many for this, but when the United States fell into anarchy and some of the smaller or newer European countries dispersed or were wiped out entirely, Father was one of the few men who could hold the public together. When cell networks and even the internet failed, he broadcasted on radio until our own network could be erected. He encouraged all to stand firm, to trust that we would make it through that trying time as one, unified Hungary.

He did better than most, but the dividing line between upper and lower class had never been clearer. Hungary was at peace, but it hadn't been an easy one since the world turned.

I suddenly realized I had been impolite. It had been a quiet drive, and I was starting to lose myself in my own thoughts, but the silence was looming palpably.

"I'll give you fair warning, Bianka. Father and Mother expected me back over an hour ago. With the weather, I'll be even later."

"*We'll* be even later," Zseid muttered.

"Did you call him to say you would be late?" Bianka asked me.

"I would, as soon as we were back on the local network, but I…actually don't have my phone with me."

"Why is that?"

Zseid chuckled wearily. "Worry not, my prince. I called and spoke with your parents for you. I told them exactly where we were, who they would be thanking for our tardiness, and why you found yourself without your cell phone."

Bianka had the slightest mischievous look cross her face when she saw how I was avoiding the topic. "Why did you find yourself without your phone, Claud?"

"It was broken."

"Oh? And how did that happen, if you don't mind my asking?"

Zseid cut in before I could explain tactfully. "It was broken by your predecessor, miss Laczkovich. While she was in something of a state, if I may say."

Bianka's only response was turning to me with an eyebrow raised sharply.

"If I may be allowed to speak, Mr. Zseid… She broke my phone because she was upset."

Bianka stared levelly.

"She was upset because I broke off an engagement of sorts."

"What kind of *engagement*?"

"An engagement of marriage."

Her lips pursed. She was silent a full ten seconds. "Well, now I must hear the entire story."

"Really?"

"You've piqued my curiosity."

"There's not much to tell, really."

"We still have some drive to fill. And you can't leave a story like that untold."

I sighed. This story was only a few hours old. As for my part, I was still trying to decide exactly how I felt about it. "As the crown prince, I have a certain duty to provide an heir for the Aba line. My parents have always had strict guidelines for who I am allowed to spend time with, so you can imagine the lengths they went to find me the *perfect* wife."

"And this last one didn't fit those guidelines?"

"Adrienne was a...nice woman. Her family lives on the other side of Hungary, and I was staying with them while arrangements were made. We were engaged for two months before I learned from one of her maids that she'd been untruthful on certain medical issues. When I told Father, he demanded that I end the relationship. Shortly after discussing this with her, I stepped away to speak with Father and arrange a flight home..."

"She stormed in and knocked your phone to the floor?"

"She threw it out a window, actually."

Mr. Zseid corrected with his usual tone, "The young duchess threw the prince's phone *through* a window. That bloody red gas shot into the room like a geyser."

"It wasn't that dramatic."

"I've told your father countless times that end of the country had a far worse environmental turn after the rain turned red. And to think of that behavior from a lady! She endangered everyone in the room and quite possibly the building. Thank God they had containment and treatment protocols."

"Was anyone poisoned?" Bianka asked, concerned.

"No, thankfully. I stayed long enough to make sure Adrienne and her family were all right. By the time everyone was cleared medically, Father's jet had arrived and I flew back."

"And then our *delay* at the public house, of course."

"I needed a few minutes to myself before returning home."

"Yes, I can see that." Zseid's eyes rolled meaningfully to Bianka and back.

"I should clarify. I just wanted to be free of you and your demands to know 'what in the Devil is going on here?' for a moment." Before Zseid could respond, I added, "Why did Father send you to collect me, anyway?"

"To—" he started with a flare of anger, but softened to resigned bitterness when he realized what he was about to say. "To make sure there wasn't any delay in your return."

"Ah, yes. But as there was such ..." I turned back to Bianka. "My father has never turned away a visitor or a friend, but he might be in something of a mood. He doesn't like to be kept waiting."

"What's his policy on throwing cell phones?"

Zseid chuckled at her jest, despite himself.

Thankfully, the Aba family had the forewarning and funds to prepare when the world turned red. The property now functions off of a private energy reservoir, collected by solar paneling. All 144 rooms are air-sealed and a dozen filters keep purity at nearly one-hundred percent. Our manor is around sixty miles from the capital, one of the three surviving estates outside of Budapest. It has been in the family since the seventeenth century but would be unrecognizable to its builders. Much of its innards had to be gutted and remodeled for the filtration, security, and surveillance systems of current need. Much of the facade has taken a heavy toll, being slowly eaten away by the same water table that used to keep the grounds lush year-round.

"It's beautiful," Bianka said as we ascended the drive.

"She has seen better days," Zseid said, craning to see the facade of the palace. "But she still has a regal sort of charm about her. A symbol of hope for all citizenry."

Bianka and I exited the limo after getting our face protection back on, but Zseid said something about 'dealing with a mess of those damn revolutionaries' and left. A doorman utterly concealed within a bulkier—but far more effective—envirosuit than either of us wore let us into the manor.

The lights in the decontamination room were soft. The LED on the handle of the door to the foyer was red.   The still air was disturbed by puffs of sanitizing mist. The sound system gently played the ambiance of local birds over *Kaiser-Walzer*.

"What's your middle name?"

"My, that's quite personal." We had to talk around our masks and over the light spurts of sanitizer, a vapor so fine there would be no need for a wipe down afterwards. "Are you sure we know each other well enough for that?"

"Ioan." A moment later. "Now you have to tell me yours."

She smiled as she said, "Josefa."

The LED on the handle lit green and I slid the door into the wall.

Bianka Josefa Laczkovich stepped into the foyer and I followed. She pulled back the hood of her suit for the first time in my sight. Thick, wavy layers of black and brown escaped the hood and fell about her ears. The brown in her hair matched the brown of her eyes exactly in the (simulated) natural lighting.

I felt, briefly, that I was the sole member in the audience of the unveiling of a sculptural masterpiece.

"You're staring a bit, your Grace," she said quietly.

I cleared my throat. "Pardon."

"Of course, your Grace."

I was starting to get the impression that I wasn't so disappointed to have to break things off with Adrienne, after all. Those familiar flutters in my belly came in waves.

I realized then I wanted to know this woman better. Not because I needed a mate or a trophy… I simply wanted to learn her hows and whys. I wanted her to learn about me as well. To understand where I come from. I wanted to show her the ascending stairways, the lavish kitchen, the enormous guest rooms…but my parents had been waiting for us to arrive, so the tour would have to wait.

Father and Mother strode into the room, her hand on his arm, both dressed in dark blue suits.

"You're a bit late, my son."

"Apologies, Father. I was sidetracked. Bianka, this is my father, Samuel II Aba, King of Unified Hungary."

Father turned to Bianka, who curtsied deeply.

"Your Majesty. It is an honor to be in your beautiful home."

Father looked her over carefully. He turned to me. "I thought you were coming home alone."

"I was. Father, Mother, this is *Lady* Bianka Laczkovich."

All the necessary pleasantries were exchanged.

"I hope you'll forgive us. When Edwin called and said he did not know when you'd return, we went ahead with dinner," Father said.

"Of course, your Grace."

"Father, Lady Bianka's auto is in need of repair. I offered her our hospitality until then."

There was a hint of reluctance when he said, "Of course."

Bianka was cautious when she responded, apparently eager not to offend. "I have no intention to intrude, your Grace, but… also, there are reports of a sandstorm possibly picking up within the next couple hours. I'm not certain when your people will be able to get to the vehicle. Would it be possible…?"

"Lady Laczkovich," said Mother, "better safe than sorry. We shall prepare a room for you."

"That is far too kind, your Grace."

Mother waved a hand. "Think nothing of it. I've apparently just lost a daughter-in-law." Now she looked to me. "It will be so thrilling to hear the story some other time, I'm sure." Back to Bianka. "It will be nice to have a beautiful young woman's presence around the manor. It's been dreary here since we've had to close up the entire place. The new lighting and ambiance help, but…" she leaned closer and pretended to speak conspiratorially. "You have no idea how *dull* the men around here can be."

A lesser man might have gotten upset, but Father, sour though he usually is, smiled not unkindly at Mother's ribbing. "Lady Bianka, you and my son should dine in the solarium. We will rouse the staff and have them see to a warm meal and a comfortable bed for both of you."

Bianka curtsied deeply again. "Thank you, your Grace."

Father excused himself. Mother walked with us a ways. "So, I understand the two of you met in a public house."

"Yes. At the oxy bar downtown."

"Let me guess. The bar was crowded but you happened to sit next to each other and strike up a conversation?"

Bianka paused. "Uh, something like that, yes."

"And neither of you recognized each other? I'm sure you've met at least once before. The Laczkovich family didn't often attend our galas, but we've attended several operas with your parents, Bianka."

"Really? I didn't know."

"That was before the red rain."

"Of course."

"Did you try anything special, dear?"

"I ordered coffee for us."

"Claud, you know how caffeine ruins your sleep," Mother responded in her most motherly tone.

"Of course, Mother. But you'll be glad to know that it wasn't any good. Neither of us had more than a sip."

She suddenly seemed more interested than polite conversation would require. "Why is that? Did they use real milk with it?"

"It was hazelnut instead of white chocolate."

"Ah, I see. Was the music good, at least?"

I shrugged. "Honestly, Mother, it all just sounds like 'Gangnam Style' anymore."

Bianka and I sat in the solarium. The table between us was full of the freshest, cleanest, most heavily modified, hydroponically grown food that our nation's brightest could produce. The projections on the walls offered a nearly-real view of a lush, green lawn. Bright monarchs fluttered between the trees and hummingbirds buzzed from flower to flower, ceaselessly gorging on their nectar. It was as close as our new world could mimic the old one.

Bianka was staring into the projections with a species of longing on her face that I knew quite well.

"Bianka. Are you all right?"

She came out of her trance and lowered the cupful of pseudo-tea that she was holding. "Yes, I'm fine. It's just been so long since I've seen a hummingbird. I must be feeling...nostalgic."

"I understand. I miss it, too."

She was looked down for just a moment, then was ready to change the subject.

"This food is wonderful. I've never tasted synth this good."

"Ah, that's because it's mostly the real thing. Here—" I picked a wedge of Romano off a tray. "The sheep that provided the milk for this cheese were genetically enhanced to produce lower-phosphate milk."

"Do sheep have the same reaction to the red rains that people do?"

"Yes, but if they're kept in controlled conditions, the poisoning and birth defects can be avoided altogether. Before the cheese is set to age, additional enzymes are added to clump the phosphorus molecules together. This reduces the odor that causes the nauseating reaction."

Bianka was giving me the oddest look.

"What?"

"Nothing. You just know a lot more about this process that I would have guessed."

I chuckled.

"Oh, I don't know any of the formulas or anything. Actually, I had to do a lot of research on it. After the change, eating was terrible. My favorite treats, like pumpkin seeds roasted with honey, would make me violently ill for hours. Mother thought I had been playing in the red dunes that were piling outside, but she and Father had similar reactions to salmon, brie, and even soy milk."

"Yes, it was like everything had been irradiated or something."

"When the official reports came out, Father dumped millions more into alternative food sources and supplements. We already had some investments in that area, so we had a head start when it came down to life or death for the people."

"All hail the mighty blue paste," Bianka said sarcastically.

"Well, the labs produced much more than the Danube Blue. It's just that the closer they made the synth to the real thing..."

"Exponential increase in cost."

"Of course. And that's just for nutrients. For the additives like phospho-resistance tabs, vitamin boosts, or even caffeine, the costs were—and are—rather steep."

"To afford it, you'd have to be, say ... a king."

I wasn't sure if the undertone of her voice had taken on a darker edge or not.

"Sadly, yes. But I couldn't get past my aversion to regular food until I knew exactly how it was processed. I found it all fascinating, how science has progressed to the point it can fix fundamental flaws in our foods or bodies."

"The manipulation of it fascinated you?"

"Well, I wouldn't say that. At any rate, we were lucky Father had already invested in alternative food sources. If soy hadn't been unusable after the rains, we might have been able to limp along. With all major food supplies contaminated or otherwise rendered inedible, we couldn't have afforded to continue as a nation without the labs modifying old foods to be salvageable or inventing new ways to mass produce nutrients for the people."

"So you see your father as the savior of Hungary?"

"In a way, yes. Without his leadership, we would have broken down into smaller city-states like most of the rest of Europe."

Bianka took a breath. I couldn't tell what, but it seemed like she wanted to say something or wanted to hide something. She was trying not to be upset for reasons I really couldn't guess at the moment.

"Bianka, are you all right? Do you feel faint?"

She cleared her throat and recomposed. "Yes, I'm quite fine. I was outside a little too long, perhaps. Nothing serious." She showed me a smile she clearly didn't feel.

"I'm sorry. If this is bothering you, we can change the subject. The growing pains we had to suffer are still near to us all."

"Growing pains?"

"Yes. During the change. But, like all people before us, we meet our adversary head on. We stare down our fate and we adapt. We change what we must to protect what we must. Nothing more."

She ran her fingers over her brow gingerly. I was starting to think she really was coming down with something until smiled again and said, "Quite right." She sipped her ice water.

A few moments passed in silence.

"Favorite television show."

"Pardon?" she asked.

"What was your favorite television show before the change?"

She thought a moment. "To be honest, I miss BBC News."

"Really? I thought they only reported on the most dreadful elements of humanity. I never saw a story in the headlines at the BBC about someone's humanitarian efforts or lifetime achievements."

"They had the highest integrity of any news channel on TV or print. They showed the world for what it was, not what their producers thought would get the best ratings."

"I see. I didn't know that labeling my father as a despot counted as integrity. And I can assure you their producers only aired the most shocking stories they could find. Because producers get ratings. That's their sole job requirement."

The discussion was about to escalate fully into an argument. I saw that look in Adrienne's eyes a dozen times, but Bianka exercised more self-control, I was pleased to note, and bit back what she was going to say.

"Sorry. I had no intention of that being..." She cleared her throat. "Anyway— what about you?"

She was mostly avoiding eye contact. She didn't want me to see the frustration there. Though I could certainly see it, I still couldn't guess the cause.

"Da Ali G Show."

The tension finally broke. She laughed heartily. "You did *not* watch Da Ali G

Show."

I laughed. "No, I didn't."

"I hope that the orchestra is not the only thing you miss. What else do you miss, since you find this morbid topic so interesting?"

"Oh, I wouldn't call it morbid. I just ... I wanted to learn more about you."

"Is that so?"

"Yes. It is so. In fact—" I stood and slid my chair closer. I leaned forward. "I hope you don't think that I move too fast, but in these times, good things need to be secured as soon as you find them."

Her breath quickened. "How do you mean?"

"I mean... I already burn for you more than any other woman I've known. And I assure you, I've known more than my fair share."

"Claud..."

"You must understand, since I became a man, my father and mother have been parading women before me—beautiful women, duchesses and princesses and countesses, women of pedigree and standing—and, for most of them, I truly, truly felt nothing. After the first, I understood how it felt and why it was being done, so I guarded myself, ready to do my duty for my Hungary."

I took her hand in mine.

"But you just sat down next to me. It was as simple as that. This family spent over a decade finding the perfect woman, the perfect *royal* woman..."

Her eyes searched. She was still guarded, but she needed to know what this meant. That the future of my family and the Kingdom of Hungary was at stake.

"And if that woman is you, one day I hope you will sit beside me as Queen."

"Claud, I don't know what to say."

"Bianka, my entire family is depending on me to find a wife who is pure, free from this sickness that ravages the Earth. The Aba blood must remain pure and strong. Unpoisoned. And if I have anything to say about it, and I assure you I do, I would like that woman to be you."

"This ...this isn't a decision that can be made over dinner, Claud. I will have to discuss it with my family."

I wouldn't say I was crestfallen, but I deflated just a bit when my eagerness wasn't reflected in her.

"Of course. Their consent will be necessary."

I wanted to say more, much more, that she had a responsibility. And if I were being honest with myself, my pride had been wounded that she hadn't taken to the idea like I had hoped. I was of the mind that we were a very compatible pair. So it seemed until the end of this conversation, at any rate.

I thought it best to let her choose her time to speak, rather than badger her with the growing insistence I felt. There was a long silence, broken only by the occasional buzzing of hummingbirds.

What seemed like far too long after, a maid finally showed up to say that

Bianka's room was finished. She said she was ready to retire immediately and I led her there. Little was said. The silence was warmer than I expected it to be, as if it were charged with something. I was starting to suspect that I offended her with the suddenness of my offer.

When we reached her room, I felt as though I couldn't let our day end on such a poor note.

"Bianka, I am truly sorry if I offended you."

She finally faced me. There was a great uncertainty in her eyes. The artificial candlelight flickered in the brown disks of her eyes and I found myself lost for just an instant.

"I only wanted to share the truth with you. I feel that we are compatible spirits."

"You mean…soulmates?"

I grinned softly. "Yes. And God willing, my Father will agree."

"Claud, I'm … flattered, but I can't make a decision like this right now. I need time."

I knew that it would be best to let it go at that. This was certainly a weighty burden to appear on a woman's shoulders so unexpectedly.

"Very well. We shall discuss this further in the morning, as long as you feel up to it."

Now that I had the light to notice again, she seemed, perhaps, a little pale.

"Yes, that sounds…that sounds fine."

"Are you sure that you're well? We have a nurse on call—"

"Thank you, but I'm fine. Truly. I just need to rest."

"Of course, Bianka. Sleep well."

"Thank you, your Grace."

I couldn't get her out of my mind. I kept seeing how she looked projected into ceiling as I laid in bed. She was struggling with the heavy responsibility of it all. That was clear on her face. But what I couldn't tell for certain—what was perhaps truly bothering me—was that I couldn't tell if she was hesitant to become *the* princess or *my* princess.

We could work with the former, so long as she were given enough time and space to adjust. The latter…I would never marry against a woman's will, but the throne tends to lean heavily on those that do not submit to its wishes, let alone its *needs*.

Perhaps it was because I was so intently focused on her that I thought I heard something from her room across the hall. I was sure I had imagined it for a moment, but then I heard a muffled grunt or exclamation.

Surely it was nothing, but I had to make sure.

I clicked on the light on my nightstand and grabbed my robe from the couch nearby. I donned it on the way to the door. I opened it the instant before Bianka opened hers and we stepped into the hall in tandem. I was almost as startled as she was.

"Claud!"

"What's wrong? I heard noises."

"It's nothing—"

"Nothing? You're white as a sheet."

"I…I think I'm having a reaction."

"To what?"

Her breath was already ragged. "I'm not sure, but I feel dizzy and itchy, like I was exposed to the red gas—"

"Christ—come with me."

"No, I—"

I strode forward and wrapped both of my arms under hers for support as I walked us towards my parents' room. "Father! Mother!"

I slammed my fist on the door to their room for a few seconds before Mother opened it anxiously.

"Mother, Bianka thinks there is a gas leak in her room. We need to get everyone to the ground floor and have this wing cleared."

Mother took this information far more calmly than I expected. Even for a woman as traditionally composed as she was. "What kind of gas, Bianka?"

"I couldn't smell anything, but I feel faint and woozy, as if I'd been outside too long."

Mother was quiet a moment.

"Rouse Father, we need to leave the wing now." I said, not possessing my mother's same calmness.

She called back into the room. "Dear, what do you think? Shall we flee?"

Father slid the door the rest of the way open. His sleeping attire was far more conservative than mine. He looked like a king even in a simple sleeping suit. He was as calm as I've ever seen him.

"No, dear. That will be quite all right."

"What do you mean? It could be dangerous here—"

He held his hand up and I stopped.

"There is no danger. Though I have to say, I'm surprised we found our results so quickly."

Bianka sounded like she would have screamed had she not been fighting waves of nausea. "What have you done to me?"

"Lady Bianka, I have just done you a great favor."

"Father, what in hell are you talking about?"

"Be calm, Claud," Mother said. "No harm has or will come to anyone under our roof." Queen Mariana Aba stared Bianka full in the face and radiated her warmest smile. "We had to be sure."

Bianka's voice was timid beneath my mother's stare, warm or not. "Sure of what—" after a moment, she remembered the obligatory, "—Your Grace."

I finally put it together.

"Bianka...I told you that I had to end things with Adrienne because she and her family lied about her medical history. I discovered that she had been struck with phosphorous poisoning several years after the red rains fell. They hid this from her history, even while they began discussions with Father and Mother about our possible betrothal."

"You broke your engagement with her because she had the shakes once?"

"The affect of the poisoning is so severe that it increases frequency and severity of birth defects upwards of fifty times. It was too a great a risk to have her—" I looked to Mother and Father for the right term, but the left me to finish my sentence, "—in the bloodline."

"So you pumped phosphorous gas into my room to make sure...what...that it would still make me sick?"

"Of course not," Father said. "I had a servant, one who already had a bit of a tolerance, sprinkle a tiny amount of diluted red phosphorus powder onto one of the bed sheets. One that would be least likely to come in contact with your skin."

"You *have* poisoned me!"

"No!" Father's answer thundered. "Calm yourself. There was nowhere near a harmful amount. We simply had to be sure that there would be a marked aversion, but no abrasive reactions should have been possible."

"Then why do I feel like I'm about to die?"

"Because you're being melodramatic?" Mother queried sweetly.

"Mother, she's truly unwell." I placed the back of my hand on her forehead. "She looks feverish but her skin is cold."

"Very well. Come in and have a seat."

She and Father moved so that I could help Bianka to a reclining couch in their room. I comforted her as best I could, but she was a rough mix of illness and bitterness. Mother collected her phone from beside the bed and called for the nurse.

"He's going to be the one asking now," I said quietly.

"What?"

"It's not going to be the prince asking for your hand. It's going to be the king. The last thing I want is for you to be upset, but now that they are certain of your purity...I doubt there's much you or your family can say to convince him otherwise."

Before Bianka could respond, as if sensing my thoughts, Father stepped up behind me.

"You must understand this, Lady Bianka: my family must be strong. My family must be strong so that Hungary may be strong. Our blood must be clean and our ties must not pollute its purity. It is clear to the throne that due to your station and good health, you shall be taken into this family as a wife to my son, and a daughter to his parents. You will never want for anything, and one day, hopefully a few good years away still, you and Claud will replace Mariana and I as rulers and protectors of this great land and its people."

Bianka was quiet. There were a range of emotions all swarming within her. Most of all, I saw doubt.

"Let me be clear. This is not a command of the throne. It is, however, a truly urgent and dire request. This family's future *must* be secured."

They met eyes for several seconds.

Finally, Bianka nodded. "Yes. The family's future must be secured."

When she said that, I grinned like a schoolboy, all the grief and worry of the last decade finally gone in a flash. A warm, rushing sensation welled in my chest and I took Bianka's hand in both of mine. She looked like she shared in my great sense of relief.

Even Father was smiling grandly when he held his hand to Bianka.

"For Hungary."

"For Hungary," she repeated. She leaned forward, despite the strain it must have placed on her belly, and gently, lovingly, kissed my Father's ring.

Shortly after, the nurse arrived and checked Bianka for serious signs of harm. She was feeling much better by then and was cleared almost immediately, on the stipulation that a new bed be prepared for her.

"See? No harm done," Father concluded. "And I should say, if anything your station has improved something dramatically. Don't you agree?"

Bianka nodded.

"Claud," Mother said, "Why don't you escort Lady Bianka to another guest room. The sheets might not be as fresh, but at least they won't be as dusty," she sent a look at Father indicating she was, perhaps, less than pleased with his plan.

Bianka no longer needed my assistance by the time we arrived at her alternate bedchamber for the evening. The color had returned to her cheeks and her mood had lightened considerably, though her voice was a little weary from the stress of these recent events.

"Thank you, Claud. For all of your help."

"Bianka, I am truly pleased that you agreed. You have no idea how wonderful this news is, especially to my parents."

"And for you?"

I smiled as broadly as I could manage. "An answer to prayers."

She laughed wearily. "I had no idea."

"With all honesty... Bianka, I—"

She silenced me by holding a hand to my cheek. Her skin was cold, but it felt like fire against mine. She leaned in gently and kissed my other cheek. "Good night, Claud," she whispered.

She slid into the room beyond, leaving nothing more than a wisp of her perfume.

"Good night," I whispered to the empty space.

I was truly on the top of the world. Never before had I felt like a prince from the fairytales, who always meets the woman of his dreams in the most unsuspected way. She was a prize, to be sure, but I was filled to the brim with desire to discover her fully. I felt the warmth in my chest spread lower...

All in good time.

I took a deep breath to recompose and went back to my bedroom. As I lay there, a giddiness I'd not known since my youth swept over me. I kept retracing our encounter, listening to the pleasing timbre of her voice, burning her profile into my memory. Feeling a brief flush as I envisioned her in her smooth, white, skin-tight suit...sliding her goggles down...pulling back the shiny hood to reveal the wavy forest of immaculate hair...and letting my imagination slide on a little further...

I eventually fell asleep with a smile on my face, expecting pleasant dreams.

I awoke shortly after with many hands holding me down and something cold and sharp pressed into my throat. I went from panic and shock directly into mortal stillness, but my blood was already thundering through my veins.

The light on my end table clicked and lit the room dimly. The face hovering over me had deeply pocked cheeks. Dark eyes under a dark brow. An odor of eggs on his breath.

"Wakey, wakey, little prince."

"What do you want?" I said, moving my jaw and throat as little as possible. I could feel the tip of the knife splitting the top layer of skin. "You wish to kidnap me?"

"Oh, no... *my friend.*" The drunk from the bar and his friends were all dressed in dark green envirosuits. Their hoods were back. They were all grinning like madmen. "You're not going anywhere."

I had to warn my family—"Bianka! Father! Mother!"—I screamed, ignoring the steel pressing into my throat. I struggled to rise—"Run!"—to fight them off, but they held me firmly, arms, legs, and torso. I hoped they could get away, warn security, anything, but all I got in return were a few dark chuckles from the men hovering above me.

A feminine voice spoke beside me. "We've already been to their room, darling."

A familiar face leaned into view. She was dressed like the others.

"Bianka—what is this?"

Her voice hissed. "This is what happens when your family uses people as their tools and slaves."

"What are you talking about? The Aba family has only worked to serve Hungary!"

Her voice was full of hate. "Your *father* has slaughtered more people than the second World War. Not to mention destroying the oceans, polluting the water table—"

"It's not our fault!" The pockmarked man spat on my face. I choked back revulsion. "The fertilizer was supposed to make food grow faster and easier—we were trying to save people, to *feed* people!"

She leaned so close to my face that I felt the heat of her breath. "You don't get to downgrade *murder* to *manslaughter*. You don't get to wipe out *half* of a population, then rule it like a god. Not without consequence."

I could only whisper, "We tried to make it right."

Bianka stared levelly for a moment.

"You failed. We won't."

She nodded to the pockmarked man and he used his free hand to pull his goggles and mask back on. Bianka and the others did the same.

I tried to call her name, but the knife cut it short. The pockmarked man pressed it into me so severely it was just about to pierce the skin. I struggled, pulling away from it, but I was held firm, even while the men were still donning their masks.

I stopped short when I saw Bianka, fully sealed again, raise the axe in both hands.

"No!" The steel axe crashed as it chopped into the wall of my bedroom where the window would have been over a decade ago. "No! Stop, please!"

Within three strikes, the wall was compromised. Red gas poured into my bedchamber. From the right, the men pushed against the bed and it slid, knocking the lamp off the nightstand. It rolled and scooted on the floor as it was trampled over, throwing light at horrible angles across the room.

No matter how hard I struggled, they held me firm beneath the fuming geyser.

I wanted to hold my breath, but after the first wisp of caustic vapor tore into my lungs I couldn't stop myself from a violent, dry coughing spell that worsened sharply. I felt the lesions stress and open in my throat, in my sinus cavities, in my lungs. When my chest tightened and my torso began to heave, my captors all sat back to watch me cover myself with my dinner.

Behind their green-tinted goggles they all observed as I slowly succumbed to my fate.

As the panic subsided and the contractions in my abdomen came slower, I realized what a fool I had been. I locked eyes with Bianka, hoping that I could understand why, but there were no answers there, only a hatred I couldn't explain.

"Death to tyrants."

Her compatriots echoed.

Even when everything else started to blur and distort, I couldn't break her gaze. Those dark brown pools stared on, devoid of any pity or regret.

In the end, they unflinchingly watched me slip away into the red haze.

ONSER VON FULLON has submitted works to the Pathfinder Chronicler and to the PAGE International Script contest. He is currently working on a series of dark fantasy novels entitled *Orphans of Endra*. The first installment, *Dark Friends*, is available on Amazon and Kindle).

He currently lives in rural Missouri as a (not so) starving artist.

Traveler

by Deborah Walker

I was mindless, a smashed vessel, empty of understanding. How long I was in this state, I don't know. Then an element of emotion slowly came to me, the fear washing over me. I was running from something. All I knew was that I have to get away.

I grabbed at the arm of a passing boy. "What is this place?"

He turned his grimy face at me, while struggling to get free. He wriggled like a worm on a hook. "It's Jaffa, sir."

I released him. He walked off, rubbing his arm. I was immediately sorry for my rough treatment and hoped I hadn't hurt him. Although from the look of him, he was a wharf rat and probably used to ill treatment. Still, I shouldn't have added to his burden. "Here, wait," I shouted. I opened my purse and held out a coin.

He turned around. His eyes widened at the glint of metal in my hand, but he said, "That's all right, sir." He ran off with a tattered dog yapping at his side.

I was at the port of Jaffa, then. At least I had a name to add to this place. I looked at the ships resting against the stone dock. Men and a few women bustled against me. I stood perfectly still, treading water in the flow of humanity. The red stone buildings seemed familiar. Had I been here before? Many doorways were framed with brightly-colored canvas. Merchants cried out their wares.

Beyond the red stone buildings, an elegant tower rose to touch the sky, patterned with a splendid intricate mosaic. As I stood and marveled, a voice sang out an undulating song. It occurred to me that I'd heard different languages spoken, and I had understood them all. Most of all I understood the meaning of the song issuing from that high tower. It was an invitation to prayer.

Another thing became clear to me. I did not belong here. Like a fish swimming through dark waters, a sliver of knowledge came to me: Tarshish. I was supposed to go to Tarshish. I was on a dock. I needed to take a ship to Tarshish.

It was in this way that my mind was returned to me, piece by piece, like the slow reconstruction of a smashed vase. The dread had not gone away. I still felt pursued and hunted, but I was no longer the mindless thing I had been. With the return of my mind came hope.

I studied the crowd I swam in more carefully. The men, who I assumed were sailors or merchants, were dressed brightly. Their heads were covered in turbans. The few women I saw were veiled and hidden from my eyes.

I stopped a sailor who was dressed differently from the rest. He seemed, like me, to be an outsider. "I want to go to Tarshish," I told him.

"Tarshish?" he replied, "I've never heard of it. What land is it in?"

I looked away, helplessly. I didn't know. I felt the weight of my purse at my belt. I grabbed a handful of gold and held it out to the man. "Look," I said. "Is this enough to take me to Tarshish?"

The sailor grinned. "It's enough to take you anywhere, my friend. But put it away. That's enough gold to get you gutted in a place like this. I would like to help you, but my ship returns to Italy."

It seemed that I must seek out some other person to help me. I needed to get away from this place, that's all I knew. Something was pursuing me. Something massive and terrible. When it found me, I knew that it would consume me.

I walked away from the sailor, searching the faces of the crowd for someone who might help me.

"Wait, wait." The sailor called me back. "Come with me, otherwise no good will come to you here. We'll talk to the captain. Perhaps we can help you. I am called Aaron. What's your name?"

I was ashamed to admit that I did not know my name.

"Hmm," said Aaron. "Every man has a name. Let me call you Traveler. It will do, for now, until I can think of something better."

Aaron took my arm and led me towards the far end of the dock. He kept up a constant stream of chatter as we walked, "We give passage to the Christian pilgrims who visit the Holy Land. This port is the gateway to Jerusalem and the Galilee. And even though Jaffa is in the hands of the Sultan, they make us welcome. We ferry pilgrims from all over: Scandinavia, Russia and Portugal, England. Often the English pilgrims decide to remain here."

"Why's that then?" I asked, barely knowing the names he spoke but wanting to make a friend of this man.

"Ah, there's plenty of trouble for Christians in England. Even under Queen Bess. A man who can't hold his tongue might be burned for his beliefs. And the

Queen is old now, who knows what the new king will do. I can see why people might choose to stay here."

"Not you, though," I said.

He laughed, "No. I'm not a man to stay in one place for long. That's why I'm a sailor, eh?" He looked around the port with an appraising eye, "But Jaffa's a hospitable place. They're starting to build Christian churches and hostels for the pilgrims. I couldn't imagine us doing the same in England, eh? If the Muslims had a holy site in England, how welcoming would we be to them?"

"It's a busy port," I said.

"Yes, Jaffa's—"

From the belly of the ship we passed, I heard a desperate sound, men's voices crying out for aid with a ragged, animal sound. I stopped walking and went over to the ship. I placed my hands against the hull. "We must help them," I said to Aaron.

Aaron shook his head. "There's no help for them, poor devils. They're oar men chained to the galleys. They must be new to the life, or they'd know enough to keep their mouths shut."

"They're trapped inside? They're chained to this ship?"

"Yes," said Aaron. "There's nothing we can do for them. It's the way of things—or at least it was."

We walked on. The fate of the oarsmen had quieted Aaron's chatter. I was deep in thought considering the souls trapped within that ship. It seemed like their fate had caught up with them, but mine still lay before me. We stopped before a fine looking vessel.

"This my ship. I'm first mate to her," said Aaron. I could hear pride in his voice. "The *Sally-Rose*. She used to be called the *Saucy-Rose*, but the captain decided that weren't a good name for a ship embarking on voyages of a religious nature."

I noticed immediately that the *Sally-Rose* was different from the other ships docked at Jaffa. She had no oars.

"She sails by the power of the wind, only?" I asked.

"Yes," said Aaron proudly. "She's Hawkins' design. You've heard of him?"

I shook my head.

Aaron smiled, "No, perhaps not. But let me tell you this, my friend. She's the way of the future. I've sailed on galleys with them poor souls chained to the oars down below in the belly of the ship. The *Sally-Rose* is a ship of the 17th Century. She's the way of the future, indeed."

The captain interviewed me in his cabin. He was less welcoming than Aaron. "You say that you don't know who you are, or where you come from? You're not running from the authorities are you? I want no trouble with the Sultan's men. It's only by his graciousness that we are allowed to dock here."

Two men stood at the captain's side: Aaron, who was vouching for me, and a black-robed priest, who had taken an instant hatred towards me.

The priest spoke, "It's bad luck to take a simpleton on board, Captain."

"His money's as good as anyone's," said Aaron, glaring at the priest. "We've got no call to cast the first stone of accusation."

The captain glanced from one man to the other, then he stared at me, "Sir, we are heading back to Monopoli. That's a southern port in Italy. Aaron told me that you're seeking to head to a place called Tarshish. You'd be better off speaking to one of the local captains."

I did not like the thought of traveling on one of those ships powered by the misery of the oar men. It seemed to me, that I didn't care where I was going just so long as I was gone from Jaffa. "I'd be grateful for passage on the *Sally-Rose*, sir." The ship was setting sail this noon. That was enough for me.

"There'll be four months of hard travel before we dock at Monopoli. We stick to the coastline to avoid the attentions of the privateers that prey upon us poor Christians."

"It makes no difference to me, sir. I just want to be gone from here."

"This ship is meant to take pilgrims to the Holy Lands," said the priest, "not bring heathens back to Italy."

"It would be Christian to give aid to a traveler in need," said Aaron.

The captain still looked doubtful. It seemed that the priest was winning the argument, so I laid out the contents of my purse onto the table and said, "Take a fair price, for I know nothing of such things."

The captain sighed, "He's money enough. He seems honest enough to me. Who knows where he's from? He speaks the Queen's English well enough. Maybe you can help him on his way, Father Alfonse."

"I doubt he knows anything of our Redeemer," said the priest.

"He's an innocent then." The captain had made up his mind about me, and none would sway him now. "Welcome aboard, Traveler. We set sail in a few hours. Aaron will show you to your quarters."

As we walked out of the cabin, Father Alfonse whispered to me. "Take care, heathen, I'm watching you."

The crew was packing the *Sally-Rose* with spices and other items for trade. For my amusement, Aaron showed me the fragrant soap that made up part of the cargo. "Apparently there was a great call for such novelties as this in Italy," he said. "Soap from the Holy Lands, eh?"

I smiled. I was grateful that I had fallen in with such a kind friend.

The voyage set out well. The skies were clear. A fine wind blew through the sails, and that same wind blew through me and alleviated my dread. I felt more comfortable now that we had set sail. I felt at home on the water, perhaps I was a sailor in my past life.

One thing saddened me: all the crew, apart from Aaron, left me alone. The talk of Father Alfonse had influenced them. I saw them casting sidelong glances at me. They were uneasy with my presence, and that was something that felt familiar.

I was watching the crew throwing bone dice on the stock when Aaron came up to me, "Do you fancy a game, Traveler?" He had not got around to selecting a new name for me, but Traveler suited me well enough.

I shuddered. "No, I do not care for games of chance."

"No?" said Aaron, "That's a shame. It passes the time on a long journey."

"Yes," I agreed. "Sailors are attracted to the whims of fate. In every age I've lived through, it is always the same." I spoke the words unthinkingly. I immediately realized that they were strange and unreasonable.

"Don't let Father Alfonse hear you say things like that," said Aaron. He was angry with me. "It's things like that that will get you in trouble. Keep your mouth shut."

He strode off, not hearing my apology, which the sea breeze snatched away.

The storm set in one week out of Jaffa. Wave after wave crashed against the *Sally-Rose* threatening to smash her against the rocks that rose jaggedly against the hostile coastline. The ferocious waves that tossed the *Sally-Rose* like a child's toy, however, were not the worst of it. When churning drills of water started to explode out of the sea, I heard the many of the crew speaking against me.

On the second day sleet ran onto the deck. It was an unnatural sign in those temperate clines. Through the icy weather I could hear the mutterings of the crew, encouraged by Father Alfonse. They called me unnatural, cursed, and perverted.

I sought refuge in my cabin, but it was not long before the captain called upon me to answer the charges made against me.

The captain, who had shown me a hearty countenance on our first meeting, looked pale and haggard. Aaron and Father Alfonse stood, once more, at the captain's side.

"There have been accusations made against you, Traveler," said the captain. "I do not believe them, but it seems like fear and superstition has taken hold of my crew. I think it best to face these accusations openly."

"This is no ordinary storm," said Father Alfonse. "We're carrying an ill-fated cargo. The Traveler has admitted that something unknown pursues him. Something unholy, no doubt. He should be jettisoned," Father Alfonse stared at me with a look of hatred on his face.

The captain turned and struck Father Alfonse full in the mouth, "Shut your coward's mouth, church man. They'll be no talk of throwing any man overboard while I'm captain. It's nonsense and ungodly to talk of curses. I should never have agreed to discuss the matter. Get out of my sight. I'm sick of you all."

I noticed that Aaron had said nothing in my defense. That saddened me.

I could feel my fate closing quickly upon me.

Aaron came to tell me that the captain was dead. He told me that he washed overboard during the night. But he would not meet my eyes. A terrible thought crossed my mind, but I could not believe that Aaron was involved in any act of treachery—he was my friend.

The unnatural storm continued to rage. Aaron locked me in the captain's cabin for my safety.

Outside I heard the men preparing to drawing lots. They sought to identify the cause of this strange storm, whoever draws the short straw will be blamed.

"It's clear who is the source of our problem," I heard the words of Father Alfonse driving the men forward.

There was silence as the lots were drawn.

I heard Aaron's voice say, "It's the Traveler."

"Was there ever any doubt?" said Father Alfonse. "Bring him to me."

They unlocked the door and pulled me towards Father Alfonse. The sleet slashed at his face as he spoke, "What are you? What are you? You're not a man. You're a Jonah. We'll do the Lord's work when we return you to the ocean."

His words were revelation. My memory returned to me.

I fell to my knees and clutched at the priest's robe. "Yes, I'm Jonah. If you cast me overboard the storm will abate. But, I beg, you not to do that. I beg you to have mercy on me."

"He admits it. He's cursed," Father Alfonse screamed.

The crew advanced towards me.

"He's-feeble brained. What are you doing?" said Aaron, but his words were weak and hesitant.

"We'll stop the storm," said Father Alfonse.

The crew laid their hands on me and lifted me high into the air. Aaron stared into the storm. He did nothing to stop them.

It's a hard thing for a sailor to cast a man into the water. They lifted me high turning their heads to avoid my face, while Father Alfonse screamed his encouragement. The storm lashed all around us.

When I touched the water the waves calmed and the storm died. I could hear words of disbelief from the crew. But I was drowning. Seaweed wrapped around my body, pulling me downwards. I saw a dark shape approaching the *Sally-Rose*. My fate had caught up with me. But I wasn't afraid.

I heard the Father Alfonse cry out, "He *is* Jonah. Lord, save us."

I am Jonah. Jonah, son of Amittai. The final piece of the vase has been returned to me, and although it is a broken thing, my mind is complete. With the sight of the great black whale all my memory had come back to me.

I remember the three days in the belly of the whale. I remember my refusal to repent. I am the other Jonah, the Black Jonah who would not accept God's commands.

I am the Jonah who is damned to repeat his story over and over again.

The whale was close to me. I turned to him like an old friend.

The movement of the whale causes the *Sally-Rose* to rise and fall, but I ignored the shouts and screams of her crew.

The great whale unhinged its rotten jaws. Inside the filth of decay beckoned me and soon I would slide inside to my resting place. This is where I would lie. The whale will sink to the bottom of the ocean. I would become part of him.

Then there will come a time when I would be reborn, my memory wiped clean. I will return to Jaffa once more, I will seek passage and try to escape my fate.

I took one more look at the *Sally-Rose* and the face of Aaron staring, horror-struck, over the railings of the ship. The shape of the ship has given me hope. It seemed to me that humanity is moving forward. There will come a day when no man is chained into the belly of a ship.

I swam into the mouth of the great whale. I became consumed by fate.

Yet it was my hope that one day I'll be taken aboard a ship and that they will know me as the Jonah, and yet they will not cast me overboard. They will take pity on me—and then I might find forgiveness for my great sin.

I will find forgiveness. My travels will finally come to an end.

DEBORAH WALKER grew up in the most English town in the country, but she soon high-tailed it down to London, where she now lives with her partner, Chris, and her two young children. You can find Deborah in the British Museum, trawling the past for future inspiration, or on her blog. Her stories have appeared in *Nature's Futures, Cosmos, Daily Science Fiction,* and *The Year's Best SF 18*; they have been translated into a dozen languages.

LINKS

http://deborahwalkersbibliography.blogspot.com
https://twitter.com/deboree

Deliverance

by Angela Wallace

DEBORAH bolted upright in bed, a cold sweat chilling her arms as the sheet pooled in her lap. The words from her dream continued to echo in her mind. *Rise up, and I will deliver your enemy into your hand.*

She shuddered as the memory of that all-consuming voice slithered down her bare arms, drawing up gooseflesh. Deborah hugged herself and willed her breathing under control. Gradually, the rushing of blood in her ears slowed and the soothing sounds of trickling water leaked back into her senses. She turned her head toward the sheet of water that ran down a vertical aperture in the cave wall of her chamber. The liquid shimmered between silver and translucent, sometimes catching splinters of color as morning sunlight refracted at a certain angle. Peeling back the rest of her bed sheet, she placed her feet on a shaggy rug and walked to the wall of water. Her eyes couldn't pierce the veil, but she knew what lay on the other side—a realm ravaged by war.

Yesterday she had stood on the mountainside and gazed across the land she called home. Plumes of gray smoke wafted like nebulous grave markers over decimated villages. Entire sections of forest had been burned, leaving a cemetery of charred trees, branches clawing at the sky like crooked bones. And sometimes a group of refugees in the distance would wind their way around Lake Argot like a line of ants, searching for a new home. They would find none, not while King Jabin terrorized the Isterian people. The Kaanites had conquered Isteria twenty years ago, and, Deborah admitted bitterly, it was their own fault. Isterians had grown lax in stewarding the Earth as Adonai had commanded. And for their disobedience, their land was given over to another, crueler master.

She shivered, and rubbed her hands up and down her arms. The aura of that dream clung to her like wispy strands of spider silk, its weight of urgency failing to disperse upon wakening. Grabbing a shawl from the back of a chair, Deborah hurried from her bedroom into the outer hall, her bare feet pattering down the earthen corridor carved into the side of the mountain. Her pace quickened around each bend until she came to the central chamber.

A large block of white marble stood in the middle of an otherwise empty room with a domed ceiling. Curved depressions in each corner of the altar cradled four, fist-sized orbs—one emerald green, one fiery red, one cerulean blue, and one silvery gray. Deborah breathed a sigh of relief. The Elemental Stones were safe, and nothing appeared to have disturbed the quiet of the chamber.

Tugging the shawl tighter about her, Deborah approached the altar and reverently ran a hand over the Earth stone. At one time, these orbs had held the power to grant Isteria prosperity in each season, back when there were enough Guardians to wield them. Now Deborah was the last. As her people's faith waned, so had the blessings from the Elemental Stones. Her only task now was to protect them from King Jabin. The man already made use of dark sorcery to twist unnatural elements to his will; should he gain the Stones, the world would crumble into chaos.

She frowned as the words from her dream filtered through her mind again. Was it a mere dream? Or something more?

Deborah startled at a warm pulse of energy beneath her palm. She snapped her hand back and her mouth dropped open. The Earth stone was glowing, bright green light swirling within its emerald depths. *How?*

She stretched her fingers tentatively toward it again. As the tips of her index and middle finger brushed the smooth surface, tingles raced up her arm, collecting in a buzz along the runes tattooed on the inside of her forearms. Pulse ratcheting up in her throat, Deborah reached for the Fire stone. Life flared within its ruby core, plunging energy into her bones. The Stones were stirring.

Deborah took a frightened step back, adrenaline surging through her veins. Now warm, her shawl slipped to the floor, forgotten. It wasn't a dream; it couldn't have been.

Adonai...

The Lord of the Elements had been silent for so long. Many believed he had turned his back on the people of Isteria, his proclaimed chosen people. Few remembered that they had first turned their backs on him and his commandments. But now? Could Deborah dare hope that he would finally answer their cries for help?

"Rise up, and I will deliver your enemy into your hand."

Deborah gasped as the voice resounded in her head, softer than in the dream, but holding the same sovereignty. The Stones gleamed as though in response.

"Yes," she breathed. Now was the time. After twenty years, it was time to stand against the evil that dominated Isteria, to reclaim its lands for Adonai, the rightful ruler.

Not bothering to dress appropriately, Deborah hurried down the hall to the outer foyer where two guards were posted. Their brows rose in alarm as they took in her disheveled state, but she ignored them.

"Summon Commander Barak," she ordered. They hesitated a fraction of a second, long enough for her to fix them with a stern glare. Just because it had been a long time since she'd functioned as Prophetess for her people did not mean she didn't still hold that authority. And based on what had just been revealed to her, it was time to take up that mantle once again.

A day later, Deborah stood in the large greeting hall, arms folded behind her back as she stared at the ornate tapestry adorning the back wall. Vibrant threads wove a tale of enslavement, deliverance, and the inheritance of the Promised Land in which the Isterian people now dwelt. Her people had forgotten their Lord's providence, but now that he was their last hope, they would remember. Isteria would return to its former glory.

Heavy footsteps signaled someone's approach, and she turned toward the open double-doors as a tall man entered. The faded black of his coat and mud-streaked pants bespoke his current living conditions. Stray strands of brown hair frizzed around his ponytail. Despite the shadowed stubble and weary lines around his eyes, he walked with shoulders back, one hand braced upon a sheathed sword at his side as he strode into the hall.

He came to a stop seven feet from her, clacking his boots together and giving a small bow. "Deborah, the message said your summons was urgent. Are you well?"

She closed the distance between them, lifting her arms to take him in a brief embrace. "Barak," she breathed, realizing how relieved she was to see him. It had been several months since he'd last checked on her. They had become friends after he helped secret her away to this mountain sanctuary for her protection. But his place was with the army, and he was often away protecting what land holdings they could.

He returned the hug for an even briefer second than she, stepping back to grip her arms and study her. "What's wrong?"

"Nothing. I have received divine revelation."

Barak's brow furrowed slightly, and she didn't miss the flash of doubt in his eyes. "Divine...revelation?"

Deborah lifted her chin. "It is time to rise up against King Jabin and retake our kingdom." A thrill pinged through her at the declaration, and she knew deep within her bones that this was *right*.

Barak stepped back and rubbed the top of his head, mussing more hair. "Deborah," he began, tone patient as though speaking to a child. "I know you must be frustrated here, but you have it a lot better than those out there."

"I know that," she snapped. God, how she had watched the gradual destruction of her home, her people, from the safety of the mountain. "I do not propose this on a whim, out of some sense of boredom or helplessness. Adonai has commanded it. Our soldiers are to gather and the Lord will deliver Jabin's army into our hands."

Barak pinched the bridge of his nose. "We do not have the means to win a war. I have ten thousand men; Jabin's commander, Sisera, has *nine hundred* chariots alone, not to mention his infantry."

"Numbers do not matter, not with Adonai on our side."

A scoff slipped past Barak's lips. "I am to believe that after two decades of silence, the Lord of the Elements wants to help us *now*?"

Deborah flinched at his crass tone. "Why do you have so little faith?"

"Why do you have so much?"

She paused. How could she explain it? It was true, she had nothing tangible to prove it, but that was the point of faith. Even when she had been plagued by what was happening outside these walls—when fear, doubt, and despair hemmed her in—she held onto her belief that Adonai would eventually deliver them. It was the only thing she had.

Deborah studied Barak's worn expression, the tightness around his eyes and the slight slump to his shoulders. The man was war-weary, as were most of the soldiers fighting a losing battle. She softened. "I lose nothing by having faith, but if I abandon hope, then I have lost everything."

Barak shook his head. "I'm sorry, but I cannot order my men into a battle we will likely lose. If Adonai wants to help us, he should just strike down Jabin where he sits on his throne, and then we will be free."

Deborah resisted the urge to fist her hands on her hips. Barak's practical attitude had often gotten in the way of faith before, and it had been a point of contention between them on the long road to bring her here. Despite their opposing viewpoints, however, the journey fraught with dangers and assassins had nurtured a trust and friendship between them. She knew how to get him to act, even as it sent a slight tremor through her.

"Disobedience is what got us into this mess; therefore, obedience is required to get us out." Barak started to roll his eyes, so Deborah pressed on. "And since you will not lead the army against Jabin...I will."

His gaze snapped to hers, eyes flaring. "Excuse me?"

Deborah pulled her shoulders back, the high stiff collar of her caftan chafing her neck. "I will march against Jabin's army." She stepped to the side and breezed past him, calling over her shoulder as she exited the hall. "Are you going to stay here or come with me?"

After a moment of stunned silence, clomping boots hurried to catch up. Deborah suppressed a triumphant grin before he came up alongside her.

"Deborah, do not be foolish."

She continued purposefully toward the guards stationed at the outer door. "I know you do not have faith, Barak, but that's all right." She flashed him a brief smile, slipping back into friendship a moment before she donned her Prophetess role once more. "I have enough for us both."

Deborah stood outside the commanders' tent, a gusty breeze off the lowlands flapping the lapels of her coat and the canvas hanging from the marquee. Her tightly-restrained curls set in a twisted bun resisted the wind's pull, yet she still subconsciously brushed a hand across her face to clear her eyes. The remainder of Isteria's army, ten thousand men, had gathered at the river Kishon upon Barak's summons. He'd had no choice, lest he abandon Deborah to face Jabin's forces alone, which of course, he could not do. She had heard the grumblings among some of the men. They believed her mad for proposing this confrontation, and some resented that their honor prevented them from fleeing. At least they still believed in that. It broke her heart to see the spirits of her people so beaten that they were beyond hope. Surrounded by such doubt and despair, she began to wonder if she was insane, if she was leading them all to their deaths.

Her hand dropped to the hilt of a sword at her hip. Then she would die with them. Though she had been trained as a warrior to perform her Guardian duties, Deborah had never utilized her skills outside a training arena. She was capable, skill-wise, but in the fervor and panic of battle, would she rise to the challenge or quail?

Have faith, she urged herself. She had been trying to convince Barak and the other commanders to do the same; she could not falter now.

Still, as the first of the enemy army crested the distant rise and began descending into the plain, Deborah's chest tightened. The Kaanite forces outnumbered them. Their nine hundred chariots carried five men—a driver and four archers. Then there were the foot soldiers swarming in and around the wheels like rodents.

Even from two kilometers away, Deborah could feel the waves of unnatural magic stemming from the advancing chariots. An Ulgorath, one of Jabin's monstrous mutilations of nature, pulled each one. At seven feet tall, the huge stags boasted bulging muscles underneath hides as hard and black as igneous rock. Fiery cracks fissured up and down their flanks, glowing as with the fires of hell. What once must have been creatures with a proud, erect bearing now marched with heads bowed forward in strain, metallic ram horns curving in coiled circles. Brimstone snorted from their nostrils, pupils flaring red with each labored breath.

Barak stepped up beside her, their shoulders almost touching. "It is too late to turn back now," he said. "But please let a few guards remove you from this place."

Deborah pulled her chin up. "No."

He let out an exasperated grunt and turned to grip her arm firmly. "There is no reason for you to risk yourself. Who will protect the Elemental Stones if you fall?"

She looked over at him calmly. "Adonai has promised; everything will work out according to his plan."

"And if that plan includes your death?"

Deborah hesitated for a moment. Yes, she'd wondered that. "Then I die in service to my Lord, just as you would die in service to me."

A muscle in Barak's jaw ticked, and his fingers tightened slightly around her upper arm. "Of all the times I hoped you would one day lead our people, this is not what I had in mind."

She smiled softly and reached her free hand up to caress the line of his jaw, scratchy from stubble. Heat filled his eyes, and her touch lingered for a moment before she dropped her hand away. They had flirted with intimacy in the past, always held back by the boundaries of their positions. Now was no different.

She slipped her hand into his and gave it a squeeze before he turned to rally their men. Deborah drew her blade and faced the oncoming army.

Jael stood on the rise of a small rolling hill, overseeing her herd of Corazon stags. A pleasant warm wind breezed through purple millet, caressing burgundy cattails in a sashaying dance. A young, honey-brown fawn snapped futilely at one of the stalks repeatedly bopping his nose. Jael smiled and descended into the small valley, walking among her creatures with ease. Though a grown Corazon stag was robust and muscular, with a height almost two feet above her own, she had no cause to be wary. Respectful, yes, of their might and prowess, but not fearful. Each of her animals recognized her as their shepherd.

As Jael strolled among them, a tremor ran through the ground, growing into a steady rumble. The stags pricked their ears erect, muscles bunching in alertness. Low, distraught noises escaped a few throats. Frowning, Jael strode toward an elevated mound, bursting into a sprint up the incline. Her sudden movement coupled with pheromones of unease sent a few stags bounding in the opposite direction, the normal beating of powerful hooves barely registering over the amplifying grumble.

Jael crested the hill and jerked to a stop. Three miles north ran the river Kishon, now surrounded on the south end by a large encampment. Gold banners flapping in the wind bore the symbols of the four elements. Why had Isteria's forces gathered at the river? Were they trying to incite King Jabin into attacking?

Jael had nothing against the Isterians; her own people, the Kenites, had a neutral relationship with both Isteria and Kaanan. She and her husband even bred strong stags for King Jabin's personal stock. Though she disliked the king's cruel treatment of the people he'd conquered, Jael did not get involved in matters beyond her ranch. That didn't mean she wanted to see the remnants of a fallen nation slaughtered in her backyard, however.

She frowned as the vibrations beneath her feet grew stronger. The Isterian army was already settled. Jael turned her head west where a huge dust cloud blotted out the sky. On the ground several miles out, she could see a line of chariots slowly making their way to the river. King Jabin's blood-red crest accented the ends of the forward lines. Adrenaline spiked through Jael, kicking up her heart rate. She needed to evacuate her herds, especially if a major battle was about to take place so close to her grazing land—and that appeared to be the case. How much time did she have?

Her mind raced through mental calculations: the location of each herd, their number of adults and young, what land further south would be safest. She uttered a small curse; of all the times for her husband to be away traveling... Jael took several deep breaths. She had no trouble controlling her animals, but they were smart, and should one get antsy at the first sign of trouble, that whiff of fear could spread like wildfire through the herd. She needed to get moving.

Launching into a run, Jael barreled down the hill and west, toward the oncoming army. There was a watering hole about halfway between her and the chariots, and at this time of morning, her Goldenrod herd should be there.

The impact of her pounding footsteps reverberated through her soles and ankles, and the stirring wind whipped about her, clogging her nose. Breathing heavily through her mouth, Jael pumped her legs harder. She rounded a small mound and nearly collapsed in relief at the sight of the herd huddled around the watering hole. Three fawns were tucked in the center of crowded does, with the male stags on the perimeter, ears and eyes shifting warily, nostrils flaring. They could sense something amiss, but with no visible predator or threat, they didn't know what action to take.

Jael put her thumb and index finger to her lips and let out a shrill whistle. From a copse of bushes ten feet from the herd, two dogs stood up. Sable hair ran down lean body frames, fanning out around their legs and tails, shining like black silk in the sunlight.

"Tish, Rhone, *izet!*"

The dogs stiffened at attention, ready to obey her commands.

"*Fieda, arot!*"

With a yip of acknowledgement, Tish leaped into action, Rhone at her heels. They circled the herd, alternating taking point as they spurred the stags into movement, driving them south toward the ranch. Once the herds were gathered there, Jael could make the effort of moving them all to another grazing area, as far from the impending battle scene as possible.

Disgruntled chuffs punctuated the clopping of hooves as the herd moved off. Confident in the dogs' ability to get them safely to the ranch house, Jael turned her thoughts to the Umber herd she'd left a mile and a half back. They might have bolted after her abrupt departure, but wouldn't have gone far. Still, it would have helped had she ridden a mount out today rather than choosing a leisurely stroll. But how could she have predicted war would come down on their heads that morning?

Jael scrambled up the tallest hill to see how much progress Jabin's army had made. Damn, they were moving fast, though it was clear they were not rushing their pace. The creatures pulling the chariots must be quite strong. Jael shuddered at the taint of evil wafting off them, even at that distance. A trace of sulfur filtered through her nose, turning her stomach sour. Never had she seen such creatures before, hard exteriors cracking with each step, orange hellfire bleeding between the splintering gaps. Their build was similar to a stag, save bulkier.

Jael gasped. No, it was impossible. Underneath the blackened hides and bowed postures, it was difficult to see any resemblance to her beloved Corazons in these monsters. But the curved horns…and the *feeling* she got as she gazed at them.

She'd heard of Jabin's dabbling with dark sorcery, of his desire to manipulate nature and the elements to his whim, but she had never witnessed the results firsthand. He *wouldn't dare*…

Jael and her husband had been supplying Jabin with Corazon stags for over a decade. The king was their biggest customer…their *friend*. Did Tynosh know this was the reason Jabin wanted the stags? To play God and master manipulator, as though the laws of nature were his to shatter?

No, her husband couldn't possibly know, would never allow it. She would rather die than sell her beloved animals into this monster's hand. But then, Tynosh had always stressed the importance of maintaining the king's favor, how it supported their lifestyle. The wealthier they were, the more herds they could raise and maintain, which was all Jael needed in life. But at this cost?

Her chest tightened until she struggled to breathe, choking sobs wracking her throat. As the wind kicked up, bringing with it the stench of evil and brimstone, Jael dropped to her knees on the hillside and wept.

The flurry of battle was nothing like practice drills. The sheer cacophony of clanging steel and gut-wrenching cries was almost enough to knock Deborah over. At first, she had to focus more on blocking it out than on her thrusts and parries. But soon, adrenaline and training took over, and she sliced through the enemy horde like a dancer, twisting and bending to avoid blows. Her steel cut through flesh and muscle, spritzing the air with a red haze.

Barak was not far, watching her back as he had done all those years ago. She caught a flash of his black coat in her peripheral vision as he darted in to impale an enemy soldier coming at her exposed side. Then he spun away to meet the next onslaught.

Ulgorath trampled over the field, leaving streaks of singed grass in their wake. The huge beasts reared up against their harnesses, belting out roars befitting large wild cats. The acrid stench of sulfur wafted through the air, plunging into Deborah's nose and threatening to suffocate her. Fighting the urge to gag, she was too slow to dodge a sword swung at her chest. She brought her own blade up at the last moment to block, rattling steel sending vibrations up her arm. She stumbled back against the overbearing weight of the soldier who had a hundred pounds on her.

For a split second, his brow quirked in confusion as he found himself fighting a woman, and Deborah seized upon the distraction to ram her knee up between his legs. Surprise morphed into agony and the soldier staggered back, dropping his sword away from hers. With one swipe, she slit his throat.

There was a brief lull in bodies being flung at her, and Deborah swept her gaze around the battlefield. For every Kaanite that fell, three more swarmed in to take his place. Arrows rained down from the sky and zinged across the field. A sharp draft of air slapping her jaw was the only sign Deborah had that a bolt had narrowly missed her neck. The Isterians were sorely outnumbered.

She lifted her gaze to the heavens. Victory would come, of that she was sure. But in what manner? And would enough Isterians be left for it to matter? Evidence to the contrary surrounded Deborah's physical senses. She had led them all here, to their deaths.

The runes on the inside of her forearms tingled. Deborah tightened her grip on her sword. Still, she would obey, to her dying breath. With a battle cry, she lunged at a group of Kaanite soldiers.

In the blur of battle, Deborah did not see beyond the next opponent within a five-foot circle around her. She did not see the Kaanite general dismount from the lead chariot and stride toward her. Barak's warning cry barely filtered through her senses before a blow struck her shoulder and she fell to the ground. Her palms scraped across charred dirt, blackening her fingers. She flipped onto her back and thrust her sword point upward to protect herself.

A broadsword swung around, impacting her blade near the hilt. The force wrenched her arm to the side and her weapon flew from her grip. She rolled to scramble after it, but a metal edge at her throat made her freeze.

"Deborah!" Barak was shouting, trying to push his way through a wall of soldiers to get to her. Three Kaanites converged on him. He blocked one's strike, but a second rammed the butt of his hilt into Barak's shoulder and he crumpled to his knees. They divested him of his weapon and held him restrained. His panicked eyes met hers.

Sounds of battle gradually died as other Isterians noticed their leaders had been subdued. Frantic eyes darted around to find the Kaanites had surrounded them.

General Sisera glanced over his shoulder at a struggling Barak with a dismissive snort. He turned his attention back to Deborah, black eyes glinting with cold malice. A ragged scar bisected one cheek, tugging his left eye into a sneering squint. "There you are, the last prophetess of a dead god."

Deborah slowly forced herself onto her knees, back straight and defiant. "My God is not dead."

"No? Will he rain fire down upon us then?" He smirked and jerked his chin toward a nearby Ulgorath. "Jabin is the King of Fire."

"Adonai is the true Lord of the Elements," she ground out.

Sisera took a step closer, and it took every ounce of her will not to flinch away. He angled his sword a little higher, level with her neck. "We shall see."

An explosion of energy sent a whomp through the air, and in the back of Deborah's mind she could see the altar in the mountain sanctuary and the Elemental Stones explode in a flash of brilliant light. The ground shuddered a moment later, and with a loud crack, a beam of white energy shot from the peak of the mountain miles away.

For a moment, no one moved or breathed. Then Sisera chuffed. "This is worse than I thought—he missed."

Deborah couldn't respond, overwhelmed by the thrum of magic racing toward her from the mountain. It drowned out her hearing in a rush of wind and water, pressure building within her chest until she thought she'd explode. And then, as clear as a glass chime, a voice broke the chaos.

"Deborah, my faithful steward, rise."

She wanted to obey, but the air was too thin, and she was split between two consciousnesses—physically kneeling in a bloodstained battlefield with a sword ready to execute her, and mentally drowning in an eddy of darkness like obsidian silk.

"Adonai, deliver us," she gasped.

"As I have decreed," the voice responded. *"Now rise, and accept the power I bestow upon you."*

Shock rippled through her, snapping her inner eyes open. A figure swathed in a billowing white cloak stood in a sea of shimmering black. Eyes glacial blue, yet filled with warmth, gazed at her. His arms spread to his sides where the Elemental Stones hovered, glowing with a radiance Deborah had never seen.

She wanted to duck her head in reverence, but she was transfixed in awe. *"I am not worthy."*

"You have kept my commandments and devoted your life in service to me and mine. That is all I have ever required. Now rise, and by my hand you shall defeat Sisera's army."

Deborah hesitated, but at a kind, encouraging dip of his head, she reached out for the Stones. The cerulean Water orb zinged forward, plunging into her tattoos with a burning fire, followed in quick succession by the rest. Her arms sizzled, painfully at first, and her head buzzed with the timbre of each element, until at last they swirled into a harmonious orchestra that swelled to fill every fiber of her being and lift her spirit in exultation. The once black runes on her forearms pulsed with color.

The outside world gradually filtered back in, and she heard the jeers of Sisera and his men as they mocked her God. It seemed as though no time had passed while she'd been frozen in that ethereal space.

Sisera turned back to face her. "As I was saying, your god has abandoned you." His gaze drifted down a fraction, and the lines of his eyes squinted.

Deborah glanced at her arms, tattoos still glowing. Confidence filled her, and she rose to her feet with such calm composure that Sisera took a surprised step back.

"No, he hasn't." She thrust her arms out to the side and called upon the earth. The ground groaned and shook with a force that knocked several men off their feet. She then brought her arms above her head with a resounding clap, and thunder cracked the cloudless sky. Lightning forked down and struck a cluster of enemy soldiers. Inhuman screeches went up with the scent of charred flesh. Sisera and those closest to him staggered back with gasps of bewilderment.

Deborah whipped one arm toward the river, connecting with the chord of its current. Yanking, she drew up a wave of water that crashed down on a group of Ulgorath. The monstrous creatures bellowed and shrieked as steam spewed from their exposed veins. Several stags burst into a frenzy, heedless of their drivers' whips as they stampeded their own infantry. Jabin's soldiers began to flee.

Deborah summoned a ball of flame in her palm and hurled it at the enemy. It exploded in a flash of fire and splintered earth, bodies plummeting through the air from the concussive force. She whirled to find Barak and other Isterian soldiers staring dumbly at her.

"What are you waiting for?" she shouted. "Victory is ours!"

Barak was the first to snap out of his daze, giving his head a small shake and lifting his sword. He projected his voice above the din of retreating soldiers. "To Deborah! To Adonai!"

Isterian men surged forward, cutting down their enemy with a speed and precision that had only minutes before been used against them.

Deborah called up a column of water, rising like a giant snake from the Kishon river. It swayed side to side as it rose twenty feet into the air before striking down upon a hundred Ulgorath chariots and sweeping them back into the deep currents. She whirled, swinging her arms around and up. Power rippled through her bones in tune with the earth, and a wall of rock and sediment shot from the ground to cut off escape on one side. Trusting her warriors to finish off the Kaanites trapped there, Deborah spun again, her fingers crackling as an electrical charge filled the air. The sky rumbled and lightning arced down, striking Kaanites leading the retreat. Rock and tree exploded with a sizzle of fire, sending the terrified enemy soldiers in other directions. Deborah clenched a fist and connected with the embers left over from the lightning. They flared to life in response to her will, bursting into a stream of fire. Twisting her arm around, she wielded it like a lasso, curtailing the Kaanites' attempt at fleeing and driving them back toward the river or Isterian soldiers.

One by one, they were all cut down, until at last Deborah stood in the midst of a calm field, bodies piled around her. The fetor of charred flesh and grass was only slightly dampened by a strong wind that tried to snatch it up and carry it away. The carcasses of Ulgorath sizzled and steamed, their unholy inner fires quenched by the river. Not one of those monstrous creatures had survived. And still as hundreds of statues all around her were her kin, stunned by this unexpected triumph— unexpected to everyone but Deborah.

She traced a finger along one of the tattooed runes, feeling the hum of energy beneath the surface. It settled within her bones, seemingly comfortable and unprepared to leave.

"Well done, my faithful servant."

She smiled. Sisera's army had been defeated, but King Jabin was still in power. It would take great effort and a large campaign, but Deborah knew Adonai had bestowed his favor on his people once more. They would win this war. She bowed her head and sent up a prayer of thanksgiving.

Hurried footsteps crinkling over seared grass interrupted her. She looked up as a soldier came to a stop, chest heaving. His eyes were round with a mixture of disbelief, elation, and perhaps a little fear.

He bowed his head. "Prophetess, Sisera has escaped."

Her brow furrowed. "What?"

The man thrust his chin toward the rolling hills south of the river. "He fled on foot once the tide turned in our favor." A glimmer of pride filled his eyes at that statement, though a second later his gaze dropped to her glowing tattoos with trepidation. "Commander Barak has gone after him," he said a moment later.

Deborah's jubilation at their victory plummeted. *No.* She whipped her head in the direction they'd gone. "Tend to the wounded," she barked over her shoulder. Her gaze landed on her lost sword, but she didn't pause to retrieve it; she had no need for such weapons anymore, not with Adonai by her side. She launched into a run, praying Barak could take down the enemy general. And if not, that she would catch up to them in time.

Jael had found the Umber herd, and with gentle nudges and encouraging clucks, had coaxed them to follow her back to the ranch house where Tish and Rhone had already driven the Goldenrod herd. Jael had then summoned all the available ranch hands to take the two herds south, sending a handful to collect the groups grazing on the eastern and western pastures. She was not taking any chances. Yes, it would be crowded, and there were bound to be some dominance challenges between head stags, even some mixing of herds, but they would handle it as best they could.

Jael oversaw the departures, making sure everything was in order before heading out last. She wondered if the battle had already started. Probably. It had taken the better part of an hour to simply pack needed supplies and hitch a couple wagons. Jael also had to give instructions to each group of handlers on which parcel to direct their assigned herds. Some of the animals had been bred for specific traits—aggressiveness being one of them—and those needed to be kept as far away from each other as possible. The handlers were skilled men, but were accustomed to following orders and preset protocols; most didn't have the foresight Jael did to avoid unnecessary complications.

Finally, as the second hour approached, Jael prepared to ride out after the last herd, but a figure stumbling over a hill stopped her short. The man was alone, half-running, half-staggering toward the ranch house. Had he come from the battle? A deserter? A lone survivor?

Jael cast a torn look toward the haze of dust that had swallowed the traveling herds. They were too far ahead for her to call a handler back to help. Besides, the stags were her priority.

Shoulders bunching with apprehension, Jael turned her dapple-gray horse around and rode back toward the house to meet the stranger. He steered to intercept her, and as Jael drew closer, she recognized the dark hair and scar-puckered face.

"*Sisera?*" she blurted as she reined her horse to a stop.

King Jabin's general planted his hands on his knees, bowed forward as he gasped for breath. "Lady Jael," he rasped.

She could only stare at him. Had the battle gone so poorly for the Kaanites? How was that possible? They had a formidable army that outnumbered the Isterians nearly ten to one.

"I would appreciate some aid," he said caustically, pulling himself upright.

Jael quickly dismounted. "Yes, of course." She offered her arm, but he shoved past her, heading toward the house. Biting back irritation, she followed. She'd rather be tending her herds than this ungrateful brute, but she couldn't desert him. He was as much a friend of her husband's as Jabin was.

The thought filled her with bitterness, the memory of those hellish stags marching across the plain...perhaps they had all been destroyed in battle if Sisera had lost. She hoped so.

Silent and submissive, Jael tethered her horse to the porch and led Sisera into her house, a two-story dwelling with bedroom balconies and fuchsia bougainvillea covering their wrought-iron railings. She guided him past the sitting room and straight to the kitchen where she pulled out a chair from the dining table. Sisera shrugged out of his dirty coat and shoved it at her. Jael smoothed the bunched folds, pausing at the bloodstains on the arms, front, and back. They looked like rusted spots against the brown leather.

"Are you injured?" she asked, draping the jacket over the back of another chair.

He shook his head gruffly and rested his arms across the table, staring at the empty hearth across from him with unnerving intensity. Jael was almost afraid to ask what had happened at the battle. Her only interaction with the general had been when he'd accompanied Jabin to inspect herds set aside for the king's purchase. Sisera always bore himself with constrained discipline, but his shrewd eyes made Jael think of a viper waiting to strike. And if he had just suffered a defeat at the hands of Isteria…then poking the coiled snake would be very unwise.

Jael snatched the flint from above the hearth and struck it until an ember caught in the dried straw. As tiny flames popped into a growing blaze, she filled a kettle with water and hung it from a bar over the fire. Then she retrieved half a loaf of bread and a wedge of cheese from the cupboard, cut up a few slices onto a plate, and set it before the stewing general. He seemed to start out of his brooding, and after a fraction of hesitation, tore a chunk of bread apart and began shoving pieces in his mouth. Jael hoped he wouldn't take offense at the meager offering; she'd sent most of her supplies with the handlers and didn't have the means to cook up a fancy meal as hospitality demanded.

The kettle started whistling as steam escaped the spout. Jael grabbed a set of padded mitts and lifted the hot cast-iron from the hearth. She poured boiling water into a ceramic mug and set the kettle on the iron baking rack. After adding a helping of crushed peppermint and sage leaves, Jael set the cup in front of Sisera. The tea's aroma, normally soothing, did nothing to alleviate the tension in her shoulders as she tried not to stare openly at the man brimming with dangerous fury at her kitchen table. Her eyes kept darting to the window, thoughts going to her herds and wondering how they were faring with the chaotic relocation.

"Where is everyone?" Sisera's low voice startled her after the prolonged silence.

"Tending the herds." Jael opened her mouth to add that Tynosh was away, but changed her mind, belatedly realizing she was completely alone with a man who looked as though he were about to come unhinged. She took a few steps back and casually set about stoking the fire, keeping her body angled so her back wasn't fully to him.

"The herds, yes," Sisera mumbled, and stuffed a chunk of cheese in his mouth. He chewed for several long moments, eyes staring ahead but thankfully not focused on Jael.

"Yes," he said again, posture straightening. "I will need one hundred grown stags in three days' time, and three hundred the week after."

Jael stiffened. "What?" she stammered.

Sisera knocked back a draught of tea. "I realize it's short notice, but you have the numbers. If you must disappoint other customers, so be it. The king's needs are more important."

Jael's knuckles whitened around the fire poker. Despite the tremor in her extremities, her voice came out calm. "The king already has a marvelous collection of Corazon stags from us over the years. What need demands such a rush now?" *Perhaps because Sisera had just gotten the king's entire stock slaughtered.*

Sisera's eyes narrowed and he rose from his chair. "The *king* does not *need* a reason."

Jael instinctively took a step back. No, he didn't, but then, this wasn't the king's orders. It was Sisera trying to make up for a colossal mistake. Not that Jabin wouldn't insist on Jael and Tynosh replenishing his lost inventory eventually.

Intense heat began searing her leg, and she realized she'd moved too close to the fire. She sidestepped left, unfortunately putting her back up against the wall.

Sisera's left eye twitched, puckering the scar on his cheek. "In fact, send for fifty stags now and your best handlers to deliver them to the capital." He retrieved his coat and roughly shoved his arms through the sleeves.

Jael's heart thudded violently. It didn't matter that Jabin was king, that Tynosh valued his favor and the resultant lifestyle such wealth afforded. She could live without it all, but she could not send more of her beloved animals to be mutilated.

"No."

Sisera froze. An icy flint entered his eyes as he fixed them on her. "Excuse me?"

Her cheeks were hot and her palms sweaty, but Jael refused to duck her gaze or fold her shoulders in submission. "I said no. There are no stags available at the moment. You will have to come back later." And later she would figure out how to tell the two most powerful men in the region that she meant never.

He took a step toward her, nostrils flaring. "Is that so?" His tone was deadly calm, and it sent a chill up Jael's spine. "Perhaps you have switched your allegiances." He took another step, now four feet from her. "Is that it? You've aligned yourselves with the curs of Isteria."

"No, that's not—"

"You plot with them to overthrow the king!"

Before she could think to run, Sisera closed the distance between them and slammed a palm against the wall, a breadth's inch from Jael's face. The impact puffed air across her cheek. He pressed his body close to hers, trapping her beneath stiff, corded brawn. Peppermint breath huffed over her mouth; the heat of it sent her stomach rolling.

Sisera leaned in, brushing his puckered cheek against hers. "I will seize them all for your treachery." He inhaled deeply, burying his nose in her hair. Jael flinched away, a whimper catching in her throat.

"In the name of King Jabin, I seize *everything.*"

He grabbed her forearms and thrust her back against the wall. Her skull smacked stone and black spots blotted her vision. Blood roared in her ears, and along with the stench of his breath and the hardness pressing against her thighs, Jael's senses were overwhelmed. She briefly forgot the fire poker still in her hand, point angled toward the floor. Her fingers spasmed around the iron, she was clenching it so tightly.

In a flash, Jael's shock at the sudden attack was replaced with hot fury. She lifted the fire poker and shoved it against Sisera's hip, prodding the point below his belt. He stiffened and glanced down.

"*Move,*" Jael hissed, increasing the pressure from the rod.

Sisera's cheeks reddened and his eyes blazed, but he took two slow steps back. Jael tore herself away from the wall and sidestepped into the center of the room, keeping the poker leveled at the general. She needed to get away from him, but where could she run that he would not follow? He would catch up to her, take her home, her herds, her life. She needed to protect herself, needed to protect her stags.

She needed to kill Sisera.

The man must have seen the determination steel her eyes because he scoffed and began to circle her. "You are no match for me, little lamb." He drew a long, serrated knife from his belt.

Jael moved to put the table between them. Belting a roar, Sisera grabbed under the top and flipped it against the counter with a crash as wood splintered and jars shattered. He charged, and Jael swung her poker. The iron collided with the side of his head, sending the man reeling back. He staggered to avoid falling into the fire. Sisera straightened slowly and touched two fingers to the side of his head. They came away gleaming red. The veins in his neck bulged and he bellowed as he launched at her again.

Jael gripped her weapon with both hands and swung, but this time Sisera caught the poker between his right elbow and ribs, pinning it. The knife he held in that hand wavered inches from her body. His other hand jerked around to clap her ear. Stars exploded across her vision and Jael dropped to her knees. Sisera grabbed a fistful of curls and wrenched her head back. She couldn't prevent a cry of pain from escaping her throat.

"I won't kill you. Yet," he sneered. "First I will round up some of your beautiful animals and carve them up like grated cheese in front of you."

Jael's pulse hammered, and a surge of rage coursed through her like an inferno. She let go of the fire poker and seized Sisera's knife. The bottom of the blade nicked her knuckles, but she ignored the sting and bent his wrist back until it cracked. His arm slackened and the poker dropped to the floor with a clatter. But he wasn't fast enough with his good hand still wrapped in her hair. Still on her knees, Jael stabbed the dagger into Sisera's chest, burying it to the hilt.

A surprised gasp issued from his lips and his face whitened. Jael scrambled back, tripping as she got to her feet. Sisera stared at the knife protruding from his chest and the red stain slowly spreading. He collapsed to his knees and didn't move.

Breathing heavily from shock and adrenaline, Jael simply stood by the door, staring, waiting for a twitch or sign that the man would get up and resume fighting. Only after the dark wine liquid began pooling a foot out from his body did she begin to breathe easier. Still, she kicked his body tentatively. He didn't stir.

Exhaustion flooded her and Jael nearly collapsed herself. Tearing her gaze away from what she'd done, she turned and fled outside.

A man brandishing a sword was sprinting up the path toward the house, and in a flash of fear, Jael wished she had grabbed the fire poker. She cast her gaze about frantically for something outside to use as a weapon, but before she could find anything, the man called out to her.

"Good lady, I'm sorry if I startled you. I'm looking for a fugitive, the General Sisera."

Jael froze. Was he another Kaanite come searching for his commander? But no, beneath the grime and bloodstains on this man's garb, he bore a patch of the four elements. Isterian then. Jael allowed herself a measure of relief, shoulders sagging.

"He is inside."

The man moved as though to charge past her.

"But you won't need that," she added, nodding to his sword.

He paused, head jerking as he finally studied her. Curious, Jael glanced down at her disheveled clothes and hands dripping with crimson. She flexed her fingers, wincing as the action split her cuts further. The side of her face also hurt, and was probably blossoming red. She might have a bruise tomorrow. But it was a small price to pay.

The Isterian soldier regarded her with a new air of respect. "Oh?"

Jael listlessly lifted an arm and gestured for him to head inside.

Deborah's legs screamed as she crested hill after low hill at a sprint. Every other muscle also ached from the strain of battle she'd subjected them to only a short while ago. Her chest burned with the exertion, but she did not slow down. Barak was a strong warrior, Deborah had no doubt, but Sisera could not be allowed to escape, not if she could help.

She didn't know how her instincts were directing her in one particular direction; everything in the rolling terrain looked the same. Credit her newly given powers or divine nudging, Deborah had learned to trust that inner voice. She would find Barak. And Sisera.

She finally traversed the last mound and descended into a large, flat clearing with a farm in the middle. Perhaps Sisera had sought refuge there. Ignoring her wheezing lungs, Deborah pushed herself harder. The farm seemed unusually quiet and empty, save for a single horse tethered to the house's front porch. Apprehension filled her as she closed the distance.

She was only ten feet away when the front door opened and Barak stepped out, followed by a woman with bronze skin and ebony curls. Deborah pulled up short to catch her breath. Barak's face had a strange expression she couldn't read, mouth pinched in thought.

"Where is Sisera?" she asked once she could breathe more slowly.

"Dead."

Deborah lifted her brows. "Then Adonai's promise has been fulfilled—not a single Kaanite warrior survived the battle. You defeated him."

Barak's brows dipped a fraction. "It wasn't me who killed him."

She shot him a questioning look before shifting her gaze to the woman at his side. Shock mixed with underlying calm swirled in the woman's eyes, her shoulders taut. She held a rag pressed firmly against the knuckles of one hand, a few drops of blood trickling down her fingers.

Deborah strode purposefully up the porch steps to stand before them. "It was you?"

The woman lifted her chin. "He threatened me. I did what I had to."

"And in doing so, you have aided Isteria in our first victory against Kaanan. The first of many," Deborah added, casting a pointed look at Barak. She glanced back at the woman. "What is your name?"

"Jael."

Deborah smiled. "Jael, Isteria will sing of your courage and great deed for generations to come."

The woman glanced to her right, as though searching the barren horizon for something. "I did not do it for Isteria," Jael said in a low voice. "I was in the pasture earlier...I saw what Jabin had done..." Her voice broke, and she returned her gaze to Deborah's. Resolve steeled her fiery eyes. "I will no longer provide stags to Jabin's army to be undone by black sorcery." She paused, brow furrowing. "I will, however," she said slowly, "contribute some to Isteria's. If you do intend to rebel against Jabin's rule."

Deborah's heart swelled with hope. "I do." Adonai had blessed them with victory today already, and now he had blessed them with a new ally.

She held out her hand. "I am Deborah."

Jael's gaze roamed over the faintly glowing tattoos. "Prophetess for the Lord of Elements," she said softly.

Deborah nodded, hand hovering. Tucking the bloodied cloth under her elbow, Jael reached out to clasp Deborah's arm firmly, and gasped as magic pulsed from one of the tattoos. Before Deborah could yank her hand away or realize what was happening, a bit of earth magic had siphoned down her fingers and plunged into Jael's forearm. The woman staggered back a step, staring mutely as black ink formed the earth rune across her skin.

"What is that?" she rasped, eyes wide as she looked at Deborah, then Barak, both equally shocked.

Deborah shook her head slowly, wrestling with the feelings and senses suddenly coming to her. Taking a deep breath, she met Jael's gaze. "You are a good steward, Jael, daughter of Jem. Adonai has declared you a Guardian of Earth, to tend his creatures as you have done for many years."

Jael straightened, and Deborah could not guess what revelations such power or connection to the Lord was given to the woman. Jael was not Isterian, but she was honorable and stewarded her land and animals with a faithfulness that most Isterians had forgotten. Deborah would not question Adonai's will in the matter.

Barak's jaw worked as though he would, and Deborah shot him a quelling look. Who were they to claim privilege when their failure had brought Isteria under Kaanite occupation? His mouth tightened, but he kept his peace. Jael still looked enthralled with her new blessing, eyes alight. The corners of her mouth lifted.

"I can hear my herds," she said breathlessly, and her smile brightened. "They are well, and are coming home."

Deborah grinned in return. She turned to Barak. "We have much work to do." They would fight against Jabin, and Adonai would deliver Isteria from the wicked king. And then they would have peace.

ANGELA WALLACE has been penning adventures ever since she was sucked through a magical portal as a child. What she saw and whom she met gave birth to exciting and complex fantasy worlds where defying the laws of physics was a bonus. She has since come back down to earth, only to discover this mortal realm has magic of its own. Now she is quite at home in the world of urban fantasy, though believes that love, faith, and hope are of a stronger magic than fire wielding and sorcery. She loves gun-toting good boys, and could have been a cop in another life except real blood makes her queasy. She'll have to stick to solving supernatural mysteries. Language is her pleasure, whether it's weaving words on a page or lassoing linguistics into translations as a sign language interpreter.

Angela is currently working on the next book in her Elemental Magic series.

LINKS

http://angelawallace.wordpress.com
http://www.facebook.com/angelawallaceauthor
https://twitter.com/AngelaRWallace

Red as Heart's Blood

by Cynthia Ward

The Princess

WHEN the queen enters her lying-in room, she tells me how she found my singular name. "I sat sewing by an open window framed with ebony," she says. "Early snowflakes were falling as gently as goose-down. They turned the castle and apple orchard white. The beauty distracted me, and I pricked my finger with the needle. Drops of my blood fell on the snow. The three colors together were so striking, I found myself speaking a sudden wish:

"'Would that I might give my dear husband a child as white as snow, as black as ebony, and as red as heart's blood.'

"Within days," she tells me, "I bore you. Your skin was as white as snow, your hair as black as ebony, and your lips as red as heart's blood. So I named you Snow White."

Then my mother tells me something else I did not know; and it weighs like a stone upon my heart.

"The king and I have always sorrowed," the queen says, "because you were alone. We rejoiced when I quickened at last."

I wish I'd known. I would have told my parents they're all the family I need. Had I known to put their minds at ease, they might not have conceived another child.

I wish with all my heart and soul they had not, for my newborn brother and my mother do not survive.

Overnight, grief ages my father twenty years. His advisors mark this. Bare days after my mother's funeral, they counsel him to remarry, so he'll not be alone. The way they speak the word "alone," the counselors make me feel as if I too have died. Or never existed at all.

I don't intend to overhear, but as I pass, their voices are raised. Once I understand what they're saying, I cannot force myself away from the door. So I hear how his advisors' suggestion enrages my father, who loved my mother more than his own life.

Then the canniest of the royal advisors speaks.

"Snow White, too, mourns," he says. "Your Highness, she is barely more than a child. She must suffer even more grievously than her father, having lost a mother's love. Do you wish her to be without a woman's care at this time?"

When my father finally makes reply, he speaks in a voice that says his advisor has broken his will; and my heart breaks anew.

"Very well, then. Find a woman fit for Snow White."

The advisor loses no time. However, I don't see my father's bride-to-be. She resides with a baron's family, for the baron's foreign-born wife is teaching her our language. One of my ladies-in-waiting is cousin to the baron and has visited his manor; she says my father's future wife is from the east.

"She is eighteen—your own age," the lady adds. "And she is more beautiful than any woman who has ever lived in the land, saving only yourself, Princess." This last I discount, as my parents taught me to assume any praise we receive is base flattery. "Her skin is as white as ivory," the lady says, "and she is as delicate as porcelain. Her eyes are like polished jet, and her hair is as black and sleek as a seal's pelt."

I know not why I'm troubled by comparison of the woman to items of the marketplace. But I do know why I'm troubled by the impending nuptials. She will wed my father not three months after my mother's funeral.

Contrarily, I don't wish my father to be without a wife's companionship. I hope his intended will treat him benevolently. Perhaps my lady-in-waiting senses my concern, for she mentions my father's bride-to-be wears a gentle mien.

As the wedding draws close, I listen by the door while my father's advisors speak to him again.

"Your bride was betrothed to the king of an eastern land," the canny advisor says, "until she was struck by tragic loss. On the night of their first meeting, the king choked upon an apple, which caught in his throat and none could dislodge it. His heir didn't want the young woman, so he sought a husband for her. She will make a fine wife, Highness. She is comely, and of royal birth, and a virgin. With her, you and your daughter will find happiness again."

Now we gather in the cathedral, and my father weds the foreign princess in a grand ceremony.

Every eye is drawn to the king's bride, including mine. She wears her ornate white gown with poise, though I've heard our clothing is outlandish to easterners. When my father removes her veil for their first kiss, the beauty of her face makes my heart trip.

With the veil drawn from her eyes, my father's new wife glances at me frequently, as if inclined to become my friend. Always, she smiles, as if the sight of me gladdens her. This lightens my heart a little.

As we leave the cathedral, I overhear some words from those watching the royal procession. They say the new queen and I must become close, if not as mother and daughter are close (for we're the same age), then as sisters are close. These words are like seeds, planting hope for my father and myself.

Other onlookers' words sow melancholy. "Now," they say, "Snow White will finally be wed."

My parents never arranged a betrothal for me, saying, "It's unwise to force marriage upon a girl before she wants it." I never found favor for any of the young men—the princes and the sons of dukes and barons—that my parents invited to the castle. Nor has my heart sped at the sight of knight or squire, or even blacksmith or peasant. I know I must marry, and hope soon to meet the man I would want as my husband. But I fear I shan't find that man before the new queen sees me wed.

She looks so gentle, I pray she understands my concern. Yet every glimpse of her increases the pounding of my heart, and makes my blood heat until I grow dizzy. I turn my eyes away, reminding myself how unmannerly it is to stare. Yet always my attention returns to her, and my heart resumes its fearful pace.

The Bride

I've always been the most beautiful woman in the land. Yet, when my new husband raises the bridal veil, and I see my new stepdaughter clearly at last, the sight of her sends the heart's blood rushing through my veins like poison. But, as my new husband kisses me, no one dreams my flush is anything other than a shy maiden's blush. No one guesses, as I smile at Snow White, that I cannot bear the sight of her.

I can't abide to see a woman as beautiful as I. But I'm just. I'll not destroy a woman for approaching me in beauty. I'll destroy her only for surpassing me.

Giving no outward sign of my agitation, I retire to the chamber in which I spent the night before the wedding. Its appointments include a mirror from my homeland. It was created by my own hand, with arts I learned from my mother's wisewoman.

Last night, I slept surrounded by my new ladies-in-waiting. Their presence had less to do with soothing my nerves than keeping my maidenhead intact. Now, when I tell my ladies-in-waiting I need a moment to compose myself before I go to my husband, they leave the chamber.

I should do what I came here to accomplish, then summon the ladies. But I'm too agitated to wait until dawn for what I most desire. So I raise the skirts of my wedding gown—it is a perverse color, white, the color of mourning—and sweep across the room.

A small frame, hanging upon the wall, is shrouded in a silk sheet the color of heart's blood. With a flourish, I pull the sheet away, revealing a mirror of polished silver. I study my reflection closely. I cannot judge if my beauty is greater.

In a voice as resonant as a sounding gong, I speak the question I've put to the mirror many times before.

"Mirror, mirror, on the wall, who in this land is the fairest of all?"

The mirror speaks as I did, in my own dear language; and the mirror's curious timbre, as always, sounds neither male nor female.

"You, O queen, are the fairest of all."

At those words, my burning restlessness eases a little. My mirror speaks the truth. I do not need to slay Snow White.

Not today.

I open the door. The chamber floods with ladies-in-waiting. They make themselves so busy preparing me, they take no notice of the ring I've just placed upon my thumb. They pay no mind to the white jade lozenge that adorns the gold band.

My ladies-in-waiting lead me to the king's bedchamber, and accompany me within. I'm glad of their presence, however much they may chatter about weddings and my future happiness as King Gottfried's wife. But when the king gestures in dismissal, they flee his chamber like startled peahens. And, as he closes the heavy door behind them, the massive slab settles with the sound of a tomb closing.

Then the king turns to me.

"Leona," he says, and thinks he speaks my name.

My name is Lienhua. The barbarians mangle it into one of their harsh words, and never seem to realize what they've done. But I don't let them see how I hate their clumsy speech and butchery of my name.

Everyone tells me King Gottfried mourns his first wife greatly. But, as I stand before the man with my head lowered, looking up through my eyelashes, I see desire kindle on his face. For all my maiden status, I cannot fail to recognize his sentiment; it inflamed the face of my late betrothed in the same manner. But that old dodderer wasn't recently bereaved.

My husband approaches, raising his hands. He cups my face, forcing my head up for a kiss. My heart clenches with revulsion at his behavior, so unseemly in a new-made widower.

"Hold a moment, my husband." Though I put all my will to the effort, I'm unable to keep the disgust from my voice; but the man only smiles. He believes the emotion is a passion to match his. "Please forgive your wife," I say. "But the door to your chamber has not yet been locked, and I—" I cast my gaze shyly downward "—I've never—"

FAIRYTALE, FOLKLORE, & MYTH. REIMAGINED & REMASTERED.

"Of course." The king turns away.

As he twists the key, perhaps he hears the sound of wine flowing. When he turns back, he sees me pouring from the bottle the royal taster must have opened and sampled, before leaving it in the king's bedchamber.

The king studies the bottle in my hand, then looks at me and smiles. "I've never seen a bottle colored or shaped in that manner, nor one marked with such curious writing. The scent is reminiscent of wine, yet I don't recognize it. What is this potation?"

"Plum wine." I smile. "It's the custom in my land for the bride and groom to drink plum wine," I tell him, "before they consummate their marriage."

Two gold goblets stand upon the table. The dark wine glimmers below the rims.

"Let us drink a toast to our life together," I say, "for as long as it might last."

The king frowns, as if he find my words an awkward way to wish for a long life together; but he knows his bride is from a far land, his language new to her.

"Does custom dictate," he says, "which goblet is the groom's, and which the bride's?"

"It doesn't matter which goblet you choose, so long as we both drink the joyful wine."

He smiles at me, and takes one of the goblets from the little table.

I take up the other goblet, and he taps the rim of his goblet to mine and says, "To our life together."

We drink.

That is not correct. We both raise our goblets to our lips, and I drink. He watches me over the rim, taking no taste while I swallow the wine.

I lower the goblet, a quarter of its contents gone, and look at my husband. "Does the wine not please you?"

"It does," the king says, and sips. Then, putting his goblet aside, he looks upon me with that repellant gleam in his eyes. He steps toward me and takes the goblet from my hand, setting it down beside his. He leans toward me, his lips parting for the kiss.

Then the king falls to the floor.

Staring up at me, he clutches at his heart. He opens his mouth. No words emerge; only a weak, pain-racked cough.

"You want me to summon help?" I ask. "But it's not dyspepsia or apoplexy that's felled you."

I touch the hollow jade adorning my left thumb, so it springs open once more.

His eyes widen, and his lips work desperately.

"I suppose you're wondering how I knew which goblet you'd select," I say. "I didn't. I took a trace amount of the poison every day, until I developed immunity. But perhaps you've already realized that. Perhaps what you want to ask is, why? Why did I poison you?

CYNTHIA WARD | 695

"Can a man understand why, though I tell him?" I ask. "I think not. Still, I will try.

"I'm tired of being bartered like a bundle of silk."

My new husband writhes with increasing feebleness on the stone floor. His eyes are wide in his empurpling face. His lips form words he cannot voice.

"I know what you want to say," I tell him. "You want to tell me it's the natural order of things, for old kings to bed young women—even girls too young to bear a babe without being grievously harmed, or dying, as my younger sister did. After all, you must be wiser than I, as you're a score of years older. No doubt you rejoiced to be rid of your first wife, once her wrinkles and gray hair and sagging flesh began to reveal themselves."

The king is shaking his head, *no*, frantically, *no*!

"You must have realized—" I snap shut the hollowed jade "—this isn't the first time I've done something like this. But I've not repeated the mistake I made the last time I was betrothed." I kneel beside my husband and put my lips to his ear. "This time," I whisper, "I've made sure to kill my betrothed *after* we're wed."

His expression changes.

"Oh, don't look so surprised," I say. "I've learned your laws as well as your language. I shall be queen of your land, until such time as your daughter finds a husband, and he becomes king. Only—will I allow your daughter to marry? It's possible—" I tilt back my head and laugh "—it's possible I'll have to kill Snow White first!"

The Princess

All in the land attend the funeral of King Gottfried. All mourn, including the new queen. From her expression, it's clear her new husband had already grown dear to her. And she sympathizes with my grief, I know, for she glances frequently at me. I glance at her as often, taking a measure of comfort from her sympathy. And, after the funeral, Queen Lienhua embraces me tenderly, speaking words of comfort, as my birth mother would have.

The Bride

I seem every inch the grief-stricken widow, until I'm alone. Locking the door, I storm across the floor and pull the silk, red as heart's blood, from my mirror. Then I speak in my own language:

"Mirror, mirror, on the wall, who in this land is the fairest of all?"

"You are fairer than all who are here, O queen. But more beautiful still is Snow White, as I have seen."

The storm of my anger rises unbearably as the mirror confirms what I observed at the funeral. Why did I not foresee that grief for her father might purify Snow White's looks like gold? That beauty rent my heart like the beauty of no other woman I've seen in my eighteen years.

I invite Snow White to the royal bedchamber (it is mine now, with that wretched old man buried). I greet her with the kisses and embraces and consoling words of one who shares her loss. Then I offer Snow White a potion.

"It will help you bear the unbearable," I say.

Snow White is trusting; she drinks the potion.

Then she puts her hands to her temples, as if suddenly dizzy.

I furrow my brow in a show of concern. "Your grief is great, Snow White. Sit, before you swoon."

She sits upon the edge of my bed; and within moments she has fallen back upon the blanket, her senses fled.

Then I wrap her in the blanket, hiding her face and form, which arouse such paroxysms of envy and resentment in my breast. Then I summon a huntsman who lives with his family deep in the woods. He does not know Snow White's appearance.

I tell him, "One of my servants has insulted the memory of my husband, and spreads lies that she lay with him, and carries his son in her womb. Huntsman, take her deep into the forest and kill her, and bring me back her heart as a token of your obedience. Then you will be well rewarded. But if you fail me in this task, you will wish you'd never had a family."

And so, understanding the lives of his wife and son are forfeit, the huntsman takes Snow White away.

The Huntsman

I cannot believe our new queen—a woman of high birth and tender years—has such evil in her heart as to kill my wife and son if I don't obey. But her expression is fierce, and I love my family; and her servant's action threatens our kingdom. So I take the queen's servant deep into the forest, nearly as far as the mountains that are home to the dwarfs. Here I unsheathe my hunting knife, and draw back the blanket. I wish to strike true. Even a servant who's behaved this wickedly should receive a quick death.

As I steel myself—I have never slain man, woman, nor child—I raise my knife to pierce the woman's heart. At that moment, she wakes. She sees my knife poised to strike like an adder.

She cries out: "Don't kill me, kind sir! Let me run away into the forest, and never will you see me again."

The sight of her face has struck me motionless. She's surely no older than my son. Whatever evil she has done, I cannot kill her in cold blood.

Lowering my knife as if it has gained a weight greater than the world, I say, "Run, child. But come no more to the castle, for the queen is set on seeing you dead."

The young woman springs to her feet and flees from me as fleetly as a frightened hind.

As I start back to the castle, my heart is leaden. I didn't slay the young woman; but she is small and defenseless. She'll soon be devoured by wild beasts.

Before leaving the forest, I kill a young boar, and cut out the heart. It looks much like the human heart. I take it to the queen as the token of her treacherous servant's death.

The Bride

The cook prepares the heart of Snow White. I've told her it's the heart of a boar. She cooks the heart slowly, in red wine, with garlic and wild onions. She seasons it with salt, lovage, rosemary, thyme, and long pepper, and adds turnip and greens to finish.

I dine.

Snow White's heart is the choicest viand I've ever eaten.

The Princess

I run. Though I grow faint with hunger, I cannot eat; I know not which forest plant is safe, and which deadly. I fear the sounds I hear; the forest has bears, and wolves, and perhaps other creatures that dine on human flesh. I scarcely pause to drink water from the streams I cross.

The sun is setting when I emerge at last from the forest. I don't know where I am; I've never been outside the town that surrounds my father's castle. But I know I'm in a meadow, and realize the mountains ahead must be the home of the dwarf folk.

In the meadow, I'm surprised to see a small cottage.

Perhaps I should pass it by. It's hardly abandoned; smoke rises from the chimney, a black line against the red glow of the western horizon. But night is coming on, and I shiver with the growing chill. I won't survive an autumn night in my tattered silk dress, even if no hungry creature finds me. And where else might I take shelter?

I limp toward the cottage, hoping its inhabitants will aid a lost girl, at least for the night. Reaching the door, I extend a shaking hand to knock. Before I can touch the wood, hunger overtakes me, and I collapse.

When I wake, I see a dwarf peering through a door at me. I shrink back from the stranger. Then I perceive that he hasn't disturbed my garments, and my wounded feet are bandaged. I lie in a comfortable bed, too, in its own little room.

"You must be hungry," says the dwarf, and, to my astonishment, he summons six others.

They say, "We wish only to help you," as they come into the room, showing open palms to indicate they mean no harm. They help me rise from the bed, and bring me out of the little room to a short-legged table (it's well I'm not tall). When I'm seated, they bring me delicious food and cool water.

The dwarfs are friendly. Dwarfs aren't subjects of my father—my stepmother—and mostly keep to themselves. They've no reason to recognize me. Likely, they've never heard my name. So, when one of the seven asks my name, I answer truly.

"Snow White."

To my amazement, they bow.

"We trade ore in the town," says one, noticing my surprise, "and know your name, Princess."

"But," says another, "why are you not at the castle? How came you to our remote and humble home?"

"My father died," I tell them.

"But surely you should be taking his throne?" one says.

Another dwarf, more familiar with human customs, says, "Surely you're betrothed or married to his heir? Was the new king cruel, that you must flee?"

"I have no betrothed or husband," I tell the dwarfs. "There is no new king."

"Then why are you here?" they exclaim.

"My stepmother sits upon my father's throne," I tell them. "When my father died, she summoned me, offering a potion to help with grief—or so she said. I fell asleep, and woke to find a huntsman preparing to kill me. He said the queen wanted me dead. But he was merciful and let me go. So I ran and ran, until I found your cottage."

Then the dwarf I saw first, who must be their leader, tells me, "You may stay with us, and heal, so you have the strength to seek allies and overthrow your stepmother. We'll tell no one you are here. But your stepmother or one of her servants may come looking for you, or discover your location by sorcerous arts. Princess, allow no one in the cottage."

The dwarfs' counsel is wise, and I agree. And, as I recover, I keep the dwarfs' house clean. Some would say this act does not befit a princess; but I must repay the dwarfs for their kindness, and this is all I have now.

I find myself thinking often of the queen. I sorely fear she'll find me; but I don't speak of my dread. I don't wish to place even more of a burden upon the dwarfs.

The Bride

I trust no man; I consult my mirror.

My mirror says, "You, O queen, are the fairest of all."

So, knowing Snow White is slain, I release the huntsman's family.

But as the days pass, I grow melancholy, wondering if a new woman has supplanted me in beauty; and I speak to my mirror.

This time it says: "You, O, queen, are the fairest of all I see. But by the hills where seven dwarfs dwell, Snow White also dwells, healed and well, and there is none so fair as she."

"The huntsman has betrayed me!"

In fury such as I've never known, I order my men to find the huntsman and his family and kill them. When my men return, they lay the heads of the huntsman, his wife, and his son at my feet. The sight should gladden my heart. Yet my fury continues unabated. Snow White still lives.

I should never have trusted a man to kill a woman so beautiful.

I mark my face with charcoal, and rub ash in my hair. Soon, I look ancient in the polished silver mirror, and cannot even recognize myself. Now, disguised as an old peddler-woman, I slip from the castle and travel to Snow White, whose location I've divined by scrying.

Reaching the cottage by the hills, I knock at the door and cry, "Pretty things to sell, very cheap, very pretty."

The shutters beside the door swing open.

My heart tightens like a fist as Snow White leans through the window.

She doesn't recognize her stepmother in the stooped and ancient hag at the door, or in the creaking and quavering timbre of my voice. Snow White is convinced the old peddler-woman is not someone she should fear. She opens the door to me.

"What have you to sell?"

"Good things, pretty things," I answer. "I have stay-laces of all colors."

I show her the prettiest, which is woven of bright silk.

Snow White stares, and says, "The stay-lace is as pretty as you say." Then she shakes her head. "I cannot buy it, though, as I've not a penny."

I say, "Child, you look such a fright, I shall *give* the stay to you."

Snow White looks down at her mended silk dress. She blushes, aware of how poorly she is dressed; she cannot even tie her stay-laces properly by herself. And, though she shakes her head at my offer, she utters no refusal this time.

I press my advantage. "Please, sweet maiden, let me give you this stay, and help you lace it up properly."

Snow White leads me into the cottage. I look around. There are many little chairs around the short-legged table, but none are occupied. No jerkins hang on the seven pegs by the door. Snow White and I are alone.

I keep my bloodthirsty eagerness buried deep within my ancient looks and sooty rags as Snow White opens her bodice and corset. Still, as I tie her new laces, my hands shake. She takes this as another mark of my advanced years.

I lace so tightly Snow White falls, to lie without moving. Swiftly, I crouch to listen, pressing my ear to Snow White's breast. I find no signs of life.

I rise, exultant. "Now *I* am the fairest in the land."

The Princess

Awakening, I find myself lying on the floor, with the seven dwarfs gathered around me. "What has happened?"

"We returned from the mines and found you lying on the floor, as still as one dead," the dwarf leader tells me. "You were laced so tightly, princess, you couldn't breathe. We had to cut the laces, lest you perish in the time it would take to untie them. How could you lace yourself so tightly?"

I tell the dwarfs what happened.

Their leader says, "That old peddler-woman must have been the queen. Trust no one who comes to the door in future, princess, for the queen must be a master of disguise. Let no one in when we're not home."

They're right. I agree to do what they say. Yet the idea that the queen might return fixes my thoughts on her constantly.

The Bride

When I arrive at my castle, I hurry to the privacy of my bedchamber and consult my mirror.

It answers: "You, O, queen, are the fairest of all I see. But in the hills where seven dwarfs dwell, Snow White also dwells, alive and well, and there is none so fair as she."

The shock casts me down in convulsions, and it is long before I'm able to rise.

Summoning a serving-woman, I send her to bring me the most beautiful apple from the orchard. Then, alone again, I lock my chamber door. I treat this apple as I treated the one I gave my betrothed, in the kingdom to the east.

It's in very different guise that I return to the cottage, riding upon a handsome horse with trappings fit for a prince. I don't go directly to the cottage, but dismount a little ways off. I stand in the shade of a lonely tree, as if I have no greater desire than a respite from the autumn sun, which pours down heat with midsummer ardor.

From the saddlebag, I draw the ripe red apple, and study it from every angle, and speak in a carrying voice. "Would that I had a companion, with whom I might share this beautiful fruit."

Directly, Snow White opens the shutter and looks out the window. She sees me, but doesn't *see* me. She looks upon a tall and handsome young man in princely garb, with a gold coronet upon his brow.

Yet she holds silent. It's clear she knows who tried to suffocate her. As she studies me, her expression is wary, though I've made the prince as handsome as disguise may make anyone. She crosses her arms and remains at the window, waiting for me to leave.

Showing no awareness of her presence, I raise the apple and study it. Then I shake my head, as if in regret, and say, "'Tis a crime I must eat so fine an apple by myself."

Now, Snow White, who was unmoved by the prince's fine looks, is moved by the apple's beauty. Hiding in this remote meadow, she cannot have tasted fresh fruit since the huntsman took her from the castle. Hunger suffuses her face, and she leans through the window.

She speaks. "I dare not."

Her rejection floods me with wrath, but when I turn my face to hers, I wear the expression of one merely startled.

Miming recovery, I address her. "Are you afraid of poison? Then you're a wise young woman. But I shall take a bite, and you shall see what befalls me."

The apple is cleverly tainted, so only the fairest cheek is affected; and I've smeared the untainted side with bright turmeric from the Indies. I hold the apple so Snow White doesn't see the mark as she carefully watches me. And she sees that no harm befalls the princely young man when he eats half the apple.

Now Snow White runs to me, stretching out her arm. Smiling, I extend the remaining half, pressing it into her hand with both my own. When I release her hand, she raises the fruit to her lips. Her face is avid. Her red lips part. The snap is sharp as her eager teeth pierce the red skin and white flesh, and she takes her first bite.

Immediately, she begins to gasp for breath. Within seconds she's silent, her eyelids fluttering. Then she falls, to lie as still as one stricken by acute apoplexy.

Gazing upon Snow White's motionless body, I laugh. "It's too early in the day for the dwarfs to return and save you again, Snow White."

I smile in triumph, and cast off the spell that cloaked me in the likeness of a man, and wipe the paint from my face.

I find myself wondering how long it will take the paralytic poison to finish its work and leave Snow White beyond all hope of revival. The thought sets the heart's blood rushing so fiercely through my veins, I fear I might swoon. What a curious reaction, I think, to seeing Snow White die at last. Truly, I've waited too long to fulfill my desire.

To cheer myself, I bring to mind the image of Snow White, still and cold, in her coffin; but, instead of joy, I feel as if I've discovered the person dearest to me in the entire world has died.

Then I understand at last the emotion that smote me like a keen-edged sword whenever I saw a beautiful woman. I fling myself down beside Snow White, my sudden movement knocking the princely coronet from my head so my long black hair tumbles around my face. I tilt Snow White's head.

The bite of apple falls from between her red lips.

My heart pounding as if it must burst, I press my ear to Snow White's bosom. I hear no sound of breath or beat of heart. The tears escape my eyes. I'm too late.

Too late.

I brush loose strands of her hair from Snow White's face, and give her a farewell kiss.

Then her breasts press suddenly against mine as she draws a tremendous breath.

Abruptly, I feel as if I were the one who ate tainted fruit, for my heart seems to stop.

With an angry cry, Snow White opens her eyes.

Her eyes need a moment to focus, yet I'm immediately struck motionless by her gaze. I should pull back from such nearness to Snow White—I should turn away— rise and be gone! Yet I cannot move, even to close my eyes.

Snow White's eyes widen to find my face so close to hers. The rosy hue drains from her complexion. She drives the heel of her hand into my breastbone.

Of course she pushes me away.

What else can she do, when she finds herself so close to the woman who's thrice tried to kill her?

The Princess

I wake to the sensations of earth beneath my back and pressure against my breasts and lips against mine. None of this makes sense. I've not even known a kiss on the lips before; I know the feel only from kinfolk putting their lips to my brow or cheek. Then I remember the princely young man. My heart races like an Araby steed at the realization that a strange man is touching me improperly. With an angry shout, I open my eyes.

I am astounded to find the *queen* pressed against me. Where did the man go? How came the queen here?

Then I see the princely trappings, and know the queen came here in disguise, bearing a poisoned apple. There's a dagger at her belt, inches from my heart. She leans intimately close so she may properly administer the deathblow the huntsman left undone—

Having no better weapon, I thrust my hand upward.

At the blow to her breastbone, she rocks back. I keep my right arm upraised in a warding gesture as I press my left palm against the ground. I'm hoping I've time to push myself to my feet before she draws the dagger, even as I know there's no time to escape her blow.

The queen only stares at me. I return her stare, stricken motionless by the sight of her face. It is, most inexplicably, streaked with tears.

My blow was weak; her breastbone settles once more upon my raised hand. Her weight presses as solidly against my palm as marble. But I don't feel a stone-cold stillness through the velvet of her doublet. Her heartbeat is like thunder. Her flesh is as hot as heart's blood.

I'm still weak from the injuries and privations of my flight through the forest. My arm swiftly tires. My elbow begins to bend under the queen.

The queen's breathing grows more rapid as she catches her weight on her two hands. This takes the weight of her body off my hand. It leaves my body trapped between her arms, which show a graceful strength against the tightness of her sleeves.

She may safely draw her dagger now. Why does she not? Why does she take no action at all, beyond drawing breath and staring downward?

She watches my face with the most puzzling and extraordinary expression, a mixture of regret and longing.

Her breastbone presses rhythmically against my palm. Her every breath seems as forceful as the pumping of a blacksmith's bellows. Finally, I cannot help but glance down.

Every inhalation presses her breasts against the binding she must wear, revealing their shape.

When I look again at her face, I understand she is quite the most beautiful woman ever to draw breath.

My hand rises to her face. My fingers trace the lines of cheekbone and jaw. My fingertip brushes her lips.

The Bride

Snow White whispers. "Finally, I understand." Her tone is so altered from her wrathful waking cry. The rose is returning to her complexion. "Finally, I understand," she says, shaping her palm to my face, "why I always open the door to you, Lienhua."

Snow White presses her lips to mine.

When next I address my mirror, I speak in the words of my new homeland, and I smile joyously at the woman by my side as the mirror replies in the same language.

"O, queen, of all in the land the fairest be not you, but the young woman who rules beside you."

CYNTHIA WARD has published stories in *Asimov's Science Fiction* magazine and *Bending the Landscape: Horror* (Overlook Press), among other anthologies and magazines, and articles in *Weird Tales* magazine and *Locus Online*, among other webzines and magazines. Her story "Norms," published in *Triangulation: Last Contact*, made the Tangent Online Recommended Reading List for 2011. With Nisi Shawl, she coauthored the diversity fiction-writing handbook *Writing the Other: A Practical Approach* (Aqueduct Press). She lives in Los Angeles, where she is not working on a screenplay.

LINKS

http://www.cynthiaward.com
http://www.facebook.com/CynthiaWardAuthor
https://twitter.com/cynthia_ward
http://www.writingtheother.com

The End

www.ingramcontent.com/pod-product-compliance
Lightning Source LLC
Chambersburg PA
CBHW071328020726
47502CB00001B/2